CW00496532

LOST GODS

The Brotherhood of the Eagle Book 3

Tim Hardie

TJH Publications UK

The characters and events portrayed in this book are fictitious. Any similarity to real persons, living or dead, is coincidental and not intended by the author.

ISBN 978-1-8381824-5-8

Cover design by Anne Hudson

For May Stapleton

MAP OF LASKAR

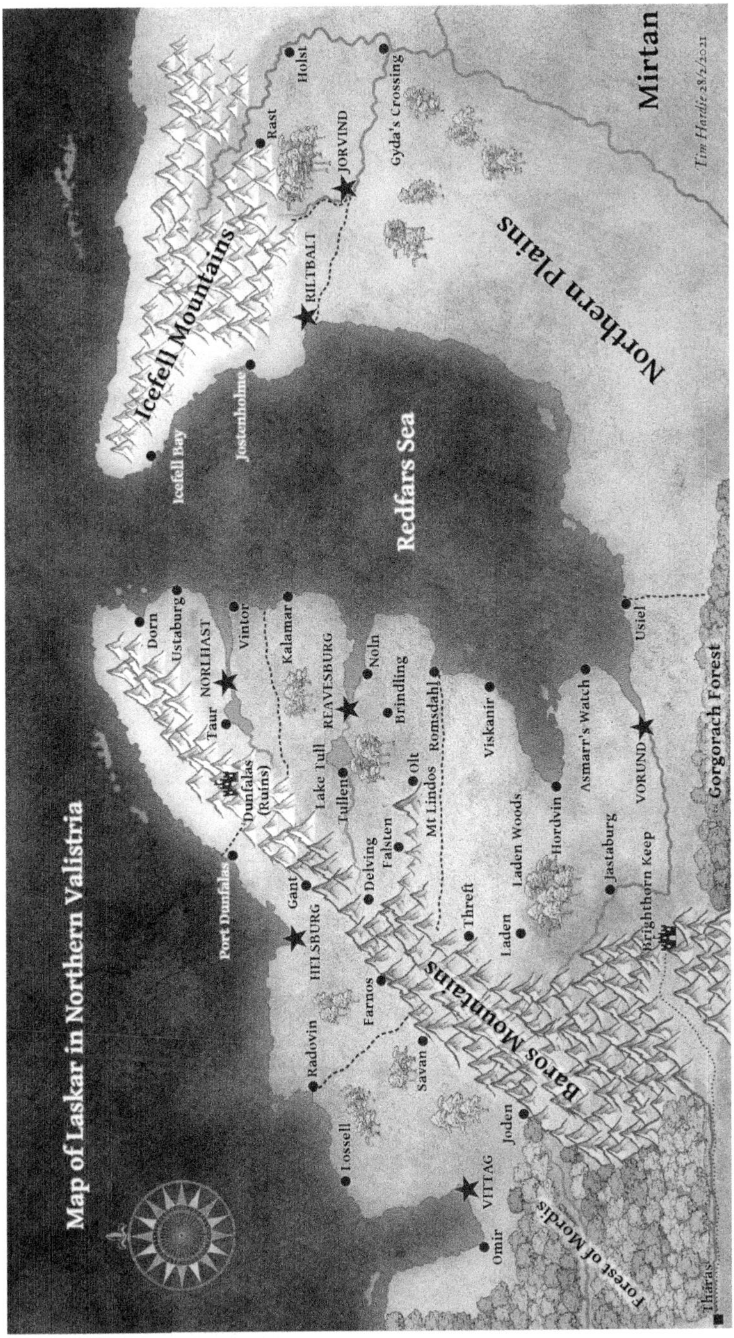

AUTHOR'S NOTE

Welcome to the third instalment of The Brotherhood of the Eagle series and the adventure set in the disputed lands of Laskar. At the back of this book you'll find a list, summarising the major and minor characters of the story, as well as their houses and their relationship to one another, which you may find useful.

PROLOGUE

Hardly able to sleep with excitement that night, I woke early and rushed to the window, where I was greeted by the morning sun glittering off the flat waters of the Redfars Sea. Father kept his promise and Brunn Fourwinds, captain of Marl's Pride, *welcomed us warmly on board. His crew scurried around him, making the ship ready. The great longship of fifty oars had been built by my father for one purpose – to strike fear and wage war on our rival clans. As its sail, emblazoned with the eagle of the Reavesburg Clan, unfurled and caught the wind we seemed to fly over the waves with each beat of the oars. We headed east down the widening estuary of the River Jelt, Reavesburg's wooden walls and the stone towers of Ulfkell's Keep rapidly receding from view.*

"You've lived up to your name this morning, Brunn!" Father remarked.

"Aye, Culdaff favours us, and no mistake," said Brunn, a wide white-toothed, amiable grin splitting his beard. The laws of Reave clearly stated the Laskan Clans turn their backs on the gods, following their failure that led to the War of the Avatars. However, sailors like Brunn still offered up their traditional prayers to Culdaff, avatar of the air and winds, and Nanquido, avatar of the waters and the seas. "So, what'll it be? The north coast to Kalamar or south to Romsdahl?"

"Neither," my father laughed. "Let's take her out into the open water and show the boy real seamanship."

I ran freely about the deck with my friend Bram, Brunn's son, both of us as at home on the water as on dry land. Brunn Fourwinds bellowed orders and his crew swiftly ran to obey his commands. My father looked on with satisfaction as the shore receded behind us and soon we were surrounded by the Redfars

Sea, with only a few noisy crows wheeling about high in the sky for company.

"Which way lies Riltbalt, Son?" my father asked as he clapped a cold hand on my shoulder. The question was an easy one and I grinned as I pointed east across the blue sea, imagining a distant coast I had never seen where the rival Riltbalt Clan's territory lay. I could see from the look Brunn exchanged with his son Bram that I was right. My father nodded in approval. "So you'll have no trouble telling me where Vorund lies."

"South," I laughed, though I felt a little uneasy. The Vorund Clan were our fiercest enemies, frequently raiding on our shores. "Father, you don't mean to set sail that far south, do you?" Seeing my worried expression, my father smiled.

"It's too late for that, Son. The Vorund Clan serve Adalrikr Asmarrson, Kinslayer and King of the North. He's a fearsome foe and not one to trifle with."

Brunn nodded in agreement. "Aye, but that didn't stop your thick-skulled brother attacking Viskanir, did it? If he'd only done the sensible thing and sworn fealty to Adalrikr then Tyrfingr Blackeyes would never have attacked Noln in revenge for his defiance. My son would still be alive."

Bram stepped forwards, his sandy head bowed. When he looked up at me he was older and I saw him as a young man in his teens, freckles standing out on his pale face, eyes staring blankly from the death mask he wore when I found him on the beaches of Noln in the aftermath of the battle. I gasped, taking a step backwards and turned to look at my father. His face was distorted, slack on one side, just as it had been in the weeks before his death. He was stretched out on the decks of Marl's Pride, *his broken body wrapped in thick furs.*

"I left you too soon," he mumbled, words slow and half-formed. "Left you and Jorik as boys with a man's burdens and troubles. And look where it led you."

"Cost me my head," added Brunn, pulling back the collar on his tunic to reveal the red cut encircling his neck, dark blood pouring from the wound.

"You traded my life for yours, by a hair's breadth," accused Bram, words cold and rimed with frost.

My eyes filled with tears as my hand moved to my neck, fingertips tracing the thin scar left by the fletching of Tyrfingr Blackeyes' arrow. He had missed his mark at Noln and found Bram instead, leaving him dying in front of me as he bled out over the yellow sand. I backed away from the scene, drawing my cloak around me. The wind had died, Marl's Pride *becalmed on the Redfars Sea beneath the bright blue sky. The oarsmen all sat idle on their benches, heads bowed in silence. A powerfully-built man turned slowly and fixed his gaze upon me and I looked into the face of my late brother, Jorik, his eyes red with grief.*

"My wife and son are dead," he whispered, blood dripping onto the deck from the stab wounds covering his body. Next to Jorik his wife Reesha sat nursing their murdered boy, Kolfinnar, blood soaking into Reesha's clothes from where Blackeyes had opened her throat.

"I'm sorry." It was all I could think to say.

"Tyrfingr told me you betrayed us," said Jorik. "You confessed as much in the Great Hall before the elders. Why? Why did you betray me? I loved you, Rothgar. You were my brother and this is how you repay me?"

I shook my head, retreating from their accusing eyes. "That's not true. I only confessed under torture – you have to believe me, I never betrayed my family."

Another of the oarsmen looked up and my grizzled old weapons master, Olfridor, spoke. "You had the makings of a great warrior, Rothgar. You would have been a fine jarl, serving your brother wisely when the time came for Finnvidor Einarrson to step aside."

Finnvidor, solemn-faced and serious as ever, even in death, shook his head. "No, you're wrong. Where this young man walks, death follows."

The rest of the crew turned to stare at me and I found myself looking into the faces of all the fallen members of the Brotherhood of the Eagle. Rugga and Patrick, amiable Ragni,

Old Gunnar, the Flint cousins. When I looked at Brandr I could hear the sounds of his widow, Maeva, weeping as she mourned. And there were more, the rows of dead oarsmen stretching back as far as I could see – a host of half-forgotten faces of those who had fallen for our cause. I wanted to run but there was nowhere to go, the still waters of the Redfars Sea encircling Marl's Pride. *The crew of the dead began to murmur, their breath smoking cold as it chilled the air.*

"Traitor."

"Arrogant fool."

"Murderer."

At the stern of the longship one man remained slumped over the oar across his knees, wrapped in a dark cloak. I took a hesitant step, trying to block out the growing noise of the crew as I approached. I recognised him even before he lifted his head.

"I'm no traitor," I said. "I didn't ask for any of this."

The Weeping Warrior, the shade of Sinarr left behind when his life was stolen by the durath, stood and reached out his hand, placing it on my shoulder. Tears ran down his face from his blind eyes and I realised he would mourn those slain by Adalrikr's treachery until the River of Time ceased its flow.

"These words come from your heart, not theirs. Your doubts cloud the truth of what is happening in the realm of the Real and beyond. You need to set your misgivings aside and hear what I need to tell you, before it's too late."

Silence. I turned and the longship was empty except for a figure standing next to the dragon-shaped prow. The sun was in my eyes and I held up my hand to shield them, bringing the dark shape of Tyrfingr Blackeyes into sharp relief. Adalrikr's jarl, the man now sitting in Reave's Chair in my old family home, swept his long, dark hair away from his face and drew a black-fletched arrow from the quiver by his side. He raised his bow and levelled it at me, drawing the string tight.

"I won't miss a second time," Tyrfingr said moments before releasing the arrow, sending it hissing through the air, unerringly towards my heart.

CHAPTER 1

I cried out in the darkness. Something was wrapped around me, pinning my arms to my chest. I thrashed from side to side, struggling to free myself and fell, landing hard. I lay there for a few moments, trying to gather my thoughts, my face pressed into the rush matting on the floor. I wrestled free of the blankets and ran a hand across my face, which was wet with tears. I could still see the faces of the dead. I missed my family so much and another sob wrenched itself free, a ripple of pain running up my back as I involuntarily moved my aching muscles.

As my eyes adjusted to the dark of my bed chambers in Romsdahl Castle I could make out the glowing red embers of the fire. Even though it was summer I shivered as I moved carefully towards the light until my bare feet felt the soft Oomrhani rug in front of the fireplace. I squatted down, hugging my bony knees against my chest, ignoring my body's protests as I rolled my shoulders to free up the knots and ease the pain running down my back. I placed another log onto the fire and watched as flames began to greedily lick around the wood. I stretched out my hands towards the glow, the welcome warmth touching my fingers. I still felt cold, a chill nestling in my heart and I rubbed the place where Tyrfingr's arrow would have struck had I not woken. I sat there, watching the log burn and the dream slowly began to fade, leaving me alone in the darkness.

***

At dawn one of the servants in Gautarr Falrufson's household brought food to break my fast. I ate the warm black bread and porridge with little enthusiasm, hardly tasting my meal as I washed it down with weak, watered wine. I was exhausted, a sense of dread settling over me as I thought about the day ahead. Joldir had once told me that when he forged a runeblade a piece of his soul went into each one. There was always a price for using magic. Now Joldir lay in the hospital, weak with fever as Arissa tended to his broken hands and, in his absence, Johan had appointed me as his artificer. I was a poor replacement but I knew the runes of warding and imprisonment by heart, so I had been put to use painting them inside Romsdahl Castle. After a week of work those symbols were all I could see by the end of the day, the black script swirling before me, even when I closed my eyes.

Outside I was met by Faraldr and Svafa, two warriors of the Brotherhood of the Eagle. After the battle of Romsdahl Johan had scoured the battlefield to find the weapons belonging to the fallen members of the Brotherhood. Joldir had worked tirelessly in the days leading up to the confrontation with Vorund's army, ensuring each blade carried by the Brotherhood bore at least three runes of power, making them too valuable to lose. Johan gifted some of the runeblades they recovered to Gautarr's warriors, a gesture that united the houses of the Reavesburg Clan still defying Adalrikr Kinslayer.

"Rothgar. You look tired," Faraldr said by way of greeting. The young warrior was one of the few surviving men from Johan Jokellsward's house of Kalamar, long since destroyed by Adalrikr's forces.

I nodded, glancing at Svafa, the runeblade of Old Gunnar hanging at his side. The Romsdahl warrior smiled, his crooked nose bent to one side of his face. Through the Sight I'd shared his experiences in the recent battle and felt a connection with the warrior, although the young man was completely unaware he possessed the gift.

"I didn't sleep well," I replied. "Let's get started."

Clutching my brushes and paint we made our way towards Gautarr's feasting hall. Johan insisted two of the

Brotherhood guarded me day and night. With Joldir injured I was the only person who could ward the castle and keep its occupants safe from the shadow spirits. After witnessing the dark magic wielded by the Vorund Clan, Gautarr insisted his family and warriors were protected. Johan had brought the portable runestones used to shield our camp during the long journey to the castle. However, Romsdahl Castle was far harder to secure and, when it became clear Joldir's recovery would take time, Johan asked for my help.

I had carefully painted the runes onto the main gates and doorways of the castle and I was now halfway through creating the intricate inscriptions around the doors and windows of the feasting hall. The durath had made no move against us since the battle, though I had no doubt they were present in the city of Romsdahl. Warding the castle to protect the Brotherhood was a necessary precaution. However, the work took its toll, sapping more of my energy each day.

As the morning wore on I could sense Svafa and Faraldr's frustration at my slow progress. I cursed under my breath at yet another mistake, taking a damp cloth and wiping away the paint, getting ready to inscribe the warding runes perfectly once more. Faraldr and Svafa glanced at each other as they watched me start again – this was the least desirable duty for the members of the Brotherhood. Magic and religion were distrusted by the Reavesburg Clan, so people were naturally suspicious after seeing how I'd used those arts to slay Sinarr the Cold One on the battlefield. With my broken body and stooped frame I no longer carried myself as a warrior, and cripples were despised in the clan, regardless of their mighty deeds.

Laughter rang out from the far side of the hall and I looked up, welcoming the distraction. Bandor entered arm in arm with his new bride, Freydja while his father, Johan, the Reavesburg Clan battle chief, followed in his footsteps, deep in conversation with Gautarr. Behind them came Damona,

Johan's wife, and Jora, the wife of Gautarr. They were guarded by more warriors of the Brotherhood, including Svan and Jolinn, their eyes watchful. Last night's dream about my lost childhood home stirred my memories as I looked at the newly-wedded couple. As the chief's son I'd been betrothed to Freydja, Gautarr's niece, since childhood. It was a strange thought that, had I not been tortured and broken at the hands of Tyrfingr Blackeyes after Ulfkell's Keep fell, I might now be looking at my wife. I reflected on how the life I once imagined for myself was gone forever and, distracted, black paint dripped from my paintbrush onto the stonework, also spattering the knees of my woollen breeches. A cornerstone of the treaty between the rival houses of Romsdahl and Kalamar was Gautarr's agreement Johan could claim Ulfkell's Keep, my former home, when the Vorund Clan were defeated and driven from our lands. Bandor saw me for the first time and smiled, running his hands through his bright red hair as the group approached.

"I'm not sure I like it," commented Gautarr, twisting his thick neck as he appraised the dark, flowing script decorating his hall. "This is my ancestral home – now one look at these wards is enough to turn my stomach."

I knew what Gautarr meant, though his words stung. When finished the runes took on a life of their own, their forms twisting and swirling as if alive when seen from the corner of your eye. If I spent too long in the hall I felt sick, so I tended to take most of my meals in my chambers, where the single ward on the outside of my door was tolerable enough.

"A necessity if your family is to be protected," Johan replied.

"Rothgar, are you alright?" Bandor asked me, looking at me with concern. The flowing script surrounding the tall glass windows of the hall crawled around the edges of my vision, making the room sway and I had to put a hand to the floor to steady myself.

"I'm fine." I bit the words off, not wanting to seem

weak in front of Gautarr as I rose unsteadily to my feet, shaking off Faraldr as he tried to take my arm. Johan asked Svafa how much I had completed this morning and I found myself unable to meet the gaze of Bandor and Freydja. I cast my eyes down, staring at my feet and the drops of black paint seeping their way between the stones on the floor. I saw Jorik in front of me, clutching his stomach in Ulfkell's Keep as his life bled away, his face full of doubt and grief as he died, wondering if I'd betrayed him. I closed my eyes, willing the image away.

"He's not well," Damona was saying. "He should take some fresh air."

"Come with me," said Jolinn, taking my arm in an iron grip as she steered me out of the hall.

Outside, the sun was shining and the courtyard was pleasantly warm. I dropped onto a bench, Jolinn taking a seat next to me as Faraldr and Svafa looked on from a discreet distance, talking to each other in an undertone.

"Myshall's bane, what's the matter with you?" asked Jolinn. Her blonde hair was closely shaved as ever, the bruises around her eye and jaw left by the recent battle starting to fade. I leaned back, enjoying the sun on my face. I took a deep breath, steadying my nerves as the nausea began to recede.

"Rothgar?" There was an edge to Jolinn's voice.

"I'm sorry. Damona was right – I needed some air, that's all. Painting those wards is gruelling. I'm sure that sounds ridiculous but I feel stretched thin, that's all."

Jolinn laughed humourlessly. "Having seen my friends possessed by the durath and fought the undead I'll not dismiss anything as mere fancy. I believe you, even if I don't understand what you're going through."

"I'm so tired," I admitted. "Sometimes I feel like the task before us is insurmountable. So many of the Brotherhood have died and Joldir's badly hurt." I shrugged. "What can one man do in the face of so much evil? I wish I had Johan's unshakeable self-belief."

Jolinn looked at me for a time. "I'm sure Johan has his doubts too, just like the rest of us. Remember, you were the one who killed Sinarr the Cold One and turned the battle of Romsdahl in our favour. Those were the actions of a true warrior, facing our enemies even when the cause seemed hopeless."

I rose from the bench and walked off, thinking about her words. Jolinn fell into step next to me, Svafa and Faraldr jogging to keep up as we walked out of the castle gates and through the city streets. We climbed up onto Romsdahl's outer defensive wall, the wind buffeting the four of us. Svafa put out a hand to steady me as I staggered towards the edge when a strong gust tugged at my cloak.

"Careful."

Faraldr scowled, face screwed up tight as we were blasted by sand and grit picked up from the seashore below the cliffs. "I'm not happy about this. This isn't the day for a pleasant stroll and Rothgar's meant to be working."

Jolinn rounded on him. "Does he look well enough to be working, Faraldr? He's exhausted – can't you see that?"

I gently shrugged off Svafa's hand and leaned on the thick walls between the battlements, peering out across the battlefield. I could see Gautarr's thralls raising a burial mound over the burned bones of the fallen Reavesburg warriors. In northern Reavesburg we simply built pyres for the honoured dead. I was unsure how I felt about this southern fashion for crumbling tombs and barrows. Other thralls were dismantling the remaining parts of the palisade raised by the Vorund Clan to protect their camp during the year-long siege. Their siege engines were also being salvaged under the watchful eye of Petr Hamarrson, Johan's loyal young second, ensuring our enemy's handiwork wouldn't be wasted.

Elsewhere Vorund's warriors lay where they'd fallen, bones stark white against the grass, picked clean by dark clouds of crows. Some birds still lingered one week on from the battle, picking over the last morsels of rotting meat left on the bodies. We estimated one and a half thousand men of the Vorund Clan died that day or soon afterwards, hunted as far as the border by Adakan's warriors. If the Vorund Clan ever dared to return to Romsdahl, they would have to cross a field filled with the bleached bones of their kin, a fate shared by the warriors of the Reavesburg Clan who'd sided with Adalrikr. Gautarr made an exception for his dishonoured bannerman from Olt; Hrodi Myndillson and his son Radholf. They had been interred in one of the vaults beneath Romsdahl Castle. Above their tomb the mason had inscribed *'Oath breakers and traitors – the house of Romsdahl never forgets'*. Jolinn, Old Hrodi's estranged illegitimate daughter, approved, shrugging off the shame on her own house with disinterest. Now she spoke for the warriors of Olt who had heeded Johan's call to arms. The rest of that divided house served her fawning nephew, Alfarr Radholfson, who had pledged himself to Adalrikr, still pronouncing him King of the North.

Neither Johan nor Gautarr knew about Haarl, another childhood friend I'd lost to war. Haarl might have fought for Adalrikr but his body resided in the Reavesburg Clan burial mound after my intervention. I owed his widow, Desta, that much. Guilt washed over me as I thought of her, far off in Reavesburg, and wondered if she'd heard the news of Haarl's death. Their son, Finn, would grow up without a father as a result of this war. How many more innocent lives would be blighted before this was over?

"Rothgar?" Jolinn's voice stirred me from my thoughts.

"I do feel better," I confessed. "I didn't realise how much I needed to be away from Romsdahl Castle. The runes ... they have an effect on me, after a time."

Jolinn turned to Svafa and Faraldr. "You two, get lost. Think of it as a day off you can spend in one of the taverns or with Ekkill's whores, if that's your fancy."

"We're here to guard Rothgar," Faraldr replied stubbornly.

Jolinn was a tall woman, six inches higher than both of them, and they shrank away as she stared down at them on that windswept wall. "I'm a speaker at the clan moot for the warriors of Olt and the mid-lands of Reavesburg, so I think my word carries more weight than yours. Do you really think anything will happen to him while I'm here?" She glanced down at the sword hanging by her side, before fixing them both with her fierce ice-cold blue eyes.

***

"Thank you."

Jolinn arched an eyebrow above her bruised cheek and temple, legs dangling over the edge of the cliffs. "You were there with me when my father died. You showed him mercy in his final moments, staying with him so he didn't die alone when I couldn't find it in myself to face him. You were kind to him, even though he betrayed you. You were kind to me. I won't forget that."

She picked up a small stone and tossed it idly over the edge of the cliff. We both watched it plummet towards the black rocks on the shore below, losing sight of it long before it reached the ground. We sat there together for a time, listening to the sea birds' calls as they wheeled in the sky, others diving into the waters of the Redfars Sea to hunt for fish. The salt-tinged air was fresh and clean and the headache behind my eyes lifted, the tension in my shoulders easing as my knotted muscles began to relax.

"I'm worried about you," Jolinn said. "It's like you're hiding in the shadows. You were the one who brought the armies of Johan and Gautarr together. You killed Sinarr the Cold One, proving Kolfinnar's blood runs strong in your veins, a worthy successor to a line of chiefs going back to the time of Marl."

"I walked away from Reave's Chair when I pledged my

loyalty to Johan Jokellsward. Ulfkell's Keep isn't my birth right anymore."

"Rothgar, you're an intelligent young man, someone of influence with rare skills." Jolinn waved a hand at the hilt of her runeblade. "I can use this but so can more than three thousand other warriors who follow Johan as battle chief. What you can do is nothing short of remarkable and yet you're letting Johan and Gautarr work you to death. Tell me, where's the sense in that?"

I sat on the edge of the cliff, leaning further back than Jolinn out of respect for the strong wind. Grey clouds scurried across the sky above the choppy waters and I could see squally showers gathering further out to sea. Jolinn gave me a crooked smile, impervious to the wind and fearless as she defied Culdaff atop the cliffs.

Jolinn looked at me for a long time. "I'm a shieldmaiden who grew up in a whorehouse, sired by a good for nothing traitor. I know how it feels to not fit in and be unsure of your place in this world. You were born to be a jarl, if not the chief of your clan. The hardships you've suffered have blinded you to what still could be, if you had the confidence to reach out and take it."

"Etta says –"

"I don't care what the old crone thinks. What do you think? What do *you* want?"

I leant my head back, letting the wind run its fingers through my hair. "Let's go back to Romsdahl. It's time I saw my friends."

Jolinn sprang to her feet and held out her hand, helping me up, her grip strong, palm calloused from hours spent each week in the sparring circle. It reminded me of Ulfkell's Keep and Olfridor's relentless training. I wondered what he would have made of me now.

As we neared Romsdahl we had to start weaving between the bodies scattered over the ground, often hidden behind tussocks of long grass waving in the strong breeze.

It struck me these warriors might still be alive if the battle had gone in Vorund's favour. They were dead because of me. Sensing a change in the weather as the rainclouds approached I glanced back, wondering if we had time to get under cover. I cried out in surprise as I saw the Weeping Warrior standing by the cliff edge, dressed for war. His back was to me, long hair streaming in the wind, cloak billowing out. He raised his finger, pointing out to sea. All I could see were the approaching showers and when I looked again at the spot where he had been standing he was nowhere to be seen.

CHAPTER 2

Nuna was wide awake despite the lateness of the hour. Her bodyguard, Brosa, stood by her side, ever watchful. She could tell he was tense as they waited down by the docks with three other guards; all men Brosa said she could trust with her life. The sky was clear and the half-moon shone brightly, washing the cobbled stones and wooden jetties with pale white light. The noise of the water lapping on the deserted quayside was loud – a constant rhythmic slap. In a few hours the docks would be full of noise, laughter and shouting as the fishermen and whalers landed, bringing their catch ashore for the morning markets. Now, though, the place belonged to them alone. Brosa and Sigurd had both argued against Nuna making the journey but she had been adamant. Her husband, Karas Greystorm, was closely watched by Valdimarr's men. As a woman Nuna was afforded less attention and someone had to speak on behalf of the Greystorm House. This moment was too important to be left to emissaries and messengers.

"I don't like this," muttered Brosa. The moonlight had turned his red hair dull silver. At twenty-four Brosa was young to hold the position as her bodyguard. He'd begun sporting a closely-cropped beard on his handsome features in an attempt to appear older.

Nuna sighed. "I'll not waste words debating the same point. Our people need to see the house of Greystorm is together with them on this and I won't have others risk their lives while I hide in my chambers."

Brosa scowled. "Coming here is hardly making my duties easier, is it my lady? I swore to keep you safe. If this is a trap …"

"Shush." One of the other warriors with them, Curren, held his finger to his lips.

Nuna strained her ears. There it was, the faint sound of an oar dipping into the water. Further out to sea a dark shadow emerged as a small rowing boat glided into view. With a soft thump it came to rest against the side of the jetty and two men swiftly climbed ashore, two more remaining in the boat.

"Are my brothers waiting for me?" hissed one of the men on the jetty.

"The Brotherhood welcomes those loyal to the cause," Brosa replied. Nuna felt proud at those words – the Brotherhood was led by the jarls of Reavesburg; her own clan. They had defied Adalrikr and as a consequence the fires of resistance were now being stoked in the Norlhast Clan.

The two men approached cautiously, hands never straying far from their weapons. Brosa stepped forwards and held out his hand. One of the visitors took it in his, shaking his arm vigorously.

"Brosa. You've grown tall and broad. That's quite a grip you have." The man pulled down his hood to reveal a tangle of long, grey hair, tied back into a scruffy ponytail. His face was craggy and scarred, although his smile was warm.

"Orglyr the Grimm. It must be ten years since we last met."

"At least." Orglyr's voice had a rough quality. "You know Fundinn, my second?"

"By reputation," Brosa replied, acknowledging the huge warrior who was keeping watch at Orglyr's back. "There's someone here you need to meet."

Nuna stepped forwards, drawing back the fur-trimmed hood on her cloak to reveal her distinctive long blonde hair. She bowed her head in greeting to one of Norlhast's most famous warriors.

"It's an honour to meet you, Orglyr. I've heard of your

deeds and welcome you to the cause of the Brotherhood. I am Nuna Karaswyfe, Lady of Norlhast Keep."

Orglyr looked at her carefully, dropping stiffly to one knee as he bowed his head and took her hand in both of his. "My lady. I heard how your marriage to our chief has restored him. I'm your servant but you should know those deeds you speak of took place many years ago. I've been tending to my flocks near Dorn these past ten years."

"Your name still carries weight among our people," Nuna told him, bidding him to rise. "My husband needs you if we're to shake off the yoke of Adalrikr Kinslayer. The Norlhast Clan is preparing to rise up and honour the promise my husband made to my late brother. Word has reached us that the Reavesburg Clan is fighting Adalrikr's army and has won a great victory in Romsdahl, slaying Sinarr the Cold One and scattering his forces. They are led by Johan Jokellsward, my brother's jarl, under the banner of the Brotherhood of the Eagle and we believe they intend to defeat the Vorund Clan once and for all. To prevail they need our aid. Karas is determined to honour his oath of alliance with the Reavesburg Clan, one that he was forced to break when Tyrfingr Blackeyes took Ulfkell's Keep. If you want to restore Karas' honour then he needs enough men to overthrow the Vorund Clan's occupation here and go to war."

Orglyr grinned, a wolfish expression on his face. "There's fire in your belly for such a young woman, that's for sure. Tell Karas I'm glad he sent for me. When Karas became chief he showed me mercy, even though I was Bekan's man. My axe might not be as swift as it was back then but there are plenty of good men who'll rally to Karas' banner if I speak on his behalf."

Nuna felt butterflies in her stomach at those words, a thrill running through her. Her husband had taken the title of clan chief from Bekan Bekansson in single combat, dividing the Norlhast Clan at the time, leaving them weakened and ultimately unable to resist when Adalrikr claimed their lands. Orglyr was crucial to their plans to unite them once more, bringing Bekan's loyal followers together under Karas Greystorm's banner. Karas' act of mercy to Bekan's former jarl might be the single most important decision he had made as chief.

"I'm indebted to you, Orglyr, as is my husband. You must raise your army in secret. When you're ready to move, send word and we will bring Valdimarr down and cast out the Vorund Clan from our lands for good."

Orglyr smiled, licking his lips, eyes glittering as they fixed on the middle distance. "I always wondered why your husband spared me. This was the reason – the banner of the whale will fly proudly once more."

"Men approach," said Fundinn quietly, jerking his head towards the far end of the docks.

"We must go," Brosa told her, gently taking her arm.

"You'll hear from me soon," said Orglyr, pulling his hood back over his head and hurrying with Fundinn back to their small rowing boat.

Brosa's warriors moved swiftly into the shadows of the alley where they had been waiting. Nuna glanced back to see that Orglyr's men had already started rowing back out to sea, the boat shrinking into the distance.

"They'll be fine," Brosa told her. "Quickly, we have to move. We can't stay here."

Brosa led them through a maze of alleys, pausing once or twice to check the way was clear as they hurried back towards the keep. He cursed as another Vorund patrol appeared in the distance.

"That moon is too bright," Curren observed. "We need to get off the streets."

"This way," Brosa replied, changing direction and making his way back towards the docks.

They reached the door of a modest house and Brosa knocked three times. Nuna held her breath, glancing around anxiously as she heard booted feet, the sound growing ever closer. There was a creak as the door opened a fraction and Luta, Kalfr's wife, peered through the narrow gap. She gasped and hurriedly ushered them inside.

"I'm sorry, Luta, we had no choice," Brosa told her.

Luta was a broad lady of small stature, although she wasn't intimidated by the warriors filling her home, jabbing a finger into Brosa's chest as she spoke in an angry whisper.

"Really? You had no choice bringing *her* here tonight? What were you thinking? What if Valdimarr's warriors find her? Everything will be ruined."

A door opened from another room in the house and a sleepy-looking Kalfr appeared, rubbing his face and patting down various spikes in his blond hair. Short but stocky, Kalfr was Sigurd's younger brother and a key supporter of Karas. Nuna had never forgotten how Kalfr had been a good friend to her younger brother, Rothgar, before his execution – no, his *murder*, by Tyrfingr Blackeyes. Kalfr's support of Rothgar when he first came to Norlhast to propose her marriage to Karas and the alliance of their two clans had proved invaluable. There was no one in Norlhast Nuna trusted more.

"Move away from the door and come inside," Kalfr said.

"Father, what's going on?" asked Tassi, Kalfr's eldest son, who was standing in another doorway looking worried.

"Hush, go back to bed," Luta told him, taking his shoulder and steering him back the way he'd come.

There wasn't much space in Kalfr and Luta's bedroom, each of them trying to be quiet and not bump into each other in the darkness. Nuna could hear Luta's voice in the room next door, softly trying to calm their four children. She felt a pang of guilt, realising she'd put them all in grave danger. She closed her eyes, offering up a prayer to Dinuvillan that the Vorund patrol hadn't seen them enter the house.

"Luta's right," Kalfr whispered in the darkness. "What's Nuna doing here?"

"It was agreed I would come," Nuna replied. "Karas and Sigurd were against it but I had to meet Orglyr and know for myself he could be trusted. Too much depends on him – I wasn't going to place my life and those I love into the hands of a man I'd never met."

"And if you'd been caught?" Kalfr hissed.

"My clandestine night time meeting with Brosa would have been a great scandal," Nuna told him. One of the warriors chuckled and Nuna could almost feel the heat from Brosa's face as he blushed.

Such a ruse was not so outlandish. Nobles often had affairs and to be accompanied by trusted guards during such surreptitious meetings was not unusual. Whilst Karas had been a loving husband since their marriage it was an open secret he was unable to perform all his marital duties. The blood plague that killed his last wife and their two children had left its mark in other ways. She was a young woman and it would not be so strange to seek solace in another man. Nuna was determined to turn anything she could to her advantage, if it meant they would be free from Valdimarr ruling their land in Adalrikr's name.

The Vorund patrol passed by Kalfr and Luta's house and a few minutes later Nuna could hear them talking with another group of guards watching the docks. Soon the voices faded away and it was silent once more, except for Luta's soothing tones as she calmed her daughter, Gilla.

"You need to get back to the keep while you can," Kalfr told her. "We'll meet there tomorrow and you can tell me everything."

Nuna nodded, reaching out to squeeze his hand in silent thanks. With Brosa taking the lead they slipped out into the darkness, sticking to the shadows cast by the moon as they hurried back to Norlhast Keep.

CHAPTER 3

Thengill laughed hard, dark brows creasing together as he slapped the table, cups jumping with the impact. Skari One-Eye shook his head, giving the leader of his crew, Ulfarr, a sidelong glance. The grin on One-Eye's face softened the scar that ran from under the eye patch he wore on his left side, almost giving him a friendly aspect. Almost.

Myr the Silent sat on the other side of the table to me, a thin smile on his lips, as he nursed his ale. The shaven-headed warrior was the last original member of Ulfarr's diminishing band. I wondered what Myr thought about recent events, watching as Ulfarr's warriors died one by one in Johan Jokellsward's service. Without a tongue he was unlikely to ever share them with me, unless I probed his mind with the Sight. I had used the ability on plenty of other people in the past but the thought of turning it on Myr felt wrong. Already mute when he joined Ulfarr, his story belonged to him alone.

Ulfarr grinned, stroking his grey-streaked black beard. This was a hard crew, each man powerfully built, veterans of countless battles and skirmishes and none of them strangers to killing. I perched on my chair, cloaked wrapped around my skinny frame to keep warm, despite the summer heat. We couldn't be more different but after everything we'd shared there was a bond between us.

"So?" pressed Thengill.

"What?" Ulfarr asked.

Thengill tutted. "You know perfectly well what. Finish the story. What happened next?"

Ulfarr sighed. "If you insist. There I was, halfway

through the window, legs dangling outside and my hand gripping the purse. Trouble was my sword belt is caught on the frame and I'm damned if I can figure out how to untangle myself. I'm using my free hand to try and unhook it when I hear footsteps and look round to see that snooty couple have returned to their room. They're both standing there, gawping at me and there's this thin, shrill noise, coming out of the woman, rising in pitch with each second."

"It served them right," interjected Skari. "They spoke to me in the street like I was dirt. Hurt my feelings."

Thengill looked unconvinced. "Hmm."

Ulfarr took a long draught of Joldir's ale and continued his story. "Going out the window wasn't an option, so I heaved myself back into the room. Didn't go too well, 'cause I landed on my backside, breaking the dressing table on my way. The woman's screaming now and as I scramble to my feet her husband is skipping about like a frightened rabbit. He knows he should be challenging me and demanding the return of his money. Instead, though, his eyes keep flicking to the sword at my side and I can tell he's crapping himself.

"In a situation like this, you have to keep your head, so while those two are flapping in front of me I got to my feet with all the dignity I could muster, brushing the dust off my cloak and pocketing their purse before their eyes. Then I gave them a short bow and said 'I'm terribly sorry for the intrusion. I don't think this is my room, after all.' With that, I strode straight past them to the door, flung it open and made my escape."

"Very calm and collected," I observed.

Skari chuckled. "Patrick was *furious* when he found out, remember?"

"Aye, that he was," Ulfarr agreed. "Up until then he'd missed the whole thing, trying to convince the serving maid at the bar that he really was a Berian knight. Think he had her believing him right up until the moment I ran downstairs, those nobles hard on my heels. They were both shrieking that I was a thief, although they were talking over each other so loudly no one could make out what they were saying."

Skari took up the story. "Patrick's face is a picture, I can tell you. While he's still trying to speak I put my hands on the shoulders of Callis and Olaf and said to them and the rest of our crew 'Drink up, lads. Time to go.'"

"It's not exactly an inspiring tale of good versus evil, is it?" Jolinn commented archly from her chair by the fireside. She was sitting opposite Joldir, who was staring deep into the flames crackling in the hearth.

"Ahh, true. This was long before we'd seen the light and become heroes of the Reavesburg Clan," Ulfarr told her. "I'm not proud of being run out of that town but I won't pretend to be something I'm not, either. The thing to remember is Johan's pardoned us for our crimes, even the incompetent ones."

I folded my arms, shaking my head. "And the moral of this story?"

"Next time someone insults Skari One-Eye, I'm just going to let it slide," Ulfarr declared.

I got up from the table, laughing with the rest of them, and wandered over to the fireside. Jolinn had been right to get me away from the castle. Here in Joldir's home, nestled under the defensive walls of Romsdahl, I felt more myself in the warm company of friends.

Joldir didn't look well, appearing older than his thirty-five years. He was still recovering from his injuries on the battlefield and the subsequent fever that wracked his body as he lay in the hospital, tended by Ingirith and Arissa. My eyes were involuntarily drawn to his hands, tucked under his armpits in a vain attempt to hide them.

"What was it you told me when I came to you last year, more dead than alive?" I said cheerfully. "'You need to give it time and let your body do its work'. Something like that, anyway."

"I don't make the best patient," Joldir replied, scowling as he put his hands out in front of him, resting them on his knees.

I grimaced as I looked down on those twisted fingers, which had been blasted and burned when Joldir fought Sinarr. The red burns were visibly healing, Arissa's poultice having drawn out an infection that might otherwise have cost him both hands. Bandages still covered his palms, where the burns had been deeper. I stared at his warped fingers as Joldir flexed them, arms shaking with the effort as he tried to draw his fingertips together. It was hard to watch Joldir facing similar challenges to my own – the cost of fighting against Adalrikr's rule had been high for both of us.

Joldir sighed. "What's done is done. Whilst I might not be much use as Johan's artificer these days I have two good apprentices in you and Leif to carry on my work. Although Jolinn tells me you've found it difficult warding Romsdahl Castle."

I nodded, my eyes drawn to the runes around the doorway of Joldir's home. The familiar flowing script was the distinctive handiwork of young Leif, the third member of our Fellowship. Joldir tutted as I explained the areas of the castle I had completed.

"There's no need for you to ward the main door to the feasting hall as long as the entrances to the castle itself have been attended to."

"Johan agreed to provide Gautarr with two lines of defence as part of their pact," I explained, glancing over in Thengill's direction as he chatted with Skari, Ulfarr and Myr. "Gautarr's still unhappy at how Thengill's life was spared and Johan didn't want to give any cause for an argument."

"Gautarr should be delighted, the amount he saved on Freydja's dowry," Jolinn said with a wry grin.

"As far as Gautarr is concerned Thengill's a member of the Vorund Clan and he thinks Johan still owes him for his clemency. He's convinced Johan was behind the scheme to make him look foolish, although I know it was Bandor's own idea. Anyway, whatever the rights and wrongs of the argument the price of keeping the peace was additional protection for Gautarr's family. Their chambers are accessed from the feasting hall and Gautarr tells me his wife sleeps better knowing the durath can't come close."

Joldir flexed his hands again, working on the exercises Arissa had tasked him to complete each day to aid his recovery. It had been a condition of her releasing him from hospital. Pain crossed his features, his eyes half-closed in concentration as he tried to make his body obey his commands.

"At least Gautarr is taking the threat of the durath seriously," Joldir said. "I thought that might be Johan's biggest challenge, persuading him to join our cause. Sinarr did us a favour in that respect, facing us on the field and revealing his dark powers."

Everyone stopped talking as a fist pounded on the door of Joldir's townhouse. Ulfarr raised his eyebrows and got up from the table to open the door. Adakan was waiting outside, arms folded, surrounded by warriors including Svafa and Faraldr, both of whom looked chastened.

"I understand Rothgar Kolfinnarson is here." It wasn't a question. Adakan's dark eyes bored into me. "I'm an elder of the eastern men and a speaker of the clan moot. I shouldn't have to run errands locating those who shirk their duties, not least when two warriors have been assigned to guard them." Adakan cast a withering look at Faraldr and Svafa.

Ulfarr looked ready to protest as I got to my feet and shuffled towards the doorway, clapping him on the back. I stretched and gave a heavy sigh as I prepared to resume the tedious task of warding the feasting hall.

***

My head was pounding once I'd retired to my chambers later that night. My eyes ached and when I closed them the runes swirled in front of me in the darkness. Poor Svafa and Faraldr had been put in an impossible position – told to do one thing by one elder, only for the command to be reversed by a second. Although Adakan had rebuked them Jolinn was right – a day's break had been enough to straighten my mind and enable me to finish the task. I doubted Adakan would see it that way.

I shivered, turning onto my side and pulling the bedcovers around me. With the key sites around Romsdahl warded by me and Leif the city was protected from the durath. Joldir's individual runestones were also deployed in the city in varying locations each day, used to discourage the durath from venturing inside. So far, none had made the attempt, which didn't make me feel safe. Sooner or later our enemies would make a move, probably when the army left to begin the next offensive against the Vorund Clan. The hospital was virtually empty, Arissa and her helpers now only tending a few warriors recovering from more serious wounds, which meant they would never fight again. The steady flow of men arriving at Romsdahl each day to join the call to arms, encouraged by our recent victory, had seen five hundred more swords swell our ranks. Now, though, that stream of warriors had become a trickle and there was talk of moving on and finding our next target before the summer season was over.

What would I do then? As a member of the Brotherhood I was entitled to break bread with Johan and his men and had always given them my counsel. However, the debilitating effects of warding the castle had taken their toll, leaving me exhausted. I'd been absent from the Brothers' Table, neglected Bandor, my oldest and closest friend, and become distant from Johan's court. I knew people were afraid of me after seeing me use magic to destroy Sinarr and I'd avoided their company, giving them what they wanted as I focused on my chores. I'd become lost in myself, until Jolinn's timely intervention. It was time to make changes and play my part once more.

I sat up in bed, waiting for the wave of nausea to subside. My bare feet touched the cold floorboards as I padded over to the cabinet, fingers tracing the door in the darkness. I opened it and paused, hand hovering over the small bottle of ataraxia I used to dull the Sight. I knew it would provide relief from my discomfort even as something stayed my hand. I closed the door and returned to bed, rolling this way and that as I tried to get comfortable. The Sight was all I had left and I wasn't ready to set it aside, even for just a few days. I reached out with it now, seizing the opportunity to escape my life in Romsdahl. I wanted to learn more about Nuna and events in Norlhast, but the Path proved fickle, drawing my mind to an altogether different place.

CHAPTER 4

Hallerna shivered as she was herded along with the rest of her frightened companions from Riltbalt, Vorund warriors flanking them as they stumbled down the stairs. The dozen tributes spilled out into a vast central chamber swathed in darkness, the light from the torches set in sconces on the circular wall dissipating within a few inches of their source. She heard footsteps and saw a young man approach, his polished steel armour reminding her of stories she'd heard of the western Berian knights. He carried a sword at his side and his long hair was framed by a silver circlet. Hallerna would have thought him handsome, but his blue eyes were cold when they regarded her and under one of them there was a weeping cut or sore, the blood oozing from the wound appearing black in the gloom. Accompanying the man were six guards, each of them wearing the traditional warrior garb of the Vorund Clan, covered in chainmail and carrying shields emblazoned with the sigil of the bear. They were wearing helmets with a full face-guard, disguising their features. As they approached the temperature dropped, the hairs on Hallerna's arms standing on end as she hugged herself, trying to shy away from her captors. Even the Vorund warriors who had brought them to this place seemed wary of the new arrivals, backing away silently, remaining at the foot of the stairs to prevent any hope of escape.

"Tributes from the Riltbalt Clan," announced one of her captors.

"Kneel before your king," replied one of the men wearing a face-guard.

All but one of the tributes followed the order instantly.

They had learned on the voyage across the Redfars Sea that any sign of defiance was swiftly punished. Hallerna held her breath, shocked as the young man, Vegrim, stood there, straight-backed as Vorund's king approached. She would have guessed that if anyone was going to cause trouble it would be him.

"I am Adalrikr Asmarrson, King of the North," the scarred king announced. "You are my subject and have been offered up to me by your clan to do with as I wish. You belong to me and you will kneel."

Vegrim swallowed, a sheen of sweat on his face as he stared back at Adalrikr. Hallerna had no time for the gods but she found herself offering up a prayer to Dinuvillan all the same. One of Adalrikr's honour guard strode up and drove a swift punch into Vegrim's gut, dropping him onto the floor, gasping and retching. Adalrikr smiled, fresh blood welling up from the wound on his face.

"This one has spirit," he said, to muted laughter from the warriors in the chamber as the man writhed on the floor, doubled over in agony.

Adalrikr bent down towards Vegrim. Hallerna thought he was going to do him some harm. Instead, Adalrikr merely squatted in front of his prisoner, a look of concentration on his face. Finally he stood up straight, shaking his head.

"Thrall," he announced. At once, one of the guards at the staircase advanced and dragged Vegrim away into the darkness, his coughing soon fading away.

Adalrikr repeated the procedure with two more of the tributes, watched closely by his personal guards. Both times he announced they were to become thralls, and the young man and woman were both taken into the darkness in the same direction as Vegrim, heading towards a life of slavery. Hallerna flinched when Adalrikr approached. His guards gave off a putrid odour, the stench mixed with cold air that flowed around their bodies, chilling her heart. In contrast,

Adalrikr's hand was warm as it gently stroked her cheek, fingers curling under her chin as he forced her to look into his eyes. Up close, the wound on Adalrikr's face writhed, the flesh surrounding the cut dead and mottled. Adalrikr had applied makeup to disguise the injury but more black blood was welling up in the wound and it dripped down his cheek, creating thin, dark rivulets.

"Now, I could feel *your* presence, young lady, from the top of those stairs. Tell me, what is your name?" Adalrikr's voice was soft and cultured, though it did nothing to put her at ease.

"Hallerna," she whispered. "My lord, please, I beg you to show me mercy and let me return home. I was taken from my family when they lost everything after Riltbalt fell …" Tears welled up as she remembered her parents pleading with her captors at the dockside as the tributes were loaded into the longship.

"It broke their hearts to see their only child board that ship," Adalrikr told her, making her start. "I know you want to see them again. Your family loved you but a new life awaits you here in Vorund Fastness. Don't be afraid, young lady. Come with me. The Calling draws you near."

His voice was impossible to resist and Hallerna found herself reaching up to take Adalrikr's hand as he raised her to her feet. She thought she heard the remaining tributes calling her name but realised she was mistaken since the sound was coming from in front of her, not behind. Hand in hand with Adalrikr, Hallerna walked into the centre of the chamber, where the darkness seemed to swell, coil and weave around her. She turned to look at Adalrikr, the only thing she could see.

"This is a great honour," Adalrikr whispered in her ear, breath warm as it caressed her cheek and neck.

The shadows in the chamber gathered, swirling around the pair. Hallerna drew in a breath to scream for help, heart pounding as panic gripped her. The shadows coiled around her, choking off the air, leaving her gasping as it knotted around her hands and feet, tightened the grip on her chest, forcing her to her knees. Hallerna felt a moment of pure terror before a sensation like hot knives drove itself into her skull –

***

I was hurled from my bed, slamming into the stone wall on the other side of my room. I saw stars as my teeth snapped together and I slid onto the floor, tasting blood in my mouth. Moments later I vomited, a blinding headache tearing through my skull as I lay curled on the floor, screaming.

***

Dawn's first watery light marked a new day, although it was a while before I felt well enough to open the shutters. By then the sun peered out between the clouds, a glittering sliver of white gold rippling as it was reflected on the sea. My two guards were waiting patiently for me – Domarr the Oak, Gautarr's broad-shouldered illegitimate nephew, and Varinn, another of Johan's warriors from Kalamar, the old man rubbing his stubbled face as he wiped sleep from his eyes. The three of us slipped through the castle gates and wended our way along the streets. Already people were going about their business, carrying wares, setting up market stalls, opening the shutters to their shops. With the vanquishing of the Vorund Clan life in Romsdahl had returned to normal, at least on the surface. While Johan's army was barracked in the city there was money to be made – until they departed to fight Adalrikr Kinslayer once more.

Domarr turned, sniffing the air and I caught the scent too – freshly baked bread. I was unable to face the thought of food, bile rising in my throat at the very idea and I hurried on, much to Domarr's disappointment.

"Where are we heading?" Varinn asked, also looking longingly behind him at the bakery.

"Etta's house," I replied.

Varinn exchanged a glance with Domarr. "Don't

expect to get breakfast there," he told him. "Not unless you like hot tea." Domarr scowled, saying nothing.

We soon reached Etta's tiny home, which was next door to the larger house Joldir occupied. The leaders of the Brotherhood and its best warriors had been found lodgings in Romsdahl Castle. The remaining people who had accompanied Johan's army on their march south were now camped outside the city walls, making use of the remains of the defensive palisade that until recently protected the Vorund Clan. A smaller number of those favoured by the Brotherhood had been found places to live within the city by Gautarr, generally in homes abandoned by those killed in the war or who had fled Reavesburg's lands for somewhere safer.

At first Etta had refused to leave her tent in the camp, telling anyone who would listen it had been good enough for her so far and she didn't much fancy being Gautarr Falrufson's guest. Exasperated, Johan had finally convinced her to come within the protection of the city walls on the pretext it made it easier for him to visit her for counsel. Joldir had agreed to take the house next door so there was someone nearby who could look out for her, a point Etta grudgingly accepted. As we approached I saw Arissa, Joldir's adopted daughter and the Brotherhood's chief healer, open Etta's door. She smiled as she saw me, drawing up the hood of her cloak to ward off the morning chill, hiding her auburn hair. I reached out and hugged the young woman.

"Arissa. It's good to see you."

"Joldir was so pleased to see you yesterday, Rothgar. You shouldn't leave it so long between your visits. Varinn, Domarr – good morning to you, too." Domarr gave a short nod, staring down at his boots whilst Varinn smiled and patted her arm.

"Off to the hospital, lass?" he asked.

"Yes, there's still work to do there and Maeva will already be waiting for me."

"Say if you need any help," Varinn told her, crow's feet

crinkling around his eyes as he grinned. "I'm on guard duty today but I don't mind lending a hand tomorrow."

Arissa took Varinn's calloused hand in hers. "Thank you. There are only a few people left to tend these days."

"Better they'd died," Domarr told her bluntly. "They'll never fight again and with you helping keep them alive they'll be left crippled and broken – less than men. I'd rather walk into Navan's Halls as a warrior with my head held high. Left to live a half-life thanks to your healing arts – that's no life at all." Domarr cast a glance in my direction as he spoke, appraising my stooped posture, his lip curled with disdain. Arissa and Varinn both stared at him and he shrugged, unrepentant.

I turned to Arissa. "Is she in good spirits?"

She arched an eyebrow. "Feisty as ever."

I nodded at Varinn and Domarr. "Wait outside while I see her."

Varinn took up his position outside the front door, Domarr at his side, as I said my goodbyes to Arissa and entered Etta's house. Inside it was well lit and Etta was sitting in bed, propped up by a pile of pillows, a bowl of steaming porridge on her lap. Etta had been bedbound for most of our journey to Romsdahl and although I had seen glimpses of her old self during the battle she had weakened once more. No one knew her exact age and Etta was never going to reveal that secret, although most agreed she had already passed her hundredth year. Despite the fire in her spirit her strength was fading.

"Rothgar. What is the occasion that honours me with a dawn visit?" Her voice was still strong, quiet yet authoritative. Her one good eye regarded me intently as I drew up a stool and took a seat by her bedside.

I told her about my dreams and visions – the images impossible to forget. The longship where I faced my regrets, Nuna's efforts to free Norlhast and Hallerna's death as the durath murdered her, taking her form as another spirit crossed from the Realm of Shadows into the Real.

"Have you eaten anything?" Etta asked me. When I shook my head she pointed to the pot warming on the fire and waited as I found two cups and poured some tea.

The first sip soothed my nerves, the warm liquid comforting as it helped settle my stomach. I sat there, letting the steam waft across my face, breathing in the pleasant vapours of this delicacy from Samarakand. My insides grumbled and for the first time today the thought of food was not accompanied by the desire to vomit.

Etta gave me a gap-toothed smile, her eyes momentarily disappearing amongst the spidery web of creases covering her face. "Nothing is as good a tonic as talking about something that's bothering you and drinking a cup of tea. You look famished. I've had enough of this porridge – here, take it and don't let it go to waste."

I thanked her, accepting the offered bowl and spoon and taking a mouthful. As I greedily ate I explained how exhausting it was warding Romsdahl Castle. I glanced about me at Etta's room and doorway, which were plain and unadorned.

"You should have asked me or Leif to pay you a visit and ward your house," I remarked.

Etta laughed. "Really? The durath favour the firm flesh of the young, as poor Hallerna discovered. This bag of bones is of no interest to them, I can assure you. No durath is going to risk their soul trying to take mine when all they would inherit is the body of a bedridden old woman. You've just told me how thin you've spread yourself this past week. You're kind, but don't waste your efforts."

I looked at her, unconvinced, saving my arguments. It was never a good idea to lock horns with Etta when her mind was made up. Instead I scraped out the last of the porridge with the wooden spoon and drank more of my tea, feeling much better when I finished.

"Anyway, you didn't come here to talk about runes,"

Etta told me, sipping her own drink. "You want me to help you unlock the mysteries of your dreams. There's something that –"

She was interrupted by voices outside. I could hear Varinn's tone, although I couldn't make out the words. Moments later Varinn opened the door, apologising for the intrusion.

"You've already interrupted us, so you might as well tell us why," Etta chided.

The older warrior opened the door wider, revealing a number of visitors had arrived. "Jora Gautarrswyfe seeks an audience with you, Etta."

Etta placed her thin hand on mine as I began to rise from my stool. "No, stay. We haven't finished our business and it might be helpful for you to hear this."

CHAPTER 5

Jora's guards remained outside with Domarr and Varinn as she walked into Etta's house, pulling back her hood. Accompanying her was Karlin, Gautarr's handsome resident bard and Jora's close confidant (and occasional lover, if the rumours were to be believed). The third person to enter was Ekkill, Etta's wiry spy and part-time scout in Ulfarr's company. He grinned at me as he closed the door, leaning against the frame with his arms crossed. Jora's eyes swept around the small room, lip curling in disdain as she took in the mean lodgings.

"Was it really necessary for me to come here in person?"

"I wanted to see you, yes," Etta replied. "Although I'd have preferred more discretion. Ekkill could have brought you here safely with much less fanfare."

Karlin took a step forwards. "You'll forgive me, Etta, if I don't trust your pet. Or you for that matter."

Etta took another sip of her tea, regarding Karlin carefully. "And what makes you think I value your opinion?" Ekkill laughed, eyes glittering with amusement at Karlin's expression.

"I trust Karlin completely," Jora told Etta. She glanced in my direction, noticing me for the first time.

"My lady," I said by way of greeting.

Karlin looked at me with contempt, hand unconsciously sweeping his long brown hair away from his face – a familiar habit. I could tell he was remembering me on the walls of Romsdahl, taken ill as battle was joined and appearing to suffer from a panic attack. Karlin had struggled with the sudden transition in my status from cowardly envoy to mysterious magic user. It was something I struggled with too.

"Rothgar. What brings you here?"

I smiled. "My work warding Romsdahl Castle is done. I'm catching up with my old acquaintances."

"Yes, you've worked hard to protect the castle and my family," Jora remarked.

"If you believe in the threat they claim they're protecting you from," Karlin muttered.

"Believe it, young man," Ekkill told him. "I've seen things that put a few more grey hairs on my head." He ran a hand through his dark curly hair, indicating the silver at his temples.

"Have no doubt, the durath are real," Etta added.

Jora put a placating hand out to Karlin. "Enough. I know your views but I heard the leaders of the Brotherhood give their testimony – they believed what they said. Believed it absolutely. Whatever your reservations my niece is wed to Johan's son and we're allies and part of the Brotherhood, both by clan and by marriage. The permanent circle of ice where Sinarr fell is proof enough there are powers in Amuran none of us fully understand." Jora's eyes lingered on me for a time before she addressed Etta. "I've come as you asked."

Etta chuckled. "I see you've become accustomed to living a life of luxury. I brokered a good match, far above your station, wedding you with Gautarr. The years have been kinder to you than to me."

"My life hasn't always been easy," Jora retorted, eyes flashing as she drew herself up; an imposing figure notwithstanding her slender frame. "I've buried my eldest son and daughter and took on the leadership of this house when Joarr killed Egill, raising his orphans as my own children, for his sake. I've done all that with the Vorund Clan on our borders. Now I have to watch as Johan plots to take my husband and surviving son to war with Adalrikr, and I'm sure *your* hand is never far away, directing their fate."

Etta frowned. "You're right, life for the privileged or the pauper isn't always easy. And I stand by my decision – you were the perfect partner for Gautarr, guiding him wisely when the responsibilities of leadership were thrust upon him. You have done well, better than I expected in fact, and Ragnar lives, does he not? You've been blessed with two grandchildren from his union with Asta. Not everyone is so fortunate. Yes, you have faced challenges and you have risen to them, Jora. I'm proud of you." Jora looked like Etta had struck her. Karlin drew her close, taking her hand as he glowered at the old woman.

"I've followed all your orders," Jora replied, "even stooping to spy on my own husband and his advisors. I don't want you to be *proud* of me, old crone. I want to be rid of you. Even now, you stubbornly cling to life, when you should have died long ago. Let's get this over with. I've brought what you asked for, though it's not mine to give. If Gautarr ever finds out my head will be on a spike on the castle walls feeding the crows. This is the last time you give me orders, Etta, and that's my price – the amulet in return for you releasing me from your service. Forever."

"I could just take it from you," Ekkill told her with a smirk.

Jora stiffened at his words, though she kept her eyes fixed on Etta. "I don't doubt your pet is right but this should be dealt with in a civilised manner. How many more times do you want me to betray my marriage, Etta? I've done everything you ever asked of me and now I want an end to this. Isn't that fair, after all these years?"

"You were nothing when I found you," Etta replied with a sneer. "A street rat, begging, thieving and whoring to survive, until I scraped the dirt off your face and ran a comb through your infested, tangled hair. It's remarkably easy to create a false lineage with a few whispers in influential ears and some fine clothes, and Gautarr swallowed it all when he first laid eyes on your pretty face. You owe me everything and you have the audacity to try and bargain? I own you, Jora. I could send you back to nothing again with a few well-placed words. You vowed to serve me until death parted us, and I never forget when someone makes a promise."

"I was just a child," said Jora, misery etched on her features as Karlin stared at Etta with undisguised hatred. "I had no idea what I was saying. I see you haven't changed in the past thirty-five years. You've acquired another young, malleable, apprentice. How old are you, Rothgar? Sixteen? Seventeen?"

I cleared my throat. "Eighteen. Etta is merely a counsellor to the Brotherhood, and I can assure you I'm not in her service."

Jora laughed bitterly. "You fool, she has you tied tight on a string and you don't even see it. Well, Etta, do we have a deal or must I call my guards outside to come to my aid?"

"There's no need for that," Etta told her. "If you've brought what I asked you'll be released from my service. Show me."

Jora looked surprised, exchanging a glance with Karlin who nodded at her encouragingly. She reached into her cloak and drew out a black velvet bag, fingers shaking as she loosened the string. I gasped when she drew out the contents, an emerald necklace draped across her palm. A dozen highly-polished stones of varying sizes were held within a delicate mesh in diamond formation. The centrepiece was a flawless green stone several times larger than the rest combined and on its own it would have been worth a fortune. Set in this sparkling cluster of gems and fine silver the necklace was priceless. The morning sun glinted where it struck the facets of the jewels, casting bright green fairy lights around the room.

Etta's face lit up, more animated than I had seen her in months, as she pushed herself upright, bony hand outstretched. "Give it to me."

Jora hesitated, doubt on her face, before she stepped forwards and carefully draped the necklace across Etta's palm. Etta gave a throaty chuckle as her fist closed around the jewels.

"You're satisfied?" asked Jora. "You'll honour our bargain?"

Etta unfolded the necklace and stared at the swathe of emeralds as she spread them out across both hands, the better to see the intricate design and admire the polished gems.

"Etta?" Jora asked again, a catch in her voice.

Etta smiled, eyes looking up into Jora's face – one dark and intense, the other milky white and dim. "You've been true to your word and I'll be true to mine. I release you, Jora. You are no longer in my service. Treasure such as this would buy the freedom of a thousand thralls. Your debt is paid."

Jora clasped Karlin's hand, still wary of the old woman wrapped in blankets on her deathbed.

"Come, Jora," said Karlin, "it's done. Let's be gone and be rid of this woman forever."

Jora nodded and without a word turned her back and walked towards the door, Karlin at her side, casting a suspicious glance back at me and Etta. Ekkill moved aside and opened the door for them.

"Jora." Etta's thin voice stopped Gautarr's wife in her tracks. She turned back, face fearful.

Etta set the jewels to one side, laying them on her bedspread where they sparkled with a cold, green light. "You're free not because you demanded it but because it's time. You've given me a lifetime of loyal service and I haven't forgotten that."

Jora glowered. "Your scheming will leave me a widow and see me bury my last surviving child. Don't pretend I should be grateful. I want you out of our lives and gone from Romsdahl. Forever."

Etta glanced down at the jewels spread out across her

bony knees, green light reflecting on her lined face. "You'll get your wish."

***

I walked back to Romsdahl Castle wrapped in my thoughts, hardly aware of Varinn and Domarr walking at my side. Etta had confounded me once again. To have someone of Jora's rank and title beholden to her was, frankly, disturbing. I couldn't quite believe Etta had allowed such a well-placed spy to walk away and I told her so after Ekkill escorted Jora and Karlin home.

"What makes you think I need to justify my decisions to you?" Etta asked with a mischievous smirk.

"She's Gautarr's wife. I still don't trust him and she could have been useful – now more than ever. Events are likely to move swiftly in the war and Johan needs to be one step ahead of the politics within our clan."

"Hmm. You heard how she spoke to me. How many times do you think her loyalties have been tested, at great personal risk, to bring me tidings of events in Romsdahl? When Gautarr plotted to kill your brother it was Jora who warned me about it. Her raven reached me too late – Jorik had already set sail."

I shook my head. "You *knew* about that and never even told me?"

Etta shrugged. "Do you think I tell you everything? When Jorik's homecoming was delayed, forcing you to challenge Gautarr at the clan moot, I thought Gautarr's scheme had succeeded. Afterwards, when Jorik returned and defeated Gautarr in the duelling circle my work was done. The fewer people who knew about my well-placed spy, right in the heart of the Romsdahl court, the better."

"You should have told me. I'm talking about being honest."

"Like you with your clandestine use of the Sight to visit your sister?" Etta replied, a wry grin on her face. "Your secrets almost got you, Joldir and Leif killed. Don't pretend we're so different."

I couldn't think of an answer, so I folded my arms as I sat on the stool, unable to meet Etta's gaze. She laughed and we both let the subject drop, Etta asking me to give her more details about my encounters with the Weeping Warrior and what I had seen in Adalrikr's underground sanctum in Vorund Fastness.

"The durath gather to Adalrikr," said Etta. "Each day we linger in Romsdahl sees him growing in power as they flock to the Calling. Johan has fulfilled his bargain with Gautarr and defended his home against the shadow spirits. Now Gautarr needs to make good on his promises and bring his warriors and ships into the battle, before it's too late."

"I agree, but what of the Weeping Warrior? What was he trying to tell me?"

Etta pursed her lips, a deep frown creasing her forehead. "He's reaching out to you still, even though you destroyed his undead form. The Weeping Warrior will not make his journey to Navan's Halls until his work in the Real is done. His purpose is something you need to uncover before Johan gives the order to move against Adalrikr Kinslayer. I know I've counselled you against this in the past but you need to use the Sight to find him. On your own if you have to. No more ataraxia to protect your mind – let him find you and reveal his intentions."

After taking my leave I found it hard to shake Jora's words. Etta's reach extended across the whole Reavesburg Clan and she had influence in high places. Did that give her the right to dictate our affairs? My grandfather had seen fit to bring her into his service but why? What means had Etta used to inveigle her way into the court at Ulfkell's Keep all those years ago? Part of me didn't want to know the answer.

CHAPTER 6

Randall's knees protested as he climbed the staircase leading to Vorund Fastness' Inner Keep. So *many* steps, it was hard to catch his breath as he walked with a score of hand-picked men, his trusted friend Kurt at his side. Randall fervently hoped he wouldn't have to speak when he got to the top. The stairway within the Vorund Clan's mighty fortress ran in a spiral, encircling the outcrop of rock on which the Inner Keep was perched, a wall of vertical smooth granite running to their right-hand side, a sheer drop to the left. Any attacking army would have to approach the Inner Keep no more than two abreast, exposed to attack from defenders above. The innermost defences of Vorund Fastness had been re-worked from the ruins of a temple shattered in the War of the Avatars. Some said it was originally dedicated to Altandu, avatar of light, while others claimed it was an abandoned relic of Tiovam's worshipers, avatar of wisdom and knowledge. Whoever it was, they'd obviously enjoyed climbing and a good view, the temple builders reaching up towards the heavens in their desire to please their gods. As Randall's thighs and calves began to burn it felt like they hadn't stopped there.

Randall glanced to his left and immediately regretted the decision, a wave of vertigo washing over him as he looked down at the city of Vorund far below, encircled by its defences. He could see tiny specks moving about on the stone walls; warriors on patrol, vigilant after the stinging defeat at Romsdahl. Their best estimates were at least fifteen hundred fighting men were dead, and at least a thousand more had deserted. Too many of the ships that set sail during the rout at Romsdahl hadn't reached Vorund to be explained by bad weather and mishap. They'd lost more than a battle that day – Adalrikr had lost his authority.

I didn't do too badly out of it, Randall reflected. He still couldn't believe that, after his dishevelled and exhausted crew disembarked at Vorund two days ago, Adalrikr named *him* jarl in place of Sinarr the Cold One. Now Randall Vorstson was mentioned in the same breath as Tyrfingr Blackeyes and Joarr the Hammer; the three great jarls of Adalrikr Asmarrson, King of the North. It didn't seem real.

Hasteinn the Cruel didn't believe it either. Joarr's favoured second, he'd been groomed to succeed as jarl for years. Randall couldn't stand the man, thinking back on how he'd tortured the Reavesburg prisoners with such relish. There was something not quite right about Hasteinn – everyone knew it, although most people were too afraid to say anything in case word got back to him. A true warrior didn't revel in a name like that.

Scrying pools and blood magic, is that what we're about now? Randall had seen with his own eyes how killing the prisoners gave Sinarr powers on the battlefield that day. He'd witnessed and heard a lot of things he'd rather forget, including Sinarr's confession that he had been one of the undead, a foul fly-blown corpse brought back to life as Adalrikr's jarl.

I served a corpse, and that's not even the worst of it, Randall thought to himself, shaking his head. He'd been afraid of Sinarr, refusing to admit what his heart had been telling him for a long time. Adalrikr was something else entirely – Adalrikr *terrified* him. He remembered the sense of dread descending on him as he stood on the deck of the longship, watching as Vorund Fastness drew closer with each beat of their oars. Six thousand warriors had besieged Romsdahl and little over half that number returned. As the dispirited remnant of their army landed their ships along the length of the shingle shore the longships carrying the surviving leaders of Sinarr's army berthed at the docks, where they received their summons from Adalrikr.

Randall expected to be executed for their failure. He'd been Sinarr's second, and had to take some responsibility for the disastrous outcome of the battle. Adalrikr had met them in his customary lair – the dank cellars of the Inner Keep, far beneath Vorund Fastness. The unnatural, swirling darkness occupying the centre of the main chamber held a horrid fascination for Randall, constantly drawing his eye. He thought he could hear voices, whispering in the shadows, and struggled to pay attention as Joarr and Hasteinn abased themselves before Adalrikr. Their king listened to their words and rambling excuses, sitting distractedly on a golden throne, flanked by a half-dozen bodyguards, each rendered anonymous by a full face guard. In the days that followed, Randall learned they were known as The Six. After Joarr had finished speaking, Adalrikr beckoned Randall to approach, his bowels turning to water as he stood before his king. Up close, Randall saw Adalrikr sported a cut on his left cheek, the wound fresh and bleeding. It was cold near the throne and the armour of Adalrikr's guards was rimed with hoarfrost.

"I knew Sinarr well," Adalrikr told him, voice soft and silky. "He was the first to join my cause in Vorund and we remained ... close, afterwards."

"You mean after he died," Randall replied. He looked meaningfully at the cold guardians surrounding the throne and knew he was right. Adalrikr was flanked by more of the undead.

Adalrikr nodded. "You disapprove? Some believe it's wrong to wield this kind of power. Such things were set aside by our forefathers when they settled Laskar after the War. Our forefathers were wrong. Amuran has always been steeped in magic; it flows through its very fabric, the indelible mark left by the avatars when they breathed life into the world. In the Age of Glory magic was as commonplace as eating and sleeping, extending people's lives until their longevity rivalled dragons. There were darker arts too. The ability to raise the undead was originally used as a punishment – did you know that? Even under torture death was no escape for the enemies of the great kingdoms of those times; not when their souls could be bound here and interrogated endlessly, until every last secret was revealed. In the past torture was a rarefied art form, and to think we hark back to those days with *regret*, thinking of them as something we have lost. It was a savage age – dark times, which called for change. *Demanded* change, and I will fulfil that ambition and complete what was started all those years ago, with all the powers at my disposal."

"Guess that's alright, then," said Randall, eying the king's icy retinue. He looked down at the ground, scarcely able to believe those words had come out of his mouth. Fear could do strange things to a person. *That's some rare ability, Randall – talking yourself straight into the hangman's noose.*

Adalrikr laughed, a cultured sound. "Indeed. Sinarr's reports were always complimentary concerning you, Randall. A man who talks sense and knows his mind. Too many flatterers, vain followers and those with naked ambition flock to my court. I need men with the true heart of a warrior. Sinarr is dead and you will replace him as my jarl, Randall Vorstson. If you serve me as loyally as you did Sinarr, you will do well, I'm sure."

Randall could feel the eyes of Joarr and Hasteinn boring into his back. His knees felt weak and he shook his head, trying to decide whether he'd misheard or if the king was toying with him.

"I give you command of what remains of Sinarr's army," Adalrikr told him. "You'll need to name a second, a man you can trust and rely upon."

"Kurt," Randall replied without hesitation. "He's more than capable."

"Your first decision as my jarl," Adalrikr said with a

smile.

After his promotion the men in his company had been elated but Randall knew he'd made an enemy of Hasteinn. Adalrikr's decision had split the loyalties of his army. In the days that followed Randall wondered if it was a deliberate move, ensuring too much power wasn't resting in the hands of one of his rivals for the throne.

Is that what I am? A future King of the North? Randall laughed at the notion.

"Nearly there," gasped Kurt. Randall was pleased his young second was having trouble with the climb too, sweating under the weight of his chainmail and helmet.

The stairs opened out onto a wide stone path leading to the iron portcullis protecting the Inner Keep. Outside two of The Six stood guard, an unmistakable stench of decay wafting over Randall's men, causing a couple to cough and gag. They remained motionless, allowing Randall's company to walk unchallenged through the entrance. The reception hall of the Inner Keep, set on its high promontory overlooking the Redfars Sea, was a welcome contrast to Adalrikr's usual gloomy lair, shafts of light from the narrow windows cut into the thick rock bathing the room in bright summer sun. The remaining members of The Six stood in the corners of the hall, one of them closing the heavy wooden doors behind Randall's company with an ominous crash. Adalrikr was sitting at a polished wooden table, platters of food set out in front of him. An attractive young woman with brown hair sat at his side and she turned and whispered something into Adalrikr's ear, both of them laughing.

"Hallerna tells me you look more like a farmer than a fearsome leader."

Randall glanced down at his travel-stained clothes, patched and mended in places, and felt his cheeks redden. "Apologies, my lord. I've been attending to so many things since I took command. Inventories of our remaining supplies and equipment, organising the men into new companies, finding warriors I can trust to lead those crews."

As he went on to explain how he was drilling those new companies Adalrikr smiled and turned to Hallerna. "This is why I chose him. While Joarr is neglecting his wife and drowning his sorrows with women and wine down in the city, Randall is preparing for war. Randall takes his duties as a jarl seriously. The men see how hard he works and their loyalty towards him grows as a consequence."

"No one is disputing he works hard," Hallerna said with a playful grin, her green eyes appraising Randall carefully as she watched him, cat like. "My point is a jarl should be an imposing sight – one that commands respect. I'll arrange for him to be taken to a tailor."

Adalrikr motioned for Randall's men to sit at the table and join him as he took his midday meal. Randall introduced Kurt and the rest of his crew as servants brought them food and scurried about their duties, shying away from the four undead guards watching from the shadows. Hallerna moved around the table, talking to each of the warriors in turn as they ate and drank with relish. She moved gracefully, light on her feet, her long untied hair brushing Kurt's cheek and shoulder as she leant across to pour him more ale from a silver jug. Several of Randall's crew were looking at her admiringly but Kurt caught Randall's eye and saw his jarl gently shake his head. As she returned to the head of the table Hallerna wrapped her arms around Adalrikr, kissing him just below the open wound on his cheek. The king smiled and the two began to kiss passionately, ignoring their guests.

Randall occupied himself with the warm bread, cheese and dried fruits and took a long draught of ale, thirsty from his long walk. The food was good, although the atmosphere in the hall was subdued, the men eating quietly. Randall looked at one of The Six, face hidden by his helmet, although the whites of his eyes were visible, staring straight at him. *A dead man's stare is certainly enough to put you off your meal,* he reflected, chewing on his bread and forcing himself to look down at his plate.

Hallerna giggled as she disentangled herself from Adalrikr's embrace, draping herself over the chair next to him in a sinuous motion. Adalrikr dabbed at the wound on his cheek with a small handkerchief, dark spots of blood appearing on the white cloth, before he stood and addressed the warriors at his table, raising his cup.

"To the health of Randall Vorstson, Jarl of Vorund." The warriors round the table cheered at that, pounding the table with their fists as they drained their cups and toasted their leader. Adalrikr waited for the noise to subside before he continued. "I've been watching you, Randall. Not many warriors live to be your age. You're canny, understand the art of war and know how to lead men – invaluable skills when war approaches. The Brotherhood of the Eagle plots my downfall and I need men I can trust and rely upon in the dark days ahead. I'm putting you in sole command of the defences of Vorund. I want you to review every inch of the outer walls and inspect my fortress. Send your men to the outlying towns and villages and take whatever provisions and materials you need with my blessing. Johan Jokellsward will rue the day he decided to oppose us. Better for him to have died that day in Ulfkell's Keep than face my vengeance."

"I'll see to it, my lord," Randall replied, mouth dry.

"I know you will," Adalrikr told him. He raised his cup to his lips and drank deeply, eyes never straying from Randall as he watched him with a smile.

CHAPTER 7

Seabirds wheeled around the towers of Ulfkell's Keep, noisily calling to each other as Djuri watched them from the keep courtyard. His clothes were dirty and travel-stained, face scratchy with several days' growth of stubble. Bjorr was nearby, shouting orders, as the three hundred Vorund warriors under Djuri's command wearily dumped their gear. They headed off in groups towards the barracks, whilst their carts were unloaded by a gaggle of servants and grooms led their remaining horses to the stables.

It had taken several days to regroup what was left of his scattered army – some two hundred dead or deserted after the disastrous battle at Romsdahl. Adakan's men had hunted Djuri as far north as Olt before turning back, killing any stragglers without mercy. Their weary trudge north had taken them a week, watching every step for enemies, amid recriminations and back-biting from Bjorr and the rest of the Vorund Clan's warriors about what had gone wrong. There'd been suggestions Djuri led them into a trap, singling him out for blame as a Reavesburg warrior. Ulf, one of Djuri's trusted shieldmen and another Reavesburg man who now fought under Tyrfingr Blackeyes' banner, stayed true, reminding everyone they were in the wrong place at the wrong time – bad luck, that was all. Everyone knew they'd had the advantage until Adakan's warriors appeared. Whilst true, there was no escaping the fact that defeat was still defeat.

And Haarl was dead, killed leading their rear guard as Djuri's forces fought to escape when the battle turned. Djuri had seen him fall, slain by Petr Hamarrson himself, leaving his young wife Desta a widow, his son fatherless. Djuri had given the order that sent his shieldman to his death.

"Djuri Turncloak returns!"

Djuri turned to see a group of men gathered at the entrance to the Great Hall. The speaker, a small man with lank, dark hair stepped forwards. His warriors shrank away as Tyrfingr Blackeyes, Jarl of Reavesburg, approached Djuri and Bjorr. At this side walked Galin Ironfist, Tyrfingr's second at Ulfkell's Keep. Djuri swallowed. *Public humiliation, then – if we're lucky.*

Bjorr sank to his knees, head bowed. "My lord, forgive us. We failed you. We gathered those who survived and returned here as soon as we could."

Tyrfingr stared at Bjorr with those completely black eyes that made Djuri's flesh crawl. The hubbub in the courtyard had died down. Everyone had stopped what they were doing to find out what punishment Tyrfingr would mete out to those who had disappointed him.

"Word has already reached me. Ravens from Olt brought tidings from our ally Alfarr Radholfson, who now rules in his grandfather's stead. Hrodi Whitebeard and his son Radholf slain, with half of Olt's warriors now fighting for the Brotherhood. Hrodmarr, one of Adalrikr's most loyal warriors, killed. Sinarr the Cold One destroyed by dark magic. Joarr the Hammer fled. We were not the only ones to suffer defeat that day and many great names are no more. Now Romsdahl is the centre of the Reavesburg Clan's rebellion, setting back Adalrikr's plans to unify the north."

Bjorr glanced in Djuri's direction. "My lord, I know you had your reasons for putting Djuri Turncloak in command of my men. However, we could have had Petr Hamarrson's head, were it not for him panicking and ordering the retreat too soon."

Djuri realised he was still on his feet as Bjorr gave his grovelling apology and tried to get him hung in the process. He'd missed his moment to bend the knee and he was damned if he was going to do that now, here in Ulfkell's Keep

– his home for so many years.

Tyrfingr turned and looked at him. "You're very quiet, Turncloak. Anything you wish to say to explain your part in this sorry mess?"

Ulf was standing at Djuri's side, hand on the hilt of his sword. They'd been through so much together – Djuri didn't want to lose him too. He wasn't convinced begging at Blackeyes' feet was the right thing to do. Instead, he decided to tell the truth and see whether the hand of Myshall or Dinuvillan steered the fates.

"Sinarr was overconfident of victory," Djuri told Blackeyes, the hushed crowd straining to hear his every word. "He gave up a strong defensive position to face Johan Jokellsward on the field. I was too far away to tell you exactly what happened but Sinarr was slain and the spirit of his men broke. Panic spread through their ranks as their courage failed and the battle turned on that moment – the instant Sinarr died a howling wind tore through our ranks and we were battered by a storm straight from legend. After that followed panic, death and defeat."

Blackeyes glanced sourly at Bjorr, who was still on his knees. "Get up. Go and make sure our surviving warriors drink their fill of ale. Have Cook give them double-rations and make sure they're barracked by nightfall. Loyalty should be rewarded. Djuri, come with me."

Tyrfingr told Ironfist to guard the door with his men and, reluctantly, Djuri followed Blackeyes alone into the Great Hall. It was gloomy inside, the feasting table running the length of the room bare, a low fire burning in one of the hearths. At the far end of the hall was Reave's Chair, the wood black and polished from over a century of use by the ruling Reavesburg chief. There was a woman lounging in it.

"I believe as Reavesburg's jarl that chair belongs to me," Tyrfingr said with a note of amusement as they approached the dais.

"I was merely keeping it warm for you."

"Djuri Turncloak, meet Nereth, one of Adalrikr's trusted advisors, recently returned from Norlhast. Turncloak is anxious to prove himself, so it's a pity his first major campaign ended in disaster, though it could have been worse. Returning here with three hundred warriors was more than I expected."

Nereth rose from Reave's Chair, drawing back her hood to reveal fine features and long, flowing black hair. She was young, although Djuri noticed she moved stiffly, perhaps carrying an injury of some kind. Nereth walked down the steps and approached Djuri, wrinkling her nose as she inspected his grimy face, making him wish he'd had chance to visit the bathhouse.

"You gave him command in place of Bjorr?"

Tyrfingr nodded. "The Reavesburg Clan need to be shown a united north. Djuri knows the land and commands respect in Ulfkell's Keep. Bjorr is no tactician and shadowing Jokellsward's forces all the way to Romsdahl and into Sinarr's hands required skill and self-control. We suffered defeat but you spoke honestly in the courtyard, Djuri. The blame for our loss falls on Sinarr's shoulders, not yours."

Nereth walked to the top of the feasting table, where goblets and a bottle of red wine were set out on a silver tray. Nereth poured three glasses and handed one to Djuri. She reached into her cloak and drew out a small glass vial, which gave off a strong cinnamon scent as she unstoppered it. Djuri took a sip of wine. He wasn't fond of the stuff, preferring ale, yet even to his untrained palate he could tell this was good. He took another mouthful, feeling some of the tension of the past few days ease as he watched Nereth add a couple of drops to the remaining two goblets and pass one to Tyrfingr.

"You don't want to make that a habit," Tyrfingr told her as he took an appreciative sip. "Look what it did to me."

"Ataraxia has side-effects if used for many years," agreed Nereth. "However, the benefits currently far outweigh the risks. Rothgar's Fellowship almost destroyed me – they've grown strong under Gildas' guidance. I need to be ready when I face them again and, until then, I have to stop him worming his way inside my thoughts."

Djuri frowned. "You mean Rothgar *Kolfinnarson*, Jorik's brother? I thought he was dead."

"The same," Tyrfingr replied. "Word of his deeds has spread since the Battle of Romsdahl. Rothgar killed Sinarr, if the rumours are to be believed."

Djuri wasn't sure how he felt at this news and took another drink from his goblet to allow him time to think. He hadn't known Rothgar well, although he'd seen the boy grow up in the keep, helping Olfridor train him. He'd shown skill with a blade in the practice courts but killing Sinarr? That seemed hard to credit for a young man of, what – seventeen? Eighteen? Although, as a chief's son, Rothgar had always been accomplished for his years.

"We can expect Johan to march on Ulfkell's Keep and consolidate his position in Reavesburg," Tyrfingr was saying. "If he does, Rothgar will be at his side and you'll have to face him."

Nereth drained her cup and refilled it from the bottle. "I'll be ready. Until then, I need rest. We'll talk more on this another time." She nodded in Djuri's direction. "I'd like you to attend my chambers later today, once you've had the opportunity to bathe. There are things I wish to discuss with you, privately."

***

Djuri felt nervous as he was escorted by one of Galin's men to Nereth's chambers later that afternoon. This was different from the tension before a battle – something he was familiar with. He'd washed in the bathhouse, scrubbing his body to remove the grime and dirt from the road and carefully shaving his face before putting on fresh clothes. Even so, he felt ill at ease and unprepared as he knocked on Nereth's door, which led to the chambers Nuna Karaswyfe had once occupied before she left for Norlhast. The guard outside smirked and patted Djuri on the shoulder as she bade him enter. Djuri swallowed as he walked into the chamber, his throat dry. Nereth was standing at the window, looking out onto the courtyard below. She'd changed and was dressed in a white gown, a stark contrast to her long black hair, which reached down to her waist. She really was very beautiful and Djuri found he was staring dumbly, any pleasantries forgotten.

Nereth arched an eyebrow, looking him up and down. "That's a welcome change from this morning," she said with a laugh, walking over to a walnut cabinet engraved with intricate floral designs. "This is where you're supposed to tell me how beautiful I look," she added, taking out two goblets and a large glass decanter filled with red wine. She set them on a small table and filled both.

"I prefer ale," Djuri said, instantly wishing he could call the words back. Too late.

Nereth shook her head. "This Sunian red would cost you half a year's wages. Kolfinnar Marlson had this imported from Vittag at great expense and, since I don't appreciate the smell of ale on a man's breath, you'll drink wine." He took the goblet with a smile that emerged as more of a leer across his reddening face. Nereth stared at him and laughed again. "Gods, you're not very good at this, are you?"

Djuri took a long draught from the goblet to hide his embarrassment now he understood why Nereth had invited him to her chambers, barely tasting the wine. How long was it since he'd been with a woman? There'd been plenty of potential suitors at his home in Olt but since arriving in Ulfkell's Keep his life as a warrior had been all he knew. Kolfinnar's jarl, Finnvidor, had no time for the whores down at the dockside and discouraged his men from frequenting them, although many still did. Keen to prove himself, Djuri had shown restraint and knew Finnvidor approved. There had been that maid who showed some interest in him a couple of years ago. Myshall's bane, what was the girl's name

...?

"Terrible, in fact." Nereth's icy words cut through his thoughts and he stared at her.

Nereth set down her wine on the table and took his goblet, placing it next to hers. She turned her back on him. "Perhaps you respond better to clear instruction? Let's see if you're capable of untying my dress."

Nereth swept her long hair out of the way and Djuri fumbled with the knotted lace cords running down her back. Part of him wanted to run out the room and his palms were sweating as he struggled with shaking hands to untie the knots. He almost cried out with relief as they came undone and he began to slide the fabric down from her shoulders. He stared at Nereth's slender back and a small gasp of surprise escaped his lips as he saw the deep long wound running from her right shoulder all the way down to her left hip, red and raw. He knew the bite of a sword blade when he saw it and couldn't believe Nereth had survived such an injury.

"I had to leave Norlhast in a hurry," Nereth told him. "Sigurd Albriktson gave me something to remember him by."

Djuri reached out, gently inspecting the scabbed wound, relieved there was no sign of infection. "It's healing well, though I'm afraid it's bound to leave a scar."

"I don't doubt it. I'm sure in your profession you sport a fair few of your own."

Djuri nodded, running his hand softly down Nereth's back, feeling her tense although she didn't move away. "I'm a warrior, my lady, not a perfumed noble."

Nereth turned, lips parted as she cradled his face in her hand and drew him into a long, lingering kiss. "We're both servants of the King of the North, which comes with a heavy price. That's why we should take our pleasures when and where we can find them."

CHAPTER 8

The sun was warm on his back as Humli Freedman pulled on the oars and steered his small fishing boat up the River Jelt towards home. Reavesburg was shrinking into the distance, Ulfkell's Keep looming over the town, set on the hill at its centre. A good catch last night and the return of Djuri Turncloak's army meant there was plenty of demand from the fishmonger with all those hungry warriors to feed. Humli's purse was heavy with the extra coin, enough that he could set a little aside to make sure his daughter, Desta, and their friend Lina would be provided for.

Humli grunted, rowing against the flow of the river, bunching his muscles as he dipped the oars into the water. Either the River Jelt was flowing faster this year or he was getting older. He found it harder these days to rise while it was still dark and take his fishing boat out to sea. He hadn't planned on having another four mouths to feed at his time of life but now Djuri was back things would be different. The word on the docks confirmed the rumours circulating for days that the Vorund Clan had been defeated. Humli didn't mind too much as long as Haarl was safe. Desta had been fretting about him constantly and their young babe, Finn, could read his mother's moods all too well. That meant crying, which started Lina's own little boy Frokn off quick enough, and a restless night for the five of them.

The war made life harder for everyone. Humli hadn't given it a second thought when he'd given shelter to Lina, a pregnant refugee, earlier that year. She'd been half-dead when he found her and had he not taken her into his home her fate, and that of her newborn son, would likely have been very different. Although Lina had never shared her story, Humli suspected Frokn's father was dead, leaving them alone and defenceless. There'd been no choice other than raising the coin to keep five of them fed and clothed – a responsibility which worried him. When Humli heard Johan had prevailed in Romsdahl his first reaction was weariness. It meant the war would continue and, much as he admired Jokellsward's Brotherhood of the Eagle, it didn't help people like him. Still, at least Haarl was back. After marrying Haarl, Desta continued working as a servant in Ulfkell's Keep. Haarl had been teased for not being able to provide for his wife but Humli saw the sense in what she was trying to do. Her friend Tola had taken care of little Finn alongside her own child, allowing Desta and Haarl to save for their own home. They still had that money and now Haarl was back they could put his coin from the campaign to good use, giving them the chance to be a proper family at last.

Humli reached his cottage, his boat bumping up against the jetty, the familiar sound signalling he was home making him smile. He jumped out of the boat, tying it to the wooden posts fore and aft with practised ease and called out to Lina and Desta. He stopped when he saw the warrior standing in the garden next to his vegetable patch. It was Ulf, Haarl's friend and one of Djuri Turncloak's shieldmen. Desta was standing next to him with Lina, who had her arm around her shoulders. One look at Desta's face told Humli all he needed to know and a sick, heavy weight settled in his stomach.

***

"Leave?" Humli couldn't believe what he was hearing.

"You should listen to her," said Ulf. "Things aren't going to change with this defeat. Tyrfingr Blackeyes is still the Jarl of Reavesburg, ruling in Adalrikr's name. If you have the chance to get away, I'd take it. Sooner or later the war will come here and you don't want to get caught up in the middle of that."

"I can't stay," Desta added, her voice thick from crying. "There's nothing here for us now, not with Haarl gone. I can't go back to Ulfkell's Keep and serve under Blackeyes and his men, I just can't."

"You don't have to. I've provided for you haven't I?" Humli told her, pride stung.

Lina laid a hand on his arm as they sat together round the table in his small cottage. "Of *course* you have, Humli, no one is saying otherwise but Ulf is right. I've seen what warriors do in the name of war, and Reavesburg isn't safe any longer."

Not for the first time, Humli was struck by how much Lina resembled his late wife with her dark hair and hazel eyes, so alike with Desta they could be sisters. He'd come to think of Lina as a second daughter, the family he might have had if his wife hadn't died bringing Desta into the world. Her words struck him, forcing him to think, as he looked around the cottage which had been his home since he'd been given his freedom. He took a puff on his pipe.

"You think I don't know about war? I was ten when I was brought here as a thrall by one of Marl Hroarson's raiding parties. I was a slave for eight years until Kolfinnar freed me as part of the year-long celebrations when he became chief. During that time I thought every day about the shores of Riltbalt, where I'd grown up. Longed to go back there, to see if I could find my friends and family, find out what happened to them, whether they were even still alive. Would have left, too, except by the time Kolfinnar gave his decree I'd met Desta's mother and fallen in love. We made our lives here and built this place with our own hands. It's all I have left of her and now you want me to leave and start again, at forty, with nothing?"

"It's what I had to do," Lina told him.

"Take your boat and go," urged Ulf. "Do it now, while you have time to plan and get ready, rather than with a horde of warriors at your back."

Humli snorted. "I thought you were an able sailor? You've seen my fishing boat. There's not enough room for five people and the sea is no place for two babies. No, we need to stay here. Our home is out of the way and I can't see it being of much interest to anyone."

Ulf shook his head. "Scouts *will* find this place and if you're lucky the warriors who follow in their footsteps will strip your home for provisions and anything else they find useful. They could even take your boat. And what do you think will happen when they find two young women living here?"

Humli let go of Lina's hand and sat back in his chair, arms folded, puffing on his pipe to avoid having to reply. Ulf pursed his lips and turned to Desta. "I'm so sorry. Haarl died a warrior's death and you should be proud of him. Just remember he did it all for you and Finn, fighting for your future. Don't let his sacrifice be wasted." Ulf took out a small purse and placed it on the table in front of Desta, the coins inside clinking. "This is yours, although I know it's not what you want. The money will be a help – whatever you decide to do." Desta patted Ulf's hand, tears in the corner of her eyes as she took the purse, not even bothering to count what was inside.

"Blood money from Adalrikr, our *king*," Humli said bitterly, letting out a cloud of tobacco smoke. "Some coin from our new ruler doesn't make up for leaving Desta a widow and Finn without a father."

"No, you're right," Ulf agreed. "Even so, it's better than nothing and it's all I have to give. You'd be a fool not to take it." Ulf stood, hugging Desta and Lina as he took his leave. "Think on what I said," he told Humli as the two parted at his front door. "I mean no insult, only that the coming months will be difficult. Make sure you do what's right not just for you but for those who depend on you."

Humli watched Ulf's retreating back as the young warrior walked down the garden and took the road leading to

Reavesburg. He drew on his pipe, deep in thought.

***

Djuri was waiting for Ulf when he saw him come through the main gates of Ulfkell's Keep late in the afternoon. He strode over and clapped him on the shoulders.

"You found her?"

"All too easily," Ulf told him. "Desta's been living with her father down by the river ever since we left for Romsdahl. There's something strange going on, because they weren't alone. There's another woman living with them, around Desta's age with a young baby boy in tow."

Djuri frowned. "Humli's remarried?"

"He swears not. Took her in as a refugee was the story I was told."

"You think otherwise?"

Ulf shrugged and the two of them headed off towards the guardroom. "I don't know. It didn't feel like the whole story."

"It's none of our business anyway. I take it they listened to what you told them? When do they plan to leave?"

"Well, Desta took the money," Ulf said with a grimace. "Her father was stubborn, though, and wouldn't hear about leaving home. All he's got left of his dead wife, or words to that effect."

Djuri stopped in his tracks. "That's not what we agreed. I told you to take my wages and put them together with Haarl's to make sure they had enough to make a fresh start. Not take the money and stay put. It's an open secret Rothgar and Desta were lovers until the night Ulfkell's Keep fell. How long do you think it will take for Tyrfingr to find out where she is now word's out that Rothgar is still alive? Her past puts her in danger, especially since Nereth has returned from Norlhast, which I don't think is any coincidence."

Ulf whistled. "This gets worse. Nereth *hates* Rothgar after what happened in Norlhast. People talk and she's bound to find out about their history eventually. I should go back again and tell them to leave."

Djuri took hold of Ulf's arm, shaking his head. "No. Your first visit was risky enough. Rushing back there now will only draw more attention to her. And if Humli's as stubborn as you say he is, he's unlikely to change his mind in the space of a few hours."

"What are you going to do? Keep Nereth busy in her bedchamber for the next few months and hope she'll forget all about what happened in Norlhast?"

"That's not funny," Djuri said, glowering at Ulf.

"Then what's the plan?"

Djuri folded his arms, shaking his head. "I don't know – not yet. We'll think of something."

CHAPTER 9

I broke the connection and lay back on my bed, exhausted. I summoned one of Gautarr's servants and ordered him to bring me food, eating the salted pork, bread and dried fruits without savouring their flavour. After my meal I felt steadier, smiling as I took a sip of watered wine. I'd ranged far by myself with the Sight, without the support of my Fellowship and whilst I could hear Joldir's admonishing words I didn't care. Nereth was too weak to use the Sight, using ataraxia to protect herself against unwanted intruders trying to break down her defences. Protecting herself against *me*. The Sight had always been a risky venture for my Fellowship with Nereth watching our every move. Now I could do so much more – and I didn't need Joldir or Leif to help me.

A dead weight settled in my stomach, the smile vanishing from my lips, as I remembered Desta was in danger back in Ulfkell's Keep, knowing I was partly responsible. We'd waited too long in Romsdahl already. Ulfkell's Keep was only defended by eight hundred men and the Brotherhood boasted four thousand warriors. It was time to take my revenge on Tyrfingr Blackeyes.

***

The noise in the feasting hall was deafening as I took my seat at the table next to Ulfarr and Myr. The fires had been lit, servant children turning spits as they roasted pork, aurochs and fowl, the delicious smell wafting through the hall making my stomach rumble. My appetite had returned and I broke apart the fresh warm loaf placed in front of me, chewing with relish. Thengill arrived amid a gaggle of warriors and I saw Joldir was with him, leaning on the big man's arm.

I jumped up from my seat and hugged Joldir, pleased beyond words to see him out of his house. "You came. I wasn't sure you'd be well enough to make the journey."

Joldir patted me on the back. "Yes, I'm here. Gautarr has summoned the Brotherhood for a reason and I'm keen to find out why."

The three of us sat back down as Ulfarr took Thengill's hand in greeting, making space so he could sit with us. As a member of the Vorund Clan, Thengill was still treated with suspicion by many of the Romsdahl warriors. Gautarr had pardoned him as one of the terms of Bandor's marriage to his niece Freydja, meaning no one would be foolish enough to stick a knife in his back. However, treating Thengill with friendship and respect was another matter, and Domarr the Oak had taken a particular dislike to my friend.

"I see you've been busy," said Joldir, his fingers awkwardly wrapped around a mug of ale. "We're still one Fellowship, even if you choose to go off by yourself. How many times must I remind you of the dangers before you listen?"

Normally I would have been stung by Joldir's rebuke. However, today I felt elated – the Path had been so clear, my experiences vivid and fresh. I told Joldir about Nereth, unable to keep the smirk off my lips.

Joldir shook his head, looking at me despairingly. "And you knew she was incapacitated *before* you set out on the Path?"

"Well, no, not exactly ..."

"Rothgar," a voice called out, rescuing me from Joldir's rebuke.

Bandor approached me, arm in arm with Freydja, her brother Throm walking alongside. I greeted each of them warmly, remembering the part Throm played in brokering the deal that kept the Brotherhood united. The sharp mind of Gautarr's young nephew was not to be under-estimated.

"You look well," Bandor told me as we embraced. "Much better, in fact."

"My uncle is pleased with your efforts," Freydja added. "Anything that sets my aunt Jora's mind at ease curries favour with him."

The pair of them looked so happy, befitting newlyweds. I cast my eye over the runes inscribed into the massive doorway of the hall, reflecting that it was indeed a skilful piece of work. As men and women continued to flock through the entrance the runes remained dark and dormant – assurance that the durath were far away.

Johan swept through the entrance with Damona, who looked radiant, her blonde hair piled high on her head and held in place by an intricate silver hairnet. It was true how a woman blossomed when they were expecting. Since Damona had shared the news with her husband, Johan's dour demeanour had lifted and he offered me a rare smile as they walked across the hall. They were flanked by Petr, Varinn, Eykr, Svan and Faraldr, the five surviving warriors of Kalamar – the men Johan trusted most within the Brotherhood.

The remaining leaders of the Reavesburg Clan took their places. There was Jolinn, speaker for the mid-lands, deep in conversation with her second, Beinir. Adakan represented the eastern lands, his influence vastly increased as a result of his deeds during the Battle of Romsdahl. Towards the empty head of the table sat the enormous frame of Sigolf, his reputation greatly enhanced by the heart he showed in leading the western men of the Brotherhood. I had grown to like him both for his honesty and intelligence. He bobbed his white-haired head to me in greeting, eyes twinkling under bushy eyebrows.

"Gautarr Falrufson, Jarl of Romsdahl," boomed Karlin's voice, cutting through the noise.

Gautarr entered the feasting hall dressed in his

armour, polished plate and sanded chainmail gleaming. He was an imposing figure, still broad and muscular despite being in his mid-fifties. Jora was at his side, dressed in rich red silks and velvet, looking entirely composed as her eyes met with mine, betraying no hint of our previous encounter. Gautarr's dark-haired son, Ragnar, followed them in the company of his beautiful wife Asta, flanked by their own chosen warriors, Tomas the Berserk and Svafa in close attendance. Domarr was already in the hall, seated some way distant and clearly still in disfavour with his uncle following his failure to capture Joarr the Hammer during the recent battle.

"He certainly knows how to make an entrance," whispered Joldir next to me as Gautarr's retinue took their seats at the head of the table.

I glanced across at Johan, who was favoured with a seat near the top of the table as befitting his station. In a time of war his rank was equal to Gautarr's, a key aspect of Throm's diplomacy. Still, we were guests in Romsdahl Castle, Gautarr's seat of power, a fact he was keen to emphasise at every opportunity. Again, I reflected that it was time to move on. The longer we remained here the more Gautarr's influence within the Brotherhood would grow at Johan's expense. I watched as Gautarr clapped his hands, silencing his audience as he stood before us with a wide smile.

"Welcome, friends, to Romsdahl Castle. There will be time to eat and drink in a moment but before we begin many of you have been asking what happens next, now Sinarr the Cold One is no more. Some counselled me to simply rid Adalrikr's scourge from my own lands and fortify our defences. I said no. Those tactics only buy us a year, perhaps two, before Adalrikr is back with an even greater army."

Gautarr began to walk down the length of the feasting hall, looking at each of us sitting there in turn. A nod of acknowledgement to some, a smile for others. He stopped when he was halfway down, shaking his head. "Hunkering down behind our strong walls makes us feel safe and might seem like the natural thing to do. However, we know the Riltbalt and Norlhast Clans have sworn fealty to Adalrikr and now call him their king. Word has reached us that the White Widow of Vittag has signed a treaty with our so-called King of the North to spare them from war. She's opened up trade with Beria to the west, making sure Adalrikr has a steady flow of equipment and supplies. The Helsburg Clan are currently under blockade, and we expect their leader, Bothvatr Dalkrson, to follow the example of the Vittag Clan in the next few weeks. That means more men and supplies for Adalrikr's cause. Only the Jorvind Clan fight on and they've retreated from Jorvind itself and are now trapped at the head of the River Holst in Rast, far to the east. They cannot help us – it's down to us to help ourselves and end this threat, once and for all." Shouts and cries of support rang out across the hall as Gautarr turned slowly and surveyed his audience. "It's time to take the fight to Adalrikr Kinslayer. We will take the siege engines his army abandoned outside our gates and we'll turn them on Vorund Fastness. This time, our ships will blockade *his* port, so no help will come from his allies or the clans he's conquered."

Gautarr drew out the sword of the late warrior Yngvarr, gifted to him by Johan and etched with three runes of power. "We have the tools to destroy him and end his fell magic. With Adalrikr gone and Vorund Fastness under our control we'll break the Vorund Clan's spirit. When we return to Reavesburg as the victors, they'll open the gates of the keeps and castles they still hold and throw themselves on our mercy." Gautarr raised his hand exultantly, before bringing his fist crashing down on the table, next to Skari and Myr. "Vengeance, my friends. The Brotherhood's time has come."

As if on cue, the sun appeared from behind the clouds, shining through the tall glass windows running the length of the hall and filling it with light. The room exploded with noise, everyone standing to applaud Gautarr's words. Johan rose and the rest of the Brotherhood followed his lead. I clapped along with the rest, trying to ignore the dead weight which had settled in my heart.

"What's the matter?" Joldir asked as I sat back down.

"Ever since this war began all we've done is march further away from Ulfkell's Keep."

The oak doors of the hall, embossed with the black iron of the Reavesburg eagle, swung open to admit three visitors. I recognised Arissa instantly, her auburn hair plaited rather than loose. Holding on to her arm, with her other wizened hand grasping her stick, was Etta. The pair began to wend their way through the throng towards Gautarr with Ekkill at their back, eyes watchful. I twisted round to look at Jora, a false smile fixed on her face as she watched Etta approach. Gautarr was standing less than ten feet from me and I could tell he was as surprised as I was by Etta's appearance. She'd been on her death bed for so long I'd almost forgotten what she looked like up and about.

There was a spring in Etta's step and she gave Gautarr a sly glance as she looked up at him with that familiar, toothless grin. "I heard the Brotherhood was gathered here this evening. What did I miss?"

***

The feasting hall became rowdier as the evening wore on, ale and wine flowing freely. Players were energetically performing music on a raised platform in one corner and, now everyone had eaten their fill, the tables had been pushed to one side and many of the men and their wives were dancing and singing. On unsteady feet I sidled over to where Johan was standing. He was smiling as he watched Freydja dancing with Bandor, Petr standing alert at his side, nodding to me as I approached.

"Where did that come from?" I said without preamble, emboldened by too much ale.

Johan raised an eyebrow. "What?"

"The plan to take Vorund Fastness. I thought we were

going to free Ulfkell's Keep and liberate Reavesburg's lands first. I have people at home that I care about – Gautarr's plan effectively abandons them."

"You think this wasn't discussed and debated?" interjected Petr. "The leaders of the Brotherhood are all agreed. Bring down Adalrikr and we have an opportunity to end this war for good. This is our best chance."

I folded my arms and frowned at Johan. "*All* the leaders of the Brotherhood? There was a time when you valued my counsel before making such decisions."

Johan smiled patiently. "Your quick and insightful mind and your gifts make you invaluable, Rothgar. Yet you're the one who's absented yourself from my court – I never pushed you away. Etta explained how your work in the castle has left you exhausted, so I left you to your own devices."

"And did you discuss this plan to take Vorund Fastness with her too?"

Johan nodded. "Yes, I did. Not that I have to give an account of every decision to you."

"No, it seems abandoning my home to suffer under Tyrfingr's rule wasn't something that merited a discussion with me at all."

Johan stiffened at those words. "Abandoned *your* home? How do you think it felt watching Kalamar reduced to a pile of rubble, seeing most of my friends and family slaughtered? Have a care, Rothgar, and choose your next words wisely. You're no longer the brother of the chief. I love you – I've known you from childhood and you're the son of my dearest friend. However, these days I see very little of Kolfinnar in you. You can't hide away in your chambers and then bemoan the fact life goes on without you."

"There you are." Jolinn interposed herself between the two of us with a forced smile. "Care to dance?"

"Not really."

"In that case, you can help me find some more ale."

Jolinn's hand firmly gripped my shoulder as she

steered me away from Johan, who shook his head and muttered something to Petr.

"What. Was. *That*?" hissed Jolinn when we reached the other side of the hall.

"What?"

Jolinn's eyes narrowed. "How much have you had to drink? You don't walk up to Johan and talk to him in that way."

"You were the one who told me I should remember my heritage and be proud of who I was," I replied petulantly.

"I told you to come out from the shadows and play your part, not kick Johan in the balls when you don't get your own way."

I rubbed my temples, unable to come up with a reply, as Jolinn poured herself ale from a jug on the table. She didn't offer me any. Through the din I heard the sharp tap of Etta's walking stick and turned to see her standing behind me, looking thoughtful.

"Etta, it's good to see you out and about," said Jolinn.

"It *feels* good. There were times I feared I'd never leave that bed. Now, though, the thought of taking the fight to Adalrikr has put some fire in my belly."

I peered closer, studying Etta. She didn't look any different – back bent with age, long white hair tied back, face lined and wrinkled. The more I looked, though, the more I felt there was something …

Jolinn was telling Etta about my argument with Johan. The old woman shook her head and reached out to take my hand, the cool touch of her papery skin soft against my flesh. "I know you want to go back to Ulfkell's Keep. That doesn't mean rushing off there is the right thing to do – we have to *finish* this. You've played enough boards of kings to know victory is long in the planning and a winning move must be executed perfectly. This is about defeating the durath and bringing an end to Adalrikr and his vision of ruling Laskar. Surely you must understand things are *different* now?"

I sighed, unable to fault Etta's logic. "I know you're right but that doesn't make it any easier and our people there need us too. What will we find when we eventually return to Ulfkell's Keep?"

Etta nodded with understanding. "There are no easy choices in war."

Feeling in need of some time alone I said my goodbyes and walked out of the feasting hall into the cool of the evening. Wrapped up in my thoughts, I almost bowled over Throm, stopping when he called my name and placed his hand gently on my chest.

"Leaving so soon? Are you alright?"

I nodded. "Fine. Just needed some air, that's all."

Throm smiled. "I know what you mean – it's intense in there. I've never been a great one for dancing and singing, if I'm honest. I leave that kind of thing to my sister."

The fresh air and the amount of ale I'd drunk made my stomach roil. I took a deep breath, swallowing hard, and leant back against the wall until the feeling subsided.

Throm looked at me with concern. "Are you *sure* you're feeling alright?"

Another laughing couple walked past us, arm in arm. It was Thengill and Arissa, the two of them utterly absorbed in each other. A few paces behind them, walking at a discreet distance, was Myr, in case the drink caused any of the Romsdahl warriors to forget the oath of protection Gautarr had bestowed on Thengill. So Thengill had *finally* worked up the courage to talk to Arissa and confess his feelings towards her. I smiled, feeling pleased for both of them and remembering with amusement Thengill's clumsy words whenever he'd previously tried to broach the subject with Arissa.

"It would appear love finds a way, despite these dark times," observed Throm as he followed my gaze. "I wouldn't be surprised if another marriage follows swifty in the wake of Bandor and Freydja's union."

I glanced towards the doors leading to the Feasting Hall, listening to the noise of the celebrations within – the sounds of comradeship and family. As I walked back to my chambers with Throm at my side I reflected we all had something we were fighting for.

CHAPTER 10

Light was fading as Fundinn crouched down amongst the heather and gorse bushes, eyeing the farmhouse and outbuildings near the town of Ustaburg. A flock of sheep milled in the next field behind a long dry stone wall, baaing noisily as they cropped the grass. His six companions were spread out either side, each of them keeping low, watchful for any sign of danger.

"What do you reckon?" he asked Orglyr.

The old warrior hawked and spat on the ground. "Doesn't look like anyone else is around, though there's plenty of places where you could hide, like down in the barn and those stables."

"That's what I thought. Hoskuldr, take a couple of the lads and check those buildings are all clear. The rest of us will call at the farmhouse, if that's alright with the mighty Orglyr the Grim."

Orglyr grinned. "Sounds like a plan. Let's go and pay Vikarr a visit."

The group split up, moving swiftly over the moorland, leather-booted feet treading lightly. Fundinn stayed close to Orglyr, voicing his worries as they ran.

"I still think we need more men. Vikarr was never happy when Bekan appointed you as jarl and always made life difficult for you at Norlhast Keep. He's going to take some persuading to join Greystorm's cause."

"That was *years* ago," Orglyr replied lightly. "Vikarr hates the Vorund Clan. He'll come over to our side, easy. You worry too much."

You don't worry nearly enough, thought Fundinn. *Too*

late to do anything else now, other than see it through. Fundinn noticed smoke rising from the stone chimney jutting out from the slate roof. *Not turf*, Fundinn noted, taking in the fact the fortified farmhouse was on two storeys. *Vikarr's done well for himself in the last few years.*

"Vikarr?" called Orglyr softly, hand on the handle of his axe.

"Orglyr, is that you?" came the reply from inside. The farmhouse door was pulled open and a round man in his mid-forties with greying hair emerged, smiling when he saw his visitors.

"Good to see you Vikarr," Orglyr said, taking his hand and slapping him on the back as the two embraced. "It's been too long."

"That's true. This must be your second, Fundinn? No mistaking a man that big, is there? Come inside – you never know who might be listening. I got your message and I'm sure you must be hungry after your long journey."

The four of them followed Vikarr into the main living area of the farmhouse, where a fire blazed in the hearth. A number of pheasants and a huge ham were hanging from hooks in the ceiling. Food was set out on a long wooden table in the centre of the room – bread, cheese, what smelled like roasted goose and a thick-crusted pie. Fundinn's mouth watered at the sight – they had been on the road a long time.

"Ale?" Vikarr asked, holding up a jug.

"That would be welcome," Orglyr said with a smile, looking around the room, his eyes also drawn to the feast. Vikarr sat down and gestured for the rest of them to join him.

Fundinn helped himself to the leg of the goose as Orglyr and the other warriors began putting food onto their wooden trenchers. Fundinn took a bite and chewed slowly, wondering where Hoskuldr and his men were. He looked back at the door, listening for any sounds from outside. Nothing.

"Clearly you got my message," Orglyr was saying to

Vikarr. "So, tell me, what do you think?"

"Wasn't sure what to make of it at first. You can't be too careful now Valdimarr rules in Karas' name from Norlhast Keep. Is it true, that you're mustering men to drive the Vorund Clan out of Norlhast for good?" Orglyr nodded and Vikarr whistled. "Never thought Greystorm would have the stones. Worst thing that ever happened to the Norlhast Clan, Karas Greystorm becoming chief. Wasn't that what you told me?"

"Aye, though Bekan wasn't perfect, was he? Always had a bad temper and he was getting fat and slow, towards the end." Fundinn winced as Orglyr took a meaningful look at Vikarr's belly.

Vikarr's eyes narrowed. "You were always Bekan's man, through and through."

Orglyr took a drink of ale and wiped his mouth with the back of his hand. "Times change."

"That's true. Now there's some bitch from Reavesburg wedded to our chief. Some say it was all a plot, lashing our chief to her, so when Reavesburg was defeated Karas had no choice other than to follow and bend the knee. All in it together, Vorund and Reavesburg, that's what people are saying."

"If that's the case, then why is the Reavesburg Clan in the middle of an uprising against Tyrfingr Blackeyes down south?" Fundinn asked pointedly.

"If those rumours are true," Vikarr replied. He took out a knife and cut a thick wedge out of the pie. "You never know what to believe any more."

"There's no doubt," Orglyr told him. "I'm no lover of Johan Jokellsward but all the tales coming out of the south say he routed Vorund at Romsdahl and killed Sinarr the Cold One. We swore an oath that united our clans. This is the perfect time to act, while their attention is drawn to the conflict on their borders we can strike and throw off Valdimarr's rule."

"You want me to risk my life for an oath our chief saw fit to break less than a day after marrying the Reavesburg bitch?" Vikarr said, taking a large bite of pigeon pie, pieces of crust falling onto the table as he shook his head.

A woman with short black spiky hair opened a door leading from another room inside the farmhouse, followed by three more men. All of them were obviously warriors, swords hanging at their sides. Fundinn and the two men with him jumped up, hands reaching for their weapons. Orglyr turned and looked at Vikarr questioningly, their host offering them a wide smile.

"This is Nimm," Vikarr said, nodding to the woman. "Best sword I have amongst the small crew I keep up here. Thing is, Orglyr, we've done pretty well for ourselves in Ustaburg since Valdimarr arrived. Like you said, times change. I could have made a princely sum, handing you over to Adalrikr's emissary. Trouble with that plan is I wouldn't have had the pleasure of bringing your head to him myself."

Vikarr moved quickly, flicking the knife over in his hand and bringing it down savagely towards Orglyr's face. Fundinn gave a strangled cry of warning as Orglyr swayed out of the way, the knife missing him by a fraction and burying itself in the table.

Orglyr glowered, staring at the vibrating blade, an inch from his hand. "So, is that a yes or a no?"

Vikarr snarled, jumping across the table as Orglyr pushed himself away, both men drawing their weapons. Fundinn didn't have time to watch how his chief was faring as Nimm advanced on him. One of Fundinn's men took a wild swing with his sword, which Nimm blocked with disdain, rolling her wrist and catching him with a counter-thrust that slammed into his arm. The only reason it remained attached to his body was his chainmail armour. As he dropped with a cry, clutching the wound, two of Nimm's warriors attacked Fundinn's other companion, a fierce axeman called Snaga, while Nimm closed in on Fundinn, the remaining man with her trying to outflank him.

"Doesn't have to be this way," muttered Fundinn through gritted teeth.

"Too late for that now," Nimm told him, sword darting out.

Fundinn stepped back and used his huge reach to clear the space between him and his enemies, sword whistling through the air. His shield was slung on his back and there was no time to use it. Instead he took his sword in a two-handed grip and swung again, keeping Nimm's friend in sight, making sure he didn't get behind him. Nimm attacked again, a series of complex, flowing movements that had Fundinn backing away, breath already whistling in his chest from the effort of parrying each blow. He felt a stinging pain as the other warrior caught him a glancing blow on his hip.

Taking too long. Fundinn dropped to his left, shoulder barging his attacker, slamming him hard into the door, which rattled on its hinges. The man dropped to his knees, dazed, and Fundinn finished him with an uppercut stroke, splitting the warrior's face in two. He felt something hit him hard in the back, Nimm's sword bouncing off his shield. Fundinn whirled around and went on the attack, trying to use his greater strength to batter Nimm into submission. She parried each blow, perfect footwork helping her absorb the energy of his attacks. Her counter-move took Fundinn by surprise, the tip of her sword nicking his cheek.

Really could have done with getting this one to fight on our side. The door flew open and Hoskuldr stepped inside, bow drawn back. He let fly and at such short range the arrow buried itself in the chest of one of Vikarr's warriors and pinned him to the opposite wall. Nimm paused for a fraction, distracted, and Fundinn took her head with a huge circling stroke. Her body dropped to the ground with a wet sound like a split gourd, blood gushing onto the wooden floorboards.

The fight turned in that moment as Hoskuldr's

companions burst into the room, Snaga bellowing a war cry as his remaining opponent was slain with a series of short brutal axe strokes. Vikarr was still duelling with Orglyr on the far side of the farmhouse, his sword striking sparks off Orglyr's shoulder plate. Orglyr grunted, spinning away, teeth bared as he raised his axe.

"Hold!" It was Hoskuldr, another arrow nocked, bow drawn and levelled at Vikarr. The grey-haired warrior paused and stared in shock, realising the rest of his crew were dead. He dropped his weapon and raised his hands.

"Now, lads, let's not be hasty about this. I'm sure we can work something out."

"On your knees!" Orglyr bellowed, nostrils flaring.

Vikarr didn't need asking twice. "Alright, now listen –"

Blood and brains sprayed from Vikarr's head, splattering the food on the table with red, dripping gore. Orglyr groaned, ripping his axe from Vikarr's ruined skull before kicking over his corpse, which lay on the floor, twitching.

Orglyr wiped his axe clean on Vikarr's jacket, shaking his head. "What a shame. Stupid mistake to come here. Vikarr always hated my guts but I figured he'd hate the Vorund Clan more."

"You were wrong," Fundinn muttered, "but we're all still alive, which is something. Can't quite believe it."

"Aye. I was born with Dinuvillan smiling down on me."

"What now?" Snaga asked.

Orglyr looked longingly at the ruined feast and sighed. "Burn the whole place and scatter the flock. Make it look like a Vorund Clan looting party, where things got out of hand. Oh, and bring that ham and a couple of those birds."

Fundinn nodded. "We'll see to it. Then what?"

Orglyr rolled his neck and rotated his shoulder, grimacing at the bruise no doubt blossoming under his armour. "We journey to Taur and seek out my second choice, Tidkumi."

Fundinn swore. "*Limping* Tidkumi? Didn't you cut off his toes?"

"Not *all* of them," Orglyr replied. "It was a long time ago. I'm sure he's moved on."

CHAPTER 11

I looked up, stiff-backed from sitting in my chambers for so long, jolted from the Path by someone knocking at the door. I'd seen enough to understand Nuna's plans and probably her life hung by a thread after Orglyr's disastrous meeting with Vikarr. If Tidkumi was unwilling to join with Orglyr, I feared there would be no aid for the Brotherhood from the north. I groaned as the knocking sounded once more. I couldn't remember which members of the Brotherhood stood guard outside but they weren't doing a very good job. I rose from my chair, stretching my aching muscles, and padded over as the banging intensified. I reached out and hesitated, placing my hand on the hilt of my sword.

"Who is it?" I called.

There was no reply from my visitor or my guards, even when I repeated the question. Heart pounding, I drew my blade and threw open the door, stepping back, sword held out in front of me. Birds sang in the forest, the fresh scent of pine and sap assailing my senses. The carpet of needles was soft under my feet as I took a tentative step through the doorway, eyes scanning the sun-dappled trees for any sign of a threat. I glanced back at my chamber, set out exactly as I remembered it. A perfect replica – everything in its place.

"You're unwise to use the Path without your Fellowship," the Weeping Warrior scolded, emerging from the pines. "I've observed many things since Sinarr was defeated. Johan treats you with honour, yet you throw it back in his face because you want to return to how things were before. You hanker after your lost life and the first love of youth when, deep down, you know such feelings must be set aside. You seek the honour and station of your old life, one that's gone forever. All this waiting and idling now the battle is over has not been good for you."

Those words struck home and I felt a hot flush of embarrassment, recognising myself in the shade's description as I sheathed my sword. "A friend advised me never to forget my lineage."

"Your friend is right – holding on to your memories and remembering where you've come from is good advice. Knowing who you are and what you're heading towards, that, young man, is much more important."

"You seem to know me better than I know myself," I muttered, idly kicking a pile of pine needles to avoid the warrior's gaze.

"Most men your age are a little lost, I think. The moody sulking of a young warrior is one thing. For a Sightwielder to lack such focus and discipline ... As I said, you should only range out on the Path with your Fellowship beside you, guiding your steps and guarding your back. Even now, they sense your absence and are searching for you, placing themselves in danger because you're so thoughtless. Are those the actions of the Brotherhood's wise counsellor and advisor? I think not."

I walked in a slow circle through the imaginary forest as I thought on his words. "I don't need them in the way I used to and Nereth is weakened and afraid of the Brotherhood. She's no longer a threat."

The Weeping Warrior sighed and shook his head. "Proud and stubborn, I see. Those are not qualities in your favour. If you make the journey north you must understand you cannot carry on like this – so reckless and self-absorbed."

"What journey?" I asked, annoyed. "Since you brought me here, you could at least refrain from speaking in riddles."

A look of anger crossed the warrior's face. "Proud and careless. This world is a construct of *your* imagination, run wild in your dreaming – one which allows others to reach you. The damage wrought by Adalrikr flows through the realms of Dream and Death, a great Tear that's slowly destroying Amuran as the realms draw closer, making it easier to cross from one to another. If I can reach you, think about who else can. Remember your encounter with Adalrikr. I may not always be there to save you."

It grew cold and I drew my cloak around me, the trees thinning despite the fact I was walking through the forest in a circle. I was standing on the battlefield outside the walls of Romsdahl, only this time it was midwinter, a dusting of snow covering the scene as the occasional flake drifted down. Corpses were scattered in every direction, crows cawing at each other as their clawed feet scrabbled over bloodied metal and leather. I didn't look at the faces of the slain – I already knew them all by name. I cursed, wishing my thoughts hadn't drawn me here.

"This is what you imagine, so this is how it is," the Weeping Warrior told me with a sad smile, staring at me with his sightless eyes. "You see your friends and allies, whilst I see all of those I failed when Vashtas, Flayer of Souls, consumed me and made me his vassal. I brought death to my ward Adalrikr when I came into his presence and the shadow spirit set my body aside and took his. I turned him into the Kinslayer, the young man with so much promise who slew his father and murdered his brothers. Had I been stronger, had I been able to resist Vashtas, none of this would have happened."

"You had your vengeance," I told him. "Sinarr the Cold One has been destroyed and you saved me from Adalrikr. Your undead form has been released, no longer a slave to do his bidding."

The Weeping Warrior laughed mirthlessly. "True but the Brotherhood's mission is doomed to failure now Joldir's staff is destroyed. Adalrikr has gathered six of the remaining Sundered Souls to him and all the Brotherhood's runeblades will not be enough to defeat them. Worse still, Adalrikr has used death magic to create The Six. Only your sword is inscribed with runes able to destroy the undead."

"You helped me once, weaving the runes of magic into my sword. Is this something you could do again?"

The shade shook his head. "Sinarr's blood magic brought the realms close, giving me the power to aid you. I can no longer fashion things in the Real, unless you're willing to embrace those dark arts? No, I didn't think so. Adalrikr now recognises the threat posed by the Brotherhood and gathers his forces, intending to face you at his stronghold. Without the weapons to destroy him and his closest followers you stand no chance of defeating him and undoing the damage caused by the Tear. You must arm yourselves anew before that fateful battle."

I frowned, hugging myself to keep warm as I surveyed the battlefield. Familiar faces looked back at me, vacant eyes fixed in death; Olfridor and Bram, Haarl and Finnvidor. Alongside them lay my friends who still walked Amuran; Bandor and Johan, Damona and Petr. Jolinn. Arissa and Thengill. Joldir, Leif in his arms. All dead. Was this the fate that awaited everyone we cared about if we were unable to defeat Adalrikr?

"What of the others? You said six of the Sundered Souls have returned to Adalrikr. Adalrikr told me eight of his kin were still loyal to him, so what's become of the other two?"

"They have travelled to Ulfkell's Keep, placing themselves at Tyrfingr's court as they search for Lina and their investigations are likely to lead on to learning of the significance of her child. Natural offspring of the durath – such a thing has never happened before and Adalrikr will want to uncover the meaning behind the child's existence, of that you can be sure. The shadow spirits' power grows in your former home and they must be rooted out before the end. In their current form they are known as Eidr and Kolsveinn. However, first you must turn your attention to

Vorund Fastness. Each of the Sundered there set aside their old form and their previous hosts were used to create The Six."

The Weeping Warrior looked up and our surroundings changed once more, Romsdahl shifting and changing until Vorund Fastness swam into view. My eyes were drawn towards the hall where I had recently seen Randall's audience with Adalrikr. "Within the Inner Keep you will find the rest of the Sundered," the warrior explained. "Hallerna is the latest form of Adalrikr's long banished lover, returned to him through the Calling. She may not be a Sundered Soul but she's his closest confidante and shouldn't be underestimated. As for the Sundered, he has been joined by Finnaril, Solvia and Heidr, the one known as the Prophetess. Orn the Giant and Vedisra fulfil the role they played during the War and act as Adalrikr's bodyguards. And then there is Nishrall, who, along with Finnaril, has taken up his original name once more."

"Is that significant?" I asked.

The Weeping Warrior shrugged. "Perhaps. The path of the durath requires them to set their former lives aside, constantly reinventing themselves. Nishrall was a great prince in the Age of Glory, so taking his original name harks back to that earlier time. Finnaril was once a priestess of Ceren. Declaring themselves so openly is an ... interesting choice."

"So Adalrikr is guarded by six Sundered Souls in addition to the undead, plus all the durath gathered to him from the Calling. Hardly comforting, especially if you're saying we don't have the means to defeat them."

"There *is* someone who can help you," the Weeping Warrior told me. "You have heard the legend of the Fire Isle, yes? On that remote island, surrounded by the frigid seas of the north, lives Bruar, avatar of fire. He raised that island from the sea during the tumult following the War and has lived there ever since, in self-imposed exile. The Creator's smith could forge the weapons you need to end Adalrikr."

I shook my head, wondering if I had heard correctly. "You want me to appeal to the gods for help?"

"Is such a thing so fanciful?" the Weeping Warrior replied. "The avatars devised the runes of power your Brotherhood now carry with such pride. It was Navan who revealed to me the runes that can destroy the undead. The durath were forged by Morvanos himself, and if you seek to defeat them then yes, you will need the gods to aid you in your struggle if you hope to succeed."

I swallowed. "Even if Bruar can help us, no one knows the location of the Fire Isle. Sigborn Reaveson was shipwrecked on the ice shelf and told anyone who would believe his tale that he couldn't remember how to return. That's if the legend is even true."

"It's true – all of it. The shipwreck; crossing the ice, which claimed the lives of his companions; Sigborn's year of solitude; slaying the dragon to earn his passage back to Laskar, where he was reunited with his father who thought him dead. All true."

I grimaced, taking a moment to reflect that in Amuran our mythology and history were really one. Reave's simple teachings had tried to draw a veil over our past and the magic of our world, a stance that left us ill-equipped to deal with the threat we now faced. Reave taught the gods and dragons alike had abandoned us and were gone forever. If Sigborn's tale was as true as Sinarr's shade was insisting, it was yet more evidence of the fact the world was a much larger and more dangerous place than we had been led to believe.

"And what makes you think Bruar will help us, when he refused to take part in the War?" I asked. "According to legend, my ancient clansman killed one of Bruar's dragon guardians – the gods have long memories and hold grudges for generations. It could be a long and perilous voyage to meet my executioner."

The Weeping Warrior smiled – an unnerving sight.

"You need to have more faith in your abilities. I heard it said you're a skilful emissary and diplomat and one of Johan's closest counsellors. You'll find a way to see this done. You must."

***

Sunlight streamed through the windows in Joldir's house as he paced the length of the room, face gaunt and worried. He clasped his twisted fingers behind his back and try as I might, my eyes kept being drawn to them. He saw me looking and scowled, turning on his heels to face me.

"Did you do this to spite me, Rothgar? Is that it? You once told me the Sight was all you had left and you wanted to use it to serve the Brotherhood – to give you a renewed sense of purpose. How do you think I feel when you treat our Fellowship with such disdain?"

Ekkill smirked, watching proceedings with a languid air as he stood protectively behind Etta's chair. It was good to see her out of bed after so long, though she still looked frail, her black cloak doing little to hide her thin frame.

Joldir spread out his broken hands. "What if something happened to you? Did you even consider the impact on me? What about Leif? He's only seven years old and after the desperate lengths we went to in order to rescue him earlier this year, you repay the sacrifice of those warriors poorly when you place him in needless danger. We're bound together as a Fellowship, stronger when we're together and yet time and again you flout our agreements and place yourself in danger. Leaving us searching for you, placing ourselves at risk because you lack the self-discipline to think about anybody, other than yourself."

I thought of Leif. Apprenticed to Curruck the smith to learn metalworking, the boy now tended to be accompanied by the smell of sweat, leather and smoke. He was being groomed to follow in Joldir's footsteps as an artificer, a pressing need now Joldir showed no signs of recovering the necessary strength and dexterity in his hands. Leif had promise but it would be years before he was ready.

"I didn't *decide* to do anything, I've already told you that," I snapped, feeling guilty.

Joldir tutted. "The Weeping Warrior came to you while you were *alone*, using the Path to spy on people like *Adalrikr* and *Nereth*. Do you understand the risks you're taking? I don't think you do, or you don't care. What's happened to you?"

"I think the boy has learned his lesson," Etta said in a kindly tone.

Joldir waved at her dismissively. "Really? I don't agree."

"This doesn't move matters on," Etta pressed. "Regardless of how he came by the information, what Rothgar has learned is important. We need to decide how best to present this to Johan and the Brotherhood."

"You take this all at face value?" Joldir asked me. "You don't see a problem with any of this? This could all be a ploy, intended to divide the Fellowship when we should be united, facing Adalrikr together."

"I've encountered Sinarr's shade before – I have no doubt it was him."

"You grew up with your sister and didn't even notice when Nereth masqueraded in her form to lure us all into a trap," countered Joldir tartly.

"There's sense in what he says," interrupted Etta. "Our strategy was based on the runeblades being sufficient to destroy the durath. With your staff and Thengill's axes we had the tools necessary to end Adalrikr. His use of death magic and the destruction of the staff changes everything. Pressing on with our tactics unchanged is folly – Sinarr's only stating the obvious, something we should have seen, if we'd been honest with ourselves."

Ekkill cleared his throat. "That may be true. However, Joldir has a point. Sinarr's counsel is we set sail and seek out the help of a god on an island that, for all we know, is nothing more than a legend. I've seen things I wouldn't have believed possible – this tale, though, it sounds more like fantasy or the ravings of a madman. No offence, Rothgar."

"Someone will need to believe the truth of such things," I said, deep in thought. "For one thing, we'll have to find enough men willing to undertake such a venture and crew a longship." My statement was met with silence. After all, who would be willing to risk their vessel and crew on the basis of such a tale? They'd have to be half-mad themselves.

CHAPTER 12

The winds were favourable, helping Humli bring his fishing boat into the docks at Reavesburg early. He knew the flow of the dawn currents in the mouth of the River Jelt, navigating the maze of sandbanks and channels without thinking after all these years. It was still dark, the first grey light struggling to appear through a thick layer of clouds. Humli was aware of the shadowy shapes of other fishing vessels returning with their catch, wind snapping at sails, oars splashing in the waters. The dockside was busy as Humli moored his ship and began heaving baskets of fish out onto the quayside – a good catch this morning. He loaded them into a small handcart and began to wend his way, bouncing over the wooden boards towards the fish market. Sissa Gamliswyfe was in her usual spot, haggling with the early arrivals. She saw Humli and waved him over, a cheerful smile on her ruddy face.

"Humli, my friend. What have you got for me this morning?"

Humli lifted the lid off the baskets to reveal his catch of mackerel and herring. Sissa reached inside and inspected some of the fish, feeling their weight and sniffing them to make sure they were fresh. She counted them out, sucking her prominent front teeth in concentration.

"I'll take them off your hands for ten coppers."

Humli sighed as they began a dance as familiar as navigating the river. "I'd be a fool to accept less than fifteen, Sissa."

Sissa breathed out through her nose, looking at the baskets and licking her lips as she considered the offer. "Not so easy to make a living these days with Blackeyes taxing everything in sight. Twelve, that's as far as I'm prepared to go."

"All those extra warriors in the keep need feeding now they're back from the battle. You're not telling me you can't sell some of my catch to the servants of Ulfkell's Keep. I'll accept fourteen for them – that's more than fair."

"Twelve is as much as I'm going to offer – I suggest you take it."

They haggled for a few more minutes, eventually settling on a figure of thirteen. Humli held out his hand and they shook on the deal before he unloaded his baskets from the cart. Twelve coppers was the price Humli had been hoping for, so the extra coin in his purse put him in a good mood. Sissa's husband started to arrange the fish on their stall and already buyers were arriving at the market, inspecting the catch and bartering with the fishmongers. One of them, a tall man wrapped in a cloak, bumped into Humli and apologised, gripping his upper arm as he did so. Humli tried to wave the man away as he leaned in close, continuing to express his regrets.

"Humli Freedman?" he asked in a deep undertone.

"What if I am?" Humli replied, wary.

"My name's Djuri, a warrior of Ulfkell's Keep. Are you Humli, Desta's father?"

Humli nodded, the man holding him in a fierce grip, his strong fingers encircling his arm. "I've heard your name; you were in command of Haarl's company. Your friend, Ulf, passed on the news that my son-in-law fell in battle."

"Aye. I'm sorry for his death. He fought bravely and with honour."

"So I've heard," Humli replied trying, unsuccessfully, to break Djuri's hold on him.

"There are things you should know," Djuri continued in an urgent whisper. "Rothgar Kolfinnarson lives and now fights as part of the Reavesburg rebellion against Adalrikr's rule. Nereth, the witch of Norlhast, has arrived at Tyrfingr

Blackeyes' court. Both of them are Rothgar's enemies. This places your daughter in great danger. I assume you know she and Rothgar were ... close?"

Humli's eyes narrowed. "I know some entitled noble took advantage of my young daughter, if that's what you're saying."

"I meant no offence. Whatever the truth, the rumours are well-known within the keep and one careless word will bring Desta to the attention of Tyrfingr. He'll not be merciful if he thinks he can use your daughter against Rothgar and the rest of the Brotherhood."

Humli felt as if everyone's eyes were on the pair of them as they spoke. He looked around at the figures milling in the market and the docks, wondering if anyone was listening to this conversation. Djuri must have had the same thought, releasing his hold and taking a step back before speaking.

"I can't stand here talking with you for long. I might be recognised, which would only make matters worse. I know Ulf gave you the coin – enough for a fresh start. Make the most of the opportunity and heed my warning before it's too late, please. I owe it to Haarl to see his family safe."

Djuri walked away, declaring loudly that he was a clumsy fool. Humli rubbed his aching arm, watching as the warrior disappeared into the crowd.

***

I rubbed sleep from my eyes as Svafa escorted me from my chambers to the feasting hall. The young man talked incessantly as we wended our way through the corridors, passing courtiers and servants along the way. Like every other Romsdahl warrior, Svafa was excited by the prospect of war and being on the move after the long siege. I'd experienced the Battle of Romsdahl first hand from Svafa's perspective – a brutal, bloody affair which had come close to turning against the Brotherhood. Clearly, in addition to his latent potential with the Sight, Svafa shared the warrior's gift of only recalling the glory of battle, setting aside the memory of the hard road to victory.

The rest of the Brotherhood arrived for the moot in twos and threes. Huge Sigolf entered, deep in conversation with Adakan and Ulfarr; Thengill, Skari and Myr close behind them. Joldir looked tired as he took a seat opposite, offering me a thin smile. Bandor arrived arm in arm with Freydja (the two of them never seemed to be apart), Throm watching protectively over them both.

"They make a lovely couple," Etta remarked, making me jump. She'd slipped into the seat on the bench next to me, Ekkill at her side.

The doors on the far side of the hall were opened by two guards and Gautarr strode into the feasting hall, Jora walking with stately grace at his side, head held high. Karlin was with them, together with Ragnar and his family, more warriors flanking them. Gautarr's guards took up their positions by the windows and tapestries, Domarr the Oak among them. Finally, Johan marched through the warded entrance with the warriors of Kalamar, Petr on his right, Damona to his left. Ingirith, Dalla and Maeva were in attendance as her maids wearing their finest gowns, hair braided in nets of silver and gold.

"Who's was the grander entrance?" Etta hissed mischievously in my ear as Johan's retinue took their places. I was too diplomatic to offer an opinion as Gautarr stood, clapped his hands and, as food and drink was served, the Brotherhood's war council began.

***

I grew bored as the afternoon wore on, with its discussions on tactics, troop and ship deployments, provisions and the weather. I stuck to red wine, drinking modestly after my recent indiscretions, keeping my counsel as Johan and Gautarr reached agreement on various matters, each treating the other with due deference and respect. The main challenge was transporting the Brotherhood's four thousand warriors to Vorund Fastness, which lay over one hundred miles south of Romsdahl, with Vorund's fortified towns of Viskanir, Hordvin and Asmarr's Watch barring the way. Gautarr's longships could carry up to eighty men and he had forty of those – half in the docks at Romsdahl, the rest hidden along the coast. Another ten were now being constructed following the announcement of the planned attack and those would be ready in two weeks. That meant the warriors could be brought to Vorund Fastness. However, there was also the matter of the siege equipment – too much to carry, even with a fleet of fifty longships.

"It takes a while to agree anything when there's no clan chief," muttered Ekkill, eating a green apple noisily and looking as bored as I was feeling.

"There's a delicate balance to be struck when two jarls lead a clan," Etta replied, glancing in Jora's direction. Gautarr's wife caught her gaze and quickly looked down at her food.

"I'll not divide our forces," Johan was saying to Gautarr. "It would take too long for an army marching overland with the siege engines to reach Vorund Fastness – they would be under threat of attack as soon as they crossed the border. Any skilled commander would allow them past Viskanir and then bring Hordvin's warriors into play, trapping them between two forces, north and south. We must devise a plan to land at Vorund Fastness with our full strength."

"The siege equipment is more valuable than infantry alone," Sigolf counselled. "Take that together with, say, two thirds of our men. We could leave half the longships in Vorund to blockade our enemy's docks whilst the rest return to Romsdahl. Our army could prepare for war on Vorund soil and be ready to attack when our reinforcements landed in a week, perhaps less if the winds are favourable."

Gautarr nodded. "We must be on our way while it's still summer, before the season starts to turn. You'll have your ships – our craftsmen down at the dockside can build them soon enough under Molda's supervision."

"We could ready twice that number, if we had more timber," added Ragnar ruefully.

Etta rapped the handle of her stick on the table, everyone's head turning towards her. "It's a sensible plan. However, there's one problem to which we do not have a solution. The walls of Vorund Fastness are thick – it could take months to breach them with the equipment we have and that would only gain you access to the city. You would still have to take the Inner Keep, which we know Adalrikr will defend to the death."

"The blockade will sap their morale and as the siege goes on the city will begin to starve," said Johan. "We can use the trebuchets and ballistae to pound a narrow section of the curtain wall and breach it. Once we have the city it's only a matter of time before the keep falls. It doesn't matter if we breach the wall in one day or three months. The crucial thing is keeping Adalrikr trapped in Vorund Fastness. It will send a powerful message to his people that he's not the invincible King of the North. Moreover, it gives us the chance to kill him and end the war with the durath."

"And defeating Adalrikr himself?" asked Joldir.

Johan nodded towards Thengill. "I have the very man for the task, wielding the axes you crafted for him, Joldir."

There was a murmur from the Romsdahl men, still unsettled at the prospect of fighting alongside even a lone warrior of the Vorund Clan. I rose to my feet, sensing this was the right opportunity.

"Adalrikr has gathered the Sundered Souls to him, allies more powerful than Sinarr the Cold One. My Fellowship has seen with the Sight that Adalrikr is also using death magic, creating six unsleeping undead guardians, watching him day and night. Johan, nine members of your Brotherhood, each of them bearing runeblades, rode out to meet Sinarr on the battlefield. Only four of them survived.

Thengill can't accomplish this task alone and unaided."

Johan sighed. "The Sight is useful at finding problems, it seems. Do you have a solution you wish to propose at this battle moot?"

"Are you saying our grand plan to attack Vorund is doomed from the outset?" mocked Ragnar as his father looked on, glowering at me.

A hush fell over the moot as I told the Brotherhood of my encounter with the Weeping Warrior and how Bruar could aid our cause. I could see Domarr talking in hushed tones to the guard standing next to him, the pair of them laughing quietly. Despite everything they'd seen, I realised how fanciful my words must sound. Joldir remained silent but I could see the misgivings on his face. I'd been too trusting before, almost costing us our lives, and I could see he was unconvinced.

Etta addressed the moot, showing her support. "Remember we fight a war on all fronts, crossing into every Realm. We need to arm ourselves for the coming battle. Anything else is folly."

Sigolf crossed his arms, leaning back in his chair. "You've just heard us discussing the challenges of getting sufficient troops to Vorund. Sending a longship north means one less crew fighting on Vorund soil or sacrificing one of our siege engines."

"It's one ship," countered Bandor.

"Really?" said Ragnar. "The way Rothgar is speaking, it sounds like he wants a fleet of his own."

"That's not what I said," I replied, although my words were drowned out as everyone started talking at once until finally Jolinn raised her voice sufficiently to be heard.

"I fought Sinarr the Cold One. Don't you remember how many of us died at the hands of the undead? The rules of war have changed with this new foe and we risk dooming everything the Brotherhood is sworn to achieve if we don't properly prepare for this war. I've heard enough and agree with Rothgar's proposal."

"So your answer is to go chasing one boy's dreams into the frozen north?" said Svan, laughing in her face. "The gods are dead – they failed us and, as Reave says, we now find strength in our own hearts. Rather than this foolish quest, why not simply find a new artificer?" Joldir looked dismayed at Svan's words, which prompted more noisy debate.

"It's a fair question," said Gautarr, his voice cutting through the hubbub. "Joldir's grievous wounds are what place us at a disadvantage. Why not seek out someone else in the real world who can aid us? I'd pay handsomely for such a service."

"Is it possible?" asked Damona. "Could we find someone else to take Joldir's place?"

Joldir raised his bandaged hand, waiting until the noise died down before answering. "The only land in Valistria where the knowledge of runes is understood is Mirtan, where I was trained. However, their understanding is incomplete. The runes used to destroy the undead were never part of my studies and I don't know if anyone in Mirtan even possesses such knowledge."

"We have the design on Rothgar's sword," Damona pointed out.

Joldir shook his head. "You must apply the words of making to imbue a rune with power. I'm sorry, even if I was whole I couldn't replicate the runes that destroy the undead. The best we could do is copy those by rote, which would at least act as a barrier, much as we have warded the castle against the durath."

"Which is why we need to find a way to fashion more," I said. "My visions –"

Ragnar spoke over me. "You've played your part in the defeat of Sinarr's army, Rothgar. No one disputes your deeds. However, on this I do question your judgement." Domarr sniggered openly at my discomfort.

Gautarr shook his head. "You're asking me to

surrender my warships, which we need for the attack on Vorund. My son is right and the answer's no. I'm not going to sanction the release of a single longship to send Rothgar on a fool's errand chasing after lost gods."

Johan remained silent during this exchange and without his open support the warriors of Kalamar didn't challenge Gautarr. Damona offered me a sad smile and I understood she and Johan didn't believe they could carry this vote. I took my seat, dismayed at the outcome.

"I thought they'd listen," I whispered to Etta.

She sighed. "The Brotherhood might have learned the value of a runeblade but their mistrust of the gods runs too deep. Don't despair. Johan didn't openly speak against you in the moot and I know the man well enough to understand he's keeping his counsel. You need to talk to him again, in private."

"And what are you going to do?"

Etta grinned. "Gautarr may not be willing to help you but he doesn't own every ship in Romsdahl. I'm going to find you a longship and a captain willing to take you to the Fire Isle."

CHAPTER 13

The brazier in Orglyr's tent blazed brightly, providing warmth and light as night fell on their camp in the foothills above Taur. Fundinn's feet ached from the long march across Norlhast, although he knew he should be grateful such discomfort was the only price of their journey. Orglyr's small crew had evaded Vorund patrols and other mishaps after their disastrous meeting with Vikarr in Ustaburg. However, simply being alive wasn't enough to repay Nuna Greystorm's faith in them. This conference with Tidkumi had to go well.

Fundinn rose when he heard the sound of footsteps. Stepping outside he saw Snaga and Hoskuldr had returned. With them was Tidkumi, a tall, thin man with a hooked nose, his stature diminished by a pronounced limp as he favoured his right leg. Once the Jarl of Taur, Tidkumi's title had been stripped from him by Valdimarr, one of his cronies taking his place. Fundinn also recognised Soma Alvedottir, Tidkumi's second, rumoured to be even more skilful with a blade than her late father. They'd come, which was a start.

Orglyr emerged from the tent, arms outstretched in welcome as Tidkumi regarded him with undisguised mistrust. The two old jarls might have fallen on hard times but their shared history meant this was never going to be a warm reunion. Tidkumi had been a rival during Bekan's bloody rule as chief, so Bekan sent Orglyr to deal with the challenge. In the ensuing conflict Tidkumi lost three of his toes duelling with Orglyr. It might have been more than twenty years ago but Fundinn was sure the memory was fresh in Tidkumi's mind. When Orglyr was exiled after Bekan's death, Karas appointed Tidkumi as jarl during the negotiations to maintain his own powerbase. Orglyr was banking that Tidkumi's loyalty to Karas still counted for something.

"Let's not stand out here in the cold," said Orglyr. "Come and share food and drink with me in my tent and the rest of your crew can take their ease with mine by the fire."

Snaga made a show of inviting Tidkumi's warriors to take a seat as their leader entered Orglyr's tent, Soma at his side. Orglyr served Tidkumi and Soma himself with a thick stew full of lentils and beans, seasoned with herbs foraged from the roadside and the last of the dried ham from Vikarr's farmhouse. Fundinn fetched a wineskin and the four of them shared this whilst sitting cross-legged around the brazier. It was still summer in Norlhast but up in the foothills of the Baros Mountains the air soon became chill once the sun set.

"Simple fare, I'm afraid," said Orglyr.

"Your hospitality is welcome all the same," replied Soma, cupping her wooden bowl in her hands. Fundinn would have guessed her to be in her late twenties. Soma had short dark hair and her intelligent brown eyes settled on him. "Have we met before?"

Fundinn nodded. "You once visited Dorn, my home town. Your father Alve was a guest of our elders."

"Times have changed since then," Tidkumi observed. His voice had a rasping quality, his expression sour. He spooned some of the steaming stew into his mouth, his eyes lingering on Orglyr.

"They have," the old warrior replied.

"They say Vikarr from Ustaburg is dead."

Orglyr set his empty bowl aside and took a long drink from the wineskin before passing this to Soma. "One tale I heard was that our friends from Vorund forgot we were allies, raiding Vikarr's farm when they should have been raising taxes. We're an occupied land, Tidkumi, and Valdimarr isn't always good at keeping his dogs on the leash."

"Is there another version of that story?" asked Soma.

Orglyr shrugged. "Others say Vikarr broke the rules of hospitality, betraying his kin after sharing food and drink with them at his own table. Tidkumi is right, times have changed in Norlhast."

"Karas must be desperate to have turned to Orglyr the Grim for aid," said Tidkumi. Fundinn took in a sharp breath but Orglyr didn't rise to the jibe.

"Karas understands the clan has to be united, if things are to change for the better."

Tidkumi looked unimpressed. "And you think a handful of warriors from Dorn will turn the tide? The people of Ustaburg were clearly unimpressed with the idea."

"More warriors of Dorn are heeding my call every day. This isn't about Ustaburg – I'm asking where the people of Taur stand when it comes to the future of Norlhast."

Tidkumi let out a short, humourless laugh. "You've some stones, coming here, asking for my help."

"To be fair, this conversation's already going better than the one I had with Vikarr."

"Valdimarr is relying on our disunity to maintain his rule," added Fundinn. "We have to rise above the old blood feuds if we're to overthrow our enemies."

"And when Norlhast is free, what then?" asked Soma.

"We honour our promises and aid Reavesburg," said Orglyr.

Tidkumi grimaced, making a show of drinking from the wineskin before speaking. "Is that what we've come to? Beholden to the Bitch of Reavesburg? Even when I was Jarl of Taur, Karas didn't see fit to seek my approval before wedding Kolfinnar's pretty whelp."

"You're talking about the clan chief," said Fundinn in a low, dangerous voice. Soma glanced between him and Tidkumi, hand straying towards the hilt of her sword. The four of them waited, Tidkumi eventually breaking the silence.

"Can Reavesburg's warriors *really* overthrow Adalrikr Kinslayer?"

"They'll have more of a chance if we're at their side," Orglyr replied. "A free Norlhast and an end to the Vorund scourge. Is that something you want to be part of?"

Tidkumi looked hard at Soma. "What do you think, Alvedottir?"

Soma grinned, her hand moving away from her sword hilt. "I think it's time the people of Norlhast rediscovered their pride."

***

Fundinn was tense as he approached the gates of Taur, Snaga at his side. Tidkumi and Soma had left at dawn, whilst they were still striking camp. If all had gone as planned they would already be back at Tidkumi's occupied castle, waiting for the signal.

"No need to look so worried," said Snaga. "What could possibly go wrong?"

Fundinn couldn't help himself as he glanced back along the column of merchants and traders snaking their way along the road. Orglyr was there, hood pulled up to hide his distinctive features. Nearby Hoskuldr was leading one of their ponies, laden down with baggage. The few score warriors of Dorn were scattered along the road, all trying to look inconspicuous. The men guarding the gate looked bored, dressed in leather armour, the bear of Vorund standing out on their shields. One of them stood a little straighter as he spotted Fundinn approach, his size making him stand out in the crowd.

"Your business?"

Fundinn's cloak covered his chainmail and hid his sword and shield. He stared at his battered boots to avoid making eye contact with the man. "We've heard they're looking for strong backs to work in the quarry. I was told to report to the overseer in Taur and sign up."

The guard chuckled, waving them through, his

attention already drawn to the people in the queue behind Fundinn. "Reckon you'll come in useful. Go on through."

"Told you," Snaga observed in an undertone. "All too easy."

The hard work's about to start. Fundinn eyed the guardhouse behind the gates, where a few men were lounging outside, enjoying the morning sun. He looked up the main road, where he could see the walls of Castle Taur. The flag of the Vorund bear stood out proudly in the stiff breeze. Other members of Orglyr's crew slowly drifted through the gates in ones and twos.

"They're not even bothering to search the traders," muttered Snaga.

"We've been under Vorund rule for over a year," said Fundinn. "People get bored and lazy. You ready?"

"I was born ready."

Fundinn nodded, unclasping his cloak so he could strap his shield onto his arm, the rest of his crew gathering around him. One of the men outside the guardhouse glanced over at them, a look of disbelief spreading across his face.

"Your business here?" said the guard at the gates, unaware of what was happening outside the guardhouse as he addressed Orglyr.

Orglyr shrugged back his cloak and pulled out his axe. "Liberating Norlhast."

There was a blur of movement as Orglyr's axe split the man's skull in two, the crowd gasping in shock. Hoskuldr put an arrow through the throat of the second guard. The man outside the guardhouse rose from his bench with a strangled cry, eyes fixed on Fundinn, as his companions looked up at the commotion outside the gates. Fundinn drew his sword, crossing the short distance with his crew. The lone guard was the only one to appreciate the danger, scrambling desperately for his spear as he shouted an incoherent warning to the rest of his company. Fundinn swung his sword, cutting the man's hand off at the wrist. He screamed in horror as Fundinn slammed his shield into his face, pinning him to the wall long enough to thrust his sword through his ribs. Snaga was at work next to him, axe rising and falling as he shattered the skull of the next man.

Fundinn growled and kicked open the door of the guardhouse. *Not even locked.* He blinked, eyes adjusting to the dim light. There were six men playing a card game around a table in the middle of the room. A couple were already on their feet when Fundinn charged them. Chairs went flying as the other guards tried to get out of the way, Fundinn bringing the nearest one down with a vicious stroke which cut through flesh and splintered bone. Snaga was at his back, the rest of his crew piling into the room as it filled with the noise of their war cry and the terrified screams of Vorund's warriors.

Fundinn advanced on the next man, who looked to be in his teens. He'd drawn a dagger, stumbling over his chair as he tried to find some free space to fight. Fundinn had to appreciate the lad's bravery as he lunged at him with a fierce cry, despite the fact Fundinn was fully armoured and his sword had greater reach. The lad was fast too, getting in close enough that Fundinn had to block the dagger with his shield. The Vorund guard's weapon stuck in the wood and Fundinn twisted his shield, tearing it from the young man's grasp. The lad looked up, eyes wide as he realised what was about to happen. Fundinn made sure his sword stroke was clean, opening his adversary's throat with a single swing. The lad dropped to his knees, hands clutching desperately at the wound in a futile attempt to stem the torrent of blood. He choked noisily and Fundinn backed away, turning to see that Snaga and the rest of his crew had already finished the fight. He glanced back at the dying young Vorund warrior, his face already a white death mask.

"You fought well," Fundinn told him, breathing in deeply as the battle rage subsided. "You'll walk proudly into Navan's Halls. You died a warrior's death." The light in the young man's eyes faded, his head drooping and he fell onto the blood-soaked floorboards with a crash.

Orglyr was waiting for them outside, the streets now filled with panicking townsfolk running in all directions. "Hoskuldr has the main gate," he said, nodding towards the gatehouse, where the flagpole was now bare, stripped of the Vorund flag. "Should have brought something with the Norlhast sigil, really."

"We making for the castle, chief?" asked Snaga, his smiling face spattered with blood. Fundinn guessed he didn't look much better.

Orglyr nodded. "Let's finish this."

The warriors of Dorn sprinted through the streets towards Castle Taur, ignoring the screams of those they were liberating as they pressed on. When they reached the outer wall of the castle Orglyr broke into a wild laugh. Fundinn looked up to see the Vorund banner had already been torn down and above the gates the Norlhast sigil of the whale was rippling in the wind. Soma was waiting to greet them when they reached the gates, standing in front of a tight knot of Norlhast warriors.

"Did we lose anyone?" asked Fundinn, sucking in a lungful of air, winded from his run.

Soma nodded. "A few but it was over before most of them knew they were under attack. One of the advantages of living under the same roof as your enemy, I suppose. Tidkumi's in the main courtyard, hanging those who surrendered."

Orglyr looked unconcerned at the casual mention of ongoing murder. "Well done. I told you, didn't I? Strike fast and swift before they even see it coming. Vorund's had it too easy for too long and it's made them slow and soft."

Soma raised her eyebrow, which was split neatly in two by an old scar. "Freeing Taur from a small garrison is one thing. Driving Valdimarr from Norlhast Keep is going to be far harder."

"Every rebellion has to start somewhere," Orglyr replied, looking up once more at the Norlhast banner with a satisfied smile. "It's time to muster our troops and march eastwards. Our chief's waiting."

CHAPTER 14

The summons to Johan's chambers in Romsdahl Castle came late in the evening. As I walked through the corridors with Faraldr and Varinn I felt a tight knot of worry in my stomach. I knew this might be my last chance to persuade Johan to support my request and I tried to imagine the different ways the conversation might go and the best arguments to use. Etta was already in attendance when I arrived, wrapped in a shawl by the fireside. Damona was sitting opposite her next to Johan, with two strangers taking up another two chairs – an older woman with greying plaited red hair, while the man next to her was a slim-built Samarak, who looked to be in his sixties.

"This is the Sightwielder?" asked the man.

"Rothgar is one of the Sight users in the service of the Brotherhood," said Johan. "Rothgar, this is Molda, Gautarr's chief shipwright and her husband, Tellian."

Varinn closed the door to ensure our private audience was undisturbed as I took my seat. Etta was making tea by the fire and I wondered if Tellian was the source of her tea leaves, knowing both him and his wife by reputation. Molda was from a long line of shipwrights, who had perfected the art of crafting the best longships in Reavesburg. Following her marriage to Tellian, a merchant from distant Naroque in Samarakand, they had amassed a fortune through his business connections and her private fleet. I glanced at Etta, hoping my guess at why they were here was right. The old woman's self-satisfied smile confirmed she had made good on her promise and found me a ship.

Etta served tea, Johan politely declining. Damona

looked warily at her cup, watching as Molda and Tellian both thanked Etta and took a sip of the steaming black liquid. As I drank my tea I was reminded of that long year in Lindos, recovering from torture and illness. There was something calming about a well-made pot of tea, which started with the act of boiling the water and letting the leaves steep. I offered Damona a smile as I took another mouthful. She followed suit, nodding appreciatively, eyebrows raised in surprise.

"Etta has always recommended this beverage," she said, "although this is the first time I've had the opportunity to try it."

"I had plans to begin importing coffee as well until Adalrikr's war intervened," Tellian replied with a sigh. "It's becoming popular in the southern cities of Harrows, Medan and Listan. So many of my ventures were disrupted during the long siege of Romsdahl, before the welcome arrival of the Brotherhood of the Eagle changed everything, of course."

"Gautarr Falrufson's commission to build ten longships goes *some* way to make up for our recent losses," added Molda, her accent speaking of money and privilege. "War can also be profitable, if you're in the right place to take advantage of those opportunities."

Etta leaned forwards, cup clasped in her bony hands. "Rothgar's proposed voyage is one of those opportunities."

Johan shifted in his chair, looking uncomfortable. "I'll admit you've outmanoeuvred me, Etta. When I said we'd discuss this further if you found me a ship, I never expected Molda and her family would be so willing to do your bidding. You're placing me in a difficult position."

Tellian looked straight at me, eyes narrowed. "When we heard what took place at the moot, I found myself drawn to Rothgar's plight. Did you know my people, the Abitek, were the first humans to serve the dragon race? The magics you northerners so despise are common in the land of my birth. You're right, Rothgar. To fight magic you must use magic – there is no other way."

I shook my head. "I realise my request must sound fanciful."

"Not to me," replied Tellian with a wide grin. "If I were ten years younger, I'd be coming with you."

"So you'll help us?" I asked, hardly daring to believe my ears.

"What of Gautarr?" asked Damona. "Won't he see this as a challenge to his authority as Romsdahl's jarl?"

Molda laughed. "Leave Gautarr to me. Our families go back to the founding of Romsdahl and he owes me a favour or two. We're not taking any of his warships, are we? This is a private venture." Johan and Damona exchanged a look and I glanced at Etta, wondering what I was missing.

"We're chartering a private vessel," Etta explained. "*Stormweaver* is captained by Aerinndis, Molda and Tellian's daughter, one of the best sailors in all of Reavesburg. I've secured her services on very reasonable terms, I might add."

"Which are?" I asked.

Johan cleared his throat but it was Damona who spoke. "Molda and Tellian will appoint their own representative to hold a permanent seat on the merchant's guild in Reavesburg, providing Ulfkell's Keep is liberated from the hands of the Vorund Clan. Docking fees will be waived at the port of Noln and we'll write them a letter of recommendation, so they can further their business interests through our allies in Helsburg, Vittag and Norlhast."

Etta smiled at me, clearly pleased with herself. "As I said, very reasonable."

"If we win the war and those clans are also liberated," I replied.

"For such a prize, we're willing to gamble on that outcome," said Molda.

Tellian nodded. "You'll ward *Stormweaver* before your departure. The durath must not find a foothold on that vessel or harm my daughter and her crew. The shadow spirits *will* try and stop you when they learn of your plan, of that I'm sure."

"And when this is done, *Marl's Pride* belongs to us," added Molda. I was unable to disguise the shock on my face at those words, and she leaned forwards, taking my hand in hers. "Before you say anything, *Marl's Pride* is far more than just your late father's ship. Egill commissioned her as a gift when Kolfinnar became chief and he spared no expense. The thought that one of the masterpieces of my shipyards is now in the hands of Tyrfingr Blackeyes is too much. If she can't be recovered, I'd sooner see her burned and sent to the bottom of the Redfars Sea."

"This was Etta's bargain, not mine," Johan replied, his voice clipped, responding to my shocked expression. "Her ingenuity has presented us with the means to reach the Fire Isle. Now we must discuss whether we should go there."

Damona rose, showing Tellian and Molda from Johan's chambers, the two women embracing as they parted. I tried to compose myself as Damona took her seat once more. What had I expected? I knew I was never going to captain *Marl's Pride* myself and Johan was merely exercising his rights, rights I'd sworn to uphold in front of witnesses, that Ulfkell's Keep was to become his new seat of power. I'd set aside my ancestral claims and yet it still hurt when I saw Johan wield his authority before Ulfkell's Keep was even free, despite knowing in my heart it was the right decision.

"What did you mean?" I asked. "Why are you even debating this, Johan? I've told you what the Weeping Warrior said."

"You're talking about dividing the Brotherhood," Johan replied.

"It's one ship."

"One ship for you. Have you thought about that? If you make this journey it means dividing your Fellowship. Joldir has explained to me how your powers to work together are weakened over distance."

I shrugged. "True, although you sent me on ahead to treat with Gautarr to agree terms ahead of the Battle of Romsdahl."

"This is different, Rothgar," said Damona.

"Why?"

"Because you could *die*," she replied, looking directly into my eyes. "This isn't a temporary parting, such as you just described, or a crossing of the Redfars Sea we're talking about. This is a journey across the northern ice shelf, a journey which killed every single one of Sigborn Reaveson's companions on his fateful voyage."

"And it means losing your Sight visions, which were crucial to defeating Sinarr," added Johan. "Even if this voyage is one I agree to undertake, why not simply send Aerinndis and *Stormweaver's* crew?"

"You don't believe me," I said, understanding at last why Johan had remained silent during the moot. "After everything I've done, everything I've seen and shown you. After helping lead you to victory, you doubt me now?"

Johan ran a hand over his weary face. "This isn't your story, Rothgar. You're a noble in the service of the Brotherhood, one with gifts we can ill-afford to lose. You don't get to decide. This latest revelation … Well, let's just say people are talking. You have a vision that we need to appeal to the *gods* and now you want to lead a crew on a journey so far north that only one man has ever been there and survived to tell the tale. People are saying by dabbling in dark magic you've lost your way."

"We're *worried* about you," added Damona.

"You're listening to the opinions of fools," Etta remarked, her sharp voice cutting through the conversation like a dagger. Johan and Damona fell silent, staring at her. "This is no time to lose our nerve. The durath are real. The Weeping Warrior is real. The threat we face in Vorund is insurmountable without aid. How can you even think to send *Stormweaver's* crew off in the hope they'll succeed on their own when the whole fate of the Brotherhood hangs on the outcome! That's where you need Rothgar's Sight focussed, so he can guide them. Who's the emissary you've always trusted? Rothgar. The Weeping Warrior reached out to him, not you. Don't you see? It has to be him."

"You're willing to risk Rothgar's life on this gamble?" asked Damona, unbowed by Etta's outburst.

"Can you say whether Johan or Bandor will survive when they go to war at Vorund Fastness? Will you live, Damona, when the time comes to give birth to your child? All of us are taking risks and now comes the time when everyone must play their part. You must strike at Adalrikr, we must go to the Fire Isle."

I frowned and turned to Etta. "We?"

Etta made an exasperated noise. "Yes, *we*. You. Me. Both of us. We're talking here about treating with a god. We'll need your gifts and instincts but it's also a matter of knowledge and lore. Who else do you think should go?"

Johan sat back in his chair, shaking his head. "You've lost your minds."

Etta lifted her chin, her gaze defiant. "I'm no fool. I know this is dangerous but I've been making preparations that will ensure this frail body won't fail me."

"I'm not even sure I want to know what that means," muttered Johan. "However, I see you're both determined. As Molda said, this is a private venture and I can't force anyone to follow me south to Romsdahl. You've secured your ship without interfering with Gautarr's plans and as the Reavesburg battle chief this is a matter over which I have the final say. If people volunteer to join *Stormweaver's* crew I won't interfere, with the exception of Thengill. His axes are the best weapons we have against the durath and I need someone who knows Vorund Fastness and the surrounding lands."

Etta gave a deep sigh. "Thank you, Johan. I know this is against your better judgement but you won't regret this decision."

"I've not finished. There's one other condition. Rothgar, if you're set on this path I need you to surrender your blade." I stared at Johan, my fingers brushing the hilt of the short sword at my side as he continued. "You've told me The Six are guarding Adalrikr. Only your blade carries the runes that can destroy the undead. I'll see you're given another weapon worthy of your status but I'll not sail south to Vorund Fastness without that weapon in the Brotherhood's armoury."

I glanced at Etta, who gave me a short nod. I understood why Johan was asking this of me and, reluctantly, bowed my head. "Of course. If I'm nothing else, I'm the loyal servant of the Brotherhood," I told him.

CHAPTER 15

Djuri opened the door for Nereth, falling into step behind her as she walked into the Great Hall of Ulfkell's Keep. She carefully hid the pain of her injury as she crossed the stone floor with confident grace, black hair piled high, held in place by more pins than Djuri could count. His duties as Nereth's favoured companion kept him busy – he'd been fortunate to find the time to slip away to pass on his warning to Humli.

Tyrfingr Blackeyes was in his customary place, slouched on Reave's Chair. The sight angered Djuri – the black wooden throne, worn smooth through the generations, symbolised the clan chief's power. The new Jarl of Reavesburg treated that honour with disdain, once complaining it was the most uncomfortable seat in the keep.

That's the idea, Djuri thought as he approached, noting Galin Ironfist, Blackeyes' second, was in attendance with two other men. Reave's Chair was set on a dais in the hall and a polished wooden table had been set in front of it. Three other chairs had been arranged around the table; two already occupied by the men Djuri didn't recognise.

"Nereth. I'm pleased you could join us," Tyrfingr said by way of welcome, indicating her to take the remaining seat. Djuri took his place standing behind her, while Galin watched over his master, torchlight reflecting dully on his metal hand.

"Let me introduce Kolsveinn and Eidr, emissaries of King Adalrikr," said Tyrfingr, waving his goblet at his guests. Some red wine sloshed over the rim, splashing on the table. Djuri caught a whiff of cinnamon as Nereth wrinkled her nose.

"Rather early to be so deep in your cups, Blackeyes?"

Tyrfingr looked unconcerned at her reprimand. "As Jarl of Reavesburg I can do as I please." He turned to Eidr, the taller of the two men with a close-cropped red beard. "She's the one I was telling you about."

Kolsveinn stood and gave Nereth a short bow. "You're the Sight user, the one Adalrikr placed in Norlhast for so long?"

Nereth nodded. "Until I was thwarted by Rothgar Kolfinnarson. That crippled boy has cost me dear, twice." She looked accusingly at Tyrfingr. "You should have killed him when you had the chance."

"Torturing him was more fun," Tyrfingr said with a shrug.

Kolsveinn, a broad man with unsettling bright blue eyes and dark hair, leaned across the table. "Your *fun* has unleashed one of the most powerful Sight users we've ever seen, giving the Brotherhood an advantage they should never have possessed. Adalrikr is our kin and, I can assure you, he is unimpressed."

Djuri frowned, wondering what Kolsveinn meant by that remark. It was well known Adalrikr killed his close relatives during the uprising when he took power in Vorund. That meant Kolsveinn and Eidr could only be distantly related to Adalrikr. However, the effect of those words on Nereth and Tyrfingr was noticeable. Tyrfingr swallowed, looking hard into his goblet as if there were something fascinating in the bottom and Nereth stiffened in her chair. Galin was also aware something was amiss, meeting Djuri's gaze with a worried expression, his hand hovering over the hilt of his sword.

"You're Adalrikr's *kin*?" repeated Nereth, her voice tight.

"I think we understand each other," Kolsveinn told her with a cold smile, looking meaningfully at Tyrfingr. It was clear something was being left unsaid but Djuri was unable to grasp the hidden meaning.

Eidr laughed. "Relax, Blackeyes. Ignoring your lapse of judgement when it came to Rothgar, Adalrikr is otherwise pleased with the service you and Nereth have given. We're here on account of another matter."

Tyrfingr took a long drink from his goblet. "I'm pleased to hear that. Tell us, how may we assist our king?"

Djuri listened with mounting horror as Eidr and Kolsveinn recounted their recent visit to Humli Freedman's cottage on the banks of the River Jelt. To his surprise it wasn't Desta but the other woman, Lina, who most interested the two men, the woman Ulf had mentioned. Djuri cursed silently, praying the stubborn old fisherman had listened to his advice.

Tyrfingr set his goblet on the table. "The name of the fisherman's daughter – Desta. It's familiar. Wasn't she a serving girl, here at the keep?"

"She was, my lord," said Galin. "She was married to Haarl, one of the Reavesburg warriors who swore fealty to you. When he went to war in Romsdahl she left the keep, taking her son, Finnvidor, to live with her father."

"She has *two* children," Kolsveinn interjected.

"At least, that's what she told us," added Eidr, deep in thought.

Galin shook his head. "No. She only has the one son. She's a pretty girl and plenty of my men were interested in her – I remember them talking about that. I don't know who this other child might be."

"Where is this Haarl?" asked Eidr.

"He's dead," Galin explained. "He was one of Djuri's shieldmen who died during Sinarr's defeat."

Tyrfingr glanced at Djuri with those black, disturbing eyes. "Do you know who this second child might be?" Djuri shook his head, mouth dry. He didn't trust himself to speak and saying nothing looked like the best option at the moment. Where was all this leading?

"There were other rumours concerning this serving girl," Galin began, hesitantly. "I didn't know whether to believe them or not. Some people said Rothgar was enamoured with her and they were once in a relationship, right up until the keep fell into our hands."

Tyrfingr frowned and turned in his chair. "You *knew* this and never thought to mention it? Do I need to take your right hand too? Perhaps Bjorr would make a more worthy second."

Galin's eyes widened and he cleared his throat before speaking. "My lord, it was common knowledge throughout the keep. I ... I assumed you'd heard these tales too. All the servants knew and I overheard them talking. I'm sure Djuri Turncloak was equally aware."

Thanks for that. "I've heard the *rumour*," Djuri told them, his voice scratchy and tight. "Never took it very seriously."

Tyrfingr looked at Djuri. "If Haarl was your shieldman then you'll recognise his wife. Do you know where to find this Humli Freedman and his family?"

"Of course."

Tyrfingr turned back to his visitors. "It appears our interests align. Djuri can help you, with a few of my handpicked men. Galin, choose half a dozen of your best warriors and pay this fisherman a visit."

"We want Lina brought back to us alive," Eidr told Tyrfingr. "Kolsveinn and I will accompany your warriors."

Tyrfingr bowed his head, taking another drink. "Of course. It is my pleasure to be of service to our king."

"We know our own," Kolsveinn added. "I'm sure this woman is Lina from Lake Tull, despite her denials. Once we found her hiding place we sent word to King Adalrikr. On his orders, Lina is to be brought back with us to Vorund Fastness, where our king has demanded a personal audience with her."

"Desta could be useful as well," said Nereth.

Eidr shrugged. "Perhaps you're right. In that case,

we'll make a gift of both of them to our king."

***

Nuna dabbed at the corners of her mouth with a napkin as she ate her midday meal, gathered in the hall of Norlhast Keep with her husband Karas and his closest advisors. She had been served the choicest cuts of whale meat and watched as her companions eagerly tucked into their food. Nuna found the gamey, fishy taste took some getting used to, drinking more than she usually did of her watered wine to wash it down. Sigurd was laughing with his father, Albrikt, while his brother Kalfr chatted animatedly with Curren. As usual, Kalfr's wife, Luta, and their children were absent. No slight was meant by this – Luta and Kalfr both agreed their family should stay as far away as possible from Valdimarr, Adalrikr's emissary in Norlhast.

Across the table it was obvious the local delicacies also held little appeal to Valdimarr. A round, bald man, he clearly liked his food but on this occasion he was pushing most of the meat around his trencher, only eating the boiled vegetables and potatoes. Nuna smiled as she watched the look of distaste on his face, making a show of clearing her own plate. She didn't want to have anything in common with the man she despised.

Her husband's loyal servant Styrman swung open the doors of the hall and Nuna recognised Vrand, one of Karas' men, as he entered together with two warriors whose shields bore the sigil of the bear. Valdimarr turned to look at the arrivals and whispered something to one of his own warriors, an ugly red-bearded man called Dromundr. Next to her Brosa gently pushed his chair away from the table, ready in case Nuna needed to be escorted from the hall.

"Visitors from Vorund, landed here this morning," Vrand announced as he approached the feasting table.

"We seek a private audience with you, Lord Valdimarr," said one of the warriors, with a brief nod at Adalrikr's emissary.

Not even an acknowledgement that Karas Greystorm is the Jarl of Norlhast. Nuna twisted her napkin in her lap, glancing at Karas. He sat there, stony faced, watching events unfold. *How does he remain so calm and composed when they slight him at every turn?* Valdimarr hurriedly stood and gave a short bow to his guests, who returned the gesture, the older of the two men stepping forwards, removing his helmet to reveal a long mane of grey hair.

"Welcome to Norlhast Keep, Geilir," said Valdimarr, eyes widening in recognition as he stared at the grey-haired man.

Geilir smiled. "Valdimarr. Dromundr." He nodded in the direction of the other warrior. "This is my second, Tryggvi. We're here on urgent private business with a message from our king. May I suggest we retire to your chambers to discuss things further?"

Dromundr and the rest of his warriors rose from their seats, chairs scraping noisily on the stone floor as Valdimarr waved at Styrman. "Find our guests quarters and bring them food and drink. After their long journey they'll want to refresh themselves." The visitors and Valdimarr's warriors left the hall without a backwards glance, Styrman closing the doors quietly behind him as he left to attend to the new arrivals.

Karas shook his head. "When did it become customary to ignore your host entirely in his own feasting hall?" He looked thin and frail with his gaunt face and grey hair.

Nuna reached over and squeezed his hand. "You play your part, as you must," she told him quietly. "Your people are loyal to you, not him. The fact they underestimate you gives us the advantage."

Albrikt nodded. "Nuna is right. We must allow events to play out and let our friend do his work behind the scenes."

Karas laughed bitterly. "Orglyr the Grim is now my friend, while I place food and drink in front of our sworn enemies and dine with them. How did it come to this?"

Sigurd was staring at the closed doors of the hall. "I wonder what this delegation from Adalrikr signifies?"

"They were tight lipped when they came ashore," said Vrand.

"This doesn't bode well," Sigurd muttered, with a shake of his head. "Vrand – make sure you keep an eye on our new guests. I want to know why they're here and what they want with Valdimarr."

CHAPTER 16

My head whirled with dark thoughts as Svafa and Jolinn escorted me through the streets of Romsdahl. It was my fault Desta was in danger and I remembered Etta's warning from years ago, wishing I'd listened back then. I should have set her aside as soon as I knew people were talking about us, but instead I'd been selfish, following my own desires, heedless of the cost. Even my journeys down the Path put Desta in danger. The Weeping Warrior was right – I spent too much time on the Path observing the remnants of my old life. I told myself I was keeping watch on Lina, since she posed a threat as a shadow spirit but this was a lie. I was there because of Desta, even though she'd since married and given birth to Haarl's child. What was I doing? That part of my life was gone forever and the time we'd shared belonged in the past.

Tellian also accompanied us, the old man walking with a sprightly spring in his step. "You seem preoccupied this morning, young man," he said, his words jolting me from my thoughts.

I looked at him, trying to see if anything else lay behind his outwardly friendly smile. "There's a lot to think about."

"I'm sure there is. Life can't be easy as one of Johan's advisors, especially for one so young."

"I've seen and done plenty of things."

Tellian's smile widened, a feat I thought impossible. "I'm sure you have. I meant no disrespect. I was merely observing the weight you carry around your shoulders. You're not having second thoughts about the voyage, are you? If such things were on your mind it would be best to speak openly now, before we waste my daughter's time."

"No. I'm the one who argued in favour of making this journey, even though many think it foolhardy."

Tellian put a hand on my shoulder as we walked. "It is foolhardy. Necessary but still foolhardy. And you would be a fool to think otherwise."

"Why put your daughter at such risk if that's what you think?"

"Aerinndis does what she wants," Tellian replied, laughing. "Etta approached us asking for a ship and a crew and when Aerinndis heard what you were trying to achieve she volunteered immediately. They call her Stormrider for good reason. Aerinndis has always wanted to be the first at everything."

"I thought Sigborn was the first to reach the Fire Isle," remarked Svafa.

Tellian wagged a finger at the young warrior. "Whilst true, there's a significant difference between being shipwrecked there and reaching the Fire Isle as part of an organised expedition, with the ability to leave at a time of your choosing. And if we're splitting hairs about such matters, Aerinndis will be the first *woman* to reach the Fire Isle's shores." Svafa remained quiet after that conversation, Jolinn offering me a wry grin.

We found *Stormweaver's* crew enjoying the late afternoon sunshine, gathered in two groups, each tending a fire on the stone quayside. A longship of twenty oars painted red and green sat out of the water for repair, resting in a lattice of wooden beams, the smell of fresh paint and smoked fish hanging in the air. As we drew near I heard laughter and the clack of horn drinking cups as the crew shared a toast. A thick-set sailor with a huge grey beard turned and set his cup aside, the conversation around the fire quietening as we drew near. He called out to Tellian and held out a paint-flecked hand to me in greeting. I took it, his grip firm, hands rough from a life pulling an oar.

"My name's Meinolf Saltbeard, first mate on *Stormweaver*. So, you're the lad looking to charter a vessel and sail into the frozen north beyond the Endless Ocean?"

"I am."

"You've chosen the right crew for this voyage," Meinolf said, gesturing to his companions with a flourish. "We've sailed the length and breadth of the Redfars Sea more times than I can count. No port is a stranger to us – we've landed at Rodil in Oomrhat, navigating the icebergs of the treacherous Locked Bay. We're frequent traders at Brear and Neem in Lagash, familiar faces in the Berian ports of Denar, Harrows and Medan. We even have a charter permitting us to dock at Listan Bay in the Kingdom of Sunis – few can claim such lofty connections. If you charter *Stormweaver* we can open up trading opportunities across the whole of Valistria, for the right price."

"But that's not what you're interested in, is it?" said a small woman, rising from her place at the fireside. Barely five feet tall, Aerinndis had the light brown skin of her father and an unruly mop of curly red hair hanging down to her shoulders which could only come from her mother. Her crew took her lead, standing as one.

"I'm not going to pretend what we're asking you to do isn't dangerous," I replied.

Aerinndis shrugged, dark eyes sparkling with excitement. "Where's the fun in always doing what's safe? Come sit with us and you can tell us why you're so keen to undertake this voyage. I might be willing to aid you but the rest of my crew have the right to choose whether or not they volunteer."

I took a seat in the circle, with Svafa and Jolinn either side of me, Tellian taking his place next to his daughter. Aerinndis passed me a cup of bitter smelling liquid. After a tentative sip I found the ale to be warm but not unpleasant. Fish was cooking on hot stones ringing the fire and this was also shared with us, served with small loaves of dark brown bread.

"I don't know where to begin," I admitted. "Everything I say will sound ... unbelievable."

Aerinndis popped a piece of steaming fish into her mouth. "If it helps, I understand the evil the Brotherhood is trying to overthrow. I know why you've been warding Romsdahl Castle and I don't think it's because Gautarr Falrufson is superstitious."

"My people, the Abitek of Naroque are the Tribe of the Dragon," added Tellian. "Our ancient history is entwined with the dragon race and the doom that befell them during the War, when the Beast was unleashed. My daughter knows the threat posed by the shadow spirits. Each generation is taught the same story, of how the durath betrayed us and how the dragons were corrupted, resulting in the chimera being unleashed upon the world."

Jolinn leaned forwards, sliding her sword halfway out of its scabbard to reveal the runes inlaid into the metal. "Is that the meaning behind the runes?" she asked, indicating the dragon and chimera pattern. I realised I'd never thought to ask Joldir the question – there was so much I still didn't understand, despite what I'd told Tellian earlier. I shook my head, appreciating that my studies in recent months had barely scratched the surface of Amuran's mysteries.

Tellian's face was sombre. "Morvanos sundered soul from flesh, thus in humans creating the durath, the foul corruption of the Sight. In dragons, he harnessed the power of the Beast within and ... did terrible, terrible things. Those dragons who followed him became the first chimera, their forms twisted and evil, nature turned in upon itself and given over to chaos. The runes undo such magic. During the Dark Night we inlaid our spears with such runes, imbuing them with power as we hunted them down, durath and chimera alike. They were born in darkness and into the darkness we cast them once more."

Aerinndis' crew listened to those words in silence,

Meinolf's face intense and brooding. Now I understood why Etta had gone to Molda and Tellian for help. They had a different perspective compared with the rest of the Reavesburg Clan. I sat there, thinking of my upbringing in Ulfkell's Keep and reflected on how narrow and insular my life had been. Aerinndis' crew had sailed around half the whole known world and *Stormweaver's* captain understood the battle we were really fighting.

"They'll try and stop us," I said, pausing to take another sip of ale. "We have to reach the Fire Isle if we're to prepare for the coming war with Vorund. No one else can fashion the weapons we need to overthrow Adalrikr. If we simply prevail on the field of battle, we'll merely allow Adalrikr and his kind to slip away, take new forms and rise to power once more."

"Exactly," Aerinndis agreed. "History will speak of this moment as the turning point, when a few brave souls took the chance to end evil, once and for all."

I didn't know what to say to that, swallowing down a lump in my throat as I silently toasted Aerinndis and her courageous crew.

***

The light was beginning to fade when we left the docks, Tellian remaining behind, talking animatedly with his daughter. Even if other members of the Brotherhood were still questioning my motives, Johan wasn't preventing me from making this journey and now I had a crew and a ship at my disposal. I shook my head, marvelling at how Etta's myriad connections had proved their worth once more.

"You can be quite charming when you want to be," Jolinn remarked with a wry grin as we walked through the streets back towards the castle.

"I'm always charming."

"Hmm."

"It's getting late," Svafa said, a note of worry in his voice. "I want us back indoors before nightfall."

"This is as fast as I can walk," I protested, ignoring Svafa's sigh of irritation.

"He's right," muttered Jolinn, looking around the quiet street. Most people were already at home, their business done for the day, although three men were standing up ahead, watching us approach. I glanced behind me and saw another group of three following us at a discreet distance. Svafa noticed them as well, exchanging a look with Jolinn.

"Do you know them?" I asked him. The young warrior shook his head and when I half drew my sword I felt a moment of panic as I saw the pale blue glow of the blade.

I gripped Svafa's arm. "Don't go any closer and draw your sword. Now."

Seeing they had been recognised, the men in front of us drew their weapons – a deadly assortment of axes and daggers. I looked behind us again and saw the other warriors closing in, their blades already out, cold steel glinting in the light of the setting sun. The street was narrow, the location of the attack ensuring there were no other alleyways or roads we could take that offered the chance of escape.

Svafa cursed, the three of us drawing our swords as we took up a position back-to-back, runeblades glowing ghostly blue as the durath approached. Our only advantage was the tight street made it difficult for our enemies to attack us. I faced one foe carrying two daggers, whilst Svafa and Jolinn took on opponents armed with axes, Jolinn shouting for help as she did so. Her voice echoed off the walls as the first of the assassins reached me and lunged forwards with his blades.

I grunted with the effort as my sword met his strokes, parrying each one as I concentrated on keeping my foe in front of me, preventing his companions getting too close. He dropped to one side, letting another man step in, his dagger blade whistling past my ear as I managed to sidestep the attack. My wrist was already burning from the effort of holding off their weapons and I was forced backwards, jostling Svafa as I did so. I risked a glance to where Jolinn was trading fierce blows with the axeman. Svafa reached out, grabbing his foe's arm, stopping him from bringing his axe down, shoving him into a doorway with a huge crash. Svafa gave a roar and drove his runeblade into the durath's heart, one rune dimming as Old Gunnar's former weapon destroyed the shadow spirit. Black smoke billowed out from the wound and flowed from the creature's mouth and nose, the foul acrid smell making me cough as the shadow spirit's body crumbled, axe falling to the ground with a loud clatter.

Another durath lunged forwards at Svafa, who sidestepped the strike at the last moment, his dagger burying itself in the wooden door. The durath shrieked in frustration, planting his foot on the door to pull his weapon free. With a loud cry Svafa brought his sword down on the back of the creature's neck.

My adversary's strokes forced me backwards, the air rattling in my lungs as I struggled to keep up. I was fighting on instinct, using those skills honed during long hours on the practice courts. However, my body was tiring quickly and the durath's dagger tip caught my cloak, narrowly missing my shoulder. There was a whistling sound followed by a dull crunch as Jolinn appeared through the smoke of the dying durath at Svafa's feet, burying her sword in the skull of my enemy with a shout. Another opponent stepped in close and I tried to take my opportunity, blade darting out, only to despair when I discovered I didn't have the strength to pierce his leather armour, the point of my sword turned away. I was forced to staggering backwards to avoid a savage cut by his dagger.

Jolinn grunted as she wrenched her sword free, one rune now dimmed, and a fine spray of blood spattered my face as she slashed the blade left and right. The shadow spirit met her strokes and I raised my sword, aiming for his throat, where there was a gap in his armour. However a blow from behind drove me to my knees and I felt hot breath on my face as arms wrapped around me, teeth snapping at my shoulder and neck. I was forced to the ground and my sword span out of my hand, clattering away, out of reach.

"King Adalrikr sends you his greetings," the durath hissed, slamming my head into the cobblestones.

I tried to roll away, cursing, his grip too strong. Blood was coming from a wound on my head and the durath turned me over onto my back as my limbs became lead weights. I blinked, everything moving so slowly, sounds coming to me as if through water. He ripped open my shirt, exposing my neck as he bared his teeth.

I gasped as blood sluiced from his throat, drenching and blinding me as Jolinn's sword swing virtually decapitated my assailant. His body dropped on top of mine, pinning me to the ground as the flow of blood was replaced by a poisonous smoke, making me gag. I felt Jolinn's strong hands under my armpits as she dragged me free, both of us coughing as we staggered back, resting side by side against a stone wall, gasping for breath.

I wiped the thick blood away from my eyes with shaking hands. Svafa stood there with a stunned look on his face, staring at the ragged remains of clothes and weapons scattered around the street, the only remaining signs we'd come under attack. I felt the back of my head, damp with blood, where a lump was already starting to swell.

"Are you alright? Are you hurt?" Svafa asked, bending down to check my wounds, eyes wide as he took in all the blood covering my clothes.

"I'm fine. It's not mine – at least, most of it isn't," I explained, allowing Jolinn and Svafa to help me onto shaking feet.

"That was far too close," Svafa muttered breathlessly. "We should have been more careful. Those were the shadow spirits Tellian was talking about, weren't they? I'd never thought ..." His words trailed off as the young warrior tried to take in what had just happened.

Jolinn nodded. "That's why you carry a runeblade,

Svafa. You did well."

I shook my head, trying to clear it and bring my pounding heart back under control. "It looks like Adalrikr really doesn't want me to reach the Fire Isle."

CHAPTER 17

The road wound its way alongside fields and through the occasional sun-dappled copse as it followed the River Jelt, iridescent dragonflies buzzing across the waters in the summer sun. Djuri caught a flash in the corner of his eye as a bright blue streak darted out from a small burrow in the riverbank. There was a splash and the kingfisher broke out of the waters, a minnow firmly caught between its beak as it flew back towards its riverside home.

A perfect summer day to take a fisherman and two young women prisoner, thought Djuri. He felt a lump in his throat as he remembered Haarl and wondered what would become of his son, Finn, when all this was over. He wished Ulf was here; he needed someone he could trust to have his back, out here surrounded by Galin's warriors. Tyrfingr's mysterious visitors hadn't said a word since they had ridden out that morning. Ten of them to capture one old man and two women seemed heavy-handed to Djuri – there had to be more to this to explain Adalrikr's interest.

Djuri absently swatted away an insect from his face, swaying in his saddle as he matched the rhythmic trot of his horse. It hadn't been easy to bend the knee to Tyrfingr in the Great Hall. It was no excuse that he'd been beaten, bloodied and exhausted after weeks spent in the cells under Ulfkell's Keep. He knew what he was doing when he pledged his cause to Tyrfingr and betrayed his own clan. Only later did he understand those betrayals were constant, one bad day leading to another. The time he spent privately with Nereth was pleasant enough, only for the fear and worry to return afterwards, like being drawn ever deeper into foul waters that threatened to cover his head and drown him.

Kolsveinn held up his hand at the head of their column and the riders halted. They were approaching the edge of the woods and Djuri knew Humli's cottage was just around the next bend in the river. They'd looked for Humli at the fish markets at dawn, waiting near Sissa Gamliswyfe's stall for him to make an appearance. When he didn't show they'd saddled their horses and made straight for his home.

"Galin, come with me," said Eidr. "Bring three of your men and we'll take a path through the woods, so we can position ourselves on the far side of the road. We don't want our friends to escape."

Djuri remained with Kolsveinn as the group melted into the trees, their horses picketed nearby. Birds sang and chattered as Djuri's mount stamped nervously. He reached down and stroked her neck as she whickered, calming her even as his own heart began to beat faster.

"Don't think I've seen you before," began one of the Vorund warriors in a low voice, addressing Kolsveinn. "Where were you stationed before this? I'm from Jastaburg ..." He trailed off as the other man glared at him.

"What makes you think I have any interest in talking to you? Keep quiet and wait for the signal."

They sat on their horses waiting in silence after that until Kolsveinn signalled the advance, waving at the others to follow him. Djuri patted his horse and set off after him, the other warriors following behind. When the small cottage came into view he knew they were too late – Humli's boat was gone, the jetty empty. Djuri quickly wiped the smile from his face, not difficult when he saw Kolsveinn's thunderous expression. One of the warriors kicked open the door and Djuri followed them into the deserted cottage with Kolsveinn. It was gloomy inside, the hearth cold and all the food gone. There were two small wooden cots in the bedroom and Kolsveinn stood for a time, hands resting on both of them, looking troubled as Galin's warriors tore the place apart. Crockery smashed, straw mattresses were ripped open, floorboards levered up.

Eidr appeared at the doorway and peered inside with a shake of his head. "Nothing?"

"No, we're too late," spat Kolsveinn. "The question is, which way did they go? Upriver towards Lake Tull or out to sea?"

"That ship was tiny," Eidr replied. "Five of them won't be able to get far in that – certainly not out in the open sea. My guess is they headed upstream."

Kolsveinn picked up one of the cots with a roar and threw it hard against the wall, smashing it to pieces, blue eyes flashing with rage.

"Kolsveinn. We'll *find* them," said Eidr.

"Tell that to our king," Kolsveinn snapped, breathing hard.

"I'll ride upriver with Galin and his warriors to begin the search," Eidr replied. "I suggest you return to Ulfkell's Keep and send out search parties to all the nearby coastal towns. If they're holed up in one of those we'll find their hiding place soon enough."

Kolsveinn nodded and clapped a hand on Djuri's chest. "One thing's for sure. They won't be coming back here. Burn it to the ground."

Djuri looked back just once as he rode towards Ulfkell's Keep with Kolsveinn. Thick black smoke was rising through the open shutters up into the sky, the crackle of the flames within the cottage growing louder despite the distance. One image stayed with him. Two little wooden horses, painted red and yellow, one smashed underfoot by Vorund's warriors as they turned the cottage upside down. He'd stood in the doorway, watching the fire take hold, flames curling around the broken horse as his matching companion looked on a few feet away.

Two horses. Two toys for two small boys would have been Djuri's guess. One for Finn and the other for – who, exactly? Haarl had never mentioned Humli having any other children, so this had to be Lina's child. He looked at Kolsveinn riding in silence and again wondered what made this woman of such interest to Adalrikr.

***

I rose from my seat in my chambers, head still throbbing from yesterday's attempt on my life. Joldir stood, stretching his back, which gave a satisfying crack. Leif, temporarily released from his smithing on Johan's orders, sat quietly in the corner in his chair by the window.

Joldir cleared his throat. "The Path guides us to old haunts and the places of our past this morning. I was hoping we'd learn more concerning your attackers."

I sighed. "There were a lot of people in the feasting hall. It would be all too easy for one careless word to be overheard by the durath hidden within Romsdahl. Perhaps this is better – we forced them to show their hand."

Leif drew his knees up to his chest, resting his head against them. I walked over, giving his arm an awkward pat, a mix of emotions surging through me.

"Leif," Joldir began. "We've talked about this before, haven't we? About Lina –"

"Don't keep telling me she's not my mother," the boy snapped. "You think I don't *know* that? You tell me she's gone all the time. That doesn't mean ..." He roughly wiped away tears with the heel of his hand.

I reflected it would have been better if Lina had died when we burned Tullen to the ground. Anders, Leif's father, had also been possessed by the durath and Leif had accepted his father's death in Tullen when we'd slain the shadow spirit. The fact one of the durath still walked Amuran in his mother's form was torturing the boy.

"I'll take him back to Curruck," Joldir told me, putting a hand on Leif's shoulder. "It'll do you good and take your mind off things. The Sight's curse is to see events far away you can't change or influence. I'm sorry, Leif, but there it is."

Leif rose in silence, although he didn't shrug Joldir's crooked fingers away.

"Are you well enough to begin your works down at the docks tomorrow?" Joldir asked me.

"I think so. The fact the durath were so keen to stop me is motivation enough."

"Good, I'll see you tomorrow morning. Call by my house on your way and we'll walk there together."

Ulfarr, who was waiting outside with Myr, smiled when I told him we were leaving. "Good. It's boring standing out here all day long." Myr nodded in agreement.

Whilst Joldir and Leif headed off to Curruck's smithy, the three of us left to find Etta. Following her rehabilitation she had taken up rooms in the castle in order to be closer to Gautarr and Johan. Gautarr was less than delighted at the presence of his new guest, although he treated her with every courtesy. Bandor had made me aware there were dark mutterings in some quarters that her rejuvenation was not entirely natural. When I mentioned this, suspecting Svan to be the source, Etta evaded my various questions. Since she wouldn't be drawn on how her health had been restored, I was unable to quell the rumours and I worried whether there was indeed some truth behind them. Despite my concerns, Etta remained tight-lipped as she focussed on exercising more influence on the affairs of the clan. She would expect a report from me on what my Fellowship had discovered – doubtless the intrigue of durath at Ulfkell's Keep and Geilir's arrival at Norlhast would be of particular interest.

***

The following morning I readied myself to begin the work of warding *Stormweaver* with Joldir. After the last attack, Johan had ordered my guard to be doubled if I was travelling to the docks. Ulfarr and Jolinn chatted as they led the way, Myr and Eykr, one of Kalamar's own, guarding our backs. Joldir looked tired and I could tell his hands were paining him. I was one of the few people who truly understood what it was like to lose so much. I placed a hand on his shoulder and the older man smiled.

Meinolf Saltbeard met the six of us down at the docks, while Aerinndis and most of her crew were away as they sought out provisions and any remaining equipment needed for the voyage. I recognised Feyotra, *Stormweaver's* diminutive navigator, talking with another woman called Matthildr and a young sailor named Jonas as they worked side by side mending sailcloth. These women were no doubt drawn to a life among *Stormweaver's* crew by the rarity of serving under a female captain and I wondered what Brunn Fourwinds would have made of such a thing. I'd noticed how Romsdahl paid less heed to the Laws of Reave compared to their strict application in Ulfkell's Keep. These southern ways still took me by surprise, although I reflected that my own grandfather had broken with tradition when Etta became his counsellor.

I ran my hand along the smooth wooden planks of *Stormweaver's* freshly painted hull – bright red and green stripes, with the green paintwork flowing up and around the dragon figurehead on the prow. Meinolf smiled as he watched me admiring his vessel, once again proudly telling me we had chosen the best ship for our journey. He set foot on a ladder and led us up onto the deck of the longship.

"What will these runes of yours do, exactly?" he asked, arms crossed as he watched me unfold the bundle of cloth in which my brushes were wrapped. Myr and Eykr set down two wooden buckets, thick black paint sloshing around inside.

"I'll establish a warded threshold," I explained, "creating a barrier around the hull of the longship that the durath will be unable to cross, at least not without great difficulty. If any of your crewmates are possessed it will also reveal them to us, weaken their powers and give us a chance to end them with our runeblades."

Meinolf shuddered. "You surely don't think that some

of us are ... what? These shadow spirits you were talking about?"

"It could be anybody," said Joldir. "It could be you."

Standing towards the stern of the ship Jolinn gave Meinolf a long stare, patting the hilt of her sword.

"Let's hope it doesn't come to that," Meinolf replied.

"There are other things I can do as well," Joldir continued. "Elemental wards and runes that can protect this vessel from the sea and storms. Further runes on the inside of her hull that will strengthen her timbers and help protect her from the damage caused by ice as you sail further north."

"Right," Meinolf said, looking sceptical. He thought better of making any sarcastic remarks as he glanced over his shoulder at Jolinn and Ulfarr. "Sounds like you have a lot of work to do, so I'll leave you to it."

I smiled as I picked up the nearest brush and began my work.

CHAPTER 18

Leif hung his head as he walked towards Joldir's house, bone tired; feet finding their own way home through Romsdahl's winding streets. Curruck was a quiet man, not given to saying much, yet Leif knew he'd disappointed the smith. Usually, his small fingers were ideal for intricate metalwork. Today he'd managed to ruin three pieces before Curruck gently placed a rough hand on Leif's shoulder and told him to work the bellows. Leif grunted with the effort, sweat pouring off him as the day wore on, as Curruck poured the molten metal into a mould, time and again. By the end of the day his shoulders ached and they had a barrel full of arrowheads to show for their labours. Readying for war could be dull work.

"Tomorrow, you'll finish the brooch Svan has asked for," Curruck said as he bid him farewell. "Get some rest and make sure you're keen and bright-eyed when you come back to my forge tomorrow."

Leif could feel Rothgar watching him as he walked – his presence like the merest stirring of the wind. Had they not grown to know each other so well through their Fellowship the intrusion would have gone unnoticed. A smile crept across Leif's face as he imagined what Joldir would say if he knew Rothgar was using the Sight more than ever. Rothgar's interest didn't really bother Leif. There was a loneliness to the broken prince and if he craved the touch of company and life beyond the confines of his empty chamber in the castle then let him share these stolen moments. Hearing laughter inside, Leif pushed open the door to Joldir's house, finding that both Thengill and Ulfarr were there as his guests that evening.

***

Ulfarr looked up as Arissa called out a greeting to Leif, telling the boy to wash his face and hands before joining them for their meal. Ulfarr leaned back in his chair at the table, taking his ease and noting how Thengill's eyes never strayed far from Arissa, the couple touching each other whenever they thought no one was looking. It was nothing too obvious – fingertips brushing as they set the table together, a hand placed lightly on Thengill's shoulder and once, briefly, his around Arissa's waist. The warriors in the Brotherhood spoke of Thengill with awe and Johan had taken to calling him Adalrikr's executioner. In Arissa's company he was a different man since the news of their betrothal and Ulfarr shook his head, amused by the mysterious power of women.

"Something on your mind?" Joldir asked Leif, his hands stained black from his work on *Stormweaver*. Leif shook his head as he trotted over to a bowl of water next to his bed, giving his face and hands a cursory wash.

Thengill's axes were set against the wall by the door. Ulfarr watched as Leif paused to look at them, the metal gleaming and sharp, wooden handles worn smooth from frequent use. Runes covered the weapons, dark and cold. The interlocking dragon and chimera pattern was etched in exquisite detail, Ulfarr reflecting that Joldir's injury had robbed Reavesburg of a master craftsman. Thinking he was unobserved, Leif reached out and ran his fingers over the design, causing a faint crackle of power to spark against his fingertips.

"You're touching history," Thengill told him, making Leif jump.

He turned round, looking guilty. "I was just looking," Leif said, relaxing a little as he saw Thengill was smiling.

Thengill raised a thick black eyebrow and his grin broadened. "You were *touching*. Those axes are no toys – they're destined to kill Adalrikr Kinslayer."

Arissa shuddered as she stood at the table, listening to their conversation. Thengill saw the expression on her face and walked over, giant arms drawing her into an embrace.

"Why does it have to be you?" she whispered.

"My people have been poisoned by the durath. It's only right I'm the one who roots them out and puts an end to the war."

Arissa looked up into his face. "Adalrikr's surrounded by the Sundered Souls and protected by foul death magic. You can't defeat them all."

Thengill sighed. "I'll have the Brotherhood at my side, but this is one battle I can't walk away from, even if I wanted to. I'm better protected than most, since the durath can't use their magic against me, a gift from the Fates I'd be wrong to spurn. Remember what you said to me when we talked about how I didn't want you to come with us to Vorund Fastness?"

Arissa stepped back and folded her arms, green eyes flashing, face framed by her long dark red hair. "I told you that the Brotherhood needs someone to run the hospital while Joldir ... recovers ... and I'm a trained healer. I can hardly stay here, knowing I could be helping tend the wounded. Maeva and Dalla feel the same way. I understand why Ingirith has chosen to remain behind – she has her children to think of. My path lies with you, at the side of the Brotherhood."

"Then you can understand why this is something I have to do," Thengill told her.

Ulfarr watched as Leif wandered over to the range, sniffing the food and asking Joldir whether the fish was ready. Johan had assigned Ulfarr's crew, including Ekkill, to join Rothgar's voyage north and Ulfarr was still trying to make up his mind whether that was a more dangerous mission than the journey south to Vorund Fastness. Leif would be travelling to Vorund with Joldir and Arissa, despite Romsdahl being safer for a boy of his tender years. Unlike Ingirith's children, Leif's abilities marked him out and Joldir was keen to continue his tuition in the Sight as well as his metalworking apprenticeship under Curruck.

Joldir hurried over, waving Arissa away as he awkwardly took the baked fish stew out of the oven. Ulfarr's stomach growled and he broke open a brown roll, smearing a pat of butter over it and stuffing it into his mouth as Joldir spooned long green beans and carrots onto his trencher.

"Fresh carrots," Ulfarr said wistfully, holding up the steaming vegetable on the end of his knife. "Enjoy it while you can. Whichever way our journeys take us, it'll be salted meat and dried provisions when we set sail. After a few weeks we'll all be *dreaming* of fresh food."

They enjoyed each other's company as they ate and talked, knowing this was one of the last times they would be together before going their separate ways. Everyone carefully avoided the fact that when Ulfarr was eventually reunited with them at Vorund Fastness, there was a chance some members of the Brotherhood would have made the journey to Navan's Halls. Ulfarr grimly reflected that could easily mean him or his crew but there was nothing to be done about that now – the Brotherhood had long ago chosen a path where there were no guarantees.

After finishing their meal, Arissa took Leif off to bed, the boy looking absolutely exhausted. The rest of them took their ease by the fire as darkness fell and Ulfarr asked Joldir what he thought awaited them at Vorund Fastness. "Things were pretty dicey when we faced them in Lake Tull," said Ulfarr. "Breaking into Adalrikr's stronghold ..." Ulfarr shook his head. "I don't want to sound so full of doubt but now the moment's come, I fear we've overreached ourselves."

"We must," Thengill replied, staring into the fire, the flickering light reflecting off the polished metal of his axes by the wall. "We must recover Vorund Fastness from the Kinslayer."

"You'd be a fool, or insane, if you didn't have doubts," Joldir told Ulfarr with a grimace. "Much depends on Norlhast joining our cause, which appears much more realistic now than it did three months ago. But yes, Ulfarr, when it comes down to it we must overcome the dark magic of Adalrikr and his allies. That will be no easy task and we must hope your mission with Rothgar helps even the odds. Ultimately, I have to trust in the wisdom of the Weeping Warrior – after all, without him, we would never have won the Battle of Romsdahl."

"Strange times indeed," muttered Thengill as Arissa took a seat next to him and he put his arm protectively around her shoulders.

"This will be a dark and bloody business but at least we're more prepared," Joldir admitted. "I had no idea what I was going to face when Serena sent me to investigate a series of murders, reportedly committed by people possessed by dark spirits. This was years ago, whilst I was a student with the Mages of Mirtan and Serena was the head of our Chapter. Serena had this giant map in her chambers and I remember her pointing to it, marking out the location of each story and tale, always heading north. Attacks in the port of Medan, followed by further incidents near the southern marshlands and then the Mirtanian port of Tivir. The latest reports placed them on the northern border of Mirtan, near the city of Okas, where members of our Chapter confronted a group of ten travellers crossing the Icefell River. They destroyed our adepts and murdered the border guards before disappearing into the Northern Plains. Witnesses spoke of the way they moved and how they fought – lightning fast, more animal than man. Throats torn out, eating the flesh of their enemies. You've seen what the durath can do for yourselves but, back then, we were ignorant and believed the tales to be exaggerated."

Joldir shrugged as he continued. "I was a student of Ramill at the time and he asked me to join the company he was putting together on Serena's orders. After all, he said, who better to act as a guide than a northman? It didn't matter I was originally from Reavesburg – the north is all the same to Mirtanian southerners. Nereth, as my apprentice, also accompanied me. We followed the trail across the plains, stumbling one day across a slaughtered tribe of nomads, killed in similar fashion to the guards at Okas. It was obvious their elder had been tortured before he died. The trail led westwards, into Vorund lands, our quarry not even bothering to try and disguise their passage. The signs were everywhere; farming families murdered in their homes, deserted villages where people had fled."

"Why?" asked Thengill. "It makes no sense. Why would they draw attention to themselves?"

Joldir shook his head. "That's something I debated with Ramill and Nereth several times on our journey. It's only a theory but I now believe the durath consume human flesh to gain power in some way. Perhaps this was necessary to enable them to open up the gateway that now exists under Vorund Fastness? Sandar built his altar after filling his long hall in Tullen with the skulls of his victims for a reason, and we may need to understand that secret before the final confrontation with Adalrikr. Back then we had Knights of the Chapter escorting us, hardened men and women familiar with war. I could tell they were frightened by what they'd seen. Ramill was too, even as he ordered us to continue, the trail taking us nearer Vorund Fastness each day."

Joldir paused, taking a sip of ale. "They attacked us one night as we camped in the grasslands south of Usiel. I woke to the sound of screaming as the durath tore apart the knights on watch. They ripped them limb from limb, laughing all the while ... There was a blazing light as Ramill stepped forwards, gathering together those who were still alive as we stared, horrified, at a scene of carnage and murder. Then a man approached us, face and hands red with blood, demanding our surrender. It was Vashtas, Flayer of Souls, the First of the Sundered. He wore a different guise back then, since this was several years before he began posing as Adalrikr, Laskar's northern king."

"What did you do?" asked Arissa in a small voice and Ulfarr realised this tale was as new to Joldir's adopted daughter as it was to the rest of them.

"Vashtas' name was a well-known legend in Mirtan and finding it made flesh struck terror into our hearts. When Ramill pleaded for mercy, Vashtas only laughed."

"How did you survive?" asked Thengill, wide-eyed.

Joldir pursed his lips. "When Ramill realised his appeal for clemency was futile, he gave the order to fight. Nereth panicked and turned traitor, stabbing Ramill in the back to try and save herself, which plunged the rest of us into darkness. The sounds that followed ... They'll never leave me. Men and women screaming as they were slaughtered, the sounds of clashing steel, breaking bone and tearing flesh. My training and magic fled my mind and I ran into the night, leaving everyone behind. I ran until I couldn't breathe and when I stopped and listened the night was quiet and still. Somehow I evaded capture and several days later I made it over the border, back into Reavesburg. Ekkill found me in Romsdahl and brought me to Etta. She offered to pay for my passage back to Mirtan to complete my studies but I was too ashamed to face Serena. I'd abandoned my master and my apprentice to certain death; I couldn't return after that. I took up a new life as a healer, establishing my home in Lindos, having no idea Nereth was still alive until my encounters with Rothgar years later drew me into contact with her through the Sight."

"Joldir, why didn't you speak of this before?" said Arissa, her hand entwined tightly in Thengill's.

"It's not a story I'm proud of. This is why I have to go to Vorund Fastness, so when I face Adalrikr next time I won't break."

Thengill's frown deepened. "We always knew this would be a deadly, hard fight but you don't have to worry about the Kinslayer. He's mine. After listening to your tale,

I'd have thought you'd want to turn north and hunt Nereth down."

Joldir nodded. "I'd like to see her and speak with her again before the end, if I get the chance."

"*Speak* with her?" Arissa looked shocked. "You surely can't believe you can be reconciled, not after everything she's done."

Joldir looked away, his gaze distant, seeing another time and place. "Sometimes we need to face the people from our past so we can close one chapter of our lives and move on. Nereth's betrayal wounded me more deeply than Ramill's death. However, I can't escape the fact I also betrayed my companions and left them behind to die. It constantly plays on my mind and ... I don't know, it feels like there's unfinished business between us."

Thengill raised his cup. "To setting aside the ghosts of our past."

Ulfarr nodded as he raised his own mug, pondering on everything Joldir had said. *Whether I go by the longer road or the shorter one, when I reach the end of it blood is going to be spilled at Vorund Fastness.* He wondered which, if any of them present here tonight, would be there when the time finally came to bring Nereth to justice.

"To setting aside ghosts of the past," Ulfarr said, and they drank once more. Sometimes, it was best to leave your darkest thoughts unspoken.

CHAPTER 19

Humli stared at his boat, moored to the jetty as it bobbed on the waves. It was raining, dawn's light little more than a pale glow as the sun struggled to penetrate the grey clouds. The town of Noln on the Reavesburg coast was a busy port, better known for its merchant links than fishing trade, although Humli's boat wasn't out of place. There were plenty of fishermen landing and unloading their catch for the morning markets and Humli had been here himself a few times, though that was years ago. He offered up a prayer to Dinuvillan no one would recognise him.

Lina and Desta stood at his side, both cloaked, hoods up to shield them from the rain, their children wrapped up and held tight to their chests. A couple of dock workers were looking at them curiously and Humli shouldered his bag, pulling up the hood on his travelling cloak as they walked away. He paused for a moment, turning and looking back at his old boat.

Funny, in all the years I worked on her I never gave her a name. No point doing that now, so why does it feel like I've abandoned a member of my family? Humli coughed and cleared his throat, pressing on as they joined a crowd of people making their way towards the market. He held his breath as they walked through Noln's gates, passing two guards carrying shields depicting a bear on its hind feet. Frokn whimpered and Lina tried to settle him, stroking his head and whispering in his ear. Humli kept his gaze forward and they passed the guards without challenge, his heart hammering until they turned a corner and were out of sight.

"Are you sure about this?" Lina asked, not for the first

time.

"If you've a better idea, I'd like to hear it," Desta snapped. "Shush, Finn, I'm sorry. It'll be alright. Hush. I didn't mean to startle you."

Lina pursed her lips, glancing at Humli. He shared her misgivings but they were desperate and former thralls didn't have many friends in high places. His boat was too small to take them far – they'd been fortunate the sea had been calm as they made the cramped, uncomfortable journey along the coast to Noln. This was the best plan they'd been able to come up with. The market square was already busy, more people arriving every minute as Humli looked at the surrounding buildings. The largest of these had two warriors posted outside the front door and Humli guessed it was the home of Lundvarr, Noln's elder. Lina hissed when Humli shared his thoughts.

"Why are there guards? How do we get past them?"

"He's the town elder. There's bound to be guards," Humli explained, trying to keep his voice calm.

Desta drew herself up straight, passing Finn over to her father. "I'll have to talk to them – there's no other way to get inside, not without drawing attention to ourselves."

It took Humli a moment to understand what Desta was about to do. "No, take the child back. If anyone's going to do this it should be me."

"And if something happens to you?" Lina replied. "What do you think will happen to two young women alone on the road? Desta's right. Let her go."

Humli watched reluctantly as Desta crossed the market square and headed towards Lundvarr's house. He wanted to go with her but if things went wrong they couldn't afford to all be caught up in whatever happened next. He gritted his teeth, desperately hoping these warriors were Reavesburg men. One of the guards walked towards Desta as she approached and the two of them spoke for a short while. Finn wriggled in Humli's arms, growing restless and

Lina held Frokn close. Finally, Desta turned and waved to them. Humli swallowed, legs feeling like water as he walked towards his daughter.

"This is Dyri, a Reavesburg man," said Desta, introducing the youthful dark-haired warrior she had been speaking to. "He'll take us to Lundvarr."

Dyri took them to the back of the house, which was obviously the tradesman's entrance. Humli's heart jumped when he saw there were already half a dozen men and women waiting there in a small walled garden. They were all dressed in fine clothes, marking them out as wealthy merchants. As they turned and stared at the new arrivals Humli was acutely aware of his patched clothes and travel-stained cloak; Lina and Desta looked little better.

Dyri entered Lundvarr's house and emerged a few minutes later, telling Humli and his companions to come inside. A number of the merchants protested as Dyri shook his head, closing the door firmly in their faces with an apologetic smile. They were escorted into Lundvarr's office, where Noln's elder was sitting in a red leather chair behind a carved wooden desk, strewn with papers, ledgers and books. He didn't rise when they entered although his face registered some surprise at the appearance of his guests. He had curly dark hair, now greying and receding. When he spoke Humli was surprised at his halting, hesitant manner – the elder of Noln lacking any natural authority.

"Dyri tells me you and your children are in need of help. How may I be of service?"

Desta stepped forwards, introducing them. "I'm Desta Haarlswyfe, widowed after my husband fell in the Battle of Romsdahl, fighting in Adalrikr's service. You may have met him when you came to Ulfkell's Keep on business. I've personally waited on you in the Great Hall when you were a guest of our chief, although I doubt you remember me."

Lundvarr's eyes narrowed. "Haarl. I confess the name means nothing to me. I'm sorry to hear of your loss but if your husband died fighting for the Vorund Clan then surely Tyrfingr Blackeyes as Jarl of Reavesburg owes you a boon. Why come to me?"

"You'll know Johan Jokellsward leads a rebellion against Adalrikr's rule," Desta explained. "One of his supporters is Rothgar Kolfinnarson, brother of our late chief." Lundvarr remained silent, listening intently as he stared, unseeing, at the papers he was idly shuffling on his desk. "I know Rothgar's name means something to you after he led the warriors who saved Noln from attack. Rothgar meant much to me as well and we were ... very close, before Ulfkell's Keep fell. My history with Rothgar places me and my family in danger, forcing us to flee our home."

"You must understand I have little *real* power here," Lundvarr stuttered. "I serve Tyrfingr. Defying him would be ... unwise. Perhaps if you explain your situation and remind him of how Haarl loyally served him this past year ..."

Humli shook his head. "Mercy and reason are not qualities Tyrfingr is famous for. Remember how Blackeyes hung Rothgar from a crows cage?"

"Do you know why he did that?" added Desta. "Tyrfingr tortured and humiliated Rothgar as vengeance for the defeat he suffered at his hands, right here at Noln. Rothgar was the only one who came to your aid when your town was attacked, fighting side by side with my husband. Without their intervention Noln would have been sacked and you would be a thrall in Vorund Fastness, rather than living in this fine, comfortable house. You're in debt both to Rothgar and my late husband and now I'm asking for that debt to be repaid."

"We're not asking you to fight," said Humli as Lundvarr hesitated, looking at each of them in turn. "We only want to be on our way. Surely you can help a small group of women and children to get away from here?"

"It's not that simple," protested Lundvarr. "If I help you I'll be defying the jarl – that's *treason*."

"Noln's a trading port," said Lina. "Ships for Helsburg and Vittag come and go from here all the time. We need safe passage on one, that's all."

Humli stepped forwards, holding out his purse. "We have money. We can pay our way if you put us in touch with the captain of a ship willing to take us."

Lundvarr shook his head. "Keep your coin – you'll need it. Whatever you have in your purse won't be enough to smuggle you out of Noln under Blackeyes' nose."

Lundvarr rested his elbows on his desk, running his hands through his hair, weighing up his choices while Finn stirred, no doubt getting hungry. Desta bounced him on her hip, telling him to keep quiet and Lundvarr looked up at the mention of his name.

"What did you say your son's name was?"

"Finnvidor, although we normally call him Finn," Desta told him. "Haarl wanted to name him after Finnvidor Einarrson, the jarl he served under before … everything changed."

"A good choice," Lundvarr said with a sigh. "I remember Finnvidor well. He was an honourable man, very close to Alaine, Rothgar's mother. He was completely distraught when she died – I remember him watching her funeral pyre all through the night, long after everyone else had left. Finnvidor didn't deserve to die that way. I watched Vorund's warriors carry his body out of the Great Hall the following morning, laughing and joking as they dumped it in the street, covered in dirt, bloodied and mutilated. Tyrfingr didn't show him the honour he was owed as a jarl."

"Please, can you help us?" Desta asked as she continued to nurse Finn.

Lundvarr turned to her, though his eyes were distant. "I saw what Blackeyes did to Rothgar," he told her, voice shaking. "He made us watch as he pressed a hot iron into his flesh, over and over. I'll never forget his screams in the Great Hall but don't you understand? If I help you and Tyrfingr finds out what I've done that would be my fate."

"If you don't help us can you live with your conscience?" Lina replied. "You speak of how much you admire Finnvidor's honour whilst displaying little of your own. You owe a debt to Rothgar Kolfinnarson's household and you baulk now the time has come to repay it?"

"I'm no warrior. I never have been."

"We didn't ask for any of this," Humli pressed. "If you can't help us I don't know who else we can turn to."

Lundvarr sat there in silence, fiddling with a gold ring on his little finger. "You can't stay here. I know the owner of one of the smokehouses who's no friend to the Vorund Clan. Remain there and when the arrangements are made I'll send Dyri to find you. You can trust him."

"Thank you," Desta said, tears in her eyes. "Thank you so much."

"Save your thanks for when you're safely on that ship," Lundvarr told her, his face full of misgiving.

CHAPTER 20

"It's going to take forever to ward my ship if all you do is stare at the paint drying on your brush."

I glanced up to find Aerinndis watching me, head cocked on one side, her curly red hair wild and unruly, tousled by the wind. She was straddling the side of *Stormweaver*, one leg swinging in empty air, the other booted foot resting on the deck.

"How long have you been there?" *How long have I been away?*

"A while," Aerinndis told me, grinning.

I glanced at Joldir, wondering if he'd shared my vision. He was busy at work, holding his brush with some difficulty as he concentrated on the intricate patterns now covering half the mast, which had been lowered onto the deck for the task. There was no indication he'd joined me on the Path and I swallowed, reflecting how it was becoming all too easy to slip away, even during my waking hours. Easy and dangerous. At least Desta had a chance, all because I'd ridden out to defend my realm and thwart Tyrfingr's attack at Noln. Those deeds had made a real difference after all, even if my warrior days were long behind me.

"Are you alright?" Aerinndis asked, a frown creasing her forehead.

Joldir looked up as I stood and stretched my back. As I tried to think of the best way to answer I heard voices below calling out in greeting. I peered over the side of the ship, where from my vantage point on top of the scaffolding I could see Meinolf talking to Molda and Tellian. Aerinndis scampered down the ladder to greet her parents as Jolinn,

Ulfarr, Skari and Myr watched them approach. Johan had assigned Ulfarr's crew to accompany me on the journey north and Jolinn had volunteered to join the mission as well. They were now my constant guards, the thinking being it made sense for them to get to know *Stormweaver's* crew. However, I also noted that, with the exception of Jolinn, all of them only carried weapons etched with a single rune. They had been with me in the castle prior to the battle of Romsdahl, so Joldir didn't have the opportunity to work on them, unlike the other members of the Brotherhood. Johan was keeping his most powerful runeblades close, most notably Thengill and his axes. Whilst I understood his reasoning I realised he still had doubts about whether I would ever return from this journey. Ulfarr and his companions looked up as Molda and Tellian crossed the runestone barrier encircling the longship, the runes etched onto the stones remaining dark and dormant. Another attack by the durath was always a possibility and we were taking every precaution.

"How's my daughter?" asked Tellian with a broad smile.

Aerinndis hugged him. "Eager to be on my way. Your idea of warding my ship has kept us in the docks for longer than I hoped."

"It's an investment in your future," Molda told her, walking over to inspect our craftsmanship.

Runes swirled along the length of the vessel, warding her against waves, ice and storms while Joldir's runes on the mast would keep it strong and channel the winds. I was busy protecting *Stormweaver* from the durath and there was just the dragon figurehead decorating the prow to finish after that, for which Joldir had special plans.

Molda was running her fingers over the runes on the keel. "Lacquered to protect them from the salt water?"

Joldir nodded as he leaned over the side of the ship. "That's right. They'll last for years if you keep applying the lacquer every time you bring her into dry dock."

Meinolf was staring at our handiwork, hands on his hips. "She looks different with all ... this," he said with a shake of his head.

"It's still necessary," replied Tellian. "You'll be going farther, pushing your ship and crew harder than ever before. This is more perilous than a voyage to the distant Emirates or the ports of Naroque." Aerinndis' father gave Molda a sidelong glance.

"All of us must make sacrifices and take risks," Molda answered without taking her eyes off the smooth hull of *Stormweaver*. "I can't think of a better person to captain the first ship to reach the Fire Isle since Sigborn Dragonslayer."

Tellian didn't reply, hugging his daughter hard once more. "I'm coming back," Aerinndis assured him. "This is a chance to write the name of *Stormweaver* and her crew into the sagas for the bards to sing about in the future. If doing so hurts Adalrikr then all the better."

"That's the kind of thinking I can understand," Jolinn said, grinning at Ulfarr.

***

Randall shivered as he descended the stairs and entered the circular underground chamber at the base of Vorund Fastness. He preferred his audiences with Adalrikr when they were held in the main hall of the Inner Keep. Down here the air was oppressive and cloying, making it difficult to breathe and think clearly.

Adalrikr was accompanied by Hallerna, long hair stylishly arranged in braids that fell down her back. She kissed her king's cheek and Randall noticed the wound was still there, showing no sign of healing. Adalrikr was flanked by The Six, ceaselessly watchful in death, the now familiar smell of death and decay hanging in the air. Six other people stood in the chamber, two men and four women. Randall didn't recognise any of them.

"Randall, your new clothes suit you admirably," said

Hallerna with a self-satisfied smile.

Hallerna's tailor had fussed over Randall for what felt like hours while he made his measurements and notes. Randall flushed, looking down at his black breeches and fine blue velvet jerkin, tugging at the cuffs of the white linen shirt. *Still irritatingly long, no matter how fashionable they might be.*

"Don't embarrass the man," Adalrikr admonished her with a smirk, waving lazily for Randall to approach his throne.

Randall bent the knee and bowed his head while the six dignitaries looked on. Each was dressed in polished banded armour, wearing finely worked leather boots and fur trimmed cloaks. Their eyes turned on him, making Randall distinctly uncomfortable under their scrutiny. Behind Adalrikr's throne the oily blackness that dominated the centre of the chamber swirled and roiled. Randall turned his head as he heard footsteps behind him, watching as Joarr the Hammer entered the chamber. He joined Randall and bowed before his king, glancing curiously at Adalrikr's guests.

Looks like Joarr doesn't know who they are either. I guess it's better that Adalrikr's treating us both the same, I suppose.

Adalrikr told both men to stand and invited his jarls to give their reports on the preparations for war. Their king listened as they detailed how the walls had been strengthened, supplies brought into the city and the warriors drilled day and night. Randall felt a sense of pride as he thought of Kurt, his young second, training the men under his command. *They put Joarr's lot to shame.*

"Excellent," Adalrikr said. "The scrying pool has revealed to us that Johan and Gautarr will soon be ready to leave Romsdahl. When their ships land on our shores the Brotherhood will find us well-prepared."

"Your king has good tidings. Tell them," urged Hallerna.

Adalrikr smiled. "I'm pleased to say we've reached

terms with the Helsburg Clan after our emissary, Finnaril, spent time with Bothvatr. Although reluctant at first, he soon came to see the benefits of being part of my northern kingdom."

The strangers laughed and one of the women, a tall lady with flowing blonde hair and a silver nose stud, stepped forwards and drew a velvet bag from her cloak. She opened it and tipped the contents out at Adalrikr's feet. More laughter echoed throughout the chamber, as The Six stood there impassively. Randall risked a glance at Joarr, who was staring, transfixed, at the pile of fingers on the floor. A single thumb had rolled away from the pile, dropping off the table and coming to rest against Joarr's boot. He moved his foot an inch or two away with a grimace.

"Finnaril had to be quite ... persuasive. I believe Falki Ruunson, Helsburg's new jarl, will be far easier to work with. The example set in Helsburg should be enough to ensure the Vittag Clan abide by the terms of their recent agreement, which means we now have control of western Laskar without bloodshed. Well, not too much bloodshed, at least."

"Good news," Randall managed to say, the words catching in his throat.

"Indeed," said Adalrikr with a grin. "The Jorvind Clan remain trapped behind their walls in Rast in the Icefell Mountains, now besieged by our new allies the Riltbalt Clan as well as our forces. When the Brotherhood has been defeated you will take your ships and sail to the eastern coast to end their resistance. Without the Landless Jarl's defiance they may lose heart entirely – his destruction is the key to establishing our undisputed rule across Laskar."

"When he lands we'll finish him," declared Joarr, studiously ignoring the severed thumb by his foot.

Adalrikr nodded. "After your failure in Romsdahl you'd better hope for your sake that's true. Until then there's one more matter we need to deal with. We have also seen through the magic of the scrying pool that Rothgar Kolfinnarson is taking an expedition north from Romsdahl, seeking out the legendary Fire Isle on a ship called *Stormweaver*. The Brotherhood believes they will find magic and weapons across the frozen northern ocean, which they intend to use against us in an effort to turn the tide of this war."

"A fool's errand, surely?" asked Randall. *Although Adalrikr looks like he's treating it seriously.*

"Perhaps. Joarr, I want Hasteinn the Cruel to take our three fastest longships and intercept Rothgar's vessel. They're to hunt down *Stormweaver* and her crew and make sure they never return."

"Hasteinn's my second," Joarr protested.

"Then appoint another," snapped Adalrikr.

Joarr bowed his head at the reprimand. "Of course, my king. I only meant that it's one ship sailing north, chasing a bard's tale. Three longships is ..."

Joarr's voice trailed off as Finnaril appeared at his side, slipping an arm around his waist, her other hand stroking his long blond beard. She giggled and reached down to pluck the thumb off the floor. Joarr squirmed, staring at the grey-tinged digit as she toyed with it before popping it in her mouth. Randall winced at the sound of bones crunching as Finnaril chewed on the mouldering flesh in front of Joarr's horrified face.

"Finnaril is easily bored," Hallerna said, perched on her seat next to Adalrikr. "She's always looking for another distraction, isn't she?"

"Very true," Adalrikr agreed with a smirk. "I believe unquestioning obedience is the best way to avoid drawing her unwanted attention."

Randall followed Joarr up the steps as they left to give Hasteinn his orders. It was all he could do not to break into a run.

CHAPTER 21

Nuna waited nervously outside Valdimarr's private chambers in Norlhast Keep as Brosa knocked on the door and asked for admittance. A Vorund warrior ushered them inside before closing the door behind them with a solid thump. Brosa glanced around the room, tense and alert. He'd advised Nuna not to go and it was obvious he thought she'd made a mistake responding to Valdimarr's summons, although there was no sign of the little bald man she so despised. Valdimarr's treatment of her husband in the feasting hall still rankled. How *dare* he issue her with a summons – she was the Lady of Norlhast Keep, wife of the Jarl of Norlhast.

"My lady, so good of you to come at such short notice."

She turned and saw Geilir sitting in a window seat on the far side of the chamber, his long hair loosely tied back in an unruly ponytail. He grinned at her, a gold tooth flashing in the corner of his mouth. He was dressed in a white linen shirt with a black jerkin inlaid with silver thread. Grapes and wine were set on a platter in front of him, both expensive imports from Sunis or Medan. Nuna couldn't remember the last time she'd seen grapes – probably her ill-fated wedding in Ulfkell's Keep. Geilir's grin widened and he stood, holding out his hand towards Nuna. Brosa took a step forwards, hand on the hilt of his sword.

"We were invited here by Valdimarr. Where is he?" he asked.

Geilir's hand remained outstretched. To avoid embarrassment, Nuna took it and watched as Geilir bowed and kissed her fingertips lightly, grey stubble rough on her skin.

"Such beauty," Geilir declared. "Karas Greystorm is a lucky man to have you grace his halls."

"I doubt he would think it appropriate I'm here alone with you in these chambers under false pretences," Nuna replied.

"We're hardly alone. Your bodyguard is a more than capable chaperone and my guard at the door will see we're not disturbed. As for being brought here on a falsehood, you have my apologies. I find these things are better done with as little warning as possible."

"What *things*?" demanded Brosa through gritted teeth.

Geilir shook his head. "All in good time. I've heard interesting rumours since I landed in Norlhast. Strange events in the north, such as Vikarr's homestead in Ustaburg being burned to the ground. He was a good Norlhast man, quick to swear fealty to his king and follow in the footsteps of his jarl. I've heard the names of Orglyr and Fundinn whispered concerning his demise. Even more worrying, earlier this morning our messengers brought word that the Vorund garrison at Taur has been attacked and Norlhast forces are mustering there. One could be forgiven for thinking your husband was plotting something."

Nuna took a deep breath to steady her nerves, praying her voice would not betray her as she took a seat by the window. "Orglyr was Bekan's jarl. Karas let him live after he took his place as chief and Orglyr was banished from court. He's no friend of my husband, I can assure you. As for this Vikarr, I confess I've never heard the name mentioned before. Should I know him?"

Geilir shrugged, leaning back nonchalantly in the stone seat opposite her. "He was a significant northern landowner in Ustaburg and Valdimarr rewarded him for his loyalty with additional property, formerly belonging to your husband. I find it odd Karas would not have mentioned this to you, as he would have signed the title papers over to

Vikarr. Perhaps he has other uses for you, if you're not one of his confidantes."

Nuna met Geilir's gaze steadily and took a handful of grapes from the platter, popping one in her mouth. It was sweet and juicy – perfectly ripe. "I find it odd I should be subjected to an interrogation by one of Valdimarr's cronies without warning. I should be accompanied by my chosen advisors for such a meeting."

Geilir took a sip of wine from one of Valdimarr's crystal glasses, before offering to pour some for Nuna and Brosa. Both politely refused. "As you wish," Geilir said. "I must correct you, my lady. I do not serve Valdimarr. I'm here on the king's business, fresh from bringing Riltbalt under his heel, and I represent his interests here in Norlhast. Consider me his voice here in your meagre keep. It follows that when I speak, you hear the voice of your king. To defy your king or to lie to him are acts of treason and I'm sure there's no need to remind you of the penalty for someone found guilty of such a crime."

"You'll show my lady proper respect," said Brosa, standing at Nuna's shoulder. She reached up and patted his forearm.

"It's alright, Brosa. We've nothing to fear from this man, since we have nothing to hide. You're right, Geilir, my husband is pleased enough when I am at his side to decorate the feasting table or to keep him company in bed. However, he has made it plain that affairs of state are not my concern, so whatever his dealings with this Vikarr might have been, I had no knowledge of them."

Geilir sat forwards, setting down his wine on the platter. "Tell me how you helped your brother, Rothgar Kolfinnarson, escape the crows cage outside the gates of Reavesburg."

Nuna had to catch her breath at those words, knitting her fingers together on her lap to hide the fact they were shaking.

"My lady? I asked you a question."

"I heard you but I confess I don't understand what you mean. Both my brothers are dead."

"Really?" scoffed Geilir. "If that's the case then why is Rothgar one of the Landless Jarl's closest advisors? He's in Romsdahl as we speak, part of the rabble calling themselves the Brotherhood of the Eagle. You're his sister and I know the pair of you were close. You were in Reavesburg when he confessed his crimes and Tyrfingr punished him. Yet, within hours of your departure for Noln, Rothgar's cage was empty and he was nowhere to be seen. I find it hard to believe there's no connection."

Nuna's mind was racing, trying to put the jumble of words she'd heard into some kind of order. "Rothgar's alive?" she whispered.

"I've just said so, haven't I? Do you really expect me to believe you didn't know?"

Nuna stood and turned to Brosa. "I need to leave."

"I haven't dismissed you," said Geilir, gold tooth glinting as he grinned at her discomfort.

Nuna glared at him. "This audience is over. I'll not sit here and be insulted in my own keep, accused of things I had no knowledge of or played any part in. Brosa, come with me."

Brosa walked towards the door where the Vorund warrior barred their passage. He looked to Geilir, unsure whether to draw steel on Brosa or let them pass. Geilir sighed and waved his hand.

"Let them go. We'll speak again soon, Nuna Karaswyfe. In fact, I think you'll be seeking me out before too long."

Nuna hurried out into the corridor, keen to put as much distance as she could between herself and Valdimarr's chambers. She was aware Brosa was speaking to her and it took a while for the words to sink in. She stopped in her tracks and turned to look at the young warrior, who had a troubled look on his face.

"I'm sorry, Brosa. What did you say?"

"I was asking you where we were going, my lady. I don't trust Geilir and you need more warriors at your side. We shouldn't be aimlessly wandering the keep."

Nuna nodded, trying to think. Was Geilir lying to her, trying to throw her off balance? She'd seen Rothgar hanging there, dying outside the gates, when she left Reavesburg for the last time with Karas. She had hardly known what to think, mourning the murder of Jorik and his family, forced to walk past their heads on spikes set on Reavesburg's walls, those terrible rumours about Rothgar's confession at having had a hand in betraying them all. She hadn't truly believed it but that didn't matter – he'd been convicted and punished anyway. Looking at Rothgar in the cage she'd known he'd be dead by nightfall, considering it a mercy. She'd seen the burns covering his body and the crows pecking at his flesh as he hung there. Was it even possible he'd survived? Yet why would Geilir lie about Rothgar when the facts could be checked? Somehow Nuna knew it was true – Rothgar was alive. She still had a brother.

"My lady," said Brosa, his tone urgent. "We cannot linger here."

"I need to talk to Karas," Nuna told him.

Together they hurried to his chambers, only to find them deserted. There was no sign of his guards or servants and when Nuna called for Styrman there was no response. They headed for the courtyard, seeking out Kalfr and Sigurd, who would normally be in charge of weapons practice with the rest of Norlhast's warriors. They found the courtyard empty, wooden training weapons in their racks, untouched. Nuna and Brosa were debating whether to head to the barracks or the feasting hall when they heard footsteps approaching them.

"Get behind me," muttered Brosa, pushing Nuna out of the way and drawing his sword. "Who's there? Answer me."

Nuna gasped with relief when she saw Sigurd and

Kalfr running towards them. She smiled and hurried forwards, only for the greeting to die on her lips as she saw the dark expression on Sigurd's face. Her husband's former jarl was always serious-minded but this was different – he looked distraught and that frightened Nuna more than anything.

"Nuna, you're alright," Sigurd gasped, drawing her into a tight embrace. "When we heard Valdimarr summoned you we feared the worst."

"It wasn't Valdimarr – it was our latest visitor from Vorund, Geilir," Nuna told them, before going on to explain her encounter.

"Rothgar's *alive*," mused Kalfr, shaking his head in astonishment as he looked at Nuna. "I'm pleased for you, my lady. It seems Dinuvillan has smiled upon your family."

"Those welcome tidings don't help us here in Norlhast," Sigurd said with a sigh. "If anything, it makes it worse. Valdimarr and Geilir will try and use you against the Brotherhood, exploiting your links to Rothgar, which places you in danger."

"Then we have to get her away from here," Brosa replied. "They know about Orglyr's army in the north and what happened to Vikarr when he tried to interfere. If one person talks they'll hang us all for treason."

"There'll be no getting me away from anywhere," Nuna told him firmly. "This is my home and I won't be driven out of it, not after everything I've done to make a new life here."

"You may no longer have a choice," argued Sigurd.

"If you won't listen to me I'll talk to someone who understands. Where's Karas? We've been looking for him all over the keep."

Kalfr stared at her, stricken. "Myshall's bane – you haven't heard? Geilir came for him this morning with that thug of his, Tryggvi. Our father insisted on going with him and we haven't seen either of them since."

CHAPTER 22

The docks at Romsdahl were busy, most members of the Brotherhood there to see *Stormweaver* depart on her voyage into the unknown. Gautarr and Ragnar were in attendance, Asta and Jora deep in conversation. Joldir and I had worked night and day to complete warding the vessel after learning Hasteinn was sailing north to find us and, although I was tired, I looked at our handiwork with pride at a job well done. Aerinndis was acting as if Vorund's ships might round the cliffs at any moment, bellowing orders to Haddr as the large sailor manhandled barrels onto the ship with the help of his crewmates Fari, Soren and Jonas.

I felt like a spare part, leaning against a wall to be out of the way whilst Meinolf supervised the dockers who were loading the last of our salted and dried provisions. Piles of thick cloaks, fur-lined boots and gloves and wolf skin coats were being carefully packed into chests for the latter part of our journey. In the warm summer sun it was hard to believe we'd need them. The members of the Brotherhood assigned for our protection were already aboard, with the exception of Jolinn. Skari was moaning that he was a warrior, not a sailor, as Ulfarr listened patiently to his protests and Myr looked on, his expression inscrutable.

Bandor walked over to me and pulled me into a fierce embrace. "Take care," he said, clapping me on the back.

"I will," I told him.

"We'll see you soon," said Freydja, taking me by surprise as she hugged me as well.

Now my work was complete, there was time to think and various doubts had begun to cross my mind. When I'd spoken to Etta about our plans she'd made it seem so sensible and plausible. Now Jora's words came back to me. *You fool, she has you tied on a string and you don't even know it.* What *had* I talked myself into?

"Stay safe and look after yourselves," I told them. "The siege of Vorund Fastness is going to be long and dangerous. Look out for each other while I'm away."

Bandor smiled. "We will."

Freydja put her hand on Bandor's arm. "I've spent long enough trapped behind these walls. Ragnar's *furious* at being left behind. He'll be poor company."

"So Ragnar's part of the second wave of reinforcements?" I asked.

"You hadn't heard?" Bandor said with a smirk. "No – Gautarr's ordered him to stay here and take command of Romsdahl's defences."

Much must have been happening at court during my short absence. "I thought Ragnar was going to be named as Gautarr's second?"

Bandor shook his head. "That's what everyone expected after Haki was killed, but Gautarr gave that honour to Throm."

Freydja swelled with pride. "Ragnar doesn't like it, though I can tell Asta's secretly pleased he'll be safe. I'm sure that's what's in Uncle's mind – he wants to make sure Ragnar's alive so he has an heir when this is all over, one way or the other."

"It's a good choice," I told her. "The men trust Throm and I know he'll do well."

As the pair of them moved off my hand strayed to the new sword hanging at my side. I could see Svafa standing in the crowd and nodded to him, the young man acknowledging me with a raised hand. He now had the honour of carrying my sword, the one I'd used to vanquish Sinarr the Cold One, and in its place Johan had gifted me Old Gunnar's weapon. The longer blade with its three runes was heavy at my side and I had some trouble shaking off the feeling that handing over my preferred sword was an ill omen. I had what I wanted – a sense of purpose and a real part to play in defeating the Vorund Clan and thwarting Adalrikr's ambitions. That didn't stop a dead weight settling in my stomach as I thought of what was at stake. I saw Arissa hanging back with Thengill, Joldir and Leif and waved them over, anxious to be rid of such thoughts. There were more tearful goodbyes and I began to wish we were at sea, finding this harder than I expected.

"Skari looks like he's about to be sick," Thengill observed with a smile. I glanced at Ulfarr's second, who certainly looked pale as *Stormweaver* gently bobbed on the high tide.

"I don't think Skari's a born sailor," said Arissa, concern on her face.

"I'll look after him," I said, making Thengill laugh.

"The distance of this journey means the ability of our Fellowship to protect each other will be diminished, until we're reunited in Vorund," Joldir reminded me for the hundredth time. "Until then, it's only safe to send the briefest of messages. Such tidings will still be important, so we know how you're faring and you can be prepared for what awaits you at Vorund Fastness."

Joldir was right – it was easier and certainly safer to walk the Path together. Our Fellowship would become more powerful once I re-joined Joldir and Leif at Vorund Fastness, where we could use our combined abilities in the service of the Brotherhood. Yet in that moment I understood that whilst my Sight visions were becoming more expansive and wide-ranging, which I put down to the magical effect of the Tear, Joldir's experiences were different. Joldir had warded himself so extensively to protect himself from Nereth's influence the gift had become stunted in him.

"I'll send word of our progress, I promise," I told my mentor. I reached into my bag, producing my bottle of ataraxia with a flourish. "I have this if I need it – I'll be fine, honestly."

"*Please* be careful," said Joldir. "Those runes on your sword can't ward against your stupidity."

"He's going to the Fire Isle," piped up Leif. "It's bound to be dangerous."

"Leif, that's hardly helpful," cried Arissa with a scandalised look as Thengill chuckled.

"But it's true. He's going to the Fire Isle. There'll be *dragons*, won't there, Joldir? That's what you said." Joldir laughed, shaking his head.

"I've heard the happy news that you're engaged," I said to Arissa and Thengill. "I've not had chance to congratulate you."

The pair of them glowed at the mention of the subject. "We plan to marry before setting sail for Vorund," Arissa told me. "Karlin's agreed to perform the ceremony. One of several, in fact."

"Lots of people are seizing the day," added Thengill. "We could be away for a long while and I didn't want any regrets before going into battle."

"I'm pleased for you both," I told them, meaning every word.

Aerinndis called out from *Stormweaver*, the last of the gear and provisions now loaded aboard. Time was short and we needed to be on our way.

"Don't get eaten," Leif said, hugging me around my waist.

Johan approached me after I had said my goodbyes, Damona at his side. "May Dinuvillan smile on you, Rothgar and Culdaff fill your sails. I'm sure Aerinndis will keep Hasteinn far behind."

"Let's hope so," I replied.

"I'll be praying for you every day," said Damona. Six months pregnant she was starting to show despite her voluminous robes, her hand clasped protectively under her swelling belly. She looked ten years younger with child. Like the marriage of Thengill and Arissa, this was another sign of hope for the future. Her babe was likely to be born in a foreign land amidst a bitter war, when she could have remained in Romsdahl with Ragnar's family and her friend Ingirith. I had to admire Damona's determination to remain at Johan's side.

"I'll be thinking of you too, my lady."

The throng of onlookers at the dockside parted and I saw Etta walking towards us, her stick tapping on the stones. Ekkill was at her side carrying two large oilskin bags, Jolinn walking closely behind with another bag slung over her back. There were some dark mutterings from certain quarters of the crowd, no doubt concerning the mysterious nature of Etta's rejuvenation. I resolved to tackle her about this subject once we were underway, since I could see the lack of an explanation was damaging the reputation of the Brotherhood as harmful gossip continued to circulate.

"The last of our passengers for the voyage," said Johan. "Etta, are you sure you won't reconsider? Your valuable counsel will be missed at the court of the Brotherhood."

Etta shook her head. "Johan, you and Gautarr understand the art of war and I have every faith in you, whilst my counsel is needed on this voyage. It would be madness to send a boy of eighteen out on his own to treat with a god. This is a task requiring lore and wisdom and no one knows more about such matters than me."

Aerinndis sauntered by, swearing at one of her men with such force even Etta recoiled. *Stormweaver's* captain turned to Johan and gave him an elaborate bow. "My lord, Johan Jokellsward, Battle Chief of the Reavesburg Clan," she said in a refined voice. "*Stormweaver* is *almost* ready to depart with the tide," she glared at her sailors, who redoubled their efforts to finish their tasks. "That's if you've finished delaying my passengers?"

Johan gave her a rueful smile. "My apologies, Captain."

Aerinndis flashed him a grin, reminding me of her father, before taking her leave.

Etta paused as Jolinn loaded their baggage and climbed aboard *Stormweaver*, inspecting the lacquered runes on the gunwale, glinting in the sunshine. She reached out, almost hesitantly, to touch them. "Excellent handiwork," she told me with a gap-toothed grin as Ekkill gently steadied her, holding her hand as he helped her aboard.

"You'd better go," Damona told me, hugging me tightly. "I pray Dinuvillan will smile upon you and your companions. This separation of the Brotherhood has been a hard choice and whilst I know it troubles Johan I think you've made the right decision. This is about fighting magic with magic, so we can all have a future." Damona cast a meaningful look at the baby she was carrying.

"I won't return until we have what we need."

Damona's eyes narrowed and she took my hands in hers. "I overheard you speaking to Joldir earlier. Think what you have already learned with the Sight – such as the three ships now giving chase to you, already out there on open water as they try and close you down on the Redfars Sea. Wouldn't it be useful to know *exactly* where they were? A matter of life and death, perhaps; one which might decide whether I live to see my child born into this world. Think on that before you surrender your advantage." I nodded, part of me relieved to hear an excuse not to set aside the Sight. "There may be a time when you must take ataraxia," Damona continued. "You'll know when it's right to do so but I know for a fact that time isn't now. Joldir wants to protect you, yet too much caution can still kill a man. Think on that as you cross the ice-filled seas."

I thanked Damona and Johan, climbing aboard *Stormweaver* and taking a seat next to Etta as Aerinndis and Meinolf gave their final orders and the crew set their backs to the oars. I glanced back at the dockside, where Molda and Tellian were watching their daughter with pride. Like

Damona, they had faith in our quest, faith I needed to repay if the Brotherhood was to survive the challenges to come. I blinked and for a moment thought I caught sight of the Weeping Warrior on the quayside. When I looked again, all I saw was Thengill's tall frame, standing with Joldir and Arissa, Leif bouncing up and down on his heels. I turned away, setting my face seawards as with every beat of the oars *Stormweaver* moved out into the Redfars Sea.

CHAPTER 23

"Go on," invited Tyrfingr with a cold smile.

Nereth leaned forwards in her chair, her face intent as she waited for one of the men to answer. Djuri saw she still favoured her back, although she disguised it well. Kolsveinn was standing in the corner of Tyrfingr's chambers, broad arms folded as he observed the two dockers from Noln standing before them.

The older of the two, with a shock of white hair and tobacco-stained black teeth, coughed nervously. "Word is you're looking for a certain family who used to live round here. Reckon we may have seen something."

"*Really*?" Tyrfingr drummed his fingers on the arm of his chair.

The white-haired docker coughed again, tried to meet Tyrfingr's fathomless black stare and failed, instead looking down at his feet. His younger companion, who had a hole in one of his old boots, revealing a grubby toe, nudged him. When the older man didn't speak he jabbed him in the ribs with his elbow.

"Stop embarrassing us," he whispered. "Speak up."

"Do you have something to say to me or not?" snapped Tyrfingr.

"That depends," began the older docker.

Tyrfingr raised an eyebrow. "It *depends*?"

Old Boots squirmed and wrung his hands as he gathered his courage to speak. "He means, my lord, there's the matter of ... Loyal subjects of the king, especially those bringing important information to his jarl ... They should be rewarded, shouldn't they?"

"Surely that depends on the information?" interjected Nereth. "It's for us to decide its value, not you. Tell us what you know and we'll decide the price. That's fair, isn't it?"

The white-haired docker nodded and opened his mouth to speak but Old Boots put a hand on his arm. "This isn't what we agreed," he hissed. "If we tell them now they don't have to give us anything."

Tyrfingr nodded and Djuri stepped forwards, landing a solid punch into Old Boots' back, above his kidneys. The man gasped and dropped to his knees and Djuri struck him again, a ringing blow to his ear that left him sprawled on the floor.

"Pathetic," Tyrfingr scoffed. "Who do you think you are, daring to haggle with me in my own private chambers?"

The older docker was staring wide-eyed at his companion. Djuri grabbed Old Boots by the shoulders and lifted him back onto his feet, leaving him swaying as he struggled to find his balance. There was a wiry strength to him, though he was clearly underfed and poor. Now the opportunity to better himself was slipping through his fingers as Tyrfingr toyed with his subjects.

"If I were you, I'd tell them what you know," muttered Djuri.

Old Boots stared sullenly at Tyrfingr, a trickle of blood running from his ear down a grimy neck where it met the sweat-stained collar of his jerkin.

The white-haired docker took a step forwards. "Please forgive my friend. He meant no offence by his words. We both have families to feed, that's all –"

Tyrfingr threw up his hands in despair. "Did I ask for your life story?" He nodded towards Djuri, who took a reluctant step forwards, muscles bunching in his arm as he balled his fist.

The older docker shrank away from him, hands outstretched. "Forgive me my lord, I forgot myself. I'll tell you. I'll tell you everything."

Tyrfingr sighed and waved Djuri away, much to his relief. There was no honour in beating the weak and powerless. Instead he listened to the halting tale as the two men explained who they had seen at the docks in Noln. As they described them there was no doubt in Djuri's mind they were talking about Humli and his family and when his eyes met Nereth's he could see she thought the same.

"So, they're in Noln – or at least they were yesterday," said Kolsveinn.

"There's more," added Old Boots. "I followed them through the markets and I saw them enter the house of our elder, Lundvarr. He could be sheltering them or giving them aid."

Tyrfingr frowned at that remark. "Lundvarr? Are you absolutely sure about this? You're making a very serious accusation concerning a man who has been nothing other than loyal to me since I became jarl."

Old Boots nodded. "It's the truth, I swear it."

Tyrfingr sat there in silence, brooding on what he had heard. Eventually the older docker coughed and tapped his friend on his shoulder. "Er. We'll be off in that case, my lord. I hope what we've told you is of some value." Tyrfingr said nothing, chin resting in his hand. Old Boots scowled and looked ready to protest as his companion tightened his grip on his shoulder and tried to steer him out of the chamber.

"Wait," said Tyrfingr. He reached into a pouch on his belt and produced two small silver coins. He rubbed them together between finger and thumb, moving them so they caught the light and glittered. Old Boots' face lit up, although the other docker took a half step backwards towards the door, still wary.

"You want these?" asked Tyrfingr with a wolfish grin.

The two dockers turned and looked at each other, trying to gauge if this was some kind of trap. Old Boots took a hesitant step forwards, putting his hand out towards Tyrfingr. "If it pleases my lord," he said, his voice tight.

Tyrfingr flicked the two coins, sending them spinning into the air. Old Boots gave a cry and caught one, the other bouncing onto the carpet and rolling towards Djuri's foot. He watched as the other docker bent down and snatched it up, pocketing the coin as he backed away.

"The Jarl of Reavesburg rewards loyalty," Tyrfingr told the retreating dockers, who were bowing and scraping their way towards the door. "You will not speak of this meeting to anyone, do you understand?"

Djuri watched as the guards escorted away the two fearful men from Noln. He closed the door and turned back towards the others in Tyrfingr's chambers.

"*Lundvarr*?" Tyrfingr was out of his chair, pacing up and down on the plush rug covering most of the room.

"It's not such a surprise," Nereth replied. "The loyalty of a conquered people is always torn. Lundvarr's weak – you said so yourself. If a family in desperate need turned up on his doorstep he'd have trouble turning them away."

"Sandar betrayed us and Hrodi's bones are scattered outside Romsdahl's walls," Tyrfingr said bitterly. "Lundvarr was the one Reavesburg elder I thought we could trust. If someone as weak as him turns against us we'll never bring this people to heel."

"I'm not interested in your problems ruling Reavesburg," cut in Kolsveinn. "We need to find Lina and Desta and bring them to our king – that's all that matters. Djuri, send a rider to call Eidr and Galin back to Ulfkell's Keep now we know they're on the wrong path. Then report back to me with six hand-picked warriors. You'll be riding with me to Noln by noon."

***

Humli gratefully drank the cup of warm cow's milk, wiping his mouth with the back of his hand. He eyed the food Dyri had brought; a ripe cheese wrapped in cloth, fresh apples and two loaves, a cured ham and dried fish. There were also dry sea biscuits – hardly appetising, although they would keep them fed for weeks. Two wineskins rested on the floor next to these provisions and the wooden milk-churn.

Lina drew Lundvarr's man into a hug. "Thank you, Dyri. This is more than we could have hoped for."

The warrior grinned. "You're welcome. Just remember this needs to last you until you reach Vittag. The captain of your ship will feed you, of course, but this will help you keep up your strength, especially with the young ones to look after. It's also a good idea to have something to barter with – you never know what you might need."

"Helsburg's much nearer," Desta said, nursing Finn on her lap. "Wouldn't it make more sense to make for there, if we could?"

"It doesn't matter where we go, as long as it's away from here," Humli replied, his hand reflexively moving to the purse containing the money Ulf had given them. Enough coin to start a new life, if they lived long enough to spend it.

Dyri shook his head. "You haven't heard? Helsburg's now part of Adalrikr's northern kingdom, although there's been rumours of unrest in some towns. News reached us a couple of days ago that their new jarl swore fealty after his predecessor's head ended up adorning the sharp end of a spike. Vittag's safer – for now. Their treaty with Vorund keeps their borders open and trade flowing freely. It'll be far easier for you to slip into the White Widow's territory unnoticed."

Desta looked up, her face worried. "I thought we only had to get to the other side of the Baros Mountains."

"Even Vittag isn't far enough," Lina told her. "It's only a stopping point on our journey and we'll need to travel further than that to be safe. We have to head south, through the Forest of Mordis, and make for Tharas in Beria. From there the roads are good and we could go on to Silvergate or Medan, cities large enough for us to be able to disappear."

"It was risky enough travelling from Reavesburg to Noln," hissed Desta. "I'm not taking Finn through that forest

– it's too dangerous. And we've no place in Beria – we'd be refugees from the north. We won't be welcomed there."

Lina shook her head. "You're not a refugee if you have coin. Beria's kingdom is ruled by fat merchants and greedy mercenaries. Trust me, as long as you have money to spend, they'll embrace us with open arms."

"And when the coin runs out?" asked Humli. "I'm no merchant and I'm certainly not a warrior."

"Medan or Harrows further south are both major ports," Lina explained. "You could find work, Humli. This is where we need to go – trust me on this."

Desta's brows furrowed. "Who put you in charge, Lina?"

Dyri opened the door to the dockside smokehouse where they were hiding, letting in a shaft of light and noise from the outside world. "I have to go. You'll have plenty of time on your journey to decide what to do. Stay here and don't go anywhere until I get back. We should be able to move you with the evening tide."

Humli felt a brief pang of worry as the young warrior closed the door and left them alone, crouched in the corner amongst the wooden racks of smoking herring. He tried to relax until a whimper from Frokn caused him to start.

"Gods, Lina, keep the boy quiet. If someone outside hears us we're done for."

Lina glared at him, eyes bright despite the gloom. "What do you think I'm trying to do? Make yourself useful and get us something to eat and drink. We may as well rest up while we can."

Humli did as he was told, sharing out the milk and some of the bread and apples for breakfast. They ate hungrily in silence, each wrapped up in their own thoughts, eyes stinging from the smell of smoke and fish hanging in the air. Finn started to cough as Desta nursed him and her eyes wandered toward the door of the smokehouse.

"Don't even *think* about it," Lina told her in a firm

voice.

"She's right," Humli agreed. "We only have to stay here for the rest of the day, that's all. Finn will be fine."

Desta nodded and tried to settle her boy, softly whispering a lullaby into his ear until he quietened. Humli reached for his tobacco pouch before thinking better of that idea. They couldn't afford to do anything that would give them away, not when they were so close to making their escape from Reavesburg. Dinuvillan had smiled on their journey so far, with Lundvarr offering to help. He felt a glow of pride as he thought of how Desta had convinced him to defy Tyrfingr.

"Just one day," he whispered to himself, settling down in the corner of the smokehouse with his back to the wall. "We'll be away come nightfall."

CHAPTER 24

I felt disorientated, taking a while to adjust to where I was as the rhythmic splash of the oars and the snap of the wind in the sail reached me. The smell of smoked fish faded and I took a shuddering breath. I knew how close Noln was to Reavesburg – I'd ridden there in haste myself when I led the warriors of Ulfkell's Keep to repel Vorund's raiders. Kolsveinn and Djuri would be there well before nightfall.

"Rothgar, are you with us?" asked Etta. She was looking at me intently, curled up at the stern of the longship, wrapped in her cloak despite the warm sun shining down on *Stormweaver* as the vessel skipped over the waters.

I nodded, recounting what I'd seen as the sailors concentrated on rowing, trying to put as much distance as possible between us and Hasteinn's pursuing ships. Ulfarr, Myr, Ekkill and Jolinn were all adding their strength to the task, allowing some of the crew an opportunity to rest, as Skari leaned weakly against the side of the ship. He'd been violently seasick as soon as we reached open water and had entertained the crew with frequent retching for the rest of the morning. He sat there with his one good eye closed, looking pale and moaning quietly from time to time.

"There's an old saying that the Sight shows us what we need to see, rather than what we want to know," Etta mused.

Aerinndis, who was at the stern of the ship next to Etta, pursed her lips. "I would have thought knowing where Hasteinn's ships are would have been important enough to draw your attention."

"It depends if there's someone open to the Sight on his crew," I explained, disliking the fact that on such a small vessel the secrecy I'd grown used to concerning matters of the Sight was virtually impossible.

"Perhaps," said Etta. "Lina and Desta have always exerted a strong pull on you. There's history there," she added to Aerinndis' questioning look.

"Our route will take us past Noln," I said quietly.

Stormweaver's navigator Feyotra sighed. "We won't get there today," she said, arm resting lightly on the steering oar. "By the time we reach Noln events will have played out and your friends will either have made their escape or else ..." Her voice faded away.

Aerinndis placed a hand on my shoulder. "I'm sorry – those are the facts. We need to stay out on the open sea, away from the coast where we'll be easier to find. Don't forget that any delay also increases the chance Hasteinn will overhaul us."

"What you've seen doesn't alter the plan," added Etta. "We have to make this crossing with all possible haste, regardless of whether we're being pursued."

I got up and walked to the prow of *Stormweaver*, careful not to jostle the crew and disturb their timing as the oars struck the waters and sped us on. Skari groaned, head hanging down and I chuckled, enjoying how the reversal of our fortunes had stemmed the usual flow of barbed comments from the warrior. I'd always been at home on the sea and leaned over the side of the ship, watching the sparkling waters parting as they flowed around our prow, one hand holding onto the rune-inscribed dragon figurehead to help me keep my balance. With each beat of the oars there was a collective grunt from the crew as their backs bent to their work. It was a task I was unsuited to, putting me into the same company as ancient Etta and seasick Skari. The crew had grumbled at that, so it would have been helpful to be of assistance in another way. Unfortunately, the Sight was proving fickle.

"Careful," said Aerinndis. "I don't want to fish you out

of the Redfars Sea."

I hadn't heard her approach, although that was no surprise. The way she moved about the ship it was obvious she had been brought up living on the waves.

"Think your friend's work will help us steer a true course?" Aerinndis asked, slapping her hand on the wooden dragon. Joldir had painted runes of finding on the creature's eyes, lacquer glinting in the sun.

"Broken fingers or not, Joldir's work is without compare. I've seen the most powerful durath held back by nothing more than paint on a stone. They'll guide you true."

Aerinndis wrinkled her nose in amusement. The sun was bringing out a splash of dark freckles across her cheeks and the bridge of her nose. "I'd rather take my course from the position of the sun and stars. Feyotra isn't happy with this particular innovation, I can tell you."

I glanced back at Etta, hunkered down at the back of the longship where she was looking out to sea. The wind was rippling through her long grey hair and with the weather set fair she looked comfortable enough. I wondered how she would cope in colder, rougher seas as we sailed further north into the Endless Ocean.

"I was surprised you didn't object more strongly to Etta joining us," I said.

Aerinndis laughed. "I admire her spirit, undertaking a journey like this at her age. Not all of us are going to survive this and Etta has as much right as anyone else to choose the risks she's willing to take. And I agree with her – I think her wisdom and knowledge are exactly what we'll need once we reach the Fire Isle.

"If she survives."

"If she survives," agreed Aerinndis. "You seem to have a soft spot in your heart for your tutor."

I pursed my lips, thinking over those words and remembering again what Jora had said during her visit. Etta was full of good advice and probably knew me better than anyone else. Why was Etta here? Didn't she trust me, despite everything I'd done for my clan? Etta glanced at me and nodded and as I waved back I felt a sense of disquiet, knowing there was something I was missing.

"She saved my life. I owe her everything."

"Yet you're not entirely comfortable with your new skin, if you'll pardon the expression," said Aerinndis, looking down at my thin forearm, criss-crossed with silver scars, the skin uneven where it had regrown over my burns. "People heard you at the feasting hall, when you were arguing with Johan. You've said all the right things since then, yet I can't help feeling you revealed your true thoughts that day."

"What's it to you?" I asked.

"I'm not interested in politics and who leads the clan when all this is over. Victory over the durath, gold and a chance to own *Marl's Pride* are why I'm here. Do you know what you want? This path is dangerous and only you can walk it. What will Bruar think if your heart is divided? Are you content to act as Johan's advisor or is your real desire to rule your clan?"

"I've never wanted to rule," I replied, needled.

"It's obvious you're unhappy at Johan's decision not to try and liberate Reavesburg. And this constant talk of Ulfkell's Keep being *your home* when everyone knows Johan's laid claim to Reave's Chair – that's tantamount to issuing a challenge at a clan moot. Listen, I don't want to be caught up in some ill-conceived plan placing you on the road to conflict with Johan. You don't have the friends or the support for such a move, which I'm sure you're intelligent enough to understand. I've invested everything in this venture, so I'm telling you I don't want to be associated with such a plot. If that's what's on your mind, you can find your own passage back from the Fire Isle."

I folded my arms and tried to meet Aerinndis' gaze. Despite her small stature she radiated strength and an iron will, leaving me in no doubt who was the captain of

Stormweaver.

"Anything else on your mind?" I came out with weakly.

Aerinndis snorted with ill-concealed laughter. "No, that's all I had to say. I make a point of preparing for a voyage and that includes knowing what my passengers are up to. Decide what you really want to do, Rothgar, because it affects all of us on this ship. My job's to help Gautarr and Johan defeat Adalrikr – make sure that's what you're focussed on too."

I watched Aerinndis as she nimbly walked the length of the ship, pausing to talk to Soren and another sailor called Aguti sitting at one of the oars. I turned and looked back out to sea, shielding my eyes from the glare of the sun. As the son of the chief I'd been brought up to understand diplomacy and the need to cultivate allies in order to remain in power. I realised I'd grown careless with my words and actions, leaving me vulnerable if people were talking openly about such things. Aerinndis saw me as a risk and potential threat, her words landing home in a way that those of my friends had failed to do.

What *did* I believe in? Of course I wanted the Brotherhood to succeed, so I could see my family avenged. Was that enough? If we were victorious it was clear Johan and Gautarr would vie for power and the right to rule the clan. Gautarr was no friend and stupidly I'd risked placing myself on the wrong side of Johan too. Why had Johan sent me? Did he implicitly believe the words of the Weeping Warrior? Was he acting out of loyalty to my late father? Was this actually a ruse to get this troublesome and unpredictable vestige of the past away from his court? It struck me my close friendship with Bandor might be the only reason I wasn't already in chains in the dungeons of Romsdahl Castle.

The Sight had given me a useful window into the wider world, whilst also weakening my focus and sense of self. Instead of planning ahead, I was reacting to events, giving little thought to the consequences of my actions. Aerinndis' words helped me understand why for the first time. I'd never properly acknowledged I'd lost Ulfkell's Keep and Desta's love forever the night Jorik died, just as Leif hadn't accepted the death of his mother at Lake Tull. There was no going back, no recapturing the life I'd led before. Desta understood this, making the right decision to leave and begin a new life, probably somewhere in Beria. I'd told myself over and over I loved her but our relationship had been that of young lovers, with no thought for the future. Desta had tried to tell me that more than once, and I'd never properly listened to her. I offered up a prayer to Dinuvillan for Desta and her companions. Out there on the Redfars Sea I finally accepted I had to let her go, once and for all, swallowing down a lump in my throat as I made peace with a fact I should have come to terms with years ago.

And what of my future? Did I want to be Johan's advisor and counsellor when all of this was over? Did I want to become his spymaster and Etta's natural successor – his secret eyes in Reavesburg and beyond? Whatever the future held, all that mattered now was completing this quest and finding the means to destroy the durath. I felt a sense of calm as I found focus and a renewed sense of purpose. I breathed out hard and looked at Aerinndis with new found respect as she leaned casually against the gunwale, joking with Aguti and the rest of her crew.

CHAPTER 25

Nuna dipped the white cloth into a silver bowl filled with warm water, steam rising into the air. The shutters of Karas' chambers were half-closed, keeping the light dim in the room despite the bright summer sun. She squeezed the cloth, watching bloody droplets fall back into the basin, turning the water pink. Carefully she applied the cloth to Karas' fingers, cleaning away more blood where his nails had once been. Karas winced, his bruised face contorted in pain as he waved her away.

"That's better – leave it there for now and it will heal," he said through gritted teeth.

"We must get these wounds clean first," Nuna insisted, continuing to attend to her husband as delicately as she could.

Sigurd and Kalfr were both standing in the chambers, the brothers' shocked expressions strikingly similar. Brosa stood guard outside the door. Styrman busied himself bringing Nuna fresh water as she worked, ignoring Karas' protests until she'd finished, applying cheap spirits to prevent infection. She'd seen this done enough times back in Ulfkell's Keep and knew exactly what to do. Karas' right hand was shaking when she had finished, fresh blood welling up on his fingers.

"Let the air get to the wound," advised Sigurd, swallowing hard. "It'll heal in time – no lasting damage, just painful."

"I didn't know if they were going to stop," Karas replied with a distinct tremor in his voice, patting Nuna with his good hand. "I've fought battles and won the right to rule my clan through trial by combat. Yet I've never felt fear like I did in those chambers, when I was alone with Geilir and Tryggvi, completely powerless."

Kalfr's voice was tight when he spoke. "Sigurd, they did this to our jarl in his own keep. If they're prepared to do that what might they be doing to our father?"

Nuna leaned forwards and kissed her husband on the forehead. The feeling of relief had been overwhelming when she first saw him, even covered in blood, swaying as he stood outside the door to her chambers. Karas told them Geilir released him without explanation, having held him prisoner for three days.

"Karas," she whispered, "I know this is difficult but what did they want to know? Why did they do this to you?"

Karas shook his head. "Geilir asked lots of questions, although most of the time I was left alone in the dark. He mentioned your brother, Rothgar – he seemed very interested to know everything about him. I kept telling him he was dead, only that didn't satisfy Geilir. He only seemed to believe me after Tryggvi ... had done this." Karas held up his bloodied fingers.

Nuna shook her head and told Karas what Geilir had said to her in Valdimarr's chambers. "When I heard Geilir say Rothgar was alive I knew it was true," she said as Karas looked on incredulously. "Somehow he escaped the crows cage and survived."

"What else did they question you about?" Sigurd asked Karas.

"He knows about Orglyr's muster in Taur. He gave me a beating concerning that, asking me for numbers and their position, wanting to know when they planned to strike. Sigurd, you were absolutely right to leave all the preparations up to Orglyr. I told Geilir over and over I had nothing to do with it and couldn't tell him anything useful – a hair's breadth away from the truth. Enough that he believed me, I think."

"Sigurd. What are we going to do about Father?" pressed Kalfr.

"*Do*? What do you think we can do?" replied Sigurd brusquely. "Geilir's here on the king's orders. Do you believe it'll make any difference if we petition Valdimarr or write to Adalrikr himself, pleading for his release? We don't even know if he's being held in the keep."

"I could speak to Geilir," said Nuna.

Her comment provoked a storm of protest, even old Styrman voicing his opinion at how foolish she was being. Nuna smiled, feigning calm as she set out her plan.

"Geilir spoke to me about the same things, whilst treating me with every courtesy. There was no doubt it was an interrogation, even as he complimented me and offered me food and drink. I don't think he'd risk physically hurting me, though."

"Why do you say that?" asked Karas. "Look what he did to me – I'm your husband."

"And I'm Rothgar's sister. They're very interested in him and the role he's playing in the Brotherhood. I think they plan to use me in some way against him and they can't do that if I'm dead."

"They can do plenty of terrible things to you without killing you," Sigurd pointed out.

"I don't think so. I don't think Geilir will risk hurting me – not yet, at least. Not with Rothgar hundreds of miles away in Romsdahl."

Nuna knew she was taking a calculated gamble. What she was completely sure about was Geilir wouldn't hesitate to torture any of the men in this room. Her position was different and there was a slim chance they could exploit that fact.

"Absolutely not! I forbid it," Karas declared.

"I agree," added Sigurd. "It's far too risky. We should be discussing another proposal – *anything* other than this foolishness."

"And what's your plan, exactly?" Nuna asked innocently.

Sigurd stared at her, jaw working although no words came out. Nuna gave him a glowing smile, the one that melted most men's hearts.

"I thought so. Listen to me – Geilir's already had me brought before him. He didn't harm me, although there's nothing to say he won't arrest me this afternoon and throw me in a dungeon. I know you mean well but don't you see? There's nothing you can do to protect me. Isn't it better to take matters into our own hands?"

"No, it's not," Kalfr blustered. Nuna waited for him to elaborate and smiled sweetly when no further useful thoughts were forthcoming.

***

Djuri tied his horse outside Lundvarr's house in the market square of Noln. Kolsveinn was already speaking to the two guards at the door as the rest of the Vorund warriors took up their positions behind him. Djuri had deliberately picked Vorund men for this task, even though he'd have felt happier with Ulf at his side. Bjorr had asked him where they were going as they got ready in the courtyard of Ulfkell's Keep, giving Djuri the satisfaction of telling him it was none of his business.

Lundvarr's guards were unhappy at allowing eight heavily armed warriors into the house but Kolsveinn didn't give them any choice as he insisted on his audience with Noln's elder. One of the men did his best to reach the door to Lundvarr's study and announce his visitors before being barged out of the way.

"Stay outside," Djuri told him, patting him on the shoulder before slamming the door in his face.

Lundvarr looked up from his desk as Kolsveinn's men crowded into his room. He stood, wringing his hands, nervously eyeing each of them in turn. Djuri noticed Lundvarr looked older, his grey curly hair thinner than last year. He'd also acquired a paunch, presumably enjoying some of the benefits of being in favour with Tyrfingr. All that was about to change.

"Gentlemen," Lundvarr said. "To what do I owe the pleasure of your unexpected company?"

Kolsveinn smiled, blue eyes boring into Lundvarr. A muscle was playing in his jaw, fluttering under the skin in a way Djuri found distinctly unpleasant. Kolsveinn walked over the desk and picked up a leather-bound ledger from the pile, idly leafing through the pages.

"P-p-please be careful with that."

Kolsveinn snorted and several of the men laughed. "Why? I confess lists of figures in date order have never held much interest for me. Hardly an occupation fit for a man, scribbling numbers down on parchment day and night."

Lundvarr glanced down at his ink-stained fingers, vainly rubbing them. "Without ledgers and contracts there would be no trade. Without trade no coin would flow into Reavesburg and you would have nothing to tax, leaving you unable to pay the wages of your men. You need people like me – it's the natural order of things, in fact. Everyone plays their part."

Kolsveinn snapped the ledger shut, making Lundvarr jump. "For the good of the king?"

"Indeed," stammered Lundvarr. "For ... for the good ... of the king. Yes."

Kolsveinn swept the ledgers and papers onto the floor with a clatter, to the laughter of the warriors in the room. Djuri took hold of Noln's elder, tying him to his chair with a coil of rope, ignoring Lundvarr's protests as he did so. The locked door shook as one of his guards tried to gain access to the room, followed by a crash as he shouldered it.

With a sigh Kolsveinn strode across the room and opened the door, timing it perfectly so that the young warrior charged straight inside, losing his footing and landing in a heap at Djuri's feet. The Vorund warriors shouted their encouragement as Kolsveinn stepped forwards, pulled out a knife and set to work on the prone young man. Djuri turned away, the guard's shrieks turning to screams as his throat was cut. He glanced out of the window to see the other guard sprinting away from Lundvarr's house towards the market, to mocking jeers from Kolsveinn's men. The dying man on the floor kicked feebly as Kolsveinn wiped his dagger on a corner of his victim's clothes. Lundvarr looked pale, staring up at the blood-splattered ceiling, a sheen of sweat on his face.

"There'll be no more disturbances," Kolsveinn told him, eyes glinting. There were flecks of blood on his face, which he casually wiped away with the palm of his hand. He licked his lips, the muscles in his face spasming, contorting his features for a moment as he took a deep breath.

"What's the meaning of this?" stammered Lundvarr, looking desperately at Djuri. "Why are you here? What have I done?"

"Who said you've done anything?" Kolsveinn replied, toying with the dagger. "What makes you say that, unless you've committed some crime you need to tell us about?"

"There's nothing. Nothing, I tell you. Please, you have to believe me."

Djuri winced. Lundvarr wasn't a good liar, especially under pressure. There was more laughter around the room and Djuri felt a sickening sensation in his guts.

Kolsveinn leaned forwards, a hungry look on his face, his eyes bright. He licked his lips. "Do you know how Finnaril, Adalrikr's current favourite, persuaded Bothvatr Dalkrson, Chief of the Helsburg Clan, to join our cause? He thought he could bargain with his king, offering him poor terms and showing astonishing disrespect. It was a strange thing in the end – every time Finnaril cut off one of Bothvatr's fingers his proposed terms improved – markedly. He was pleading for death by the end and Finnaril granted him his wish."

Lundvarr's arms were tied to the arms of his chair. He swallowed hard as he tested Djuri's bonds – too tight to offer even the slightest purchase. Kolsveinn stroked his prisoner's hand, fingertips moving lightly over Lundvarr's skin as Noln's elder shuddered and closed his eyes.

"That's the fate of a potential *ally*, one who failed to show proper respect and understand his place," continued Kolsveinn. "Imagine what I would do to a traitor. If you shelter fugitives from the king's justice that's what you are, so think carefully before giving me your next answer. A criminal family, fleeing Reavesburg's jarl, was seen entering your house only yesterday. Now, unless you wish to end up like the man lying on the floor of your study, you will tell me where they are."

CHAPTER 26

Humli's heart hammered in his chest as he hurried away from the smokehouse in the dark, the heavy sack of food slung over his back as he followed Dyri, with Lina and Desta bringing up the rear. The docks ahead of them were deserted as they flitted between the warehouses, their way illuminated by the thin light of the moon. He stank of fish, nose stinging and eyes watering from being holed up in the smokehouse all day. Dyri held up his hand as they reached the corner of a building and the group came to a halt.

"All clear," the young warrior whispered as he peered round the corner.

"Is the ship waiting for us?" asked Desta.

"I can't see it from here. We need to get down to the quayside. Wait for me here and I'll come back for you when I know it's safe."

Humli pressed himself against the wooden wall of the warehouse as Dyri left, crouching as he ran across the road before disappearing into the shadows. Desta and Lina stayed close, even their breathing sounding loud in the silence. Finn gurgled as he stirred in the cloak Desta had carefully wrapped to form a papoose, making it easier for them to move at speed. She stroked his cheek and the boy settled once more – only then did Humli realise he was grinding his teeth.

Not cut out for this, that's for sure, he thought, trying to steady his breathing and slow his pounding heart. Humli's bowels churned and he was afraid he'd embarrass himself before all this was over, even though he'd made water a dozen times already whilst waiting in the smokehouse. There was a scrabbling nearby which made all of them start. Humli's hand reached towards the small knife on his belt before he realised it was a large black rat feeding on some rubbish on the other side of the road. It glanced at them, pausing to clean its whiskers, before rooting through the pile of rotting fish guts once more.

"Just vermin," Desta whispered, her voice wavering.

Lina patted her on the shoulder. "I know you're scared but we're almost there. Once we're aboard ship we'll be free of this place and on the way to a new life."

Desta looked at her, eyes wide with fear. "How can you be so calm?"

Lina gave her a crooked grin. "You'd be surprised at the strength you can find in yourself, when you have to. We're going to get away from here, do you understand? You, me, our boys and your father. We're all going to make it, if we just stick together."

Humli had never spoken to Lina about her past. When he'd asked her questions as she recovered in his cottage after her rescue she would only shake her head, telling him none of that mattered now. There had been dark news from the western lands – tales of Vorund's warriors burning villages, robbing and stealing from helpless people. Sometimes worse. Humli found himself wondering what Lina had seen before reaching safety in Reavesburg, no doubt leaving her family and the father of her child behind. *Perhaps she's drawing strength from whatever she'd been through before finding that boat and casting herself adrift on the river*, Humli pondered. *She's a survivor.*

They remained in hiding, the moon disappearing from time to time, obscured by the occasional passing cloud. The rat was joined by more of its kind – there was more than enough food to go round as they rummaged through the stinking pile of fish. Humli strained his ears as he thought he heard approaching footfalls.

"Do you hear something?" he whispered.

Lina nodded as she crouched there, tense and ready to run, Frokn wrapped around her chest in the same manner as Finn. The rats scattered, vanishing into the darkness as a figure emerged next to the building opposite. Humli almost wept when he recognised Dyri.

"Captain Elfradr is waiting for us," he announced as they huddled around him in the shadows. "We have to go, quickly, before the tide turns. Stay close and follow me."

Hardly daring to believe everything was going to plan they set off, wending their way between the dark buildings until they reached the stone quayside where the merchant ships lay docked. Dyri led them towards a smaller vessel where Humli could see six or seven sailors were waiting on the deck. One of them saw them approach and climbed up onto the quay, hand not straying far from an axe hanging from his belt.

"This is Elfradr," said Dyri as he introduced them. The ship's captain had a long black beard, streaked with grey and banded with iron rings. Humli didn't like the look of him, swallowing hard as he realised it was much too late to back out now.

Elfradr nodded and held out his hand. "Pleased to meet you all. Time's pressing, so we need to be away while Nanquido's waters still favour us. Five silver crowns, one for each of you, and you can step aboard and stow your belongings for the voyage to Vittag."

Dyri shook his head. "No, that wasn't what we agreed. Lundvarr has already paid you well to delay sailing until tonight."

"The terms have changed," Elfradr said with a shrug, provoking laughter from his crew as they looked on.

Dyri glanced at Humli, reaching for the hilt of his sword. Humli put a hand gently on his arm. "No. We need them."

"Wise decision," Elfradr added, hand still outstretched.

Humli stepped forwards and dropped three silver coins into his calloused palm. Elfradr stared down at the money with disdain. "What's the matter, can't you count?"

"I know the difference between a man who honours his word and one who doesn't. Three silver crowns is more than a fair price for five passengers, as well you know. Now, you've been paid twice and handsomely at that for helping us out of this bind. Are we going to make our way or would you rather risk spending more time standing here, waiting for the next Vorund patrol to round the corner?"

Elfradr's eyes narrowed and Humli looked straight back at him, hoping he couldn't tell how dry his mouth was or that his bowels felt ready to release at any moment. The bards never sang about this side of their heroes' adventures. His small taste of the experience so far left Humli firmly of the opinion the sooner it was over the better. He had to muster all his strength not to sink to his knees when Elfradr closed his fist and pocketed the money.

"We've all got to make a living," he told Dyri, who was glaring at him. "Please, step this way and come –"

There was a thrumming noise and before Humli could move Elfradr was doubled over, clutching his stomach and screaming. A black-feathered shaft was buried deep in his guts, blood welling up between his fingers faster than he could stem the flow, soaking his jerkin and breeches. More arrows flew through the air, over Humli's head, dropping onto the deck of the ship. Two of the sailors died as Humli looked on, horrified, while the rest of their companions tried to take shelter.

"Father, come on," called Desta as she began to drag him away. Humli tried to move, his legs like water, unable to take his weight as he sagged onto the floor, struggling to breathe.

"What's the matter? Is he hurt?" called Lina.

"Go," Humli wheezed, shocked at how suddenly his strength had left him. He glanced up to see a group of men appear from the shadows by the nearest warehouse, four carrying bows and another four drawing axes and swords as they approached, barring their way and trapping them on the quayside.

The archers loosed more arrows at the crew as they tried to untie the ropes and make for the sea. Humli heard more screams and Dyri drew his sword and charged the four warriors running towards them. Their leader was a stocky young man, axes held in each hand. His eyes glittered in the moonlight and he pointed straight at Dyri.

"Kill him."

Two of the warriors advanced on Dyri, swords and axes raised. Humli could see the sigil of the bear on their shields. The third warrior, who dwarfed his leader and carried a shield with the Reavesburg eagle, held back, his sword lowered and pointing towards the ground. With a jolt, Humli recognised it was Djuri, the warrior who'd warned him to leave Reavesburg. The shorter man in command paused and stared at him with his bright eyes.

"Djuri. Kill that man and help capture the others or –"

"Or what, Kolsveinn?" asked the giant Reavesburg warrior, taking a deep breath and standing his ground.

Dyri was already fiercely fighting against the two Vorund warriors, feet away from where Humli had sunk to his knees. He turned towards the ship as Desta tried again to haul him to his feet. The crew of Elfradr's ship lay dead or dying, one of them trying to crawl along the dockside, two arrow shafts in his back. He left a trail of blood on the ground, black and shining in the moonlight. The archers were advancing towards them as Lina crouched down, whispering to Frokn as she clutched him tightly to her chest.

This is the last time I'll hear that little boy's name. It's all over. Humli glanced at Desta's tear-stained face, seeing despair and misery etched upon it. Everyone was moving so slowly; Dyri trading blows with his two opponents, Kolsveinn and Djuri squaring up to each other and the four archers advancing, calling out to their commander for orders. With a crack the noise of battle and dying men reached Humli's ears and he forced himself to his feet.

"Run," he shouted at Desta. "Take Finn and run. Don't look back."

Stepping towards Dyri, Humli swung his sack of food at one of the warriors he was fighting. There was a dull *thunk* as the wooden churn inside connected with his helmeted head, bursting open and drenching him in milk as he tumbled to the ground. Dyri took the opportunity to swing at the other distracted warrior, sword cutting deep into the man's neck and dropping him.

"Ha!" shouted Dyri, sword darting out again, stabbing the milk-soaked man on the floor as Humli staggered away, unbalanced by the force of his own swing.

You've got a knife, you idiot. Use it. Humli dropped the sodden sack and drew the small blade from his belt. He could see Desta was cornered by two warriors, clutching Finn tight as one of the men took hold of her arm and tried to wrestle her to the ground. Lina stood nearby, warily circling the other man as Desta cried out in fear.

"Dyri help me," Humli shouted as he ran towards the women.

Dyri was a few paces ahead but the young man came to a sudden stop, his sword clattering onto the cobbles as he tumbled to the ground. Humli stared in shock at the arrow protruding from Dyri's neck and it took him a moment to fully register what had happened. Another shaft passed so close to Humli's head he felt the breath of wind as it vanished into the darkness and buried itself into the mast of the ship. Humli ducked and charged towards Desta and Lina, screaming in terror and rage, a primal feeling as blood pounded in his head. He reached Desta first, driving his knife into the back of the warrior grappling with her. Humli gasped in horror as the blade feebly caught in the warrior's armour, snapping off at the hilt and spinning away onto the ground.

The man half turned towards Humli and Desta struck him across the face. Humli leaned in, locking his arm under the man's neck and dragging him off his daughter with all his strength, squeezing tight as he did so. The warrior started to choke, fumbling at his belt for his sword. Desta reached down and drew out the man's dagger, punching it hard into his stomach, piercing his chainmail as Humli hauled the man backwards, lifting him and forcing him to arch his back, leaving him prone. He felt the strength ebbing from the Vorund warrior as Desta struck again and again, until he gasped and went limp. Humli dropped the lifeless weight to the floor with a wet thump. Desta was screaming, Finn wailing too, both of them covered in blood.

"It's alright," Humli told her. "It's over. He's dead, my love. Come on, we have to get away from here."

Humli glanced over to where Lina had been fighting the other archer and his veins turned to ice. Lina, the woman Humli had started to think of as his second daughter, was covered in blood but that was where the resemblance to Desta ended. Lina's face was slicked with gore as she bit out the throat of the other warrior. He was lying still and dead on the ground, limbs broken and twisted, his pale face frozen in an expression of absolute terror.

CHAPTER 27

This wasn't the smartest move you've ever made, Djuri thought as he traded blows with Kolsveinn, parrying one axe away as he blocked the other with his shield. Kolsveinn's face was contorted in rage, veins bulging. Djuri took a step back, absorbing the energy of Kolsveinn's strokes, trying to keep calm and conserve his strength. After rebuffing another frantic flurry of attacks, Djuri took the opportunity to counter with one of his own, forcing Kolsveinn wide with a shove of his shield and nicking his shoulder with his sword, drawing a gasp of pain from his foe.

With Dyri dead Djuri knew the odds of surviving this fight were slim, even if he managed to kill Kolsveinn. He didn't care. The image of what Kolsveinn had done to Lundvarr in his study was burned onto his mind. By the time they slipped away from his house later that evening they knew when Lina's vessel would be leaving and exactly where to find them. However, his full, terrified cooperation wasn't enough to save Lundvarr's life. Kolsveinn had … feasted on Lundvarr at the end, as Djuri and his companions had looked on in shock and horror. *Looked on and done nothing, like the coward I am.*

Djuri had hoped the pleading, the shouting and, finally, the high-pitched screams from Lundvarr's house would have been enough for someone to send a warning to Dyri they had been discovered. Clearly the folk of Noln were too afraid of the Vorund Clan to take such a risk. He'd prayed to Dinuvillan they would be too late, only to find Elfradr and Humli haggling over the price of their passage, unaware they were being watched as Kolsveinn closed in with his men.

"I should have known you'd betray me, Djuri *Turncloak*," spat Kolsveinn as they exchanged blows once more.

"Clue's in the name," grunted Djuri, turning Kolsveinn's axe and striking him on the thigh, driving him backwards.

No more night time trysts with Nereth. He'd taken pleasure in those moments, although he wasn't sure how much he meant to her. *Now she's someone else I've let down, I suppose.* He wondered what she'd think if she heard he'd killed Kolsveinn. Would she be impressed or merely dismiss him as a traitor? Right now, none of that mattered.

Kolsveinn's axe whooshed over Djuri's head. He backed away to buy more time and felt a splash across his cheek. Sticky and warm, an iron tang in the air, he realised he was covered in blood. For a moment he thought he or Kolsveinn had been injured, although his opponent looked equally confused. Djuri could hear a woman screaming – a sound of pure terror. It almost cost him his life as Kolsveinn attacked once more, axes combining in one flowing move after another, numbing Djuri's shoulder as his shield took the force of each blow.

Over to his left there was a tearing, rending noise, followed by a man's agonised scream, cut short by a wet spattering sound. Kolsveinn attacked again, although Djuri was ready for it this time, blocking more quickly, the tip of his sword cutting his opponent's wrist. Kolsveinn sprang away with a snarl.

"That's three touches," mocked Djuri, careful to keep his shield up as he baited Kolsveinn. "Care to concede?"

Kolsveinn swore and threw his axes to the ground, leaving Djuri confused. He thought he was about to surrender and lowered his guard a fraction, sucking in a deep lungful of air. It was a mistake as Kolsveinn roared and sprang upon Djuri, his face twisted by savage fury, giving him the appearance of a wild animal. Djuri had never seen a man move so fast and in that moment, as he desperately managed to interpose his shield between them, he clearly saw the evil creature who had slowly stripped Lundvarr's flesh from his bones. Djuri was the larger of the two men, yet Kolsveinn forced him back, his boots scraping along the cobbles of the dock. Djuri thrust with his sword, only for Kolsveinn to seize him around his wrist and he felt his bones grinding together as the Vorund man began to squeeze.

"Traitor!" spat Kolsveinn, teeth snapping an inch away from Djuri's nose. "You'll plead for death before I'm finished –"

There was a blur of movement as Lina sprang on Kolsveinn from behind. She locked her leg around his neck as her fingers clawed at his eyes through his helmet. He stumbled, releasing his grip and Djuri leapt forwards, cutting off one of his hands midway between wrist and elbow. Kolsveinn's scream of pain was cut short as Lina bore him to the ground, crushing his windpipe with the leg she had wrapped around his throat. Taking both hands she gripped Kolsveinn's head and with a savage cry she twisted, his blue eyes bulging as the bones in his neck popped and snapped one by one. Kolsveinn went limp as Lina released her grip, screaming directly into his face.

Djuri gasped, making sure he kept his distance as the young woman slammed Kolsveinn's head into the stones. Once. Twice. Three times. He glanced to his left and saw a jumble of broken flesh and bones that had once been a Vorund warrior. One of the men Djuri had chosen for this mission. Slowly he scanned the quayside, taking in the bodies – or things that might once have resembled bodies – strewn in every direction. Djuri turned back to Lina, who looked up at him with a feral snarl, face covered in the blood of other men. Djuri's blood ran cold as Lina dropped Kolsveinn's broken body and began to crawl towards him.

"Wait. We're on the same side," he shouted, panic rising.

Lina paused as thick, green smoke began to pour out of Kolsveinn's mouth, nose and ears. It gathered around his body, which began to crumple with a hiss, limbs twitching as his flesh dissolved into a slick of dark oily liquid. A black shadow rose up from the corpse and in moments Djuri was surrounded in darkness, a rushing wind battering him as he cried out in terror.

***

Blinking, Djuri looked up at the pale opalescent sky. The clouds were thick and featureless, no hint of blue, the light bleaching any colour from the stony ground. He was dressed in simple travelling clothes, sword hanging from his side and shield slung over his back. Of the Noln dockside and the battle he'd been embroiled in there was no sign. Djuri gently ran his hands over his body, carefully checking for any sign of injury, and that was when he knew something was wrong. After every fight there were always bruises, cuts and knocks that only became apparent after the action was over – in his case there was nothing.

Djuri scanned his surroundings once more with a sense of unease. Other than the sound of his boots on the ground it was silent – not even a breath of wind on his face. The land in front of him gently sloped downwards, a worn path wending its way between the rocks and thick tussocks of grass. In the distance he could see a wide river, its waters dark and sluggish. A tall wooden bridge spanned the waters and beyond he could spy an enormous feasting hall, the only building visible in any direction. Behind him the path led uphill, towards a dark and uninviting forest. As it was the only sign of habitation Djuri started down the path towards the hall. Peering closer he thought he could see a figure standing at the entrance to the bridge. As he squinted he saw them raise an arm in greeting, beckoning him forwards. Warily he continued to walk down the path, hand tapping the hilt of his sword, reassuring himself it was still there.

He stopped. He couldn't say why he turned back

towards the forest. There was another man sitting on a rock a few feet away, watching him from under the hood of his cloak, face hidden. Djuri gave a strangled shout of surprise as he drew his sword and unslung his shield.

"Who are you, stranger?" he asked, heart pounding in his chest. He took a few slow, deep breaths to steady his nerves as the hooded man watched him in silence.

"I asked you a question," said Djuri, slowly advancing on the man. "Where are we and what are you doing, watching me?"

The hooded stranger gave a shrug, remaining seated on a flat stone by the side of the path. "I was here first. I could ask the same of you."

Djuri licked his lips as he thought about that. He didn't like the stranger's answer because it highlighted the fact he had no idea where he was or how he'd got there. He looked back towards the bridge and the hairs on the back of his neck prickled. Something was wrong with all of this. The stranger stood and lowered his hood, revealing white, blind eyes. Djuri's breath caught in his throat and he took a step backwards, although he didn't flee. Something held him back from attacking as the man looked directly at him, despite those blind eyes.

"Answer my question," Djuri said with more confidence than he felt.

The man waved at Djuri. "Put your weapon down if you wish to talk. I'm no threat and your blade will do you no good here."

Reluctantly Djuri did as he was asked, taking a seat on another stone near the man. He glanced about him – there was no sign of anyone else nearby. Only the figure down on the bridge, who Djuri was sure was watching the two of them.

"My name is Sinarr, although the Brotherhood of the Eagle calls me the Weeping Warrior. I mourn for Vorund, led astray by darkness, its people bleeding for a struggle that's not even theirs, misled by the lies of the usurper who sits on the throne."

"Sinarr? As in Sinarr the Cold One, Adalrikr's fallen jarl?"

"Close to the mark. The man I once was, called Sinarr, died long ago, his body possessed by shadow spirits known as the durath. I was one of Asmarr's bodyguards and the leader of the durath consumed me, my spirit cast into a realm between life and death. He used my form to get close to Adalrikr Asmarrson, stealing his soul and using his position to take control of Vorund. I couldn't cross the bridge to Navan's Halls because I failed my chief and now I'm still bound here, trying to undo the damage wrought by Adalrikr's magic. He's unleashed a rent through the very fabric of Amuran – the Tear, which now threatens to destroy everything."

An uncomfortable silence settled between the two men as they sat opposite each other in that bleak landscape. Djuri felt cold and when he looked again at the bridge he knew the man was there for him. It was Navan, waiting to guide him over the river and into the Halls of the Dead.

Sinarr spoke softly. "You see? You already knew the answers to your questions. Your mind simply refused to accept the truth."

"I'm dead?" Djuri replied. Giving voice to the idea made it real and tangible, even if it wasn't as frightening a prospect as Djuri had expected. However, as he sat there Djuri remembered the dark, coiling smoke from Kolsveinn's corpse, choking him as it enveloped his body.

"Kolsveinn. Is he one of these ... durath that you spoke about?" Djuri asked.

Sinarr nodded. "One of the oldest of their kind – one of the Sundered Souls who were drawn to Morvanos in the very beginning."

Djuri sat there in silence. Lina might have snapped Kolsveinn's neck but his evil spirit was now taking hold of

Djuri's body back at the docks in Noln. Instead of helping Humli's family he was going to turn on them. Everything he'd tried to do to right the wrongs of his life would have been for nothing. He sat there, head bowed, despair gripping him until the rest of Sinarr's words settled in his mind.

"If I've not crossed the bridge to the Halls of the Dead then what is this place? Am I between life and death?"

"You're not a shade yet, although your spirit is failing. Kolsveinn is dividing your soul from your body and that struggle goes on in the Real. Your mind is trying to make sense of what is happening to you, leading us here."

Djuri's head snapped up. "So there's still a chance I could survive this? That I could help Desta and her companions?"

The blind warrior looked up the hill, towards the forest. "You face a choice. Do you want to live after what you've done? Turncloak isn't a name anyone would choose for themselves – I suspect it will be impossible for you to shake it."

"I won't betray those I'm trying to help."

The shade looked at him with those sightless eyes. "Kolsveinn is adept at taking new forms. He's done so countless times but that doesn't mean you can't defeat him. This struggle within your mind is about the desire for life and is ultimately determined by whichever person has the strongest will to survive. If you take the difficult path, away from the bridge, perhaps you will succeed."

"In some ways, it's no different to any other contest on the battlefield," mused Djuri.

The shade nodded. "In understanding that, you have an advantage over most victims as the durath prefer unsuspecting prey. May Dinuvillan smile upon you, Djuri Turncloak."

Djuri stood and, without a backwards glance, he left the shade and began to head up the hill towards the forest. The path leading there was steep and before long he was sweating with the effort of the climb. He pressed on, scrambling over rocks and squeezing between boulders, slipping on loose scree as the path continued to steepen before it disappeared into the trees. Up close, Djuri saw that they were ancient, some of the trunks as wide as houses, thick with ivy and brambles. Within the forest the path vanished completely after only a few feet. Inside it was dark and the now familiar silence of this world between life and death hung there like a weight, pushing down on his shoulders. Djuri felt thorns snagging his clothes and cloak, scratching his skin around his calves and thighs as he forced his way through the dense undergrowth, the tree canopy far above him cutting off almost all the light. He drew his sword and began to use it to cut a path through the forest, grunting with the effort, sweat running down his face. Time lost all sense of meaning as he struggled on and, after a while, it dawned on Djuri he had no idea where he was. He cast about him, the trees little more than shadows in the dusky half-light. Even the passage he had cut through the thorns had vanished behind him.

"I hacked through there just a moment ago," Djuri said to himself, his words falling flat, swallowed by the silence.

There was a creak and the earth beneath his feet shook. Djuri looked around wildly as the noise grew louder. Something slithered over his boot and he lashed out with his sword, feeling it snap back. All around him the thorns were growing and twisting as they rose up and encircled him, pressing in on all sides. At his feet the roots of the trees were moving, shaking free of the packed soil and wrapping themselves around his feet as he desperately tried to hack them away. Djuri's arm caught on a thick thorn-covered branch, holding him tight and tearing through his flesh, blood dripping onto the tangle of roots snaking around his knees and thighs, drawing him down into the ground.

Djuri opened his mouth to scream as the forest consumed him, sharp thorns scratching his face, threatening to put out his eyes as the roots clamped around his chest. Muddy tendrils sought out his mouth and began to worm their way down his throat, causing him to panic and thrash as he fought to free himself. His desperate efforts opened up deep cuts and lacerations all over his body, blood flowing freely now as he was pulled to the ground in agony. Damp earth and roots closed over his head, drawing him under, blocking out all light. The roots balled in his throat, preventing him from taking a breath and Kolsveinn's face floated in front of him, grinning in triumph. Djuri stared back and he found himself thinking of his last visit to Olt, when he'd returned to his father's house, empty and abandoned. On the floor he remembered finding a bundle of letters he'd written, kept safe by his father and carefully tied together with ribbon. Djuri wrote those when he'd been a warrior in Kolfinnar Marlson's household in Ulfkell's Keep. He remembered his father's pride the day when Finnvidor Einarrson recruited him. Would he meet them all again in the feasting hall if he crossed over the bridge with Navan? Would Kolfinnar and Finnvidor look on him with pride and invite him to take a place at their table? Djuri knew no such welcome would await him as a traitor – those last few moments turning on his comrades in Noln wouldn't be enough to undo everything that had happened before.

"Why do you continue to fight me, Turncloak?" Kolsveinn asked with a hungry look in his bright blue eyes.

Djuri felt tears coursing down his cheeks. *Because I'm not done yet.* Djuri held on to everyone he'd ever cared for and everything he wanted to be. Kolsveinn frowned as Djuri met his gaze, defiant and determined not to be cowed.

I know what you are and you'll not take me.

Kolsveinn remained in front of him but Djuri also felt his presence within his mind. He tried to resist and deny Kolsveinn, feeling the grip of the roots around his body slacken, just a fraction.

Your journey is over, foul demon. This is one battle you're not going to win, because my will is stronger and I reject you.

The roots released their grip and Djuri spat out the tendrils probing down his throat, gasping as he managed to raise his head above the loose soil and breathe once more. Kolsveinn was staring at him, a shadow of doubt spreading across his face as he hesitated and Djuri struggled to assert his will one final time.

In that moment, Kolsveinn's spirit shattered.

CHAPTER 28

Nuna gathered her skirts as she hurried up the steps towards Geilir's chambers, her maid Katla and bodyguard Brosa at her side. Kalfr had argued the longest that she needed more protection until Karas finally interjected to end the discussion.

"This plan of my wife's will only work if it appears she's acting of her own accord. If we send her with an honour guard at her back it will be obvious her mission is not a secret and we will gain nothing. We either proceed with this plan or resign ourselves to doing nothing at all until Orglyr's forces arrive, which could be months off now Geilir knows there's a threat. What's it to be?"

Kalfr cast Sigurd a dark look and folded his arms, reluctantly acquiescing to the scheme. The trouble was part of Nuna actually agreed with Kalfr. Her plan *was* risky and she felt a wave of nausea as she drew closer to her destination.

"Wait here," she whispered to Katla. "Listen carefully and if anything happens you must go and tell my husband immediately. Don't try and interfere – I shan't forgive myself if anything happens to either of you on my account."

Brosa stared at her, misgiving written all over his face and Katla reached out, clasping her hands. "Dinuvillan smile upon you, my lady," she whispered before hurrying to her hiding place farther down the corridor, disappearing into a shadowy alcove.

Nuna walked the length of the corridor towards Geilir's chambers, looking directly at the guard on the door, her head held high, watching as he straightened when he saw them approach. She was only a dozen paces away from him when Valdimarr emerged from the room and almost bumped straight into her. He stepped back with a mumbled apology and Dromundr, the repulsive commander of his warriors, interposed himself between them, warty face glowering at Brosa.

"Step back," Brosa snarled, nerves already on edge.

"Gentlemen," interjected Valdimarr. "We are all friends here, are we not?"

Up close Nuna noticed Valdimarr was sweating, beads of it running off his bald head, gathering in the creases of his furrowed brow and neck. Clearly his audience with Geilir hadn't gone well, a fact which made Nuna smile. Valdimarr misread her expression, leaning in towards her conspiratorially.

"My lady, the hour is late. What brings you here at such a time?"

"I could ask you the same question," Nuna replied, her eyes twinkling. She'd perfected the look after a year toadying up to the odious man.

Valdimarr nervously smiled and his eyes flickered to Geilir's door. "If you're intending to pay our friend a visit, I wouldn't recommend it. He's in a foul mood. Most ... well, let's just say his demands are ludicrous. I told him our people can't be ruled with sharp steel alone. They need to believe their ruler cares about them and only wants what's in their best interests. That's all I've tried to do here. Apparently, despite raising the king's taxes and keeping the peace, it's not good enough."

Nuna thought of the whalers Valdimarr hanged merely for speaking out of turn at a tavern one night. Or rather, how he'd manipulated her husband into ordering their execution. She could scarcely believe he was trying to paint himself as being on her side, although with Valdimarr she'd found her expectations were always set too high.

"Now it's my fault, according to Geilir, that Orglyr the

Grim has mustered an army," continued Valdimarr in a lower voice, wringing his hands as his eyes flicked to the door once more. "How is that my fault? If a tree produces one bad apple you don't cut it down, do you?"

"Some people can be so short-sighted," Nuna replied, gently patting his arm even as her insides squirmed with revulsion. "Now, if you'll excuse me, I do have some business to attend to with Vorund's latest representative in Norlhast." She made to disentangle herself from Valdimarr's sweaty grip but he held on to her tightly.

Brosa stepped forwards. "The lady asked to be excused. You'll make way."

Dromundr growled, hand moving towards the axe at his belt and the guard took a step forwards. Fortunately, Valdimarr released Nuna as if he'd been scalded.

"Apologies, my lady. All I was trying to say was that if you intend to pay Geilir a visit I'd do so on another day. I fear you won't be well-received this evening."

"Geilir has made it clear he is the king's representative. Are you saying I should ignore his summons on account of the hour?"

"No. No, no, no. Of course not," Valdimarr blustered, eyes widening in fright. "No, please don't misunderstand me, I'm trying to look out for your best interests, my lady, that's all. Nothing more. However, if he has called you here *himself* ..."

Nuna had heard enough from Valdimarr and walked past him with a brief farewell. Even so, she was wary as she knocked on Geilir's door, wondering at whatever had taken place between them to leave Valdimarr so terrified. Politics were being played out in Norlhast and Nuna didn't like the fact she couldn't see all the pieces on the board.

Geilir looked up, surprised, at Nuna's arrival, closing the door firmly on Brosa as he ushered her inside. Geilir's grey hair was loose, flowing down over his shoulders and he had another day's worth of stubble on his chin since they'd last met. His sword belt lay on the bed, although Nuna's eyes were drawn to the long dagger hanging at his hip, the handle polished with use.

"The Lady of Norlhast Keep returns. I thought you would, although I confess I hadn't expected it to be so soon. How's Karas?"

Rage boiled up in her at the casual mention of her husband's torture. Nuna clenched her jaw tight until she trusted herself to give a measured answer. "As well as can be expected."

Geilir shrugged and walked to a cabinet in the chamber from which he removed a decanter of red wine and two crystal glasses. "The world is a savage place. Sometimes one must be cruel for the sake of the rule of law and the good of the people. I'm sure you understand. Some wine? I'm no expert but ever since Helsburg fell into line we've had all manner of goods delivered here. The men of Beria are soft but they produce good wine, so I'm told. This is a Medan red – well worth trying."

Nuna took a seat and the proffered wine, taking a small sip as she looked across her glass at Geilir. He was right, the wine was delicious, superior to what was served in her own feasting hall. Geilir didn't take his eyes off her as he took a longer draught. She felt colour rising in her cheeks and looked away.

"So here we are. Alone together in my chamber, with your man keeping watch outside," said Geilir. "Last time we spoke you were busy protesting at the inappropriateness of it all – yet here we are. Why the change of heart?"

"My brother. I can't stop thinking about what you said the other day. I lost my whole family, or so I thought, the night Tyrfingr took Ulfkell's Keep. Now you've told me my brother's alive and I want to help him, if I can. I don't know how Rothgar has become involved with the Brotherhood of the Eagle. You're close to the king – you've said so yourself. With your influence you could say something to Adalrikr –"

"*King* Adalrikr," Geilir reminded her.

"My apologies. I was wondering if it would be possible to persuade King Adalrikr to spare Rothgar's life, assuming it was worth his while?"

Geilir frowned, looking at her intently. "I thought you said your husband doesn't involve you in matters concerning the state?"

"Karas doesn't know I'm here. My husband is a broken man and was all too willing to do Valdimarr's bidding before you even set foot in Norlhast Keep. Do you know what I felt when I saw him this evening, after he'd spent a few days in the company of your man, Tryggvi?"

Geilir looked irritated. "I've already told you why that was necessary. If you've come to remonstrate with me you must understand he only suffered those injuries because he wasn't being cooperative. Lesser men would have been treated far more harshly."

"You mistake my meaning. I *despise* what Karas has become. Nothing remains of the man who killed Bekan Bekanson. Jorik married me off to a wreck of a man, twice widowed and drowning in grief for his lost children. It's as you said; I adorn his feasting table and warm his bedchamber but it's not a marriage and it never has been. I'm married to a coward, afraid of his own shadow, who only carries out the bidding of other men. I was born to be more than that."

Nuna watched Geilir listening to her lies. Speaking of Karas whilst actually thinking of everything she despised about Valdimarr made them easier to tell and, she hoped, more convincing. It also helped she was telling Geilir what he wanted to hear.

Geilir flashed her that annoying grin of his, gold tooth catching the light. "And if Rothgar was spared and brought to you, how would my king benefit from such an arrangement? What does he get in return?"

"I've worked hard to win the trust and respect of the Norlhast Clan," Nuna told him. "The Laws of Reave might state a jarl should be a man but times change. We're not in Reavesburg now and no one would dare suggest Ingioy the White Widow isn't the rightful ruler of Vittag. I could be King Adalrikr's Jarl of Norlhast in more than just name, which is all Karas is content to be. Bring my brother safely to my side and I'll give you the loyalty of my people and help you quell this northern rebellion."

Geilir took another long sip from his glass, the wine almost gone. "What do you know of Orglyr?"

"Did you know Karas was secretly *pleased* when you linked him to Orglyr's uprising? The truth is he has nothing to do with it – nor could he. The idea the people would rise up in his tarnished name is laughable. The root of this trouble won't be found in Norlhast Keep. More likely Valdimarr has had an inadvertent hand in things by dealing poorly with the redistribution of land and titles in the north, reopening old wounds and past rivalries. Orglyr has enough of a following as Bekan's former right hand man to raise his own army. He might not even be planning to attack you – perhaps taking Vikarr's lands and livestock was enough to settle things."

"I'll not leave some savage with his own private army running around, whether he's happy with his lot in life or not," Geilir replied. "It's interesting, though. What you've said accords with what your husband and Albrikt told us. Sometimes, when you deal with conspiracies and plots all your life, you see more than there is."

"I can help you," Nuna said. "However, you need to offer me a sign I can trust you. Start with telling me where Albrikt is. He's a well-respected member of the Norlhast Clan and the longer you keep him imprisoned the more ill-feeling you'll stir up. If you want to maintain control in Norlhast you need to avoid giving the people cause to rise up against you."

Geilir thought for a time as he sat there, finishing the last of his wine. "Come with me," he said eventually.

Together they left his chambers and, accompanied by

his guard and Brosa, Geilir led them out of Norlhast Keep. More Vorund warriors joined them at the main gates, until Nuna and Brosa were surrounded by more than a dozen armoured men. She caught Brosa's anxious stare, unspoken understanding passing between them that it was too late to do anything without causing more suspicion. Eventually Geilir led them to a small house on the outskirts of the town, where Tryggvi was dozing outside the door, his breath reeking of ale. Geilir wrinkled his nose in distaste as Tryggvi looked up in surprise at the arrival of so many visitors. When he saw Nuna his eyes widened further.

"What's she doing here?"

"What gives you the right to ask me anything?" Geilir retorted. "Is the prisoner still inside?"

Tryggvi scowled and nodded as Geilir pushed past him and opened the door. It was dark inside and as Nuna approached the smell hit her, almost making her gag. It was a foul stench – excrement, urine, blood and vomit all mixed together to create a sickening miasma Nuna could taste in the back of her throat. Next to her Brosa uttered an oath and a number of Geilir's guards moved away, covering their faces.

"Bring me a light," ordered Geilir and one of his men obeyed, stepping forwards with a torch.

Nuna steeled herself and took a step inside, blinking as she took in the filthy form of a man, slumped naked and chained to a chair in the middle of the room. Albrikt's portly flesh quivered, his white beard dark with blood and snot from his broken nose. Nuna gasped as she saw a dozen broken teeth piled up on a wooden table by the door, scattered around a pair of dirty pincers. There were wounds all over Albrikt's body – too many to count and Nuna suspected many more were hidden under the muck and blood covering him.

Geilir took in the sight of Albrikt and turned to Tryggvi, his face full of rage. "I leave you alone and *this* is how you treat the jarl's closest counsellor?"

"You told me to get him to talk," Tryggvi replied obstinately. "I got him to talk. Job done."

Geilir took a long breath in through his nose. "Job. Done."

"Think you'll be interested in what he had to say," added Tryggvi, looking pleased with himself.

Geilir glanced at Nuna and Brosa, ushering them outside before talking to Tryggvi in low tones. Nuna couldn't hear what they were saying, although the few words she caught from Geilir were enough to confirm he wasn't pleased with Tryggvi's work.

"Gods," muttered Brosa next to her. "What have they done to him? You should never have come here."

"Hush," Nuna stroked his strong arm. "We're here now. Let's just get Albrikt away from here and be gone."

Eventually the door swung open and Geilir stepped outside, making a show of breathing in the fresh air. A cursory attempt had been made to clean Albrikt and he stood dressed in a dirty smock, swaying as Tryggvi took his weight, holding him around the shoulders. Blood and drool poured from his ruined mouth and he appeared unaware of anyone else around him, even when Brosa rushed up to help carry him back to the keep.

Geilir caught Nuna by the arm as she turned to leave. "Don't you want to know what Albrikt said through that shattered mouth of his?"

Nuna met Geilir's stare and held it. "I'm sure it accords with everything I've already told you."

"Quite so," Geilir said. "Tryggvi went too far and for that I apologise. However, Albrikt is alive and turned over into your care, just as I promised. I'll expect you to honour your side of the bargain when the time comes, for the good of Norlhast."

Nuna and Brosa wended their way back towards Norlhast Keep, finding Albrikt so heavy they had to stop at Kalfr and Luta's house for help. Luta's face was a stony mask as she hurried to tend to her father-in-law whilst her children looked on, the youngest of them, Varinn, weeping at the sight of his grandfather. Kalfr and Sigurd arrived a short time later, brought there by a white-faced Thyra, Kalfr's eldest daughter.

"You need to leave," Sigurd told Nuna. "You have my thanks for helping my father. We can manage things from here and tend to his wounds. It's not a good idea for you to be seen here come the dawn."

Brosa ushered Nuna to the door, where Thyra, who was only a few years younger than her, took her hands. "Thank you for helping Grandfather. That was very brave of you. My uncle is grateful, I know it. He's just not very good with this kind of thing."

Nuna kissed the girl lightly on the cheek and headed out into the night, hood up to hide her face from any onlookers. Brosa accompanied her back to the keep in silence. Despite achieving her goal Nuna felt empty as she got back to her chambers, where Katla began to fetch hot water so she could bathe. Nothing could wipe away the image of Albrikt in that room, made less than a man by *King* Adalrikr and his followers. If Nuna's lies were discovered nothing could protect her from the same fate – or worse. Later that night Karas entered the room and found her crying, silent tears rolling down her cheeks. Without a word he enfolded her with his scabbed hands, hugging her tightly.

CHAPTER 29

I awoke, my arms wrapped tightly around me in an echo of Karas' embrace. For a moment I couldn't understand why I was lying in the darkness, bright stars wheeling slowly above my head. It took the sound of the waves lapping against the hull to bring me back.

"He's awake," came Jolinn's voice from the shadows.

I struggled to sit up, feeling drained and weak as I untangled myself from my cloak. The air was fresh, a stiff wind filling our sails and causing me to shiver. I pulled my cloak around me once more, drawing my knees up to my chest.

"Are you alright?" Jolinn whispered.

I sense movement in the darkness and felt a hand press on my arm. I thought it was Jolinn until Etta spoke. "Rothgar. We were worried about you, my boy, you'd been gone for so long."

"I'm fine. I saw ... many things. Events move and Norlhast, where Nuna's playing a dangerous game and Desta's attempt to escape Noln came undone." I went on to explain what I'd seen in hushed tones as Etta and Jolinn listened in the darkness.

"Geilir," whispered Etta after I finished my tale.

"You know him?" asked Jolinn.

"Only by reputation. Geilir led Adalrikr's forces to victory over the Riltbalt Clan and will be unswerving in his purpose in Norlhast. Nuna faces a dangerous foe."

"What about Djuri? He broke Kolsveinn's hold. The death of a Sundered Soul is no small matter."

"Yes," Etta mused. "That was something I didn't

foresee and it could change things. We need you to venture out onto the Path once more to learn what's happening in Reavesburg."

"Is that such a good idea?" whispered Jolinn. "He's only just come back to us."

"I'll not face our enemies blind," said Etta, voice sharp as a blade. "My role is to watch *all* the pieces that are part of this game. Why do you think Rothgar is so important?"

We settled into an uncomfortable silence. I was stung by the casual way Etta spoke about my role, whilst seeing the truth in her words. Following her logic her presence on this voyage made more sense – I could see further than Joldir or Leif and Etta was there to study every piece of information I brought back. I stared at Etta's shadowy form, outlined by the stars, noting how bright and alert she sounded, whilst I felt incredibly weary from my journey along the Path.

"So," I asked her in a low voice, "now we're out here and away from Romsdahl, are you going to share your secrets?"

"My secrets? What could you possibly mean?"

"Don't dissemble. People have been talking in Romsdahl about your restored ... vigour. Not all the comments I've heard concerning this are complimentary."

"Are you sure you want to know the answer?" asked Etta, voice quiet in the darkness before dawn.

I swallowed hard. "Why? What makes you say that?"

"I don't want to lie to you, Rothgar, but neither do you need to know everything concerning my business. And that's what this is, my business and no one else's. What I will tell you is I've done what was necessary to enable me to help you on this voyage. Have I ever led you wrong?" I shrugged, thinking Etta would miss the gesture until she gave a *tsk* of annoyance. "I'll pretend I didn't see that. Concern yourself with the part you're playing in this quest and let me worry about my own affairs."

I knew that note of finality and dropped the subject

with a sigh. Looking around I saw that most of the crew were asleep, huddled under cloaks and blankets as they lay on the deck. Aguti was on the night watch, his hand resting lightly on the steering oar. Despite the darkness he noticed me staring at him.

"Good weather for keeping on course," he declared, nodding up at the stars. "Keep the northern constellation of Elphinas in your sights and the rest is easy."

"Until it clouds over," said Jolinn.

"Aye. Then it does become trickier, I'll give you that," Aguti agreed.

"I'm sorry Desta wasn't able to make it away from Noln," Jolinn said to me in a lower voice as I watched the stars sparkling in the black velvet sky. "I know she means something to you."

I sighed. "She's in trouble because of me. The worst thing about the Sight is you see events you can't influence. For Etta, knowing what's happening is all important. She doesn't understand what it's like to experience events as if they're happening to you, as if you're fighting for *your* life in those moments. People's fears, loves and passions – I feel them all."

"I can't really imagine what that must be like. You must wish things could be as they were before."

I shrugged and, unable to think of a reply, said nothing, watching the stars as *Stormweaver* skipped over the waves.

***

Dawn broke, Altandu's bright star to the east giving way to her gift of the sun as the first slivers of that glowing disk emerged above the waters. There were no landmarks – we were surrounded by the sea in every direction. Aerinndis approached and gave Aguti a slap on the back, acknowledging the fact he'd kept us on a true course through the night. Aguti rubbed his tanned face as he gave up his position to a sleepy Feyotra.

"Go and break your fast," Aerinndis said, indicating the pot of porridge oats Haddr was cooking on the small stove.

"Where are we?" I asked.

Aerinndis flashed me a grin. "You're awake. I thought you might have slipped away to Navan's Halls – we've been unable to rouse you for a whole day."

"I'm still in the land of the living. So, where are we now?"

"We've left the Redfars Sea behind," she told me. "You're looking out across the Endless Ocean."

I frowned. "How can you tell? There's nothing to see."

Haddr laughed as he piled steaming porridge into a bowl and passed it to me. My stomach growled loud enough for the whole ship to hear and a few of the crew sniggered.

Feyotra looked up from her food. "The number of days we've been at sea for one. A better guide, though, is the feel of the wind on my face. It's noticeably colder already and in another day or two you might even see icebergs."

"We're not alone," announced Aguti, his soft words cutting through the chatter in an instant.

Aerinndis set aside her breakfast and hurried to the stern where Aguti was standing. "Show me what you see."

"There, there and there," Aguti's finger indicated three separate points, close together on the horizon to the south.

I squinted, trying to make out anything against the ever-shifting waves. After a moment I saw three square smudges on the horizon – the red sails of longships in close formation. I caught a glint either side of them, flashing briefly before vanishing. It appeared again a moment later, part of a rhythmic pattern as I continued to watch.

"Those are oars," I said.

Aerinndis nodded. "You've got sharp eyes. That's right, they're rowing towards us and fast, even though the wind is favourable."

"Chasing us, you mean," said Ulfarr, who had joined

us, quickly spooning porridge oats into his mouth.

"Hasteinn," I muttered. "Vorund is miles away. How have they got so close?"

"My guess is Hasteinn the Cruel is living up to his name and his crew are rowing night and day to close the distance between us," said Aerinndis, pursing her lips as she scoured the horizon.

"And that's why the Sight is so important, alerting us to this threat," added Etta.

"I don't need the Sight to recognise when someone's chasing me," Aerinndis retorted, turning towards the rest of her crew. "We've got company and they're rowing as if Rathlin himself was on their tail. Everyone to their oars – we've a long day ahead of us."

"Can we keep ahead of them?" I asked Meinolf.

Aerinndis' first mate shrugged. "They're far away but my guess would be that Hasteinn's sailing with war ships. They can carry plenty of crew, enough to row in two teams. Although that gives them one advantage, Stormweaver's a smaller, faster ship. All we need to do is keep ahead of them until we reach the ice floes – that'll give us a chance to lose them."

***

Aerinndis set every strong back to work on the oars, even Skari lending a hand despite his sea sickness. With each stroke he cursed someone – the sea, the Brotherhood, the Vorund Clan, Adalrikr, Johan, Ulfarr, Aerinndis. The list went on. I sat at the back of the ship with Etta, the two of us unable to help. For want of anything else to do I looked behind us, the sails of the pursuing ships stubbornly remaining fixed on the horizon.

"They don't seem to be closing us down," I said.

"Hmm. We aren't losing them either," Etta remarked sourly.

"Hasteinn must be driving his crew with a singular purpose," said Feyotra as she continued to steer the ship.

I nodded towards the crew, backs bending as they worked as one, oars dipping into the water with precision, driving us forwards. "How long can we keep this up?"

Feyotra scowled. "If they've worked that hard to bring us into sight it means we're the fresher crew. That'll count for something."

As the day wore on the weather began to change, clouds gathering above us as and releasing fine rain showers. Out at sea it was possible to see the individual weather patterns, although Aerinndis didn't trouble herself to try and avoid them, Stormweaver cutting an unerring course north. As the weather worsened we lost sight of our pursuers, although no one doubted they were out there, hunting us down. I did what I could to be useful, handing out watered wine, ale and rations of hard sea biscuits dunked in brine and salted fish to the crew. They ate silently as they sat on their benches, too tired to complain. Ekkill's hands were blistering and I offered to bind them.

"No," he shook his head. "I'm fine."

"You don't look fine. Let me help – if that wound gets infected ..."

"I'll clean them at the end of the day. A few more days of this and they'll be calloused over, fit for the task at hand. Some of us aren't afraid of hard labour."

I ignored the jibe as I worked my way to the front of the ship, noting Ulfarr and Jolinn were also nursing their hands. At the prow Aerinndis took a swig from the waterskin, her eyes never wavering from the sea. She occasionally spoke to Feyotra in low tones as they checked our course against the position of the sun, watching its journey as it flitted in and out of the rainclouds. Up ahead, the sky looked darker and I could feel the change in the temperature now, the air noticeably colder.

"What does the Sight have to say about our current situation, Rothgar?" asked Aerinndis.

"Nothing," I confessed. "If there's anyone on

Hasteinn's crew open to the Sight I haven't detected it so far."

"In that case, it's down to a test of seamanship to determine whether Hasteinn's ships overtake us on the open water."

"It won't come to that," I said, with more confidence than I felt.

Aerinndis turned and flashed me a grin, the wind running through her curly hair. "That's the spirit. And if you're wrong and it comes to blade work, those extra hands you brought aboard my ship will have to earn their keep."

CHAPTER 30

Djuri washed his hands in the stream, the dirt and blood carried away by the water, revealing pink skin underneath. His clothes were just as filthy but there'd been no chance to change. After the fight on the dockside they had stolen the horses belonging to Kolsveinn's men. Unfortunately, since Noln was only a half day's ride from Reavesburg, they'd carried scant provisions and equipment, riding through the night for as long as they could before sleeping uneasily under their cloaks, huddled in a ditch next to a field for a few hours before dawn, with their horses picketed nearby. The rest of the group were now awake, making breakfast with the last of their food. The only good thing was they had enough coin to buy more, including fresh clothes. Spending it in another town would be a risk, since they could easily be recognised by a Vorund patrol. However, without the proper gear and more food no one would survive the journey, meaning there wasn't really any choice to be made.

Journey? Journey where? That was the question rattling around his mind as he splashed water on his face. What were they going to do? He glanced up and saw Desta Haarlswyfe was sitting on the bank of the stream a few feet away, watching him. There were scratches around her neck and cuts and bruises blossoming on her face. The least he could do was see she was safe for Haarl's sake – her and the baby. He glanced up at Lina, tending to both children as the old man looked on, busy dividing up the last of the milk-sodden loaf from the sack he'd been carrying. Although she'd also tried to clean herself, Lina's clothes were blood soaked. The brown smear on her hairline spoke of what took place last night, a cursory wash failing to erase the evidence.

Desta followed his gaze. "She was fighting to protect us and her child. She saved us all." Djuri couldn't tell if she was trying to persuade him or herself.

"I don't think that's how your father sees things," Djuri replied. "You understand, don't you? You know what she is? A skin thief – she's taken that young woman's soul and now she inhabits her stolen body, just like Kolsveinn tried to do to me. She's no angel. You can't trust her."

Desta pressed her lips together, wrapping her arms tightly around her chest to ward off the morning chill. "I'm just glad she's fighting on our side."

"Is she?" Djuri asked.

***

Humli winced as Frokn began to cry, the sound carrying far and wide. Lina took the little boy and began to nurse him, letting him suckle greedily on her milk.

Altandu, Mother of Light, protect us. Like most men of Laskar, Humli had little time for the gods. What was the point of offering prayers to the avatars when the Creator had banished them to the Void? Reave's teachings were the same as those Humli had been schooled in back in Riltbalt; the gods were only concerned with their own ends, not the affairs of humans. Godless he might be, but Humli decided this situation demanded prayer and addressing his supplication to Altandu felt right. Humli had seen a terrible darkness and animal rage in Lina as she'd torn those screaming men apart with her bare hands. Those same hands were now smoothing her babe's hair as she crooned over the infant in her arms.

They hadn't spoken much after their desperate flight from the docks. Everyone was exhausted, only desiring to put many miles between themselves and Noln, anxiously watching over their shoulders for any signs of pursuit. Now, though, Humli knew they needed to deal with what had happened. What would Lina do now they knew what she was? Not that Humli really understood her true nature – only that when he looked at Lina he felt afraid.

The big warrior, Djuri, came back from the stream, looking slightly less bloody, Desta in his wake. This was another thing that left Humli worried. He knew next to nothing about this man, other than if he turned on them there wasn't much Humli could do to stop him. An evil mist had poured from Kolsveinn when he died, surrounding Djuri as he lay on the floor. The warrior *seemed* normal enough, appearing to suffer no ill-effects, yet no one really knew for sure what had happened to him.

"We need to talk," said Humli as the warrior took a seat next to him and began munching on the damp bread with little enthusiasm. Humli gulped, surprised the words had left his lips.

"We do," agreed Lina. "Decisions need to be made, for all of us."

"Let's start with you," Djuri spoke in a deep rumble, eyes fixed on Lina. "When Kolsveinn attacked me I found myself ... I'm not even sure I know how to describe what happened. I was in another world, between life and death, in some sort of spirit plane, where I learned ... things." The man shook his head. "I don't even know where to begin."

Humli and the rest of them listened in silence as Djuri told them of his meeting with the Weeping Warrior and what he'd learned of the durath. Humli felt ice in his veins as Djuri explained the nature of these shadow spirits and how Adalrikr Kinslayer was one of them. A sense of horror and powerlessness fell over him and he stared at his boots. *Myshall's bane – I'm a fisherman without a boat. What am I doing mixed up in all of this? This can't be true. It just can't.*

"Kolsveinn's focus was on you, Lina," said Djuri as he finished his tale. "However, Adalrikr also wants Desta so he can use her against Rothgar in some way. Our mission was to capture both of you."

"Yet you defied your orders," said Desta.

Djuri nodded, his dark eyes unable to meet her gaze. He rubbed a big hand over his tired face, stroking the shadow of stubble covering his chin. "I made the wrong decision when Ulfkell's Keep fell, I've known it all along and I kept trying to follow the path I'd chosen until I saw how they murdered Lundvarr." He sighed. "I thought I was helping to unite the clans and prevent further bloodshed, only to learn we're actually serving the evil ends of these shadow spirits."

"That's the story of Djuri Turncloak," said Desta. "What about you, Lina? Who ... what are you? Why did you lie to us and worm your way into our home?"

Lina looked at them, her face defiant. "Not all the durath are sworn to Adalrikr's cause. This upstart King of the North is placing us on a path to conflict and when you can live forever the one thing you come to treasure above all else is life. After more than two hundred years of searching the Sundered Souls finally found the means of creating a bridge, linking the Real to other realms. Adalrikr began summoning his lost followers from the Shadow Realm back to his side." Lina's face became distant. "We'd spent centuries in a dark place, formless shadows. Living in the Real once more, experiencing life fully ... you've no idea what that was like. Many of my brethren were driven mad during their exile while others, weakened and diminished by the ordeal, itch and burn in their new-found skin. Then there were those who have returned stronger, hungry for power and fresh meat. The flesh is both a pleasure and a curse for the durath."

Humli stared at Lina with mounting dread. She looked normal enough and before he'd seen those ... things on the docks, he'd have thought she was raving. His mouth was dry and he took a drink of water, trying to order his thoughts.

"This has never been about clan rivalries or uniting Laskar," Lina continued as Frokn snuggled next to her, sleepy and full of milk. "Adalrikr was once emperor of all Valistria and he means to restore everything he lost at the end of the War. However, not all the durath believe in Adalrikr's vision and Sandar Tindirson offered us another way. He was one of the first to be restored to Adalrikr's side through the Calling and learned how he'd bridged the two worlds. Sandar opened an alternative gateway to Amuran, enabling some of us, including me, to return in secret, beyond Adalrikr's gaze. We might have continued to grow in power, only for Johan's Brotherhood to put an end to those hopes. Johan has declared war on the durath, forging magical weapons which can destroy us forever. By razing Sandar's stronghold in Tullen to the ground he's forced the durath who remain in the Shadow Realm to Adalrikr's side. He's actually increased the power of the one he's fighting. Now thousands of our kind gather in the shadows, waiting to return to Amuran."

"You keep telling us that you're not one of Adalrikr's supporters," said Humli. "But that didn't stop you taking the form of the woman sitting before us. How is that right?"

"Can you stop being what you are?" Lina replied. "The Calling is irresistible, drawing us back home to Amuran, but we can't survive here for long without a host. If we fail to take possession of our new form we die, just as when Djuri managed to fight off Kolsveinn. That was no mere feat – the Sundered are adept at taking a new form and are one of the few shadow spirits who do so willingly if it suits their purposes."

Djuri cut a piece of ham off the joint Humli had brought with them. "Sitting here now, I don't feel very special. I don't know what else to say."

"And if that's what you are, Lina, what's the nature of your child?" asked Humli, staring at the innocent-looking boy in her arms, his flesh crawling.

"I don't know, and that's the truth," Lina replied, cradling Frokn. "A durath has never given birth to a child before. Frokn means courageous and bold, a fitting name for a child who bears the hopes of both our races. Sandar might have been able to uncover more but his knowledge died with him in Tullen. All I know is I don't want Frokn to fall into Adalrikr's hands, so our interests align. We need to escape from Reavesburg together and make our way to a new life, somewhere far away from Adalrikr's growing kingdom. We can help each other."

***

Djuri sat there, eating his slice of ham, thinking on all that Lina had said. Part of him wanted to reach for his sword and strike down this creature that took human life so casually. Yet if he spilled Lina's blood she would try and take possession of one of them, perhaps even him. He couldn't be sure he'd be able to fight her off as he had Kolsveinn. Instead, he kept his sword in its scabbard, pushing back the impulse, trying to think of the best way to deal with the situation. As he finished his food he reached a decision.

"I'll come with you," he announced. "Tyrfingr's grip of the western lands is weakened after Johan's rebellion – I've heard the talk at Ulfkell's Keep. They'll be watching the ports after your attempt to gain passage on a ship, so change your plan. We have good horses we can use to travel swiftly west to free towns like Delving. From there it's possible to take one of the passages through the Baros Mountains and reach Vittag's lands. The White Widow's treaty with Vorund keeps her borders open so trade can flow and we can take advantage of that."

Lina looked thoughtful. "I don't think you should come with us. A warrior's skills could be helpful but you'll be a wanted man, easily recognisable on the road. We'll look more like another band of refugees without you, better able to blend in and travel unnoticed with the others heading in the same direction."

"You're sending away the only fighting man we have?" Desta protested, shaking her head. Humli looked unhappy at his daughter's words, although he said nothing.

Djuri frowned. "I don't understand. Are you

suggesting I return to Ulfkell's Keep after what's happened?"

"There are no surviving witnesses to what took place in Noln," Lina explained. "You could return to Ulfkell's Keep, report on the battle at the docks and tell them you were the only survivor. You could even set them on a false trail; say we were headed south towards Romsdahl to seek passage on another ship. Buying us time would be far more helpful than having one warrior with us, only to be outnumbered if we're discovered by one of Tyrfingr's patrols."

Djuri sat there, deep in thought. There were risks with the plan Lina was outlining. Tyrfingr might not believe his story for one thing. *But is this my chance to make amends? Is this the better course, rather than fleeing Reavesburg and the consequences of my choices?*

"I know my kind," Lina continued. "When Kolsveinn and Eidr came to our home, I knew both of them were Sundered. If you return to Reavesburg you must be careful around Eidr. He's a more dangerous foe than Tyrfingr Blackeyes, believe me."

"Let me worry about Eidr and Blackeyes," said Djuri, reflecting on all he had seen in this world and the one beyond. "I'll find a way to buy you the time you need to safely reach Vittag."

CHAPTER 31

Fundinn walked through the Norlhast camp that night, checking everything was in order. Many of the warriors were still outside, despite the rain, gathered around cook fires, drinking and swapping stories rather than taking shelter in their tents. Several called out greetings to him and he slapped a few shoulders and backs as he passed, calling them by name where he could. Two thousand had heeded Orglyr's call to arms in Taur – enough to retake Norlhast Keep.

"One more victory, that's all we need," Orglyr told him. "One victory and those who were undecided before will want to be on the winning side. Taking the keep is all that matters. It's time to send word to Karas Greystorm that his army awaits his orders."

They were ready to move, the last supplies and equipment arriving that afternoon, though Fundinn wished they had struck camp and left Taur two days ago. Every hour they stayed in one place risked discovery, something which preyed on his fraying nerves.

There was a commotion at the edge of the camp and Fundinn headed off to investigate. A crowd had gathered and Fundinn saw Limping Tidkumi's distinctive figure cutting through the throng, torchlight reflecting off his bald head, his second Soma following in his wake.

"We've got a visitor," announced Tidkumi in his rasping voice, stepping aside to reveal another man; short in stature with brown hair, about thirty years of age. Fundinn peered closer. His face was familiar and after a few moments Fundinn was able to place him.

"I remember you," he said. "You were one of the Lady

of Norlhast's guards that night at the docks."

The man nodded. "That's why Nuna chose to send me, so you'd know the message I carry comes from her. My name's Curren and I bring urgent news from Norlhast Keep. I was asked to give my message directly to Orglyr the Grim."

Fundinn nodded and together they headed to Orglyr's tent, where they were ushered inside by his guards. Orglyr ordered food and drink for Curren as the warrior explained the reason for his visit.

"The Vorund Clan know about your muster, although the hand of the chief and his advisors is only suspected. They've decided to move against you now, to bring a swift end to the rebellion."

"Valdimarr's no soldier. I'll crush him on the battlefield," Orglyr boasted, looking around at his companions for their agreement.

"Valdimarr is no longer running things in Norlhast," Curren told him. "Adalrikr has placed Geilir Goldentooth in charge. He's already set forth from Norlhast Keep, leading an army of Vorund warriors and Riltbalt conscripts westwards to face you. Geilir has two thousand men on foot and another five hundred on horseback, all well-armed, little more than a day behind me."

"Those numbers don't sound so different to ours," said Orglyr, his face lighting up at the prospect of battle.

Soma arched an eyebrow. "Perhaps not, though many of our men are untried in battle and lightly armed. Do they know our position?"

Curren nodded. "Unfortunately. Darkness has halted their march but they're ready for battle."

"They think they have the element of surprise," said Orglyr. "We can use that to our advantage."

Tidkumi looked sceptical. "Or we retreat and wait until we have a better opportunity. There was always a risk we would be discovered, assembling this many men. It's a miracle it hasn't happened already. Those numbers sound too close to me."

"The arrival of the warriors from Riltbalt took us by surprise when their ships landed," added Curren. "This move against us has been long in the planning. Geilir is a cunning foe and it would be no disgrace to retreat and regroup, so we can strike when the odds favour us."

Orglyr gave Curren a wicked grin. "You don't know me, so I'll forgive you for suggesting that. This is our chance to strike a blow against the Vorund Clan. I'm not called Orglyr the Grim because I run away from battle. We'll face our foes in the field and make them wish they'd never come to Norlhast."

"We can't help the Greystorms if we're dead," Tidkumi complained, shaking his head.

"Then we'd best win," Orglyr retorted.

***

By the time dawn broke the Norlhast warriors had already struck camp and were moving into position, trying to outflank Geilir's approaching army based on the information on their position brought to them by their scouts. It was all getting frantic, with conflicting accounts and half-garbled messages not helping Orglyr and Tidkumi marshal their forces.

We're rushing this Fundinn thought as he brought his own crew into position on the edge of a ridge above a steep-sided valley east of Taur. Curren crouched a few feet from him, wanting to make himself useful in the coming fight. Fundinn needed as many experienced hands as he could get and was pleased at how Curren was with the men, especially the younger ones – laughing and joking to keep their spirits up. Making your men believe they could win was half the battle.

"I see them," called out Snaga, from further up the line.

Fundinn looked towards the head of the valley, where a long column of troops had appeared as they wended their way along the road running below them. He could see their banners – a hammer set above a single star, the sigil of the Riltbalt Clan. He watched from his vantage point as the column continued its advance, making sure his crew couldn't be seen on the ridge. They didn't want to give away their position.

"Remember to wait until they're bottled up at the base of the valley," he told his crew. "We'll lead the charge from this side and pincer them with Tidkumi's men opposite ..."

His voice died in his throat as he saw the Norlhast warriors break their cover at the other end of the valley, the very stones ringing with their war cry. In the vanguard the few horsemen the Norlhast Clan possessed were charging – an arrowhead shaped wedge, with Orglyr clearly recognisable at their head, white hair streaming out beneath his helm; axe and shield raised high in the air.

"What's he doing?" cried Curren in dismay.

"Getting bored," Fundinn grunted, after he'd finished uttering a string of curses.

Across the other side of the valley he heard a horn blowing, Tidkumi signalling his warriors to attack. They began their charge down the valley, now running at a diagonal rather than straight ahead as planned, trying to get into the fight and still use the higher ground to their advantage. Hoskuldr's archers sent a volley of arrows arching over the Norlhast cavalry into the Riltbalt ranks, shrieks and cries from wounded and dying men drifting up into the air. They continued loosing arrows as the Riltbalt forces began to spread out, pulling their own bowmen into position and trying to form up a defensive line to meet Orglyr's charge.

"Do we go?" asked Snaga.

"Not yet."

A sick feeling was spreading through Fundinn as he watched events unfold. Foremost on his mind was the fact there was no sign of Geilir's warriors and as he crouched on the ridge the hairs on the back of his neck prickled. He spun around to see a wall of horses charging them from behind, the riders bearing the Vorund sigil of the bear on its hind legs. No battle cries, just the simple murderous intent to smash them to pieces as they lay there exposed on the escarpment. Ahead of the horsemen he could see one of his scouts desperately running, his screams of warning just carrying to them as a faint, despairing whisper. A spear brought him down and he vanished under the horses' hooves as they plunged towards Fundinn's men.

Fundinn grabbed the man next to him, dragging him round so he could also see the threat. "Signal the retreat," he bellowed. "Warn them to pull back before it's too late. We've been outflanked ourselves. If we engage with the Riltbalt Clan they'll trap us in this valley and cut us to pieces."

He scoured the opposite ridge, where he could see Tidkumi's warriors continue to flow down the side of the valley. Behind them were more Vorund riders, warriors on foot chasing hard on their heels. There was nothing he could do other than hope Tidkumi and Soma could fight their way out as the horn blared the retreat signal next to him. He had enough problems of his own, as he only had a few seconds to decide whether or not to face his enemies on the ridge. His men were on their feet, understanding they were under attack and, to their credit, they stayed still, waiting for Fundinn's order. If they ran down the sloping sides of the valley they would be cut down but remaining on the ridge meant they were too exposed. Fundinn glanced to his left, spotting a dense patch of woodland nearby and made his decision, an idea forming in his head.

"With me. Run and fall back to the trees. Now, come on. Move!"

He hurtled towards the woods, trying not to lose his footing on the uneven ground or break an ankle on the rocks strewn in his path. Behind him the horses made contact with his men, a sickening crunch of metal, bone and horseflesh before screams of panic and fear filled the air. Further back he could see warriors on foot charging them, giving voice to the Vorund war cry now the need for stealth had passed.

Fundinn reached the woods and wended his way between the boughs of the trees, weaving left and right, his warriors spreading out as they sought their own paths. He was pleased to see the trees became denser as he ran further inside, brambles and thorns catching his clothes and scratching his legs. Behind him he heard horses shriek as their massed ranks tried to negotiate the confined space, forcing them to slow down. He risked a glance backwards and could see some of the riders in pursuit. However, most of the horses had been brought up short as the way through narrowed unexpectedly, causing the cavalry charge to falter. Riders cursed as their mounts skidded to a halt, caught up in the growing mass of cavalry trapped on the edge of the treeline.

Fundinn's foot caught in a hidden tree root, tripping him over. He landed on his back, stars blurring his vision as he fought to catch his breath. He rolled onto his side and saw a lone Vorund horseman charging him down, spear levelled towards him. There was a *whup, whup, whup* sound off to his left and the rider slumped over, sliding from his saddle with a cry, his steed jumping over Fundinn and disappearing into the trees. Snaga appeared, a wolfish grin on his face, and pulled Fundinn to his feet, drawing another throwing axe from his belt.

"Thanks," Fundinn gasped, staggering after his men as the woods slowly began to fill with Vorund warriors behind them.

"What's the plan, chief?" asked Snaga as they ran.

"Let's start with staying alive and figuring it out as we go along," puffed Fundinn. "If we can get down onto the road I'll wager we'll find more of Geilir's men blocking Orglyr's retreat. Giving our warriors a safe route out of the valley sounds like a good thing right now."

Deeper into the wood they passed the bodies of some of Fundinn's men, as well as more riderless horses. The pair of them came across Curren fighting alongside a dozen or so of his comrades, two Vorund riders harrying them. Fundinn stepped in, springing up and sweeping his sword round, taking off most of one rider's leg below the knee before he even had time to register more warriors had joined the fight. Snaga's throwing axe found the face of the other. The group of Norlhast warriors ran on into the wood, leaving the Vorund man Fundinn had maimed yelling for help, the strength in his shouts already fading as he bled out onto the forest floor.

Slowly what remained of Fundinn's crew gathered around him, moving downwards through the forest. They could hear the shouts from the Vorund Clan behind them, loud enough to tell them they weren't far away. Up ahead the unmistakable sounds of battle grew louder.

"Looks like you guessed right," said Snaga.

Fundinn slowed his run, peering through the trees where he could see Hoskuldr fighting with his sword, cutting down a Vorund spearman as his men were pressed back by a solid wedge of enemy warriors. Fundinn burst from the woods, his men following him screaming so loudly it caused the Vorund ranks to stop in their tracks, one young man gasping in horror moments before Fundinn cut him down. The Vorund warriors wavered at this unexpected attack and some of them broke, dropping their weapons and running. Fundinn took the chance to hack his way towards Hoskuldr, fighting side by side with Curren and Snaga.

"There's more Vorund warriors right on our tail," Fundinn yelled, smashing his sword down onto the head of Hoskuldr's opponent. "Get any bowmen you still have and break off. We need to cut them down as they come out of the woods and buy time for Orglyr to retreat."

Giving the order was the easy part. The road was narrow and disentangling Hoskuldr's men from the remaining Vorund warriors took forever. Fortunately, more Vorund warriors were fleeing – losing heart whilst they were outnumbered. Fundinn knew they had a small opportunity to break free before more enemies arrived – he could hear Tidkumi's warriors also signalling the retreat, which meant they would also be coming this way. For now, he needed to concentrate on staying alive.

A big axeman, red beard flowing out from underneath a brightly polished helmet spattered with drops of blood, led a group of Vorund warriors out of the woods and into the fray. He killed Snaga with a brutal upward stroke, shattering his jaw and face. Fundinn bellowed in fury and swung his sword at the axeman, cursing as he blocked it with his shield. The two traded blows, finding themselves evenly matched as Curren guarded Fundinn's back. Fundinn hacked at his opponent's feet, forcing him to step back and he stumbled over the body of a fallen Vorund spearman. Pressing his advantage, Fundinn's next strokes were aimed high, one of them slipping through the warrior's defences. His sword glanced off the man's helmet, the momentum carrying Fundinn in too close. The red-bearded man caught him in the ribs with the pointed head of his axe, crunching into chainmail and knocking Fundinn down onto one knee. His body screamed in protest as he brought his shield up just in time to ward off an axe blow to the head.

Curren's sword cut through the air, taking the axeman in the throat, dropping him in a shower of blood, eyes wide with surprise. Fundinn groaned as he got back onto his feet, glancing down at the blood seeping through his chainmail. It felt like a rib was cracked and he gasped in pain as he took a breath. He could hear pounding hooves and heard Hoskuldr shouting out orders, his bowmen still forming up into a ragged line further back from the main battle.

It's taken too long. They've made their way through the woods …

His thoughts trailed off as horses burst onto the road

rather than from between the trees. At their head was Orglyr, axe red with blood, shield dented. He bent low in his saddle and shattered the head of a Vorund warrior in his path. The arrival of Orglyr's warriors was enough to break the spirit of the remaining Vorund men, who turned and fled this new threat. More Vorund warriors were now appearing at the tree line, men on foot scouting the base of the valley, rather than a blind cavalry charge. Hoskuldr's archers loosed their arrows, driving them back into the cover of the woods.

"Fundinn," Orglyr shouted. "This is a right mess. We're falling back. Follow me – the Riltbalt Clan are on our heels."

"That's the first good decision we've made since this started," muttered Curren, his blade dripping with blood.

Fundinn nodded and, wincing as he clutched his wounded side, he ordered the retreat, his men following Orglyr's riders as they cut a path down the road. Hoskuldr's archers kept the flanking Vorund forces pinned down in the woods, giving Tidkumi's ragged warriors enough time to reach the road. Gritting his teeth against the pain as he ran, Fundinn cursed Geilir and Orglyr's name in equal measure as they fled westwards. The Vorund Clan would be right on their tail and Fundinn knew this day was far from over.

CHAPTER 32

I was grateful for my furs as we sailed further north. The winds turned against us, a bitter northerly that dusted the sail, ropes and planks with frost. The only way we could progress was with oars, taking a north-easterly course which Feyotra assured us would bring us to an ocean current that would speed us on our way once more. I'd never heard of rivers of water flowing within the great seas, although I recalled Brunn Fourwinds talking of currents close to the coast when he taught me how to sail on the Redfars Sea. The wind brought a further gift of squally showers which left us thinking wistfully of the frost, the rain freezing on contact and covering *Stormweaver* in a thin layer of polished ice which made every task on board difficult. Skari slipped moving about the ship and almost went over the side, Haddr's strong arms catching him at the last second.

"You don't want to touch the water," he said as he lowered a green-faced Skari onto his bench and put an oar in his fur-gloved hands. "If we fish you out of there, you'll never get warm again. You'll drift off to sleep and never wake up."

I glanced at the sea, noting it was now covered in small chunks of ice, even in midsummer. These grew larger as the day wore on, the crew's breath steaming as they rowed northwards, Feyotra keeping our course true, never leaving the steering oar. When the sky cleared I looked back for any signs of our pursuers, relieved to see there was nothing on the horizon.

"They're still close by," Aerinndis told me, wrapped in layers of furs so thick she was twice as wide as when I met her in Romsdahl. "I can feel them. Hasteinn won't give up, although I think changing course has thrown them off our scent for now. I reckon they've kept heading due north. This is the longer way as the crow flies but after we pick up that current we'll pass them by, you'll see."

The monotony of the day wore on, the crew rowing to keep warm as well as drawing us closer to our destination. Jonas started a song, its rhythm in time with the beat of the oars, Matthildr and Aguti joining in, Meinolf lending his deep bass after the first couple of verses. Aguti had a fine voice and I wondered if he'd ever considered life as a travelling bard. Etta remained quiet, wrapped up in furs and piles of blankets. She caught me looking at her.

"No, I'm not dead yet," she quipped.

"I never said you were," I replied, aiming for mock outrage and coming out with cold, shivering exhaustion.

I thought back on everything I'd seen with the Sight, wondering how Nuna was faring since Orglyr's defeat. I thought of Desta and her family on their journey to Vittag. So much had happened to both of us in the past year since I'd escaped Ulfkell's Keep. Our time together felt like it belonged to another age in this alien, icy world. A sense of disquiet settled over me as I wondered why Lina had been so insistent about sending Djuri away. Was she right his presence would have placed them in greater danger? I turned my thoughts to Bandor, getting ready with the rest of the Brotherhood to land at Vorund Fastness, all of them counting on me. Eventually, as dusk began to steal the light by slow degrees under the grey rainclouds, I felt the ship pick up speed. I glanced at Aerinndis, who gave me a knowing wink.

"The current has us in its grip. No one knows how to read the waters as well as Feyotra. Now all we have to do is make sure it doesn't smash us straight into an iceberg."

"I *think* I can manage that part," remarked Feyotra with a knowing smile, Matthildr laughing at the joke.

Meinolf ordered the crew to ship their oars and take some rest, the crew too tired to grumble or complain. Most curled up and went to sleep straight away, Feyotra and Matthildr sharing their furs, Ulfarr snoring loudly before too long. As the light faded I saw shapes on the horizon. I jumped up with a start, thinking Hasteinn's ships were upon us and almost lost my footing on the icy planks of the ship.

"Relax," said Aguti, now at his customary place on the night watch as he steered the ship. The man seemed to hardly need any sleep. "Those are bergs. It's a good sign. Means we'll reach the ice-shelf soon." He gave a short laugh. "Then you'll know what cold means."

***

Djuri lay next to Nereth's unconscious form in her chambers, unable to sleep. Washing away the grime from the road and battle had revealed a number of cuts, scrapes and purple bruises, all of which helped lend credibility to his story. The marks on his right wrist were the most obvious, the black bruise of Kolsveinn's handprint standing out clearly on his flesh – Djuri had never felt strength like it. The bones in his arm still ached.

He'd arrived at Ulfkell's Keep earlier that day, where Bjorr met him at the gates and brought him straight to Tyrfingr. Eidr had been present – looking down his nose at Djuri, his red hair and neat beard immaculately groomed as always. Djuri was aware he was filthy and stank, something Nereth confirmed when she swept into the chamber and put a hand up to her nose, face wrinkled in disgust.

"From the look and smell of you this can't be good news," she remarked.

Eidr was staring at Djuri. "Where's Kolsveinn? What happened?"

"Kolsveinn's dead, as are the rest of my men." Djuri began to tell his story, the one he'd agreed with Lina before they parted ways. He spared no details as he outlined how Kolsveinn had tortured and killed Lundvarr to reveal the location of Lina and her companions.

Tyrfingr's face darkened at that news and he gave Eidr

a sour look. "I wanted Lundvarr punished for his treachery, not torn apart in his own house. What was Kolsveinn thinking of?"

"Treachery must always be dealt with firmly," Eidr replied with a smile. "If the people don't know fear more will follow his lead. Such thinking needs to be ... aggressively discouraged."

"Taxes must be paid," countered Tyrfingr. "King Adalrikr is most specific on that point. Lundvarr's contacts with the merchants are vital to the trade flowing in and out of Noln."

"Find someone else to count your coppers," snapped Eidr. "None of this is my concern."

"Go on," said Tyrfingr to Djuri, clearly unsatisfied.

Djuri explained what took place at the docks, although in his version of the tale he had battled with Lina and been overpowered by her before she fought Kolsveinn. As agreed, he told them their quarry was last seen heading south, rather than west, hoping it would buy them time. Revealing Lina to be durath made sense, as everyone except Djuri had been aware of her nature when Kolsveinn had set out to capture her. It also gave him the chance to play upon his ignorance.

"You let us walk into a trap," Djuri said as he finished the tale. "You never warned me this Lina was some kind of monster. She tore my men to pieces – almost killed me. It was as if she was possessed by some evil spirit."

"Kolsveinn should have been more than capable of handling her," interjected Eidr.

"Well, he wasn't," Djuri retorted, putting as much indignation into his voice as he could muster.

"The most important thing is Lina and Desta's escape was foiled," said Nereth. "We need to keep watch on the coastal towns and villages further south. There's still a chance we could capture them both. Nothing is lost."

Eidr nodded towards Bjorr. "She's right. We need to find them and quickly. Ready twenty of your men and have them join me. We'll take the road to Noln before nightfall and pick up their trail from there."

As Bjorr left to carry out his orders Tyrfingr whispered something into Nereth's ear and she nodded, looking at Djuri. He felt uncomfortable under her gaze and looked away, trying to straighten out his clothes.

"That's enough for today," said Nereth, rising from her seat. "Come with me. You need to bathe and tend to those wounds."

Djuri was grateful to leave Tyrfingr and Eidr behind, although he struggled to relax in Nereth's company. The woman was a witch and now Djuri knew she consorted with the durath and worked for them or, even worse, perhaps she was one of them. *What am I mixed up in?*

"Djuri?" He started as he realised Nereth had been speaking to him.

"I'm sorry, I'm tired."

Nereth took his arm and steered him towards her chambers, where she ordered her servants to draw him a bath and fetch him clean clothes. Djuri dumped his sword and battered shield in a corner with the rest of his gear. He washed in the warm water, leaving a black tide mark on the bathtub that would soon have the servants grumbling. As he dried himself Nereth inspected his injuries, dabbing some concoction onto the cuts and bruises on his body.

"Looks like you got away lightly," she told him, dark eyes looking up into his.

"You call this lightly? I thought Lina was going to tear my hand off."

Nereth's fingers gently traced the bruising there as she applied more ointment. "Lina certainly has a strong grip – sizable hands too, wouldn't you say?"

"I wasn't trying to gauge her ring size. I tried to bash her head in with my shield and managed to free her grip. She threw me against the wall and they fled into the night. I was too dazed to do anything but I saw them making for the southern road with our horses. When I'd recovered enough to follow I saw what had happened to Kolsveinn and the rest of our company ... That's when I knew I'd been lucky."

Up close with Nereth, he caught the cinnamon scent of the drink he'd seen her and Tyrfingr share before. Djuri became very aware that he was naked, a point which Nereth also appreciated with a smile.

"I'm glad you're back," she told him, her arms sliding around his waist and exploring his body.

Afterwards, as they lay entwined together on the bed, Djuri wondered what he was doing there. Having planted the false trail, he'd formed a vague plan of trying to find the opportunity to strike at Tyrfingr and Eidr. However, Eidr had already left Ulfkell's Keep and he had no idea when he would return. They lay there in silence and Djuri thought Nereth had drifted off to sleep until she spoke.

"I don't blame you in the slightest."

He tensed. "What for?"

"Running away from Lina. Kolsveinn *should* have been able to deal with her. If you'd stood your ground and fought Lina you'd be dead, like those other warriors on the docks."

"How did you know?" he breathed, embracing the opportunity presented by her misunderstanding.

"Something about your tale didn't ring true. I've been trying to work out what."

"I thought I'd taken your mind off such things," he joked, rolling over onto his back so he could look at her. "I didn't want to admit my weakness in front of Tyrfingr. It's taken months for me to win his trust as a Reavesburg man – I don't want to lose my position."

"That won't happen," Nereth assured him.

"You don't know what it was like, being there, seeing those ... creatures. I've been in battle and believe me, this was far worse. Even her companions were terrified of her. When I saw what she did, I ran and let them go. I'm not proud of it."

"Pride can get you killed – you made the right decision. I know exactly what it's like to face creatures such as Lina. Why do you think I serve Adalrikr?"

"What happened?" he asked.

"Another time," Nereth told him, patting his chest and settling down to sleep.

Djuri continued to lie there long after Nereth had drifted off, turning over their conversation in his head, trying to work out if she still suspected him. He'd never thought of himself as an accomplished liar, yet it seemed Nereth and Tyrfingr had believed both versions of his story. In the darkness he stroked Nereth's back, tracing the scar left by Sigurd's blade.

What am I doing here?

Djuri rose and padded over the floor to gather up his fresh clothes. He slipped out of Nereth's chamber and walked back through Ulfkell's Keep to his own room, wrapped in dark thoughts.

CHAPTER 33

Randall stared down in horror from the battlements. Beyond Vorund Fastness he counted forty ... No, make that *fifty* longships either beached or on the waters at the estuary of the River Vorund. A defensive palisade had been hurriedly constructed in a crescent on the northern side of the river, encircling Vorund Fastness and preventing access to the city by land. Some of the longships on the open water were moving into formation, establishing a blockade. There was a hammering noise, shouts drifting on the wind towards him. Beyond the palisade he could see engines of war being assembled, the men moving like insects as they hurried to their task.

"You know what makes this even worse?" said Joarr next to him, tugging at his blond beard, a frown creasing his forehead.

"No. What?"

"That's our gear, from Romsdahl. Johan's brought our own siege engines and plans to use them against us."

"Same tactics as in Romsdahl too," Randall observed. "Cut off the city by land and sea to stifle our supplies."

"Good tactics. I'm guessing the Landless Jarl isn't stupid enough to give up his position on the field like Sinarr did. That's the advantage of not having a complete nutter in command, who took more notice of a tepid bowl of water than listening to what his men were telling him."

Randall looked at Joarr, trying to gauge if that had been a joke. He didn't like the man but there was nothing like a common enemy laying siege to your city to help you set aside your differences; at least for now.

"Where are they going?" Joarr was pointing out to sea.

Randall squinted, making out a small group of ships in the estuary heading for open water, more following them. "My guess is they didn't have enough ships to land all their men. They're sailing for reinforcements."

"Question is, does Johan have enough warriors to hold this position until they arrive?" Joarr was grinning now, seeing an opportunity to regain Adalrikr's favour.

"Hard to guess their numbers from here," Randall did a swift count based on the number of warriors each ship could hold, although some of those would have been carrying cargo. "My guess, Johan will have some two thousand swords down there waiting for us. They'll be tough to shift."

"We've twice that number behind these walls," argued Joarr.

Randall folded his arms and shook his head. "Maybe. There's no one else, though, is there? Geilir's taken his army north to Norlhast and the rest of our forces are either laying siege in Jorvind or establishing our hold in Helsburg now they're part of our new northern kingdom. We could simply sit this one out – we have supplies and enough fresh water to keep our army provisioned until next summer. Johan can't have that many more warriors to bring to our shores, even when the reinforcements arrive. There's no way they can take the city and the longer we wait it out the weaker they'll become. Once Geilir returns from Norlhast and our business is done in Helsburg and Jorvind, we'll crush them easily."

The grin on Joarr's bearded face grew wider, his eyes bright. "I suppose we'll have to take this matter to King Adalrikr, since his two jarls can't agree. Let's see what he thinks of your cowardly idea."

Randall followed Joarr with a deep sigh as he hurried off towards the Inner Keep. *Setting aside our differences lasted about five minutes ...*

***

Leif peered out over the palisade wall, trying to take in the scale of Vorund Fastness. Thengill had said it was the mightiest fortress in the whole of Laskar. Leif hadn't really understood what that meant, until now. It dwarfed Romsdahl, a tall inner keep standing proud on a sheer outcrop of rock rising up behind thick curtain walls, the battlements crawling with warriors.

We're really going to attack that?

Curruck was busy helping erect the palisade, which they'd started in darkness as soon as they'd landed and were now hurriedly trying to finish before the end of the day. Then they'd dig a trench to protect their position and begin bombarding the walls – at least that's what Thengill told him. That meant there was no smithing today, so Leif had been promoted to keeping watch, in case the Vorund Clan tried a swift counter-attack. Joldir told him this was a really responsible job and he was on watch with Faraldr on his section of the wall, two pairs of eyes to make sure they didn't miss anything. The trouble was Leif hadn't had much sleep, his eyelids getting heavy as he stifled a yawn. Next to him Faraldr was squinting in the morning sun, scouring the land for any signs of danger. Leif closed his eyes for a moment, head nodding forwards.

A commotion below woke Leif from a guilty nap. He glanced down, rubbing sleep from his eyes to see Johan, Gautarr, Petr and Throm hotly debating something as Damona, Bandor and Freydja looked on. A groom was leading out two horses from the makeshift stables as Leif strained to catch what they were saying. There was too much noise and activity for him to make out the words, so he probed out with the Sight, trying to find a way into the conversation and find out what was going on.

***

"... there's simply no way Adalrikr will agree to such a thing," Petr was saying. Freydja had to admit he was probably right.

"Perhaps not," Johan replied. "Even so, we should try.

If nothing else, it will give me the measure of the man we're fighting."

Throm sighed. "What Petr's too polite to say outright is Adalrikr might use this chance to kill us all."

"I'll not be called a coward," Gautarr, Johan and Bandor cried out simultaneously.

"No one is calling *anyone* a coward," said Freydja, trying to keep the irritation from her voice, keen not to undermine her young husband in front of all these older warriors. "My brother's simply reminding everyone Adalrikr is treacherous, famed for killing his own father and the rest of his family. Any parley has to be treated with caution."

"My niece speaks sense," Gautarr told the group. "However, we need to set out our terms. Otherwise, all this is nothing more than a raid."

Freydja sighed, realising she and Throm weren't going to get their way. She touched Throm's arm and as their eyes met she saw he'd reached the same conclusion. Now the argument began about which houses should be represented in the parley. The eventual outcome was *all* of them and the groom went to fetch more horses. Whilst Freydja loved her uncle she wished he wouldn't constantly vie with Johan – as Battle Chief it made sense to let him treat with Adalrikr. Gautarr's lack of trust in Johan and his desire to be involved in everything resulted in all of them heading out towards the Fastness under the flag of parley: Johan and Bandor representing Kalamar, Gautarr for House Romsdahl and Throm due to his position as Egill's son (as well as ensuring Romsdahl had two representatives to match those of Kalamar).

"Not you, Freydja," Gautarr told her.

Freydja bridled. "Egill was my father too. I represent the unity of the houses of Kalamar and Romsdahl. If you think I'm leaving my husband's side, Uncle, you're gravely mistaken."

"I'm also riding out with you," added Damona and

Freydja was unable to hide her smile at Johan's expression. "I want to look on the face of the man who ordered the murder of my daughter and grandchild. We're all here because of him and I'll not hide behind the stakewall during this parley."

Johan gave a curt nod in agreement, whilst Freydja's argument with Gautarr and Bandor took a few short moments longer before the groom was dispatched to fetch two more horses. The warriors of the Brotherhood paused in their work as their party rode through the entrance in their defences and headed towards Vorund Fastness. Freydja turned back and saw Petr watching them anxiously before the gates closed behind them.

"Remind me never to cross you, my love," whispered Bandor next to her with a forced grin, trying to make light of their disagreement.

There were times when Freydja wondered if she'd made the right decision to travel to Vorund, rather than staying in the safety of Romsdahl with the rest of her uncle's family, under Jora and Ragnar's protection. Bandor's constant desire to keep her safe was beginning to grate and she decided she would speak with him tonight. You didn't grow up in Romsdahl without learning how to wield a blade. In the relative safety of northern Reavesburg, where a weakened Norlhast had posed less of a threat, the old traditions of Reave held far more sway. Down in the south boys and girls were both taught how to bear arms, as had been the case when Romsdahl was a separate clan. If you didn't know how to defend yourself you had no business living on the border with Vorund. Freydja pursed her lips, reminding herself she had as much right as her brother to see their father avenged.

Their party stopped well outside bow range and it didn't take long before the massive reinforced iron gates of Vorund Fastness swung open. Freydja could make out nine figures on horseback, riding towards them, the white parley flag raised. As they got nearer she recognised the broad form of Joarr the Hammer with his long, blond beard – the man who had killed her father. Next to him was an older warrior, grey-haired and as he drew closer she saw he had an open, honest face. Only his eyes revealed the steel in this one – they were a bright, piercing blue. At the front of the group, riding a huge black destrier, was a man dressed in the fashion of a knight of Beria, breastplate polished to a perfect sheen, plate armour covering the rest of his body. He was a handsome young man with blond hair, the only blemish was a scar under his left eye. By his bearing and the deference shown by his companions, Freydja would have known Adalrikr without Rothgar's description. Behind Vorund's delegation rode six armed guards, faces hidden behind the steel of their helms. Their steeds were skittish, uncomfortable carrying these warriors for some reason. As they drew close Freydja felt the temperature drop a few degrees, an odd sensation in the heat of the sun.

"Johan Jokellsward, leader of the Brotherhood of the Eagle, I welcome you and your companions to Vorund Fastness," said Adalrikr with a smile. "You know Joarr the Hammer, I believe, and this is Randall Vorstson, my second jarl, who now commands Sinarr's forces."

"We fought at Romsdahl," Johan replied.

Randall was watching warily with those blue eyes. "I remember – you fought bravely that day," he acknowledged, his rough accent marking him out as a common man, rather than noble-born.

Johan introduced his companions and Freydja noticed how Adalrikr's gaze lingered on Damona as he addressed them. "Interesting you came here with your extended family. Personally, I find they bring all sorts of baggage with them. I see your wife is with child. I would have thought after seeing so many members of your family die you would have wanted to protect her, at least."

Damona's face was white as she spoke. "I wanted to see your fall for myself, Kinslayer. You murdered your way to power in Vorund and you've cast a long shadow killing innocent people across Laskar. I'm here to see you pay for your crimes and have justice for my daughter and grandson."

"Are we really here to trade insults, Johanswyfe? I won't disown the choices I made to attain power. That's the reason why I'm the king and you're married to the Landless Jarl."

"You're not a king and you have no right to rule," Johan replied, ignoring the insult. "We're here on your shores to dispute that fact. Your unwillingness to step aside and relinquish your claim to the lands of Laskar has caused countless people to needlessly suffer."

Adalrikr laughed, dabbing at his cheek as the wound on his face bled a little. "I know what the Brotherhood is and why you're here. You're sworn to put an end to the durath and you think this is your moment, deluding yourselves this won't all end in failure and defeat. You couldn't take the Fastness with ten times the number of warriors under your command. This is the only warning you'll receive from me. Abandon your defences, set aside your siege engines and flee to your ships by nightfall, otherwise you and every one of your followers will be slaughtered. Your family will be left where they fall for the carrion crows to feast upon, their bones picked clean, serving as a warning to all who defy me. Your legacy as Battle Chief will be watching your loved ones die."

Johan sat straight on his horse, wind rippling his long hair. "I've lost too many who were close to me already. You mounted the heads of my daughter and grandson on the walls of Ulfkell's Keep. You think that can go unavenged? This can only end with your death and the destruction of your kind. Vorund Fastness will fall and the Brotherhood will never rest until we have hunted down every last one of you. Make no mistake, Kinslayer, we have the means to destroy you."

Adalrikr shook his head with disdain. "We are

wasting each other's time – I'll not set aside my claim to the throne and you're determined to wage war upon me. When I saw your parley flag I had hoped for a more constructive discussion."

Johan's face was a stony mask. "It's far too late for peace. I only wanted to look on your face and know my enemy. When we next meet, I'll end you and avenge my people."

"You would be well-advised to heed my warning," Adalrikr replied. "Otherwise, you'll lead everyone following you to their death."

Johan turned his horse and led them away without another word, Gautarr on his right and Damona on his left. Freydja kept her eyes straight ahead as she rode in silence with Bandor and Throm, watching as the palisade walls grew closer. Behind her, she could feel the gaze of Adalrikr and his jarls as they watched them leave.

CHAPTER 34

Humli emerged from the river, shivering, and quickly dried himself off on his old travelling cloak. As he rubbed his face dry he could hear days of stubble scratching against the cloth.

"You should burn that too," Lina told him, nodding towards the cloak and the pile of discarded clothes at his feet, blood-stained and tattered.

"Can we risk a fire?" asked Desta. "I've already tempted Myshall visiting the village to buy fresh clothing and supplies. What if Blackeyes' men spot the smoke?"

"Chances are they'll think it's the fire of a group of travellers. Many are on the road at this time of year but we're the only ones covered in our enemies' blood. Now do as I say – burn them all."

Desta muttered under her breath as Lina headed down to the riverbank to wash and change. Humli grimaced as he pulled on the brown woollen breeches, linen shirt and dun jerkin his daughter had purchased. The days were shortening and autumn would be upon them in a few more weeks. He kept his new travelling cloak rolled up and stowed it into one of his horse's saddle bags, knowing he'd need it before long.

"Do you want a hand?" he asked his daughter, crouching down beside her as she blew onto the small flame flickering under the twigs she'd piled on the ground.

Desta shook her head. "I know what I'm doing. I'd rather you didn't meekly follow *her* every word, though."

Humli glanced over at Lina, whose back was turned to them as she vigorously scrubbed herself clean. He swallowed, remembering her soaked in blood after Noln. There was no way Lina could have gone into the village this morning, looking like that. Humli wondered if it was possible to wash that much blood away.

"Are you going to answer me or just stare at her while she's got no clothes on?" snapped Desta, irked by his silence.

Humli turned back to her and put his arm around her shoulders. "I'm sorry. My mind was elsewhere … back in Noln. When I look at Lina, I don't know what to think anymore."

"I wish Djuri was here," said Desta. "Haarl always said he was a good man but she was quick enough to persuade him on his way back to Ulfkell's Keep, wasn't she?"

"What's done is done. And Lina was right, he's too easy to recognise, big fellow like that …"

"Stop taking her side all the time. You're the elder, Father, so why don't you act like it?"

Humli sighed. "We have to stick together and Lina's right – those clothes need to be destroyed, before they betray us. I don't pretend to like any of this but I know it wouldn't be right to leave her. She saved our lives in Noln and now Blackeyes is hunting her and she has Frokn to think of."

"You're talking about the child of a *demon*," hissed his daughter. "What makes you want to protect *that*?"

Humli glanced at his daughter's bruised face. "I'd rather have her on our side," he said, with little conviction. "Crossing her would only serve to make our troubles far worse, I'm sure of that. We don't need any more enemies."

As the fire caught Desta stood and brushed her hands on her skirts, face taut with strain and worry. There were dark shadows under her eyes, betraying the fact she'd slept little last night.

"Perhaps we can help each other," she agreed. "We need to get Finn to safety and I guess you're right – we have a better chance with Lina at our side. Once we reach Vittag, though, I want her gone. We can't trust her, not after what we've seen and been told."

Desta walked away to change, leaving Humli in charge of the fire. He began to put their old clothes onto the growing flames, taking care not to smother them as he added each garment. He threw two more logs into the fire, watching the flames dancing, feeling the warmth begin to work its way into his tired bones. He felt weary and exhausted and they'd only come a few miles from his old home. *Not cut out for deeds like this,* he reflected, poking the fire with a stick to make sure the last traces of their old lives were completely destroyed.

***

Nuna was nervous when she reached Kalfr's house, even though she was accompanied by her husband and had Brosa and Sigurd at her side. A small crowd had gathered and a few Vorund warriors had stopped and were huddled together, talking in low tones and pointing in her direction. Nuna raised her chin, set her face and stepped forwards to knock on the door. Luta opened it, eyes wide when she saw her visitors. She recovered quickly, inviting them inside, little Varinn and Gilla dashing about the room and darting between their heels.

"Out you three," Luta barked, though her eyes twinkled as she looked at her children. "Yes, you too, Tassi. Take them to play somewhere else while we have guests."

"You don't have to send them out on my account," Nuna told her.

Luta shook her head. "They've been cooped up too long, my lady. Let them enjoy the last days of summer before the sun becomes a stranger."

Kalfr strode forwards, drawing his brother into a tight embrace.

"How is he?" asked Sigurd.

Kalfr's scarred face grimaced. "No real change. He's resting in bed."

Karas led the way into the children's bedroom, which

had been given over to their grandfather. Albrikt lay under the covers, propped up by a mountain of pillows. He looked thinner than the last time Nuna had seen him, eyes sunken in their sockets, white beard clean yet ragged, bald in patches. He looked up at his visitors, or so Nuna thought. It took her a few moments to realise he was looking past them, seeing something other than what was in the room.

"Albrikt?" Karas said, sitting next to his old friend. "Albrikt, it's Karas and Nuna. We came to see how you're doing. Is there anything you want or need?"

An uncertain smile crept over Albrikt's face, revealing his ruined mouth. A trickle of blood ran down his chin. Thyra, who was tending her grandfather, reached out and dabbed it with the corner of a cloth. The old man flinched at her touch, batting her hand away with a cry.

"Nurgh. No, don' toth me. No, don' toth me, pleasthe."

"He's still there, trapped in that room with Tryggvi," Kalfr explained. "He hasn't said anything else to me, Luta or the children since he's been with us."

"Landths," Albrikt was muttering. "It's all to do … with a disthpute … over landths."

"Is there anything *you* need?" Nuna asked Luta, her voice quavering. She gave a small cough, trying to hide her distress.

Luta shook her head. "No, thank you my lady, we have everything we require." She cast Karas a dark look. "Our family has fallen on hard times before. We know how to look after our own."

Karas understood her meaning. "I've made mistakes, Luta, and listening to Nereth's coven was one of them. I'll always regret banishing Albrikt from my court. It's the measure of the man that he had no qualms when I asked him to return as my advisor."

"Better you had never brought him back to your side," Luta replied. "It would have spared him this torment. You should have risen up against that worm, Valdimarr, long ago, before Geilir came here with his army. Now, the odds are stacked against us and if you fail, you'll drag all of us down with you."

"Luta, that's enough," Kalfr said in a tone that brooked no argument. "You're talking to our chief! Fetch our guests some refreshment, please."

Luta glowered before leaving the room and Kalfr began to apologise, only for Karas to hold up his hands, the tips of his fingers dark where they had scabbed over his missing nails.

"Don't beg my forgiveness. Your wife's right – what happened to your father happened because of me. If I'd acted sooner ..."

Nuna reached out and put an arm around her husband's thin shoulders. "You did what you could to keep your people safe, Karas."

Karas looked at her, doubt written across his face. "And if Orglyr is defeated? What happens then to those close to me?"

Sigurd was staring out the window, a muscle fluttering in his jaw. "You'll send word? If he recovers or there's any improvement?" He bit off each word, looking anywhere other than at his insensate father.

"Of course," Kalfr told him.

"I need to get out of here," Sigurd muttered. "I can't stand seeing him like this."

Kalfr didn't try and stop his brother, awkwardly patting him on the shoulder as he pushed his way through the door. The rest of them spent a while sitting in Kalfr's house, gathered round his fire, sharing watered ale as they listened to his three youngest children playing in the street outside. Nuna steered the conversation onto inconsequential things, talking of the weather and the preparations for the coming winter, which always came early this far north. No one quite relaxed, even though Nuna thought of Kalfr's family as friends. She glanced across at

Karas and saw him staring at his feet, lost in thought.

When they finally took their leave Luta showed them out, gently touching Nuna on the arm as they reached the door. "Begging your forgiveness, but don't come here again, my lady," she whispered. "It only draws the attention of Valdimarr and Geilir's men. I don't want them thinking Albrikt's still counselling your husband. It's better for him to be forgotten in these times."

"He's never forgotten," Nuna replied, squeezing Luta's hand. "Though I see the wisdom of your words."

Sigurd was waiting for them outside and they returned to Norlhast Keep in silence. Their mood darkened further when they saw that Valdimarr was waiting for them at the gates, a score of warriors in attendance.

"Valdimarr," Karas called out in greeting. "Good to see you on this fair summer day."

Dromundr laughed, revealing his gapped teeth, large as tombstones. "He doesn't know."

"Know? What is there to know?" Karas asked. Nuna felt her stomach knotting and it took all her strength to set her face in a mask of indifference as Valdimarr spoke.

"Word has reached us from the west that Orglyr the Grim was defeated at Taur, his army scattered. We've been fortunate with this so-called uprising – a few farms torched, nothing more. It seems Orglyr's reputation was more fearsome than his skill on the field of battle."

"Good news indeed," said Sigurd. "Geilir should be our honoured guest in Norlhast Keep this evening, to celebrate his victory, in the name of our king."

Valdimarr paused, looking uncertain for a moment. "Geilir has not yet returned. Word reached us from one of his messengers earlier today."

Sigurd smiled. "All in good time, then. We look forward to his return."

"That we shall," Valdimarr exclaimed, clapping his fat hands together with enthusiasm. "That we shall. We can plan the festivities when we eat together this evening."

Karas nodded and made to walk past Valdimarr, his progress halted as Dromundr interposed himself in front of Norlhast's jarl. Karas glared at him and Valdimarr gave a delicate cough, jowls wobbling, before speaking.

"I should add how sorry I am, Karas, for the misunderstanding that took place when you were questioned concerning Orglyr's intentions."

Karas' face darkened as he held out his bloodied fingers, making Valdimarr flinch. "This was no *misunderstanding.* My loyalty to our king remains undiminished but please don't pretend to offer your insincere apologies for my treatment at the hands of Geilir's henchmen. It's obvious you have no control over him – just pray you don't find yourself in disfavour."

"Your jarl wishes to enter his keep," Sigurd growled in Dromundr's face.

Nuna clenched her jaw, reaching for the small dagger she kept at her hip ever since Nereth had tried to kill her. Dromundr glanced at Valdimarr, who shrugged.

"Let them pass. We'll talk more this evening."

"I look forward to it," Karas replied, pushing past Dromundr.

Karas walked hurriedly to his chambers without a word, Nuna almost running to keep up. Inside they found Styrman tidying the room – the poor man jumping a foot in the air as Karas bellowed at him. His servant fled, slamming the door shut in his haste to leave.

Karas jabbed a finger at Brosa's chest. "Stand outside and let no one inside."

"We've discussed this before," Nuna began, gently touching Karas' arm. "You have to play your part –" Karas shook her away, leaving Nuna stung. Whatever else he had been, her husband had always been gentle and kind to her.

"Yes. I've heard you say it a hundred times. 'Be the meek jarl for the sake of your people. Obey Valdimarr, help buy us the time we need.' Well, I've played my part, ruined what was left of my reputation – and for what? So that odious man can mock me on the threshold of my own keep. Orglyr has failed us and all my people can look up to now is old, tired, Karas Greystorm, the chief who bent the knee."

"Orglyr never was a master tactician," Sigurd observed, taking a seat with a sigh.

Karas rounded on his friend. "You mention this now? Are you *mocking* me?"

Sigurd frowned. "No, of course not. Geilir's arrival has changed everything – he's rising in power within the Vorund Clan and he's seized the chance to prove himself. Does that mean our plans have unravelled completely? I'm not so sure."

Karas took a breath to steady himself. "Go on."

"Where's Geilir? If Orglyr's forces have been crushed then why isn't he here, crowing over his victory? Where are the bodies of Orglyr or Fundinn if they've been killed? The fact Geilir hasn't returned tells me matters aren't as settled as Valdimarr would have us believe. He's still out there, trying to end the uprising. Orglyr isn't a strategist – he had Bekan for such things. No, what matters is Orglyr's still a *name* in the north, still a name the Norlhast Clan will rally around and follow. That counts for something."

"There's hope, then?" Nuna asked.

Sigurd smiled. "Hope is a strange word to use in such terrible times, my lady. Is there hope? Yes, I believe so, whilst Orglyr lives."

"Your sage counsel is Orglyr the Grim's name is the one that inspires courage. Not Karas Greystorm," Karas muttered, standing by the window looking out across the bay. "Get out, both of you."

Nuna had never seen Karas in such a dark mood before and she quickly took her leave, returning with Brosa to her own chambers, where she threw herself into Katla's arms. As her maid rushed off to fetch her some wine Nuna sat in her favourite chair by the fire, head in her hands. She wanted to believe Sigurd, yet she couldn't help feeling their plans were unravelling. Orglyr was meant to be sweeping into Norlhast Keep, driving the Vorund Clan from their lands, not fleeing westwards. Instead, Nuna was afraid it would be Geilir returning in triumph, and when he did she knew he'd intend to collect on her promise.

CHAPTER 35

Freydja woke with a start, Bandor grumbling in bed next to her as he turned over on his side and went back to sleep. She reassured herself it was only a dream, although her heart was racing. For a moment, she had been convinced they were under attack and for some strange reason she'd been with Joldir and Leif, Curruck's apprentice. It was dark, the camp shrouded in silence save for the wind stirring the canvas of their tent. Freydja wrapped a shawl around her shoulders and went to make water, knowing she would find no more rest that night. She dressed in the darkness of the tent, a growing sense of unease creeping through her. She opened the tent flaps and found Svafa outside standing guard, looking bored.

"My lady, are you alright? It's still an hour until dawn."

"I couldn't sleep," she told him.

Torchlight caught her eye and she looked up to see Joldir hurrying towards them, Leif trotting along at his side. The boy fixed her with an intent gaze and Freydja shivered again, feeling a strange connection with Joldir's adopted orphan.

"Are you absolutely sure it was Freydja?" Joldir asked Leif, looking in her direction as the boy nodded. Freydja couldn't help glancing down at Joldir's broken fingers. The injury which had robbed the Brotherhood of their ability to make more runeblades and ultimately sent Rothgar on his quest north.

"You felt it too, didn't you?" Leif asked her without preamble.

Freydja frowned, knowing what Leif was talking

about without fully understanding why. "I woke from a frightening dream," she replied. "You were both there."

"And in your dream we were under attack?" Joldir asked. "What did you see?"

Joldir's statement took Freydja aback and she stared at the careworn man, unsure how to reply. "I can't remember," she confessed. "All of a sudden I was awake and at first I thought something was wrong – that we were in danger and Vorund's army was approaching. But then I realised I'd been dreaming. That's all it was, wasn't it? A dream?"

"If not, surely our men on watch would have seen something," said Svafa.

"I think the Vorund Clan is moving against us," Joldir replied. "Svafa, please listen to me. Go at once to Johan and warn him we're under attack. We need to ready the men. I'll head to the palisade wall and try and see what's happening. Leif, go and find Arissa and stay with her." Svafa hesitated until Freydja nodded at him and he headed off in the direction of Johan's tent.

"We'll talk more later," Joldir said as he ran towards the palisade, vanishing into the darkness.

Freydja glanced down at Leif and the strange boy looked up at her with wide eyes before scampering off towards Arissa and Thengill's tent. After watching him go Freydja hurried inside, rousing Bandor as she pulled on her armour and buckled her sword to her side.

***

Randall cursed as he stumbled, pain jarring up his knees. All around him he caught the sound of muffled swearing, dull clanks of equipment and the rattle of armour as two thousand warriors attempted to sneak up on the Reavesburg defences under the cover of darkness. He looked to his right, where the sky was beginning to brighten, a pale smudge against the starless sky. The clouds that had rolled in overnight finally settled the argument in Joarr's favour, prompting him to launch his dawn raid without the treacherous light of Ceren's moon to betray them.

Being undetected was all well and good. Unfortunately, creeping forwards in the darkness without the aid of torch or lantern, Randall had no idea how close they were to Johan's army. At least they hadn't had time to finish digging the ditch around their wall – Randall didn't fancy ending his days stumbling into a pit of sharpened stakes. Mind you, clattering into the palisade and taking an arrow to the face also sounded like an ignominious way to go.

Damn it. How much ground have we covered? It was impossible to say, moving at such a slow pace. Randall reckoned they must be at least halfway by now. Joarr was further up the lines, leading the attack, so it would be his call when they broke into a charge and began to scale the walls.

A trickle of sweat ran down Randall's face. The light to the east was slowly brightening and if he squinted he thought he could make out a darker smudge against the faint grey of the grassland beyond Vorund Fastness. How far was that? Close enough – closer than he'd expected, in fact. As the first sliver of the sun began to emerge from the waters of the Redfars Sea a soft susurrus rippled down the ranks either side of Randall, as the men realised they were nearing their goal. The noise lowered in pitch as figures emerged at each of the gaps set in the top of the wooden walls, a few cries of surprise escaping from the Vorund army as they began to understand the truth. Randall gasped as he heard bowstrings stretching. They were released as one, the air suddenly thick with deadly shafts that punched into their front ranks. The man next to him fell, shrieking, clutching at the arrow protruding from his chest. Randall slipped over onto his face as he was caught by the dying man's thrashing legs. More bodies fell on top of him as the Vorund army pressed on, screams filling the air as another wave of arrows found their mark.

Randall coughed, the air forced out of him as his face was pressed into the grass – sweet-smelling and damp with dew. He was kicked in the head, the blow ringing off his helmet and making his teeth rattle. Randall gasped, starting to panic as the weight on top of him increased, making it difficult to breathe at all. Desperately he tried to claw his way forwards, wriggling out of the pile of bodies already soaking the grass with their blood. Another booted foot missed his outstretched hand by inches. Moments later a warrior fell right in front of him, an arrow through his throat. Randall found himself staring into the eyes of a dying man, a young lad with scraggly wisps of beard, barely out of his teens. The young man mouthed something at his jarl, flecks of blood snatching away the words he was trying to form. He died in front of Randall with a look of surprise fixed on his pale face, only for the scene to vanish in blackness as another body fell on top of them both.

Buried in that heap of dead and dying men the sounds reaching Randall were muffled and dim, as if the battle was taking place many miles away, distant war cries and the wailing of the injured carried to him on the wind. Fighting down his fear, Randall redoubled his efforts, clawing his way out, no longer caring he was kicking and elbowing his own comrades as he fought to escape. He gasped as he forced his way to the top, dragging the air into his lungs, as arrows rained down on them from all sides. Grunting, Randall slid his arm out of the straps of his shield, which was stuck beneath him, and he grabbed another from a fallen warrior, raising it above his head and wincing as an arrowhead bounced off the wood. *Timed that well. Might just live long enough for the sun to rise above the sea at this rate.*

Dawn's faint grey light revealed a wall of bodies, where the Vorund Clan had been cut down on the exposed grassland. The rest of the army had surged forwards and the first few warriors were almost at the wooden walls, most of them falling to the ground as the Brotherhood's archers loosed another deadly volley at close quarters. Randall caught sight of Joarr, *Foehammer* raised, in the middle of the seething mass of Vorund men as they pressed ahead. Randall made use of the respite as the archers concentrated on the enemy closing in on their wall, dragging himself clear of the dead. He called to an assortment of stragglers, those who had either fallen behind during their march or else had been caught up in the chaos of that initial assault. With a crew of around fifty he got them into formation, shields raised and spears at the ready as they began their own advance to support Joarr's attack. Up ahead, Vorund warriors were trying to climb the walls, hands scrabbling to find purchase between the sharpened stakes. Johan knew his warcraft – the palisade had been built with a raised platform behind, which allowed his men to stand above the height of the stakewall. The archers made way for axeman, who hacked and cut down the first of their attackers. Randall could hear Joarr shouting his orders, the press of men behind forcing those at the front to climb the palisade or be crushed to death.

Randall heard the sound of yet another volley of arrows and swore as he saw the shafts arch up at a steep angle from behind the walls. "Raise shields," he shouted, swinging his own into position, wincing as pain stabbed through his ribs from a blow he must have taken earlier.

A few of his men were too slow to react, brought down by the indiscriminate fall of the arrows. Most of them found their range further ahead of Randall's men, one of them striking Joarr in the shoulder, causing him to let out a bellow of rage. More arrows fell as the Brotherhood's defences held, although up and down the wooden walls Randall could see a few knots of men who had managed to gain the other side, now engaged in fierce hand to hand combat. There was a mighty crash as the gates swung open. Before Randall had time to fully register the arrows had stopped falling a mountain of armoured horseflesh burst through the gates. They attacked with such force that those unfortunate enough to be in their path were trampled beneath their hooves or cut down as they tried to flee. Randall recognised

Gautarr at their head, axe hacking down left and right as he cut a bloody path through the Vorund lines. At his side were Johan, Throm and Bandor, all yelling battle cries as more cavalry poured through the gates – hundreds of riders spilling onto the battlefield.

They were waiting for us to attack. The realisation felt like he'd been punched in the guts and Randall slowed his advance. His men weren't yet engaged in the battle and the tide was already turning. Their own riders remained behind the walls of Vorund Fastness, too far away to help them now. A ripple ran through the Vorund warriors as they became aware of their new foes, their attack on the wall slowing as Joarr shouted his orders to get his men into formation to face this new threat. Gautarr and Johan didn't give him the time he needed, smashing into their ranks, scattering men before them as even more riders took to the field, flowing out left and right from the gates, clearing the walls of their attackers. Randall understood now what Gautarr's objective was as his riders formed a wedge and punched their way directly towards Joarr's position. Joarr's men formed a shield wall around their jarl, spearmen trying to get into the path of the charging cavalry. A rider next to Throm was flung from his saddle as his horse shied away, pitching him, screaming, onto the spears. Gautarr and Throm broke upon the half-formed shield wall moments later, shattering it as they ploughed on, undaunted as some of their companions met their end on Vorund spears and swords. Johan blocked an axe with his shield, his son cutting down his father's attacker.

Joarr shouted a challenge of some kind, the words not reaching Randall. Gautarr and Joarr met in the chaotic centre of the battle, each trading savage blows. Joarr stood his ground as *Foehammer* whirled, smashing into Gautarr's shield, almost knocking him out of his saddle. Throm closed in, his sword hacking away at Joarr's guards. Gautarr rocked back on his horse, his destrier rearing as Joarr forced him onto the defensive, even though he was on foot. Randall hadn't always seen eye to eye with Joarr yet his admiration for him as a warrior grew as he saw him face death with honour and bravery.

Gautarr blocked with his shield as his axe parried *Foehammer*, already tiring with the effort. Joarr raised his hammer again, looking for an opening, only for Throm's sword to cut off his right hand at the wrist. *Foehammer* spun away and Joarr turned to look at Throm, clutching the stump, fingers red as a fountain of blood poured from the wound. Throm's sword cut through the air and struck Joarr on the head, splitting his helm in half. The Vorund Clan gave a collective groan as their jarl died, drowned out moments later by the cheer ringing throughout the Reavesburg ranks.

"What do we do, chief?" shouted one of Randall's men, looking at him with fearful eyes.

Randall swallowed, looking at the steady flow of warriors who were already fleeing the battle. The Brotherhood had regained control of the palisade wall and he could see their archers taking their positions once more. He shook his head, a sick feeling in his stomach as he slung his borrowed shield over his back.

"Run."

CHAPTER 36

I stirred under my blankets and furs, covered in sweat, heart racing. I lay there, expecting to feel an arrow in my back as I tried to remember where I was – *who* I was. Slowly, things fell into place and I sat up, head brushing the canvas cover *Stormweaver's* crew had erected to ward off the snow and keep them warm. I headed out to the stern of the longship where Meinolf Saltbeard sat, taking his turn at the steering oar. It was already a bright morning this far north, miles from Vorund Fastness where the dawn sun was just rising over the battlefield. Etta had once explained to me why the sun rose at different times, depending on where you stood on Amuran. I confess that lesson had escaped my full attention.

"Morning," said Meinolf. "You alright? You look exhausted."

I gave him a weary nod as I took a seat next to him, rubbing my arms to get the blood flowing, thinking on all I had seen. Our struggle against the durath remained finely balanced. I worried how Nuna would fare under Geilir's rule now Orglyr and his followers were on the retreat, shivering with revulsion as I remembered what they'd done to poor Albrikt. Despite those setbacks in Norlhast, the Brotherhood had stood their ground in Vorund thanks to the power of the Sight, and Joarr's death would be a serious blow to both Adalrikr and his people. The Brotherhood had to maintain their stranglehold on the Vorund stronghold until our return, and I knew Adalrikr wouldn't make that task easy for Johan and his allies. The grim truth was that with Hasteinn hunting us down our safe return was far from guaranteed, although there was no sign of his pursuing ships that morning.

Snores from the crew drifted up from where they lay sleeping, exhausted from rowing. Even with the ocean current speeding us towards our destination Aerinndis kept her crew at work, as much to keep them busy and warm as to gain more time over our pursuers. I sat there for a while, brushing a dusting of snow from the edge of the canvas. I watched, entranced, at our strange surroundings as *Stormweaver* sailed in the company of giant icebergs, many larger than castles, floating on the freezing waters of the Endless Ocean. With the winds from the south filling our sail we were speeding past these leviathans of ice, Meinolf taking care to give them a wide berth lest hidden ice below the water tear through our hull.

"There's a sight," Jolinn pronounced as she emerged from the canvas cover and joined us.

"The bergs calve and flow south initially," Meinolf explained. "Some of them get caught in the northern current and are carried back towards the ice-shelf, like wandering sheep returning to their flock. Most avoid that fate and their journey takes them into the southern seas, where they melt under the sunlight and vanish."

"Hard to believe something so vast could simply disappear," said Jolinn, her breath smoking, blue eyes like chips of ice, reflecting the bergs she was looking at in wonder.

The crew stirred into life and we ate a breakfast of fresh fish, caught on lines trailing behind us during the night, together with dried oat cakes. I munched my food, stomach aching with hunger from the cold as we continued to journey through our fantastical surroundings. Seabirds wheeled above us and Feyotra caught me looking at them.

"A good sign," she said with a grin. "It means land is maybe one or two days sailing from here, depending on exactly where we joined the current."

"So close?" I was surprised our voyage was already

coming to an end after less than two weeks.

Aerinndis laughed. "Don't get too excited. First we have to cross the ice-shelf, just as Sigborn did all those years ago. There's a way to go yet."

"What do you think we'll find?" Jolinn asked me, popping a steaming piece of white fish into her mouth.

"In truth, I don't know," I admitted. "It seemed so clear back in Romsdahl. Out here ... it feels like another world. I have to trust the instincts of those who've guided us and helped us so far."

Jolinn grinned, her face framed by her fur-lined hood, nose pink with the cold. "That sounds like my kind of plan. Find land and see what happens next."

I laughed, realising how close to the truth she was. I would have to find a way to engage Bruar and convince him to take an interest in the wider world after two centuries of self-imposed exile, a task that would require all the powers of persuasion Etta and I possessed. However, I couldn't shake the nagging doubt that if Bruar refused to aid us, our dangerous journey would have been for nothing.

"I've never thanked you," I told Jolinn.

"Thanked me for what?"

"Volunteering to join us on this voyage. You could have stayed with Johan and travelled with the rest of his army to fight Adalrikr."

Jolinn gave me a sidelong glance. "What makes you think I wasn't trying to get out of that? This quest might be a fool's errand but it's probably safer than trying to breach the walls of Vorund Fastness."

"I saw you fight at Romsdahl – I don't believe that excuse for a moment."

Jolinn laughed and took a swig of water from her cup. Aerinndis gave the order for the crew to take their seats and begin another day rowing at sea. Jolinn groaned along with the rest of them and rose to take her place next to Myr as *Stormweaver's* sailors rolled up the canvas. She looked back at me before she left, a mischievous smile playing on her lips.

"We're making our own story out here on the sea. Who wouldn't want to be a part of that?"

***

The clash of wooden practice swords rang out across the courtyard of Ulfkell's Keep, Djuri's wrist aching as he traded blows with Galin. The Vorund warrior fought hard, having adapted to losing his left hand last year. Despite being maimed there was strength in his shield arm and he used it well, knocking Djuri's sword wide and opening up his defences for a counter attack. Djuri skipped backwards, drawing cries from the watching crowd as his feet skirted near the edge of the white chalk circle marking out the boundary for their contest. He jinked sideways, using his strength as he brought his wooden sword crashing down against Galin's weapon. His body felt good – strong, the various wounds he'd suffered in Noln virtually healed. Fighting felt good too and Djuri laughed in Galin's face, enraging his opponent. He knew what to do when he was holding a sword – it was when he wasn't duelling with his fellow warriors that things were more complicated.

"Hah!" Djuri gave a shout of triumph, the noise from the crowd immediately distinguishing the Reavesburg and Vorund men. Cries of victory from Reavesburg's warriors were met with groans of despair by Galin's supporters, as his practice sword bounced over the cobbles and Djuri raised the point of his weapon to his throat.

Galin blew out hard, red beard dark with sweat. "Well fought. Another time you won't be so fortunate."

Djuri laughed and turned his back on his vanquished opponent, facing the baying crowd, arms raised. "Who's next?"

Ulf stepped forwards, a grin on his face. "You sure you don't want to give the circle to someone else? You look shattered."

"Choose your weapon," Djuri told him.

Ulf walked over to the wicker basket and picked out a sword, testing its weight and length before setting it aside and choosing another. Djuri rolled his shoulders, shaking away the tiredness in his muscles as he got ready to fight his friend. Ulf was a few years younger and Djuri generally had the measure of him in combat. However, their last two contests had been very close. Djuri made up his mind to show Ulf who was the better warrior today, even if it meant bruising a few ribs. As he stood waiting the noise of the crowd changed. Ulf heard it too and looked round to see Tyrfingr Blackeyes approaching the circle, Nereth walking beside him. As far as Djuri could recall he'd never seen Tyrfingr train with the men.

Tyrfingr waved Ulf aside and stepped into the circle. "Turncloak. Would you care to show your jarl the measure of your skill?"

"All are welcome in the circle and those who enter do so as equals," Djuri replied, recalling late Olfridor Halfhand's words as he taught the youngsters in the keep. Was that really only a year ago?

Tyrfingr drew out his short sword, the metal ringing as it left the scabbard. With his other hand he drew a long dagger, holding the hilt loosely. Galin took a hesitant step forwards.

"My lord, is that wise?"

Tyrfingr glared at him. "Do I pay you to *think*, Ironfist? I find my skills stay sharper when I train with my own blade. I'm sure Djuri has no objections."

Djuri shrugged, though he felt uneasy. "As my jarl wishes." He set aside the practice sword and fetched his longsword, giving it a few swings as he stepped back into the circle. Ulf watched anxiously, talking in hushed tones to a few Reavesburg warriors.

Tyrfingr was waiting for him, his dark hair framing his face and those hideous black eyes. "Best of three touches," he said. "Try and get close to me."

Djuri raised his shield and levelled his sword at his opponent, a half-formed thought running through his mind. Was this his opportunity? It wasn't uncommon for people to die in the training circle in accidents and Blackeyes had chosen steel rather than a wooden weapon. Djuri knew if Tyrfingr died the Vorund warriors would lynch him on the spot. Did it matter? There was still Eidr, out there somewhere hunting down Lina and her companions and weren't the durath the real threat here?

Tyrfingr sprang forwards, sword and dagger snaking out, seeking out any gap in Djuri's defences. He gasped, cursing his lack of focus and finding his longsword and shield both slow and heavy as he tried to counter the attack. Djuri was a foot taller than Tyrfingr and had a far greater reach. It should have been an easy contest but every time he swung his sword he found Tyrfingr had already spun away and was coming at him from another direction. Sweat broke out on Djuri's forehead and the muscles across his shoulders soon began to burn. Tyrfingr was lightning fast, his dagger catching Djuri just below the knee as he tried to fend off another flurry of blows.

"All too easy. Are you going to try and make this into a contest?" Tyrfingr mocked as the Vorund warriors jeered.

Djuri shrugged off his shield, dropping it with a clang onto the stone. It was slowing him down too much. He took his sword in a two-handed grip and began circling Tyrfingr, his knee stinging from the shallow cut. Blackeyes kept his distance, matching Djuri's pace. The noise from the crowd faded, everyone holding their breath as they watched. Djuri charged forwards, lowering his shoulder as he made to barge Blackeyes straight out of the circle. Tyrfingr stepped aside, sword cutting down towards Djuri's neck and he only just parried the blow, provoking a few angry shouts from Ulf and his supporters. Djuri snarled, lashing out with his sword and watching in dismay as Tyrfingr swayed to one side. He let the momentum of the blow carry him away, out of Blackeyes' reach as he tried to collect his thoughts. If there was going to be an accidental death it was likely to be his own, unless he could find a different way to breach Tyrfingr's defences.

"Try and get close to me," said Tyrfingr softly from the other side of the circle.

His men laughed at those words and before the sound had died on their lips Tyrfingr's dagger was whistling through the air, aimed straight at Djuri's face. He brought his longsword up by reflex even before his mind had registered what was happening, deflecting the weapon. It flew into the crowd, burying itself deep into the shoulder of a Vorund man, who fell to the floor with a shriek. Djuri looked down to see Tyrfingr's sword resting against his throat. He hadn't even seen the man move.

"Two touches," Tyrfingr declared, with a hint of a grin. "Thank you for the practice."

Djuri was still shaking his head in disbelief when Galin patted him on his back with his metal hand as he passed, laughing as he shared a joke with Tyrfingr. Nereth regarded him with sympathy.

"There's only one word for that, my love – humiliating." Her inflection in the word 'love' gave it a barbed edge, wounding more deeply than Blackeyes' two touches.

"Glad to see I have your support," he gasped, too winded to say much more.

Nereth arched an eyebrow. "Few can match Tyrfingr Blackeyes with a blade. You're honoured he chose to fight you in the first place – it shows how much he rates your skill."

"I don't feel honoured," Djuri complained, wincing as he put weight on his injured leg.

Nereth laughed as she took his arm. "Someone has to lose in the sparring contest – don't pretend this is the first time this has ever happened to you."

They walked back to the keep arm in arm. Nereth stumbled slightly, her ankle turning over on an uneven cobble and Djuri saw her grimace as a ripple of pain flowed up her back at the sharp movement. She took a deep breath, face relaxing as the moment passed.

"Are you alright?"

"I'm fine. It's you who needs to be careful. Tyrfingr was making an example of you in the ring. Reavesburg is under Vorund rule and its warriors are the strongest, Blackeyes being the best of them. I saw you were thinking this was your chance to avenge the wrongs he had done to your people. Your face changed when he drew steel on you. Blackeyes was testing you and at the same time he taught you a lesson."

"I don't know what you think you saw," Djuri mumbled. "Fighting with sharpened steel is different, that's all."

"Liar. I know you too well, Djuri Turncloak. When a warrior's blood is up, the truth soon comes to the surface. Don't give Tyrfingr a reason not to trust you. I've seen him in these moods before, where he gets bored and looks to toy with someone. The games Blackeyes plays are dangerous and always have high stakes. I've enjoyed your company in recent months and it would be a shame if things had to change."

Djuri looked at Nereth, unsure what to say. "Don't think too hard," she told him with a wry grin, tugging his arm tighter. "You'll do yourself an injury."

CHAPTER 37

Randall walked under the open iron portcullis and the doors to the Inner Keep swung wide as he entered the hall. The sun had risen higher into the sky, bathing the hall in pearlescent light. The table was set for feasting, although it was not yet noon. In keeping with his mood the place was subdued as the servants hurried to complete their work. One of The Six blocked his path, hand resting on his sword hilt, bloodshot eyes staring at him from behind his helmet. Randall was so tired he couldn't even muster up enough strength to feel fear at being confronted by the undead.

"Adalrikr summoned me," he told the creature. It stared at him for a long moment before stepping aside and allowing him to pass.

Adalrikr swept into the hall, resplendent in flowing white robes, silver circlet on his brow, flanked by four of his undead guardians. Hallerna walked by his side, wearing a tight-fitting green dress that matched her eyes, holding his arm possessively. Behind him walked the rest of his new companions, who had appeared at his court with so little warning. Joarr had complained to Randall about that, privately asking who they were and why Adalrikr did not consult more with his jarls.

That doesn't matter now. Joarr's dead.

Adalrikr looked up at Randall and smiled. "Come and sit. You must be hungry."

I may as well eat one last fine meal before they take my head. Adalrikr might have forgiven one defeat but I'm sure he won't excuse a second. "It would be my honour, my king."

Randall wasn't disappointed. The food and drink

was delicious, although Adalrikr and his companions were restrained, talking little. Randall watched them carefully – there were two men, whose names he didn't know. One was broad and dark-haired, with a trimmed beard and brown eyes. The second was a giant – there was no mistaking the build of a warrior, even wrapped up in a noble's finery. His hair was close-shaven, leaving dark stubble covering his thick skull and square jaw, his huge hands dwarfing his goblet. Where his strong arms poked out beyond his sleeves Randall could see the dark ink of the Vorund Clan bear tattoo.

To Adalrikr's right sat Hallerna, daintily putting morsels into her mouth. On his left sat the blonde lady called Finnaril – the one who had cut off the fingers of the last Helsburg chief. She was watching Randall, only eating distractedly. He swallowed and quickly returned his attention to his trencher.

"Tell me, Adalrikr, why are we eating with this old man?" asked Finnaril.

"There's more to Randall than meets the eye, isn't that right, my friend? That's why I named him jarl."

"I do what I can," Randall replied, eyeing her warily.

"You are the true heart of the Vorund Clan," announced a blonde woman in the middle of the table with a plain face and large grey eyes.

"Honestly, Heidr, what rubbish is this?" snapped Finnaril.

Randall couldn't tell if Heidr heard the remark as she stared at him, her eyes deep and knowing. "Randall Vorstson, Jarl of Vorund, the men speak your name with respect. They see you as one of them and follow you willingly into battle. More importantly, I see your loyalties lie with your clan, rather than any desire to wield power for your own ends. I can see why you chose him, Adalrikr." Finnaril snorted as the rest of the group round the table all looked at Randall, making him feel increasingly uncomfortable.

"You seem to know a great deal about me," Randall said at last to end the silence. "Yet, I don't think I've been properly introduced to the new companions gracing the court of the king."

"He's an impudent one," hissed Finnaril.

"He asks a fair question," Adalrikr told her. "After all, we'll be residing together in Vorund Fastness for some time after this morning's defeat. I believe you already know Hallerna and Finnaril. The lady who sees so clearly into your soul is Heidr, although we have come to call her the Prophetess over the years. It was she who taught me the arts of the scrying pool."

Adalrikr gestured to the remaining four members of the group. "This is Solvia, Heidr's good friend." A young lady with dark hair nodded in greeting. "Vedisra is a shieldmaiden, sworn to defend me, as is Orn, the large fellow here. The gentleman sitting next to him is my old friend, Nishrall."

Nishrall, the man who sported a black beard, gave a thin smile before turning to Adalrikr. "Forgive me, my king, but whilst you promised this was our time recent events are not a ringing endorsement of such a view."

Adalrikr ignored Nishrall's words and turned back to Randall, dark eyes glittering. "The Landless Jarl will break himself on our walls, Nishrall. When this is over the spirit of the Brotherhood will be shattered and Laskar will be our kingdom."

"My king, why am I here?" Randall asked. "Joarr is dead, along with over six hundred of our men. Don't you want a report on the attack and what went wrong? Am I supposed to give you an account? Do you want me to plead for your forgiveness?"

"Was this morning your fault?" Adalrikr asked.

Randall hesitated. Joarr had taken his plans for the dawn raid to Adalrikr when Randall had refused to support him, fearing they would rush headlong into a trap. *Fearing exactly what happened, as it turned out.* Adalrikr had overruled Randall and ordered Joarr to lead the doomed attack. *Pointing all that out doesn't seem like a good idea.*

"My king – if the attack had been successful we would have prised our enemy out of their positions before they completed their defences. It was worth the risk, especially as we know they are still awaiting reinforcements. It was the right time to strike but victory was never assured."

"And what is your counsel?" Adalrikr asked.

Randall had been thinking about little else since the gates of Vorund Fastness had closed behind him. "We could attack again. We still have the numbers but it will be bloody work – Johan and Gautarr are no fools and have organised their men well. They will use the open ground against us, as they did this morning and the palisade wall is strong. I believe we would win such a fight, although it might take more than one attack to take those defences. We will lose many warriors."

"A price worth paying, if it ends the Brotherhood," interjected Vedisra. She looked uncomfortable in her flowing gown, the muscles across her shoulders straining against the soft fabric.

Adalrikr shook his head. "I cannot rule a kingdom without an army at my side. Joarr had his chance. Randall, you advised me to wait them out, even though we expect more Reavesburg reinforcements to land. Is that still your opinion?"

Randall nodded. "Although their defences are strong, ours are stronger, whilst the days are shortening and winter will soon be here. Waiting outside our walls for months in the cold with poor food and nothing to do will sap their strength and resolve. Believe me, I know – I was there at Romsdahl last winter and it's not an experience I wish to repeat."

Adalrikr took a drink of wine, the liquid dark on his pale lips. "Geilir wages war in Norlhast and things go well for us there. I have already sent messenger birds to Norlhast Keep naming him my new jarl, entitling him to take up Joarr's old seat of power at Jastaburg. After Norlhast's rebellion is finally quelled we will gather our allies and strike against Johan in the spring. Until then, let him wait out in the cold."

Geilir Goldentooth, Jarl of Jastaburg – wonderful. I miss Joarr already.

"Geilir is a good choice," Randall told his king. "I think the plan is sensible. Johan cannot prevail against the combined might of Vorund, Norlhast, Riltbalt and Helsburg."

"What of Hasteinn's mission?" asked Nishrall. "Rothgar Kolfinnarson still works to destroy us. I don't like the thought of sitting here for months waiting for him to devise the means to kill us all."

"I'm sure the Prophetess can tell us," Finnaril sniped.

Heidr shook her head. "The scrying pool only shows me the icy waters of the north – of Rothgar and Hasteinn there is no sign. The ways of the gods are always difficult to discern."

"Of course they are," sighed Finnaril, shaking her head.

"The success of Rothgar's quest is by no means certain," Adalrikr told her. "The northern seas are treacherous and Hasteinn will never give up the search. Even if by some miracle he does gain the aid of Bruar they must still bring the battle to us, here in Vorund Fastness. Where could be safer, Nishrall, than here in the Inner Keep, behind the curtain walls of the Fastness?"

"It puts me in mind of livestock, penned in and waiting for slaughter," Nishrall replied sourly.

"What's done is done, Nishrall," Hallerna told him, stroking Adalrikr's arm. "We hold out here and wait for Geilir to return with his warriors from the north. We've waited so long already – what difference does a few more months make?"

***

Randall was glad to take his leave, although he didn't relax until he reached the bottom of the winding staircase encircling the rock upon which the Inner Keep was perched. As he reached the base he found Kurt waiting for him. He drew his second into a firm embrace, patting him on the back, before telling him what had happened at his meeting with the king.

"Meldun's opened an ale keg back at the barracks," Kurt told him. "Most of the men are there, drowning their sorrows after the disaster this morning. Sounds to me like you need a drink."

Randall nodded. "Lead the way."

He felt his spirits lift as they headed down the hill towards the guardhouse. Adalrikr's methods scared him and he didn't much care for his new advisors at court. However he could see Vorund was poised to unite the Laskan clans, wielding real power. It was time the mighty kingdoms of Beria, Mirtan, Lagash and Oomrhat took more notice of the people of the north and Randall felt pride at being part of that.

A noise like a thunderclap rang out as if the sky had split, stopping Randall and Kurt in their tracks.

"What was that?" Kurt gasped, looking around. Further away, Randall could hear sounds of alarm rising up from the city.

The two men hurriedly climbed the city walls, looking out in the direction of the noise. Kurt swore and pointed north across the open ground, towards the defences of the Brotherhood. Randall squinted, his eyes not as good as those of his younger second.

"What is it ...? No, wait, I can make it out now. Myshall's bane."

Behind the palisade wall were a row of siege engines – huge trebuchets being wound back and loaded with stones. As he stood there one of them launched an attack, the sound of the snap of ropes being released reaching them moments after the rock was hurled high into the air. It fell short with a crash, bouncing along the ground. Two more stones were released as they watched, their range more accurate. One slammed into the side of the curtain wall with a percussive boom, causing the men on the walls to cower. The second cleared the wall and landed on top of a house, smashing through its roof and demolishing the entire building, which vanished in a cloud of dust. More shouts of alarm drifted up from the city.

Kurt turned to Randall. "It's what we should have done to Romsdahl last year when we first landed. If we'd pounded Gautarr's stronghold into the dust we wouldn't be watching them doing this to our home."

Randall straightened his back as he took a deep breath, finding strength he didn't know he possessed. "Come on, we have to get closer. Adalrikr put me in charge of the city's defences and I need to see what sort of damage those engines are doing to the walls."

CHAPTER 38

Humli's aching buttocks had become the centre of his universe as he rode his stolen courser westwards into occupied Reavesburg. He knew a true hero would be on the lookout for pursuit following the massacre in Noln and that his first worry should be Desta and her vulnerable child. He needed to be watchful of Lina, a shadow spirit riding in their midst, who had torn grown men to pieces with her bare hands. All of this was true, yet none of it could compare to the exquisite *agony* produced by days of riding when he wasn't a natural horseman. A cart he could cope with – they had a normal seat after all, whereas this was ... intolerable.

Not for the first time Humli reflected how in the sagas the act of riding from place to place was spoken of lightly by the bards. It was mentioned in passing; mere links as they put the story together. Humli was beginning to wonder how he would be able to endure this journey, his mood darkening as it started to rain, the weather beginning to turn. Little things, such as the shortening days, the chill in the morning and the reddening of the leaves on the trees all whispered of autumn creeping over the land. Humli knew the weather would be worse in the mountains, so they needed to keep moving. At least they still had a decent stock of provisions and their route along the River Jelt gave them a plentiful supply of fresh water. Humli had fashioned a fishing line from their supplies, which he left out at night when they camped. Most mornings that meant fish for breakfast, which made him feel useful. However, that sense of purpose swiftly evaporated when he eyed his horse and knew another day of riding lay ahead.

Late that morning the river began to widen and Humli realised they were at the head of Lake Tull. Lina stopped her horse, patting her neck and looking out across the waters. Her face was distant and Humli glanced at Desta. His daughter shrugged, clearly as baffled at the reason behind this pause in their journey as he was.

"What is it, Lina?" asked Desta, Finn wrapped in close to her chest, fast asleep.

Lina stayed quiet, staring out over the grey waters of the lake as the rain continued to fall. Humli hesitantly approached her, offering up silent thanks as his horse drew alongside and he was able to stop riding, even if it was only for a few moments.

"Have you seen something?" he asked.

Lina shook her head, dark eyes looking out at the distance. "It's nothing. I didn't expect to find myself back here again. Tullen, or what's left of it, lies on the other side of the lake."

Did the durath feel things like loss and fear? Humli looked at Lina's face and had his answer.

"We don't have to follow the road," he told her. "The ground's wide and level by the river – we could circle round and pick up the path further westwards."

"And waste another day? No, we'll ride on. There's nothing there now, only charred timbers and cold ash."

***

It took most of the day to ride along the northern shore of Lake Tull. Humli watched a pair of white herons wading in the shallows as they hunted for fish, unperturbed by the rain, which was soaking its way through his new riding cloak, water dripping down his neck. The light was fading early, the sun lost behind dark grey clouds and Humli was starting to think about where would be best to make camp when he heard voices up ahead. His heart was in his mouth at the sound, momentarily pushing aside the discomfort of another day's ride.

Desta had heard the noise too. "We could skirt round them while there's still enough light to ride."

"No," Lina replied. "We don't know who they are and leaving an unknown enemy behind us could be just as dangerous. We need to find out more."

Both women turned to Humli, each holding their infant children close. Humli sighed, knowing he didn't have much choice. As Lina and Desta picketed their horses some distance from the road, Humli nudged his own forwards to investigate. As he rounded a bend in the road the sounds grew louder and he could see half a dozen tents encircling a roaring fire. He nearly cried with relief when he saw there were women and children in the group – several families on the road together, cooking food, laughing and singing.

For a moment he hesitated. *Am I right to involve them in our troubles?* He thought of how Dyri had died trying to help them. He remembered Elfradr's look of shock when the arrow struck him on the docks – the rest of his crew massacred by the Vorund Clan. *It would be different if it was just me – those two girls have small bairns to care for. We need all the help we can get if they're to survive.*

Decision made, Humli urged his horse on and called out a greeting.

***

Gathered round the warm fire as darkness fell, Humli felt safe for the first time in days. He had called himself Gamli, taking inspiration from Sissa in the fish market – her husband's name the first one that came to him. He'd introduced Desta as Sissa and Lina called herself Eyja, pretending to be his wife. The group of travellers were led by an old pot-bellied man called Rollef and his wife Sunnifa.

"Reavesburg lands are no longer safe for folk like us," Sunnifa told them as they shared their meal. She was a kindly woman, deep laughter lines around her eyes.

"It's why we're heading west," Humli told her. "I want to believe Johan can free us from Adalrikr's rule but he can't protect us while he's fighting down in Vorund. I have my family to think of."

Rollef nodded. "All the young men have gone to fight. More heeded the call and went south once news reached us that Romsdahl had been freed. Word is that Sigolf Admundson is setting sail with a second fleet of ships bound for Vorund Fastness in the next few days. I admire those lads who've gone to fight – it's the right thing to do. It poses some difficult questions, though, for those of us left behind."

"You talk about Reavesburg, yet you're not from around here, are you?" asked Almarr, a young man travelling with the group who was missing his left leg below the knee.

Humli silently cursed, hoping this wouldn't lead to trouble. "That's true – I was brought here from Riltbalt when I was just a boy. Kolfinnar Marlson made me a freedman the year he became chief and I decided to stay here and make Reavesburg my home."

"If it was good enough for our late chief then it's good enough for me," said Rollef, staring hard at Almarr. "We've gathered up various people along the road as we've made this journey. It's safer for all of us if we travel together, so you're all welcome to join us, Reavesburg born or not. I'm not sure there's all that much difference between the clans these days, not since Adalrikr made his bid for power."

"We take care of one another on the road," Sunnifa added. "Vorund's warriors have used the uprising of the Brotherhood as an excuse to interrogate and attack anyone they find in the western lands. I've heard more tales of raids and reprisals than I can count. With our warriors gone we've been left vulnerable, so we decided to make the journey before summer came to an end."

Humli raised his cup and took a sip of watered wine. "You have my family's thanks for your kindness and hospitality. I'm glad we found you on the road."

After their meal he went to tend the horses with Lina. Almarr limped up to speak to them, using his crutches with some difficulty, clearly still adapting to his injury.

"I used to work at the stables of an inn on the road, before the Vorund Clan burned it to the ground. I know good horses when I see them – coursers, the horse of a warrior intending to travel at speed. How did a group of refugees manage to afford three fine beasts like these?"

"What does it matter to you?" snapped Lina, glaring at him.

Humli held out his hand. "Hush, Eyja, it's a fair question. My wife's brother breeds horses, up near Ulfkell's Keep. He's supplied some of the best to Tyrfingr Blackeyes now he's Jarl of Reavesburg. However, when he knew we were planning to leave he gifted us these fine animals. I only wish he'd been able to come with us too."

"Really? What's his name?" Almarr asked.

Humli hesitated and knew that gave him away before the words even left his lips. "Dyri. He holds some land north of Ulfkell's Keep."

Almarr looked at both of them, unconvinced. "I can't say I've ever heard of him. I'll be watching you, Gamli. These are good people, who've taken you in and offered you food and shelter. I hope their trust isn't misplaced."

"He's trouble," Lina whispered as Almarr limped away.

"He can tell we're lying," Humli agreed. "It's hard to make up a whole life and stick to the story. You can be betrayed by the smallest details."

"I still believe we're safer in a larger company. We need to keep to ourselves while we're with them – and as far away from Almarr as possible."

"I know. We need to be careful. It's only going to be for a short while, until we've crossed the mountains."

Lina walked off towards the edge of the camp and Humli followed her, reminded again of how much like his late wife she looked with her dark hair and that oval face. *Best not to think too much about that part of our story. Maybe I thought about that possibility once but now I don't know who she is at all.*

"What's the matter?" he asked as she stood there in silence, looking into the growing darkness, facing away from the light of the fire. Lina turned to him, her eyes deep pools of shadow, two small pinpricks of light in their centre where they reflected the orange glow of the flames.

"Do you think the sins of the past can ever be forgiven?" Humli stared at her, unable to think of a reply and a coldness crept up his spine as he wondered what Lina was referring to. "I've done things, back in Tullen. I was free after centuries of darkness and thought nothing of taking the poor woman brought to me when I crossed back into Amuran. She already had a child, Humli – a small boy. I was cruel to him and I took his father away from him too, leaving him all alone, imprisoned in our house. He probably died when Johan attacked. Back in Tullen our leader, Sandar, thought nothing of sacrificing men, women and children, using blood magic to open his gate into the Shadow Realm. We believed we were doing the right thing, trying to escape from Adalrikr's influence, yet we never gave any thought to the cost of our freedom."

Humli took an involuntary step away from Lina, wishing desperately she would stop telling him these things. *I don't need to know this. I don't* want *to know any of this.*

"Why speak of this now?" he whispered. "What good does it do to talk about things that can't be changed? The Creator judges our actions at the end of time after we've been called to Navan's Halls. It's not for me to forgive sins. You frightened us all back in Noln and what you told us afterwards. I know you're not like us, although I believe you're trying to help. Isn't that what matters? What you do next, rather than what you did in the past?"

Lina shuddered. "The durath think of humans as lesser beings – mere vessels used to clothe our lofty spirits. Humli, I want you to understand that's not how I view you and Desta. You helped me, took me in and showed me kindness, without ever asking for anything in return. Having my child made me realise I have to be better, to raise him well and give him a future with hope, one where he can be happy. I want that for Frokn and I want it for you, Desta and Finn as well. Do you believe me?"

Humli stepped in close and, after hesitating for a moment, he drew Lina into an embrace. She felt soft, warm and small, unlike the monster he'd seen on the docks of Noln. *Am I comforting a woman or a demon?*

"We're in this together," he whispered. "I have your back and you have mine. Together we're stronger and we'll get through this."

He wanted to believe those words, even as a cloak of fear settled over his shoulders whilst the last sliver of sun slid below the horizon.

CHAPTER 39

Freydja hesitated, pretending to watch as the siege engines were prepared for another day pounding the walls of Vorund Fastness. Johan had been there at first light, inspecting the ropes and giving instructions. Petr was busy too, organising the men into gangs, allocating them to their tasks as they scurried around the giant machines of war. Moments later there was a mighty snap and crack as the first trebuchet was released, the stone missile flying towards its target. It struck the fortified wall, about halfway up, producing a puff of dust, the sound of smashing stone and falling masonry reaching them a few seconds later. After three days the walls of Vorund Fastness stood firm and it was becoming clear it was going to take weeks, or perhaps even *months*, before the outer wall was breached.

The siege engines started their morning assault in rapid succession, the noise deafening this close. Freydja saw Bandor hurrying towards her and sighed, knowing there was no avoiding the difficult conversation that was about to follow. She turned to look at her brother, as Throm stood on watch at the palisade wall – menial duties for her uncle's second and she knew the reason why he was there.

"You ready?" asked Bandor over the din.

Freydja nodded and the pair of them approached the palisade, calling out a greeting to Throm as they drew close. He turned to look at them, eyes distant and a grimace crossed his face. He looked like he hadn't slept all night.

"There you are. We were worried about you," Bandor told Throm as they climbed up the steps and joined him on the platform. Freydja felt a chill as she looked out over the battlefield, the scene of their recent victory over Adalrikr's forces. The heads of their defeated foes had been mounted on spikes. There was row upon row of them, the hundreds of dead facing Vorund Fastness, staring in silent recrimination after Joarr's doomed assault. Johan's losses had been light in comparison, some fifty men killed or left with injuries that meant they would never fight again. It had been a great victory, yet Throm looked like he'd suffered a terrible defeat.

"I just needed some time alone," Throm explained. "I didn't mean to speak to your father that way. I was ... out of sorts. I'll apologise to him today."

"It should have been a time of celebration, Throm," said Freydja.

Throm peered through a gap in the stakewall, nodding at Joarr's mangled skull. "Not a day went by when Uncle didn't speak of how our time for vengeance would come for the murder of our father."

Bandor put his arm around Throm's shoulders. "And it did. You fought bravely at my side and they're calling you the Hammerbreaker for striking such a mighty blow against the Vorund Clan. You should revel in such things – it makes you a *name* in Reavesburg and gives the men who follow you heart that this fight can be won."

Throm turned to look at them, face etched with misery. "If that's true then why do I feel nothing?" Bandor stared at him, lost for words as Throm gave a mumbled apology and set off towards Johan's tent in the centre of their encampment.

"Let him be," Freydja told her husband, putting a hand on his arm as Throm walked away.

Bandor looked at her questioningly. "He's a strange one, your brother."

"He thinks deeply. Surrounded by the madness here, that can be a disadvantage."

Bandor took a few moments to understand Freydja's double meaning before a hesitant grin spread over his face.

"Why you … You should show me some proper respect," he joked as Freydja laughed.

"It's different for Throm. I wasn't even two years old when my father died, so I don't remember him at all – just the stories my uncle told. Throm was six and idolised him and he's grown up thinking it was his duty to kill Joarr the Hammer. I'm glad he's dead but it doesn't change the sorrows we carry with us. I think Throm's only just beginning to understand that."

"I keep my blade sharp to avenge my sister and nephew. Are you saying I'm wrong to seek redress for the crimes done to my family?"

"No, not at all. Adalrikr and his followers have to pay for their crimes. Think about this, though – how would you feel if you killed Tyrfingr Blackeyes? Would it bring Reesha and young Kolfinnar back from Navan's Halls to be with you again? No, of course not. If vengeance is all you have then what remains once it's been exacted?"

Bandor stood there for a while, thinking about his answer. "I have you and perhaps by this time next year we might have children of our own to care for, as well as my new brother or sister. I think I see what you're telling me."

Freydja nodded. "Throm has no one. He's never really seen eye to eye with his uncle, so we have to look out for him. We're all he has."

***

"You with us?"

Ulfarr's face swam into view, grey-flecked beard crusted with ice. He looked worried and I realised I'd been gone for a long while. As things came back into focus I caught the noise and buzz of excitement around the ship. I could hear Aerinndis shouting orders, gear and weapons being stowed. I took Ulfarr's outstretched hand and let him haul me onto my feet. In front of us lay a vast ice sheet, sloping into the sea, *Stormweaver's* hull bumping gently against the ice stretching out underneath the water. Her crew were packing away the sail using intricate, careful folds whilst Meinolf tested the ice with a long pole. He looked at his captain and nodded, Aerinndis breaking into a wide, satisfied smile.

"Meinolf, drop the mast and make her ready for an overland crossing. Haddr, take four crew and some rope so we can start hauling *Stormweaver* out of the water," she shouted.

"I'll do it," growled Skari, desperate to be off the ship as soon as possible.

He joined the first group of sailors who splashed through the shallow icy water and teamed up to begin pulling *Stormweaver* onto the ice. Slowly the ship slid forwards, the ice making some alarming cracking noises as *Stormweaver's* hull scraped along the surface. More crew jumped ashore and joined their fellows pulling the ship clear of the sea, until Aerinndis called a halt and they dropped to the ground, gasping for breath.

I stood on the ice, watching as the crew laboured, feeling surplus to requirements. The ice sheet met the sea in an irregular pattern, in some places forming shallows, in others towering cliffs reared up, preventing any landing. Further north the white expanse was featureless, too bright to look at directly for long as the sun shone down. Skari was on his knees, laughing and crying at once, as Matthildr found him fresh boots, explaining he'd lose his toes if he didn't change into dry ones. Ulfarr, Myr, Jolinn and Ekkill spread out, keeping watch on our new surroundings, still wary.

Etta hobbled over, looking thin and pinched, though her good eye blazed with energy and purpose. "We're here. We made it."

I could already feel the cold radiating from the ground, working its way through my fur boots. I stamped my feet to keep the circulation going and shook my head in admiration. "I've seen the Redfars Sea freeze solid in winter, yet even that doesn't compare to this. It's a land of ice – another world."

"One of the wonders of Amuran," Etta replied.

I looked at Etta, wondering how to tackle the subject foremost on my mind. "The going will be hard – more difficult than when we were on the ship."

"Which is why Aerinndis has brought a sled, as we've discussed before, although I think she also had *you* in mind when she purchased it."

"The woman thinks of everything," I replied, watching as the crew brought out wooden rollers, which they laid on the ground as they made their final preparations for the next stage of our journey. I looked again to the north and saw a faint haze in the distance – a dark smudge against the horizon.

"Do you see that?"

Etta nodded. "The smoke from Ballung Mountain; the great volcano at the heart of the Fire Isle spoken of in the legend of Sigborn. If Dinuvillan favours us with clear weather, it will guide us straight there."

"It looks so close."

"Hmm. The smoke rises high in the air. We're still some way from our destination and much depends on how easy it is to cover the ground."

"If we can see that, so can Hasteinn. It will lead him straight to us."

Etta shrugged. "You're right but what can we do?"

Aerinndis wasted no time readying *Stormweaver* for her overland crossing. Etta climbed onto her sled, young Jonas taking the first turn at pulling the contraption. The rest of Aerinndis' crew began the task of hauling *Stormweaver* over the ice, an aspect of our journey we had planned well in advance. The technique was used frequently when transporting a ship from one river to another overland but it had never been applied to such harsh and challenging conditions. However, after much debate, it was decided that this was the only way. If we left *Stormweaver* out on the ice at our landing point our small crew could be overwhelmed if

Hasteinn's ships found us. All they had to do was torch our longship and we would be trapped. If I disembarked with my companions and *Stormweaver* left us and set sail then we would have the challenge of being able to find each other again. We had no idea how long we would need to spend on the Fire Isle. This way, we brought our ship with us, allowing us to carry more gear and also giving us the option of leaving the ice shelf from a different location to where we landed, posing more difficulties for our pursuers.

On the smooth ice this method of transportation proved to be effective. One group of sailors pushed the ship, another up front pulling on ropes, whilst a third group acted as runners, picking up the rollers left in *Stormweaver's* wake and bringing them back to the front of the ship. After a while they would swap roles to give the runners a break. Up ahead Meinolf tested our path, looking out for hidden crevasses and other dangers. Flanking us, Ulfarr and the rest of the warriors in our company kept watch, making sure we weren't being followed.

The shoreline vanished behind us after we headed down a short incline, making it impossible to gauge our true speed and rate of progress. I lent a hand with moving the ship when I could. However, it wasn't long before the cold took its toll and I fell back, walking behind *Stormweaver*. I glanced at Etta's sled, knowing it was big enough to carry two. Stubbornness kept me putting one foot in front of another as the sun continued its march across the sky, the snow on the ground so bright I had to screw my eyes half-shut to avoid being blinded. By dusk the smudge of smoke from Ballung appeared no closer. We used the canvases we had brought to erect tents to give us some shelter from the wind, burning charcoal to cook our food and keep warm. Spirits were high after reaching our goal, even if the day's work had been hard. I looked back the way we had come and wondered if Hasteinn's preparations had been as thorough as Aerinndis'. This was a harsh, unforgiving place, where the smallest mistake would mean death.

"You did well today," Jolinn told me, huddled next to the fire, hood up despite being under canvas.

"I do feel some of my old strength returning," I admitted. "I couldn't have done this last year. Today, I just looked at Etta's sled and thought to myself 'There's no way I'm riding with her.'"

"Don't be too quick to say that," said Ulfarr. "There's going to be a few folk praying for the chance to take a rest on that contraption before this journey is over."

One of our crewmates returned to the tent, a gust of wind blowing through the opening. This directed a fine sprinkle of light snow into the fire, where it sizzled and steamed on the coals. I glanced through the tent flap before the sailor tied it fast once more, the constellation of Elphinas glinting brightly in the clear night sky, marking our path northwards. I closed my eyes, resting against Ulfarr and Jolinn for warmth, falling asleep within moments.

CHAPTER 40

Fundinn walked into the tent and without ceremony threw himself onto a threadbare blanket on the floor. Retreat had been an ignominious and disorganised affair and the resulting loss of supplies and equipment meant these accommodations lacked most of the trappings associated with an army commander. Orglyr, sitting on a crate, looked up at him with a blank expression. He rubbed a broad hand over his rough features, shaking his head.

"How many?"

"Half," Fundinn replied.

Orglyr cursed. "So few? What a disaster."

In the shambles following defeat at the hands of Geilir it was impossible to be certain of anything. The only thing Fundinn knew after carrying out a swift headcount at their new encampment was they had little over a thousand men left under their command. Many lay dead in the valley where Geilir had sprung his trap. However, Fundinn guessed a good number had slipped away, ignoring their orders to regroup at the foot of the Baros Mountains, west of Taur. After watching their friends butchered, who could blame them?

"Anything useful in that crate?"

Orglyr laughed, stood and reached inside. He produced two bottles of Berian beer and pulled out the corks, passing one to Fundinn, who took it gratefully. After a long, slow draught, life didn't seem quite so bad.

"I'm sorry about Snaga," said Orglyr after a while.

"The bastard who killed him almost got me as well," Fundinn replied, rubbing his tender ribs. He'd been lucky in the battle. A few more inches one way or another and it could have all been over. "Curren did for him."

"The Lady of Norlhast sent one of her best swords to us, clearly. I like Curren but I'll miss Snaga. He was brave and loyal. We need more warriors like him."

Fundinn sat there, wondering whether Orglyr was feeling guilty. Was he looking for Fundinn to say something to make him feel better? *Does he want me to forgive him after this monumental disaster?* Fundinn was bone-weary after days on the run but as he swallowed another mouthful of beer he felt a spark of anger. He'd known Snaga from a boy and as Orglyr's second it had been his responsibility to train him. All that promise squandered because Orglyr hadn't been patient and launched his attack too soon.

"I know what you're thinking," said Orglyr. "Why not say it?"

Fundinn wiped his mouth with the back of his hand, looking hard at the older man. "You sure you want me to?"

"Say it."

"Alright. Snaga's dead because of you. We've probably lost a thousand warriors, either dead or deserted, because of you. We're on the run in our own country, because of you."

Orglyr lifted the bottle to his lips, taking a long draught, his eyes watching Fundinn. "You're right. I made a mistake and we're paying dearly for it. Like I said, I'm sorry."

"Is that it?"

"What more do you want me to say? Nothing I can say or do will change the situation we're in. Unless you think you could do a better job? Is that it? Is that what this is about?"

Fundinn breathed in slowly through his nose, letting Orglyr wait as he turned the question over in his mind. *Do I want this? It's a pretty poor time to become chief with Geilir out for our blood. I'd probably only be in charge for one battle and that would be a short one.*

Orglyr laughed. "Doesn't look so appealing when you think about it, eh?"

Fundinn was still mulling over how to answer when Tidkumi thrust the tent flap open and limped inside, Soma and Curren right behind him.

"Drinking? That's your answer?" spat Tidkumi, looking at the pair of them in dismay.

"The Berians are masters when it comes to fashioning tempered glass," Orglyr replied, as if his conversation with Fundinn had never happened. "This is ale in a bottle, a remarkable innovation. Do you want one?"

Tidkumi didn't see the joke. "It's over. Geilir's hard on our heels with heavy horse, better gear and more supplies. There's no way we can fight them and win, even with your wonderous beer crate from Beria – the only thing you appear to have salvaged from our retreat. Another tactical masterstroke? After all, who needs weapons or food?"

"That's true enough," muttered Orglyr, taking a swig.

Fundinn watched as the flush of colour rose past Tidkumi's neck, his cheeks reddening. "Do you think this is all a *jest*?"

"I'm not jesting – I'm agreeing with you. This fight is over, for now."

"For now?" asked Soma, head cocked to one side as she watched Orglyr with curiosity.

The old warrior nodded. "How many fighters did you say we still have, Fundinn?"

"A little over one thousand," Fundinn told him. "Although many of them are hurt. Some don't even have any weapons."

"Still, they came, didn't they?" Orglyr pointed out. "This crew is hard. These are the ones who had the chance to turn tail and run home to safety. They knew we couldn't win and they still came. These are the ones we want, the ones who can't stand being under the yoke of the Vorund Clan any longer."

Soma frowned. "I don't see how that helps. Bravery alone doesn't win the battle and Geilir has us where he wants us."

"No, he doesn't. I'm not planning to stand and fight. We need to withdraw – head into the mountains and conserve our strength until spring. Then it's time to fight a different sort of war."

"How does that help our people in Norlhast Keep?" asked Curren. "Karas is counting on us to break Adalrikr's rule. How can we do that hiding in the mountains?"

"This war is bigger than Norlhast," Orglyr explained. "Adalrikr's holed up in Vorund Fastness fighting the Reavesburg Clan. He needs Geilir's army back south to help him kick Johan and Gautarr off his shores. Trouble is, he has an inconvenient uprising in Norlhast to worry about as well, meaning Geilir can't leave until things are under control here. The last thing Adalrikr can afford is to lose any territory when he's under siege. He can't risk Norlhast becoming another symbol of resistance, so Geilir has to finish the job."

"It's not all about winning today," Fundinn said, understanding what Orglyr was driving at. "You're talking about buying Johan time to defeat Adalrikr."

"It's not the plan we started out with but it's the best we've got. Who knows what will happen over the next few months? If Johan is successful or if he simply avoids defeat people here will start to believe Adalrikr isn't unbeatable. That might rally more swords to our cause, especially if we plan some well-timed raids from the mountains to help keep Geilir busy. We know the mountain paths and passes – Geilir doesn't. We can use this land as a secure base and wait him out."

"It *could* work," mused Curren.

"Better than surrendering or fighting a battle we can't win," Fundinn agreed, reappraising his assessment of Orglyr. Tidkumi was less impressed.

"And you really think you're the man to lead us, after all this?" Tidkumi said, throwing his arms wide. "Look at what we've been reduced to because of your unwillingness to listen."

"I don't see anyone else queuing up to take my place leading this crew," Orglyr replied, voice low and dangerous. Tidkumi's hand settled on the handle of his axe. Fundinn watched Soma move to one side, creating space to draw her sword and defend her chief. Fundinn slowly stood, placating hands spread out wide.

"Easy now, everyone," he said. "The last few days haven't been the best. Last thing we need is to start fighting amongst ourselves." He glanced at Curren. Whilst there was no question which side Soma would support the young warrior from Norlhast Keep was harder to read.

Orglyr gave a deep, throaty chuckle. "Fundinn's right, Tidkumi. You can't afford to lose any more toes to my axe, can you?" Fundinn winced. *That* sounded an awful lot more like the Orglyr he knew. Tidkumi gave an inarticulate growl and raised his axe. Fundinn was reaching for his own blade when Hoskuldr burst through the tent flap, gasping for breath.

"What is it?" snapped Tidkumi, rattled by his sudden entrance.

"Scouts have reported sight of Geilir's warriors," Hoskuldr gasped. "An advance party, no more than an hour away."

Everyone turned to Orglyr, who sat back casually on his beer crate, tipping up his bottle to drain the last dregs. When he finished he tossed it aside and smacked his lips.

"Time to head into the mountains lads. Only bring what you can carry." He stood and shouldered his crate, shoving past an open-mouthed Tidkumi as he left.

***

Freydja rose early, before first light, hurriedly dressing. There was a growing buzz drifting up from the camp of the Brotherhood – new arrivals, the first of Sigolf's ships from Romsdahl bringing reinforcements. On the other side of the tent Bandor was cursing as he fumbled with his belt buckle in the dark. Once they were ready they met Thengill, who was standing guard, and hurried to the eastern side of the camp, following the first light of the sun.

Thengill made a path through the gathering crowds. She counted eighteen longships being drawn up onto the beach and she could see more at sea, sails emblazoned with an eagle in flight. Hundreds of warriors were disembarking, splashing through the waves as they helped haul their ships out of the sea. Others had formed a line and were passing bundles of clothes, boxes, crates and barrels along its length as the fleet disgorged its cargo.

"Quite the sight," said Thengill. "They've brought a lot of warriors here – more than I was expecting."

"There's Father," Bandor called out, pointing at the crowd.

The three of them hurried to where Johan was standing, flanked by Petr, Varinn and Svan. Sigolf was puffing with exertion as he made his way towards them with Beinir of Olt.

"Sigolf, you're a welcome sight," Johan called out, giving the big man a firm hug.

"I think you'll find one thousand three hundred swords are even more welcome than one old man," Sigolf replied with a grin, looking tired from his days at sea.

"So many?" asked Johan in surprise.

"News of Romsdahl's liberation has spread throughout the land. Once people heard you'd set out for Vorund a steady stream of warriors passed through Romsdahl's gates each day. We've come here on every fishing vessel and rowing boat Ragnar could lay his hands on."

"I see Ragnar's kept us well provisioned as well," added Varinn, nodding at the flow of goods still coming off the ships.

"Sigolf! What news from Reavesburg?" asked Gautarr, emerging from the crowd with Throm and Domarr. "How do things fare back in Romsdahl?"

"Your family are well and send you their greetings, Gautarr Falrufson," said Sigolf. "I bring letters from Jora and Ragnar." Freydja's uncle eagerly seized the sealed parchments from Sigolf, stowing them in a pocket of his cloak, no doubt intending to read them in private. "Ingirith has written to Damona as well," Sigolf added, handing another letter into Johan's hand. Freydja's heart sank as she realised there were no messages for her. After saying her goodbyes she walked in silence back towards their tent with Bandor, knowing the rest of the day would be spent disembarking crew and cargo. They left Petr organising where their new arrivals would be barracked.

"What's wrong?" Bandor asked after a time, noticing her mood had changed.

"I was just a little surprised Jora and Asta didn't send word. We'll be here for months and this might be the last chance we have to correspond properly in a long while."

"I think they're making a point," Bandor replied with a rueful smile.

"We're still family. I didn't expect my letters to go unanswered."

"No, that's just it. Now you're part of House Kalamar."

"Our marriage was about *uniting* our houses," Freydja pointed out.

"Yes, for now. But we both know at some point the rivalry between your uncle and my father will have to be settled, once and for all. You're Freydja Bandorswyfe and as far as Jora and Gautarr are concerned, you've declared which house you're supporting."

Freydja reached out and took Bandor's hand, Thengill walking at a discreet distance behind them. "It shouldn't be about making a choice concerning houses. It should be about bringing together the Reavesburg Clan to defeat our enemies and rise above such things."

"I know he's your family, Freydja, but Gautarr's cut

from a different cloth to your father. Even while we're at war, the game of politics is still being played."

Freydja didn't reply, drawing Bandor close as they wended their way through the busy camp arm in arm, her heart troubled.

CHAPTER 41

The wind blew from the north, icy fingers probing my furs, stealing away my warmth and energy. A huge crevasse had opened up in front of *Stormweaver* the previous day, diverting us westwards as we tried to find our way around the yawning chasm. The snows deepened, making progress slow. Twice *Stormweaver* sank into the drifts, Aerinndis and Meinolf shouting orders as their crew fought to free the vessel. The second time we had to break out shovels and dig her clear before mounting *Stormweaver* back onto her rollers, now slippery with a thick coat of compacted snow and ice.

The wind picked up loose snow from the ground, throwing it in our faces, stinging our eyes. I glanced at Etta, crouched under a mound of blankets as she rode on the sled, pulled along by Haddr, head bowed as he set himself against the gale. Etta had defied all my predictions but the longer this detour took the more worried I became for her. The freezing temperatures could easily cost you fingers or toes to frostbite – at night I gratefully counted each of mine as we sheltered under the tents, huddled together to keep warm. When I stopped walking my thoughts would wander to my friends, far to the south in Vorund. I thought of Throm, expecting his life to change after slaying Joarr in battle, only to find it hadn't brought him any measure of peace. There was Freydja, shunned by the family who had raised her. Images of the Weeping Warrior filled my mind, my heart heavy as I turned his words over in my thoughts.

"You torture yourself to no purpose," Etta counselled me that night as I confessed my worries whilst the wind howled outside our tent. "You'll find no answers to such things on the ice of the Endless Ocean. None of us know what will happen when we reach the Fire Isle."

"All we can do is complete the task set before us," added Jolinn, breath misting in front of her. "The Weeping Warrior wouldn't have sent us on this quest if he didn't believe it could be done."

Was that true? Etta was wise and I didn't doubt Jolinn's courage but would we really be able to persuade Bruar to help us? Whether we returned to the Brotherhood in triumph or failure, I knew we had no choice other than to carry on.

"The crevasse *is* narrowing," Aerinndis was saying to Ulfarr and his companions on the other side of our tent.

"Yes, but each day we lose means less food and no progress towards this accursed isle," grumbled Skari. "How much further do we still have to go?"

Aerinndis wrinkled her nose and looked at Skari with exasperation. "I have as much idea as you. The currents, winds and waves I can read. Out here on the ice, it's a different story."

Skari cast me an ill-favoured look with his good eye. "Runes of finding, eh, Princeling? Looks like they've led us into the frozen wastes of hell."

"I think I preferred it when you were puking your guts up," replied Ekkill, provoking chortles of laughter from *Stormweaver's* crew.

***

The next morning I rose and after eating breakfast I carefully adjusted my furs, preparing for another day walking west along the edge of the yawning crevasse. I was now sporting a patchy beard and moustache, which I told myself was helping me to stay warm. Ulfarr joked he had more hair on the back of his hand and other, less wholesome, parts of his anatomy. I grinned wryly at the memory, shielding my eyes from the glare of the sun as I tried to see whether there was any sign of the crevasse closing. The ice cliffs were tinted pink as the sun rose behind me, a beautiful sight were it not for the fact we were trapped. Would we find our way across today or did another week of trudging through the snow lie in front of us? Should we have turned eastwards instead of west? I set my shoulder to the side of *Stormweaver*, gloved hand placed against one of her lacquered runes, and helped the crew push her forwards, others hauling on ropes as the longship made its slow crawl along the ice. At least the wind had dropped. It was a perfect, clear day, although bitterly cold, the sun giving no warmth as it rose into the blue sky.

After a while I fell back, taking a break from pushing the ship as others took my place. I trudged behind *Stormweaver*, dark thoughts banished as all my concentration was channelled into keeping moving, wading through the snows where they deepened, watching my footing where the packed ice was exposed by the wind, slick and treacherous. Breaking a leg or spraining an ankle would have dire consequences out here. I paused, peering out over that vast expanse of white wilderness. Was the wind picking up again? I frowned, feeling uneasy although I wasn't sure why.

Jolinn jogged up behind me. "What's the matter?"

I held up my hand and she stopped. "I'm not sure."

Jolinn frowned, both of us looking out across the ice, mittened hands shielding our eyes against the dazzling landscape. I blinked, thinking I'd seen movement – a black dot creeping over the snows, vanishing into a dip. Had I imagined it? I gasped as several more dark shapes emerged, disappearing just as quickly into the same depression in the ground, another row behind them. All of them were moving in the same direction, directly towards us.

"Did you see that?" I hissed.

Jolinn nodded. "We've got company," she called out.

Aerinndis gave the order to halt and her crew hurried to gather their weapons, hilts wrapped in leather to avoid the cold metal taking off their skin. Ekkill and Ulfarr took up a vantage point on *Stormweaver*, busily unwrapping their bows and strings from their protective canvas.

"Time for you to earn your passage on my ship," Aerinndis called out, her eyes watching the approaching group warily.

"And there was me thinking all that rowing, pushing and hauling counted for something," Ulfarr told her.

Feyotra and Matthildr embraced each other briefly, before the navigator scrambled up into *Stormweaver* to fetch her own short bow. Matthildr joined the rest of Aerinndis' crew as they formed a protective half-circle around the ship. I drew my sword, Svafa's longer, unfamiliar blade feeling clumsy in my cold hand, Jolinn standing next to me. Skari and Myr moved forwards, Meinolf and Haddr flanking them, shields raised, as the approaching figures began to resolve into the shapes of men. They were thickly wrapped in furs, carrying spears, swords and axes and were running straight at *Stormweaver*, faint war cries drifting towards us on the wind. Hasteinn's warriors had found us.

"No intention of a parley, clearly," muttered Jolinn next to me. "You need to fall back."

I reluctantly followed her instruction, moving over to the sled, where Etta was watching proceedings as if sitting on a throne of furs. I took up a position next to her.

"Oh good, I feel so much safer," she quipped, making Aerinndis laugh as she rushed by, bow in hand, Aguti next to her similarly equipped.

"Hold steady," Aerinndis shouted, pulling back her hood so she could see better. Her hair was tied back in a loose ponytail and she flicked a stray strand out of the way as she crouched down, bow already strung, half a dozen arrows placed in the snow in front of her. Several other sailors were joining her, readying their own bows.

"How many do you count?" Aerinndis asked Aguti next to her.

Aguti scrunched up his ruddy face, cheeks cracked by

the wind and sun. "At least thirty. Maybe thirty-five. Hard to be sure when they keep vanishing in and out behind those low hills."

A silence settled over *Stormweaver's* crew as we waited for Hasteinn's men, broken only by a creak as Ulfarr tested his longbow. We could hear the shouts of the warriors as their slow jog became a run and they began their charge. There was a snap as Ulfarr loosed an arrow, which arched over the ice and found its mark in one of the leading warriors. He gave a cry and went down, dropping his spear.

"We have them in range," called Ekkill, drawing an arrow from his quiver.

"Ready," called Aerinndis to her crew, taking aim.

Above her on the ship I saw Ekkill draw back on his more powerful longbow, side by side with Ulfarr and Feyotra. All three released their arrows at the same time, each finding their mark. Three more men fell into the snows, one thrashing as he clutched at the arrow protruding from his stomach, a red stain spreading out over the snow as he screamed in pain. The Vorund warriors' shouts grew louder, drowning out the sounds of the dying man as they charged us.

"Come on!" roared Skari, legs set wide apart, whirling his warhammer as the warriors continued to close the gap.

Aerinndis' sailors released a volley of arrows. Their aim was more wayward, only three arrows finding their mark, just one of those a killing strike. Our archers standing on *Stormweaver* struck their targets with greater accuracy and more men fell, motionless, in the snow. I knew Ekkill and Ulfarr were deadly with a bow and my admiration for Feyotra grew each time she found her target, matching their skill. As the Vorund warriors drew closer I could see they were struggling to cover the distance between us and as I watched one disappeared into a hidden drift, two more tumbling over him. They already looked exhausted and they were still some fifty yards out, caught on open ground, as more arrows thinned their numbers. By the time the first few warriors had reached us they were panting and gasping. Their leader raised his sword and his head exploded as Skari's hammer connected with it, sending his corpse skittering away.

I watched Jolinn kill three men in quick succession, carefully choosing her ground so they could only approach her one at a time before opening them up with swift, precise strikes they were too tired to defend. One man threw a spear at Meinolf, who was knocked to the ground as he blocked it with his shield. He struggled to find his footing as the Vorund warrior drew his sword and charged. Myr intercepted his attacker, silent as always, cutting low with a powerful stroke of his two-handed sword. The blade punched through the furs and leather armour underneath, burying itself in his enemy's guts. Another thrown spear took Jonas in the shoulder. He stumbled and accidently released his arrow straight into the neck of young Soren next to him. Aerinndis cursed and her crew loosed another volley, bringing down their attacker and two more men next to him before they could get any closer.

Haddr, Jolinn, Skari and Myr killed anyone unfortunate enough to get into close quarters, moving with a deadly purpose as Ekkill, Feyotra and Ulfarr's arrows continued to kill those attempting to join the fray. Blood dripped like crimson rain onto the virgin white snow, before it was churned up by booted feet and the thrashings of dying men. The air rang with the sound of clashing steel, blade on shield, war cries and screams. In minutes the attack was over, one Vorund warrior dropping his shield as he ran, whilst Myr took the head of his last opponent. Ekkill casually drew back on his bow and let fly, his arrow thudding deep into the fleeing man, right between the shoulder blades. He fell flat on his face, sliding several feet before coming to a stop, unmoving.

I gasped with relief, feeling the tension leave me as I

thrust my sword back into its scabbard. I hadn't even had to swing it at an enemy and somehow we'd managed to come through the attack almost unscathed. Only one member of *Stormweaver's* crew had been killed – poor Soren, while Jonas sat next to him, ashen and shivering as he bled heavily from the spear wound in his shoulder. Otherwise, we had survived the attack unhurt and elsewhere the sailors were congratulating themselves on their good fortune, slapping each other on the back and hugging their friends with relief. I saw Ulfarr and Jolinn approach one of the Vorund warriors lying on the ice and I hurried over to join them, Aerinndis at my side.

"Who sent you?" Ulfarr was asking the prisoner as we approached.

I looked more closely and could see the broken shaft of an arrow protruding from underneath his ribcage. The man's furs were dark with blood, which was leaking out onto the ground as he gasped, his beard frosted with ice.

"Where's your ship?" Aerinndis asked. "Where did you land?"

The bearded warrior stared up at her with glazed eyes, blood trickling from the corner of his mouth. "I'll not tell you ... anything. Hasteinn ... When ... Hasteinn finds you ... then you'll know ... why he's called ... The Cruel ..."

The man coughed up blood over his front and cried out in agony, clutching at the broken arrow protruding from his stomach with blackened fingers. He shook and curled over onto his side, blood smoking on the ground before it froze. The warrior's breath no longer misted above his face, his eyes fixed in his skull.

Aerinndis wasted no time as we searched the bodies of the fallen, thirty-four in all, stripping them of anything useful. They had meagre provisions and carried no tents or other form of shelter, only their cloaks and furs. Several had blackened fingers, hands and feet. All of them were thin and emaciated. We left the dead where they fell, knowing the snows would soon cover them. Myr bound Jonas' wound while Matthildr crouched next to him, stroking his cheek, Feyotra standing over the three of them, looking worried.

Nearby, Aerinndis gave her dead crewmate the briefest of funeral rites before drawing Soren's cloak over his face and covering his body with snow. "May Culdaff and Nanquido guide you on the swiftest path to Navan's Halls," she said, hugging herself tightly, voice wavering.

Meinolf put a hand on her shoulder. "There were always going to be risks with this journey."

Ulfarr shook his head, looking at the bodies of the fallen Vorund warriors, his expression grim. "Even if they'd killed us out here, they weren't in any state to survive the journey back to their ship."

I nodded. "This crew has been driven hard since they left Vorund Fastness. Hasteinn worked them to death to catch up with us."

"None of that will matter to Hasteinn," Etta said, having ventured out from her sled onto the ice. "This move was worth the risk, sending these poor souls out onto the snows so lightly equipped. If we'd faced fresher warriors perhaps a day or two ago with luck on their side, outnumbering us almost two to one, we could have been defeated. Merely killing enough of us to make it impossible to reach the Fire Isle or, more importantly, return afterwards would have achieved their objectives. It doesn't matter this ploy failed, not when the rest of Hasteinn's warriors are out here somewhere, continuing to hunt us. I'm afraid crossing the ice with *Stormweaver* has given them the opportunity they needed to catch us up."

I glanced in the direction of the smoking Ballung Mountain, vaguely visible on the horizon, a dark smudge underneath the grey plume drifting into the sky. "If we can see that smoke, so can Hasteinn. As long as he knows where we're heading this isn't over."

CHAPTER 42

Djuri downed another ale, sitting in a darkened corner of the Great Hall, Ulf at his side. His head felt fuzzy from too much drink and he hadn't heard a word the Vorund man opposite was saying. Tyrfingr made a point of ensuring the Reavesburg and Vorund warriors ate together every day, slowly working to weave them into a single unit. It was too soon for the old clan rivalries to vanish but many of the Reavesburg warriors were now friends with their Vorund counterparts. Having betrayed their clan, there was no going back and, like Djuri, they'd embraced the unwelcome fact Tyrfingr ruled Ulfkell's Keep. Many Reavesburg folk still thought of them as traitors, although none said so to their face for fear of reprisals.

In many ways everyday life hadn't changed much from the time when Reavesburg was ruled by Kolfinnar or Jorik. Trade came in via the busy docks as before since the merchants lived to make coin and it didn't matter if they traded with Vorund, Helsburg or Vittag. The various clans had all warred with one another in the past, yet Reavesburg's history was also one of alliances and treaties. Sigborn Dragonslayer had united the Reavesburg and Romsdahl Clans peacefully during his twenty-year rule. Pengill Svennson, the wisest of the Reavesburg chiefs, brokered the first trade links with the Vittag and Helsburg Clans; profitable arrangements for all concerned, which had endured for nearly one hundred years. And of course, there had been Jorik's ill-fated pact with Karas Greystorm and the Norlhast Clan; seeing his sister married off to a man more than twice her age, only for that plan to meet with disaster.

Life moved on yet people still wanted *something* to focus their anger upon and somehow the name Djuri Turncloak had stuck. Perhaps it was because he was the leader of the Reavesburg warriors, even if Tyrfingr didn't officially recognise the distinction. His was the face of the Reavesburg defeat and their servitude under King Adalrikr and he could only count Ulf as a real friend. People were fickle, bemoaning his choices, whilst at the same time behaving as if Adalrikr had ruled them all their lives.

Maybe Tyrfingr senses the conflict in me – the name Turncloak *is apt enough. I came here plotting murder and revenge, although I've done precious little about it since.* Not for the first time, Djuri sat there wondering what he was doing in Ulfkell's Keep. He thought of Eidr, out there somewhere with Bjorr and the rest of his men, hunting Humli's family down. He'd done as he was asked and planted his false trail. What now? Kill Tyrfingr? He glanced at the Jarl of Reavesburg, slouched as always in Reave's Chair. After his experience in the duelling circle was the task too difficult? *Or am I just a coward, finding excuses and all the while doing nothing?*

Djuri waved his mug in the air and a servant refilled it. He took a long draught, laughing at Ulf's half-heard joke whilst watching Nereth. She was sitting next to Tyrfingr, his head close to hers, his greasy black hair brushing her shoulder. Darri was entertaining those gathered in the hall, using sleight of hand to make three brightly coloured leather balls vanish and appear at will in all manner of unlikely places. Djuri preferred Darri's singing, although these days his voice had acquired a melancholy lilt, as if the pain of Reavesburg's defeat needed expression whenever he performed. His trickery kept his audience amused, putting smiles on their faces this evening.

After they had eaten Djuri said goodbye to Ulf and weaved his way back to his chambers; another perk, his rooms in the keep reflecting his rank as one of Tyrfingr's senior warriors. He crashed down on the bed and attempted to remove his boots, giving up the task as sleep took him. He couldn't tell how much later it was when the knock on the door startled him awake. He heard the latch lift and someone came inside.

"There's a sight for sore eyes." Nereth's voice.

He groaned and rolled over onto his side, chilled from lying on top of his bedcovers. With an effort he sat up, head thumping. Nereth perched on the end of the bed, pale skin illuminated by the candle she had brought, which she'd set on the mantelpiece above his cold fire.

"The hour's late," he told her, not in the mood for romance.

"I know," Nereth replied, wrapping her cloak more tightly around her shoulders. "I just needed to get away from Tyrfingr. He's in a foul mood."

At this *time of night?* Djuri wondered what had been going on between them and Nereth's dark eyes met his as she sensed his thoughts.

"We received reports from the north, if you're interested," she told him. "Geilir's army defeated an uprising by the Norlhast Clan."

Djuri frowned, sending a pulse of pain racing across his forehead. This was the first he knew of an uprising and yet the news did not surprise him. It was almost as if he'd heard it before, words mentioned in passing and somehow forgotten until now – a strange, disorientating feeling.

"Were Karas and Nuna involved?" he asked.

Nereth shrugged. "Geilir's report mentions his suspicions but he has no proof. Karas was a weakened ruler of Norlhast, his clan lands divided into various factions, including one led by Orglyr the Grim, Bekan's former jarl."

"There can't be much love lost between him and Orglyr in that case."

"Perhaps, although Karas also spared Orglyr's life, allowing him to live in exile. Equally, it's possible Orglyr mustered his army to challenge Karas. Greystorm's foreign wife is popular but if Orglyr married her that could strengthen his position."

"I thought you said he'd been defeated," asked Djuri, confused.

"Although he lost the battle he survived, as did most of his key leaders," Nereth explained. "They've retreated into the Baros Mountains. Geilir suspects they may be trying to find a passage through to Vittag."

"Those clans are sworn enemies," Djuri pointed out.

"The murder of Bothvatr by Adalrikr's emissary in Helsburg changed things. Adalrikr's trade settlement with Ingioy technically makes Vittag part of his kingdom, whilst giving her more power than other Laskan jarls. However, I imagine the White Widow won't be so keen to let Adalrikr's messengers enter her halls after the way Bothvatr was executed. That was badly handled and sows the seed of doubt, making it hard to know exactly who we can trust now Norlhast has rebelled."

"Things don't always go according to plan. I don't see how any of this affects Tyrfingr's rule of Reavesburg."

"Geilir is Adalrikr's creature and he sent him to report on Valdimarr's performance in Norlhast. The fact his orders bring him next to Ulfkell's Keep hasn't been lost on Tyrfingr. Don't forget the Brotherhood sprang up here in Reavesburg, right under Tyrfingr's nose."

"No king can be too trusting," Djuri mused, "although, the loss at Romsdahl was down to Sinarr's failure, not Tyrfingr."

"Geilir's dangerous and ambitious and Adalrikr has named him Jarl of Jastaburg following Joarr's death. Trust me, that won't be enough for Geilir, who will have designs on increasing his influence further. If he can find a way to weaken the position of Valdimarr and Tyrfingr in Adalrikr's eyes for his own advancement, he will. Remember, he led the army that conquered the Riltbalt Clan."

"Joarr's dead!" Djuri exclaimed, wincing with regret as his raised voice sent a pulse of pain through his eyes. "When were you going to get round to telling me that?"

"Word only just reached us," Nereth replied, giving him a reassuring pat on the thigh. "He died leading an unsuccessful attack against Johan's army, trying to breach his defences before they were fully dug in."

Djuri lay back on his bed, thinking on what he had heard. "Things are more complicated than ever. Adalrikr's plans to conquer the Laskan clans could still come to fruition, although it's hard to see that happening now before next year."

"You're right," Nereth agreed. "Gunnsteinn Haddison, the Riltbalt chief, or Jarl of Riltbalt to give him his new title, sent all the warriors he could spare to Norlhast with the plan of crushing the rebellion. The rest are needed to keep the Jorvind Clan pinned down in their fortress at Rast as that siege drags on. The fact Geilir's forces are now trapped up in Norlhast over the winter is a blow. Geilir was meant to bring his army south along with Riltbalt's warriors and help Adalrikr break the siege of Vorund Fastness. He can't do that and leave Orglyr's challenge unresolved, so we may now have to wait until spring before matters are resolved."

Djuri rolled over on his side to get more comfortable, looking closely at Nereth. Her expression was hard to read – was she worried by the latest turn of events? Why was she sharing this with him in the dead of night? He would hear of all this in the morning – word would get round Ulfkell's Keep soon enough. He reached over, pulling her close and Nereth uttered a gentle sigh, her head resting against his chest.

"What's the matter?" he asked.

"I'm tired," Nereth admitted. "I'd hoped after coming to Ulfkell's Keep and resting I'd begin to feel more like my old self."

"An injury like that doesn't heal overnight and many people wouldn't have survived such a wound. It might take you a year or even longer to fully recover."

Nereth placed her hand over his, their fingers entwined. "That's not what I mean. Your friend Rothgar broke me, shattered my Sight magic and left me weakened in Norlhast. The truth is I became careless. I'm vulnerable using the Sight without my sisters, the ones Rothgar killed. Alone, I would have defeated him but I didn't reckon on the combined power of his Fellowship – those three used their skills to overpower me. If I use the Sight against him again I fear they'll overwhelm me, so I'm reduced to taking precautions."

Nereth produced a small crystal bottle from her robe and uncorked it. Djuri caught the scent of cinnamon and remembered the same smell in Tyrfingr's chambers. "I've seen this before. What is it?"

"Ataraxia – it's used to blunt the abilities of one with the Sight, rendering them unreachable to those walking the Path. However, there are some side effects, with prolonged use. Tyrfingr has become addicted to ataraxia, leaving him with his ... unique appearance. Part of him loves the stories people tell as a result – nonsense such as him being half-demon and the like. The true story is he's terrified of the power of mages and Sight users. My reliance on ataraxia is only temporary, until I've joined once more with others who share the skill and can restore my powers. It takes time and trust to use the Sight with another person and creating a Fellowship is not lightly done. Whilst working with someone similarly gifted makes you more powerful it also leaves you vulnerable as well."

"Tyrfingr doesn't look a well man, Nereth. There must be another way?"

"As you said I'll recover in time and then I can set ataraxia aside. I'll not be reduced to this forever." Nereth smiled in the light of her flickering candle. "The time will come when I'm ready to walk the Path once more. When I do, I'll not make the same mistake and I'll confront Rothgar with my own Fellowship. The time will come when he'll pay dearly for everything he's done to me."

Djuri felt a stab of worry through the haze of drink as Nereth helped him undress. She leaned in and kissed him and for a time, while they spent the night together, all his questions and concerns fled from his mind.

CHAPTER 43

Leif blew on the piece of sausage perched on the end of his knife, steaming hot and dripping with gravy. He took a bite, closing his eyes in anticipation, crunching through the blackened, crispy skin into the delicious soft meat inside. Curruck had worked him hard in the smithy – despite eating every morsel of the lunch Arissa packed for him he felt like he'd not been fed for a week. The wind outside rippled the canvas of their tent as he sat at Joldir's table with Thengill and Arissa. Bandor and Freydja were also their guests that night, old Varinn joining them as Bandor's bodyguard. Varinn turned his wrinkled face to Leif and reached out with his knife, spearing a sausage on Leif's plate and popping it into his mouth. Leif stared at him, horrified, as Varinn chuckled, unrepentant.

"I thought the Brotherhood was sworn to act with honour in all things," Arissa scolded, Thengill smiling and shaking his head.

"They're good sausages," Varinn replied, as if that justified everything.

"Joldir, Varinn stole my sausage," Leif told his adoptive father, concerned no one was taking the injustice seriously.

Thengill stood up, ruffled Leif's hair, and spooned another black sausage from the dish in the centre of the table onto Leif's plate. "It's the warrior's code, son. Only the strongest survive. Keep an eye on your food from now on."

Leif glared at Varinn, pulling his trencher closer to his edge of the table. Joldir's meal of cooked sausage, black and smoky from the charcoal fire, boiled potatoes, beans, swede and rich gravy was worth fighting for, even if it meant taking on a warrior of Kalamar.

"Simple fare," Joldir was saying to Freydja. "I'm sure you're used to eating finer dishes at your uncle's castle than what my crooked fingers can conjure out here."

Freydja smiled. "Good food and good company are all anyone could desire."

"If you don't like it I could always have some of yours," Leif told her. Everyone laughed at that, Thengill slapping the table. "Rothgar's almost reached the Fire Isle," Leif added, causing everyone to pause and look at him. While it didn't have anything to do with what the grown-ups were saying, it was far more interesting.

Bandor's face brightened. "So close?"

"And there was a *fight*," Leif declared with growing excitement.

"I can't tell you much," Joldir explained. "I receive only the briefest of messages from Rothgar using the Sight, no matter how dramatic Leif may make it sound. One of Hasteinn's longship crews found them as they were crossing the ice shelf. However, they proved no match for Ulfarr and the rest of his warriors. Rothgar reports they're nearing the island itself."

"Such an incredible gift," said Freydja. "It's hard to credit such things."

"I must confess, Freydja, it was one of the reasons I invited you both to dine with me tonight," Joldir replied. Freydja looked quizzical and Bandor stiffened, face suspicious as Joldir continued. "The Sight is a powerful gift, one the Brotherhood is unable to use to its full extent whilst Rothgar is away. However, one of the strange phenomena of these times is the Sight is awakening in more people with increasing frequency, even though it has lain dormant until now. Leif made an extraordinary discovery only a few days ago –"

"It's her, isn't it?" Bandor was on his feet, moving so quickly his chair fell to the floor.

Joldir held out his shattered hands. "Please, this isn't of my choosing. Freydja needs to know as much for her own protection as anything else. Untrained, she's in danger from our enemies. There are others too –"

"And you want her for your Fellowship," Bandor snarled. "She's my wife. If there are others, why not use them?"

"I'm capable of speaking for myself," Freydja interjected, not bothering to hide the irritation in her voice.

Bandor glowered, taking a deep breath before answering. "You know the risks. Rothgar almost died the last time Nereth attacked him with the Sight. I never wanted you here, Freydja – things are already dangerous enough. Now Joldir wants to use you for some … foul magic. It's too much to ask."

"If someone spoke about Rothgar like that, you'd be the first to defend him," Freydja replied, also on her feet, hands on hips.

"This isn't what I wanted for you," Bandor told her. "Come with me – we're going."

Freydja looked like she was about to argue. Bandor was already standing at the entrance to the tent, face thunderous as she hesitated. Varinn grimaced and also stood, placing a gentle hand on Freydja's shoulder.

"Best be going now," he told her. "We can talk this through once everyone's had a chance to cool down and think things over."

Freydja sighed. "Yes, Varinn, you're right, of course. Joldir, Arissa – thank you for your hospitality. My apologies – it's been a difficult day."

Bandor held the tent flap open for her, following her out without a word.

"The lad's worried for her," Varinn said as he took his leave. "Give him some time to think things over and talk to his wife." The old warrior popped half a sausage into his mouth with a nod and hurried after Bandor and Freydja.

"That could have gone better," Thengill said as the footsteps of their guests faded into the night.

"He's young and newly wed," Joldir counselled as they ate the remains of their meal. "The recent attack has left everyone on edge and they weren't ready to hear what I had to say concerning Freydja's abilities. I'm just worried – all it would take would be for Nereth to walk the Path and we would have an unwitting spy in our midst. One placed at the heart of the Brotherhood."

"You both spoke the truth, though it could have been handled better," Arissa added as Thengill stood and began clearing up the dishes. "Varinn's right. You need to give them time to think on what you've said. After all, they're not the only young married couple in this camp. I married Thengill under the shadow of war while Svan and Dalla are trying for a child. No one is safe and we all need to play our part. I understand Bandor's worried but he's also being selfish."

"You spoke of others with the gift," said Thengill as he returned to the table. "Who did you mean?"

Joldir nodded. "Anyone with a modest amount of talent can be reached through the Sight and we can't hope to train them all. However, Rothgar told me the strongest of these was Svafa. He discovered the young man had the gift during the Battle of Romsdahl. Now I'm regaining my strength, I think it's time we added Freydja to our Fellowship but if she refuses or we're unable to establish a deeper bond, Svafa would be my next choice."

"Bandor won't like it," Thengill mused.

Arissa chuckled, reaching across the table as she wrapped her hand around Thengill's. "You're right but did you see the look on Freydja's face? I don't think he has much choice in the matter."

***

After finally reaching the end of the crevasse, *Stormweaver's* crew toiled to move their precious vessel northwards once more and watched with grim satisfaction as the plume emanating from Ballung Mountain grew larger; a dark, coiling monster, tainting an otherwise clear blue sky. The summer days were long this far north, allowing us to make good progress until the sun began its descent in the west, turning the ice-shelf blood red in its wake. Jonas, the sailor injured in the recent battle, rode with Etta on the sled, wrapped up next to her in furs as Haddr and Aguti took it in turns to pull them over the ice. Myr was skilled in treating wounds and had cleaned out Jonas' shoulder carefully after the battle, bandaging his arm to avoid him suffering too much discomfort as the sled bounced over the packed ice. Despite there being no outwards sign of infection Jonas grew weaker each day, muttering in his sleep and sweating in his furs.

As dawn began to creep over our camp I rose and went to make water. This task took an inordinate amount of time as I worked my way through layers of furs, which now felt like a second skin. Jolinn was standing some way off, keeping watch in case bears or another group of Hasteinn's warriors attacked us. She allowed me to preserve some modesty, turning her back as I finished my business, although not before making some lewd comment. I was too cold to give a witty reply, hurriedly dressing again before the frost took hold of my intimate parts. Once I was decent I joined her and the two of us watched the red smear of light to the east slowly grow and brighten.

"Another quiet night. We should be thankful," I said.

Jolinn nodded. "Etta says when winter comes this far north the sun never rises. Everything is plunged into eternal night until the spring. Is that true? I never know with that old crone whether she's jesting."

"Saltbeard said the same thing," I told her. "I've no intention of wintering over on the Fire Isle. We have to get back to the Brotherhood."

"You might not get much choice. Aerinndis and her crew are resourceful but they can't travel in darkness."

I'd not considered that possibility, staring at the sunrise and thinking how light was a precious commodity out here. The rest of the camp was beginning to rouse, a few other sailors emerging from the tent to relieve themselves some distance away, the gloom their only source of privacy on the featureless landscape. Ulfarr approached us and as he drew closer his bearing made me realise something was wrong.

"Jonas passed into Navan's Halls during the night," he told us. "Aerinndis wants to say a few words."

***

We left Jonas' body wrapped in his cloak, the wind tugging at one corner as we covered him with snow. Matthildr and Feyotra stood together, hand in hand, crying softly and I remembered the first time I met the young man, mending sailcloth with them on Romsdahl's quayside. Aerinndis described it as a burial at sea as we laid the second member of her crew to rest on this journey. Afterwards we began the arduous task of moving *Stormweaver* northwards, the wooden rollers ice-caked and heavy, the going slow. I helped push the ship, keen to have something to occupy my mind, the mood of the crew sombre. As the afternoon wore on I thought I could see a grey streak on the horizon, although against the white glare it was difficult to be certain. When I mentioned it to Aguti he nodded.

"Aye, that's land. We're getting close. Perhaps two more days at this pace, maybe three if the ground is treacherous, or the weather turns against us."

"Don't waste your breath talking," Aerinndis called from further up the line. "It's a heartening sight, true, yet there's work to be done before we get there."

Eventually I grew tired and fell back, walking behind *Stormweaver* as she made her slow progress. My breath fogged the air as I laboured on, wondering how Desta was faring as she crossed Reavesburg with Rollef and his companions. I knew she was another part of my old life I needed to let go, a fading memory of a romance when we had been little older than children. If that was in the past, what would the future hold? I grunted with the effort of keeping up, Etta's sled bobbing through the snow ahead of me. There was no point thinking too far ahead. All that mattered for now was reaching the Fire Isle –

The sky pitched and twisted as the ground gave way beneath my feet. I threw out my arms, clutching at the snow, panicking as it disintegrated as my gloved hands scrabbled to find purchase. There was a rushing noise as the snow and fragile ice poured into the hidden crevasse beneath my feet and I fell into the darkness with a terrified cry.

***

I opened my eyes and coughed, wiping snow away from my face. I was lying on my back in a twisting, white tunnel, its walls rising steeply on either side. Their surface was smooth, offering no prospect of climbing out and when I looked upwards I could see a thin faint slice of light, far above. The ice behind me had formed into a smooth chute, turning what would otherwise have been a fatal fall into a relatively gentle landing in a soft bank of snow at its base. Gingerly, I checked myself over, finding no bones had been broken, although my back ached and I was sure there would be bruises forming under my furs. I breathed a sigh of relief, knowing I'd been extremely fortunate.

The bottom of the crevasse was narrow – barely enough space for one man to stand, arms outstretched. The ice chute was too steep and slippery to attempt a climb, while ahead of me the crevasse levelled out, bending round to the left. I tried to work out how far I'd travelled away from the spot where I'd fallen. Would it be obvious to *Stormweaver's* crew I was still alive? I blinked, frowning as I noticed a dark shape standing at the corner. A man, wearing a long dark cloak rather than furs, his face shrouded in shadow under his hood. He walked towards me and my heart beat faster as I realised I was trapped.

"Who are you?" I called out. "Declare yourself. I'm armed."

The stranger didn't slow his pace as he pulled down his hood, revealing the handsome face of a warrior, his eyes blind. I relaxed, moving my hand away from the hilt of Svafa's sword as the Weeping Warrior drew close.

"You could have announced yourself," I breathed, feeling the air cool even further, if that were possible.

"I see you've not lost your talent for finding yourself in trouble, Rothgar."

I grimaced. "I'm only in this predicament because of you."

The warrior looked at me with those disconcerting sightless eyes, head cocked to one side. "Your mind swirls with so many thoughts and feelings. You're distracted, drawn to your former home, the fate of your first love, events at Vorund Fastness and your sister in Norlhast. Joldir warned you not to range with the Sight and yet what have you done?"

"I can't control it," I protested.

"You choose not to. My revenge lies in the hands of a noble who's not yet seen twenty summers, more concerned with his past life and glories. This is no game of kings, played to pass the time. You must set aside all distractions because when the time comes, Bruar will test you. You must bring the Sight under control and focus on what lies ahead. Everything depends on this."

I threw out my hands in frustration. "That's easy for you to say. How does anyone prepare for a task like this? I've given up everything for the Brotherhood, risked my life more times than I can count and still I have to give more."

"I'm the one who's given up everything," countered the Weeping Warrior. "If we can't undo the damage being wrought by the Tear none of your other concerns will matter any longer. Don't lose sight of that."

I started as a rope hit my face. Glancing up, I could see

dark figures moving about at the edge of the crevasse, calling my name. Wearily I shouted back and took hold of the rope, fingers numb from the cold. Relief washed over me, yet at the same time I felt a knot of worry as I thought about the challenges ahead. When I glanced back at the spot where the Weeping Warrior was standing, he was gone.

CHAPTER 44

Fundinn raised his hand and the small band of warriors came to a halt. The blasting wind battered them into the side of the Baros Mountains, the narrow pass channelling the gale straight down their throats. Curren Redblade said something, his words snatched away. Fundinn cupped a hand to his ear and shouted at the warrior to come closer.

"I thought I saw a light," Curren bellowed, pointing. "Up there at the head of the pass. One moment it was there – the next, it vanished."

The wind brought intermittent snow showers and they were in the middle of one now, making it hard to see far ahead. Only a couple of hours of daylight remained before the setting sun plunged them into darkness on the exposed side of the mountain. Dunfalas pass should have given them shelter at this stage of the climb. Culdaff had other ideas, his northerly winds driving them backwards, making the ascent both exhausting and treacherous. Up there somewhere was the abandoned ruin Tidkumi had told them about – Dunfalas, an ancient fortress, a remnant from the Age of Glory. When the avatars rained fire down from the heavens they'd sent most of it crashing to the bottom of the mountainside. Decades ago the Norlhast Clan had rediscovered Dunfalas' snow-covered broken walls and leaning towers, rebuilding parts of the lost city. Once it was of strategic importance; both as a refuge and an outpost where they could watch the neighbouring Helsburg Clan. However, the remoteness of Dunfalas made it expensive to man and maintain so, as the Norlhast Clan's fortunes waned, it gradually fell into disuse.

Soma was one of the few in Orglyr's company who had ever been there and she led them along the next stage of their climb, head bowed against the wind and snow, Hoskuldr at her side. Fundinn reflected on what Curren had said, fearful they might be walking into a trap. However, if Dunfalas was occupied by someone else they still had to know. Fundinn fervently hoped that light was nothing more than Curren's imagination as he glanced up the darkening pass, wondering if their bad luck at Taur was following them into the mountains. Had someone else already returned to Dunfalas? It was possible and any claim Norlhast had to the outpost could be disputed. After all, they'd abandoned it themselves in the time of Bekan's father. *Only one way to find out.*

They rounded a bend in the pass where the wind wasn't so fierce and hunkered down, pausing to take a drink and something to eat. Fundinn sat next to Soma, breathing hard. Her lips were blue from the cold as she huddled against a rock, knees drawn up to her chest to keep warm.

"How much farther?" he asked.

"Not far. Another hour at most, perhaps less."

"What about the light Redblade saw?"

Soma shook her head. "I can't believe anyone would be sheltering up here. We're only doing it because we're desperate." She stopped short, avoiding criticising Orglyr directly.

"Plenty of desperate folk about these days," Fundinn told her. "The roads and mountain passes to Vittag and Helsburg have never been so popular."

"True. However, this pass only leads to Dunfalas – it's a dead end, so if anyone else is trying to cross the mountains why come here?"

Why indeed? There were only eight of them and if Soma's hunch was wrong and Dunfalas was occupied it wouldn't take many warriors to outmatch them.

Fundinn nodded up the pass. "Let's go. We've not got much sun left."

Another snow shower slowed their progress and Hoskuldr slipped on the icy rocks, fortunate not to break his leg despite his cursing. They inched their way forwards, Fundinn spying the remains of a broken wall to his left, weathered stone stubbornly clinging to the mountainside. They passed half a dozen shattered buildings, their roofs long gone, walls sagging or missing completely. Soma held up her hand and the group paused, Hoskuldr moving forwards to scout the ruins. Fundinn watched the warrior move methodically through each building, bow held ready in case of attack. Eventually he reappeared and waved them forwards. Fundinn breathed a sigh of relief and hurried on, keen to reach Dunfalas as soon as possible.

The pass twisted left and right, narrowing until they could only walk two abreast, sheer rock rising up on either side of them. Eventually the path widened as they turned another corner, opening out onto a level piece of ground, blanketed in smooth snow. Soma held up her hand again, bringing the party to a halt as she scoured their surroundings, crouched down against the rock. Up ahead rose the walls and outer gate of Dunfalas. The smooth stone comprising the lower section had been patched above with work of far poorer quality, constructed by the Norlhast Clan during their last occupation. The wooden gates, reinforced with thick bands of black wrought iron, were closed, the windows dark in the towers standing on either side. The wind keened, whipping up the snow into fast-moving flurries, which whirled about the open space before settling once more.

"Doesn't look like anyone else is here," Curren said, nodding at the virgin snow in front of them.

"I don't like it," Fundinn replied. "That ground is very exposed. The snow could have fallen *after* someone got here – there's no way they won't see us approaching."

Soma shrugged and stood. "We can't exactly go back and tell Tidkumi we didn't like the look of the place. I'll go. You lot watch me and keep your eyes out for any sign of trouble."

Before anyone could protest Soma pulled up her hood and ran towards the gates, crouching low, leaving a cloud of powdery snow and deep footprints in her wake. Hoskuldr raised his bow, two of the other warriors with them doing the same, each of them searching the walls and surrounding mountainside for any sign of a threat. Soma reached the fortress, pressing herself up against the stonework, listening carefully as she edged forwards. She put her hand against the wooden gates and pushed, cursing as they stood firm, before setting her shoulder against the banded metal and shoving at them again, straining without success. Soma stood back, panting, hands on hips, with a look of frustration.

"Could be iced up," Curren muttered.

"Might be," Fundinn said. He turned to the two bowmen. "Stay here and watch out for any signs of trouble. The rest of you, come with me."

Those gates looked brand new, which bothered Fundinn as he jogged towards Soma. How long had Dunfalas been abandoned? Twenty years? Twenty-five? Yet the wood didn't look weathered and grey, no signs of rust on the black iron. Someone had been here recently.

"Need some help?" Hoskuldr asked Soma with a grin.

"Shut up and help me push," she told him irritably.

The six of them set their hands against the wood, cold even through their gloves, and pushed. Fundinn grunted with the effort as the gate started to shift. There was a soft clunk and the gates moved no more than half an inch, Fundinn feeling the resistance on the other side – the gates were barred.

He turned to Curren. "Looks like we're going to need some rope."

Curren looked at him. "If the gates are locked then there must be someone inside."

Fundinn nodded. "That's right. Time to find out who's

been looking after the place for us."

On the third attempt Fundinn felt the cloth-wrapped hook catch on the stonework between two battlements. He tested the rope, pulling hard to ensure it would take his weight, before planting his feet firmly on the wall. He started to climb, shoulders and his sore rib soon burning with the effort as he scaled Dunfalas' defences. Once at the top he hauled himself onto the parapet behind the battlements. Puffing with the effort, he slowly found his feet and looked around in the dusk light. Beneath him he could see the courtyard, surrounded by various buildings in a much better state of repair than the ruins they had passed earlier. His heart missed a beat as he registered the various sets of footprints and the fact the parapet had been swept clear of snow.

"Don't move." A man's voice from behind him with a western accent. Fundinn slowly raised his hands, feeling the cold edge of a sword against his neck.

"Easy now," Fundinn said, trying to turn round to get a look at his captor.

"I said don't move. Try anything and I'll slit your throat."

"Fundinn," Hoskuldr called softly from below. "You alright? You going to give me a hand up there?"

"Fundinn?" asked the man. "Orglyr's second?"

"What's the right answer?"

The man laughed. "The truth?"

"Alright," muttered Fundinn. "I'm with Orglyr. That going to be a problem?"

"Hardly," replied the man. "We've been waiting for you."

***

Fundinn sat in a circle around the fire pit with his companions, warmth spreading back into his fingers and toes. Rasmus, the warrior who had captured him on the wall, watched him from the far side of the room, arms folded.

Several other warriors stood with him, all eyeing their guests suspiciously, the crest of a wolf's head on their shields. The Vittag and Norlhast Clans had never been allies – not until now.

Soma was deep in conversation with Valka, the leader of Vittag's warriors, a young woman with long blonde hair and blue eyes. Both shieldmaidens, Fundinn supposed they had more in common than most although Valka's status in her clan put her well beyond Soma's usual circle, despite the fact Soma was several years older than their host. Soma's leader was Tidkumi, a renowned warrior of the Norlhast Clan, which afforded her considerable respect. However, Valka was the daughter of Ingioy the White Widow, Chief of the Vittag Clan, and served as her closest advisor and jarl. Fundinn couldn't imagine what had brought her here, into the Baros Mountains and skirting Helsburg territory.

"Are we prisoners or their guests?" whispered Curren, breaking off some bread and dipping it in his soup bowl, his eyes darting towards Rasmus' warriors.

"We've already shared their bread and ale," Fundinn replied. "If they were going to do anything to us they'd have done it by now."

"Who knows what goes through the mind of a Vittag warrior?" said Hoskuldr.

"Drink up and be polite," Fundinn told him.

"Word of the deeds of Tidkumi and Orglyr has reached my mother," Valka was telling Soma. "You're standing up to Geilir and his Riltbalt cronies, which deserves our respect. When we heard the news of your recent defeat we knew Dunfalas was one of the few places within reach where you might seek sanctuary."

"And here you are, waiting for us," Soma replied.

"In the spirit of friendship," Valka told her, narrowing her eyes as some of her men muttered at her words. "Do you take issue with my mother's decision on this matter, Rasmus?"

Rasmus stepped forwards and shook his head, his men falling silent instantly. "Of course not. We serve Ingioy and the Wolf Throne – if that means helping our old rivals, so be it. Better that than helping the Kinslayer gain more power. No one wants to suffer the same fate as Bothvatr."

Valka's gaze lingered on Rasmus. "Good. These are difficult times and if we're to survive we face choices many will find uncomfortable. Norlhast allied itself with Reavesburg and our friends at Ulfkell's Keep – that should not be forgotten."

"Is the Vittag Clan joining this war and breaking their pact with Adalrikr?" asked Fundinn. "We need more swords to oust Geilir from our land."

Valka turned to Fundinn. "You heard of Bothvatr's fate when he crossed King Adalrikr? The king's emissary, Finnaril, cut off his fingers and toes, one by one as he watched. All because their trade negotiations did not meet with her approval. Falki Ruunson, Adalrikr's puppet, now rules in his stead, with Helsburg declared part of his northern kingdom. I have no intention of my mother meeting the same fate. Our lands are more extensive and Adalrikr needs our trade and coin, as well as the tall timbers from the Forest of Mordis for his ships and war machines. My mother has agreed terms that ensure her rule continues, whilst Adalrikr receives what he needs to wage war on the other clans."

"Doesn't sound like the White Widow is much of an ally to Norlhast if she's giving that much aid to Adalrikr," Hoskuldr remarked.

"And where's Karas Greystorm?" Valka asked.

"Karas is looking after his people, influencing events where he can and tempering the worst aspects of Valdimarr's rule at Norlhast Keep," Soma explained. "He's purposely distanced himself from our rebellion whilst secretly helping influence and orchestrate it."

"Likewise, my mother plays her part," said Valka.

"The people of Vittag already have the Kingdom of Beria encroaching on our borders and the prospect of another conflict with them looms. We don't need open war with Adalrikr, no matter how much we may despise him. However, there are other ways to influence events more subtly to achieve the outcome we all want."

"If you're not offering us your swords then why are you here?" Soma asked.

"Dunfalas has been abandoned for many years," Valka explained. "I doubt the young king of the north is aware of its existence and Orglyr's army could winter here, which I assume is your plan? We've already brought provisions and we could fetch more before the snows cut off the pass. I understand your army retreated in some haste – this is an opportunity for you to restock your supplies and recuperate."

"That's very generous of you. However, if word were to slip out concerning where we were sheltering, that could be awkward," Hoskuldr observed. "The only route out of Dunfalas is back down the pass – there's no other way out."

"Your point?" asked Valka.

"My point is this could be a trap. Handing Orglyr over to Geilir might be the price of the White Widow retaining control of Vittag."

Valka snorted. "You'd be holding a fortress only accessible up a narrow mountain pass. That's hardly the best place for Geilir to attack you – even if he knew where you are. However, if you have a better idea of where to see out winter then I won't take offence if you decline our offer."

Soma looked at Fundinn. "I say we offer our thanks to Ingioy and bring the rest of our army up here before the weather turns. However, you're Orglyr's second, so this is your decision. What's it to be?"

Fundinn sighed, the weariness from his climb and the long flight from Geilir's pursuing warriors settling like a heavy weight as he took his ease by the fire. His rib still ached, not helped by the cold and his recent exertions. They were at the end of the road – what other choice did they have? He stood and reached out his hand towards Valka, placing his other hand over his heart.

"The Norlhast Clan will remember this day, when former enemies became allies and you aided us against our common foe. We'll winter in Dunfalas and we're thankful for your hospitality in making this ancient fortress ready for us."

Valka smiled, taking his hand in hers. "You owe us a debt. When the time comes my mother will expect the Wolf Throne to be repaid in full."

"You have my word on that," Fundinn told her.

CHAPTER 45

Randall's knees jabbed with pain every step, his back aching as he moved between the teams repairing Vorund's walls. He wanted nothing more than to sit down and rest. *If I do that, there's no guarantee I'll get up again. Can't have the men seeing weakness from their jarl.*

Instead he called out a jovial greeting to Meldun with enthusiasm he didn't feel, asking him about the repairs. Meldun was quick to take a break from the backbreaking work, eagerly explaining how everything was going to plan. Behind him wooden cranes were employed lowering stones down to the masons, who were perched on the outer walls on swaying rope ladders. It was dangerous work and several men had already died. However, building scaffolding beyond the city would take too long and was pointless, since the Brotherhood could destroy it from distance at their leisure.

Randall glanced up at the long crack on the inside of the wall, running from the broken battlements halfway to the base. The trebuchets had found their range and every day they pounded the same section of wall relentlessly. It was slow work, yet this part of Vorund's defences was beginning to crumble, since it was impossible to repair all the damage in the space of one night. The breach would come – all they could do was delay when it happened. Not for the first time, Randall wondered if he'd given Adalrikr good counsel. Whilst winter would be their ally when it came, there was a risk the Brotherhood would be in a position to launch an attack on the city before autumn ended. Another attack on the palisade where Joarr lost his life might be necessary to ensure Vorund Fastness was safe. *I think I can guess who'll have the honour of leading the attack.*

The buildings in this part of Vorund had taken severe damage, roofs torn off, walls smashed in, some houses obliterated completely. It provided ample building materials for the repair of the curtain wall – scant consolation for those left homeless as the Brotherhood continued their attack. *Still, you have to take the positives where you can. A siege will grind you down otherwise.*

Randall took his leave from Meldun and climbed to the top of the wall. He looked out from the ramparts towards the army camped outside. It was still dark and all was silent, although he could see torches flickering in the distance. He thought back to the day he'd seen more Reavesburg ships land, disgorging another horde of warriors. The Brotherhood's army now numbered some four thousand men by his estimation, roughly the same size as the one under Adalrikr's command. It meant attacking Johan's defences was all the more hazardous, whilst the Brotherhood didn't have the numbers to take Vorund easily. *A stalemate, for as long as Geilir is in Norlhast and the Jorvind Clan resists us.*

Some distance away Nishrall was climbing a staircase leading to another section of the defensive wall, Heidr following closely behind. Curious at what Adalrikr's new advisors were doing this far from the Inner Keep, Randall wandered towards them, taking advantage of the darkness to remain unseen. Nishrall was leaning on the wall, his broad frame taking up most of the space between the battlements. Heidr held back, looking nervous.

"It's higher than it looks," she muttered, a gust of wind catching her hair and drawing it across her face. She flicked it back, cautiously moving away from the edge.

"What do you see?" Nishrall asked her.

Heidr walked over, brushing down her skirts as another gust of wind tugged at them. She shivered, her grey eyes glassy and unblinking as she set her hands on the stonework and peered out over the ramparts. She tilted her head back, closing her eyes, the wind catching her hair and sending it streaming out behind her like a white-gold pennant. The ground lurched beneath Randall's feet and his thoughts swam, jumbled memories jostling with each other – his first raid against the Northern Plainsmen when he was only sixteen, pissing himself as he ran into battle ... His father, waxy skin stretched tight over his bones, coughing up blood as he lay dying in his bed, Randall at his side, holding his hand ... Ellisif's pretty face formed in front of him, the young woman he'd been courting in Hordvin more than thirty years ago. He blinked back tears as her face twisted in grief, shaking her head as he explained he was leaving for Vorund Fastness to serve their chief. *I told her it was no place for a farmer's daughter. She said I was a coward, fleeing my responsibilities and my father's death at home.*

Heidr's voice broke into Randall's jumbled thoughts and he had to hold on to the wall to steady himself. "I see it clearly for the first time – Rothgar Kolfinnarson is the catalyst. Now I understand why Adalrikr is so obsessed with him – events swirl and form around this young man. He is the pebble that causes the mountain landslide, the first spark that lights the fire. He sees far whilst understanding nothing. And there is more – he's accompanied by ... something ... something wreathed in shadow ..."

"Yes?" Nishrall's face was hungry, eager to hear more.

Heidr took a shuddering breath and put a hand on Nishrall's shoulder. "I can see no further tonight, Nishrall. We must return to the keep, since Adalrikr will want to know of these things."

"The shadow," Nishrall pressed. "What was it? What did you see?"

Heidr shook her head. "Only shadow – doom walks at Rothgar's shoulder. More than that, I cannot say."

Randall watched the pair of them leave, remaining in his hiding place, shaken by the overwhelming wash of memories from his past. *What was that? This strange obsession with Rothgar continues. I just hope Hasteinn finds him and finishes the task Adalrikr set for him.*

***

I started awake, clammy and drenched in sweat despite the cold. I tried to speak, making a strangled sound as I tried to draw breath.

"What's the matter with him?" Ulfarr's voice.

"He's fitting," Etta told him. "Ekkill, get that piece of wood between his teeth or he's going to bite off his own tongue."

Firm fingers prised open my jaw. I wanted to scream as my whole body spasmed, twisting and contorting my limbs in silent agony as I arched my back. A wooden bit was jammed between my teeth as I started to choke.

"He's going blue."

"Did he injure himself when he fell?"

"Rothgar," Etta cried. "Rothgar, can you hear me? You're safe. You're here with us. Come back to me, boy. We're almost there. You can't do this to me – not now."

"Move, let me get him on his side," Ekkill shouted.

I vomited onto my bedding, the stench so bad it stung my eyes. There was a blinding flash in front of my eyes followed by what felt like an ice pick being driven into my brain.

***

I was sitting on baking sand amid a towering sea of dunes, the sky a brilliant cloudless blue, sun scorching hot on the back of my neck. Tellian wore a loose red robe, bare arms adorned with gold bracelets and bangles, a necklace of white stones hung around his neck and he held an unusual spear, sharp at one end, a wide blade fixed to the other. Upon seeing my expression, he sank the pointed butt into the sand and walked towards me, leaving it behind.

"A thousand apologies. Old habits die hard and the traditional garb of a Samarak warrior is not complete without a spear. I mean you no harm."

My eyes narrowed, trying to stay focussed on Tellian despite the glare. "I thought you were a merchant."

"Just so. However, among the Abitek everyone is a warrior. When a man or woman comes of age they put on the red of war, they take up their spear and they stand tall with their brothers and sisters. Have no fear, Rothgar, I have no intention of fighting you. You can put down your sword – you won't need that here."

The wind whipped up a cloud of sand, dry grit and dust hitting my face and forcing me to shut my eyes. When I opened them again we were inside a large tent, made from bright colourful fabrics, weaved together in no discernible pattern. It was cool in the shade and Tellian was sitting cross-legged at my feet, tending a small black metal pot resting on a charcoal fire.

"I believe you have been introduced to the wonder of tea?"

Tellian reached out and held up a small china cup, filled with steaming black liquid. I sighed, slid my sword back into its scabbard and sat down, nodding in thanks as I took the proffered cup and crossed my legs in a similar fashion. The skin around my thighs and calves stretched, knots of scar tissue and damaged muscles twisting in unfamiliar ways. I shuddered and reached out with the Sight, working within this world. Tellian's eyebrows rose as I transformed into the warrior I had been before Tyrfingr broke me; wiry yet strong, my armour a perfect fit, fashioned according to my size, my old sword by my side, though still etched with the runes my blade carried in the Real.

"I was a warrior once," I told him, enjoying his surprise.

"So I see."

We sat there for a time, drinking tea and listening to the wind outside, sand occasionally raining down on the tent roof. I closed my eyes and breathed in the scent, recalling the time in Lindos when Etta first introduced me to Samarak tea leaves.

"This Rothgar I prefer," Tellian told me, draining his cup and pouring himself another with a smile.

"You mean the warrior?"

"The *warrior*? Ha, not so, young man. No, no, no, I mean the steady, quiet Rothgar. You are wary in my company yet remain composed, thoughtful, watchful and you treat me with deference and respect. These are good qualities, reflecting how you were raised and what you were taught." I finished my tea, frowning at his words. Tellian poured me another drink from the pot, white teeth flashing as he smiled.

"I didn't know you had the gift of the Sight," I said, taking the cup.

"Ah, you mistake what is taking place. This is your world and your creation, Rothgar, where I am merely giving voice to your deepest thoughts. Rothgar the warrior sits before me because in your heart you want to return to how things were before. You hanker after the lost love of your youth, when you know deep down that you should set such feelings aside. You seek the honour and station of your old life, one that is gone forever."

Those words, echoing the criticism levelled at me by the Weeping Warrior, stung and I felt a hot flush of embarrassment, recognising myself in Tellian's description. "A friend advised me never to forget who I was. Those words helped me find myself, when I was in a dark place."

Tellian looked at me with a sad shake of his head. "The Sight is a dangerous gift – all too easy to wallow in precious, happy memories whilst, back in the Real, you would waste away with a vacant smile on your face. Your friend is right – you should hold on to your memories, that much is true. Knowing where you have come from and who you are – yes, that is good advice. Knowing who you are and what you are heading towards, that, young man, is much more important. That was the lesson Jolinn was trying to teach you."

"I never said it was Jolinn."

Tellian flashed me a grin, hands wrapped around his tea cup. "You didn't need to. This is taking place in your mind. This world is your creation with the Sight and you've brought everything of yourself into this place."

"Letting go is harder than I expected," I muttered, staring at the hot coals to avoid Tellian's gaze.

"Jolinn was trying to help you with that. This is about looking forwards, not looking back. She's a remarkable and perceptive young woman, wouldn't you say?"

I frowned, pondering Tellian's words as he busied himself putting a new pot on the coals and watching as the water began to bubble. He threw various ingredients into the water – a black root, dried green leaves, flakes of bark and a pinch of sand. He breathed in the vapours and drew out a clean china cup, filling it with the dark liquid.

"The Fire Isle draws near. You must clear your mind and return to your friends, who watch over you anxiously. Remember how you defeated Sinarr in the Battle of Romsdahl. Not everyone has the skill to fashion the Realm of Dream as they see fit. This is the way. This is the true path you seek and you must follow it all the way to the very end, painful as it will be. Embrace who you are and embrace the Sight."

I sniffed the concoction, wrinkling my nose in distaste. Tellian was watching me and I took a sip, the bitter flavour instantly numbing my tongue.

"Drink it all, quickly."

I did as instructed, grimacing as I swallowed the last of the potion. "You couldn't find a way to make that more pleasant?" I asked.

"It's what you imagine it to be, so this is how it is," Tellian told me with a smile.

My face felt numb, colours dancing on the edge of my vision as Tellian's blurred face swam in front of me. I turned to look at the entrance of the tent and the bright light outside, a mountainous golden dune rising up towards the sky. Thanking Tellian I lurched to my feet and walked out of the tent. The cold took my breath away and I staggered in the wind, trying to keep my balance on the ice. The sun reflected in the ice crystals, every colour of the rainbow filling my vision as images swam before my eyes. I reached out with the Sight, trying to understand where I was. What I was.

The bear shook his head, confused for a moment as the connection was established between man and beast. Ahead lay three beached longships, drawn up onto the ice, the waters of the sea lapping nearby. The bear lifted his head, sniffing the cold air. It padded closer to the frozen vessels, all of them half covered in drifting snow. In front of the ships was a tent, fabric flapping in the breeze and the bear crept closer, fear and hunger both warring for control. The scent of humans hung in the air. The bear feared few beasts except for these strange two-legged creatures that sometimes hunted on the fringes of the ice. For them to make their home here, though, was unusual – they did not belong here.

Slowly the bear approached the tent, hunger gnawing his stomach. He sniffed the air again, pushing his head through the opening. Several men were slumped around a cold charcoal fire, cloaks and furs heaped on top of them. Not enough to ward off the cold. Not enough to prevent them from freezing to death as night came, the temperatures plummeted and their supplies ran low.

The bear sniffed the nearest corpse, already cold. There was a shield nearby, the symbol of a bear on its hind legs holding meaning for the man melded with the mind of the polar bear, even if the animal did not fully understand its significance. For the bear, this was a rare opportunity for an easy meal as he eased his bulk inside the tent, fear overcome by the desire to eat and stay alive.

***

I woke to the sound of the sled rushing over the ice,

its smooth runners bouncing lightly on the terrain. The sky above me was pale blue with a crossed patchwork of shredded white clouds carried on the wind. Next to me I could see Etta, wrapped up in her furs, sat upright and staring straight ahead. I felt too weak to speak, so I lay there, watching the clouds and listening to the sounds around me as *Stormweaver's* crew continued their long march. After a while Etta glanced down and noticed I was awake.

"Dinuvillan be praised, you're back with us," she said, smiling warmly. Her words were followed by an uncharacteristic pat on my arm.

"I'm back," I whispered. I was in the damn sled after all, and of the two of us I knew who looked better.

"Sit up," Etta told me. "You're going to want to see this."

I forced myself upright, resting on my elbows. Ahead I could see land – a dark smoking mountain rising up to greet us, swathed in a green pine forest at its base.

"We're here," Etta breathed, eyes bright with excitement. "The Fire Isle."

I laughed, wondering for a moment if this was another Sight vision. Yet I knew this was taking place in the Real. Unlike Aerinndis, Hasteinn had left his ships out on the ice, their guards dying from the cold as they awaited their chief's return. Had their sacrifice been worthwhile? There was no turning back from the Fire Isle but what awaited us there? When we set foot on solid ground, would it be Bruar's guardians or Hasteinn's warriors who greeted us?

CHAPTER 46

The late summer sun was warm on Humli's back as he rode, far more comfortable in the saddle after two weeks travelling with Rollef's company. Each day the Baros Mountains drew closer and spirits were high at the thought of leaving Reavesburg behind. He glanced behind him and saw Almarr sitting in one of the carts, glowering at him. Humli flashed him a grin and turned around, muttering under his breath.

"What is it?" Lina asked, riding alongside, Desta a few paces behind them.

"Almarr," Humli answered. "The lad's eyes never leave us. I heard him the other night, talking to Rollef, still arguing he shouldn't have let us join."

"Yet here we are," Lina replied. "That shows who Rollef trusts."

Humli sighed, unconvinced. Rollef hadn't abandoned them – the old man had a kind heart and wasn't the sort who would turn two young women with babies out into the wilds. However, the leader of their expedition to Vittag had asked Humli plenty of questions as they sat around the camp fire. Humli, posing as Gamli from Ulfkell's Keep, had done as well as he could, explaining how Sissa was the daughter from his first marriage – that part was the truth. When it came to explaining how he'd met and married Eyja he'd been less convincing, breaking out into a sweat before Lina interjected. She'd smoothly slid her hand around his waist and the fireside tale of romance she spun had Humli so entranced he'd half-believed her lies. Desta watched them from the other side of the fire, eyes narrowed, as Lina kissed Humli on the mouth, whispering in his ear how much she loved him as they parted.

Humli swallowed, thinking back on that night and how Desta had been quiet ever since. He'd asked her what was wrong, even though he knew full well. His daughter pretended nothing was the matter and an awkward silence settled between them, an unspoken heavy weight. All the while Lina, or *Eyja* as he had to think of her now, never left his side, taking every opportunity to caress him. The other part of the lie he hadn't considered until afterwards was their sleeping arrangements. Lina now shared his blanket, the boy Frokn nestled between them. A few of the men in their company eyed Eyja jealously, probably wondering what she was doing with a man like him. *If only they knew.*

Those damn horses had given them away, his lack of experience around them made all the more obvious whenever Humli tried to dismount – never an elegant sight, especially if a groan of discomfort escaped his lips. However, even if Rollef and Almarr had their suspicions, the days passed and they continued westwards together. Humli knew their coursers could easily leave this party behind but he preferred their company – this way, they had a chance to blend in. After all, there were many groups like theirs, all making their way towards Vittag and the chance of a new life. From Rollef's point of view a larger group meant safety, even if he privately thought Gamli and his family were riding stolen horses.

Soon it won't matter. Another few days and we'll be in the foothills of the mountains and can strike out for the pass near Delving. He glanced at Lina, who turned and smiled at him. *Once we're in Vittag we can go our separate ways. Until then, I can manage to share my bed with ... a ...*

His mind wrestled, trying to find the word. Perhaps it was best if he didn't think of one.

***

Nuna sat in her chamber with her maid, Katla, idling away the hours before their evening meal by lacemaking. Nuna had never enjoyed needlework but the days spent waiting for news were intolerable and she had to fill her time somehow. Katla was a pleasant enough companion, always able to make Nuna smile when they talked of people they had known in their previous life, back in Ulfkell's Keep. It felt like another world after living in Norlhast for more than a year. Despite all the challenges she was happy here, growing to love both her husband and his people as she got to know them. Yet Rothgar intruded into her thoughts most nights, often causing her to wake, shivering from strange dreams filled with ice and blood. Nereth had once tricked Nuna into believing she had the Sight – dreams like those were enough to make her fall for the lie all over again. How could those vivid visions feel so real? She'd been so *cold* when she awoke.

There was a knock on their door and Brosa poked his head into her chamber. "Forgive the disturbance, my lady. You are needed by your husband. Geilir and his army have returned to Norlhast Keep."

Nuna hurried to the feasting hall with Brosa and Katla, heart fluttering. Karas was waiting for her, flanked by Sigurd and Kalfr. Nuna felt a pang of regret at Albrikt's absence, missing his company at court, a lump in her throat as her thoughts strayed to the torture chamber. She pushed those memories aside, straightening her back and squaring her shoulders, moving gracefully into the throng of warriors, nodding in greeting at those she knew. Valdimarr was standing in the centre of the room, laughing at some joke of Geilir's, who scowled at Vorund's emissary with open contempt. Next to him was Lefwine, the handsome bearded leader of Riltbalt's warriors, now fighting in the service of Adalrikr. Karas was exchanging pleasantries with him as Nuna approached. Norlhast's jarl turned and smiled when he saw her, kissing her lightly on the cheek and wrapping his arms around her. Nuna caught Geilir's glance and stiffened, pretending her husband's touch was unwanted and gently breaking the embrace, Karas' hurt expression telling her she played her part well.

"What news?" Nuna asked with forced brightness. "The return of Geilir and his brave warriors must signify the defeat of Orglyr's rebellion, surely?"

"Lefwine was telling me they drove those traitors westwards and out of Norlhast's lands," Karas explained.

"So, Orglyr is defeated?" Nuna asked, inwardly cursing as her voice rose in pitch.

"Exactly, my lady," Geilir told her with a wide smile.

"If you've defeated our foes then where *is* Orglyr?" Sigurd asked sardonically.

Geilir's smile briefly faltered. "We crushed his army and they fled before us into the mountains, where we could leave the cold and the snows to finish our work. They won't return and if they're foolish enough to attempt anything I've left Tryggvi in command of a company of warriors, watching the pass."

A dozen questions filled Nuna's head. She guessed the unenviable task of spending a winter in the foothills of the Baros Mountains was Tryggvi's penance for his treatment of Albrikt, although he'd got off lightly with such a lenient sentence. Nuna's fingers brushed the hilt of her dagger as she thought of what she would like to do to Tryggvi, given the chance.

"You mean you haven't caught him yet?" Sigurd pressed. Dark shadows under his eyes told the story of troubled nights, his face gaunt and pale.

Geilir glared at Sigurd. "We left more than a thousand traitors dead on the field of battle, food for the crows. It matters little Orglyr escaped if his army has been destroyed. We've sent word to our allies in Vittag and Helsburg – so if Orglyr does cross into the western lands he'll find their warriors waiting for him."

"A matter for celebration, surely?" said Valdimarr, eyes darting nervously between Sigurd and Geilir.

"Indeed," Geilir replied, turning his back on Sigurd.

"Karas, my men are tired after the long march back from the mountains. Food, drink and the hospitality of your hall would be most welcome."

Karas motioned to Styrman, who hurried to order the keep's servants to prepare a feast to mark Geilir's return. As the tables were set and music began to play Nuna found Geilir barring her way as she went to take her seat at Karas' side.

"I would speak with you, my lady. Privately."

Nuna nodded. "Of course."

"Not here. Come to my chambers this evening."

***

It was dark when Nuna left her room, a cloak wrapped over her dress to ward off the cold. Brosa remained behind, pretending to guard her chambers, the look on his face telling her exactly what he thought of the idea of her walking the keep alone.

Geilir had changed out of his travelling clothes when Nuna reached his chambers. He was dressed in the fashion of a noble; fine dark woollen breaches, soft black leather boots, white linen shirt and a black jerkin decorated with an intricate fleur-de-lys pattern. Nuna thought the style more closely resembled a Berian or Sunian merchant, rather than a Vorund warrior. Only the bone-handled dagger at his side spoke of his true profession. Geilir smiled when he saw her at the door and ushered her inside.

"You came. I wasn't sure that you would."

"Why not?" Nuna replied, closing the door softly behind her. "I want to continue the conversation we started before you rode westwards to fight Orglyr."

Geilir raised an eyebrow, his gaze lingering on Nuna for a time, making her feel uncomfortable. She was glad when he turned away and poured her some wine, taking a breath to steady her nerves as she reached out and took the goblet.

"You still have ambitions to rule over this northern

outcrop?" Geilir asked her, smiling as she nodded. "It's yours, if you want it. However, I'd be foolish to put such trust in you without being confident of your loyalties. One advantage of my wintering here is I'll have chance to test this for myself."

Nuna tried to keep the shock from her face. "I thought you said *Tryggvi* was remaining behind."

"He is. That crude idiot gets to shiver in a tent while I enjoy the ... well ... meagre yet preferable hospitality of this hall. As your friend Sigurd was so quick to point out, I haven't captured Orglyr. I have to finish this, which means his head adorning a spike before I return to Vorund. With luck, the Helsburg Clan or the White Widow's warriors may find him if he crosses the border and save me the trouble. Otherwise, I'll have to hunt him myself, come the spring."

A dead weight settled in Nuna's stomach as she listened to Geilir. She sipped her wine, wondering how best to deal with this turn of events. This far north the Baros Mountains were already choked with snow and travelling in them was dangerous, even for those who knew the paths well. No army could fight Orglyr if he was sheltered there so Geilir had made the right decision and was happy to wait things out. Nuna realised she shouldn't underestimate Riltbalt's conqueror.

Geilir spent some time recounting his victory over Orglyr, a wolfish grin on his face as he described the aftermath. A valley littered with the dead and dying, the slain the price of Geilir's rise in power and influence. Whilst Valdimarr was ambitious he had none of Geilir's animal cunning and warcraft, making him a far more dangerous foe. Having him here in Norlhast Keep would make it much more difficult to plan the spring uprising – assuming Orglyr returned to take up arms against their oppressors. Perhaps Geilir was right and Orglyr intended to cross the mountains and escape. If that were true then all their scheming was for nothing.

"A raven brought me news from Vorund Fastness,"

Geilir was saying. "Joarr the Hammer has fallen in battle against the Brotherhood and King Adalrikr has named me as his jarl, with the associated titles and land in Jastaburg. There's a wife too, I believe. Anyway, it's important things go well for me here and I'll not return to Vorund Fastness with my work in Norlhast half-done. No, I will arrive in triumph, the northern rebellion crushed, and my warriors will turn the tide of battle against the Brotherhood and end this costly war. I'll need your help and support to keep the people with us on this – they must see Orglyr as a traitor, only fighting against us for his own ends, rather than his clan. His name carries weight in the north and it must be blackened before he is defeated."

"Orglyr and my husband were never friends," Nuna replied. "It won't be hard to start those rumours."

Geilir nodded. "Good. A few well-placed whispers will undermine him as he hunkers down in the mountains."

"That's if he hasn't fled," Nuna pointed out.

"I'm not sure that will happen," Geilir said with a grimace. "The man is a warrior and my guess is he won't back away from this fight. All we have to do is draw him out, at the right time. With his reputation in tatters few if any will flock to his banner, making it all the easier for my army to destroy him."

"With Orglyr gone Valdimarr will expect to rule, using my husband as his puppet."

Geilir's gold tooth glinted as his smile widened. "And you see yourself as a more worthy candidate?"

Nuna hesitated, wondering if this was a trap. Whatever Geilir might think of Valdimarr, the man was still the king's emissary. Speaking against him was treason but she had to gain Geilir's trust. "In Ulfkell's Keep I watched my brother rule our clan, where the only thing that qualified him to become chief was his broad back and skill with an axe. He led us poorly, placing us at risk and drawing King Adalrikr's wrath. His decisions led to his own death and the murder of half my family."

"All the more reason for you to hate our king, surely?" asked Geilir, watching her carefully.

"My point is a weak ruler is bad for their clan. I loved Jorik but I'm wise enough to understand he wasn't the right person to be our chief. Valdimarr is loyal to our king, of that I have no doubt. However, he's a vain man with little intellect, preferring to rule through fear. The people loathe him and because Karas doesn't stand up to Valdimarr, they hate him too." Nuna took a sip of wine, knowing if she spoke the words there was no going back. "You need someone fit to rule, a person who can draw the people together and show them times have changed. My family thought so little of me they married me off to a man I didn't even know to seal their doomed war pact. I want more for my life – more than Karas can offer. The Lady of Norlhast Keep is ready to rule, if you'll help me rid this land of those clinging to the past."

Geilir laughed, toasting her health as their goblets chimed off each other. "My lady, I think I shall enjoy working with you. For the glory of our king, of course."

CHAPTER 47

The campfire crackled, flames licking the bottom of the iron cook pot as Meinolf supervised the preparation of our evening meal. My mouth watered at the thought of fish stew, a tremor running the length of my body, the last vestiges of my fit leaving me weak and frail. Spirits should have been high with the achievement of our goal. Instead *Stormweaver's* crew spoke in low tones, casting fearful glances towards the mountain as the setting sun wreathed it in deepening shadow. We were camped on dry land at the mouth of a river, which disgorged its clear waters into a pool. This vanished under a lip in the ice shelf, while sea lions and seals were gathered on the nearby rocks. Presumably the waters carved a channel under the ice which met with the ocean somewhere further out, providing them with a source of food.

There was a warmth in the air, emanating from the very rocks under our feet – enough for us to shed the thickest of our furs, even though the ice shelf was a mere hundred yards from our camp. Farther inland there were thick green and yellow tussocks of grass interspersed with white flowers, whilst beyond was a dense pine forest covering most of the island, which rose about halfway up Ballung Mountain. I licked my dry lips, staring at the smoking top of the mountain, and knew that was where I would find Bruar. Assuming I was fit enough to make the journey.

Etta was sitting next to me, warming her thin bones as she held out her gnarled hands towards the flames, the only one of us who didn't seem to feel the warmth of the island. In an undertone, I continued to tell her what I had seen with the Sight whilst unconscious on her sled.

Etta sighed. "Heidr worries me. Sinarr the Cold One used scrying magic to track your progress towards Romsdahl. Heidr uses the same skills, though her abilities far outstrip anyone else because she can perceive the past, present and future. You'll recall me telling you Adalrikr was known during the War as Vashtas Flayer of Souls, the First of the Sundered? His right-hand man was Nishrall, one of the Sundered now gathered to him in Vorund Fastness. It's interesting he's chosen to use his original name. I wonder what Adalrikr thinks of that."

"Did you say Heidr can see into the future?" I asked, working through what Etta had told me. "Doesn't that mean she can see Johan's every move in the coming battle?"

"To an extent. However, the future is extremely hard to read, unlike the past, which is fixed and set in stone. The ability to revisit the past is still useful – you can learn from your mistakes and understand exactly what transpired at a particular moment. The future is yet to happen and is affected by a great many things. This is the problem with scrying when you look to the future – it's all possibilities, no certainties. Heidr was known as Celembine during the War of the Avatars and was one of Vashtas' closest advisors. Her skills made her a powerful ally but Vashtas understood her limitations. The future is never pre-determined – it's important you understand that. Your actions matter, always."

Meinolf and Matthildr were dishing out bowls of stew and I gratefully took mine, greedily spooning fish, potatoes and onions into my mouth. I felt some strength returning to my limbs, clearing my bowl before they'd finished serving the rest of the crew. I thought on Etta's words and on what Heidr had said – *events swirl and form around this young man. He is the pebble that causes the mountain landslide, the first spark that lights the fire.* It was strange to be spoken about in this way and disquieting to think what else Heidr might have seen. *Wreathed in shadow.* Was she talking about the Weeping Warrior or something else?

Ulfarr and Myr returned from scouting the land around our camp and sat down to eat with the rest of *Stormweaver's* crew, while Skari and Jolinn took their turn on watch. With questions swirling around my mind I rose and walked over to Jolinn, falling in step with her as she started her patrol.

"No sign of Hasteinn's crew," I said.

Jolinn shook her head. "Perhaps we'll be lucky. Maybe they died out there on the ice."

"Perhaps. I had a … strange encounter, through the Sight, whilst I was away …"

"You're not dreaming about me are you?" Jolinn asked with a sly grin, which widened when she saw my embarrassed expression. "I'm sorry – that was a joke and I'm not even sure I want to know the answer. Please, forget I said anything."

"No, I mean I found myself sorting through the past and what led me on my journey here. I've spent the last year looking back at what happened to me and what I've become, as well as the people I cared about who've died. I keep trying to feel comfortable in my new skin but it's not as easy as I thought."

Jolinn stopped and turned to look at me directly. "The past shapes us whilst our choices define who we are. I was raised in a brothel in Olt and that could have been my life. Instead, I chose a different path, proving my skill with a blade and even earning the name Hrodidottir from my worthless father."

"I like that. Our choices defining who we are, rather than what happened to us. While I was … away … I realised I needed to apply that lesson to my own life. No more looking back."

"Exactly. I know there's a heavy weight on your shoulders but that's why we're here. Me, Ulfarr, Ekkill, Etta and the rest of Aerinndis' crew. We're all here to help you carry the burden."

I had to swallow down a lump in my throat at Jolinn's words, feeling unworthy of such loyalty and their faith in me. "Thank you."

I returned to the camp, deep in thought. People looked at Jolinn and saw the fierce shieldmaiden but she was insightful and perhaps understood me better than anyone else here on this island. Aerinndis' crew had put up tents and, bone tired, I thought of clambering straight inside to sleep. Instead, I stared up at the sky, watching the stars emerge as dusk crept across the island. Nearby Matthildr was sitting with Feyotra, her head resting on her shoulder as they also drank in the view together. The northerly constellation of Elphinas was lost beyond Ballung's smouldering top. However, I could make out the bright stars of Altandu to the west and the dense cluster of red that marked Ceren's constellation to the east. A full moon rode low on the horizon, bathing us in its yellowish light.

Eventually, weariness fell upon me and I retired to one of the tents, leaving *Stormweaver's* crew chatting in low tones as they sat around the fire, reflecting on their journey and discussing their plans for exploring the island. I wrapped myself under my blankets, trying to get comfortable. In moments I was asleep and for once the Sight did not intrude on my dreams. Instead, when the camp was quieter and most people had retired for the night, I stirred as a hand stroked my shoulders, tracing through my furs the long scars left by Tyrfingr's hot iron. Jolinn's arm wrapped itself around my chest.

"Sorry, did I wake you?" her voice whispered in my ear.

"Yes, but it's alright."

"You looked cold."

I placed my hand over hers and the two of us slept side by side, each keeping the other warm during the long night.

***

The following morning our exploration party was ready to travel long before dawn, giving us plenty of time to argue. Matthildr and Feyotra were sitting nearby, watching proceedings with wry smiles.

"I'm not saying that. I'm saying this isn't the place to take a woman … of … advancing years," Ulfarr explained, clutching at his hair in frustration.

"Perhaps you'd like me to tend your cook fire? Maybe I could make you something nice for when you return?" Etta replied tartly.

"Ekkill?" Ulfarr appealed.

The curly-haired warrior laughed and shook his head, not willing to get into an argument with his paymaster. Ulfarr turned to me, pleading. I chewed my bottom lip, sharing Ulfarr's misgivings. I'd expected Etta to remain in the camp and act as our advisor, not find her dressed and ready to travel into the interior of the island when we rose to break our fast.

I took a deep breath. "Etta, is this really wise? Ulfarr's right. We don't know what the going will be like or how far we'll have to travel. If the terrain is difficult it might be … hard for you to keep up."

"Humph. Based on that analysis you shouldn't be going either. You've barely recovered from your fever and *your* weak constitution might mean adding several uncomfortable nights to this journey." That stung. We wouldn't be here if it wasn't for me and now Etta was suggesting I was the one they should leave behind. Her good eye twinkled with mischief as I found myself lost for words.

Aerinndis laughed. "Anyone with any sense is going to remain here, with the ship. If there's any sign of trouble I'll be ordering my crew back onto the ice and away from this accursed place."

"That may be so. However, I'm coming and that's final."

Ulfarr looked nonplussed as he let the matter drop,

his glare leaving me in no doubt he thought I could have argued his case more strongly. I busied myself checking I had everything in my pack, Jolinn next to me with a smirk on her face.

"Let's get going," muttered Ulfarr, shouldering his gear.

***

Ekkill led the way into the forest, towards Ballung Mountain, scouting ahead and soon vanishing completely once he entered the tree line. Ulfarr led the rest of our group at a more measured pace, Skari at his side, Jolinn and Myr watching our backs. Etta and I were herded into the centre of our small group – obviously we were the ones who needed protection. I glanced back at Jolinn, wondering if that was how she saw me. We'd shared our blankets and furs for warmth throughout the voyage north but last night had been different. Had she been trying to make me feel better after her careless remark?

"How are you doing?" I asked Etta.

She glared back. "That's the third time you've asked me and our camp is still in sight. I'm. Fine. You should be the one worrying. You've already broken into a sweat."

I watched Etta move with both surprise and envy. Although she relied heavily on her stick it didn't prevent her maintaining a steady pace and she never lost her footing on the uneven ground. I found myself reappraising her, wondering if she really could be as old as people thought. Had she lied about her age, perhaps to appear wiser when she first came to the court of my grandfather? She'd been described as old back then, and that was over fifty years ago. I sighed, reflecting that whichever way I looked at things, Etta was far older than me and, frankly, her early pace was starting to show me up. I thought back on our conversation aboard *Stormweaver*, feeling uneasy as I remembered how evasive Etta had been about the reasons for her improved health. Why would she refuse to tell me about that? I knew

Etta was prepared to use whatever means were necessary in her fight against Adalrikr but normally she was open about her underhand methods and tactics. The fact she had refused to divulge this particular secret must mean she knew I wouldn't approve, and that worried me.

I wiped my brow and concentrated on keeping up with Ulfarr as we continued through the forest. Walking under the canopy of the tall fir trees I caught a glimpse of the green necklace Jora had given Etta back in Romsdahl, one edge slipping out from inside her jerkin, bright even in the gloomy light of the forest. Etta furtively tucked the jewel away, glancing at me as she did so.

"Say nothing," she hissed.

"Myshall's bane, why would you bring something so valuable out *here*?" I whispered.

"Safer here where I can watch it, rather than with Aerinndis' crew. I wouldn't want to put temptation in their way. Plus, you never know when a fabulously valuable necklace might come in handy during our negotiations."

I frowned. "That wasn't part of the plan."

"It doesn't hurt to have something to fall back on," Etta replied, with a knowing look.

The air in the forest was close and warm, a thick layer of pine needles carpeting the ground and softening our footfalls. Where the trees were thinner ferns and grasses sprang up, reaching for the meagre northern light. Already some of the ferns were dying back, many of their leaves brown and curling, reflecting the short summer season. Birds sang as they marked out territory, hidden in the branches, occasionally flitting from tree to tree.

After a short while Ekkill appeared, shinning his way down from one of the taller pines. "Nothing ahead of us that I can see. No signs of habitation, just these woods as far as the eye can see till we reach the mountain."

Ulfarr nodded in the direction we'd been travelling. "We on the right track?"

"The mountain is dead ahead, although I don't think we'll reach it before nightfall."

We moved deeper into the forest, resting at noon to eat while sitting on the trunk of a fallen tree. There was a quiet beauty to this place and I felt a quiver of excitement knowing I was following in Sigborn's footsteps. I took another bite of freshly baked bread, cooked by Haddr that morning before we'd left camp. It wouldn't be long before our fresh stores were depleted and we'd be on dried rations and anything we managed to catch in the forest. I savoured the food, grateful to rest my aching feet until Ulfarr gave the order to move on.

We wended our way through the trees in single file, this time Ekkill leading the way whilst Ulfarr scouted further afield. None of us spoke as we headed deeper into the woods and under the dense tree canopy it didn't take long before the light started to fade, draining everything of colour. Up ahead we could see there was a clearing, illuminated by a shaft of light from the setting sun. A figure appeared in front of us and my hand was halfway to my sword before I recognised Ulfarr. He raised his hand as he jogged towards us, his face drawn and tense.

"What is it?" asked Ekkill, peering behind Ulfarr to see if he was being followed.

"You'd better see for yourself," Ulfarr replied, looking grim.

We walked slowly towards the clearing, my heart beating hard. There was a smell hanging in the air, growing stronger with each step – putrefying flesh. I swallowed hard. The space in the woods was thick with flies, their buzzing setting my teeth on edge.

"Gods," muttered Jolinn, staring around her, eyes wide with horror.

I trod on something soft and glanced down, stepping back with a sharp cry. My foot left an imprint in a pile of matted blood-soaked hair. What had once been a head lay smashed to pulp on the ground, a trail of teeth and brains leading to a twisted broken body, missing half its limbs. A cloud of flies rose into the air at my intrusion, flying around my head, forcing me to swat them away.

"Welcome to the Fire Isle," breathed Skari, hammer ready in his hand.

We counted a dozen corpses, although in their mangled state it was hard to be sure. Several trees were snapped in half – their trunks rooted firmly in the ground, terminating in a mass of shattered wood and jagged splinters. Huge furrows had been ploughed into the centre of the clearing, piles of freshly upturned earth mixed with body parts and the shredded canvas of a tent stretching out in front of the broken trees.

"Only one thing could have done this," Etta muttered.

"Dragons," I said, pointing towards the broken firs. "They were attacked from the air – the beast burst through the trees and was on them before they even knew they were under attack."

"Vorund Clan," added Ulfarr, lifting up a broken shield painted with a black bear.

I swore. "Wonderful. Hasteinn's here already."

"They gained ground as we feared, by abandoning their ships on the ice," said Etta. "We were also unlucky, having to work our way around the crevasse. If they chanced on a more direct path they could easily have overtaken us."

"Looks like their luck ran out," observed Skari, wrinkling his nose at the smell.

"Is Hasteinn among them?" Jolinn wondered, gingerly rolling over a corpse with the toe of her boot.

"My guess is this was a scouting party," Ulfarr said. "They're only wearing light leather armour, not the expensive equipment you'd expect to see on a future jarl. He'll be somewhere else on the island, well-guarded by his crew if he has any sense."

"We have to move on," Ekkill said, pocketing some

coins from the purse of a fallen warrior. “It’ll be dark soon and we need to find somewhere to set up camp.”

“They obviously thought this was a good place,” Skari remarked, spitting on the ground next to him.

Ulfarr glanced at his friend. “Let’s go.”

CHAPTER 48

Randall and Kurt followed the winding staircase down into the bowels of Vorund Fastness. *Not exactly my favourite place. Still, you don't get to decide the location of the meeting when summoned by your king.*

Adalrikr was waiting for them, standing in front of the coiling shadows that dominated the centre of the underground chamber. The Six stood guard, each of them holding a prisoner. The flow of tributes from conquered clans had ended with the siege; the dungeons where they were being held almost empty. Randall caught one woman looking at him, her face tear-stained. He turned away, swallowing as he walked past. *Can't help you, my love, not even if I wanted to.*

"Randall, Kurt, welcome."

"Sire," Randall bowed low, ignoring the protest from his knees. Kurt followed suit.

Adalrikr was surrounded by his now familiar companions at court, his consort Hallerna ever-present at his side. Finnaril gave Randall a disquieting grin whilst Heidr, Solvia and Nishrall stood together a little way off, whispering in the shadows. Vedisra, standing to Adalrikr's right, was watching them with narrowed eyes. Behind Adalrikr, Orn towered over them all, his face impassive, arms folded over his massive chest.

Adalrikr dabbed the wound on his cheek with a handkerchief as he beckoned them closer. *Why* hasn't *that healed yet? Is there something wrong with him?* Randall kept his eyes fixed on his king, avoiding the swirling darkness behind him, as one of the tributes started to cry, mumbling incoherent words as they pleaded for mercy.

"Tell me, how goes the defence of our city?" asked Adalrikr, ignoring the prisoner.

Randall and Kurt gave him an honest account, detailing how the night time repairs were slowing the breach of the wall. The implications were clear – if this stalemate continued the Brotherhood would eventually break through, leaving the city of Vorund vulnerable to attack and potentially forcing them back to the Inner Keep.

"How long?" asked Nishrall.

"Impossible to say," Randall explained. "Most likely this will go on for months."

"We should attack them and end this now," counselled Orn in a low voice, grating like crushed stone.

Adalrikr shook his head. "We've discussed this before and my answer is the same – no. Our armies are similarly sized and Johan's defences well dug. Even if we win the battle the cost will be too high. We will act as planned, waiting this out. They'll not breach the wall before winter, will they, Randall?"

"Not unless they increase the rate at which they can reload their machines of war," Randall replied. "Our walls will see winter come, I'm sure of that."

Adalrikr turned to Orn. "You see, Cousin. We have time yet to weaken the resolve of our foes as they shiver, sheltering against the wind and snow. When the time is right and Geilir's army is with us, we will strike."

"And if we strike now?" pressed Orn.

Heidr stepped forwards, long hair unkempt, those wide eyes giving the impression her thoughts were elsewhere as she spoke with a soft, ethereal voice. "Launch the attack before winter and there will be blood."

"*Meaning*?" Orn snorted, shaking his head. Vedisra sneered, looking at the other woman with contempt, although Heidr appeared unconcerned.

"Whoever leads the charge will die. The Brotherhood

love Johan the Landless Jarl and will fight to the death to defend him. We might prevail, although in the aftermath I see a field of corpses, stretching out beyond the walls of Vorund Fastness. Broken warriors and blood-soaked earth leading all the way to Johan's lines, Vorund's strength spent."

Randall exchanged a look with Kurt. *That doesn't sound good.*

From the expression on Orn's face, he clearly thought the same. "And if we wait for Geilir to return from Norlhast?"

Heidr shook her head, absent-mindedly sweeping her long hair out of her face. "Events in Norlhast are finely balanced, with many possible outcomes. I would need to spend much more time scrying to be able to tell you anything with greater certainty."

"You tell us precious little, for someone of such supposed skill," mocked Vedisra.

"This debate is over," Adalrikr declared, ignoring her remark. "There will be no attack against the Brotherhood before Geilir lands on our shores and we have enough warriors to ensure the outcome of the battle is in our favour."

"What if Geilir doesn't return?" asked Nishrall.

A shadow passed across Adalrikr's face. "I am unaccustomed to every decision I make being challenged. I am your king – you would all do well to remember that."

Nishrall was unbowed. "You gathered your court together to act as your advisors. We would be remiss in our duties if we didn't explore every possibility."

Adalrikr's eyes narrowed, distorting his handsome features. "You have advised. I have decided. This conversation is at an end. Randall, return to the walls and continue to supervise their repair. Guards, bring the tributes forward."

Randall and Kurt ascended the steps as quickly as they could without seeming indecorous. Slowly, the fearful shouts, cries and screams of the tributes began to fade.

"Gods, what're they doing to them?" hissed Kurt,

slowing his climb.

"You want to go back down and find out?" replied Randall. "We have our orders."

Kurt hesitated. A man gave a long chilling wail of despair, his thin voice reaching them from the depths below. The noise suddenly stopped, the silence that followed somehow far worse.

"Come on," said Randall. "I don't pretend to understand everything I see. All I know is our king uses magic to build his kingdom and secure our victories. We rule Riltbalt, Reavesburg, Norlhast, Vittag and Helsburg. Name me another clan chief who's achieved more."

"This is blood magic," said Kurt.

More cries reached them as they stood on the staircase – a woman this time, the words indistinct. *I don't need to make out the words to understand what she's saying. She's pleading for her life.*

"Joarr was right," Kurt continued. "None of Adalrikr's advisors are from the leading houses of the Vorund Clan. Who even *are* these people?"

"We were there tonight," Randall countered.

"To receive our orders," the younger man replied.

Randall placed a hand on Kurt's shoulder, gently turning his second so they were looking eye to eye. "You need to have a care. We've served together for a long time and I know you have my back, so let me give you a piece of advice. Adalrikr is our king. If you criticise his decisions or those he chooses to surround him at court, that's treason. Do you understand what I'm telling you?"

Kurt swallowed. "Randall, none of this is right. You know it as well as I do."

The two men climbed the rest of the stairs in silence.

***

I stirred under my blanket, the intrusion of Randall's encounter with Adalrikr leaving me cold. Jolinn mumbled something next to me, turning over in her sleep. I blinked, eyes adjusting to the darkness and the light from the moon filtering down through the trees. A little way off, Ekkill was watching the camp as the rest of us slept. I rose and began to buckle my sword belt, the sound waking Jolinn.

"What are you doing? It's still dark."

"I can't sleep. I need some air."

"And what if you run into Hasteinn during your stroll? Stop. You're not thinking straight."

Jolinn's eyes were bright despite the gloom of the forest, their blue hues washed white by the moon. She reached out and took my hand in hers. Without thinking I stepped forwards and kissed Jolinn for the first time, there in that forest filled with danger and death. Her lips parted in an 'O' of surprise, warm and soft against my own. I kissed her again, firmer this time, before leading her by the hand deeper into the forest. Ekkill watched us with a smirk as he waved us on, allowing us some privacy as we vanished into the trees.

"You're full of surprises," Jolinn muttered, breaking away from my hold when the two of us were alone. She stood there with her hands on her hips and a wry grin on her face. "So, what is this? A kiss and a warm embrace are all very well but is this just a stolen moment?"

"I've been living in the past for such a long time I'd forgotten how to live. We understand each other, and that's a rare thing. It's taken me until the last few days to realise this."

"You're not as smart as everyone makes out, are you?" Jolinn replied, eyes glittering.

"I'm not ... Always myself," I explained. "I experience so many other lives through the Sight. It's hard to hold onto everything and remember who I am amongst all those other people. Sometimes I feel lost and it's a struggle to retain a ... a sense of myself."

"And what does Rothgar Kolfinnarson want?" Jolinn asked, moving in closer.

"This," I told her, leaning upwards and kissing her.

Jolinn was strong, pushing me backwards against a tree as she returned my kisses with her own. My hand traced the back of her head, her normally close-cropped blonde hair grown longer during our voyage. She pulled me closer, bodies touching, her breath hot on my face.

"You can be very manipulative," she whispered between her kisses. "The trouble is, I don't mind."

***

I disentangled myself from Jolinn's long limbs, rose and dressed, aware we needed to be back at camp before morning. I paused, remembering Ekkill had seen us leave together. He was no fool, although he wasn't exactly a gossip. Keeping secrets was second nature for a spy and I doubted Ekkill cared who I slept with. Anyway, it would be impossible to keep my relationship with Jolinn secret whilst we were all travelling together. I smiled as I realised I didn't care.

In the heat of passion I hadn't been concerned when Jolinn saw the wasted state of my muscles and how they twisted my back out of shape. I remembered her eyes widening as she removed my clothes, fingers tracing the web of scars, uncovering a story of torture and torment written large across my body. She hadn't shied away from me but now I felt self-conscious, noting how I compared so ill-favourably to Jolinn's lithe, athletic build.

Jolinn sighed, covering herself with her travelling cloak, rolling onto her side to look at me. "Going so soon? There's still a few hours before the sun rises."

"We should get back to the camp. Like you said, we don't want to run into one of Hasteinn's patrols."

Jolinn propped up her head under her hand, bathed in the patches of moonlight that reached us through the trees. "What's wrong?"

"Nothing's wrong," I replied as I turned my back on her and pulled my shirt over my head. I felt cold and exposed all of a sudden and I tensed when Jolinn padded across the forest floor and put her arms around me.

"Does my touch appal you so much? You weren't complaining earlier tonight."

I turned and embraced Jolinn, the thrill of desire warring with a sense of revulsion at how I saw myself. At how she must see me. I knew I should answer her question but the words wouldn't come and I turned my head away, a flush of embarrassment colouring my face. Jolinn's hand slid under my shirt, tracing my twisted spine.

"Look at me." Her eyes softened as I looked into her face. "Do you think this matters to me?"

"It should. The Laws of Reave are clear where my place is these days. Chief, jarl, warrior, noble, karl, merchant, tradesman, thrall ... They all come before a cripple. You could do better."

"According to the Laws of Reave I shouldn't bear arms," Jolinn replied. "Don't quote tradition at me and tell me what I should do and think. Times are changing, Rothgar. I choose you. I choose the person who understands me."

"You have terrible taste," I told her, finding my voice despite the lump in my throat.

"Let me be the judge of that," she whispered, drawing me into a long, lingering kiss.

CHAPTER 49

Djuri rose at dawn, leaving Nereth sleeping in her chambers. He returned to his own rooms where he washed, making himself presentable for his duties as Tyrfingr's guard. It was a task he shared with a number of warriors, including Galin Ironfist, but Djuri was the only member of the Reavesburg Clan afforded the honour. *A perfect opportunity to strike at the Vorund Clan.* Another part of Djuri told him this wasn't the time. He still burned with shame whenever he thought about how easily Tyrfingr had bested him in the duelling circle and sighed deeply as he finished dressing.

A servant had prepared Djuri's breakfast, which he ate without enthusiasm, hardly tasting the eggs or fresh bread. Full of melancholy, he walked to Tyrfingr's chambers, relieving the Vorund warrior on guard outside as he took up his position. Servants came and went and Djuri's legs grew stiff as he continued to stand at the doorway until, eventually, Tyrfingr emerged. With his long, lank hair he was unprepossessing at first sight, until you saw those eyes. Djuri was now sensitive to the scent of ataraxia and he caught the familiar cinnamon notes on the jarl's breath as he greeted him. Together, they walked towards the Great Hall, where Tyrfingr took his seat on Reave's Chair, a table with a bottle of wine and ornate crystal glass set at his side. A servant poured some of the wine and Tyrfingr beckoned Djuri over to taste it. A fine vintage, Djuri had no doubt, though he preferred ale. The crystal glass, a prized relic from the Age of Glory that Tyrfingr had brought with him from Vorund, was worth more than the contents of the cellar under the keep. Djuri took great care when he set it back down on the table.

This morning Tyrfingr was fulfilling his duties as jarl by hearing any disputes amongst the clan. Djuri groaned inwardly as the doors swung open to reveal a long queue of farmers, merchants and even a couple of Vorund warriors, all waiting to plead their case. Tyrfingr took a sip of wine and waved the first of his visitors forwards. Djuri didn't really listen to what was being discussed, focusing instead on how each person bore themselves and whether they carried any weapons. The guards outside should have done their job and searched each person – Djuri was there to ensure Tyrfingr's safety in case anything had been missed. He smiled to himself, appreciating the irony.

The morning wore on, full of boundary disputes, grazing rights and, in the case of the two Vorund warriors, which of them had won the right to propose to a merchant's daughter in Noln. Servants brought food and more wine to Tyrfingr as he heard each case and dispensed his justice. Some left the Great Hall happy, others cursed their ill-fortune. Aside from the small morsels Djuri tried as his taster, no one offered him anything as he continued to watch. The final visitor was an old woman, bent with age, long white hair a flow of tangled curls down her back.

"Ingunn, mother of Lundvarr of Noln," announced one of the guards as the old woman walked the length of the hall. Tyrfingr's head snapped up at the mention of her name.

"Ingunn, welcome to my hall," he said, standing and offering her a short bow – more respect than he had shown anyone else that day.

"Blackeyes," she replied, her voice thin. "I think you can guess why I'm here. I demand justice for my murdered son."

"Lundvarr wasn't murdered," Tyrfingr corrected as he took his seat. "He was found guilty of aiding the escape of fugitives. Fugitives whose capture I had ordered, personally. He betrayed his king and paid the price for treachery against the crown."

"You lie," Ingunn hissed. "My son was loyal – loyalty that came with a heavy price. He was ostracised in Noln for pledging himself to Adalrikr. Despite that, he kept the port open and trade flowing, to your benefit, until your men killed him. That was no execution – I saw the body of my son. He had been ... defiled, the body desecrated and ... left mutilated beyond recognition. Do you know how I knew it was him? The ring, the one my son wore on his little finger since the age of thirteen. His face was ... gone ... but that ring – I'd know it anywhere."

Tyrfingr invited Ingunn to take a seat at one of the benches arranged in a semi-circle in front of the dais. Ingunn remained standing.

"The men who ... interrogated your son did so under my command. If you denounce their actions you, by implication, criticise me. Since I rule in Adalrikr's name, you are challenging the power of the throne itself."

Ingunn gave a long wheezy chuckle. "Why should I care about that? What could you do to me that's worse than what's already been done? I buried my husband twenty years ago and now I've lost my son and, with him, my future."

A trace of a smile played on Tyrfingr's lips. "You have more spirit than your son. Lundvarr's sentence of death was justified, on that I will hear no argument. However, the manner in which it was carried out was ... unfortunate and, for that, I'm willing to apologise. I can do nothing more, because the man who killed your son died shortly afterwards in an ambush, launched by the very people they were sent to capture." Ingunn stood there, glowering at Tyrfingr, trying to work out if he was mocking her.

Tyrfingr looked at Djuri. "You were there, weren't you, Turncloak? Would you say Lundvarr received a fair hearing?"

Djuri stared at Tyrfingr, grinding his teeth as he fought to prevent himself drawing his sword and stabbing him as he sat in Reave's Chair. His mind swirled with images of Lundvarr, trapped and terrified, being eaten alive by Kolsveinn. *Those screams, they were hardly human by the end.*

"Djuri, I asked you a question," Tyrfingr said, his voice taking on a hard edge.

Djuri cleared his throat. "Lundvarr was guilty. He told us exactly where the fugitives would be and we caught them in the act of buying passage, just as Lundvarr had said. He helped them charter the vessel, of that I have no doubt. We tried to capture them but in the fight that followed Kolsveinn and the warriors under his command were killed. I was the sole survivor."

"You see, Ingunn –" Tyrfingr began. Djuri raised his voice and spoke over him, addressing himself to the older woman.

"What happened to your son, it was wrong. He'd earned a quick, clean death after helping us. Instead, Kolsveinn went too far and tortured him beyond anything I've ever seen or wish to see again. I stood there and watched it all happen and didn't act to stop it. I should have done something – I wish I could go back and put that right."

Tyrfingr looked sidelong at Djuri with those awful black eyes. "As I was saying, I am willing to apologise for the manner of your son's death. The man responsible is dead, I can do nothing more to hold him to account." Ingunn's eyes flicked to Djuri. "No," said Tyrfingr, guessing her intent. "Kolsveinn was the man in command and it was his responsibility."

"I demand restitution. Our family built up our business in Noln over generations and now we've lost everything. The tolls Lundvarr exacted for unloading cargo and the mortgages on the trading ships should have passed to me. Instead, they've been seized by the Vorund Clan, often going unenforced or, worse still, pocketed when they should be filling your coffers. Tell me, how has the flow of coin between Noln and Ulfkell's Keep fared since the death of my son?"

Tyrfingr sat in silence for a time. "Such things should not have happened. Your son's property should have passed to you as his family, in accordance with the law. I can rectify this ... oversight, if you ensure Noln's taxes are paid in full. As Noln's elder, you would be well-placed to restore order in the town and see such things put right."

Ingunn was taken aback, finally sitting down on the bench as she mulled over Tyrfingr's words. "Noln's *elder*?" she whispered.

"That's right. I can think of no one better qualified to handle such matters than the woman who helped build Noln into the trading port it is today."

Djuri imagined Ingunn's expectations of what would happen when she met Tyrfingr in the Great Hall were low. Tyrfingr was offering her blood money in recompense for her son, although it was little more than she was entitled to. Ingunn's frown deepened as she considered the weregild.

"Is that a yes?" Tyrfingr asked gently.

Ingunn nodded and rose. "I'll have those terms in writing, if it pleases you, my lord."

Tyrfingr nodded and called for paper and ink, sealing his decree with the mark of his own ring. Djuri could see the emotions playing on Ingunn's face as she stood there, waiting for Tyrfingr to finish. Djuri took the parchment and handed it to the woman, who snatched at it, as if worried it would disappear if she hesitated.

Ingunn spat at Djuri's feet. "Shame on you, Turncloak. It's down to people like you that we're forced to scrape, bow and beg to the likes of him. You're not welcome back in Noln, not as long as I'm its elder."

Tyrfingr chuckled quietly as Ingunn made her slow way to the door, clutching her precious parchment. "A little unfair, I suppose, although you *did* watch the murder of her son." Djuri licked his lips, unsure if Tyrfingr expected him to reply, feeling sick to his stomach, hating what he had become. "All this will pass," Tyrfingr continued. "A time will come when all anyone can remember is the rule of Adalrikr, Laskar united as a great northern kingdom rivalling Oomrhat, Mirtan or Beria. How do you think those countries came into being? It always begins with conquering, the spilling of blood and the strong exercising their might to rule over the weak. Try not to look so uncomfortable – you've chosen the right side."

Djuri said nothing, the day wearing on until Galin relieved him before the evening's feasting in the hall. Djuri saw Ulf waving to him, although he merely nodded in greeting before walking out into the night, having no appetite or desire for company. Outside it was raining and he raised his hood as he walked the walls of Ulfkell's Keep, looking out over the town of Reavesburg below. He watched the yellow glowing lights emanating from various houses and inns, signs of other lives, making the best of things under Vorund rule. *Am I any different to them?* Djuri stood there for a long while, lost in thought as the rain continued to fall.

CHAPTER 50

"He's back with us." Skari's voice, not bothering to hide his irritation. I coughed and sat up, rubbing sleep from my eyes. I felt exhausted.

"Every day we lose like this puts us in danger," Skari was saying to Ulfarr. "We're out here in the wilds, exposed and vulnerable, and the Princeling here decides to take a nap for a whole day. It's madness."

"You would do well to remember this is Rothgar's journey, not yours," Etta retorted.

Skari hawked and spat on the ground. "I haven't forgotten. I just wish I'd stayed with Johan."

Jolinn passed me a waterskin and I took a few sips, my throat parched. "I'm sorry. I didn't realise I'd been away for so long."

"Can't it be controlled?" asked Ekkill. "I thought Rothgar had a potion that dulled his abilities? Skari's right, we need to keep moving. It was one thing while this was happening on the ship but out here on foot it's a different matter. Are you expecting us to carry him all the way to Ballung Mountain?"

"There are advantages to being able to see more than what's in front of your face, Ekkill," Etta replied.

"I can speak for myself," I said, taking another sip of water as my head began to clear.

Skari laughed. "Great. You can speak but you can't walk – ideal for an expedition into dangerous territory. This is like heading into Tullen all over again."

"That's enough," snapped Ulfarr. "Don't forget it was the same ability that saved our lives on our mission to

Romsdahl."

Skari shook his head and stalked away as Ekkill walked by, clapping me on the shoulder. "Makes a change for me to be the popular one. Keep aggravating Skari and that vein in his forehead might just explode."

"Wonderful," I muttered. I didn't even care that Ingunn was now the elder of Noln – what did that matter to me, far away in the frozen north? The harsh truth was the Sight was growing harder to control, if I ever truly had mastery of the gift. I was placing my companions at risk and we were none the wiser about the dangers surrounding us. Much as I didn't like to admit it, Skari was right.

"Don't even *think* about taking ataraxia," said Etta, as if reading my thoughts. "We need to be able to communicate with Johan's army. We can discuss this again once our quest is complete. A few extra days in the wild are worth the risk."

I glowered at her as she looked back at me, defiant. "Aren't you concerned at how hard it's become to control?"

"Even that tells us something, namely that the walls between the realms grow thin as the Tear widens. As your connections between those with the Sight strengthen you're drawn away more frequently."

"Is that helpful?"

"It is if you want to know what's happening in the wider world. We need to know what awaits us on our return from the Fire Isle."

I didn't reply as I quickly packed away my bedroll and ate breakfast; dried fruits and the gloomily familiar sea biscuits soaked in water, Haddr's fresh bread a distant memory. With first light we continued our circuit of the mountain and I fought to remain in control of the Sight.

***

"I was worried about you," Jolinn said quietly as we walked through the forest with Etta, Myr at our back, Ekkill and Ulfarr ranging further ahead.

"That's very sweet but I'm fine," Etta quipped, Myr's

sombre face breaking into a rare smile.

"I'm alright," I told her, giving Etta a dark look as she grinned back. I reached out and took Jolinn's hand, a gesture that surprised both of us. She gave my hand a gentle squeeze before releasing her grip.

"What?" I muttered as I caught Etta's sidelong glance.

"Nothing."

We walked in silence for a time, Ulfarr and Ekkill just about remaining in sight, moving through the forest, bows ready in case we encountered more of Hasteinn's men. Etta leaned heavily on her stick but she still moved quickly, the old crone less of a handicap on this journey than I was. I shook my head, my thoughts drawn to Jora's emerald necklace, which Etta had been so insistent on taking with her. There was a reason why she'd asked for that specific piece before leaving Romsdahl. Something told me there was no chance she would barter such a thing away, in the unlikely event it was of interest to Bruar in the first place. Once again Reavesburg's spymaster was keeping secrets from me.

A shadow passed quickly overhead and I looked up, peering anxiously through the trees, heart hammering.

"What was that?" gasped Jolinn.

I pressed my back against the trunk of a pine, all of us scurrying to find shelter as we peered through the branches. I could see a patchwork of blue sky between the tops of the firs, clear and cloudless. My mouth was dry and it took me a few moments to slow my breathing. I waited, hand on the hilt of my sword more for the sense of comfort than for any practical use if this came to a fight. Time was measured in the powerful beats of my heart, a rushing noise filling my ears as I found the strength of will to stay still. The wait stretched on, no sign of the creature returning. Slowly, I felt myself grow calm, part of me wondering if I had imagined the whole thing. I shook my head, prising myself away from the tree, rolling my shoulders and stretching my back to undo the kinks from remaining in one position for so long. I took a few hesitant steps, careful that my footfalls made no noise as I crept forwards.

Ekkill and Ulfarr had both returned, their ashen faces proving what we had just seen wasn't the work of my over-active imagination.

"Did anyone get a proper look at what that was?" asked Ekkill.

Etta shook her head. "No, although I think we all know."

"Let's keep moving," said Ulfarr. "Standing still cowering in the forest won't do us much good."

The trees started to thin as we nervously climbed higher into the foothills, Etta panting with the effort although she shook her head when Myr offered her his hand. I glanced back, taking a brief opportunity to catch my breath as I looked at the dense green forest. A few birds wheeled, high in the air. Higher still, I thought I saw an eagle circling the mountain, great wings outstretched as it rode on invisible currents of air. I thought of Sigborn Reaveson, trapped on the island with no means of escape. Had he felt the same fear as he explored the Fire Isle, the last survivor of his doomed expedition? Nearby, Skari was making use of an outcrop of rock to empty his bladder as we all paused our climb. I hoped it wasn't some sacred stone, dedicated to Bruar. That would be a disastrous start ...

We moved on through the foothills once more, looking in vain for some sign of a path leading up into the mountain. Occasionally, I cast a nervous glance behind me or up at the skies but aside from the eagle, soaring high above, we appeared to be alone. It was well past noon and the sun was starting its journey westwards. I refilled my waterskin at a stream and rested for a moment, eating some of my provisions as I tried to work out how much further I would be able to go before dark. Whilst I didn't want to admit Etta's stamina outstripped my own I was going to have to concede defeat soon. As I stared at Ballung Mountain it belched forth more smoke, the ground trembling under my feet.

By early evening we started to look for somewhere suitable to make camp, aware the light was fading, the sun low on the horizon above the distant ice shelf. I found a small rocky ridge which provided shelter from the wind, surrounded by trees to help hide our presence. A fire was out of the question with Hasteinn looking for us but when I placed my hand against the rock it felt warm. This whole island was an oasis in the desert of the sea ice, a green jewel full of life in the far-flung north. We decided to stop there, although there was still enough light to travel. We were unlikely to find a better spot and, with a weary sigh, I dropped my pack and sat down. I ate some hard cheese with a few strips of chewy dried meat, which hardly made the meal more inspiring. I washed it down with water, thinking about making my bed for the night.

"I wonder what Alcor is going to make of you?" said a woman, sitting cross-legged in front of me.

I sprang to my feet with a high-pitched shriek, cracking my head on the stony outcrop under which I was sheltering. Jolinn dropped her waterskin and Ulfarr looked stunned at how the woman had slipped past him whilst he was patrolling the camp. Only Ekkill remained calm, snatching out his bow and training an arrow on our intruder's heart.

"And who do we have here?" the young woman asked, head cocked on one side, long black hair hanging loose over one shoulder. Her eyes were a striking deep purple, which glowed softly as if lit from within. She was dressed lightly, in a white blouse with a green jerkin and breeches, tall brown leather boots completing the practical outfit.

I blinked, seeing stars, and rubbed the back of my head. "I'm Rothgar Kolfinnarson. I'm here with my friends, seeking help for my people."

"Please, relax and sit down," the woman replied. "Put

your weapons away. If I wanted to do you harm, you'd already be dead."

"Who are you?" I asked. There was something … unnerving about this woman, besides the fact she'd just admitted she was debating whether or not to kill us. I reached out with the Sight, confirming this *was* the realm of the Real, although I wasn't sure that made me feel any better.

"Jade," she told me with an engaging smile. Those eyes were unlike anything I'd ever seen, drawing me in. Two beautiful orbs set in an attractive oval face. I tried, unsuccessfully, to tear my gaze away from her as I remembered the story of Sigborn and *Jade*, the dragon who helped him escape. My mouth went dry and all other thoughts fled from my mind as I sat there, transfixed.

Etta was the first of us to find her voice after that revelation. "We're here on an urgent mission. Are you able to help us find Bruar? Events are moving quickly in Amuran and we need his assistance, whilst there's still time."

Jade ignored Etta as she continued to look at me curiously through half-closed eyes, a small frown creasing her forehead. "What *are* you, Rothgar Kolfinnarson?"

"What … what do you mean?" I stammered.

"You're not like those other men," Jade told me, her expression impossible to read.

My blood froze. "Other men?"

"The warriors I found in the forest a few nights ago. They made all sorts of … unwholesome suggestions as to how we should pass the evening. They laughed and taunted me. They're not laughing now." Jade's eyes glittered, their purple iris deepening in colour. She casually flicked her dark hair away from her face as she spoke.

"Let's try not to annoy her," Jolinn breathed in a small voice.

"Agreed," Ulfarr replied, turning to me. "Right. You'd better tell her why we're here."

CHAPTER 51

Nuna walked through the halls and corridors of Norlhast Keep with Katla and Kalfr, Brosa a couple of paces behind in his customary place. They passed the courtyard where Sigurd was sparring with Vrand, wooden swords clacking as the pair exchanged a flurry of blows. Sigurd's face was creased with concentration, driving the younger warrior back with his aggressive attacks. The crowd of onlookers gave a shout as Vrand's wooden sword was sent spinning into the air, Sigurd using the flat of his blade to knock his opponent onto the floor with a vicious stroke.

"Ouch," muttered Brosa, half in admiration, half commiserating with Vrand's painful defeat.

"There's a dark mood on your brother these days," said Nuna.

"You know the reason," Kalfr replied as Sigurd stalked away from the training ground.

"You think I don't understand the pain of living under Vorund rule?" Nuna replied. "We've all suffered. We've all lost people we loved. At least your father still lives."

"Does he?" Kalfr asked with a heavy sigh.

They walked in silence for a time, passing Styrman, who was hurrying to prepare the evening feast. They would be entertaining Valdimarr, Geilir and Lefwine tonight, making polite conversation with their enemies, carefully ignoring their slights. It promised to be another interminable evening.

"You're quiet today, Kalfr," Nuna said after a while.

The warrior nodded. "Please forgive me, my lady. I was thinking about something my brother was saying the other day."

Kalfr looked embarrassed when Nuna asked him to elaborate. She realised she had put her faithful friend in a difficult position when she eventually persuaded him to answer.

"Sigurd finds the lack of action concerning our father ... regrettable," Kalfr explained. "All we've done since his release is share our food and drink with Geilir, swallowing his insincere apology and pretending to be grateful Tryggvi will suffer a *cold winter*. It's not enough."

Nuna reached out and patted Kalfr on the shoulder. "It's not forever," she whispered. "This is part of the sacrifice we have to make if we are to be free. Justice will be done, both for your father and everyone else who has suffered wrongdoing under Vorund rule."

Kalfr stopped and looked at her, the scar on his face twisting as he grimaced. "Are we going to be free? Can you honestly say that? That's the question Sigurd posed to me, gathered around the fire in my home with our father moaning and crying out in his sleep next door. We denounce Orglyr's rebellion publicly and tell ourselves our words mean nothing, that this is all for show. What happens if Geilir defeats Orglyr come the spring? What if Orglyr doesn't return at all and flees westwards instead? What happens to us if the pretence becomes the reality and this is the future of the Norlhast Clan?"

"Geilir has to trust me for this plan to work," Nuna replied, her heart heavy.

"My lady," interrupted Katla. "Is it wise to discuss things so openly? We should carry on this conversation in private, back at your chambers."

Kalfr nodded. "Your maid's right. This isn't the place to be talking of such things. Pay my words no mind, my lady. I spoke out of turn."

Nuna put her arm in Kalfr's as they walked on, wishing there was some way she could make all things right for the people she cared about.

***

"You were gone for a while, there," said Jade, her words bringing me back to my surroundings.

I was sitting on a black basalt rock, the Fire Isle's forest stretching out below us. I was exhausted from the ascent and I took another drink from my waterskin, hoping we would find another source of fresh water soon. The Sight had ensnared me unawares and I felt rattled at the intrusion, knowing how important it was to keep my wits at such a crucial time. Jolinn had remained behind, her eyes watching Jade warily. Up ahead, I could see Ulfarr leading the rest of our party, Etta still resolutely refusing any offers of help as she stoically continued her climb.

"I'm sorry," I gasped, trying to catch my breath. "It's further than it looks."

Jade scowled, purple eyes narrowed. "That's not what I meant, and you know it. What just happened?" I decided to answer honestly – it was best not to lie to a stranger when I needed their help.

"It's been a long time since I've met a Sightwielder," Jade said after listening to my explanation, eyebrows raised. "Once all of Amuran was connected using such skills, the vast kingdoms of the Enlightened Age ruled through a network of Sight users. The world is so quiet now – it's like there's no one out there."

"You know about the Sight?" I asked. She looked to be in her twenties, although I knew from legend a dragon's lifespan was measured in centuries.

Jade raised an eyebrow. "Rothgar, dragons *taught* humans how to use the gift in the first place. Remember, we were the firstborn." She was staring at me with those fantastic purple eyes, flecks of gold dancing in them, face haughty and proud.

"I didn't mean to cause offence."

Jade stared at me and shook her head. "You're young.

Just make sure you show deference and respect when you meet Mendaleon and Alcor. They're from an older time and such things are important to them."

"Are you ready to continue?" Jolinn asked, offering me her hand. I nodded, letting her haul me onto my feet.

"So that's your secret," said Jade. She looked at my companions, who had now halted so we could catch them up. "What about her?"

"Etta?"

"She's not exactly your typical old woman, is she?"

I glanced at Jolinn, unsure how to answer Jade's question. "She's a remarkable person," I said at last. "Etta's advised our clan since the time of my grandfather and I think the chance to meet Bruar has given her a new lease of life." So much for being honest with strangers, but what *could* I say?

Jade laughed at me. "If you say so. You don't have to share all your secrets with me. Just remember, I offered no guarantees. I said I'd bring you to the gates of our city and then it would be a matter for Mendaleon to decide. Any ... unwelcome surprises might count against you, but that's your decision." With that she shrugged and set off up the mountain, leaving me standing there with Jolinn.

"Something's not right," muttered Jolinn, staring at Etta as she waited for us on the mountainside. "I overheard your conversation with Etta aboard *Stormweaver*. The fact she didn't answer your questions at the time troubled me and I don't like being kept in the dark."

"I think she's channelling some sort of magic," I said, shaking my head. "I don't really understand it but I can't think of any other explanation."

Jolinn breathed out slowly through her nose. "I hope she knows what she's doing. With magic, there's always a cost."

I re-stoppered my waterskin and scrambled after Jade, panting to keep up as she stepped nimbly from rock to rock until we reached the others. We continued our climb in silence, Jade moving further ahead while I struggled on behind. The sun was bright overhead, dazzling me, so I stared at my feet as I worked my way between the black rocks. Without warning my foot gave out under me and I pitched onto my front with a cry. I slid a few feet, stretching out my hands and feet until I managed to catch hold of a lip of rock. For a few moments I lay on my front, breathing hard, drenched in sweat, head resting on the stone. I rolled over and sat up, rubbing my knee, which was red and bleeding where I had scraped it raw, my breeches torn. There was also a deep cut on my palm – I squeezed it tight, wincing with the pain as I watched blood welling up between my fingers.

Jolinn scrambled back down with Myr, cleaning out the wound with some water while I fumbled with the straps on my pack to find a strip of cloth to bandage my hand. A shadow fell across my lap.

"Here, let me." Jade's voice was soft and calm as she deftly wrapped the bandage around my hand, fingers light and delicate, as Myr and Jolinn looked on. Could this woman really have killed those men in the forest? Looking at her now it didn't seem possible.

"Thank you," I mumbled, flexing my fingers. Nothing was broken, though my hand stung.

"Take my arm," Jade told me. "The next stretch is more treacherous. It would be a pity for you to have made it so far, only to topple off the mountainside."

I accepted the offer and, with my good hand clasped tightly in hers, we began our ascent once more. Jade's skin was soft and warm, her grip strong. I was grateful for the help, although I had the impression that to Jade I was little more than a curious plaything, rather like a mouse gently carried in the jaws of a cat. For now I was safe, until the cat grew bored.

I was drenched in sweat, knee throbbing, by the time we reached a narrow path, cutting its way steeply up the mountainside. The air radiating from the top of Ballung

Mountain was warm, smelling of sulphur and other noxious fumes. I leaned against a rock, rubbing my leg with my good hand. The cut on my palm was burning, the bandage sodden with blood. Jade sat next to me and carefully changed the dressing, pocketing the bloody rag in her jerkin, which she had now unbuttoned.

"You don't have to keep that," I told her. "Cast it aside."

Jade shook her head. "There's power in blood, Rothgar, and it would be unwise for this to fall into the wrong hands. Anyway, I don't want to leave any sign of our passage. We're almost there."

"Where?" asked Ulfarr, arms outstretched as he stared at the barren mountainside.

Jade turned and pointed towards a fissure in the black rocks. I stared, trying to see anything significant, wiping sweat from my face with the back of my hand.

"I can't see it," I admitted.

"Come with me," said Jade, pulling me to my feet with strong arms.

We followed the path, which was easier to walk on than the rocks below. We rounded a corner and arrived at the fissure Jade had shown me, which up close only opened out a few feet before ending in a smooth blank black stone wall, with the path snaking on around the mountain.

"Do we go on?" I asked.

Jade shook her head and led me into the fissure, raising her free hand and pressing it against the stone. It shimmered and Jade stepped forwards, pulling me through before my mind had chance to register what was happening. It was like stepping under a warm waterfall, on the other side of which was a wide stone staircase. The walls were decorated with sinuous carvings of dragons in their traditional form, talons and sharp teeth raking the flesh of their enemies who, disconcertingly, were human warriors, fighting them with pikes and lances. On each step was set the familiar warding rune against the durath – the dragon and chimera set in a circular design, sinewy forms entwined, frozen in the act of battle.

The rest of my companions appeared behind me, looking confused and disorientated. Skari's brows narrowed and when I turned around I realised we were not alone. Four people, two men and two women, were standing at the entrance, each of them carrying a long spear strapped to their backs. It resembled the Samarak fighting spear I'd seen Tellian carrying in my vision, one end tapering to a sharp steel point. At the other end was a curved blade, resembling a half-length scimitar like those carried by Oomrhani horsemen. One of the four approached us, an older man in banded silver armour who appeared about sixty, though still trim and fit. He had a long mane of white hair flowing down his back and the dark skin of a Samarak. His eyes were silver and power radiated from him. I found myself sinking low onto one knee, gasping under my breath as the bruised joint touched the stone.

"Jade. The exile returns, bringing us these ... ragged creatures."

I glanced at our guide. "You're not *welcome* here?" I whispered.

Jade glanced at me, unrepentant, arms folded across her chest. "It's a long story."

CHAPTER 52

I rose awkwardly to my feet, head swimming with tiredness after the climb and the heat. My carefully rehearsed words of introduction hadn't catered for this embarrassing situation. Did Jade's presence mean we were about to be *refused* entry? It seemed unthinkable.

Jade addressed the older dragon with silver eyes. "Alcor. It's been such a long time. I'd hoped we could move on from what happened and renew our old friendship. There was a time when we were inseparable."

Alcor regarded her coldly, choosing to remain silent. Unabashed, Jade turned to a slender woman with braided blonde hair. "Mendaleon. It's so good to see you."

"You shouldn't have returned," Mendaleon replied. Her eyes were of a golden hue, like a bird of prey and just as calculating. Alcor watched them both, his face unreadable.

"I know you were expecting me," Jade answered, unruffled, those fabulous purple eyes wide and innocent. "Why else would you have arranged this greeting party?"

Mendaleon sighed. "The scrying pool reveals more important matters than your personal concerns, Jade. Events move quickly, after centuries when Amuran was in balance and all was as it should be. The Tear widens, and it's no surprise that humans have set foot on the Fire Isle in such times. They always bring death and destruction with them." Her golden eyes flicked towards me as she said those final words and I had to fight the urge to shrink away and hide.

"The pool revealed you were making your journey here," added Alcor.

Jade offered a hesitant smile. "I've missed you all.

Mendaleon. Alcor. Ralina. Sirion." She nodded to each in turn. "To see your faces after so long and –"

Alcor cut across her. "I didn't say you were welcome. I said you were expected."

Jade's poise faltered. "Alcor, it's been over one hundred years."

"Ample opportunity to reflect on your actions and their consequences, yet the woman I see before me is unchanged and unrepentant. It appears you need more time."

Jade glanced at each of them, looking for some signs Alcor's companions had a different view. If they did, they hid it well as an uncomfortable silence stretched on. Alcor walked towards me, looking me up and down as if appraising livestock he was contemplating buying. His sombre face suggested that if he made an offer, the price would be low.

"Your name?"

"Rothgar Kolfinnarson." My voice was cracked and dry from the climb. I coughed and repeated myself more firmly, taking the time to introduce each of my companions.

Alcor's face was one long sneer. "There are other warriors exploring the forests and the foothills, searching for something. I believe that something to be you. Why are you here?"

I looked into Alcor's silver eyes with as steady a gaze as I could muster. "That's a matter I must discuss with Bruar and Bruar alone." Alcor's face twitched and he glanced at the sword hanging at my side. His hand touched the handle of his spear, lightly resting there, a potent threat.

"We are Bruar's guardians," Mendaleon said as Alcor stared at me in silence. "We have sworn to serve and guard him since the end of the Enlightened Age. Bruar sees no one unless we permit it."

"He'll want to see us," I told them. "Surely this matter should be decided by your master, rather than the servants at his door?"

"Why would he want to see ... you?" Alcor stretched out the final word, dripping with contempt.

"We have a common enemy. Bruar will want to hear what we have to say, I promise you."

Mendaleon gave a short nod. "These are strange times. We will permit you, and you alone Rothgar Kolfinnarson, to cross our threshold. Your companions will remain here until our business is done."

"What?" Etta cried. "No, please. I *need* to be there. This shouldn't be left in the hands of a young man who's not yet seen twenty. We've come so far and I'll not be denied at the very gates of Bruar's kingdom. Everything depends on this."

"You will wait outside, as I have instructed," Mendaleon replied, her voice reverberating inside and around me, causing me to stagger. "Yes, Etta, you're right. Everything depends on this. I have seen the waters of the pool and Rothgar is the one who must be tested. You cannot help him – none of you can."

"No," Etta breathed, crestfallen. "You don't understand. He's just a boy."

I reached out and took Etta's thin hand, giving it a gentle squeeze. "I'll be fine. Wait for me here and I'll return to you soon enough." I spoke with more confidence than I felt and Etta nodded once, offering me a thin smile that I imagined she thought was encouraging. It was the first time I had ever seen my mentor lost for words.

***

I arrowed a brief Sight message across the hundreds of miles separating me from Joldir. He and Johan needed to know we had reached our goal, even if the outcome of Bruar's test, whatever that might be, was still uncertain.

His response was immediate. *Dinuvillan will smile upon you. I have every faith in you, Rothgar. Take care.*

As quickly as it had been established, the connection was broken and I walked up the ornate staircase feeling completely alone. We entered a cavernous room, a vast cave cut into the black rock, held up by tall pillars. Some were decorated in geometric patterns, others in random sworls of bright colour and no two were alike. Jade walked at my side, Ralina and Sirion at our backs while Alcor and Mendaleon led the way.

"How many of your kind live here?" I whispered to Jade.

"Only the five of us," she replied.

I stared in astonishment at the underground chamber, which would have swallowed Ulfkell's Keep many times over. "All this for ... *five* of you?"

Jade looked at me with haunted, sorrowful eyes. "When Bruar raised the Fire Isle we joined him and helped fashion this place as a refuge, waiting for more of our kin to join us. Mendaleon left and searched Amuran, to bring word to our kindred. She found ... Terrible, terrible things. Our time was over, the ancient cities of the dragons destroyed or empty, devoid of life. Our battle with the chimera and the Beast Within during the War of the Avatars cost us dear. Dragon blood was spilled on both sides, some fighting for Morvanos, others resisting him. Those few Mendaleon found refused to come, nursing their hurts and grief in far-flung places. We were the only ones who remained loyal to Mendaleon, so we made a pact to serve the remaining avatars and guard against another cataclysmic war. We divided ourselves into four groups, each sworn to one of the remaining avatars still on Amuran. Six of us remained here with Bruar, whilst the rest of our kind sought out Culdaff, Nanquido and Rannoch."

"Not Dinas and Navan?" I asked, my voice echoing and small in that vast space.

Jade shook her head. "The Halls of the Dead need no guardian. As for Dinas, if he walks amongst us here on Amuran he does so in secret."

Something in what Jade had told me made me stop

and think. "There's something else I want to ask you, concerning Sigborn."

Alcor stopped walking and turned to look at me at the mention of my clansman's name. Ralina hissed and took a step towards me before Sirion placed a hand on her shoulder.

"Never speak that name in these halls," Alcor told me.

"My apologies," I replied, swallowing hard. "It won't happen again."

"Who is that liar to you?" asked Ralina, a red-headed woman with piercing green eyes who looked a few years older than Jade.

"I'm from Laskar," I explained. "The man we're speaking of is a figure from our history, the son of our first chief."

"He was a snake," Ralina spat the word, looking darkly at Jade. "A traitor and a liar. Like all men."

"Enough of this," said Mendaleon and her companions fell silent at once. My heart was heavy as we continued our journey. The legend of Sigborn told how he'd killed the dragon Tanios to earn his freedom. I'd never even considered that with their extended lifespan, those events of the distant past had taken place in the living memory of my companions. My life and those of my friends hung in the balance, depending on the outcome of this encounter, and I felt distinctly unprepared.

We walked through a tall wooden gate, exiting the chamber and passing into an enormous cave. The setting sun's red glow shone through the entrance, illuminating a city built on a terrace under a vast overhang of rock within Ballung Mountain. Each building would have put the finest of human palaces to shame, streets dressed in granite wending their way elegantly between them. It felt like we were walking through a cemetery, each building a monument to those long dead and gone. The six of us walked through the silent, oppressive city towards a circular building in the centre.

"Is this where Bruar lives?" I asked, my words small and insignificant in this place.

Mendaleon glanced back at me. "No. This is where we see into your heart."

We entered the windowless building, its door guarded by two stone dragons, rearing on their hind legs, jaws gaping wide in a silent, frozen roar. Inside the single room was softly lit from lamps set in the wall that burned without a flame. A circular pool, perfectly matching the contours of the room, took up more than half the floor, its surface mirror smooth, reflecting the ceiling above. The effect was disorientating, making the space appear larger than it was.

The dragons spread out around the edges of the pool, moving with a reverence and care that I copied as I approached the waters. Peering over the low stone wall holding them back I saw my reflection. A dirty face looked back at me, my chin covered with a scraggly unkempt beard, dark hair a tangled mess. I'd been grateful for it while we crossed the ice – now it gave me a feral look. My clothes were the ones I'd been wearing since I left Romsdahl, travel stained and smelling both of sweat and sea salt. I looked even thinner than normal and in my tiredness my stoop was more pronounced. The grand emissary of the Brotherhood of the Eagle sent to treat with the gods looked like a beggar in need of a hot meal and a bath.

The waters turned black and I gave a small cry of surprise. Now a younger man looked back at me with proud eyes and a handsome smile, my missing front tooth back in place. My tongue probed the spot, finding the gap I had grown used to this past year and a half. This version of myself was wiry yet strong, dressed in warrior's chainmail, my old sword given to me by my father strapped to my side. This was a man with ambitions, a future jarl of the Reavesburg Clan, descended from a line of powerful chiefs. My old life.

Hooves beat out a thunderous drum as I led the charge

of Reavesburg's warriors over the sands towards Noln with Bandor, Bram and Haarl at my side. My heart ached for my lost friends, victory against the Vorund Clan turning sour as Tyrfingr Blackeyes killed Bram, Olfridor comforting me as the funeral pyre blazed for the fallen. That was the day I became both a man and a warrior. A little over two years had passed and now I felt a hundred years older. The pool shimmered, showing my bittersweet triumphant return to Ulfkell's Keep, finding Reavesburg in silence and my father struck down by a palsy. One from which he never recovered.

The faces of Nuna and Jorik floated past, as well as Olfridor, Etta and my father. Outside Jolinn was standing a little way apart from her companions, looking at the spot on the mountainside where I had vanished from her sight. Our vantage point rose higher in the air – far below I could see *Stormweaver's* crew camped on the beach, sat around a fire cooking their evening meal. Further away, on the other side of the island was a larger camp, patrolled by warriors, flying the flag of Vorund's bear. Their young leader, a dark-haired man with a haughty expression, Hasteinn, watched as a group of men returned from a fishing expedition. The men looked tired and relieved as they dumped their catch and gear, perhaps wondering what had become of their missing scouting party.

The image shifted and Desta's face appeared, an expression of pure misery etched on her features. I was hanging in the crows cage, half-dead, as we said our final goodbyes. I saw her now, with Humli and Lina, making their slow way towards Delving and the pass to safety through the Baros Mountains. A few miles distant a score of Vorund warriors were quickly closing down upon them on the road, Eidr at their head, Bjorr at his side. Clearly Djuri's ruse had not been successful, and Desta's pursuers had come westwards, perhaps guessing Vittag was their most likely destination.

The scene changed once more and Tullen burned,

Sandar dying before the archway into the Shadow Realm, our first small victory against the evil of the durath. The Brotherhood was born and I saw Johan in counsel with his followers as they continued the siege of Vorund Fastness, waiting for news of my return, all of them counting on me. In his chamber, buried deep under his fortress, Adalrikr brooded as more durath flocked to him from the darkness, heeding the Calling and crossing over from the Shadow Realm into the Real.

The pool went black and I thought the vision was over. However, the waters coalesced into a different time and I saw the dark shapes of twisted trees, stark against the starlit sky. Etta and Ekkill were trying to save my life as they fled from Tyrfingr. *'You want to* poison *him? A blade would be cleaner,'* said Ekkill, before being persuaded by Etta to help pour her foul-tasting medicine down my throat. Everything had changed from that moment. Instead of making the journey to Navan's Halls to be with my mother, father and brother I became the man I saw today. I felt all those I was connected to through the Sight – Nuna, Joldir, Leif, Ulfarr, Freydja and the rest. Nereth looked up at me, her beautiful features marred by hatred and when I blinked her face shattered. In its place, my reflection stared back at me, the pink tip of my tongue worrying at the gap in my teeth. I shuddered and walked away, feeling cold and exposed.

Alcor turned to Mendaleon. "What did you see?"

Her golden eyes were fixed on what I now understood must be a scrying pool. "This one is strong in the Sight. A broken warrior, moulded into something else entirely – a deadly weapon against the durath. The Sundered have returned, which is why he's here. There's something else, something his mind has turned away from. A dark night and a betrayal, the first of many. I saw powdered mushrooms, the shadow root herb and a cup. When Rothgar sipped from it one door opened as another closed."

"What does that mean?" I asked, perplexed.

Mendaleon looked at me. "I think you already know, although you've closed your mind to that night for so long it's buried deep."

I frowned, hands clasped in front of me to stop them shaking after such an intrusion. I thought back to the night I was rescued from the crows cage in Reavesburg. Etta had spoken to Ekkill of using gildcrest mushrooms and shadow root to put me into the dreamless sleep. It had saved my life on my journey to Lindos, where I had met Joldir for the first time and he had treated my wounds. Why would this moment be the one Mendaleon and the scrying pool would focus upon?

"And what was revealed to you, Alcor?" asked Sirion, a handsome man who looked about thirty with short red hair of the same hue as Ralina's. Like the other dragons his eyes were his most striking feature. Sirion's were yellow, glowing bright in the subdued lighting of the room.

Alcor ignored Sirion's question as he stared intently at Jade, who took a few hesitant steps away from the poolside. "You saw only yourself, didn't you Jade? Nothing has changed. The anger, the pride, the envy – they continue to define you. The Beast always lurks near the surface, waiting for the chance to tear down all we have built. Wasn't Tanios' death enough?"

Jade glared at him. "You see only what you wish, Alcor."

Mendaleon shook her head. "No. You refuse to see what you really are. I had hoped for more, Jade. I really did. Ralina and Sirion, keep her here in the city and watch her closely. Rothgar will come with me and Alcor. You'll get your wish to meet with Bruar and he can decide your fate."

"Thank you," I replied, scarcely able to believe my good fortune.

Jade turned and looked back at Alcor before Sirion and Ralina escorted her from the scrying chamber. "You never answered Sirion's question, Alcor. What did you see?"

Alcor looked at Jade with utter contempt. “Do you think I would share such personal things with you? Go, and consider yourself fortunate to be spending a single night under the roof of our great city.”

CHAPTER 53

It was still dark when Humli went down to the banks of the River Jelt to check his fishing lines. It had been raining and he slipped once on the wet grass as he headed away from the camp. Lina had offered to come and help, leaving Desta nursing both infants in their tent. When they had first joined the group of travellers Rollef had been delighted to learn Humli was a fisherman, producing a handful of fish hooks from a box stowed in his cart.

"Never had much luck catching fish," he confessed. "Perhaps you'll do better?"

The three long lines Humli had fashioned carried several hooks each. Left out overnight, if Dinuvillan favoured him, he could catch a sizeable number of fish. It was his way of contributing and fresh fish for breakfast always signalled a good start to the day. Certainly preferable to Almarr's beans.

He tested the first of the lines, hauling it ashore, pleased to feel the weight and see a number of fish wriggling in the lamplight. Some were a fair size, others smaller – a good enough catch and if the other two lines were similar Rollef's party would eat well this morning. A murky grey dawn light was creeping over the river, mist hanging in the air, still damp from the rain last night. They were in the shadow of the Baros Mountains and the sun would take time to clear their jagged peaks. Rollef and Sunnifa were excited now they were only two days away from the pass, their good spirits lifting the rest of their party. Humli looked at that huge dark mass, thinking there wouldn't be any fish (or much of anything else) once they started that climb. He wasn't looking forward to the next part of their journey, knowing it would be cold and dangerous, particularly for the children. He could lose his grandson trying to get them all to safety.

"Are you going to help or stare at the mountains all morning?" Lina gently chided.

"Sorry," Humli apologised, shaking those dark thoughts from his mind as he pulled the last of the lines out of the river.

Lina gutted the fish as Humli packed the lines away, whistling to himself. It was better when he had a job to do. He knew worrying didn't help and he wondered what joke the gods were playing, pitting him against the Vorund Clan and Tyrfingr Blackeyes. The camp was quiet as the pair of them walked back with their catch, the bucket heavy in Humli's hand. It was still early and people would be stirring soon, another day's travelling ahead of them. As they got nearer Humli spotted the portly figure of Rollef standing by the camp fire, tending the flames. Humli raised a hand in greeting and Rollef saw him. He didn't smile in return, his face tense, and they slowed their pace.

Lina turned to Humli, looking anxious. "What's wrong?"

Humli opened his mouth, words dying on his lips as other figures emerged from the shadows. Warriors, dressed in chainmail and armed with swords and axes appeared from behind the tents, some dragging people with them. He saw Sunnifa being held by one man with a knife to her throat and Humli dropped the bucket as he considered running. He looked back the way they'd come, choking off a cry as four horsemen blocked his path, one of them laughing at him.

"Humli Freedman," called the man holding Sunnifa captive. "We have your daughter and her son. If you do anything to defy us I'll kill the boy, do you understand?"

The speaker was a tall young man with red hair and a close-cropped beard. Humli recognised him as Eidr, the man who had visited his house with Kolsveinn, back when all of this first started. Lina had said he was one of the durath, the one Adalrikr had sent looking for her.

"Humli?" It was Almarr's voice. "He told us his name was Gamli. He's lied to us right from the start. We're not in league with them, I swear."

"Come forward. You too Lina," ordered Eidr, nodding at one of his companions.

Desta was dragged from her tent, one eye swollen and bruised, a cut on her lip. Finn and Frokn were clutched in the arms of two more warriors. Neither man looked very comfortable threatening the life of a child, although Humli had no doubt they would follow Eidr's orders if it came to that. Reluctantly, he walked forwards, trying to look brave for Desta's sake.

"You've been harbouring criminals, wanted for the murder of my men in Noln," Eidr hissed. "Do you expect me to believe you knew nothing about this?"

Rollef sank to his knees, pleading with Eidr to release his wife. "My lord, we only offered them hospitality on the road. I promise you, we had no idea they were fleeing justice. I'm telling you the truth."

"You met them on the road," Eidr repeated. "And what is *your* band of travellers doing on the road, exactly?" He glanced meaningfully in the direction of the mountains. "Heading for Vittag, perhaps? Abandoning Reavesburg's jarl without his permission? Why flee, unless you had reason to do so?"

Humli glanced at Lina, seeing the wild expression on her face; rage and fear playing out across her features and he remembered her attacking the men at the dockside. *If she tries to fight now a lot of people are going to die.*

"Remember your son," he whispered to her. "They've got Desta and Finn as well. If we resist, Eidr will kill them. You know this."

Eidr smiled, eyes bright with triumph as he saw the

fight leave her. "King Adalrikr is very anxious to meet you, Lina. Bjorr, bind them. We'll take them all back to Ulfkell's Keep."

Humli didn't resist as his hands were tied in front of him. Somewhere out of sight a woman was crying while the rest of Rollef's band watched silently, too afraid to do anything as Bjorr led the five of them away. The warrior tied Desta and Lina in a similar fashion, nodding in satisfaction as he checked the knots were tight.

"I'm sorry," Desta whispered. "They were inside the tent before I knew what was happening."

"It's going to be alright," Humli told her. "They want us alive, that's something."

Rollef was back on his feet, talking to Eidr, who still had hold of Sunnifa. "We've done everything you asked of us. I swear we knew nothing of what they'd done. Now they're your prisoners you can let my wife and the rest of us go."

Eidr smiled, slipping his knife back into its sheath on his belt, although he kept a firm hold of Sunnifa. Her friendly face was strained, the cords on her neck taut as she tried to pull her head away from Eidr's face. He leaned in closer, whispering something into her ear and her eyes widened.

"Rollef," she said, her voice shaking. "I love you so very much but you need to run. All of you. Now."

Rollef looked shocked. "Run? What? No! No, we had an agreement. You promised us safe passage onwards, if we cooperated."

"Run!" screamed Sunnifa, crying out in fright as Eidr pushed her down onto the ground.

"Don't hurt her," Almarr shouted, charging forwards awkwardly using his crutch. He didn't manage to get more than two steps before an axe split his skull wide open. He dropped to the floor without a sound.

The camp erupted in panic and screams as the Vorund men attacked. Bjorr watched dispassionately as he stood with the warriors holding the infants, keeping a firm grip on the ropes binding Humli and his family.

"Don't look," Humli told Desta. He turned away and closed his eyes, although that didn't stop the terrible sounds reaching him. Sunnifa was screaming, whilst Rollef's loud protests were silenced with a sickening wet thud.

I'm a coward, no point pretending otherwise. Yet what else could I have done? I have to keep Desta and Finn safe – what good would getting myself killed achieve? Humli told himself he was doing the right thing as the shouts and screams of his travelling companions were silenced one by one. Someone was sobbing nearby until after a while that noise also ceased and the camp was quiet and still.

Humli opened his eyes. Desta had followed his advice, her eyes still screwed tightly shut. Lina was staring past Bjorr, her face a cold pale mask. Humli turned and saw she was staring straight at Eidr, who was eating something. *I don't want to know …* Despite himself, Humli's gaze fell first upon Rollef's face. His eyes were fixed in his skull, white beard matted with blood where a blade had almost parted his head from his neck. Next to him Eidr was devouring Sunnifa, taking strips of her flesh and putting them into his mouth as if they were dainty morsels. Humli turned away and retched bile onto the grass, drawing a curse from Bjorr as the contents of his stomach spattered near his feet.

"Watch it," snarled Bjorr, jerking on the rope and almost knocking Humli over

Eidr looked up, eyes bright, wiping some of Sunnifa's blood from his face. "Careful. They have to make it back to Ulfkell's Keep in one piece."

"Are you … done?" Bjorr asked, face twisted in distaste.

Eidr laughed, looking at Lina as she continued to glare back at him. "That was for what you did to my men on the docks. Their deaths are on your conscience."

"This isn't over," hissed Lina.

"Oh, I think it is."

Eidr walked over to the bucket lying on its side,

picking it up with blood-soaked hands as he inspected Humli's morning catch. "Thoughtful of you to provide breakfast. Bjorr, have the men search the camp and take anything of value, starting with those horses," he nodded towards the three coursers Humli, Lina and Desta had been riding. "If you find anyone else still breathing, kill them."

***

I started awake, unable to breathe, tearing at the covers. It took me a few moments to remember who and where I was. I sat on the edge of the bed panting and shaking, naked, clammy and cold. Feet aching, I limped over to a dresser on which was set an empty bowl, a copper pipe protruding above it. Sirion had explained how it all worked last night. I placed a stopper in the bottom of the bowl and turned the handle above the pipe, watching in amazement as steaming water poured out. No need for servants running around with jugs heated by the fire. It had something to do with the volcano and deep underground pipes to gather the hot water – exactly how it all worked was a mystery.

I washed myself down, dried off, straightened my untidy hair (which was in desperate need of a trim) and dressed in the clothes Sirion had provided; black breeches and tunic, a white shirt and comfortable brown leather boots. The garments I had arrived in had been taken away, presumably to be washed or maybe even burned. My remaining possessions had been placed in an open chest at the foot of the bed. My sword, backpack and the stoppered vial of ataraxia were all there. My travelling cloak was rolled up and carefully placed to one side. I stared at them and decided to buckle my sword to my hip. The ataraxia I left alone.

Desta and her family were in terrible danger and there was nothing I could do about it. I sat back down on the bed, trying to clear my head. Lina was also his prisoner. Had Leif seen the same events? I'd come to realise the boy saw and understood more of what I experienced with the Sight than

I'd first thought. I tried to connect with Joldir but the Path, so clear in my dreams, proved elusive in the Real and after a few attempts I gave up. I was unable to concentrate properly, rendering the simple task impossible in my current state. My head throbbed and I tried to calm down. I couldn't help Desta and told myself the important thing was that, for now, she was safe. The only way to help her was to end this war, and for that I needed Bruar's assistance.

There was a knock at my door and when I opened it Mendaleon was outside. There were no servants in their city – just the four of them living in this cavernous place. A city built to rally the last of the dragons, only there was no one left to heed the call.

"Are you hungry?" Mendaleon asked, golden eyes glowing in the soft light of the corridor, dimly lit by more of those strange cold yellow lamps.

I'd been exhausted last night, hardly remembering falling into bed after Sirion led me to my chambers. Mendaleon showed me to a feasting hall, our steps echoing as we walked its length towards a table set for two at the far end.

"All this," I gestured at the polished marble floor, high decorative wooden ceiling and windows – no, I realised it was more of those strange lamps, cunningly fashioned to look like an opening to the outside world.

"Yes?"

"Doesn't it get ... lonely? The four of you here, all by yourselves?"

"We value our privacy," Mendaleon told me, the corner of her lips hinting at a smile. It was, on reflection, a rather personal question.

Breakfast consisted of soft bread and butter, served alongside grapes, apples and other oddly shaped sweet fruits I'd never seen before. After so long eating the same dry and preserved foods it tasted finer than a banquet in the Great Hall. I stopped, thinking once more of the past, the sharp memories fading, so many of the people I shared them with gone.

"Is something the matter?" asked Mendaleon.

I shook my head. "I'm sorry, I was lost in thought, that's all." I took a drink of watered red wine, feeling calmer and ready for what was to come next.

Mendaleon popped a piece of yellow fruit in her mouth, closing her eyes as she savoured its sweet flesh. She'd called it a mango, a delicacy normally only found far to the south in Samarakand. What one was doing growing on this green island in a sea of ice was beyond my comprehension.

"You understand the honour we are affording you, allowing you to meet with Bruar? When you set foot on the island the scrying pool rang like a bell, drawing us all to its side. Does your presence mean good or ill, I wonder?"

"I'm trying to do the right thing," I replied. "You mentioned the Tear that's running through the different Realms. That's Adalrikr's doing and we have to find the means to stop him."

"If Bruar decides," said Mendaleon, popping another slice of fruit into her mouth. Her gesture reminded me of how Eidr had killed Sunnifa and my appetite vanished.

I sat back, swallowing down both fear and revulsion as my encounter with the gods drew near. Keen to think of something else, I asked a question which had been puzzling me. "Why is Jade still here – on the island, if you've exiled her? If she's banished, couldn't she have chosen to go anywhere?"

Mendaleon shrugged. "I'm not her keeper. Jade does what she wishes, hoping one day we'll forgive her for what happened the last time a human lived amongst us. She's mistaken. Jade betrayed her own husband, allowing herself to be seduced by Sigborn's flattery and lies as he tried to manipulate his way home, despite the fact the Fire Isle's existence was a closely guarded secret in those times. When Tanios discovered the truth he was enraged and, affording Sigborn more honour than he deserved, demanded restitution through single combat. Sigborn accepted the challenge, on the understanding that if he was victorious we would allow him to return home. I thought the outcome was a forgone conclusion but Jade …" Mendaleon took a deep breath, setting aside the rest of her meal. "Jade poisoned Sigborn's fighting spear, allowing him to take Tanios' life through base treachery and claim his prize of freedom. Take care when you're with Jade. Don't be disarmed by how pretty she looks – the violence of the Beast is never far from the surface. You don't want to see that other side of her."

There was a finality in Mendaleon's tone that ensured I steered clear of the subject for the rest of our meal.

"When do I meet with Bruar?" I asked as I finished the last of the fruit.

"We can go there now. Alcor, Ralina and Sirion will accompany us."

I rose, wiping my fingers on a napkin and brushing crumbs from my shirt and jerkin, heart hammering in my chest. The moment had finally arrived, the fate of the Brotherhood hanging on the outcome.

CHAPTER 54

Alcor led the way through the hidden city with his companions, their armour polished to a dazzling sheen, fighting spears strapped to their backs, making me feel more like a prisoner than their guest. We walked past the cave opening, looking out across low terraces and a patchwork of walled fields, orchards, vineyards and pastures where livestock – goats, sheep and cattle – were grazing. A high wall rose up at the far end of the terrace, hiding the agricultural land and the city behind from view. We arrived at a narrow staircase, winding down into the mountain. As we approached the ground under my feet trembled, the five of us pausing as we waited for it to pass.

"The mountain anticipates your arrival," Ralina observed. It was impossible to tell if she was making a joke, so I simply smiled politely as we continued our journey.

The descent down the spiral staircase took several minutes. My knee began to ache with each step, the pain gradually building until, swallowing my pride, I called a halt, gently massaging my injured leg. The dragons regarded me curiously – perhaps unused to any display of physical weakness. The heat was oppressive and I was sweating into my fine clothes, the cut on my palm stinging as my knee throbbed. Mercifully, the stairs came to an end before I had to stop again, opening into a winding chamber that resembled the burrow of some enormous worm. At the far end there was a faint orange glow, light reflecting off the polished stone walls.

Alcor placed a hand on my shoulder. "We go no further. Follow the tunnel and it will lead you to Bruar."

With some trepidation I reached out with the Sight, unsettled I was still unable to find any trace of the Path. Although there was no sign of him, I wondered if the Weeping Warrior was following my progress. The responsibility of speaking on behalf of the Brotherhood, all of them depending on me as they fought against Adalrikr, felt greater than ever. I remembered the outrage on Etta's face as she was denied entry to the city – dealing with Bruar on my own had never been part of the plan.

The orange glow ahead became brighter as I approached, the air so hot I had to undo the buttons on my jerkin with sweating hands. The tunnel opened out onto a wide tongue of black rock, entirely surrounded by molten lava which, even at a distance, felt scorching on my face. Standing on the outcrop was a silhouetted figure and as I drew closer Bruar's features resolved themselves – a plain older man, who looked to be in his mid-fifties. His short grey hair was receding, the red light from the lava casting an orange nimbus around his head, and he was dressed simply in a loose brown woollen tunic, breeches and sandals. I felt somewhat underwhelmed.

Bruar smiled as I bowed at his feet. "You have travelled a long way to find me, Rothgar Kolfinnarson. A pity you will be returning to your friends empty-handed."

That rich voice undid me, my prepared speech dying on my lips as I looked into those old, brown eyes. They looked back, deeper, and I had to turn aside my gaze because I couldn't bear the scrutiny. I used all my Sight skills, walling myself in against the intruder, as an immense weight pressed down between my shoulder blades. It was all I could do to hold Bruar at bay, for now.

"Nothing to say?" Bruar asked, his voice kind. I felt sympathy and concern wash over me for my wasted journey and the dangers I would face on my return. In my mind's eye I saw Johan and Bandor's disappointment when I told them I had failed. Vorund Fastness reared up, dark and forbidding, its thick walls resisting our assault. To the north Geilir's ships landed, Norlhast already conquered. Lefwine's Riltbalt warriors marched with deadly purpose towards the camp of the Brotherhood, Geilir's army at their side as the gates of Vorund swung open and Adalrikr's men charged. The battle that followed was swift and bloody. Thengill fell, pierced by half a dozen spears. Varinn was cut down by Randall as he defended Johan's back. Adalrikr slew Bandor and Svan, revelling in the chaos. Screams drifted up as the Brotherhood's camp burned, Arissa and Leif running towards the ships beached on the shore, choking on the smoke as they tried to get away. I gasped, realising Bruar had breached my Sight defences, and redoubled my efforts to place my mind beyond his reach.

"These are the affairs of men," Bruar told me. "The Creator forbade those of us remaining on Amuran from interfering in such matters. I feel your pain and understand the love you have for your friends. However, why should I intervene in the outcome of this battle? Why not turn aside the armies of Lagash that even now break upon the great wall of Oomrhat? Unchecked, events are conspiring to cause war to break out between Beria and Mirtan. Should I try and stop this? Why do your personal feelings and concern for those you love carry more weight than those dear to Adalrikr?"

I screwed up all my courage to look Bruar in the face. "This isn't just a battle between the Laskan Clans. Adalrikr has opened up a gateway to the Shadow Realm, which is disturbing the Real, the Realm of Dreams and the Realm of Death. All of them are being slowly torn apart by the Tear. Its root is found in the darkness growing beneath Vorund Fastness and our leader, Johan, is the only man trying to stop it. He can't hope to succeed without your help. There's a reason the Realm of Death and Dream both reached out to me. If the bridge the durath are using isn't broken then Amuran will be destroyed, your handiwork lost forever."

A cold wind blew around the chamber, tousling my

hair, its touch welcome on my face. The world shifted and the cave disappeared, replaced by verdant fields and rolling hills. In the distance I could see thick forests and rising from the centre of one of them was a tall tower, fashioned out of a single flowing piece of steel rather than stone. I could feel the power of the Sight running through my mind, although we were the only people in this place. We were standing in a deserted land, an echo forming part of the endless, shifting Realm of Dream.

A frown creased Bruar's forehead. "*Our* handiwork. I didn't build Amuran by myself. I set in motion the living fire beating in its heart, gifted the first spark that warmed the dragons and humans as they huddled in their caves. Amuran was fashioned from the work of all the avatars – such a song of beauty, when Morvanos and Elphinas worked together. A song that will never be heard again, the great world we built brought low by our pride and stubbornness. As the cracks running throughout Amuran and the other Realms widen, I wonder if this was how things were meant to end."

"The Creator intervened in the War of the Avatars to *preserve* Amuran," I argued.

"Yes, and with most of the avatars banished and the dragons slain it was handed over to humans. What have they done with their freedom, other than shed blood as they scrapped like dogs over the vestiges of their once-great kingdoms? Why do they deserve to live? Perhaps this is the Creator's will and when this world is swept away his work will begin anew? Amuran, born again, as fresh and as perfect as when Altandu's feet first touched its soil."

"Where are we?"

"Vestiges of the Enlightened Age. Pockets of the true Realm of Dream, before the souls who once inhabited this world were destroyed when their bodies were consumed by the ravaging fires of the War of the Avatars. Such was their power the world they fashioned here endured, though the Tear is now slowly breaking things apart, as you say. There is knowledge and wisdom here, for those who know how to find it."

I turned to the tower and drew us both closer, crossing the forest in moments, watching in surprise as the gates at its base swung open to welcome us inside. With Bruar I entered the tower, my footsteps echoing on polished marble, tall windows throwing light onto an enormous library, every wall covered in leather-bound tomes of all shapes, sizes and colours. Several winding staircases led upwards, and I gasped as I realised the true scale of this place. All was quiet and still, the library deserted and although I was drawn towards the books on the shelves I couldn't help shake the impression we had entered a mausoleum.

"You navigated the forest with ease and the gates of the library opened upon your arrival. How did you do that?" asked Bruar.

I turned to the ancient avatar, pondering his question. "I'm not sure. I wanted to explore this realm and ... it happened that way."

A look of respect passed over Bruar's face. "The lost Palaces of the Mind recognise your gift. Interesting. I see why Mendaleon allowed you access to my halls. Even Sigborn Reaveson was not so favoured. You're a catalyst, Rothgar, and events flock to you, weave themselves around your destiny and the fate of the world shifts in accordance with your actions. Morvanos was the same, and his path led us to a ruined world, a pale shadow of its former self. You come here seeking power and knowledge and I have to ask myself what the consequences would be if I agree to aid you."

"If you don't, Amuran will be doomed," I replied, my heart heavy, head aching from the effort of keeping Bruar at bay. With a sigh I gave in, feeling Bruar's mind touch with mine, sifting through the jumble of my memories – those I had loved and those I fought against, shattered dreams, my hopes for the future rising from the ashes. All my failures and desires laid bare, my motives weighed and measured.

The vortex of memories coalesced around the combat circle in Ulfkell's Keep, although it was merely a replica, the world I had created when I fought Sinarr the Cold One in the Battle of Romsdahl. I watched as Sinarr faced me, trapped by my Sight magic before I brought my sword down. He shattered beneath the blow, utterly destroyed, as the outcome of the battle turned on that moment back in the Real.

"Your Sight skills are impressive," Bruar commented, his expression thoughtful. "In the Enlightened Age you would have led a Fellowship of twenty to thirty Sightwielders. To be able to maintain connections with so many without losing yourself is no small feat, although it places you and those you love at risk. You could use ataraxia and keep them safe – why don't you take the easy path?"

"It's all I am," I whispered. "All I have left."

"A dangerous man, with nothing left to lose and a single purpose in mind." Bruar folded his arms, regarding me intently. "One final question for you to consider. Why did the scrying pool show you the night you took Etta's potion of shadow root and gildcrest? It marked the start of a long journey, one that has ultimately brought you here, seeking weapons of great power."

I looked at him, confused. "I've no idea. What's that got to do with anything?"

"You need to ask Etta," Bruar replied. The library vanished and we were back in the stifling heat of the chamber. Bruar turned away from me to look out over the lava flows as they oozed past. "After all, she's placed us both in a difficult position. I will help you but it will take time to fashion what you need and, even then, the outcome will not be guaranteed. Perhaps that's as it should be. You and your companions can remain on the Fire Isle under my protection until I complete my work."

I bowed low as I offered my thanks, scarcely able to believe my ears as relief washed over me, mixed with confusion at Bruar's remarks concerning Etta. "We're not alone," I ventured. "Some of our enemies have also landed on the island, led by a Vorund warrior called Hasteinn the Cruel. One of Adalrikr's agents."

Bruar kept his back turned to me as he replied. "Jade can deal with them."

CHAPTER 55

Almarr's cart bounced on the bumpy road, swiftly heading towards Ulfkell's Keep with its miserable prizes. It was an uncomfortable journey, the wooden benches hard and unyielding, and Humli stared down at his bound wrists, sore from being knotted so tightly. He flexed his tingling fingers as he tried to get the blood flowing. Across from him on the other side of the cart Lina and Desta were similarly tied. At least Eidr allowed them to be released each day so they could nurse their children, under his watchful gaze. The rest of the time Finn and Frokn rode in Rollef and Sunnifa's cart, used to carry the travelling party's stolen possessions, the warriors assigned nursemaid duties the regular butt of their companions' jokes. Humli found it hard to listen to their good-natured banter, thinking back to the scene on the banks of the river. The bodies of innocent men, women and children lying broken, twisted and abandoned where they fell, denied a decent burial and left as food for the crows and scavengers, while everything they owned was looted. Humli remembered watching Bjorr that day holding a child's toy in his hand; a rag doll. He'd choked back tears as Bjorr tossed it aside, the warriors treading the once-loved object into the mud as they tore through the rest of the camp.

They're dead because of us. We as good as killed everyone the moment we asked to travel with them. Almarr was right not to trust us – if Rollef had listened to him they'd still be alive. Humli hung his head, exhausted with guilt, grief and terror at what awaited them in Ulfkell's Keep.

"You need to be brave," said Lina in a low voice.

"What?"

"You need to be strong. This isn't over, not yet," Lina told him.

"Hard to feel strong when you're tied to a bench in a cart," Humli replied.

"Haven't you been listening to what they've been saying?" Lina asked. "They need us alive. If they wanted us dead they'd have killed us with Rollef and the others."

"But ropes can't hold you, can they?" said Desta, raising her tear-stained grimy face and looking squarely at Lina. "You're one of those creatures, so what's stopping you stealing the spirit of one of these warriors and slipping away in the night?"

Lina stared at Desta, incredulous. "And leave Frokn? What do you think I am? The boy needs his mother – you've heard our children crying in the other cart. They don't want to be left with strangers. Besides, if I fail to take possession of another, I die and that's not a risk I'm prepared to take. Eidr knows this, which is one of the reasons why our children are still alive."

Humli asked a question that had been bothering him for some time. "Eidr ... what he did to Sunnifa ... he's like you, isn't he? A shadow spirit."

Lina glared at them. "He's *nothing* like me. What happened in Lake Tull ..." she fell silent for a time. "I was a different person back then and ever since I've tried to find a new path and set my past aside."

"You *murdered* the woman you inhabit," Desta said, her voice full of loathing. "Don't you understand? That's not something you can simply fix and then find solace by worming your way into our affections with your lies. How dare you sit there, telling my father how he needs to be strong, like you ever cared for him or any of us at all. I don't know what you think is going to happen when all this is over but we're not your family and I don't want anything more to do with you or that demon child you're raising."

"That's enough," said Humli, louder than he intended

to. The driver of the cart turned round, scowling at them.

Lina was staring at Desta, emotions crossing her face. There was anger, defiance and hurt, each one casting their own shadow. Humli had once thought of Lina as family but what he'd seen on the docks of Noln and how Eidr had attacked Sunnifa changed his mind on that score. Even so, he didn't want Desta to make an enemy of Lina. *We've got enough of those already.*

***

Nuna was wrapped in thick fox furs as she rode at Geilir's side, Kalfr, Brosa and a dozen Vorund and Riltbalt warriors forming a loose circle around them, protecting them at a discreet distance as they explored the moorland above Norlhast Keep. There was a stiff breeze blowing in from the sea, a taste of autumn in the air as Norlhast's farmers brought in their crops and stocked up on provisions, ready for the coming winter.

"Valdimarr told me an interesting tale today," Geilir said, giving her a sidelong glance as he pretended to admire the bleak scenery.

Nuna pursed her lips. Nothing good could come from a tale involving that loathsome little man. "Really? What did Valdimarr have to say?"

"He brought me a report from one of the dockside drinking houses, where Dromundr overheard some Norlhast folk talking about Orglyr."

Nuna's hands tightened on the reins of her horse, the reflex hidden by her soft leather gloves. "Go on."

"Two men in the tavern were saying they hoped Orglyr would return. They were whispering there are plans afoot to oust the Vorund Clan and, this is the really interesting part of the story, that Orglyr has support from *within* Norlhast Keep. Your husband swore to me he had nothing to do with Orglyr's uprising, considering it to be as much a threat against him as it is to the rule of our king. I began to wonder if he should be put to the question once more, to be sure nothing has been overlooked, but then I considered how there are other possibilities. If there was truth in the rumour, could someone else be working for Orglyr within the keep? Your friend Sigurd, for example? I've made allowances for the sake of his father and your husband – perhaps he doesn't appreciate how understanding I've been?"

Nuna arched an eyebrow. "So Valdimarr's story concerns the tale of someone reporting something someone else half-heard in a tavern? Forgive me, Geilir, this is hardly compelling evidence of any kind of plot. Dromundr hasn't apprehended Orglyr's scouts carrying secret messages intended for a nest of conspirators in Norlhast Keep, has he? He's heard the ramblings of two men, probably deep in their cups. People will gossip and speculate about anything – that doesn't mean there's any truth in what they are saying. I don't doubt Sigurd's loyalty to our new allies and I've given you my open support in court, as has my husband, denouncing the uprising. Is it so surprising not everyone is ready to embrace Vorund's rule?"

Nuna felt ashamed as she thought back on the declarations she and Karas had made in Norlhast Keep. She'd seen the faces of the servants and warriors, standing there listening to her words as they openly mingled with their occupiers. The hope faded in their eyes as they listened to their leaders speak of Adalrikr as their king, the future of Norlhast entwined forever with his expanding northern kingdom. Orglyr was denounced as a rebel, an easy lie to believe with his history opposing Karas and Sigurd. Geilir looked pleased as he sat there at her side on the high table and he should have been – after all, he'd written her speech.

Geilir looked thoughtful. "Of course you could be right. The men have been apprehended and taken to the dungeons. I'll put them to the question personally, once they've had time to consider things in the darkness of their cells."

"Do I know these men?" Nuna asked, aware there was a risk in posing such a question. "I need to know if it concerns someone close to me at court. Such a thing could embarrass me and my husband."

Geilir shook his head. "Dromundr apprehended two fishermen – one of them a Helsburg freedman – named Skefill and Kofri. Have you heard of them?"

Nuna didn't recognise their names and she shook her head, relieved. It was probably a case of idle gossip; two fishermen stumbling unfortunately close to the truth within earshot of Dromundr. She swallowed, the guilt returning. There was nothing she could do to help them without drawing Geilir's suspicions.

"Be sure to tell me if they have anything meaningful to say," she said. "I'll not see Norlhast torn apart by a war it can't win. As I said at court, we have to build our future together. My marriage allied the Reavesburg and Norlhast Clans, proving that times change. Now that alliance grows more powerful – a future Laskan kingdom which will rival all the others in Valistria. An example should be made of those who refuse to embrace the ideals of progress and unity."

Geilir smiled at her, eyes glinting. "I'll be sure to give you a full report, my lady. If nothing else, it will be a good opportunity to discourage such thinking amongst the peasants."

Nuna dropped back from Geilir as they continued their ride, her horse falling into step with Kalfr's steed, his much-loved gelding called Swift. In low tones, she recounted what Geilir told her, Kalfr's face hardening as he listened.

"Foolish folk," he muttered. "Their names mean nothing to me either. Geilir won't tolerate that kind of talk in public – he'll want to punish them."

"And we'll have to sit idly by and watch," Nuna added, hands twisting her leather reins.

Kalfr turned to her. "There is nothing any of us can do. If we move against Geilir too soon everything is lost."

"That's why Geilir told me," Nuna replied. "He's testing me, trying to gauge where my loyalties really lie."

Kalfr nodded, sighing heavily. "Those prisoners are pieces in a game of kings. Sometimes you have to sacrifice a piece to win the game."

"You speak lightly of such things," Nuna said quietly, nodding as a Vorund warrior drew close, smiling at her in greeting. She waited until he was out of earshot before continuing. "Those men will have wives and families depending on them."

"Forgive my boldness, my lady, but I understand this far better than you. You've already asked me to do exactly the same thing, taking no action concerning the unjust treatment of my father. These men are simply another sacrifice, one that's necessary if we're to wait for the opportune moment to make our bid for freedom."

They fell into an uneasy silence as they continued their journey, their horses taking them back towards Norlhast Keep in a wide, sweeping circle. Kalfr rode with his head bowed, face sombre as he patted Swift's neck, whispering something to her. Nuna sighed, wishing she had chosen her words more carefully. After a while she nudged her own horse forwards, arranging her face into a smiling mask as she resigned herself to exchanging more pleasantries with Geilir.

CHAPTER 56

I stirred under the covers, muttering Nuna's name as I came to, my head aching. I opened my eyes, finding myself in the same chamber I'd slept in before, the dim wall lights giving off enough illumination to make out the shape of the room. As I swung my feet onto the warm floor the lights brightened, suffusing the chamber with a soft yellow glow. I blinked rapidly, waiting for my eyes to adjust. How long had I been here? Had I actually met Bruar in person or had the whole encounter taken place in the Realm of Dream? I rubbed my face, trying to sort out the jumble of memories, making sure I was recalling everything correctly. It didn't really matter. He'd agreed to help us.

Gingerly I rose from the bed, catching sight of my naked skinny frame in the mirror of the dressing table. I paused, looking at the patchwork of puckered flesh and silvered scars, a network of pain tracing itself over my body. My injured knee was red and swollen, although it felt better as I put some weight on it. I washed, my cheeks red and stinging as I applied cool water to my face. The itching cut on my palm had started to heal and was beginning to scab over. My travelling clothes had been returned to me, cleaned, dried and neatly folded on top of a chest at the foot of my bed. As I dressed in my familiar, comfortable garments I took it as a sign I would soon be leaving.

Sirion was waiting for me outside. "You look better," he said in a friendly voice, yellow eyes narrowing as he smiled. "Are you ready to travel?"

I nodded. "How long have I been here?"

"You've been asleep for a day since meeting Bruar and

it's now long past noon," Sirion told me. "We have prepared food and drink for you. After you have had your fill, Mendaleon thinks it best that you return to your friends."

***

Alcor and his companions escorted me to the gates in silence as we descended the stone staircase leading to the hidden mountainside entrance, the reliefs on the walls representing a journey through the history of Amuran. I could make out the first cities of Rannoch, founded for humans and dragons at the dawn of the Age of Glory, carved in exquisite detail. I peered closer, wondering if Lindos, my home until the spring of this year, was portrayed somewhere in the story.

As we descended more recent events were portrayed. I recognised Balvarran, his whispering lies fanning the flames of greed and envy in the minds of kings and queens. Aros was in the foreground, entertaining children with his stories, oblivious to the lies dripping into the minds of their parents as Morvanos' agents prepared for war in the shadows. Bruar was depicted, a muscular smith in this version of history, fashioning a huge metal horn fitted to the gates of some great city, now reduced to ash and rubble. Culdaff looked on from the sky, riding on the winds as Nanquido stirred the currents of the seas. Altandu was shown setting the sun in the heavens, whilst Ceren looked on darkly from the opposite wall as Altandu's tears became bright stars, sullying the deep night she had lovingly woven. I paused, fingers gently brushing the stonework, which was warm to the touch, as if the reliefs were alive.

"Do you understand what you're looking at?" Alcor asked me.

"Yes. Scenes from the Age of Glory, before the fall. There was always conflict between the avatars, even back then."

"He has much learning for one so young," Mendaleon observed.

I smiled, thinking of Etta and wondering what she

would make of this encounter. "I had a good tutor."

Alcor smiled humourlessly. "The avatars mirror each other in many ways. Could Myshall have existed without Dinuvillan? Fortune and misfortune go hand in hand, do they not?"

Alcor showed me through the secret doorway at the foot of the staircase, where I bade him and his companions farewell before leaving the hidden city.

"Thank you for your hospitality," I said to Mendaleon.

She bowed her head, golden eyes reflecting on her silver armour. "You have been granted a great honour. Since Bruar has deemed you and your cause worthy, we will respect his wishes and aid you in any way we can."

I walked through the secret doorway that led back onto the mountainside. Jade was sitting on a rock when I emerged with Alcor. She was wearing the same clothes as before and looked tired, as if she hadn't slept since we parted ways in the city.

"I thought you'd be here," said Alcor, his voice devoid of any warmth. "I have a job for you – one suited to your particular talents."

Jade looked at us both uncertainly. "What is it?"

"There are more intruders encamped on the other side of the island. Bruar has granted Rothgar a boon and agreed he and his companions can remain here in safety while he works to aid them in their war against the durath. These other visitors are led by a man called Hasteinn, who intends to cause harm to Rothgar and his friends. That must not be allowed to happen."

"And if I do this, will it ... count in my favour?"

Alcor laughed – a horrible, mocking sound. "You think more blood and slaughter is to your credit? I'm asking you to do this because giving in to the Beast is all you're fit for. I know you've already killed Hasteinn's scouting party – tell me, what was your excuse to end their lives?"

Jade's purple eyes blinked rapidly and part of me felt

sorry for her – another part afraid as Alcor goaded his younger kinswoman. I could feel the hurt and anger, the fury and barely contained power radiating from the young woman.

"See to it and Mendaleon will consider your position," Alcor told her. He turned on his heel and walked back through the hidden entrance, leaving the two of us alone.

"I'm sorry," I told her. "This is all my fault. They're only here because of me."

Jade glared back. "What have you got to be sorry about? Alcor will never forgive me for siding with Sigborn against him."

"Hasteinn has many more warriors with him than the group you fought in the forest. Don't you need Alcor's help to deal with them all?"

Jade's purple eyes flashed and there was a hunger there, swiftly hidden as she smiled. "Alcor broke my fighting spear when Tanios died but there are other ways to kill a man. Let me worry about Hasteinn. First of all we need to return you to your companions. They're camped at the foot of the mountain."

I decided to take Jade at her word as she led me down the steep path towards the forest. The sun was lowering in the sky, beginning its descent westwards. I wanted to be under the shelter of the trees before it was dark, hobbling after Jade as quickly as I could on my injured knee. From our vantage point I saw Ulfarr and the rest of my scouting party camped out on the edge of the woods and Jade led us towards them, making no effort to disguise our approach. Ekkill noticed us first, calling to the others who stood up and watched us draw closer. My knee was starting to ache by the time the ground levelled out and we weaved our way through the smaller pine and fir trees on the edge of the forest. Ulfarr and his companions walked towards me, Jolinn's eyes narrowing as she watched Jade walking at my side.

"You're alive," Ulfarr called out with a grin, unable to

disguise his relief.

Etta walked forwards, looking tired as she leaned on her stick. "Yes, yes. He's alive. What happened? Where have you been? Did you find Bruar? What did he say? Will he help us?"

I embraced Jolinn, ignoring the look Skari exchanged with Myr. When I recounted the events of the last few days Etta's face shone with undisguised delight. Ekkill listened impassively as he maintained a patrol around our group, keeping watch for any signs of Hasteinn's warriors.

When I finished speaking Etta reached out, taking my hand in hers. "You did it. Dinuvillan be praised, the Weeping Warrior guided us true and with Bruar's aid we finally have an opportunity to defeat Adalrikr. I'm so proud of you, Rothgar."

"It wasn't what I expected. I thought I'd have to argue with him and plead our case. But ..." I shook my head. I was missing something. Something important. "It doesn't really matter. We'll have to wait whilst he completes his work and he warned that would take time."

"And what about Hasteinn and his companions?" asked Ulfarr. "It's only a matter of time before they find our camp."

I explained how Jade had been given the task of dealing with that threat. She was sitting cross-legged on a tree trunk and Jolinn hadn't taken her eyes off her as I'd told my tale. Now everyone in our camp looked at her more carefully, understanding exactly who – or what – was among us. Skari looked wary as Jade stood and walked over to him, looking him up and down. She approached Jolinn next and the two stared at each other, Jolinn's bright blue eyes unflinchingly meeting her purple gaze.

"Jade, what is it?" I asked, an uneasy feeling settling in my gut.

Jade turned her back on Jolinn as she stared at the rest of our party. "Something isn't right, I can feel it."

"There's no one nearby," said Ekkill, although he drew an arrow from his quiver all the same, holding his bow ready.

"It's not that. It's here, among us. Right here where we're standing."

Everyone stepped back from Jade as she continued to prowl between us. Her fingers lightly brushed Ulfarr's chest and she spent some time looking at Myr the Silent, pausing when she moved on to Etta, the old woman's wrinkled face creased in a deep frown.

"What is this?" asked Ulfarr.

"Draw your sword," Jade replied

Ulfarr hesitantly slid his blade from its scabbard. I sighed in relief as I looked at the rune of power, cold and dark.

"What's the matter?" I said, confused.

Jade smiled, her pretty face taking on a hungry aspect I didn't like. "You have no idea, do you?"

"No idea about –" I didn't have chance to finish my question as Jade's hand whipped out towards Etta, snaking into the folds of her cloak. There was a green flash as Jora's jewelled necklace was caught by the rays of the setting sun.

"No!" Etta raised her staff, trying to knock Jade away. The younger woman grimaced, her hand twisting around the necklace and with a snap the chain broke. Jade stepped back with a look of triumph, holding the glittering emeralds aloft in her fist.

Etta shrank back, moaning – a noise of mingled grief, pain and fear. For a moment I couldn't understand why everybody was looking at me. I glanced down at Ulfarr's sword and choked off a cry, staring in disbelief at the dragon and chimera rune, which was glowing bright blue.

CHAPTER 57

The edge of the forest rang with the sound of steel as Jolinn and Myr also drew their weapons, comprehension dawning on Ulfarr's face as he stared at his glowing sword. Ekkill's bowstring creaked as he pointed a rune engraved arrow straight at Etta's heart. Skari growled, planting his feet wide as he hefted his warhammer into the air, the cruel head glowing blue in the fading light. Etta shrank back, clutching her stick as if this could ward off her assailants. A sick feeling settled in my stomach as I stared at the woman who'd helped raise me, a thousand memories of my childhood poisoned by the knowledge Etta had been consumed by the durath.

Jade dropped the emerald necklace at my feet. "An almost perfect disguise. I've never seen one of these, only heard of them in legend."

I struggled to find words, thinking back on Jora's visit to Etta's house in Romsdahl, when she'd handed over the necklace. Had Etta been one of the durath even then – using the necklace to move freely among us? *Stormweaver* was warded perfectly and despite that Etta had boarded our ship without any difficulty. I swallowed back bile as I realised if Adalrikr possessed something similar the durath could already have slipped past Johan's ring of runestones and into his camp.

"How long?" asked Ekkill, his voice choked with shock, bowstring quivering.

Etta gave him a pleading look, small and vulnerable as we all levelled our weapons at her. "Ekkill, I'm sorry. This isn't how it seems."

"You're a skin thief," hissed Ulfarr, taking a step

forwards. "What else is there to know?"

"Answer Ekkill's question," I said. "How long have you been walking among us as a shadow spirit?"

Etta turned to me, despair and defeat etched over her face, which had been aglow with success a few short moments ago. "You're a bright lad. You already know the answer."

Etta had been so ill during the march to Romsdahl, never leaving her tent so Johan had come to her when he needed her counsel, meaning she'd never had to cross the circle of runestones. Yet Etta had made such a remarkable recovery after Sinarr's defeat, finding a new lease of life and eventually making the arduous journey to the Fire Isle. Had she been feigning sickness all that time? As I thought back I remembered how Joldir's house in Lindos had been warded, although I'd not recognised the runes for what they were at the time. I tried to remember if Etta had ever left her cottage in the mountain valley to visit him – trying to recall her joining us around Joldir's fireside with Arissa and Thengill. I knew she'd never been there.

"So long?" I gasped. "You've been one of them since this war started, avoiding the runes protecting the Brotherhood all this time, until Jora's necklace gave you the ability to walk freely. You've had a hundred chances to kill Johan or any one of us – why haven't you acted sooner?"

"That's a good question," Etta replied, regaining some of her poise.

Jolinn moved to my side, watching Etta carefully over the top of her shield. "Don't talk to her, Rothgar, she's no longer your tutor from Ulfkell's Keep. We should kill her now – we've all seen what the durath can do."

I swallowed hard. "No, she's *always* been my tutor. What I never realised was I was being schooled by Etta the durath."

Etta bowed her head. "You're right, but before you try and bring me down remember I could have struck at the heart of the Brotherhood at any time. I had ample opportunity, after all. Think back on everything I've done and where my counsel has brought us. Yes, I'm one of the durath but that doesn't mean I'm on Adalrikr's side. Think back to what you learned in Tullen – there are different factions to this war and I'm on your side."

Jolinn shook her head. "I find that hard to believe."

"Is it so unlikely?" countered Etta. "I've advised the Brotherhood well and we've thwarted Adalrikr's ambitions many times by following my counsel. He's as much my enemy as he is yours – in fact, I have more reasons to hate him than you do. You're my true allies, not him."

"You're a skin thief." I spat the words, raising my sword. "You took Etta's form and murdered the poor woman you now inhabit."

Tears welled in Etta's eyes, my words wounding her more deeply than I expected. When she spoke, her voice was a whisper. "No. That's not true. Think anything else you wish about me but not that. This body was a gift, freely given out of love, the last thing my precious Etta did, to give me the chance for revenge against Adalrikr. Don't sully her memory and make her a victim – this was her choice, not mine."

Something in Etta's words made me stop and think. Did I really believe her? My head was starting to throb, sword arm aching from holding my weapon aloft. I let it drop to my side, trying to understand – wondering if I wanted to believe what she was telling me. If she was lying we could dispense summary execution, ridding the world of another enemy. If she was speaking the truth …

"If you're not Etta then who are you?" I asked.

"Long ago I was Merinia, the youngest daughter of the Emir of Zirhidan," Etta replied. "I was there at the very beginning, during the Enlightened Age, when Adalrikr was still known as Baltus, before he became the First of the Sundered and consumed the emperor Vashtas. I was among the first Sight users, including Nishrall and Celembine, who followed him and survived the Dividing. That was when I cast aside my life as Merinia to become a Sundered Soul, taking the form of a young prince of Valistria called Andros. Working together in our new guises we began to build the alliances that would eventually become Morvanos' army, planning to overthrow the ossifying rule of Vellandir and his cronies, who were slowly smothering Amuran. I did what I thought was right but when war came and I saw the death and destruction that followed ... By then it was too late."

"So how does Etta come into this?" I asked. "What became of Prince Andros of Valistria?"

"The surviving members of the Sundered were scattered at the end of the War. Prince Andros became a beggar, walking barefoot through the destruction and misery left in its wake. I'd craved power and immortality, thinking myself worthy to be one of the gods. Now, I couldn't die and possessed nothing, the clothes on my back little more than tattered rags. I watched as Valistria's fledgling kingdoms formed, thought fleetingly about stealing the life and hard-won power of another. I could have made myself a master of one of Mirtan's magical chapters, become a prince of Oomrhat or a warrior of Lagash. Then I met Reave, Harvaan and Norl, Laskar's founders. It was another period of civil war and they were gathering people to them, planning to head north to escape the fighting and start a simpler life. As Andros I followed in the footsteps of Reave, the father of your own clan, and I even knew him a little. He was a great man and although I couldn't wash away the blood staining my hands he gave me hope and a fresh start, where I could live out my days in the north in solitude."

"Yet you ended up guiding our affairs at the court of our chief," I observed. "Rather different to the simple life you describe."

Etta nodded. "I lived the life I wanted, farming in a remote mountain valley in Lindos for a time, moving on when the town of Olt was founded. During that journey I met Etta and the two of us married, living in a solitary homestead near Delving. We were happy, although Lamornna never blessed us with children. Perhaps that was for the best, as Etta slowly grew older whilst I remained unchanged. Eventually, I had to tell her the truth, thinking she would tell me to go …" Etta paused, taking a deep breath, more vulnerable than I had ever seen her. "I was wrong and she chose to stay at my side. As she grew older we had to move again, this time our new neighbours thinking she was my mother rather than my lover. It was there that Vashtas found us."

Etta bowed her head, grasping her stick tightly in both hands as she composed herself. "Morvanos' dark lieutenant had not forgotten the pain of defeat, Celembine using her scrying skills to find me. They set about reuniting the surviving Sundered and wanted me to join their cause, believing they could still win the war after all this time. When I said no Vashtas ran me through, a fatal wound. As I lay there dying he tried to force me to embrace what I had once been and steal another soul. When I refused they left me there to die, seeking out the rest of Vashtas' surviving followers, perhaps thinking I might change my mind, take a new form and join them after all. Yet he made a mistake that day, for Etta watched everything, hiding out in the fields. She ran to me and offered me a chance of life and the opportunity for vengeance, choosing to sacrifice herself so I might live."

"I'm sure you didn't take much persuading," I told her, taking perverse pleasure in how my sharp words etched misery and grief across Etta's face.

"There are so many days when I wish I'd not agreed to such a course but there was no going back after that moment, when I took her and I felt the woman I loved die, her soul scattering to the wind. Afterwards, I was determined Etta's sacrifice would not be wasted, adopting her guise for over forty years. In my new form I established myself as Marl's advisor and applied the knowledge and skills of my former life to build a network of spies and contacts, seeking to uncover Vashtas' plans and thwart them."

"You expect us to believe this outlandish tale of love and self-sacrifice?" Ekkill's lip was curled in disdain. "Your whole life has been a lie. You're the spy, planted right in our midst, directing our affairs as you pursued your own, selfish agenda."

"I care about all of you. Ekkill, you were my first apprentice – my most deadly weapon. Do you think I wasn't proud of everything you achieved? Think on all you've done for the Reavesburg Clan, unseen and unrewarded, except by me."

"You've always been one of them," Ekkill said softly. "You've been a shadow spirit from the very beginning, using me. Manipulating me."

Etta nodded. "Yes, but from the time of Marl, when I first came to his court, I've always worked for the good of Reavesburg. It was my way of giving something back to my wife's clan, working to protect her home and the people she loved. She was already old when I took this form, so no one noticed when I didn't age as the years passed. It was easy to appear unkempt and dishevelled, allowing my fine clothes and garments to become threadbare and careworn. People saw what they expected to see, thinking I was ageing when in fact there was never any change."

Etta stood up, straightening her back, raising her head proudly. Was I looking at a woman over one hundred years old or someone in their late sixties? Everyone at Ulfkell's Keep said she was ancient and I'd seen what others had told me, not what was before my eyes. I took a deep breath, trying to weigh the truth of Etta's words. Her story had woven a spell around my companions as they all listened to her tale. Jade was watching our encounter with a nonchalant air, arms folded across her chest and a wry grin on her face, and I wondered if she was enjoying the mischief she'd caused.

"Ekkill, you and the others I gathered to my side knew

what you were getting yourselves into," Etta continued. "My true nature wasn't relevant to the choices you made. I raised you up from poverty, made you wealthy and gave you a place of honour as one of the first members of Johan's Brotherhood. Would you rather have your old life back?"

"You haven't delivered on my latest payments," Ekkill snarled. "It doesn't look like you'll be good for the money now. You've played me and all the rest of us for fools."

"I did what was right," Etta told him. "For years the trail went cold and for a time I thought I had found my place, first serving Marl, then Kolfinnar and finally Jorik. However, my network began to bring me rumours once more of events that I suspected involved the rise of the durath. I had placed Joldir in Serena's chapter in Mirtan and called in that favour, asking her to send Ramill, Joldir and Nereth to investigate."

"Nereth was one of yours?" I asked.

Etta shook her head. "No, she was simply Joldir's apprentice, although I admit by sending her into the confrontation with Vashtas where Ramill was killed I inadvertently set events in motion that turned her over to Vashtas' service. A few years later Adalrikr rose to prominence after usurping his father and declared himself the King of Laskar. I knew then that Vashtas had assumed Adalrikr's form and now ruled Vorund, once I'd pieced things together from what I could learn concerning the death of Asmarr. After Ekkill found Thengill and I heard his tale my suspicions were confirmed and I knew this was where my enemy was building his power."

"Why Laskar?" I asked. "Why not rule one of the more powerful southern kingdoms? The Lagashans still follow the ways of Morvanos, so why not seize control there?"

"The Sundered believe themselves and all durath to be superior to humanity," Etta explained. "Their interest is not ruling human kingdoms. Ever since the end of the War, Vashtas has been seeking a way to bridge the gulf between the realm of the Real and the Shadow Realm, returning the host of banished durath to Amuran. Even now, I don't fully understand how he has achieved this but something he discovered in Vorund Fastness has given him the key to this knowledge – something Sandar stole from him and replicated in secret in Tullen. This is why Vorund Fastness must be taken, so we can close the gateway and undo the damage wrought by the Tear."

"So you engineered a war between Reavesburg and Vorund, drawing Norlhast into your plot as well," I said.

"I united the Reavesburg Clan in the fight against evil," Etta replied, her face defiant. "I'll make no apologies for doing that."

Jolinn swore. "I've heard enough. We're sworn to destroy the durath and this one's lied to us countless times over. It's time to end it."

"Killing me serves no purpose," Etta argued. "We can still work together – I know everything concerning the Sundered Souls. If the Brotherhood stays true to its purpose you *need* me."

"The Brotherhood's purpose was what you made it," I said, raising my sword once more. "We can't allow –"

Etta reached into her cloak and threw something onto the ground, where it exploded in a bright flash. I fell to the ground, ears ringing and eyes blinded, the world disconnected and distant from my senses. It took a few moments before I could see again, Jolinn looming above me, her strong hand grasping mine and hauling me to my feet.

"Where is she?" Skari was shouting, looking around wildly and I realised Etta had escaped. Ulfarr was on his knees, shaking his head, Myr sprawled on the ground nearby, moaning softly. Only Jade appeared unaffected.

"She went that way," Jade indicated with a lazy thumb over her shoulder.

"You didn't try and stop her?" I asked, dumbfounded.

Jade shrugged. "Why? Your companions are all under the protection of Bruar. This is a matter for you to decide amongst yourselves – it has nothing to do with me."

My jaw worked, my lips trying to form a reply. Ekkill growled, keeping his bow low as he set off on a loping run into the woods. "I'll find her," he shouted over his shoulder.

"Ekkill, wait!" Jolinn shouted, cursing as he vanished amongst the trees.

"We can't let him go on his own," muttered Ulfarr, looking at Skari as he helped Myr back to his feet.

"I need a moment," I told them, exhaustion and shock washing over me. I sank to the ground, resting my back against a tree. My breath was coming in shallow, rapid gasps and my head was spinning. I needed to be away from here – away from Etta's lies and manipulations.

"Alcor has given me a task," Jade told the others as Jolinn crouched down at my side, looking concerned. "I suggest you return to your ship and wait for me there and I'll let you know when it's done."

With that, Jade strolled into the forest as Jolinn put her arm around my shoulders. I closed my eyes, trying to comprehend the depths of Etta's betrayal.

CHAPTER 58

The golden eagle wheeled high on the thermals wafting off the face of the volcano, steering away from the foul sulphurous fumes, searching out his prey. Far below, men crawled on the surface of the land; a rare sight. Like all wild animals, the eagle had an innate fear of humans and kept a watchful distance, choosing his hunting ground well away from them. The first touching of minds was subtle, a gentle breath that felt like it ruffled the feathers on the back of the eagle's neck as the man who saw things through the eyes of others first reached out. Moments later, the eagle banked north, flying towards the place where the larger group of humans were camped. Far below tents were spread out on the edge of the forest and a number of trees had been cut down, wooden stakes driven into the ground to form a semicircle around the camp. More men were working on the timber of fallen trees, stripping off the bark and sawing the trunks into more stakes to complete their defences.

There was something else, deeper into the forest. The eagle felt a primal rush of fear, more powerful than the wariness associated with human interlopers. It stared down, its amazing eyesight peering between the trees, seeking out the cause. A pair of purple eyes met its gaze, framed in the face of a young woman, who was nothing of the kind. A creature of power from a time when the world was young, her savagery barely held in check. The eagle wanted to turn away and the man sharing his mind experienced the same desire. With an effort, he mastered the wish to flee and the eagle flew in a steady downwards spiral towards the men and the watching dragon.

The woman undressed, carefully folding her clothes into a neat bundle that she stowed by the bole of a tall pine tree. She stretched her back and neck, reaching up high and looking into the sky above her, purple eyes spotting the eagle as easily as it had found her. They both shared that in common – an ability to see their prey before they were aware of being watched. The woman set off at a run towards the camp, sunlight catching on her pale flesh where the bright shafts made their way through the thick canopy of trees. In the distance men were laughing as they worked on the timber, sharing a joke as their doom approached.

The pines and firs shook beneath the eagle, smaller trees folding over, snapping like twigs underfoot. Birds broke for cover, rising up in a thick squawking cloud of frightened feathers. Down on the beach the basking seals and sea lions looked up from their slumber, calling out to each other in alarm as they lumbered into the safety of the water. The laughter faded, the men looking in the direction of the trees, murmuring questions as the forest trembled, trunks of great pines splitting as they fell to the ground with a shower of needles.

The dragon burst into view at the edge of the forest, fifty feet of shining purple scales, iridescent in the sunlight. It planted its front legs into the ground, six-inch claws raking the soil as its huge wings flapped once to slow its advance before snapping back and folding tight along its sinewy back. The dragon stood there, proud and hungry, roaring its challenge to the intruders on the island, the sound like a thunderclap, splitting the air and shaking the stones for miles around. The workmen nearest the creature began shouting in horror, some falling to their knees in fear, others cowering behind the trees and workbenches. Those with more sense turned and ran as the beast sprang upon the rest of their working party, teeth and claws ending lives in gouts of blood, torn flesh and broken bones. The dragon's head snapped up, purple eyes glittering as it eyed the men fleeing the scene and it sucked in a deep breath, long neck rearing up as it towered over the survivors. Shouts of fear turned to screams of pain as they were engulfed in flames, stacks of timber igniting like kindling around them as they died.

In the main camp men were stumbling from their tents, staring in shock at the wall of flame burning at the edge of the forest. The dragon burst through the fire with another ear-splitting roar, rising into the sky with two mighty beats of its great leathery wings, before launching itself into a stooping dive. It cleared the pitifully inadequate wall of stakes with ease as it landed in the centre of the camp, smashing several of the tents to the ground with the battering wind of its wings. The creature's tail whipped round, knocking over half the stake wall and sending sharpened timbers flying. Several of these hurtled through the camp itself, spearing one unfortunate man and crushing two of his companions. Others were trampled by the dragon as she reared and brought her forelimbs down, raking through the flesh of fleeing men, demolishing another tent as she advanced.

On the far side of the camp, one man had maintained his composure. He was young, with a shock of black hair and the beginnings of a dark stubbly beard. He was calling out orders, bringing a group of bowmen forwards as others scrambled to ready themselves, seizing weapons and strapping shields to their arms. A few arrows skittered around the dragon, most of them wide of the mark, a few bouncing ineffectually off her scaled hide. Moments later the entire camp was ablaze, a ball of fire exploding outwards as the dragon took to the skies, riding on the screams of the dying. Some of the warriors gathered around their leader lost heart, turning and running towards the beach and the relative safety of the water. The dragon rose higher, forcing the eagle to avoid her as she hurtled into the sky, lazily turning to survey the destruction. Far below, a small knot of defiant warriors awaited her return, trembling with fear as she reached the apex of her climb and began a slow drop towards the ground once more, gathering speed as she folded her wings behind her. Arrows zipped past her as she stretched out, an amethyst spear thrown by the gods. At the last moment she opened her wings with a leathery snap, turning sharply, grasping two men in her front claws. The momentum carried her out over the ice, where she turned in a wide arc, dropping the warriors onto the frozen shelf with a distant thud. Neither of them moved again, limbs spread at unnatural angles, spattered blood radiating out from the points of impact on the unforgiving white ice.

On the next run she took another warrior in her jaws, knocking the others to the ground with the wind generated by her passing. The dragon landed this time, turning to look at them with the broken body of the man hanging in her jaws. She tipped her head back, long neck stretched out, as she gulped him down, drawing a cry of despair from the watching men by the shore.

Their young leader shouted more orders and everyone fled towards the water, running as fast as they could, hoping to swim across the narrow channel and reach the ice shelf. The dark-haired man looked back over his shoulder, watching in horror as the dragon took to the air once more. Whilst there was no escape doing something, no matter how futile, was better than cowering, waiting for the end. The eagle or the man (it was hard to tell which) felt a grudging respect for Hasteinn as the shadow of the dragon fell over him and his few remaining warriors. Liquid fire consumed them, choking black smoke filling the air, thick with the yells of the dying and the smell of burning flesh. Now indistinguishable from one another, a few human torches staggered onto the beach, those furthest ahead dropping into the ice-cold seawater.

The dragon returned to the camp and snapped its jaws around one man still staggering over the stony beach, biting him off at the waist, smoking legs collapsing onto the ground. Some bodies were carried off by the icy waters, hissing as the fires were doused. The camp was silent except for the sound of the flames, timbers charring and snapping at the site of the working party. Another roar, softer this time, issued out over the scene of carnage as the snaking form of the dragon prowled amongst the wreckage, casually killing two more half-dead survivors. All else was still, the fires burning down as they greedily consumed their fuel. Once more those purple eyes locked with those of the watching eagle, high above.

Is this what you wanted to see?

***

"It's done," I gasped, awakening from the Sight, drenched in sweat. The others were gathered around me, their expressions a mixture of fear and distrust. There was no sign of Ekkill.

"Hasteinn?" Jolinn asked.

"He's dead. Jade destroyed the entire encampment. None of them survived."

"Good job she's on our side," said Skari, the joke falling flat.

"What about Etta?" asked Ulfarr.

"I didn't see anything of her or Ekkill. I've never been able to reach either of them with the Sight – I think that's why I was drawn to Jade. Gods, I hope we never anger her."

"We heard it from the other side of the island," Jolinn told me with a shudder.

"Be grateful you didn't see what happened." I lay back against the tree, exhausted.

"We should get moving, whilst we still have some light," said Ulfarr, casting a nervous glance at the forest.

Skari frowned, ugly face twisting around his eye patch. "Where to? Do we go after Ekkill and Etta or back to the camp?"

Ulfarr glanced at me for direction and sighed, seeing I was too far gone to care. "We'll make for *Stormweaver*.

They'll be wondering what's happened and I don't want Aerinndis to leave without us. They'll have heard the same sounds as we did – if I was them I know what I'd be thinking. As for Etta, we've no idea where she's gone. Ekkill was our best tracker – let him find her and work out what to do next."

What to do with Etta? That thought struck me hard as Myr and Jolinn lifted me back to my feet. I found myself questioning everything we'd done up until now – all the sacrifices, the risks we'd taken, the battles we'd fought. I thought it had been for me – my vengeance for the murder of my family and the breaking of my body. I didn't know any more. Etta had been there from the very beginning, whispering in my ear. Were my thoughts and feelings my own or had they been part of Etta's secret agenda all along? Joldir would be waiting for another message from me but how could I tell him about this?

CHAPTER 59

Djuri was sparring with some of the men when he heard the noise of horses and carts approaching. The gates to the keep swung open and Eidr rode through them, the tall man sitting high in the saddle of a courser, a satisfied expression on his face. Djuri despaired as he recognised the horse as one of those he'd given to Humli's family. The warriors with Eidr were in good spirits, Bjorr calling out to Galin, pointing towards a covered cart bouncing over the cobblestones.

"They're back," muttered Ulf, stowing his wooden training sword in the basket and wiping sweat from his face.

"So I see," Djuri replied, walking over with the rest of the warriors to see what was behind the commotion, although in his heart he already knew.

Eidr swung down from his horse as his men pulled the occupants out from the cart – Humli, Desta and Lina, all bound and looking exhausted. Fear could do that to anyone, even one of the durath, and Djuri understood at once why Lina looked so terrified. From another cart two more warriors were climbing down, each one carrying an infant.

Galin Ironfist clapped Bjorr on the shoulder. "A successful mission. Tyrfingr will want to hear of this straight away."

"We'll need a wet nurse for the children," Bjorr replied.

"Where are you taking them?" shouted Desta, struggling in the grip of one warrior who was trying to drag her towards the Great Hall.

"I know somebody," interjected Djuri. "There's a lady called Tola – she used to be a servant here at the keep and she already knows the boy. She's cared for him before, so it would make sense to take him to someone familiar."

Bjorr nodded, pleased to have a solution presented so quickly. "Alright. Go with my men and find this woman. She'll have to care for the other child, Frokn, too." He cast a dark glance in Lina's direction.

Djuri led the two men to Tola's house, ignoring Desta and Lina's protests. Finn had started to cry as they left, the noise grating in Djuri's ears as he tried not to imagine what might be happening in the Great Hall to the child's mother and grandfather. He knocked on the door, relief washing over him when Tola answered. She was a young woman with a round figure, brown hair and a kindly face, with a splash of freckles running across her nose and cheeks. Her welcoming smile faltered as she saw the warriors standing behind Djuri, Finn wailing and red-faced.

Tola nervously invited the men inside and Djuri quickly explained what had happened. From another room in the small cottage her husband, Boddi, emerged, looking frightened and confused at the appearance of Vorund warriors in his house. The noise stirred Tola's own daughter in her cot and she also started to whimper. Tola took the child in her arms, trying to comfort her as she listened to Djuri's story.

"It's not that I don't want to be helpful," Tola told Djuri. "I cared for Finn so Desta could work at Ulfkell's Keep."

"Now she really needs you," Djuri pleaded.

One of the warriors grunted and shifted the wailing Finn in his arms. "I've heard enough. Here, take him." He thrust Finn into Boddi's hands and walked out.

The other warrior stared after him, glancing down at Lina's infant. He turned to Djuri. "Looks like you have everything sorted out here." He passed Frokn to Djuri and followed his friend outside, the two of them laughing loudly as they walked away.

Djuri turned to Boddi and Tola. "I'm sorry about this. You were the first people I thought of – I know you were friends with Desta and I wouldn't ask if there was anyone else."

Boddi turned to Djuri, looking uncertain. "What kind of trouble is Desta in? Lots of folk have headed west to make a new start. Why has Tyrfingr ordered her to be brought back?"

"There's Drifa to think of," added Tola. "We need to keep her safe. If this could put her at risk then we can't do this."

"No, it's nothing like that," Djuri explained. "You'd be helping Tyrfingr, if anything. He's arrested Desta and her family and he wants the children kept safe while he ... talks to them. I don't know what's going to happen, but your help will reflect well on you and your family, I promise."

"Who's this?" Tola asked, looking at Lina's child in Djuri's arms.

"The boy's name is Frokn, Lina's son. She was staying with Humli, a refugee from the west."

Tola leaned closer, stroking the child's cheek whilst gently bouncing Drifa on her shoulder. "He's a handsome boy, although he has such a serious look on his face. He'll cheer up soon enough, living with us."

"Who says he's staying here?" Boddi replied. "Finn is one thing – we know Desta but I don't know this Lina at all. What's this got to do with us?"

"He reminds me of your father, Boddi," Tola replied, as if she hadn't heard. She glanced at Boddi, eyelashes fluttering and Djuri had to bite his lip to stop himself smiling as he saw her husband's objections melt away.

"I don't make much coin as a fisherman," Boddi said quietly, fixing his eyes on the floor as his cheeks began to colour.

"I'll personally make sure you don't go short," Djuri told him. "Coin is easy enough to find. An able and willing nursemaid, that's more difficult." He reached into his pouch with his free hand, drawing out a single silver crown.

"That'll be enough to cover this month, I'm sure."

Boddi's eyes widened and he took the coin before Djuri had chance to change his mind. "I'm sure it will, sir. That's very generous of you."

Djuri passed Frokn over to Tola, who had returned a now settled Drifa to her cot. She took the boy in her arms, crooning softly. "He's so *small*," she whispered. "Look at those dark eyes – this one sees more than you think, Boddi."

Boddi smiled weakly, happy to have pleased his wife whilst also clearly concerned about what they were getting into. "Finn and Frokn – it sounds like something from the old sagas, doesn't it?"

Djuri watched Tola and understood why Desta had entrusted Finn to her care. Haarl had complained about it enough times, forgetting Desta's wages would have enabled them to buy a homestead and land of their own in another year or two. Tola had that rare ability to love without effort and share it freely, Frokn sensing this, his tired watchful eyes closing as she wrapped him in her arms, his head resting on her breast. For the first night in a long while these boys would sleep without fear and that was something to be grateful for.

"Your kindness won't be forgotten," Djuri told them as he took his leave. "Keep the children safe and I'll try and visit as often as I can. I hope their mothers will soon be free ... and then ..." He trailed off, finding it difficult to say those words when he knew a favourable outcome for Desta and Lina at Tyrfingr's hands was unlikely. *I tried to help them and I failed in that too.*

"Djuri Turncloak."

Djuri looked up at Tola when she uttered his name. It sounded like a rebuke, even when the words were spoken kindly. "That's what they call me."

"That's what people call you these days," Tola corrected. "The Reavesburg warrior most favoured by Tyrfingr Blackeyes, one of his guards and the leader of what remains of our men. I've heard the stories but I see a different side to you now. Haarl always spoke highly of you and he was a good judge of character. I thought you should know that. The fact you cared for his son and made sure he was safe, that's the mark of a good man."

"I try," Djuri replied, not daring to say more as his throat tightened.

"They'll be alright, won't they?" asked Boddi. "Desta, and this Lina?"

Tola and Djuri shared a glance, understanding passing between them. *It's likely this family will raise these boys to manhood. Not sure Boddi's ready to hear that just yet.*

"I'll head back to the keep and find out what I can," Djuri replied. "Perhaps this is all a misunderstanding. Haarl fought at my side in Romsdahl – that might count for something if I vouch for his widow."

Tola patted him on the shoulder. "I know you'll do what you can. The boys will be safe with us until then."

Djuri walked back towards the keep, deep in thought. Helping Finn was one thing but he knew Haarl would have wanted him to keep Desta safe too. That was more difficult now her link to Rothgar gave Adalrikr a way into the Brotherhood of the Eagle, something he wouldn't surrender easily. Similarly, Adalrikr had personally asked for Lina to be presented to him and that interest wasn't going to go away. The two women were beyond his help and Humli – well, he wasn't needed by anyone at all, which didn't bode well for his future. He caught sight of the two warriors who had been nursing the children, sitting at the window of a tavern, drinking ale. They saw him and called out, inviting Djuri to join them. Djuri's hands bunched into fists and he had to make an effort to relax them, wave apologetically and move on. Those men didn't care about Desta or Lina and their families – why should they?

Ulfkell's Keep loomed over the town of Reavesburg, a black outcrop of rock – its walls a sheer cliff face of stone.

Desta and her family would be within those walls, thrown into the dungeons to await their fate. Eidr was back at Tyrfingr's side and Djuri considered striking at them now. He had a chance to redeem his name and cut off the head of Vorund and durath leadership at the heart of Reavesburg – after all, he'd managed to kill Kolsveinn, so perhaps he could repeat the same feat with Eidr? Escaping alive after committing such acts would be impossible but it might be enough to change his name in the eyes of his clan. *Djuri the Avenger – that would be something to make my father proud. Trouble is, they're just as likely to keep calling me Djuri Turncloak. After all, it would mark* another *betrayal. That's not the stuff of legends – it's the actions of a traitor.*

Did that matter? Was doing the right thing more important? Djuri thought of how he had felt bringing Finn and Frokn to safety. Perhaps there was something he could do for Desta and her family. Was there a way he could free them and still take his revenge against Tyrfingr for turning him into what he had become?

Perhaps. Perhaps there was.

CHAPTER 60

"What are you thinking?" Jolinn asked me. It was dark, the days growing shorter now summer had given way to autumn. Down below us laughter rose up from the camp fire, its flickering orange glow casting shadows onto the warded hull of *Stormweaver* as her crew celebrated our safe return. And Etta's fate? It hadn't been easy to find a way to tell the truth. Ulfarr spoke with brutal honesty, setting his emotions aside when he explained what had happened.

"If you see that old crone, kill her. She's one of them – has been all along. A shadow spirit, one of the durath."

While Ulfarr dealt with the noisy interrogation that followed his announcement I established a circle of runestones, taking each smooth warded stone and setting it carefully in place, feeling the power of the magic imbued in the runes crackling against my fingertips. I stood in the middle, inviting Aerinndis and her crew to join me, one by one. Everyone passed the test, the runestones staying dark and confirming the durath hadn't further infiltrated our camp. Afterwards, I'd walked away from the storm of questions, heading back to the edge of the forest where I sat down, completely exhausted. I thought of Desta, imprisoned in Ulfkell's Keep because of me and closed my eyes, feeling helpless.

"Rothgar?"

I turned to Jolinn. In the dark skies above us the stars shone through a green and red curtain of light. It moved and shimmered to no discernible pattern, bright one moment, fading away to nothing the next. Every time it vanished I wondered if the spectacle was over, watching in awe as colour blazed across the night once more.

"I'm tired," I told her.

Jolinn took a seat next to me. "There's more going on in your mind than that."

"I hope Ekkill finds her and kills her." The words were harsh, full of bile and hatred. Etta had always been difficult but I'd loved her all the same. She had been part of my family – one of the last surviving links to my old life. All of it a lie.

Jolinn sat in silence next to me, watching the sky shift from red through to green and into a deep purple, the stars glittering in the background. The effect was so entrancing the noise from the camp quietened as everyone stopped to watch this miracle of the Creator.

"And if he succeeds?" asked Jolinn. "If Ekkill returns and tells you Etta's dead, what then?"

I cursed, picking up a small stone next to me and throwing it into the forest. "I don't know. I don't know what to think about any of this. Why we're here, whether the Brotherhood is doing the right thing, why we're even fighting Adalrikr. Etta put us on the path to war for her own personal reasons. How many people have died because of her? We've all been part of it. The things I've seen ..."

Jolinn reached out and took my hand. Her touch was gentle, although her skin was rough and calloused from days of rowing and years of swordplay. I put my hand on top of hers, feeling its warmth, appreciating her being here with me.

"I used the Sight to see what Jade did ... I saw her kill Hasteinn and his men, experienced what happened to them as if I was there. I could hear their cries, smell the blood and burning flesh. I know what Hasteinn was but does it mean he and everyone with him deserved to die like that? Hasteinn and his crew wouldn't have been here at all if it wasn't for me – more people dead due to Etta's scheming. How can I trust *anything* she's had a hand in?"

"You're thinking too much about all of this," Jolinn

told me in soothing tones. "Whatever Etta is, the durath are an evil that has to be stopped. The idea of the Brotherhood came from Johan, not Etta and, if you recall, he actually spurned her counsel for a time. You told me yourself how Johan changed after Tullen. Just because Etta isn't what you thought doesn't mean our cause isn't right. I know what I saw in Romsdahl when Sinarr the Cold One died. If that's the power behind Adalrikr's throne then it has to be stopped."

I reached into my pack and pulled out the emerald necklace. The glowing skies were reflected in the cut jewels spread out over my hand, making the object even more beautiful. "I saw Jora bring this to Etta. All that time she was pretending to be bed-bound, a ruse to evade our runestones. When I asked her to explain how her strength had been restored I suspected something was amiss but never in my wildest dreams did I imagine this. What a fool I've been."

Jolinn squeezed my hand tighter. "She made fools of all of us. That doesn't change what we set out to do and Adalrikr still has to be defeated."

I heard the crunch of boots on stone and turned to see Ekkill emerging from the line of trees, head bowed. I glanced at Jolinn as we both got to our feet, each of us with the same idea. We drew our blades, glancing down anxiously at the runes etched on our weapons, which remained dark.

"It's alright, it really is me," Ekkill declared, his voice weary.

"Did you find her?" Jolinn asked.

"No. I followed her tracks for a time but that woman is fast. She moves ... well, she moves like *they* do and she gave me the slip at a shallow stream. I searched up and down the banks for a time, trying to see where she'd climbed out until eventually it grew too dark to continue the hunt."

"You shouldn't have gone after her on your own," Jolinn admonished.

Ekkill smiled, white teeth glinting in the light from the heavens. "I can look after myself."

Jolinn shook her head. "Etta is dangerous. We'll form a search party and scout the woods again tomorrow at first light. Together."

"No," Ekkill replied. "This is personal. I gave the best years of my life to her service, risking my neck countless times on her account. Yet all the coin I earned doesn't pay for the fact she was taking me for a fool, never seeing what was right in front of me."

I'd never warmed to Ekkill, yet in that moment I felt for the man and without thinking I gave him an awkward hug. "We've all been betrayed."

Ekkill gently disentangled himself from my embrace. "Do you really think this changes anything? You're still the one Etta was grooming to take my place, so don't expect me to forgive you for that."

"Replace you?"

Ekkill sighed in frustration. "For someone with the Sight how is it you never see what's right in front of you? How could I compete with the gifts she uncovered in you? I thought I might one day become spymaster in her place, although I realise now she'd have outlived me anyway. What am I even doing out here? I've enough coin to start a new life anywhere I want, yet that old crone persuaded me to come to this accursed isle as her *protector*. I've been an idiot – Etta's always been the mistress of manipulation and it turns out none of us are immune to her tricks."

I didn't know what to say as Ekkill's jealousy boiled over. I cursed my own stupidity for not fully taking into account the feelings of those closest to me and the Brotherhood.

"There's something else you should know," Ekkill told me, his shadowed face briefly illuminated by the flickering green sheets of light coursing across the night sky. "I had a hand in creating the person who went on to supplant me."

"What do you mean?"

Ekkill laughed mirthlessly. "Gildcrest and shadow

root."

"What?"

"You heard me. Etta had me prepare that potion and pour it down your throat that night."

"To put me into a dreamless sleep for the journey to Lindos," I replied, wondering where Ekkill was going with this. A feeling of dread ensnared me as I remembered Bruar speaking about that night, revealed by the mysteries of the scrying pool. Why was this so significant?

"Joldir never mentioned this?" Ekkill asked. "I didn't think so. Have you never wondered *why* the Sight only manifested itself fully after Tyrfingr tortured you?"

"That's not right," I corrected him. "I first experienced the gift when I was recovering from Nereth's poison in Norlhast."

"Which you subsequently told Etta about."

"If you've something to tell me, get on with it."

"In sufficient quantities gildcrest mushrooms can awaken the Sight in a person, when combined in the correct proportions with shadow root. The process is dangerous, especially for someone as badly hurt as you were. I've seen it used twice before with people Etta thought had ... promise. Both of them died. Etta knew there was a strong possibility you had latent abilities and she was prepared to risk your life to fully awaken them. She might have raised me up from the gutter, yet despite your noble birth you're even more her creature than I ever was. Etta needed someone to help counter Nereth's power and she was prepared to put your life at risk to wage her war. Whether putting you into the dreamless sleep saved your life on the journey to Lindos, we'll never know. What is certain is that by giving you that potion Etta knew your life would never be the same again."

"I think you've said enough, Ekkill," Jolinn interjected. "Go down to the camp, take some rest and have something to eat. We'll be along in a moment."

Ekkill pushed past us and made his way down toward

the longship. "You had a right to know," he called without a backwards glance.

"Are you alright?" Jolinn whispered.

"I don't know," I replied, reaching out and gently taking Jolinn's hand once more.

"Ekkill was saying those words to hurt you. But think, if you'd been given the choice of living with or without the Sight, which would you have chosen?"

I thought on that for a time. "I *should* have been given the choice – now there's no going back to change things. I know what you're trying to say. This way I can use my gifts and play my part in ... whatever this is."

I drew Jolinn into an embrace, hand stroking the nape of her neck as my other arm wrapped around her waist. As we kissed it felt like the only thing on the whole of Amuran that really mattered. Here was something honest and true, discovered and treasured amid a tangle of lies and deceit.

After a time Jolinn pulled apart from me. "You need to come back to the camp. Eat, rest and sleep. Everything will seem better in the morning, I promise."

I let her lead me down to *Stormweaver*, where Aerinndis and Meinolf were in a heated discussion about who had drunk more in the port of Tandos to win a bet with a Samarak sultan. Bone-weary, I ate and drank, not really tasting the food. Nearby Matthildr was sitting next to Feyotra, hands entwined as they listened with wry grins to the argument, while overhead the skies continued to glow with ethereal light as we sat under the stars, camped at the very edge of the world.

CHAPTER 61

Meldun leaned out over the walls, hawked and spat. His round face was encircled by a ring formed by his curly beard and receding hairline, giving him a kindly look. However, he was one of the more experienced warriors in Randall's company and looks were deceiving.

"Another night repairing the walls, eh chief? Gets boring doesn't it?"

Randall nodded, watching the masons dangling from their ropes and ladders, trying to shore up the widening cracks in the outer wall. Three days ago Thengill, the axe-wielding Vorund traitor who now fought for the Brotherhood, used the cover of darkness to lead a raiding party, attacking the workers and killing several of them. By the time the alarm had been raised the Brotherhood's men had melted away and returned to their camp. *There weren't so many volunteers the next night to help protect our city, even with the watch doubled. Can't say I blame them.*

Adalrikr ordered Randall to gather any able-bodied men not already in service defending the walls to help the stonemasons. Tonight was a good night – no one had died. Randall shivered as he recalled the scream of the young man crushed to death last night, when one of the ropes on the crane broke, sending half a tonne of stone crashing to the ground below. *Let's hope that won't be repeated.*

Meldun carried on grumbling, Randall half-listening and making the appropriate noises as and when necessary to feign interest. Eventually he made his excuses and left the wall, walking back to the Inner Keep. One of the problems of being a jarl was everyone wanted to complain to you about something. Back at the keep, he could escape from it all, even if it was only for a few short hours. All was quiet when he reached the gates and Randall noted The Six were nowhere to be seen. When he asked one of the regular guards where they were he was answered with a shrug, which he could understand – no one wanted to spend any time with Adalrikr's unnatural guardians if they didn't have to. He walked inside and hesitated at the staircase leading up towards his chamber. *What's the matter with you? Afraid of a good night's rest?*

The stillness in the keep bothered him, as did the absence of The Six. With a sigh, Randall took the other winding staircase, the one leading down towards Adalrikr's underground chamber. Something wasn't right, and he knew he'd find no peace until his questions were answered. When he realised the warriors who should have been stationed along the way were missing from their posts Randall quickened his pace, taking care to quieten his footsteps as he drew closer to the main chamber and his sense of dread began to grow.

As Randall crept forwards, keeping to the shadows at the bottom of the stairs, he saw The Six weren't guarding the entrance. They surrounded two score of tributes, Randall recognising some of their faces, Adalrikr standing in front of them with Heidr and Nishrall. Some looked apprehensive, while others appeared proud and defiant as their king began to address the group, talking about bravery and sacrifice. One woman started to giggle, a high screeching sound, making Randall wince. The woman shuddered and fell silent, her body twisting into an unnatural shape, before straightening her posture with an effort as Nishrall glared at her.

"You risked all to heed the Calling," Adalrikr was saying, "and now I ask more of you. Shed these forms and strike fear into the Brotherhood. They are warded and prepared against attack but if you succeed in killing Johan

Jokellsward the Brotherhood's spirit will shatter once and for all. Who here is willing to undertake this great task and serve their king?"

The robed tributes shouted their support, the giggling woman laughing wildly, once more contorting her body, eyes starting from her skull. She stared directly at where Randall was crouching in the shadows and he pressed himself back against the stone wall, hardly daring to breathe.

"Rise up," Adalrikr commanded. "Rise up and destroy the Brotherhood's champion."

Randall blinked as the tributes screamed, some pounding themselves on the head, others throwing themselves to the floor, prostrate before their king, a few pleading for mercy. The giggling woman was dancing, her high, girlish laughter rising into the air, increasing in intensity as she whirled and cavorted in front of Adalrikr. Randall's mouth fell open as a dark, shadowy cloud boiled out from the dancing woman's mouth. She screamed as if she were being torn apart, shaking and trembling as the cloud gathered above her and rose up, shrieking, into the night. The woman dropped to the ground with a sickening crunch, head striking the stone floor, her eyes fixed in their sockets. The cries from the remaining tributes grew louder as more shadows rose from them in twos and threes. One by one, the young tributes fell to the ground, all of them unmistakeably dead, whilst the strange shadows circled the ever-present darkness in the centre of the chamber. Eventually, only one tribute was still alive, weeping as he knelt before his king, as Adalrikr looked down on him with undisguised contempt.

"Was the honour of serving me this night not enough? Was there another more worthy cause? You disgust me."

The young man cowered before his king, tearing at his robes with shaking hands. "My lord, I've spent so long in the cold and the dark. I'm not strong enough to take another form so soon. Please, I'll serve you in any other way,

I promise you. Just not this – please, don't make me do this."

Nishrall smiled as he stepped forwards. "I understand you're afraid. There's nothing wrong with fear. Nothing at all. The question is how you respond to fear – how you channel it and use it to your advantage."

The weeping man nodded, raising up his face hopefully as he knelt before Nishrall. He gave a shout of surprise as one of The Six stepped forwards and placed his frosted hands firmly on either side of his head. Randall winced as the undead warrior twisted the man's head, his flailing limbs falling limp as the bones in his neck popped and snapped. The warrior released the dead man's head, which lolled for a few moments at an unnatural angle before he fell onto his side.

"Channel your fear," Heidr told the corpse in a soft voice. As Randall watched another dark cloud rose with a despairing wail from the man's body. It joined the others, circling the room for a few moments and then as one they arrowed towards the staircase, hurtling straight past Randall as he covered his face with his hands.

***

Leif woke screaming, fists pounding Arissa as she tried to comfort him. It took him three attempts to get the words out clearly enough for her to understand. Joldir groaned, rousing himself from the bed on the far side of the tent.

"The durath are coming for Johan," Leif gasped, finally managing to free himself from the choking fear and horror of his vision to explain what was happening.

Screams were drifting over the camp as Thengill sprang from his bed, cursing and swearing as he pulled on his breeches, the tattoo on his chest stretched across rippling muscles and scar tissue. Arissa turned to him, face full of fear.

"I have to go," he explained as he pulled a shirt over his head, hefting his hand axes. They were already glowing pale blue in the darkness of their tent. "The durath can't touch me. I have to protect Johan." Thengill pushed open the tent flap. "Leif, stay here with Arissa – keep each other safe."

Leif sat on the bed, Arissa's arm around his shoulders. "It'll be alright," she told him, her other hand gripping a long knife, the three runes on the blade shining with a pale blue glow. Leif's thoughts turned to the deaths of his sisters in Brindling, his father too afraid to move from his hiding place as their home burned. Hot tears ran down his cheeks as he listened to the frightened cries and the sound of battle.

***

Svafa gasped, struggling to fight off the clawing fingers of the man he had been on patrol with. He knew enough of the durath by now to understand his companion was already dead, the skin thief trying to bite at his face.

"I'm so hungry," hissed the warrior, his face a mass of twitches and uncontrolled tics. "It burns. The hunger has to be sated."

Svafa headbutted the other man, hard enough to break his grip and send him crashing onto the ground. Myr would have been proud. He drew out Rothgar's glowing runeblade and advanced, noting the warrior's own sword was forgotten, still sheathed at his side. The creature writhed, overcome by pain that wracked his whole body. Whatever was wrong didn't concern Svafa as he drove the point of his sword straight into the throat of the skin thief, watching with relief as the creature crumbled to dust in front of him.

"To Johan. Protect your chief!" It was Petr, calling the Brotherhood to defend their leader, his sword held aloft, six runes running its length glowing bright blue in the darkness. He was standing behind the ring of runestones encircling Johan's tent. Svafa could see Johan at his side, two-handed greatsword drawn as he stood there in his nightshirt.

A warrior hurtled towards the pair of them, screaming incoherently, flinging himself at Petr. He stopped in mid-air, the warded barrier crackling as the durath tried to cross the threshold. He was sent reeling backwards as a dome of magical energy briefly flared and vanished. A shadow enveloped a man next to Svafa, who clawed at his face, shrieking in terror and pain as the durath consumed him. He growled as the durath took possession of its new host, standing up straight and looking at Johan. The first durath warrior was already on his feet, hurling himself headlong at the invisible barrier once more. His companion joined him, straining to push his way through and more arrived all the time, the runes blazing constantly as they repelled the attackers.

"What do you think you're doing standing there?" snarled Thengill as he charged past Svafa, almost knocking him off his feet. "With me –"

There was a moment of absolute night as another coiling shadow wrapped itself around Thengill. Svafa gave a cry, backing away as Thengill crouched down, roaring in defiance. Throm and Bandor arrived, stopping in their tracks and staring in helpless shock as Thengill fought against his foe. The shadow became fast-moving tendrils of darkness, wrapping themselves around his limbs, snaking into his mouth, nose and ears. Thengill's whole body stiffened, hands white as the handles of his axes burned with a blue fire. There was a pulsing sound, which grew louder until the shadow spirit shattered, dissipating with a despairing howl. So the stories were true – Thengill, the man Johan had dubbed Adalrikr's executioner, couldn't be possessed by the durath.

Thengill sank to his knees, exhausted by the effort, and turned to Bandor, Throm and Svafa. "What are you all staring at me for? Defend your chief."

By now more than a dozen durath were battering the barrier, Petr's sword snaking out, lopping off a hand trying to clutch at Johan. Gautarr charged, bringing his sword down on the head of one, splintering it as it turned into a statue of ice, the water boiling as it hit the stones, covering the whole scene in a dense fog. Svafa could hear Tomas the Berserk, fighting alongside Gautarr as his shieldman. As the mist began to clear Svafa could see him fiercely trading blows with another warrior now possessed by the durath. Most of the shadow spirits continued to throw themselves at the barrier, more joining them, their skin peeling and clothes smouldering as they tried to force their way through. Throm and Bandor hurled themselves at the enemy, their swords cutting two of them down. Svafa joined them, sword stabbing at the back of another, the durath rolling away at the last moment.

There was a cracking noise as one of the stones turned bright red. The durath moved as one, targeting the point of weakness in the circle, their leader pressed into the barrier by his fellows behind. The sheer weight of numbers forced him into the circle, the glowing barrier bending around him, light criss-crossing over his body. There was a blinding flash as Petr charged his foe moments before the durath disintegrated and a hundred smoking pieces of charred flesh were blasted across the camp. Petr skidded to a halt, Johan at his back, Svan and Varinn joining them. There was a thunderous boom and the weakened runestone broke apart, creating a gateway for the durath.

Petr brought down the first two shadow spirits to scramble through the gap before the number of clawing hands and stabbing blades pressed him to the ground. Johan snarled, beheading another durath who died in a shower of soot and ash as Bandor and Throm reached his side. Thengill was there too, axes moving too fast to see – swathes of blue light ending the shadow spirits one after another. Johan locked swords with the last of them, shoving his foe backwards, who screamed in defiance as Thengill's axe took his head from his shoulders. The durath's corpse dropped to its knees, dissolving into white dust, the human shape disintegrating in the wind.

"Johan," Gautarr called out. "Are you hurt?"

Johan dropped his sword to the ground. "No ..."

Svafa approached, pressing towards the front of the gathering crowd. Johan was kneeling by Petr, Varinn busy tending to his wounds. As Svafa drew closer he couldn't take his eyes from the deep wound pulsing in Petr's neck. One of the durath had bitten out his throat and dark blood was welling up around Petr's hand as he tried to stem the flow.

"Just hold on, Petr," Varinn was saying as a hush fell over the camp. "I need something to staunch the bleeding. Someone get me some cloth."

Bandor began tearing at his shirt, handing the strips to Varinn as Johan took Petr's hand. "You fought bravely," Johan told him with a grim smile. "You've always stood by me, the one I could always depend on. First among my brothers, my right hand through all the dark days since Kalamar fell."

Petr's eyes were full of fear and pain. He tried to speak, blood welling in his mouth, his hand held tightly in Johan's. He let go of his neck, turning to look at Varinn, the old warrior choking as he tried to say something of comfort to a dying man. Petr's blood-soaked hand wrapped itself around Varinn's bent arthritic fingers. With a bubbling sigh, his chest stopped moving and Johan and Varinn both bowed their heads.

CHAPTER 62

Bandor stared into the fire burning outside their tent, Freydja watching him anxiously, wrapped in a fur-lined cloak to ward off the evening chill. She wanted to say something to make all of this right, knowing there were no such words. The Brotherhood grieved for its fallen and somehow tried to get past the horror of cutting down their own family and friends. *Skin thieves.* Freydja had never understood the truth of that description until now. They were fighting something truly evil and monstrous. She shuddered, drawing her knees up to her chin as Bandor turned to her.

"Are you alright?"

"I was just thinking," she told him.

Bandor nodded. "I keep going over what happened in my mind, trying to see if there was anything I could have done differently. It was all over so quickly. More than a hundred of our people killed. No one able to completely trust anyone else. Petr ... gone. Murdered in front of us."

Freydja suppressed a sigh, dreading the same conversation they had been having all week since the attack. "Bandor, we've been over this. There was nothing you or anyone else could have done."

Bandor glanced down at the sword lying across his lap. "I don't feel worthy of this." He was looking at Petr's sword, a blade that had been handed down through generations of the Hamarrson family. Petr had died unmarried and without an heir, his ancient sword carrying its six runes a prized possession; the same sword that had saved Petr's life in Lake Tull. Now Petr had been placed on the pyre constructed to honour Johan's loyal second his sword had been passed to Bandor.

"You *are* worthy," Freydja insisted, placing her hand on her young husband's shoulder. He seemed to crumble under the weight of her expectations, diminishing before her. His features were cast into odd relief by the flickering of the flames, his eyes lost in shadow.

"Why am I still alive? Six warriors – all that's left of once-great Kalamar. Six of us. Why do I live when so many others have died? Rugga's young children have been left fatherless, Maeva lost her husband when our own people turned against us, Eykr's wife and child didn't survive when they fled Kalamar the night it fell. Everyone looked up to Petr all through those hard times and now he's gone."

"He's gone to Navan's Halls, with great honour and the respect of everyone in the Reavesburg Clan. Few will be counted more worthy than Petr Hamarrson at the time of judgement. He's one of the founders of the Brotherhood of the Eagle and his name will live on in legend and the bards' tales."

"I feel ... guilty," Bandor admitted. "I feel like I've stolen someone else's life and I don't deserve to be here, while so many others have been placed on the funeral pyre. I don't know if I'm strong enough for what's to come."

Freydja whispered his name as she drew him towards her, kissing his face, running her hands through his hair. He felt cold and lifeless, her kisses returned without passion before he disentangled himself from her embrace and stood up.

"I need some time alone."

Freydja watched him walk into the darkness and, despite his words, she still considered following him. She glanced at the precious ring of runestones set around their tent – protection most of the Brotherhood had to do without. Were more durath hiding in their camp? Johan had ordered everyone to walk through the ring around his own tent, the task taking all night, more important than attending to the dead or the wounded. Whilst no durath had been found everyone knew they could slip inside the camp at any time without warning. Freydja took a breath, shivered and stepped outside the circle, Faraldr following her silently at a discreet distance, her guardian for that day.

A hush hung over the camp like a shroud. A few fires flickered, people cooking food or warming themselves, talking in low tones, as if afraid their words would conjure more horrors of the night. There was no sign of Bandor and Freydja walked without purpose, finding herself wending her way towards Joldir's tent. She hovered outside the entrance, wondering whether they were already sleeping. She gave a short cry of surprise when Leif's head popped out, a mischievous grin on his face.

"Freydja's here."

As she stepped inside she found Joldir and Arissa sat cross-legged next to a small brazier.

"Where's Thengill?" Freydja asked.

Arissa looked up, face drawn and tired from days working in the hospital tent. "He's out patrolling the palisade with Varinn. He's hardly slept … since Petr …"

Freydja took a seat as Joldir invited her inside before dragging a protesting Leif back to bed.

"Varinn's a good choice," said Joldir in a whisper, taking his place and waving a wine bottle under Freydja's nose. She hesitated, then nodded, drinking deeply after he awkwardly poured her a cup, sighing as she began to relax.

"I don't think Varinn wanted to be Johan's second," Arissa replied. "He just didn't know how to say no."

"That's not necessarily a bad thing," countered Joldir. "The warriors respect him and whilst he's no politician he's shrewd and understands people. He won't let Johan down, and that's the most important thing right now."

"Any word from Rothgar?" Freydja asked.

Joldir shook his head. "Nothing recently. They're still on the island, waiting for Bruar to finish fashioning what we need to destroy Adalrikr. Who knows how long the gods will take?"

"I know how Hasteinn got killed," piped up Leif from his bed, ignoring Arissa's scolding.

"*Really*?" Freydja indulged, shrugging off Arissa's glare.

"Rothgar set a dragon on Hasteinn and his warriors and it ate them all up," Leif declared, miming the vicious events with much arm waving as he wriggled out of his blankets, bouncing on his bed with excitement.

"Leif. If Rothgar had a *dragon* to do his bidding, I think he'd have mentioned that small detail to me in his reports," Joldir replied with a note of finality. "Now get to sleep."

"It's true," muttered Leif as Arissa tucked him back under the covers.

"So all we can do is wait," said Freydja.

Joldir shrugged. "Life during a siege is all about waiting."

They drank in silence for a time, listening as Leif's breathing became regular and shallow. Arissa spoke in a whisper when she was sure the boy was finally asleep.

"I still can't believe what happened. The durath came so close to killing Johan."

"Adalrikr is willing to sacrifice his own kind so casually," added Joldir, shaking his head. "The attack on Rothgar in Romsdahl and now the one here. It's an uncomfortable truth but both of those involved lesser durath, their abilities and mind both weakened from centuries in the Shadow Realm." He sighed. "There are times when I fear we've overreached ourselves."

"Bandor's really struggling to deal with all of this," Freydja told them, before recounting their earlier conversation.

"Bandor looked up to Petr," Arissa said. "It's natural he'll feel lost without him. I was worried Johan would name him as his second. I love Bandor but I don't think he's ready for the responsibility."

Freydja sighed. "I'm glad you said that because I thought the same. Just the weight of carrying Petr's old sword seems to be crushing him, although he won't set it aside for fear of dishonouring his memory and offending people."

"Give him time," Joldir counselled. "He's strong and he has you by his side to support him. He'll recover, I know he will."

"I want to do more than just support him," Freydja replied. "Throm is now my uncle's second and earned the name Hammerbreaker, avenging our father's death. I want to be more than Freydja Bandorswyfe."

"Is that why you're here tonight?" Joldir asked with a knowing look.

Freydja shrugged. "Perhaps. I've been thinking on what you told me, about how I'd be in danger if Nereth makes use of the Sight once more. I know Bandor won't want me to do this but he doesn't have to know. Over the last few days we've seen the power of magic and since Adalrikr isn't afraid of holding back neither should we. I want you to train me so I can join your Fellowship and help fight Adalrikr."

Joldir sat quietly, thinking on her words. "Such a large secret to carry in a young marriage. Is that wise?"

Freydja narrowed her eyes, bridling at the remark. "You were the one who approached me concerning this. My marriage is none of your concern."

"I'm not sure that's how Bandor or his father would see it," said Joldir. "I'd prefer it if you spoke to Bandor about this and got his approval –"

"I don't *need* his approval," Freydja snapped. "I'm the daughter of Egill Falrufson, descended from noble Reavesburg blood and a line worthy of leading our clan. I know my own mind and this is something I am resolved to do. Are you going to help me?"

Joldir bowed his head. "As you wish, Freydja. As you

wish."

***

It was late when Freydja left Joldir and Arissa. Faraldr didn't complain at standing guard for so long as he escorted her back to her tent.

"I need to ask you something," Freydja began. "Did you overhear what we were speaking of this evening?"

Faraldr was only a few years older than her with an open, friendly face and he looked embarrassed at being asked the question. However, she had to be sure – she didn't want Bandor hearing of her decision from someone else. Faraldr was also close with Svan, and he was no friend to Joldir's Fellowship and the use of magic in general.

"I was busy keeping watch, my lady. Not eavesdropping, I assure you. I only heard the low murmur of voices, that's all. I couldn't make out the words."

Freydja looked hard at the young Kalamar warrior, his features lit by the silver light of the moon. She wanted to believe what he was saying and had no real reason to doubt him. Still, a feeling of unease nagged at her, despite his answer. They walked on in silence and she crossed the warded threshold of her tent, finding Bandor sitting on their bed. He'd cast his armour aside, dumping it in an untidy heap on the floor along with Petr's sword. He cast her a dark look as she entered.

"Where have you been?"

Freydja knew he was worried and tried to hide her annoyance. "I only went to see Joldir and Arissa. I needed some company and Faraldr was with me – I was perfectly safe."

"No one in this camp is 'perfectly safe'. You shouldn't have set foot outside the runestones."

"And you can?" Freydja replied, temper rising. "You think Petr's runeblade can ward off the durath if they try to possess you? No one is safe until this is all over and Adalrikr and his followers have been destroyed. Until then, what do you expect me to do? Hide in my tent for the rest of my life? Listen to yourself – I'm the wife of a warrior and I won't be cowed by our enemies or cossetted by you."

Bandor stared up at her, as if seeing her for the first time. "I'm sorry. I love you so much and I don't want anything to happen to you, that's all."

Freydja walked over and kissed him gently on the forehead. "And I love you, you fool. Tomorrow is a new day, and we'll face it together, as man and wife."

Bandor wrapped his arms tightly around her after she slipped under the bedcovers. She held his hand in the dark and in time Bandor fell into a deep sleep, snoring gently in her ear, finally at peace. Freydja lay there in silence, listening to him breathing and trying to ignore the secret that now existed between them.

CHAPTER 63

The mood around Johan's table was sombre as the Brotherhood discussed the progress of Rothgar's expedition far to the north. Winter would soon come to the Fire Isle and each passing day made it less likely *Stormweaver's* crew would be able to return before the favourable weather in the spring. The facts solidified a truth Freydja had understood for a while, without ever giving voice to it. There would be no quick, easy victory over the Vorund Clan.

"This changes nothing," Gautarr was saying, arms folded across his broad chest as he rocked back in his chair. "If Rothgar arrived here on the morrow with one hundred god-forged runeblades capable of destroying the undead what would we do with them? Our engines of war are months from breaking through those walls."

Throm nodded. "We should be rejoicing at this news. The avatars themselves are aiding us in our war against the evil of the durath. No one ever pretended the road we set out on would be easy but now we have a real chance to end this, once and for all."

"Assuming Rothgar returns," Gautarr muttered. His remark drew some dark looks and he held out a placating hand. "All I'm saying is it's one ship, charting a course home through the Endless Ocean. It's no easy journey and we shouldn't pretend otherwise."

Damona glared at him. "You should have more faith in Kolfinnar's son."

"The aid of the avatars doesn't keep us fed and warm," mused Sigolf, keen to change the subject. "If we're wintering in Vorund we'll need to send some of our ships home to bring more supplies before the weather turns against us."

Johan nodded. "Do it. In the meantime, Varinn, we have to maintain the bombardment of the city walls. Vorund mustn't be given any chance to shore up their defences."

"We'll attack them every daylight hour," Varinn promised, still unaccustomed to his position as Johan's second.

Freydja looked at her father-in-law, noting the lines on his face, his long greying hair. He looked careworn, Damona looking at him with worry. Bandor sat next to her quietly, listening to the discussion as he absently tapped on the hilt of Petr's sword strapped to his belt. Freydja reached out and took his free hand under the table, giving him a reassuring squeeze.

"We mustn't underestimate what Rothgar has achieved," added Joldir. "His messages to me have been short, as we agreed. However, I think they've gone through more than he's revealed. I've known him long enough to be able to sense when he's holding back."

"Why would he do that?" asked Svan.

"Remaining on the Path too long is dangerous. I meant nothing more sinister than that."

Thengill held up his cup. "A toast to Rothgar Kolfinnarson. May Dinuvillan smile upon him and *Stormweaver's* crew and bring them safely back to us."

Everyone drank to that before Johan dismissed the gathering and the Brotherhood walked out into the night, the siege engines having fallen silent. Adakan took up the honoured place of first night watch outside Johan's tent, dark eyes watching carefully for any signs of threat, hand on the hilt of his sword. Svafa joined him at his post, whilst Svan left with Dalla as they spoke in hushed tones, his arm protectively wrapped around her waist. Nearby, Varinn was speaking to Thengill, as Arissa and Joldir looked on. Freydja glanced towards Vorund Fastness, its walls whitewashed by the moon. She could spy people moving around, ropes dropping from the ramparts as they began work to repair the long dark crack that ran half its height.

"Sister. Brother." Throm embraced her and Bandor in turn. It had taken a while for her brother's melancholy air to lift after killing Joarr, the Brotherhood now calling him Throm Hammerbreaker in recognition of his achievement in defeating Adalrikr's jarl. Privately, Throm confessed to Freydja he preferred to be known as Egillson.

"You were both very quiet tonight," Throm said, patting Bandor on the back. "Rothgar has done well, better than we might have hoped, and this will give the Brotherhood heart. We've repelled Vorund's warriors and their skin thieves whilst keeping our camp safe. Things go as well as they can during a war."

Bandor threw an arm around Throm's shoulders. "I'll drink to that. Some of Beinir's men have a stash of whisky they promised to share with me."

The two men headed off arm in arm, Freydja standing there, forgotten. She pursed her lips as she watched them go.

"Are you alright, my lady?" asked Svafa. "Shall I find someone to escort you home?"

"It's alright," Freydja told him, walking with purpose to where Joldir and Arissa were standing. Let Bandor and Throm enjoy their drink. She had other work to do if she was to master the gift of the Sight.

***

Nuna listened carefully to Geilir and Dromundr's discussion at their feasting table that evening. Geilir and his cronies were less guarded in their comments these days, no longer seeing the subjugated Norlhast Clan as a threat. The latest reports confirmed Vorund Fastness was still under siege, the two sides deadlocked. A similar situation was playing out in Jorvind, where Onundr Arisson's men continued to defy Adalrikr at their holdfast in Rast. Karas sat at the head of the table looking glassy-eyed and weary, paying little attention to the conversation. Nuna worried for her husband and at how the part he was playing was taking its toll; diminishing his self-respect as his people no longer looked upon him as their true leader. Geilir was wearing his favourite black jerkin with silver thread, thinking it made him look dashing and noble-born. In Nuna's opinion it resembled the outfit of a pirate in a children's story – *Goldentooth the Pirate*. She smirked at the idea and Geilir looked up.

"Something amusing you, lady Nuna?"

"I was recalling a conversation with my maid Katla earlier this morning," Nuna lied. "I doubt such trifles concerning the ladies of this court would be of interest to a warrior of Vorund."

Geilir grinned and turned his attention back to Dromundr, Nuna breathing out slowly with relief at not having to weave a more complicated fabrication. These evenings entertaining their honoured Vorund guests were interminable. She had to stifle a groan when Valdimarr entered the hall, the short man sweating profusely, mopping his balding head as he trotted towards the table.

"You're late this evening," Geilir commented.

Valdimarr nodded as he took a seat. "Apologies. The administrative affairs of running a principality of our king are endless."

Geilir gave Dromundr, who was Valdimarr's man, a sidelong glance. "I wouldn't know."

Valdimarr called to a nearby maid. "Young girl – some wine over here. And bring me some food. I'm famished."

Nuna arranged her features into a pleasant smile as she spoke to Valdimarr. "What's kept you from our table this evening?"

Sweat was already beading on Valdimarr's forehead once more and he blinked rapidly as a droplet ran into one of his eyes, giving him a suspicious air. Valdimarr had been on edge ever since Geilir's arrival, fussing and fretting over small details, fearing a negative report to his king would see him removed from his position governing Norlhast. "Trade with Noln, my lady. Since Tyrfingr replaced Lundvarr with his mother she's proved adept at bargaining for our goods. The price of our shipments of whale oil have almost halved since she took control of the port. I thought the point of establishing one Laskan kingdom was to share our wealth. Now Ingunn is the elder of Noln I'd almost rather be dealing with Reavesburg raiders."

Valdimarr laughed nervously at his own joke whilst Geilir frowned, looking less than amused. "We need those shipments sold at a fair price. You can be sure Ingunn will turn a profit on our wares when she sells them on throughout Reavesburg. When I return to Vorund with the king's taxes he'll expect to see full coffers, not an empty chest and a list of your excuses."

Valdimarr cringed, looking towards Dromundr for support, which was not forthcoming. The big man scowled, showing no concern for his master's plight.

Nuna saw an opportunity and spoke up. "Did you say that Ingunn is Lundvarr's mother?"

"That's right," Valdimarr said, looking at her hopefully. "Lundvarr was executed on Tyrfingr's orders for trying to smuggle someone out of Noln. From what I hear Tyrfingr then made the strange decision to appoint her as elder."

"It will have been a weregild," Geilir observed. "Reparations for the death of her son, who would have been supporting her in her later years. Tyrfingr needs the port of Noln open and trade flowing freely – who better to run things than Lundvarr's own mother?"

"I wish he hadn't made such a generous gesture," Valdimarr complained. "The woman is a nightmare to deal with."

"I might be able to help," Nuna offered.

Valdimarr's eyebrows shot up in surprise. "How so?" he asked, clearly half-afraid she was making fun of him.

"Lundvarr was in my brother's debt, so her family is

honour-bound to help mine. I could write to her before winter comes and remind her of that fact. A fair price for the goods traded out of Norlhast is one way to recognise what she owes my kin."

"And what did Jorik do for this woman?" asked Geilir.

"It wasn't Jorik, it was Rothgar," Nuna corrected. "You'll recall Tyrfingr Blackeyes tried to sack Noln two years ago. My brother led the warriors of Reavesburg against him and drove the attackers from our shores, saving Noln from destruction and its people from slavery. You'll find the name Rothgar Kolfinnarson still carries much weight in Noln."

Geilir ran his tongue over the tips of his teeth, regarding Nuna intently. "Is that right? Rothgar is a sworn enemy of our king, yet you would cite his victories against my clan to curry favour with this woman? It's a strange way to help our cause, wouldn't you say?"

Nuna smiled sweetly. "A debt remains a debt, no matter what the cause. In business, one must make use of every advantage, much like the arts of war. Would you like me to put ink to parchment?"

***

Both Brosa and Karas were angry with her, although they waited until they were in her private chambers before speaking their minds.

"You're fortunate that turned out well," Karas told her, not for the first time since they'd entered her room. "You had no idea how Geilir would take your proposal."

"I saw an opportunity and I took it," replied Nuna, annoyed.

"My lady," Brosa interjected. "We're living in a den of vipers. I cannot have you needlessly risking your life –"

"We were having our evening meal, not duelling in the circle," Nuna snapped. "I am the lady of this keep and I will behave as such, rather than shrinking away as if we don't deserve a place at our own table."

Karas' anger flared. "This was not an evening dining

with friends. Our lives and the lives of my people are at risk every day. One wrong word is all it takes. One remark that causes offence and Geilir will not hesitate to pay it back tenfold. Remember what happened to those fishermen, Kofri and Skefill? Hung outside our gates, merely for *talking* about Orglyr. What could I do? Nothing. What do you think would happen if Geilir took insult at your words? What could I do then to help you?"

Nuna saw the wretched helplessness in her husband's face, lurking behind the anger. She murmured soft words to him as she drew him into her arms, feeling his heart beating hard against her chest. She reminded herself Karas loved her and was speaking out of worry for her safety.

"Geilir and Tyrfingr are rival jarls, not friends," Nuna said gently. "Noln was Tyrfingr's greatest defeat and his reputation within the Vorund Clan suffered. I could see Geilir thinking on my words and he saw this as a way of indirectly getting one over on Tyrfingr, whilst improving his own position. Norlhast's taxes swell at the expense of Reavesburg – so who is the more powerful jarl?"

"*I'm* Norlhast's jarl," Karas reminded her. She felt a stab of pity at those words, cursing herself for being so careless.

"No, you're the clan chief and one day you'll bear that title openly once more."

Karas sighed. "It was a well-played move," he conceded. "I'll confess, you're better at this game than I am. This cloak of subterfuge is taking its toll. Every night when I try and sleep I worry our scheme will be uncovered. My dreams are filled with ... well, what does it really matter? They're only dreams."

"Dreams are important. Our people took heart at the news there had been an uprising, even though Orglyr was defeated. They'll be looking to his return, a threat Geilir takes seriously otherwise he wouldn't still be here. I'm happy to break bread with him at our table over winter if it means he's swinging from the scaffold come the spring. The crucial thing is he mustn't suspect we have a part in this plot."

"He already does," Karas replied, rubbing his hands, the tips of his fingers still black and scabbed where his nails were regrowing. "The man trusts no one, which is why our position here is so dangerous. A firm connection between us and Orglyr is all it would take."

"Then we will give him none," Nuna reassured him.

"That's easy enough to do now. Come the spring, when Orglyr leads his army back down from the mountains we'll need to take more risks."

"If he returns," said Brosa.

Nuna frowned, surprised at such doubts from a man she counted amongst her most loyal supporters. "What makes you say such a thing, Brosa?"

The warrior looked at her guiltily, nervously tugging at his red beard. "I'm sorry my lady. It's just we're setting such great store on Orglyr. If the reports are true and Orglyr and Tidkumi are hiding in the Baros Mountains then I worry they won't survive the winter, let alone mount an attack come the spring."

"You should never be afraid of speaking your mind, Brosa," Nuna told him, taking one of his hands in hers. "You can be honest with us, there's no shame in that. All I can say is *something* tells me Orglyr is biding his time and making ready for war. I've no proof I can show you to sweep away your doubts. I just know that he's out there, somewhere, and we have to be ready for his return."

As Nuna spoke those words she knew she believed them – utterly and completely. Why? Was the alternative too much to bear? Perhaps. Yet she had a feeling, deep inside, that she was right. Was this the same hope that fuelled Johan's Brotherhood or Onundr's resistance in Rast? Nuna knew it was more than that. She knew in her *bones* she was right and Orglyr would return.

Karas nodded in agreement, as if he'd been listening to her thoughts. "You're right. If we lose hope in Orglyr, what's left for any of us?"

CHAPTER 64

Djuri's footsteps rang out in the gloomy corridor leading to the dungeons under the keep. They were always full these days, shouts and groans coming from the cells. He ignored the desperate pleas for help, as his passing torch briefly sparked hope in the hearts of the prisoners. He pressed on, deeper into the dungeons where the more secure cells held those of special interest to Tyrfingr. People like Humli, Desta and Lina.

The gaoler looked up briefly as Djuri approached, face slack with boredom and pale from lack of sun. His eyes brightened as he recognised Djuri and saw a fleeting opportunity to break the monotony of his job.

"All quiet today," he told him. "Does Tyrfingr want one of the prisoners?"

Djuri shook his head. "I'm just checking on them, that's all."

The gaoler looked hopefully at Djuri, keen to continue the conversation. Djuri held out his hand and the gaoler reluctantly passed him the keys. He turned his back on the man and put the key in the lock, the well-oiled mechanism opening with a satisfying click. The room inside was sparse – three cots pushed up against the walls. Tyrfingr had ordered the family be kept together and whilst it appeared a kindness, Djuri knew better. *Tyrfingr has something over them now. If they don't cooperate he'll threaten to separate them. They're drawing strength from each other, something that can be turned into a weakness.*

Humli looked up, wary until he saw who was coming through the door. He looked even whiter than the gaoler, his face pinched and lined, greying hair growing long and unkempt. Desta had her hands clasped together, kneading her fingers with worry. In contrast, Lina was full of energy, standing when Djuri entered and running over to him, taking his hand in hers. Her grip was uncommonly strong, dark eyes boring into his. Djuri hesitated, reminding himself what she really was.

"How is he? How's Frokn?" Lina asked, a hint of desperation creeping into her voice. She narrowed her eyes, breathing in deeply through her nose as she struggled to regain her composure.

"He's fine," Djuri assured her. "Both boys are thriving under Tola and Boddi's care. You don't need to worry about them – they're safe."

Lina's eyes flashed. "Safe? Tyrfingr could order them killed at any moment. How, exactly, is that *safe*?"

"Lina, stop it," Desta complained from a corner of the cell. "Don't talk that way, please."

Lina glared at her. "It's the truth. Why are you so desperate to ignore the facts?"

Humli's shoulders sagged and he clutched his head in his hands. "Enough! Enough from both of you. All this bickering gets us nowhere so if you can't speak without arguing then say nothing at all, for the sake of my sanity if nothing else."

"I have some news," Djuri told them in a hushed voice, trying to steer the conversation away from the argument. "Tyrfingr doesn't want to risk bringing Desta and Lina south to Vorund until the siege is over. That's good because it buys us some time."

"We're waiting until the end of a *siege*?" Humli muttered. "We could be stuck here for months. Years."

Desta stifled a sob. "I can't be separated from Finn for that long. I haven't seen Rothgar in over a year and a half so what can I possibly tell them? I didn't even know he was *alive* until you told us."

Djuri winced, glad they didn't have an audience for this discussion. "Have a care with your words. Your past relationship with Rothgar is what's keeping *you* alive."

"No, it's putting me in danger. If it hadn't been for him, I wouldn't be here now."

"No point complaining about it," Djuri replied. "What's done is done. We have to make the best of things and find a way through this."

Lina stood there, her arms folded across her chest as she listened to Djuri's story. "Who's this *we*? Why are *you* here?"

Djuri frowned. "What do you mean?"

"Is it such a difficult question? What are you doing here? You act like you're our friend, bringing us news from the keep and showing concern for our sons. Yet you're working with them – serving the man keeping us prisoner. Does coming here make you feel better about the part you're playing in this?"

It took a great effort for Djuri to speak softly. "I'm trying to keep you alive. I've protected you and done all I can. I'm your only ally in this keep and I'm trying to find a way to get you out, reunite you with Finn and Frokn and secure you safe passage away from Reavesburg. Otherwise, what's been the point of any of this?"

Djuri knew he needed help to get these three to safety. With Haarl's widow and son safe he'd have nothing to lose and could redeem his name, taking action against Tyrfingr. He left the cells with an idea forming in his mind, thinking through each of the steps as he strolled through the main courtyard. *It's dangerous – trusting anyone is dangerous in these days. Yet I can't do this alone.*

"Djuri," Nereth called out as she walked towards him. She smiled as he held out his arm, taking it in hers as they continued around the courtyard together.

"A word of caution," Nereth whispered. "Your frequent visits to our prisoners haven't gone unnoticed."

"You know Desta was Haarl's wife. He died on account of me, and I promised I'd look after their child," Djuri told her.

"I don't doubt your motives but the issue is how it appears and there are other ways to bring Desta and Lina news of their sons. Have Tola come and visit them – Tyrfingr will permit it, I'm sure. It will be a reminder of all they have to lose if they don't cooperate."

"Why hasn't Tyrfingr put them to the question?" Djuri asked. "They've been here long enough."

Nereth tutted. "They're not his prisoners, are they? They belong to Adalrikr and he doesn't want them spoiled before their audience with their king. Their capture stands to Tyrfingr's credit when so much is going awry elsewhere, so he won't risk anything happening to them. Their presence here in Reavesburg may prove very useful, depending on the outcome of the wars in Norlhast and Jorvind."

"Why not use the Helsburg Clan? Falki Ruunson must be keen to prove himself as Adalrikr's new jarl. Why not bring their forces into the fight to help end the siege?"

"Adalrikr needs his new ally watching the western border. The Vittag Clan is powerful and although the White Widow is trading with him, Ingioy remains unpredictable and powerful enough to upset his plans. She's always played a careful game and Adalrikr will need to unite Laskar behind him to ensure Vittag remains loyal."

Djuri thought on Nereth's words as they walked arm in arm. The season was changing and summer had given way to autumn, the green leaves on the trees slowly turning amber, gold and red. This war of the Laskan clans looked set to end in a stalemate, at least until the spring, although that did at least give him time to firm up his plan. *Or is that more time to come up with excuses not to act?*

"You're moving better," Djuri commented.

Nereth smiled, stretching her back. In their bedchamber Djuri had seen the vicious scar knitting itself together, now a silvery line running from shoulder to hip tracing a story of violence, one of the few parts of Nereth's history Djuri knew. How was it possible to be so intimate with someone, whilst knowing so little about them? His liaison with Nereth had earned the grudging respect of the warriors in the barracks, as they admired his conquest. However, Djuri disliked all the boasting talk, trying to change the subject whenever it was raised.

Am I undone by Meras? Being fond of this woman is one thing ... Anything more, well only a fool would say they loved a stranger.

"What are you thinking about under those knotted brows?" Nereth asked with a playful laugh. "It looks like hard work."

"I was thinking that I have the rest of the day off and I'm free to spend it how I wish, with whomever I wish," Djuri lied.

Nereth arched an eyebrow, a playful smile curling her lips. "Is that so? I can think of a number of pleasant ways we could spend this afternoon."

I'm a fool.

***

One advantage of facing winter on the Fire Isle with *Stormweaver's* crew was they knew how to work wood. First of all they felled some of the nearby pines to fashion a boat house, Meinolf and Aerinndis carefully inspecting every inch of the building to make sure the structure was weathertight before rolling *Stormweaver* inside. Only when they were satisfied that their precious longship was protected from the elements did they turn their attention to building a long house to replace our tents. The lack of daylight as winter returned to the isle soon became our main challenge, limiting the amount of time we could spend working. Aerinndis drove everyone hard, raising a building large enough to house us all in fifteen days, topped with a warm turf roof in the Norlhast and Riltbalt fashion.

The work was too physical for me to offer much

practical help. I fetched and carried to make myself useful and prepared the meals, Haddr showing me how to bake bread in his portable oven. Mendaleon gifted us both fresh and dried fruits and more flour, providing some welcome variety to our diet. Fari and Matthildr proved adept at scaling the cliffs to the south of the island, the seabirds they caught providing a change from fish and seal meat. Even if none of it was the richest fare, when you're hungry after a day of hard work any hot food tastes like it was fit for the chief's table.

Some of the crew grumbled the dragons lived in a city large enough to house hundreds of their kind, while we toiled to build our own home with our bare hands. Aerinndis wouldn't countenance such talk for long, understanding as well as I did that we did not belong there. The dragons only tolerated our presence in their home whilst we were under Bruar's protection. When I remembered the way Alcor had looked at me, I knew Aerinndis was right.

Ulfarr and the other warriors continued to scout around our camp, looking without success for any signs of Etta. The lengthening nights curtailed their efforts, although Ekkill would sometimes range out on his own in the darkness. When Ulfarr counselled him against taking such risks, Ekkill merely patted his quiver of rune-tipped arrows. "One of these is marked for that treacherous crone's heart. The northern lights are all I need to find her."

The sun's path across the sky became lower and lower as we waited for word from Bruar, until it barely rose above the horizon, those strange shimmering curtains taking its place to provide a more familiar, if inconstant, source of light. One evening I brought Jolinn into the boathouse to show her something I had noticed, leaving the doors open so they framed a square of inky blackness interspersed with a bright swathe of stars.

"If you want companionship, we could do that just as easily under the blankets in the long house," Jolinn remarked with a knowing look.

"Wait," I told her. After a few moments the sky lit up, sheets of green wavering with an ethereal glow. Jolinn frowned, only noticing the effect this was having on the lacquered runes painted on the hull when I pointed to them. In the gloom of the boathouse, we could see each of them shimmering with the same green glowing light cast across the sky.

"A reflection, surely?" said Jolinn, eyes wide with wonder.

I shook my head, closing the boathouse doors, the green pulsing glow of the runes running along *Stormweaver's* length warding off the darkness. Jolinn gasped as the colours shifted into red and then purple. Although the doors remained closed I knew the runes were mirroring the changing colours outside.

"What does it mean?" asked Jolinn.

I shrugged, at a loss for an answer. "I've no idea. I noticed it before when *Stormweaver* was resting up on the beach but like you I thought it was merely reflecting the lights. If Etta was with us still I'm sure she'd put forward a theory. I've been thinking about reaching out to Joldir. I know I promised him I wouldn't do so until we were making ready to leave but I can't help feel this could be important."

"Does anyone else know about this?"

"Only you."

Jolinn smiled, her face lit with soft purple light. "You're full of surprises."

We kissed for a time, enjoying the privacy of the boathouse. "I'm glad you came here," I said as we drew apart at last.

Jolinn laughed in the half-darkness. "Don't flatter yourself I chose to join *Stormweaver's* crew just because of you. Being a speaker for my people showed me how hard it is to be an elder and I see now how Father made it look so easy. Settling disputes between the warriors of Olt is wearing and Beinir is far better suited to the task than I ever was. I've left our people in good hands with him."

"That's told me where I stand," I replied, Jolinn laughing again as she playfully slapped my chest.

"No, this gave me a chance to *do* something – I can make more of a difference here than sulking outside the walls of Vorund Fastness. We've done something incredible – no, let's be clear, you've done something incredible by persuading Bruar to help us. Our journey to the Fire Isle has given us the chance to win this war and for our deeds to be remembered through the ages. That'll be something to look back on, when all this is over."

I sighed. "When all this is over. Honestly, we've been fighting for so long I can't imagine what I want for my life afterwards."

Jolinn stiffened at my words, taking a deep breath before she replied. "You don't have *any* thoughts about that?" As she began to pull away from my embrace I realised how thoughtless my words sounded.

"I'm sorry, that came out wrong. Just because I haven't thought about it doesn't mean it's not something I want. What I'm saying is my life has *become* this war. I don't know who I'll be or what I'll do when it's over."

My hand reached out, gently touching Jolinn's fingertips. She drew her hand away, walking towards the door before hesitating, speaking in a low voice. "Becoming a warrior was a way to escape the life I'd been born into but that doesn't mean it's the only life I can imagine leading. I've no desire to die a violent death, like my poor Karl. Making the journey to Navan's Halls with all the honour achieved through death in battle is overrated. There's a reason you don't see many greybeards in the Brotherhood. I want a house of my own, perhaps some land and some animals, somewhere to raise my children when the time comes. A life free from Adalrikr's rule – a full, normal life that isn't defined solely by the violence I inflict on other people. That's why I'm fighting – because I want more than this."

I walked over and drew Jolinn into my arms, feeling chastened. "Jolinn, I'm sorry. I've spent so long dwelling on what I've lost, I never had the wit to appreciate what I had. What I *could* have."

"You've some brains, after all," Jolinn conceded with a smile.

"Ah, so that's the answer. It's my peerless mind that drew you to me."

Jolinn gave me a sardonic look. "I said you had *some* brains. Perhaps less than I first imagined."

Did I want all those things Jolinn was talking about? Why not? Didn't we both deserve some measure of happiness when all this was over? I felt guilty, recalling my recent visions of Desta trapped in the dungeons. Was it right to even think about the life Jolinn talked about while she was in prison because of me? I kissed Jolinn again, trying to picture it all in my mind. The road we were on seemed so long, yet Jolinn was right to ask the question. What did lie at the end of it? What was it all for?

Kissing Jolinn stopped me saying anything else stupid to ruin the moment. After a time we let each other go and walked back outside, hand in hand, pausing to take in the breathtaking display above us. Fragments of splintered rainbow interspersed themselves amongst countless bright stars.

"If the stars are Altandu's tears shed at Ceren's betrayal then what do the legends say concerning *that*?" asked Jolinn in a whisper, eyes wide with wonder.

"I don't know. Perhaps we'll be the first to bring back the tale and those legends will start with us."

Jolinn squeezed my hand. "Come on, it's getting cold. Let's go back to –"

We both saw the shape on the ground at the same time, stopping in our tracks. Over by the tree line a body was sprawled on the ground. Even at this distance I could tell from the way the limbs were splayed and the odd position at which the figure's head lay that he was dead. We approached hesitantly, a gasp of shock escaping my lips as I recognised the mop of curly hair. Ekkill's empty eyes stared into mine, his lips slightly parted in a look of surprise.

Jolinn's drew her sword, eyes scanning our surroundings for any sign of Ekkill's attacker as I crouched down. His bow and rune warded arrows were gone, as was his short sword and dagger. The back of Ekkill's skull had been smashed in, a smooth round stone nearby, covered in blood. Jolinn's sword reflected the aurorae, the runes on the blade showing no sign that the durath were nearby. Etta was long gone.

"We need to tell the others," I said, my voice small.

Jolinn looked down at Ekkill. "Now do you understand what I was saying? Close his eyes. I can't abide that look."

CHAPTER 65

Despite the icy wind tugging at his cloak Fundinn leaned out over the walls of Dunfalas, eyes straining to pick out any signs of movement along the mountain pass leading to the fortress' gates. The winter snows had fallen thick and heavy, choking the road and making any attempt to reach their refuge foolhardy in the extreme. However, it was better doing something and Dunfalas offered little in the way of entertainment besides drinking and dice. Soma had cleared the courtyard of snow countless times to create sufficient space to drill the warriors and keep their skills sharp with sparring and archery practice. It helped the men expend some of their pent-up energy, although as the weeks and months wore on and food had to be carefully rationed people became less restless and more concerned with keeping the cold at bay.

Valka had been as good as her word, bringing sufficient food, live animals and, most importantly, firewood to enable them to see out the winter. She'd arrived after Orglyr's army had reached Dunfalas and when Tidkumi saw the number of Vittag men wending their way through the mountains he mistook them for a Vorund attack. The reality was it took a huge amount of provisions to feed nine hundred men for four months and keep them warm. The generosity of Ingioy's gesture was not lost on Fundinn – they really were in the debt of the White Widow after this. Fundinn wondered what her price would be when she eventually called in her debt.

Their main enemy was boredom and keeping the warriors' spirits up. Not everyone who fled with Orglyr after their defeat chose to make the journey into the Baros Mountains. Many slipped away in small groups as they made their westwards journey. Of more concern to Fundinn were the fifteen men who had changed their minds after reaching Dunfalas and the reality of wintering there sank in. They'd waited too long before making the decision to leave, the snows already falling heavily when they opened the gates and stole through them late at night. Hoskuldr headed out in the morning, after the snowstorm abated, to see how far they'd got. He'd found three bodies, frozen in the snow not half a mile from Dunfalas. Of the rest there was no sign, although the pass was so thick with snow it was impossible to believe they were still alive. Fundinn knew not all the warriors sheltering in Dunfalas would see through the winter. There was no option other than to light fires in the main hall and the buildings they had converted into barracks, the Norlhast warriors gathered round as close as they could, shivering in the cold. On clear days the smoke would be visible for miles, revealing their presence, even if they were safe from attack until the spring. The choice of freezing to death or sending up some smoke wasn't really a choice at all.

"Anything?" asked Curren, joining him on the walls.

There's no one else alive up here. "Nothing. All quiet, just how I like it."

"The Vorund camp's still out there," said Curren, pointing eastwards into the distance. Far below the mountain range on the rolling hills of western Norlhast there was a dark smudge on the green grass and Fundinn thought he could see smoke rising from camp fires. Whilst Geilir's main army had retreated he had left a small force behind to watch the mountain pass.

"Geilir's not leaving anything to chance. They'll be there all winter, expecting us to return the same way we left."

"It's a pity there's only one way back to Norlhast from here," Redblade sighed, breath steaming in the cold.

"Unless we go further west," Fundinn replied.

"West? Into Helsburg? You can't be serious?"

Fundinn's hand traced the western path that led between the mountains into Helsburg territory, outlining a half-formed plan. Like the eastern route, it was also blocked by the snows and currently impassable. Yet come the spring Tidkumi said the western path tended to thaw first. Would it be possible to round the Baros Mountains by marching through Helsburg and re-entering Norlhast from the north, far beyond Dorn? Curren listened to Fundinn's proposals, his face impassive. Long before Fundinn had finished talking he knew he'd failed to persuade him.

"Helsburg's part of Adalrikr's territory now," said Curren. "There's no way a force as large as ours could make the journey northwards unseen. At best Ruunson would send word to Geilir and we'd find a welcoming party when we reached the coast of the Redfars Sea. Even worse, he might see it as an opportunity to curry favour with Adalrikr and attack us himself. The only other option would be to head south over the mountains until we reach Vittag, although I don't think we'd receive a warm welcome from the White Widow. Aiding us with provisions on the sly is one thing – giving sanctuary to a Norlhast army in her own lands is something else entirely."

Fundinn cursed with frustration, knowing Curren was right. "We'll never make it down from Dunfalas and back into Norlhast without being seen by Vorund's scouts. By the time we do Geilir's going to send reinforcements to that camp and they'll be waiting for us."

Curren looked thoughtful. Fundinn liked the man from Norlhast Keep. He'd been brave making the journey on his own to warn them about Geilir's army, even if Orglyr had squandered that advantage in the subsequent battle. Curren had still distinguished himself that terrible day, earning the name of Redblade for the way he'd fought. As important in Fundinn's eyes was the way he had with the men, keeping their spirits up after the battle as they made their hurried retreat, always ready with a joke. He looked at him now, wondering if the man had an idea that could enable them to escape their predicament. Curren was staring down the mountains towards the Vorund Clan.

"How many people do you think Geilir left behind?" Curren asked.

Fundinn puffed out his cheeks, a plume of steam misting in front of him. "Hard to say. A camp big enough to be visible from this distance? Seventy swords? A hundred?"

Curren nodded. "It would need to be a force sufficiently large to discourage a direct attack. If they've fortified the camp they could hold it with about a hundred men, with the rest of Geilir's army including his horsemen back at Norlhast Keep. You're right, though, they won't want to face us on their own so when we begin the march out of the mountains they'll send runners or riders eastwards to Geilir, calling for aid."

Fundinn realised where Curren was going with this. "If we send a smaller party ahead of us, there's a chance they could slip by the Vorund watch, especially if we make a big performance of our main army marching down the pass, moving slow to give them time to get into position. The advance party could intercept the scouts and ensure word reached our own people in Norlhast Keep, rather than Geilir. Instead of reinforcements arriving to swell the Vorund ranks they'll be entirely on their own. It'll be bloody work taking a fortified camp but the numbers would be on our side."

"It's a plan," Curren said. "It's not without its risks."

"It would have to be you," Fundinn told him. "You know the route to Norlhast better than any of us and the Greystorms trust you."

Curren nodded. "I thought you might say that."

***

Djuri felt a chill run down his spine, although he was well wrapped in furs and his long travelling cloak. The docks of

Reavesburg were becoming less busy as the morning market traders began to close their stalls. The fish market was Djuri's destination and he spied the woman he'd been told about, recognising her from the unflattering description of her horsey front teeth. He pretended to be interested in the smoked herring, waiting for the buyers she was speaking with to purchase their wares and move on. Sissa was pocketing the coins as Djuri sidled nearer, a frightened look crossing her face as his shadow fell over the stall.

"How can I help you sir?" she asked, eyes darting nervously left and right.

"I'm not here to cause trouble," he assured her in a soft voice, smiling as warmly as he could. The effect was undone by him being a foot and a half taller than the fishmonger. Sissa shrank away from him, babbling as she described her wares, both of them knowing he wasn't interested in buying anything.

"Do you know who I am?" he asked her in hushed tones, pretending to examine some fresh shellfish.

"Of course. You're the Turncloak, though I don't hold much store by that name myself, sir. We're all finding our way as we live under Blackeyes' rule – isn't that right?"

"It is, Sissa. Your name was mentioned to me –"

Sissa's face crumpled in misery and with her unfortunate front teeth she resembled a rabbit caught in a trap. "I've paid everything I can, I swear it. I know we're behind with the guild's share and I'll make it up with Gamli's next catch, I promise. We've had ... a difficult few months, that's all. It's nothing we can't deal with."

It took a few moments for Djuri to understand what Sissa was talking about. "No, this has nothing to do with the guild's share or the king's taxes. This is something else entirely."

"What's he done now?" growled Sissa, the colour of her ruddy face deepening as her expression changed in a flash from worry to anger. "He's not in one of the cells is he? I need him out there to bring in the next catch by morning, or so help me ..." Sissa's hands bunched into fists and she had to make an effort to unclench them.

"Your husband?" asked Djuri, trying to guess at the cause of the misunderstanding. "No, this has nothing to do with Gamli."

Sissa breathed out through her nose, trying to regain some composure. "Good. I've told him before, he likes the drink too much. It gets him into trouble and that's the last thing we need with Vorund warriors crawling all over our town. Meaning no disrespect, sir."

"None taken. I'm here about something else. I've been speaking to people over the past few weeks and I've heard your name mentioned a few times."

"My name?" Sissa looked worried and her eyes darted to a sharp knife on her stall. She glanced back at Djuri, the colour draining from her ruddy cheeks. "*My* name?"

"Put any thoughts of reaching for that knife out of your mind. I mean you no harm, Sissa. I've not come here to drag you to the dungeons. I need your help."

Sissa remained wary. "Unless it's fish you want, sir, I'm not sure what help I can offer."

Djuri frowned and leaned closer, whispering into her ear. "You help provision people when they're heading west for a new life – at least, that's what I've heard."

"That's not a crime," Sissa pointed out. "People buy things from the market. Where they choose to go next, well, that's up to them, isn't it?"

"Your name has come up as someone who helps people slip out of Reavesburg," Djuri pressed. "I'm not asking about this because I'm here to arrest you. I need to know if you can help me."

"You'll pardon me for saying this, but isn't that what you'd want me to admit before you arrested me?"

Djuri smiled, acknowledging Sissa had a point. "You have me there. In your line of business you're always having to trust people, aren't you? It can't be easy, helping them escape from Blackeyes? I'm not asking this for myself. There are three prisoners and I believe you know two of them. Humli Freedman used to sell you his catch and I'm sure you're acquainted with his daughter, Desta."

"Prisoners?" Sissa's eyes widened. "Helping prisoners of the jarl to escape would be treason, as you know perfectly well. What makes you think I'd be part of such a plot?"

"Money, plus the fact you hate the Vorund Clan as much as I do. There, I've said it. Now who's the traitor?"

Sissa looked at him for a time and Djuri felt uncomfortable under her gaze. *Have I made the right decision in trusting her? It's too late to back out now if I have.*

"Who indeed?" she said after a while. "Some people say Djuri Turncloak is a good man. I heard what you did for Desta's child – Tola will raise Finn well. Many folk would say you've already helped her enough by looking after her boy. Am I to understand you're wanting to help his mother as well?"

Djuri nodded. "If I could bring Desta and her father and the woman they were travelling with to you, would you be able to get them away from Reavesburg?"

Sissa's eyes narrowed. "They won't go anywhere without their children. Does Tola know about this?"

"Not yet."

"Keep it that way. Tola's a lovely girl but she can't keep a secret to save her life. My Gamli can get them away, although it won't be easy."

"Name your price."

"Two silvers now buys my silence. Six silver crowns purchases your friends safe passage from the docks when the time comes. You too, Turncloak, if you need to get away."

Djuri pursed his lips. "One silver should be enough for your discretion, four when I bring the prisoners to the docks."

"One now, five on the day they depart," Sissa

countered. "You have my word I won't say anything about this."

You won't need to unless I figure out a plan to get them out of the dungeons that actually works. "Done. I'll let you know when we're ready to act. Until then, neither of us will speak of this again."

Djuri passed Sissa some coppers, hiding the silver crown between them as he slid the coins into her palm to pay for two smoked herring. He'd take them to Cook, who'd know what to do with them. They'd make a fine supper for a man plotting to betray his master.

CHAPTER 66

Although it was traditional to cremate the dead, we decided to raise a cairn for Ekkill on a small rise at the forest's edge, overlooking the bay and our new long hall. Ulfarr took responsibility for placing most of the stones, although Ekkill had never really been one of his company.

"We shared some long journeys together," was how Ulfarr put it and everyone understood what he meant.

Skari and Myr shared in Ulfarr's work until the mound was piled high. I watched with Jolinn and Aerinndis, waiting until Ulfarr stood back from his handiwork, stretching tall as he rubbed his back. As one all of *Stormweaver's* crew stepped forwards, creating a line wending its way towards Ekkill's resting place. Each of them placed a small stone on top of the cairn as they passed before stepping back and forming a circle with Ulfarr and the others. I found a smooth dark grey pebble down on the shore, shot through with veins of white. It was warm in my palm by the time I placed it on the cairn and joined the circle, Jolinn holding my hand.

"Would you like to say a few words?" Aerinndis asked Ulfarr.

Ulfarr shrugged and stroked his thick beard. "Rothgar knew him the longest. You anything you want to say?"

I stepped forwards, placing my hand on the cairn. Seabirds squawked above us, the light already fading fast, the sky turning red. "Ekkill wasn't the easiest man to like and he didn't set much store on making friends. He was always honest, speaking his mind without fear or favour to chief and thrall alike and not everyone liked what he had to say. Yet I owe him my life, because he rescued me from the gates of Reavesburg – an act of daring carried out under the noses of the Vorund Clan. He was our best scout and I've never met someone so capable or deadly with a bow. I'll never forget how he killed Sandar Tindirson in Tullen." At those words Ulfarr and Skari both nodded appreciatively. "So much of what he did went unseen and the Brotherhood doubtless owes him more than we'll ever know. I'm proud to have shared his final voyage and we'll all remember how he bravely defended us during our journey to reach the Fire Isle."

My fingers touched the stones on the cairn, already cold as the temperature dropped with the setting sun. "In many ways this is a fitting resting place, since Ekkill was always a man apart. When the time comes to leave he'll remain here alone, as he always preferred it, resting on an island steeped in the legends of our clan. This cairn will act as a memorial for his sacrifice as well as Soren and Jonas, who lost their lives on the journey north."

Skari joined me, raising his hammer, its rune cold and dark. "He was a good warrior and deserved a better fate. We'll find the old crone and brain the bitch, I promise you." Myr was behind him, arms folded, nodding his bald head in mute agreement while Ulfarr stood nearby, staring at the ground.

As we made our way back to the long hall I sought out Ulfarr, placing a hand on his shoulder. "Are you alright?"

He glanced up at me with empty eyes. "Those were good words. If it comes to it, I'd like you to speak at my funeral."

I laughed. "I hope that won't be necessary."

"No, I'm serious. You were right, Ekkill was one of the best of us and the durath killed him all the same. Most of my crew have died fighting them and there's been a fair few times I've thought I was next. I was twenty-seven when I took to this life and now I've seen forty summers I know how this story ends. I watched Callis, Olaf and Patrick die and there's only Myr and Skari left from my company. I'm not complaining about being given a second chance by Johan. It's just ... I don't see all of us making it through to the end of this war."

"Gods, Ulfarr, you're maudlin at funerals," said Skari, walking a few paces behind us. "We're warriors. We live fast and die young, ushered into Navan's Halls with our heads held high, isn't that right, Myr?"

Myr raised a sardonic eyebrow. Whatever counsel he might have shared remained a mystery.

"Don't forget how our story started," Ulfarr replied. "We weren't always warriors. We were thieves and robbers."

"And who decided that? Johan declared us as outlaws from his lofty position in Kalamar Castle. Then later on, when he was desperate enough and he really needed us after Kalamar fell, we became 'warriors of the Company of Shadows'. It's a grand title but what's the difference? The opinion of one man, who stopped being quite so fussy after Sinarr the Cold One deposed him as jarl."

Ulfarr looked as if he was about to argue with Skari. Instead, he shook his head and trudged on down towards the long hall in the gathering darkness. Skari clapped Myr on the back as the pair followed him down the hillside.

Jolinn spoke to me as I stood there, wrapped in thought. "Skari's not listening, even though Ulfarr's right. There's only one way the life of a warrior ends. That's what I was trying to tell you earlier."

***

There's only one way this is going to end. Randall gently brushed his hands over the sightless eyes of the young mason's apprentice, ending the lad's silent rebuke. *Well, I sent him to his death, after all. He's every right to look annoyed.*

Randall's back protested as he gripped the dead boy under his armpits and lifted him up, Meldun grasping his ankles, round face red with sweat. *Six dead and I can't see a damn bit of difference in that crack. If anything, it's* wider *than the day before.* This was the last body resting at the base of the wall of Vorund Fastness and Randall knew he was pushing his luck venturing out again. The grey light of dawn wasn't far off and would herald another day of unforgiving rock raining down from the skies, breaking down the wall inch by inch, slowly prising an opening through which the Brotherhood could launch an attack.

Mason's apprentice wasn't exactly the truth, either. No one in their right mind *volunteered* to work on the wall and most of those truly skilled in stonework were already dead. Badly mixed mortar and ill-fitting stones, ineptly stuck together in the dead of night by people who wouldn't know how to build a pigsty, their handiwork left Vorund Fastness defaced by a lengthening grey festering wound. Now it fell to the young or those unfortunate enough to have gotten on the wrong side of Adalrikr and his cronies. There were frequent accidents as men dangled from ropes or perched on rickety ladders in the pitch black. Last night the Brotherhood had used their siege engines to attack the workers; an infrequent but effective tactic that meant those pressed into the repair gangs were always jittery. This latest attack had left six men dead and prevented any more repairs that night. Randall had sent them to their deaths and felt he had no choice other than to volunteer for the grim task of recovery in the still hour before dawn. He breathed a sigh of relief as he and Meldun reached the postern gate, the reinforced iron door as comforting as being sealed in a coffin as it slammed shut behind them.

"Looks like he's sleeping," muttered Meldun as they set the boy's body down next to the others.

Randall could see what he meant, although the odd shape of the boy's head showed how he'd met a violent end, his skull crushed. *It would have been quick, at least.* Some of the others were in a worse state, parts of bodies piled up and now hidden under rough sackcloth. They'd been scraped off the rocks as best as Randall could manage. He took a deep breath, fighting against rising nausea. Without a backwards glance at Meldun, Randall ran through the chamber and out into the city, gasping as he vomited over the broken wall of a burnt out building. He staggered back, coughing and choking, hands shaking. Behind him the curtain wall shook as the first missile from Johan's siege engines found its mark and dawn heralded another day's bombardment.

Just made it back in time. That was close.

"You did a good thing, Randall."

Randall looked up at Heidr, Adalrikr's seer, and rose, self-consciously wiping away strands of sick from the front of his jerkin. Nishrall was with her, making no effort to disguise his disgust at the state of the Jarl of Vorund. Next to him Orn glowered, his massive body towering over the three of them.

"I sent them there. I had a responsibility to bring them back," Randall explained. Heidr's protuberant grey eyes blinked once, slowly and deliberately. Randall didn't want to look into them too closely – Heidr always saw too much.

"The dead are dead," rumbled Orn. "Let them look after themselves. Good jarls are harder to come by."

Randall cleared his throat. "It's not safe here. Our king wouldn't be happy to lose three of his advisors as they chatted idly with his jarl. We should –"

Right on cue another rock slammed into the wall, high up and right above where they were standing. One of the battlements shattered and lumps of stone rained down on them. Heidr cried out in alarm, raising her hands above her head as she cowered under the shower of stones. Orn glared at the interruption, casually dusting himself off.

The four of them moved back into the city of Vorund, weaving through the broken remnants of this district, its inhabitants long since fled as their homes had been burned or crushed by the siege engines. People had scavenged anything of value from the rubble. Randall spied the shattered remains of a rocking chair under fallen masonry and thick timbers. Someone's favourite resting place of an evening, now reduced to cheap firewood. If he'd been on his own he'd probably have stopped to take it back to his chambers – nothing could afford to be wasted as winter settled over Vorund and the city's supplies grew scarce.

"I suggest you return to the Inner Keep," Randall told them once he was confident they were out of range of the Brotherhood's war machines.

Heidr shook her head. "Today isn't the day any of us are fated to die. I came to see you, Randall."

That doesn't sound good. Randall glanced up at Orn, the huge man standing uncomfortably close. *I wonder what Orn would say if I insisted I had to be on my way?*

"You were there the night some of our brave tributes sacrificed themselves for our king," said Nishrall.

How could I forget? I saw one of The Six break the neck of the man who refused. "I was there," Randall admitted, deciding it was pointless to lie. Another wave of nausea hit him, making him feel weak and he licked his lips, his mouth tasting dry and foul. He remembered fleeing the Inner Keep after watching the tributes sacrifice themselves, grateful for the fresh air as he ran into the night. It was then that the screaming started, the distant sound coming from the other side of the wall – from Johan's camp. Despite being sworn enemies, Randall had felt a pang of pity for the Brotherhood as they fought for their lives against dark magic.

"The people begin to doubt their king," Heidr said, her words like a jug of cold water in Randall's face, bringing him back to the present with a start.

Nishrall gave her a sidelong glance. "The people, or one person in particular?"

Heidr sighed, giving Nishrall a withering look. "Randall is true of heart and he isn't the only one to have doubts as this siege drags on. That is Adalrikr's greatest weakness. He doesn't understand the hopes and fears of the common folk."

"If you know I was there then why don't you tell me what happened that night?" Randall asked.

"We're at war," Nishrall said patiently. "We have to use every means at our disposal to win. You're a practical man, Randall. You organise our warriors, maintain our defences and keep Vorund safe. We have other talents, which we won't shirk from using if it helps end the threat to our king's vision of a united Laskar."

"Makes sense," Randall answered, more aware than ever of Orn's presence at his side.

Heidr looked at him sympathetically. "You don't have to like it Randall. You only need to understand that we're all on the same side. People listen to you. A few words in support of our king will make all the difference. You'll do that for us, won't you? As the king's jarl it's your duty to bring the people together against our enemies. If Randall Vorstson tells folk he's behind King Adalrikr and supports his decisions people in this city will feel better. I know you have doubts after what you saw but a fearsome king is needed to win this war. And we will win, with the Vorund Clan united behind us."

Heidr gave Randall's hand a gentle squeeze before setting off in the direction of the Inner Keep with Orn and Nishrall. Randall watched them go, arms folded across his chest. It was beginning to cloud over, the air cold and sharp. He glanced up at the sky, sensing the first snows of winter would soon be falling.

CHAPTER 67

As the days passed on the Fire Isle I watched with fascination as the sun continued its daily retreat. Eventually it became a dull red disc, which crawled along the horizon at dawn, barely casting enough light for us to see. It was like watching the legends from creation playing out in front of me as Ceren battled with Altandu for supremacy, darkness slowly swallowing the light. Finally the sun set and never rose again, the new day signified by nothing more than a faint reddening of the eastern sky.

By now the Fire Isle was no longer immune to the effects of winter, a blanket of snow covering the island, whipped into thick drifts by the wind. The location of the dragon's city, nestled under its vast overhang of rock within Ballung Mountain, made perfect sense as the weather worsened. The main tasks in our more exposed camp became looking after the animals Bruar had provided for us during our stay, managing our provisions and cutting down trees in the darkness to keep the fires burning in the long hall. We huddled around the flames, wrapped tight in our furs and cloaks, waiting for Bruar to complete his work. Whenever I ventured outside my eyes were always drawn to Ballung Mountain, the orange glow at its peak the brightest source of light now the sun had vanished. On some days I could see grey plumes of smoke rising from the mountain, illuminated from below, and occasionally the ground shook beneath my feet, the vibrations shaking loose snow from the roof of the long hall, which fell with a soft thump onto the deep drifts around the building. Ekkill's cairn had long been hidden under a white shroud, lost somewhere up on the rise as the Fire Isle was enveloped in constant darkness.

Aerinndis had a strange circular metal device covered in glass that she proudly told me came from Port Eledar in Oomrhat and was worth as much as *Stormweaver*. Its edges were inscribed with numbers and set within were other circular designs around which thin slivers of metal moved in a circular fashion to point to different symbols. Aerinndis explained she could use this device to count the days and mark the seasons and on one occasion she let me hold the shiny object. It was heavy despite its small size and when I lifted it to my ear I could hear a faint ticking sound, as if it possessed its own tiny beating heart.

Storytelling and singing became the main source of entertainment during those sunless days. *Stormweaver's* crew came armed with a ready supply of both, some tales more outlandish than others. Aguti's fine voice reminded me of Darri and Arissa and he would have been a fine bard had he not chosen to make his living on the seas. Ulfarr had shaken his melancholy spirits and recounted stories of his past and the deeds of his company before they met with Johan. Matthildr spoke of the various lands she had visited, explaining the differences in the customs of the people of distant Samarakand. Feyotra told us about her childhood in the town of Omir in Vittag and how her father first taught her to use a hunting bow in the forest of Mordis. When it was my turn I spun tales of horror and magic intended to chill the blood. I proved to be more popular than I expected, finding I was always in demand at the end of the day. I was particularly proud at how they listened in silence over several nights to the tale of freeing Norlhast from the grip of Nereth's coven of witches. I didn't even mind when Meinolf and some of the others scoffed at the (true) part where Nereth had almost murdered me with poison before invading my dreams. I also told them of the fall of Ulfkell's Keep, Sandar's death at Tullen in his Hall of Bones and how Sinarr the Cold One was defeated in the Battle of Romsdahl.

After I had finished that last tale Ulfarr came up to speak to me. "I never had you down as a storyteller. Yet the way you describe those events, it's as if you were there."

"That's the point – I *was* there," I replied with a grin.

Ulfarr looked thoughtful as he stroked his beard, which had grown long during the winter. "No, that's not what I mean. Some of what you spoke about tonight matches events as I *personally* saw them, on the battlefield at Romsdahl. Like when Sigdan fell and I had to take command of the Romsdahl archers or how Patrick died attacking Joarr's warriors. I don't recall telling you all the details of that particular story."

I shrugged, trying to disguise my sense of discomfort as I realised I'd been thoughtless, revealing events I'd seen through Ulfarr's eyes using the Sight. "I saw the battle unfold from the walls of Romsdahl and listened to plenty of fireside tales afterwards concerning what happened. I have a good memory, something Etta instilled in me, and apparently the skill also lends itself to fireside tales."

Ulfarr narrowed his eyes as he weighed my words. I made an excuse that I had to visit the latrines before retiring to bed, Jolinn catching my eye and rising to join me. Outside the air was bitter, the wind sharp as a knife. Both of us shivered, pulling up the hoods of our cloaks and wrapping our furs tightly around our bodies.

"Everything alright?" Jolinn asked through chattering teeth.

I nodded, before taking a deep breath and explaining to her that Ulfarr's guess was right. "I don't think he understands how the Sight works or that he possesses the gift. I was so wrapped up in the story I didn't realise I was straying into details only he knew about."

Jolinn peered at me, her face mostly covered by a woollen scarf. "It's hard to imagine such a life – experiencing things through the eyes of others. When you said the Sight gave you visions I thought … Well, I don't know what I thought."

"It's like you *are* the other person," I explained. "That's what can be so hard, sometimes, because you can lose hold of yourself. I've shared the lives of our friends and enemies, warriors, fishermen, adults and children, men and women. It's hard to explain – I feel like I'm part of all of them. That I *am* them."

"Am I one of those you've reached with this gift?" Jolinn asked, words turning to steam in the frigid air.

"No, which I'm glad about, although I've seen events concerning you, experiencing them through the lives of others. At the Battle of Romsdahl I saw through Yngvarr's eyes how bravely you and the rest of the Brotherhood fought against Sinarr the Cold One. When Yngvarr died it felt ..." I swallowed at that disturbing memory, coughed and continued. "It was as if I'd died, only to wake up in the body of another person."

Jolinn shook her head and drew me into an embrace, her body warm despite the thick layers of clothing. "I had no idea."

"You're the only person I've told. Even Joldir doesn't have any idea how many people I'm connected to through the Sight and how frequently I walk the Path. It's so easy I don't think twice about doing it."

Jolinn drew back from me. "I thought Joldir warned you against that. Isn't that why you carry a bottle of ataraxia with you everywhere? Shouldn't you use it to stop this happening?"

I felt guilty at her words, knowing she was right. "Nereth's the only one who can harm me when I walk the Path and through Djuri I can keep an eye on her. She hasn't dared to use the Sight since she was defeated in Norlhast."

"And your sister? Does she know how you share the events of her life?" Jolinn asked.

"She's no idea. Nereth told her about the Sight but Nuna thinks it was a ruse used to trap her. The best lies always have an element of truth woven into them."

Jolinn looked at me, saying nothing and I felt a scarlet flush creeping up my neck as I realised how my words sounded. I was glad I was so wrapped up in my furs she couldn't see my face.

"Are you coming back inside?" Jolinn asked me eventually.

"No. I really do need to pay a visit to the latrines. I'll be back in a moment."

I trudged towards the low outhouse, following the route of compacted snow and ice formed by countless journeys before mine. The cold air inside made me gasp in shock as I undid my breeches. At least the freezing winds blowing in off the ice shelf had the benefit of warding off the worst of the smell.

My conversation with Jolinn had left me thoughtful. She was thinking about her life after all this was over and I'd allowed myself to imagine we could share it together. Could we? My world was so different from hers. Jolinn could hang her sword above the fireplace and think about the future. Could I set aside the Sight? I could blunt my abilities with ataraxia, I supposed but then what would I be? Jolinn's crippled husband. I scowled at the thought as I dressed and hurried back towards the long house, looking forwards to the warmth of the fire. I had my head down, walking carefully on the frozen ground, and only heard the sound of approaching footsteps at the last moment. I glanced up to see a shadowy shape rushing me and the unmistakable noise of a steel blade cutting through the air.

I dived out of the way with a loud cry, my assailant's momentum carrying them past me as they crashed into the bank of snow that had built up on either side of the path. I tried to rise and draw my own sword, only to slip over on my side, the blade stubbornly sticking in its scabbard. My attacker rose to their feet and I expected to see Etta's face as they turned towards me. Far above our camp Ballung

Mountain erupted into life with a low rumbling boom that I could feel in the pit of my stomach. The orange flare lit up a stranger, whose ghastly disfigured face resembled cooked meat. The hood of his cloak had slipped back and the hair on one side of his head was gone, the other half dark and matted with dirt. His eyes looked at me with pure hatred.

"Hasteinn?"

The Vorund warrior snarled as he regained his feet and I realised he was carrying Ekkill's blade. "You've grown careless. I've been waiting for this chance to finish you."

He raised Ekkill's sword above his head and charged. Again my feet slid out from under me and with a shriek of fright I managed to free my own sword at the last possible moment. Steel rang as I parried Hasteinn's blow, rolling away to try and get some distance between us as I shouted for help, only for another boom from Ballung Mountain to drown out my words. Hasteinn was almost on me as I scrabbled away, only for him to lose his own footing on the ice and fall flat on his face, sword spinning from his grip. He growled, sucking in air as he pushed himself up onto all fours with shaking limbs. Keeping my sword in front of me I advanced towards him, taking care not to fall, willing the distance to shrink between us so I could finish him before he could stand. I found myself wondering how he had survived out here – pushing that thought aside at once. It didn't matter now.

I kicked away his sword as I approached and Hasteinn looked up at me, eyes defiant in that mangled travesty of a face. Up close he reeked of rot, his neck gaunt and thin where it emerged from his thick furs. I realised the man was dying, intent on taking me with him so he could complete Adalrikr's mission. Killing him would be a mercy and I raised my sword as he crouched there, gasping in air, too winded to fight.

My sword cut down, striking the ice where Hasteinn had been moments before, my enemy rolling away at the last second. His leg snaked out, catching my ankle, and I went down on my back with a crash, head striking the ground hard. I saw a flash of light and my hands became weak, sword tumbling from my fingers even as I ordered my hands to grip it tight. There was a warm sensation around my ear and I could smell blood. I groaned, trying to rise, falling back again and then there was a crushing weight on my chest as Hasteinn pinned me down, the stench of rotting flesh even worse up close, causing me to gag. Hasteinn held my own blade to my throat, trapping me easily despite his emaciated condition as I feebly struggled to fight him off.

"I could have been a jarl in a new kingdom had I not been sent here after you," he growled. "I've lost everything. Now it's your turn."

With a wild grin of triumph distorting his hideous face, he drew back my sword and I waited for him to strike the killing blow. His eyes widened and I saw another hand gripping his sword arm. Both of us turned to see Jade standing behind him, dressed in the same light clothing as when I had first met her, her jerkin and breeches dusted with crystals of snow and ice. She smiled at me, purple eyes glimmering with their own light and I heard a cracking sound as her hand crushed the bones in Hasteinn's forearm. He screamed as he dropped my sword, the blade falling inches away from my face.

"This one's mine," Jade told him, releasing his arm and placing both hands around his head, bodily lifting him off me. Hasteinn tried to fight her off with his unbroken arm as Jade's grip around his skull tightened.

"No. Let. Me. Go," gurgled Hasteinn, helpless.

Jade raised an eyebrow, her beautiful face looking puzzled. "Why?"

He stared at her in horror as she squeezed harder, Hasteinn giving a long, terrified scream as the bones in his skull were crushed in a series of sickening, loud cracks. Jade sighed and dropped his lifeless body onto the frozen snow. I heard the door of the long hall bang open, people having finally heard the commotion outside now Ballung Mountain had fallen silent.

"He wanted to kill you," Jade told me, fingers gently pressing the back of my head as she inspected the wound.

"There's a lot of that ... going around ..." I mumbled, wondering why I was seeing two Jades.

"You've always been kind to me," Jade replied, stroking my face with her hand. "You're like Sigborn. He was a good man – always thoughtful and gentle with me. I was married to Tanios yet my husband never had a good word to say to me after the fall. He became so bitter, mourning for his lost family and friends. I loved him once, yet that time belonged to another world and I didn't think I would ever feel that way again until I met Sigborn. He promised he'd come back for me after I helped him escape. Why did he never come back?"

"I ... I don't know. He died ... in battle ... many generations ago."

"It seems like only yesterday," replied Jade, looking downcast, "and yet my time on this wretched isle passes so slowly."

"You're a dragon," I pointed out. "You could change form and leave here forever."

Jade shrugged, purple eyes distant. "Why leave to be alone somewhere else?"

"What are you doing? Leave him alone." Jolinn's distant voice, sounding both frightened and angry.

Jade looked up. "I've just saved his life. He's hurt and needs your help."

Hands lifted me up, the world around me pitching and rolling violently, my head stabbing with pain. I felt the warmth of the fire on my face as Jolinn pulled back my hood and cleaned blood from my hair, her worried face swimming into view. Jade stood in the doorway, apart from all the others, watching as they cared for me. The next time I looked up she was gone.

CHAPTER 68

"Djuri? Are you even listening to me?"

Djuri blinked at the mention of his name, recognising from Nereth's tone this wasn't the first time she'd tried to get his attention. He rolled over in bed, running his hand over the pale flesh of Nereth's shoulder. She made an exasperated sound, shaking him off.

"Is that all you can think about? I'm asking you a question."

He flopped onto his back with a sigh, head full of his own worries. He'd spent weeks planning how to free Humli and the others at the midwinter feast, when the Vorund patrols would be less frequent and they could make best use of the cover of darkness. The only part of the plot he hadn't figured out was how to get them out of Noln once Gamli brought them there. Humli and his family wouldn't be able to make their escape on foot, so he needed a ship. He'd expected to have the chance to reach out to Ingunn for help when Tyrfingr sent him to collect the monthly taxes from Noln. He'd made the journey every month he'd been in Ulfkell's Keep, so why had Blackeyes decided to send Bjorr instead? Did Tyrfingr suspect something? Djuri knew the chances of his scheme succeeding were slim. He'd been at the bloodbath in Noln, Elfradr bleeding to death on the cobbled street with the rest of his crew. The only way this would work was with a distraction – that was easy enough and was the main part he would play in the plot once Desta, Lina and Humli were safely on their way.

If I see this through, it'll be the end of me. Now I'll have to wait for another opportunity to travel to Noln. It's strange how being given the chance to live longer makes me feel like I've lost something. He glanced at Nereth, who was watching him with a shrewd expression. In another world this might have been a good match and they could have built something together with their lives. She had more than enough brains for both of them to rise to high places in Reavesburg but he couldn't afford to think like that now. Maybe it was safer this way. The seas were always treacherous in winter and there was no prospect of Geilir returning to bring the prisoners south. There would only be one chance to do this and it had to be done when the time was right – there was no point trying to force things.

"Olt can't be that bad, surely?" asked Nereth, stroking his chest, softening her tone. "Is that what's on your mind? Did you and Alfarr fall out when you rode to war together?"

Djuri sighed. "Alfarr's a spoiled brat – a product of Old Hrodi's favouritism and a rather queer urge to spite his last surviving son. Poor Radholf put up with all of that for years, waiting for his father to die so he could take his rightful place, only for them to die on the same day."

"How old is Alfarr? Twenty? Twenty-one? Certainly young to be named elder."

"As I said, he didn't get it on merit. Everyone else was dead after the Battle of Romsdahl."

Nereth chuckled. "There's nothing wrong with a talent for survival."

"No, that's true. That doesn't qualify Alfarr to run things in Olt, though. He never had Hrodi Whitebeard's sense for business or diplomacy – why would he? All he had to do was ask his grandfather and he got whatever he wanted."

Nereth laid her head on Djuri's chest. "I keep forgetting you grew up there. Aren't you glad to be returning to your childhood home?"

"It hasn't been my home for years. How would you feel if you were told you had to return to ... Where *did* you grow up?"

Nereth raised her head. "Tivir on the shores of the Sea of Mirtan. I see your point. There's nothing there for me now, not after all these years."

Djuri ran his hands down Nereth's back, glad she was going to accompany him to Olt. Tyrfingr had chosen him because he still knew many of the people there, even if he didn't expect a warm welcome. Nereth's presence at his side was in part a tacit recognition of their relationship, by now an open secret in Ulfkell's Keep, as well as her sharp mind. If Alfarr was cheating Tyrfingr and taking an illicit share of the king's taxes then Nereth would get to the bottom of it soon enough. Was Alfarr stupid enough to cross the Jarl of Reavesburg? *I suppose when you've had everything given to you on a plate for so long, you think you're entitled to do anything.*

"This could be good for us," Nereth purred. "Tyrfingr's placing his trust in you. If Alfarr is pilfering from the king's coffers he'll lose his head. If he's not and he's awful at collecting taxes, well, perhaps he should still lose his head. You could run things in Olt."

"I don't want that," snapped Djuri.

"Alright, although you might not get a choice," replied Nereth, stung.

"I'm sorry. It's just that being a warrior is everything to me and returning to Olt is the last thing I want to do. Last time I was there ... You should have seen how people looked at me. At least here in Ulfkell's Keep I command some respect."

Nereth kissed him on the forehead. "Then that's what we'll do. Let's finish our business in Olt as soon as we can. Just remember, you can't be a warrior forever. Sooner or later, you'll have to set aside your sword."

Djuri drew her into a tight embrace, kissing her lips and face and trying hard not to think of Lina, Humli and Desta shivering in the cold cells far beneath their chamber.

***

Freydja felt the connection break, the Path dissolving before her eyes, the gossamer strands snapping the instant she tried to take hold and follow one of them. Next to her Joldir sighed, unsuccessfully trying to hide his frustration. She saw Leif watching as Arissa placed a comforting hand on Freydja's shoulder, reflecting that it was a strange thing. According to Joldir, Leif could make a strong Sight connection with her without any difficulty, but they didn't appear to be able to find the Path together as a trio and Joldir was at a loss to explain why.

Thengill grunted sleepily as he rolled over in bed and Arissa glowered at her husband. "I think it's time you dragged yourself out of bed and helped me with breakfast."

"Great warriors need their rest. I need to be in peak condition to face Adalrikr's hordes when the time comes."

"You'll be facing him without your stones if you don't get out of that bed."

Freydja had to stifle a laugh as Thengill grumbled and began fumbling around for his clothes, complaining at how cold it was. She found herself swallowing down a lump in her throat, missing the good natured bickering between man and wife. It was days since she'd woken up with Bandor at her side. He spent more and more time these days drinking with Beinir and Sigolf and would be sleeping it off somewhere in the camp. At least it made it easier to pay these dawn visits to Joldir, although she was always accompanied by one of the Brotherhood after the last attack by the durath. Eykr was outside the tent now, no doubt wondering what she was doing inside. Freydja had pretended she was going to visit Arissa, which wasn't really an untruth as she liked the girl and there were precious few women in the camp she could be friendly with. She hoped the pretence wouldn't draw any unwanted attention.

Arissa spooned out hot porridge oats into bowls for all of them, making sure Leif got a larger portion. The boy was still scrawny, although his body was acquiring a layer of wiry muscle from his work at the smithy. This was no place for a child but where else could Leif go? Joldir and Arissa were his family now.

"What you're trying to learn isn't easy," Joldir was saying, attempting to be encouraging. "Everyone learns at their own pace and without Rothgar our Fellowship is less balanced. When he returns I think things may go better."

Leif looked at Joldir. "Rothgar's hundreds of miles away at the moment, yet I can feel he's reaching out with the Sight, even now. He walks among our camp and even within Vorund's walls. Why is he able to do that on his own when we're finding it so difficult to work together?"

Joldir looked at Leif with a shocked expression. "Are you speaking the truth, Leif? Rothgar knows better than to walk the Path unprotected by his Fellowship."

"Of course it's the truth! This is *Rothgar* we're talking about and when has he ever listened to you? Anyway, Nereth's too busy rolling around in bed with that big warrior – the one who should be freeing my mother. I don't trust him."

Joldir sat in silence, the rest of his food uneaten, as Arissa gave Leif a wrinkled apple and a black bread roll for his lunch. The boy took them gratefully as he rose to head off to work at Curruck's smithy.

"Have I gotten Rothgar into trouble?" asked Leif.

"Never mind that," Joldir barked, making the boy jump. "Why didn't you tell me this earlier? I swear, you're as wayward and disobedient as he is!" Leif hurried out of the tent without a backwards glance.

"You didn't have to say that," Arissa told him afterwards.

"I'll make it up to him later," Joldir replied, finishing his porridge without enthusiasm. "It's Rothgar I'm angry with – he sets a bad example for the boy. I've allowed both of them to explore the limits of their powers when they're much too young to understand the consequences."

"You didn't answer his question," said Freydja.

"About what?"

"Maybe I'm not gifted enough in the Sight to be of use to you." Joldir's face was blank and Freydja realised her lack of ability was the furthest thing from his mind. She repressed the feelings of anger and frustration this stirred. "You're worried about Rothgar," she said instead.

Joldir sighed. "I'm sorry. Yes, you're right. He's growing so careless. I thought the short messages he sent to me were as far as he was straying with the Path. How could I have been so stupid? Leif's right – when did Rothgar ever listen to me?"

"Is he in such danger?" Thengill asked, wiping his mouth with the back of his hand. "The last time Nereth attacked you she was well beaten and barely escaped with her life. Will she really risk herself in that way again?"

"Perhaps not – at least, not without a strong Fellowship," Joldir replied. "That's not the only thing I'm worried about. If Rothgar's ranging as far and as wide as Leif's saying then there are other dangers."

"Such as?" said Thengill.

"Becoming too close and entangled with those he's connected to. He's stretching himself thin and there's a risk he could lose himself, no matter how much natural talent he possesses."

Freydja felt guilty, although she was unsure why as she knew none of this could be her fault. This world she was exploring was strange and confusing. "I wonder if this really is my place," she said, setting aside her bowl. "I'm struggling with this and you have your own troubles and worries. Perhaps I shouldn't be adding to them."

Joldir gave her a kindly look. "No, I won't hear of that. Untutored, the Sight represents a risk to you and those you're close to. I want to see you here again tomorrow morning, and I won't take no for an answer."

CHAPTER 69

It was several days before I began to recover from Hasteinn's attempt on my life. Or was it hours, weeks or months? In the constant darkness it was impossible to tell for certain, other than by relying on Aerinndis' mysterious time keeper. When she told me I had been lying there for two weeks I had no choice other than to believe her.

I slept for much of that time, my dreams a jumble of images stolen from other lives. Humli praying to long-forgotten gods in the dungeons as Desta sobbed softly nearby. Djuri saying his goodbyes to Ulf as he made ready to leave with Nereth for Olt. Freydja arguing with Bandor, his breath reeking of stale ale and whisky. Randall, bone tired, inspecting his lined unshaven face in the mirror in his chambers, fearful for the future. Nuna and Karas grimly entertaining Geilir, talking to him whilst wearing fixed smiles as he and Valdimarr drank their wine cellars dry, secretly counting down the days until spring when the pass to Dunfalas would reopen. Fundinn maintaining his constant watch from the mountains, thinking of the two men they had buried that morning, dying overnight in their sleep, their lips blue with the cold.

When I stirred my head throbbed and even the dull light of the fire hurt my eyes, making me nauseous. I struggled to keep any food down and I caught snatches of conversation between Ulfarr and Jolinn, who were clearly worried the blow to my head was more serious than they first thought. Maybe they were right – although there wasn't much to be gained by worrying. The next time I woke my head felt clearer, although there was a residual thumping sensation at the back of my skull as I sat up. Jolinn was resting nearby, wrapped in her furs and sleeping deeply, her back resting against the wall of the long hall. I felt dizzy as I tottered to my feet, the room swimming before me.

"The Princeling's awake," Skari said, poking Ulfarr in the ribs. "You gave us quite the scare – we thought Hasteinn might've bashed your brains out."

I gingerly rubbed the back of my head, which still felt tender. "No, I think they're still in there."

"Not sure you're ready to be up on your feet," said Ulfarr, taking my arm and holding me steady. I didn't protest as he helped me sit back down, the effort sending a stab of pain through my head. Jolinn stirred at the noise.

"Back in the land of the living?" she asked, moving over with a yawn and sitting by my side. "You had us all worried for a while."

Skari was watching us, shaking his head as if he couldn't believe of all the men on *Stormweaver's* crew Jolinn had chosen me. He had a point. Next to him Myr raised his cup in silent congratulations. Whether it was to my recovery or to wish us happiness as a couple I had no idea.

"Drink this," Ulfarr told me, offering me a cup.

I sniffed it. "Water?"

"Melted snow," Ulfarr confirmed. "We're rationing out what's left of the ale for midwinter. You roused yourself just in time."

I took a few tentative sips, not entirely certain I wanted to think about the prospect of drinking ale. The water was cool and refreshing, easing my parched throat and the dull ache in my head.

"You were talking in your sleep," Jolinn told me in a low voice. "Nothing that made much sense. Desta's name came up a few times. And Freydja."

I affected a nonchalant air. "Really? My dreams were a tangle of all sorts of lives – were they the only ones I was talking about?"

"They were the ones I noticed in particular," Jolinn replied, taking a sip of water from her own cup.

"What happened to Hasteinn?" I asked, worried my head would explode if I didn't change the subject.

"You mean after Jade crushed his skull with her bare hands?"

I nodded. "I meant, what happened to his body? Did you see what he was carrying?"

"Ah, yes, Ekkill's sword and bow. We pieced it together afterwards. Hasteinn must have killed Ekkill, rather than Etta. Meinolf was saying it doesn't prove the two weren't in league with each other, although I don't know about that. Etta's never been a friend to the Vorund Clan, even if she did lie to us from the very beginning."

"No sign of her?"

Jolinn shook her head. "It's too dark and cold to try and track her down. Something tells me she isn't far away."

We sat together in silence for a time, Jolinn fetching me some more water. I felt better, my thoughts becoming more focussed. "So, what happened to his body?"

"We didn't waste the time and energy to bury him, if that's what you mean," Jolinn replied. "We took everything of use, burned the rest and left his body farther up the shore. Aguti says he saw white bears hunting nearby – the body was gone a short while later. Not that there was much meat on him. I can't believe he managed to survive such injuries and cross the island to find us. His toes were black and frostbitten and he looked half-starved. If Etta was helping him she didn't do a very good job."

"If there are bears nearby I guess that means I shouldn't go outside unaccompanied."

Jolinn gave a throaty chuckle. "No. That wouldn't be the best way to go after everything we've been through. I don't think Johan would see the funny side of such a demise. Listen, I'm sorry. I shouldn't have left you outside on your own in the first place. I didn't think – there'd been no sign of Etta for so long I'd grown complacent. And what did you think you were doing, trying to take him on?"

"I *almost* had him," I told her, irritated by the remark. "I was moving in for the kill when he caught me out."

"Almost is the difference between alive and dead. I never thought I'd say this but I'm grateful Jade is out there watching over us. She seems to have a soft spot for you. She's been back, you know. She came to ask after you and see if you were recovering."

"She's lonely," I said, thinking back on Jade's words that night.

"Well don't grow too attached to her. Once Bruar's finished we'll be gone for good."

***

The reality was that if Bruar completed his work tomorrow we would be stuck here for a long time. The winds picked up, howling across the ice, making any journey south impossible to contemplate. No one ventured outside unless they really had to, the weather too extreme to even set a watch for our camp. I waited for the weather to clear, hoping in vain to see the strange lights in the northern sky. Instead, the weather turned worse, snowstorms battering us every day, forcing Aerinndis' crew to work in shifts to prevent the long hall and boathouse from being completely buried.

Bruar's work showed no signs of being finished, the ground continuing to rumble and shake beneath our feet. We mined our stock of stories and tales until they were exhausted, after which we asked each other for a retelling of our favourites. As we roused each morning Aerinndis would inform us how many days were left until midwinter. When I stirred myself on the day of the midwinter feast I couldn't understand at first what was different and it took me a few moments to realise the winds had died down.

I ventured outside with Jolinn, gasping when I saw the skies had cleared, the constant velvet night shot through with stars glinting like jewels of ice above the frozen wilderness. They were wreathed in the shimmering curtains of the aurorae, the colours shifting from purple through to red, orange and green. Those columns of light stretched upwards to the heavens and touched Amuran's horizon, where their colours were dimly reflected, giving the ice shelf an ethereal glow.

"That's ... amazing," Jolinn breathed next to me, her hand in mine.

I looked at her, swaddled in her cloak and furs so thickly there was no indication of the shape of the woman within. We more closely resembled two bears, one considerably shorter and smaller than the other. I grinned at the thought and although my mouth was covered by my scarf Jolinn must have noticed the gesture reaching my eyes.

"What's amusing you?"

"Nothing really. I was thinking how incredible this place is and how lucky we are to be seeing this. I'm glad I'm sharing it with you."

"That's lovely. However, you'll be sharing it permanently if you continue to stand outside much longer," Aerinndis told us as she tramped back from the snow covered outhouse. "Keep moving, otherwise you'll both freeze to death."

We spent the rest of the day in the shelter of the long hall, the pleasant smell of baking bread from Haddr's oven wafting through the air. Our stores of grain and oats were being carefully rationed but today Aerinndis allowed more food to be used as we prepared to celebrate the passing of one year and the start of another. The easing of the weather enabled Aguti, Feyotra and Ulfarr to lead a hunting party, returning later that day with seal and fish. Back at home I would have preferred roasted beef or pork – now my mouth watered at the prospect of fresh food, cheering along with the others at their successful expedition.

"There's a patch of open water farther out on the ice where the seals gather to catch fish," Feyotra explained, playing down their efforts. "I'm guessing it must be linked to those hot springs we've found on the island. The seals don't show any fear of humans – I reckon we're the first ones to ever hunt them."

"This island may be a bleak place in winter, yet it still provides for us," Meinolf observed.

Aguti smiled, pulling out his long hunting knife. "We'll eat well tonight. It augers well for the coming year."

The last of the ale barrels were opened on Aerinndis' orders as Haddr and Aguti prepared our food. The crew became boisterous under the effects of drink, playing games and singing songs as the long hall filled with the smell of cooking meat and fish. I found myself wondering whether Etta was nearby and whether she could really have survived out in the forest all this time. The thought occurred to me that she might have abandoned her host and found another, although I had warded the entrance to the long hall and those runes remained dull and inactive. I placed my hand on my sword, sliding a few inches of steel out of the scabbard. There was the dragon and chimera runes, all dark and black. Whatever Etta's fate had been, she hadn't returned to hide amongst us.

"It's nearly midnight," Aerinndis announced, when the long house was quieter and everyone was feeling full from meat and drink. "It seems fitting to me to greet a new year in the open air."

We pulled on our furs, cloaks, scarves and mittens and followed the captain out into the bitter night, huddled together under the stars. The aurorae continued to flicker over our heads, although it was less powerful than the dawn display.

Aerinndis inspected her timekeeper before tucking it deep into her furs. "The two hundred and tenth year of the Fallen Age saw us rise up as a clan once more. All of us are here because of that fight and not everyone has survived our journey north. We remember Ekkill, Jonas and Soren who died on this quest, as well as those who laid down their lives in battle at Romsdahl so we could make this voyage. We say farewell to them as we look back on those deeds as the year comes to an end. Now we greet a new year, one which arrives unheralded in the absence of the dawn in this strange place. May this year see us return in triumph, Adalrikr defeated and the Reavesburg Clan free once more."

Her crew cheered her words and they would have toasted them too, were it not for the fact that their ale would have frozen in their cups and on their lips. Instead, we returned to the warmth of the long hall, heartened at the thought of returning home, even though that reality was only a single day closer.

I sensed movement in the corner of my eye and hesitated at the doorway. Jade was crouching nearby in the snow, still dressed in her light garments despite the bitter temperatures. Her purple eyes met mine, glittering like two pinpricks of captured aurorae from the sky above. Jolinn followed my gaze and she started as she realised who was with us.

"We should go inside," she told me, looking warily at Jade.

"It's fine. She saved my life."

"She almost ripped Hasteinn's head from his shoulders," Jolinn countered, unmoving.

Jade rose and came towards us, moving lithely through the snow and a few more people became aware of her presence. Meinolf, Ulfarr and Skari waited with me and Aerinndis reappeared, asking why we weren't already inside. When she saw Jade her voice faltered, eyes narrowing as the pair faced each other.

Jade looked at *Stormweaver's* captain for a time, her expression hard to read. She turned to me, purple eyes flashing with their own inner light. "I was drawn to the voices and the sound of singing. It's so long since I heard such things." She glanced in the direction of the boathouse.

"Tell me, Rothgar, was it you who warded your vessel?"

I nodded, wondering why Jade asked such a question. "Much of it is my work, with some help from my teacher."

"It's skilfully done," Jade declared. "The runes absorb the magic of this island and, having imbued the power of the aurorae, their protection will carry you safely back to land when the time comes."

"And when will that be?" Jolinn asked, mittened hand on the hilt of her sword.

"Bruar doesn't share his secrets with me any longer," Jade replied. "He'll come to you when he's ready and his work is done. When that happens, you'll be gone and the singing on the island will be lost forever – only living on in my memory."

The statement hung in the air, a frozen thought suspended in the icy night. As I stood there I wondered if Jade was trying to ask us something. "You know we have to leave if our quest is to have any meaning. You still have a choice. What if you were to come with us?"

"*What*?" Jolinn and Aerinndis exclaimed together.

"Jade could help us," I explained. "When we reach Vorund Fastness we still have to breach the walls and fight our way to Adalrikr. Think what we could do if we had a dragon fighting on our side."

"I *could* help you, but the answer is no," said Jade, a mischievous smile playing on her lips. "You've always been kind to me but my place is here, with my own people."

"Mendaleon has banished you from her city and I've seen how Alcor talks to you. He's never forgotten what took place between you and Sigborn and it's obvious they'll never forgive you."

Jade looked at me thoughtfully. "You tell me I'm lonely as if it's some great revelation only you can see. In the Fallen Age all of my kind feels this way. Humans are always quick to use clever words to get what they want, like Sigborn, who lied to me, promising he'd return. You're no different – I don't belong with you any more than I do here, living out my life in exile within sight of the last of my kin. Yet there's someone else you *could* take with you, someone whose help you really need. Etta is staying with me and she has asked me to pass on a message to you, Rothgar."

I felt my throat tighten. I tried to speak and found I couldn't. Etta was alive – I didn't know whether I was relieved or horrified at the news.

"You judge her harshly," Jade continued. "Etta is also under Bruar's protection, so I was honour bound to offer her shelter. We have spoken much during the long night and I've learned a great deal. You say you need my help in the coming battle. Perhaps you do. However, you need her more than me if you're to win this war."

With an effort I found my voice. "Tell Etta ... Tell her I'll never trust her again. She's lost any right to be part of the Brotherhood and if she comes anywhere near us ... we'll kill her."

"That's a shame. She's very fond of you, in her own way," Jade said before turning and walking away, trudging through the snowdrifts and disappearing into the trees without a backwards glance.

Aerinndis and Jolinn both rounded on me the moment the long house doors were closed behind us. "Myshall's bane, what did you think you were doing?" cried Jolinn, angrier than I'd ever seen her.

Aerinndis clapped a firm hand on my shoulder as everyone turned to look at the commotion. "*Stormweaver* is my ship, lad. You've bargained for your passage, nothing more. I'm the captain and *I'll* decide who joins us on this voyage, not you, so don't ever forget that."

"I've seen what she can do and I know how long it will take to break Vorund's walls without her," I retorted. "I saw a chance to gain an advantage and I took it. I'm not going to apologise for that."

"You remind me of someone else when you say such

things," Jolinn told me in a cold voice. "Etta's schooled you well."

CHAPTER 70

"You're dead," I told Ulfarr for the fourth time. "Just accept it and concede defeat."

Ulfarr's brow furrowed with concentration as he stared at the kings board, trying to find some hidden pattern in the pieces no one else had seen. "Give me a moment."

"You've had plenty of moments," Aerinndis told him, leaning backwards with a self-satisfied air, hands behind her head. "It's high time you allowed me mine, so I can savour my victory."

Ulfarr scratched his beard, looking at me for inspiration. "What if I move here?"

I shook my head. "Aerinndis controls all four corners, so she'll take you here, here and here. Honestly, Ulfarr, it's hopeless. I don't think I've ever seen someone play kings so badly – at least not since they came of age." Skari snorted, enjoying Ulfarr's discomfort even though he had no idea how the game was played.

The keening wind picked up, rattling the door. There was a soft *shump* as snow slid off the roof and landed on the ground. With a sigh Ulfarr rose from his stool, made from the thick trunk of a tree, reached out and offered his hand to Aerinndis. "Well played, Captain."

Aerinndis grinned, eyes gleaming with pleasure through the unruly mop of curly red hair that now reached down well below her shoulders. No one cut their hair in this cold with the exception of Myr, who still scrupulously shaved his head every morning. "You're an awful player, Ulfarr. I *knew* we should have wagered money on the outcome."

I took Ulfarr's place and began to arrange the pieces on

the board, ready to start a new game. "Another challenger?" Aerinndis asked with a raised eyebrow. "Willing to stake some coins on who will be the victor?"

"Win or lose, what would be the point?" I said with a laugh. "Where could you spend them?"

"We're not going to be here forever. I can think of a few places in Romsdahl where a fat, bulging purse would be more than welcome."

I grinned. "I know better than to gamble with you."

Aerinndis' reply died on her lips as there was a pounding at the door. Everyone jumped at the sound, so long had we been alone in the long hall. Jolinn was the first to recover her poise, walking towards the door with her hand on the hilt of her sword, Myr at her side.

"Who's there?" Jolinn called, raising her voice to be heard above the howling wind.

"Bruar wishes to speak with Rothgar." Alcor's voice, muffled yet distinctive.

Jolinn slid away the beam barring the door and Myr swung it open. Bruar entered first, surrounded by a whirlwind of snowflakes and freezing air. The four dragons were with him, stepping over our threshold with the poise and watching eyes of wolves entering a sheep pen. Mendaleon's golden eyes met mine and I gave her a faltering smile as I rose from my seat. Myr shut the door with a solid crash, blocking out the worst of the wind as our guests brushed snow from their cloaks.

Bruar's lined face looked tired, wispy white hair stuck up at odd angles as he took down his hood, his cloak patched and mended in places. Only his dark brown eyes hinted at his true nature, glinting with energy as he took in his surroundings and *Stormweaver's* crew. At his side Alcor licked his lips, not bothering to hide his disdain at our meagre dwelling.

I swallowed and stepped forwards, dropping on one knee. "Bruar, avatar of fire and the forge, we are honoured by your presence. May we offer you and your companions food and drink after your journey from the mountain?"

"They offer our own food back to us," Alcor observed.

"A gift we gave freely," Bruar replied. "Whilst we live with plenty they must make do with what little they have, and they offer to share that with us. Don't go looking to take offence, Alcor, it reflects poorly on you."

Alcor stiffened at the rebuke as Bruar gestured for me to rise. "When the storm dies down we will send you more supplies. Although my work is done it will be some time before the spring thaws come and it will be safe for you to take to the seas."

"Done?" My mouth felt dry.

Bruar smiled, eyes twinkling. "Done. It's been a long time since I laboured at the forge and I had no idea how much I missed the swing of my hammer. To be back at work gave me a great deal of satisfaction and I have you to thank for that."

"I'm truly honoured. You have our eternal gratitude for aiding us."

"Sigborn wronged us yet now we reward his short-lived children," muttered Alcor, shaking his head. "The 'eternal gratitude' of these Reavesburg men is quickly forgotten as your generations come and go."

Mendaleon turned to him. "Have you seen nothing of what the scrying pool revealed? Didn't you hear what Rothgar told us and how Amuran itself is in danger from the Tear? Helping the Brotherhood is the least we could do – some might say we should do more."

Alcor glowered. "You may command here but we're still bound by our oaths to guard this island. Have you forgotten how the Sundered broke the promises they made to Elphinas when he first taught them to use the Sight? My oath still counts for something."

Bruar watched this exchange in silence and I was reminded of how my father sometimes looked when I was bickering with Jorik and Nuna. An image swam into my mind, a ghost from my past, as I thought of the Great Hall in Ulfkell's Keep, roaring fires in the hearths keeping us warm as we played at my father's feet. The dragons were a proud race, whose accomplishments far outstripped our own, yet Bruar listened to Alcor and Mendaleon in the manner of a long-suffering parent. His eyes met mine and I had a disconcerting experience as understanding passed between us. Bruar smiled at me, crow's feet crinkling around those ancient eyes.

"Alcor, you know I would never keep you here forever. You chose to be bound to me and I would willingly release you, if asked."

Alcor was unable to meet Bruar's gaze, his master's words shaking his usual self-confidence. "You are kind, my lord," he said at last. "However, our place is here, at your side. One day the rest of our people will return to the city we have built. We must be here to welcome them, when that time comes."

"Those days are over," Bruar pronounced. "They will never return."

A silence fell over the long hall and Bruar nodded to Ralina and Sirion, who stepped forwards, each of them carrying a bundle wrapped in oilskins. With care they laid them at my feet and Bruar turned to Alcor, who unslung another long thin bundle strapped over his back, which he also placed on the floor. I tried not to flinch as he glared at me, resentment bubbling up within those chilling, silver eyes.

"Open them," Bruar commanded. "They were made at your request, so it is only right you should be the one to see them first."

The first object was large and round and as I unfolded the cloth I saw Bruar had fashioned a black metal shield, formed from a series of circular bands radiating out from a polished silver boss in the centre. I picked it up by the edges, finding there was no discernible way in which the metal bands had been joined together. As I slipped my arm through the leather straps I found it sat comfortably, as if made to measure. My broken body lacked the strength to carry a shield in battle but Bruar's handiwork was astonishingly light.

Bruar shrugged, as if apologising for his gift. "I'm afraid I'm a metalworker, not a wordsmith. I pondered on its name for many long nights and all I came up with was *Defender*. It's a sensible enough name for a shield, I suppose. This one will protect the bearer from possession by the durath and will also weaken any magic they work against you. The undead under their command will shrink from *Defender,* for to them it will be as if the wearer carries the light of ten suns.

I stared down at the shield, reappraising its value. As I looked an image flowed out from the silver boss, the black metal changing colour as the image of a white eagle in flight appeared on the shield.

"The eagle is your clan symbol, is it not?" Bruar asked. I nodded, staring in wonder at the object as a murmur of astonishment rippled through *Stormweaver's* crew. "Whoever bears the shield imbues it with their own sigil," Bruar explained. "Using this, it should be possible to get close to Adalrikr, even if he is guarded by the undead under his command."

"We shall call it *Eagle's Defender,* in honour of the Brotherhood for which it was forged," I declared and Bruar smiled with approval.

I laid the shield aside, watching in fascination as the eagle folded its wings and flowed back into the silver boss, leaving it black and undecorated once more. Ralina's bundle had an unmistakable shape and I was unsurprised when the layers of oilskin were removed to reveal a gleaming sword, polished silver steel shot through with a blue sheen despite the gloomy light of the long house. The hilt was in the form of an eagle, wings outstretched, its head set in the centre, beak open as it called out its silent challenge. At first I started, thinking the blue light emanated from the runes on the blade and the durath were amongst us. However, it was a quality of the steel itself, the runes running along the centre of the blade dark and inactive. I recognised some of the runes – there was the dragon and chimera, repeated at least two dozen times over both sides of the blade. These were interlaced in equal number with the runes of crossed spears and locked castle gates. I knew from my encounter with Sinarr that these would destroy the undead before banishing their spirits forever to the Realm of Death. In contrast to *Eagle's Defender*, this weapon felt heavy in my hand. My shoulder ached as soon as I lifted the sword for all to see and my hand stung as if I were grasping nettles. I quickly set it down on the floor, hoping this did not make me appear ungrateful.

"Just the *one* sword?" hissed Skari. His churlish words carried further than he intended, the dragons casting him a baleful look. Skari didn't quail, folding his arms and puffing out his broad chest. "There's an *army* waiting for us in Vorund Fastness. While we've been gone Adalrikr could have created hundreds more undead to stand alongside The Six. You're expecting one warrior to carry that sword into battle and defeat them all?"

Bruar looked at Skari, unruffled. "It wasn't my intention to decide the outcome of this war, only to give the Brotherhood a chance of victory. Doing more would upset the balance that has been in place since the end of the War of the Avatars. I'll do nothing to alter that, no matter how worthy I deem the cause. That was the error Vellandir made when he decided to fight directly against Morvanos' uprising. Countless millions died as a result of his decision – one I have no desire to repeat. Amuran's fate lies in your own hands and I will not interfere further."

Jolinn stepped forwards and picked up the sword, with

no signs of the discomfort I felt as she tested the weapon, cutting through the air with a swish of her wrist. "It's a fine sword. I've never seen workmanship of this quality."

"Its name is *Death's Gift*," Bruar told her. "The weapon is designed to work in partnership with *Eagle's Defender*, although I doubt one warrior could use both of these creations together. Each draws power from their bearer and not all are compatible or possess the strength necessary to carry them into battle."

I crouched down and with trembling fingers I unwrapped the gift Alcor had presented last of all. In front of me lay a long silver spear, wrought of a single piece of metal and beaten at one end into a wide flat head, its edges razor sharp. Inlaid into the shaft were countless runes, the object thrumming with power as it reflected the orange glow of the firepit. I reached out, feeling a crackle as my fingertips brushed its surface. I lifted it with two hands and let out a gasp of surprise at its lightness. I'd mainly learned to fight with sword and shield in Olfridor's fighting circle but even to my untrained hand it was obvious this weapon was perfectly weighted and balanced.

"You hold *Lightning's Fire*," Bruar explained. "Adalrikr is the First of the Sundered, the Flayer of Souls and your runeblades may not be powerful enough to kill him. *Lightning's Fire* and *Death's Gift* have both been fashioned to slay Adalrikr and the rest of the Sundered and their undead followers. However, *Lightning's Fire* has another singular purpose. Cast *Lightning's Fire* into the gateway binding Amuran to the Shadow Realm and it will close forever, enabling you to undo the damage being wrought by the Tear."

"Easy words to say. Not so easy to accomplish," I mused.

Bruar's expression softened. "I can't say whether you will prevail in your war with the one who now calls himself Adalrikr. I have thought long and hard as to whether I was right not to fight when Morvanos first rebelled against the Creator. I found I was confronted with the same doubts and questions when you came to this island. Having power doesn't mean it's right to use it and I stand by my choices then and now. This way, whatever the outcome of the coming battle, the Creator's will shall be done."

"Thank you," I replied, lost for words. "I wish there was something I could do for you in return."

"Strive to stop Adalrikr and save my creation," Bruar told me, placing a hand on my shoulder. "That will be thanks enough."

I stood outside, watching as Bruar led the dragons back through the swirling snow towards Ballung Mountain. I looked towards the trees and, as I expected, there was a hint of purple light in the shadows – Jade watching over us as usual. I wondered how much she had heard of our meeting with Bruar. Jolinn stood at my side and I could hear the murmured conversation emanating from the long hall as everyone inspected Bruar's gifts. Were the bearers of the sword, shield and spear standing in that room? Had I already shared bread with the one destined to kill Adalrikr and end this war?

"You did it," breathed Jolinn, blue eyes bright with excitement. "We fought our way here and we succeeded. It's ... incredible. This is the stuff of legend and we're the ones living it."

"When the Brotherhood needs something doing that concerns the stuff of legend, it's me they turn to," I said with a wry smile, enjoying the moment.

Jolinn laughed, mittened hand stroking my shoulders. "Do you want to know something else?"

I gave Jolinn a sidelong glance, detecting a note of mischief in her voice. "Go on."

"No one else has been able to so much as touch *Eagle's Defender*. It belongs to you."

CHAPTER 71

"Is it done?" asked Djuri, looking over Nereth's shoulder as she sat at her writing desk. He laid a hand gently on her, the tips of his fingers brushing her smooth neck.

Nereth looked round, placing her quill into the inkpot. She wrote with an elegant, flowing script, detailing where Olt's taxes were gathered, the costs of the garrison of warriors stationed there and how much Alfarr had kept for himself in order to maintain his own household. There was nothing wrong with the elder of the town doing such a thing, of course. Alfarr was the king's representative and it was important he made a show of power in keeping with his station. The question was whether such a display crossed the line and when Djuri and Nereth had arrived in Olt it was obvious Alfarr had shown scant restraint as the king's coin flowed into his coffers. Such conduct, barely excusable in peacetime, showed 'poor judgement' during a time of war, as Nereth had succinctly put it.

Alfarr had been warned of their visit, offering hospitality to his guests with a fixed grin and a nervous laugh, which grated on Djuri's nerves before he'd finished his first cup of ale. Both being Reavesburg men, as well as having a shared history with Olt being their home town, should have given Djuri and Alfarr more of a connection. After several days Djuri concluded there was a more powerful force at play that worked against what they had in common – he couldn't *stand* Alfarr. He had to remind himself the lad was young and the responsibilities of leadership had been thrust upon him early. Not that Alfarr gave that impression – he'd always been arrogant and had an eye on his grandfather's position from the very beginning. That didn't mean he was ready to take it.

Alfarr knew his situation was vulnerable so on the face of things he had welcomed his guests, who were there with the authority of Tyrfingr Blackeyes, Jarl of Reavesburg. The fact Tyrfingr felt it necessary to intervene was a source of deep shame and it wasn't inconceivable Alfarr could lose his head, depending on what Djuri and Nereth reported back. However, despite Alfarr's entitled airs and poor treatment of his own people, this was something Djuri was keen to avoid. He couldn't forget the look on Lundvarr's face as he'd been killed in front of him and how Kolsveinn's lack of control had turned the people of Noln against their new jarl. Alfarr might not be well liked in Olt but that didn't mean they wouldn't rally around him to defend one of their own. No – if this state of affairs was to be resolved they needed to avoid bloodshed if at all possible.

The task of working through ledgers and accounting for the wealth of the neighbouring landowners in the midlands was taking an inordinate amount of time. This wasn't something Djuri was well suited to and he was glad Nereth was with him. It was made more complicated since many of the nobles had joined Johan's army when Jolinn and Beinir had sided with the Brotherhood, rather than riding to war under Hrodi Myndillson's banner. This had led to all manner of disputes concerning property, livestock, workers and thralls, all of which was taking an age to unravel. Alfarr hadn't helped matters, granting goods and land to his cronies and favourites over people with a better claim. The more they delved into such matters it became clear that, whilst Alfarr was enjoying a life of luxury at the king's expense, the lack of coin flowing to Reavesburg owed more to the myriad of disputes he had created rather than his pilfering.

Here I am, standing around trying to resolve how much tax Olt's elder owes, while Humli's family rot in prison. The thought was a bitter one and Djuri felt useless.

Nereth smiled at him as she steered his caressing hand away. "I'll be working on this for the rest of the day. Beinir's lands are forfeit for his treachery against the king – that's the easy part. The problem is Alfarr seems to have bequeathed those lands to two different people. He's an idiot."

Djuri nodded. "There's no arguing with that."

"You can't help me with this," she said, passing him a list of names on a piece of parchment. "Why don't you head out from the fort and gather these people together. I want to meet them round Alfarr's table this evening before I decide whose claim is more compelling."

"I thought you said Alfarr's cronyism was the reason everything was in such a mess," Djuri said with a frown.

"It is. However, I don't think we want a sympathiser of the Brotherhood of the Eagle to inherit Beinir's lands, do we?"

"That only wrongs such people again and pushes them towards Johan's cause."

Nereth hesitated before answering. "Be careful when you say such things. People have to understand there's nothing to be gained from supporting Johan and it's only a matter of time before we gather our forces in the spring and crush him. I've met Adalrikr and I can promise you the Laskan clans will all bend the knee to him when this is over. When you speak in this way it sounds as if you have doubts over the outcome. That's dangerous. We have a difficult job to do here and I wouldn't want Alfarr to muddy the waters by questioning your loyalty to divert attention away from his own failings."

Djuri swallowed. "I've made my choice and I know who I fight for."

"Good," Nereth said with a smile, "so go and gather our guests for tonight's feast. The prospect of roasted meat in the feasting hall should hasten their arrival if you send word this morning."

Djuri left their chamber with a heavy heart, wrapping his winter cloak around himself as his words to Nereth ate away at his insides. *When did lying to the woman I care about become so easy?*

***

There was an excited buzz as Freydja waited for everyone to gather around the Brothers' Table. Joldir was already in his seat, sitting opposite Johan, Freydja and Bandor at his side. Everyone of significance was there – Gautarr and Throm, Sigolf, Beinir, Varinn and the rest of the Kalamar warriors, Dalla, deep in conversation with her friend Maeva. Adakan was standing nearby with Svafa and Tomas, holding a cup of ale from which he drank sparingly. Thengill joined the table with Arissa and the young woman gave Freydja a friendly smile. Finally Damona, now great with child, took her place by Johan, her hands absent-mindedly stroking her stomach. Her time was drawing near and not for the first time, Freydja saw the mixture of pride, love and worry cross Bandor's face as he considered the prospect of his new baby brother or sister being born in the middle of a battlefield.

Johan rose to his feet and addressed those at his table. "Joldir has important news concerning Rothgar's quest. It's been a long winter and I know we could do with some good tidings to give us cheer as the days drag on. What Joldir has to say will give each of us heart, for the gods themselves have been good to us."

A hush fell across the table as Joldir stood and explained Bruar's work was done and Rothgar now possessed the means to kill Adalrikr and his undead guardians. Under her breath Freydja whispered the names of the artefacts Bruar had fashioned. *Eagle's Defender. Death's Gift. Lightning's Fire.* She could picture each of them in her mind, almost feeling the coldness of the metal and the crackle of magic as Rothgar's fingertips brushed their surface, gifts from the hands of the gods. Their cause no longer felt so hopeless, even if Rothgar and his crew were still hundreds of miles away, hunkering down in the perpetual night of the Fire Isle. For the first time, Freydja felt confident that

Rothgar would return to them and, when he did, Adalrikr would wish he'd never roused the anger of the Landless Jarl.

Bandor turned and looked at her, his eyes bright with excitement. "He's done it!" he whispered in her ear, squeezing her hand. "He's actually done it."

Joldir's words were greeted with roars and cheers, hope giving heart to the battle weary and the grief stricken. The noise was deafening, only subsiding when Johan stood again and thanked Joldir, raising his cup to those gathered with a wolfish grin. "Our siege engines have been quiet for long enough this morning, Varinn. It's time to set them to work once more. When Rothgar returns I want him to see the walls of Vorund Fastness split wide open."

CHAPTER 72

I watched as Meinolf took *Eagle's Defender*, thoroughly wrapped in protective oilskins for its journey across the sea, holding it as if afraid he would break the god's handiwork with his clumsiness. He passed it reverently to Fari, who was standing on the deck of *Stormweaver*, helping to load the last of their possessions on board. In a few moments we would be ready to cross the narrow channel of water separating the Fire Isle from the vast plains of ice. No one was relishing the prospect of the difficult return journey but there was no other way to return to the Redfars Sea.

The sky was blue, the sun having finally returned with spring after the long winter, white clouds scudding along, borne on a stiff breeze. The lacquered runes on *Stormweaver's* warded hull had been polished by Aerinndis herself until they gleamed in the morning light. I glanced back at the long house, a faint wisp of smoke trailing through the opening in the turf roof. The firepit inside had been doused and I felt more emotional than I'd expected at the prospect of leaving our home of the past few months. Towering high above us, Ballung Mountain was quiet, although it too issued smoke from its flattened peak. I'd wondered if Bruar and the dragons would bid us farewell but there was no sign of them. However, I knew Jade would be out there somewhere, watching us.

Remembering how she spoke of her loneliness on the island I didn't want to go without saying goodbye. Casting a quick glance over my shoulder to make sure Jolinn wasn't watching I slipped away towards the woods. Sure enough I found Jade waiting for me, sitting on a rock, watching with fascination as a column of ants marched past her foot.

"It's time for us to leave," I said.

Jade looked up, her expression blank. "Goodbye, Rothgar Kolfinnarson. It was good to meet you and touch the outside world once more."

"It was good to gain your friendship, Jade. Without your help and protection we wouldn't be leaving with what we came for and I won't forget that."

My words had more impact than I expected. Jade's large eyes welled up with tears and she turned away from me, wiping her face with her green sleeve. "Amuran has become a friendless place for me. Your kindness means a great deal and I'll remember your words, even after your spirit has passed to Navan's Halls. That's my real curse – not living in exile but to live on through the ages. I love Sigborn still, even though I know he's long dead. If Meras is the avatar of love then she must have been cruel to make it possible for me to love someone with such a short span of years, whilst I endure."

"Better to have known love," I told her.

Jade smiled. "Wise for one so young. Now, tell me, were your goodbyes really for me or were you actually looking for her?"

Jade looked over her shoulder and I saw Etta was standing nearby, leaning on her staff. Seeing her again after all this time drew the breath out of my body, making me feel weak. So much time spent together, planning, plotting, scheming and working towards Adalrikr's downfall. Etta might not be part of my future, yet here I was about to set sail to destroy Adalrikr, the man she wanted dead more than anything else in the world. Was I really free from her web of deceit or had Etta found a way to manipulate me still, even now I knew who and what she was?

I looked at the old woman and hardened my heart. "If you try and set foot on the ship, they'll kill you. I should kill you." My hand strayed to my sword and I slid it from its scabbard. The blue glow lit up the forest as Etta stood there, small and hunched as she placed all of her weight on her stick.

"You don't have to pretend to me," I snapped. "I've seen how the durath move. You're not a vulnerable old woman, so don't act as if you are."

Etta straightened at my words, resting her stick against the trunk of a tree. "Have it your way. You can put your sword away. I haven't come here to hurt you."

I slid the blade back into its sheath, wary of any sign of betrayal. "Why are you here?"

"I could ask the same question of you," Etta replied, with that familiar toothless grin. "*Stormweaver* is ready to depart, yet here you are."

I wanted to yell and scream, all the while keenly aware of how much I missed her counsel. I had to suppress the urge to draw my sword and run her through. My feelings left me standing there mute, unable to decide what to do or say.

Etta moved closer, sending a shiver of revulsion up my spine. "I can help you, Rothgar. You're about to face Adalrikr but you're not ready for this and neither is the Brotherhood. You know I'm speaking the truth – you've met him before but I know him of old. I can help you. You *need* me."

I finally found my voice. "Despite all your supposed insight and cunning, that didn't stop him murdering you and forcing you to take the body and soul of your own wife. If that story is true."

Etta bridled. "True? How dare you ... I haven't shared that with anyone before ..."

"Until you were forced to," I finished. "Forgive me, Etta – after all the lies, it's so difficult to know what to believe any more."

For a moment I thought Etta was going to attack me. Her face hardened and her body tensed, as if she were readying herself to pounce. Jade stood, interposing herself between us in a smooth, fluid motion in the time it took me to blink.

"Etta," Jade's voice was cool, calm and clear. "You know if you threaten him I'll be forced to intervene. He is one of the Bearers of Bruar's gifts."

Etta sighed and hunkered down, resting her back against a tree. She closed her eyes, face tilted upwards. "It's all such a mess. I never meant for any of this to happen."

"Yet here we are," I muttered.

"And now you're going to abandon me, alone on this island with no means of escape?" It was one of the few times I'd heard Etta sound frightened but I pushed any feelings of pity aside.

"You won't be alone. You'll have Jade and perhaps in time Mendaleon will relent and allow you access to the city, although I doubt that very much. Anyway, why not flee your current stolen form and take another? You're not really trapped at all, so don't try and fool me into pitying you."

Etta looked at me shrewdly, although her voice still had a quaver of fear when she spoke. "I'll never take another human life as a skin thief. Never. Whatever our differences, we share a common enemy. Let me help you to prevail over them and I don't care what happens to me afterwards. Etta gave me her life so I would have the chance to take my revenge and the need for vengeance is something we both understand all too well. If you want to defeat Adalrikr, you need me."

My patience was worn thin. Something had changed and it was no longer unimaginable being without Etta as our counsellor. "Have you listened to yourself? You took the life of your own *wife* to survive and thought nothing of it. You wormed your way into the confidence of my grandfather with your lies. I know who I want at my side when we go into that final battle with Adalrikr – people I can trust."

I turned to go, pausing when I realised there was something else I needed to say. "Ekkill's dead. I wasn't sure if you knew."

Etta's familiar short temper flared. "Of course I knew! I saw you raise the cairn and I heard your words at the funeral. My most gifted pupil, he had a bright future in front of him."

"The one you determined. Has it occurred to you that he'd still be alive if he hadn't been out here, searching for you? Too many people have died because of your thirst for vengeance. No. We don't need you any more, Etta. You stopped being my tutor a long time ago."

I stalked back to the shore, heart pounding as I waited for Etta to call out after me but she never uttered a word. When I reached the others I ignored Jolinn's questioning glance as I climbed aboard *Stormweaver*, Matthildr's firm hand helping me over the gunwale. I looked back at the long house, Ballung Mountain rising up to dwarf our small winter home, thick forests covering the mountain's skirts. I knew that somewhere inside those woods Etta and Jade were watching us leave.

Nearby Skari was already groaning, even though the waters were still and flat. "Come on. Let's get this over with."

Ulfarr chuckled. "I swear, you're the worst sailor Reavesburg has ever seen. We'll be landing on the ice shelf in a few moments."

"What's on your mind?" Jolinn asked. "I was beginning to worry when you vanished. Where did you go?"

"I just needed a moment to myself. This may be the last time in a while when there's chance to think and reflect on what's happened and what's still to come."

Jolinn looked at me, opening her mouth to say something more when Aerinndis interrupted us. "Take your places," she bellowed, "all able hands to the oars. It's time to say goodbye to the Fire Isle and head home."

I sat down at the rear of the ship next to Skari, both of us knowing we wouldn't be much use as with a groan *Stormweaver's* crew bent their backs and pulled on the oars. The longship skimmed out across the narrow channel, the oars splashing rhythmically as they beat in time, the ingrained familiarity of the task immediately returning to the crew despite months ashore. I glanced back again at the island, catching sight of a pair of eagles riding high on the winds, circling the mountain. I felt a lump in my throat and turned away.

"Not feeling so good?" asked Skari, his scarred face already taking on a green hue.

"Not really," I admitted.

"It's no good ... I ... wurgh ..." Skari scrambled unsteadily to his feet and vomited hard over the side of the ship. His indignity provoked gales of laughter, upsetting the timing of some of the rowers. Several oars clashed and *Stormweaver* lurched to one side, her steady progress unsettled as Ulfarr's oar dragged in the water.

Stormweaver's captain wasn't amused. "Ulfarr – get that out of the sea. You've all gone soft lounging around on land for so long. We've a hard journey ahead of us – every bit as difficult as the one that brought us here. If we don't work hard and behave like one crew all this will have been for nothing. Careless sailors die and I've already lost enough of you, so put your mind to the task and bring us home."

"You heard the captain," roared Meinolf from his bench. "Bend your backs and get to it."

There was a collective grunt as the regular beat of the oars was restored and the vast realm of ice loomed ahead. A few lazy seals watched our progress from the shallow shelf we were aiming for, where we would drag Stormweaver out of the water and begin the grinding job of moving her on rollers across the pack ice. Aerinndis was right – we were still far from home and a long way from safety. I closed my eyes, catching a few more moments of rest before the grim task of crossing the ice began.

CHAPTER 73

Orglyr waited for the signal confirming the Vorund camp was surrounded before stepping forwards to address its commander. *He's learned the lesson from his last defeat* Fundinn reflected. *Sometimes it pays to be cautious.*

The Norlhast warriors didn't move with the same well-drilled speed of last summer. Months spent wintering in Dunfalas on dwindling rations had robbed them of their strength. Almost fifty men had died in the mountains, the cold seeping into their bones until they drifted into a dreamless sleep, never to recover. Five more had died falling to their deaths in two separate accidents on the treacherous path through the pass, still icy in early spring. Orglyr knew they couldn't afford to lose any more warriors – a force of little more than eight hundred wasn't going to fill Geilir's heart with fear. However, that was all they had and they weren't going to waste any lives on this latest encounter with the enemy.

"Who's in charge here?" Orglyr shouted, once his men were finally in place.

Silence greeted his words at first. Eventually someone emerged, poking their head above a wall of wooden stakes.

"Who is that?" Orglyr called out. "Do you speak for those behind that wall?"

"Who wants to know?"

Orglyr spat on the ground. "I've spent months shivering in those mountains and it's left me a little short on patience. My name is Orglyr the Grim, warrior of Norlhast and at one time I was Bekan Bekanson's jarl. We're here to reclaim our lands from Adalrikr, the so-called King of the

North and you're in our way."

"Tryggvi, Geilir's second," shouted the Vorund man in the camp. "Your words condemn you and your men for treason and rebellion against your rightful king. Your own chief bent the knee and swore fealty to keep his lands and reclaim Kalamar from the Reavesburg Clan. Is this how you repay your king? Do the words of your chief mean nothing?"

Orglyr gave Fundinn a sidelong glance. "Defiant words from someone surrounded and outnumbered."

Fundinn nodded. "No one else is coming to their aid – if they were, they'd already be here. Curren's advance scouts did their job well and they must have successfully intercepted Tryggvi's messengers. If Dinuvillan smiled on Curren then his party should already be in Norlhast Keep, ensuring they're readying for our arrival and preparing for war."

"All the more reason to get on with things," Orglyr muttered. "You're on your own, Tryggvi," he called out in a louder voice. "No one's coming to help you, so spare everyone some trouble and surrender. It'll go easier on you if you do."

Tryggvi swore back at Orglyr, with defiant shouts rising up from his fortified encampment. "I'm not going to throw my gates open to anyone, least of all you. You want us out of your way, you'll have to come here and settle things the Laskan way."

"Last chance, Tryggvi," Orglyr shouted back. "I don't have time to waste talking to you. Surrender or you and all your men are going to die."

"I'd rather die with a sword in my hand than cowering over the executioner's block," Tryggvi told them. "Come on. Let's get this over with."

Orglyr sighed. "So be it." He turned to Hoskuldr. "Archers forwards. Light your arrows. Fundinn, raise the shield wall."

More shouts rose out from the camp and a few of

Tryggvi's warriors released arrows at their attackers, all of which fell short. With a loud *clack* Fundinn's warriors formed up in front of Orglyr's army, shields raised to create a solid line. At his back, Hoskuldr's archers readied their bows and fell into step as Fundinn's warriors advanced. More arrows whistled through the air, landing closer as they drew into range. One thudded onto Fundinn's shield, skittering away.

"Nearly there," Fundinn called out. "Form up and hold steady."

Behind him Hoskuldr was giving more orders and Fundinn caught the smell of burning oil as his archers lit their arrows and took aim. Vorund's bowmen launched another volley, peppering the shield wall. An arrow landed a few inches from Fundinn's exposed foot and he bellowed at Hoskuldr to hurry up. Hoskuldr gave the order and, as one, the fire arrows of the Norlhast Clan launched into the air, arching high. Tryggvi's camp was the target rather than his warriors, making it virtually impossible to miss. Cries drifted up from behind the wall as they found their mark.

"Again," roared Hoskuldr. Another volley flew up into the air and the Vorund Clan's arrows stopped as their bowmen tried to take cover. A third and fourth wave quickly followed and as Fundinn peered over the top of his shield he could see parts of the camp were already ablaze, the earlier cries of alarm soon replaced by the screams of those inside.

Fundinn hunkered down behind his shield, shoulder to shoulder with the men either side of him as Hoskuldr continued to rain down death from the skies on Tryggvi's warriors. There was nothing to be done now other than wait for it all to be over.

***

"You're sure?" Nuna asked.

Kalfr nodded, the thin white scar running from his lip to his cheek wrinkling as he grinned. "Curren's back with a handful of scouts. I've seen him with my own eyes early this morning."

Nuna was talking to Kalfr in her husband's chambers, Karas listening carefully to every word as he sat in his chair by the fire, wrapped in thought. Brosa stood guard outside, making sure they weren't disturbed. Sigurd was standing on the other side of the fireplace, arms folded across his chest as he listened to his brother's story. He looked lean and muscular, the result of long days spent training in the circle sparring with his men. However, the dark rings under his eyes were less wholesome and spoke of long sleepless nights, giving him a feverish look. A change had come over Karas' quiet, dependable friend since Tryggvi broke his father's mind and Nuna wasn't sure she liked the transformation.

"It's not all good news," Kalfr explained. "Many of Orglyr's warriors were killed or fled following their defeat last year and more died while they were sheltering in the mountains. Curren tells us that Orglyr and Tidkumi's combined forces number little more than eight hundred."

"That's not enough," Sigurd muttered.

Kalfr grimaced. "They might gather more as they move eastwards towards Norlhast Keep. Curren reports their supplies were running low and they'll be marching straight for the keep. Orglyr intends to end this, one way or the other."

"Then he's going to die and get the rest of us killed alongside him," said Sigurd.

Kalfr shrugged. "It is what it is. It's too late to back out – Orglyr's on the move and we have to stand and fight with him, despite the odds."

Sigurd's bloodshot eyes flashed with anger. "Don't mistake me for a coward. I intend to fight, have no doubts about that. I've lived long enough as a dog, cowering on Geilir's leash, our father unavenged."

"I'm sorry," Kalfr replied. "I didn't mean to suggest –"

"No, I'm sorry," Sigurd said, stepping forward to give Kalfr a bone-crunching hug. "I spoke thoughtlessly."

"You spoke honestly," Karas corrected, hunched in his chair. "Geilir has more warriors under his command, four hundred of them with heavy horse. Lefwine has a further eight hundred Riltbalt men. They outmatch us – it's a simple matter of numbers."

"How many can we muster here?" Nuna asked, fearing the answer.

"We have some two hundred men within Norlhast I can trust to be ready when the time comes," Sigurd replied. "Depending on how Geilir decides to defend the keep that should be enough to at least make a fight of it."

"Won't he just wait in the keep and defend his position from here?"

Karas shook his head. "No. Geilir will want to avoid another protracted siege – he plans to return to Vorund Fastness and go to Adalrikr's aid. Orglyr's low numbers invite immediate attack and Geilir won't want to waste this second opportunity to crush the Norlhast rebellion, even if it costs him more lives."

"He'll put Lefwine in the vanguard of the attack, I guarantee it," added Kalfr. "He won't waste Vorund men when he has the conquered warriors of Riltbalt at his disposal. From the accounts I've heard he used the same tactics when he fought Orglyr last year. Even if Geilir takes to the field Orglyr's never going to get near him."

Karas turned to Nuna. "This is going to end badly but Sigurd's right. Every day we've delayed this fight makes us less than we were and I can't play this part any longer and continue to live with myself. You need to leave, before Orglyr's army arrives, so I can keep you safe and away from all of this."

"I can't *leave*," Nuna argued, her voice rising with indignation. "If I do, Geilir will know we had something to do with this plot. We're supposed to be playing our parts as the allies of the king – doing anything other than that will only arouse his suspicions. We have to stand with the Vorund warriors and pretend we'll defend the walls alongside them."

Karas sat there, weighing her words before turning to Kalfr. "Luta and your father should leave, at least. This is no place for your children."

"And the rest of our friends and their families? Will they benefit from the same warning?" Kalfr replied, looking guilty. "This could end with Norlhast in flames – no one will be safe."

"You know we can't risk telling anyone else until Orglyr's army is at our walls," Sigurd told him. "If you feel guilty at receiving special treatment then do this one thing for me. Spare my nieces and nephews from what's about to happen, so all this will have been for something."

Kalfr hung his head, embracing Sigurd once more. "I'll send them northwards, up the coast to Ustaburg. I'm not abandoning you, though – do you understand? We'll fight side by side when the time comes."

"Time is short, so go now," Karas told them both. "Make your arrangements and bring me word when Orglyr arrives. Until then, we won't speak of this again. Nuna, please, stay with me for a few moments longer."

Nuna said her goodbyes to Sigurd and Kalfr, wondering if Karas was intending to try and persuade her to follow Luta's example and leave Norlhast. When they were alone she steeled herself for an argument.

"Nuna, have I been a good husband?"

Whatever she might have expected Karas to say, it wasn't that. Nuna was thrown and it took her a few false starts before she could find the right words. "What? Why are you asking me this now? Of course you have. You've welcomed me into your home and made me part of your family. I couldn't have asked for more."

"Our marriage began under a terrible cloud. Jorik and his family were murdered hosting our wedding. I made you walk past Rothgar at Reavesburg's gates as he hung in that crows cage, a spectacle for all to see. I brought you home to an occupied land after bending the knee to our oppressor. What kind of a man does those things?"

"The man I love," Nuna told him, bending down to kiss his pockmarked cheek. He felt cold, despite being so close to the fire.

Karas' eyes were distant as he spoke. "Sometimes I wonder, especially when you act so convincingly as the bored wife in front of Geilir. After losing Katrin, I never thought I'd find love again. Thora confounded my expectations and gifted me two beautiful daughters, helping me to be strong when I fell into disfavour and Bekan threatened my family. I fought for them in the duelling circle, rather than the right to rule our clan. I could have fled into exile but instead Thora convinced me I could rule fairly and with honour. And for a time all was well, until our hopes and dreams for the future were dashed when the blood plague struck. I was too weak to even light the funeral pyre for Thora and our daughters as I lay on what I believed was my deathbed. Those duties fell to Sigurd, who has done more for me than any loyal friend should ever be asked to do."

Nuna reached out and took hold of Karas' thin hands, enfolding them in her own. Why did he feel so cold? "Karas, I don't understand. Why are you telling me this?"

"We both know I've not been able to give you a child to further strengthen our union," Karas replied, staring into the fire. "The blood plague ... left me less of a man. I sometimes wish you could have met me as Katrin and Thora saw me – a young warrior in my prime. The man who killed Bekan Bekanson, who acted with mercy sparing the life of Orglyr the Grim and who ruled his people wisely. That man is gone."

"You're the man I married. I'll admit I did my duty when I married Karas Greystorm. That marriage came from a union of two clans, forged on the hope we could defeat our mutual enemy. What I also remember is the man I married had the foresight to set old enmities aside and look to the future, putting his people first even when the choice was hard. When my home was destroyed you made a new one for me and if I were given the choice again I would still choose to be the Lady of Norlhast Keep."

Karas turned to her. "My people ... No, *our* people love you, Nuna. The frightened young noblewoman from Reavesburg has become the Lady of Norlhast Keep, that's certainly true. I only wish I was stronger and my clan was able to shake off the shackles of Adalrikr Kinslayer."

Nuna felt a jolt of understanding as she pieced together Karas' meaning. "You don't expect to live through this, do you?"

Karas shivered. "A chief has to lead his warriors into battle. When the time comes I'll fight with Sigurd and Kalfr to reclaim my own keep. I'll be fighting for you – I just wish I could keep you safe. If we fight and fail, as looks likely, then I know our people will still look to you to lead them when all this is over. If ... If ..."

"You don't have to honey your words," Nuna told him. "You mean to say if I survive. No one is safe anymore, you and me least of all."

Karas fixed his gaze upon her, watery eyes reflecting the orange glow of the fire. "Brosa is under strict orders never to leave your side when the fighting starts. I'll feel better knowing you're safe behind the walls of the keep with him guarding you. When all this is over, whatever the outcome, Norlhast will have to find a way to survive. Stay safe and our clan will be yours. They couldn't be in better hands, Nuna."

Nuna rested her forehead against Karas' head. "Come back safely to me, and we'll rule them together," she told him. Whilst she didn't believe her own words the lie gave them both some comfort as the storm clouds of war gathered over Norlhast Keep.

CHAPTER 74

The winds howled across the unbroken tracts of the vast frozen shelf, battering us as we crawled southwards, *Stormweaver* lumbering along on her rollers. Our furs and cloaks were soon encrusted in ice, the weight making it even harder to walk. The chill gnawed through my flesh, seeping deep into my bones, sapping my strength. After two days I was unable to lend a hand pushing *Stormweaver* and two days after that even walking behind, following the flattened path she left in her wake, became impossible. Realising I was slowing our progress, Aerinndis ordered I ride in the sled. Whilst it was humiliating to admit I lacked the strength for the journey I knew I was putting everyone in danger and had no choice other than to agree. It fell to Ulfarr, Myr and Skari to take turns hauling me over the ice as I shivered under a mountain of blankets and furs, sleeping more and more often as we left the Fire Isle behind us. Eventually, Ballung Mountain was nothing more than a black smudge on the edge of the horizon.

The world of ice shifted and changed, so even though we tried to follow our original route we found our way blocked by great chunks of ice, carved by the wind and snows into a maze of narrow channels too small for Stormweaver to pass. As we worked our way around the edges of this field of boulders a crevasse opened up, swallowing Fari without warning. We never found his body. Two more sailors died from exhaustion as the weather worsened into a snowstorm and the driving winds took their toll, slowing our progress to a crawl. I felt guilty when we camped that night, listening to Matthildr sobbing over her lost friends, Feyotra too tired to be able to offer meaningful comfort.

My dreams with the Sight provided respite from the cold, even Humli's experiences providing a welcome relief as he spent countless days in the dungeons under Ulfkell's Keep with Desta and Lina, their hope in Djuri's promises wearing thin. I felt Nuna's fears for the future keenly and I had to swallow down the lump in my throat as I considered the prospect I might never see her again. Was it enough to have brought Bruar's weapons and the shield back with us? Was this the part I'd been destined to play, my journey ending here on the ice? I thought of Ekkill's cairn, Petr's death defending Johan, how Patrick, the Flint brothers and so many other members of the Brotherhood had fallen in the Battle of Romsdahl. I was no different to any of them – they had crossed over to Navan's Halls and one day I was going to follow them.

Jolinn's anxious face loomed over me as we camped one night, watching me with concern. She spoke and I tried to answer, my tongue like a lead weight in my mouth. Her features blurred and shifted before my eyes, transforming into Sinarr's shade, his normally blind eyes glowing white like ice crystals.

"The time for grief is over," the Weeping Warrior told me, voice dry and thin, barely audible above the wind howling outside our tent. "Now is the time for war."

"We're dying out here."

Sinarr reached out and put a chill hand on my shoulder. "The strength to survive comes from within. The seas of the Endless Ocean lie a mere two days from here. You will live to see it – you must. Only you can bear *Eagle's Defender*."

"I'm so cold."

"Death is colder," Sinarr replied. "When all this is over, perhaps we will cross over into Navan's Halls together. Your time isn't now – you must finish what you started and bring Bruar's gifts to the Brotherhood. You're one of the Bearers and you can die when your task is complete."

I closed my eyes, fearful that if I went to sleep I would never wake. I was so tired, even breathing was an effort. The cold touch of Sinarr's hand on my shoulder began to burn, ice cold fire that pierced my skin and sent pain lancing into the marrow of my bones. I woke with a cry, throwing off my blankets as I sat up, rubbing my shoulder. The pain was unbearable, taking me back to the dark place in the Great Hall of Ulfkell's Keep. I saw Tyrfingr's face, lit with a ghastly red glow as he turned the hot coals with his poker, its tip white hot.

"What is it?" Jolinn said, stirring under her furs next to me.

I pulled my clothing open, gasping as I felt the frigid air on my pale skin. On top of my right shoulder there was a red palm print, fingers and thumb marks radiating out as livid welts, ice cold and sore to the touch. Even as I watched the mark faded, red turning to black like a primitive tattoo.

"What is that?" asked Jolinn, eyes wide.

"The Weeping Warrior reached out to me," I said, teeth chattering with the cold as I hurriedly dressed again. "We're only two days away from the sea."

"How do you know that?" said Aerinndis from the other side of the tent. "You've been asleep for days."

"How did I know to come here in the first place?" I countered. "You followed my quest here, so listen to what I have to say on our return journey. Take heart – we're close."

Jolinn was looking at me, brow furrowed. "What's happened to you? I thought you were going to die."

I dropped my voice as I replied. "Sinarr brought me back from the brink. He hasn't finished with me yet."

We settled down to sleep together, the canvas over our heads snapping in the wind. I put my arm around Jolinn's shoulders and even through the layers of blankets and furs I could feel the knots of tension in her back.

***

By morning the weather had cleared, raising our spirits as we resumed our journey. I clambered aboard the sledge, still tired but more awake than in days. Myr nodded to me and offered me a rare smile as he got ready to haul me along. The white expanse was dazzling when the sun shone, forcing me to squint and shield my eyes with a gloved hand. There was a difference in the air and I wasn't the only one to notice the change.

"Smell that?" said Meinolf, pulling aside his scarf to reveal his grey beard, rimed with frost. "There's a taste of salt on the wind – that's the smell of the ocean."

Heartened by the news *Stormweaver's* crew set to work and Sinarr was true to his word. Two days later we reached the edge of the ice shelf where it met the sea, the waters filled with icebergs breaking off with the spring melt. Aguti sank to his knees, tears of joy falling down his ruddy face. Only Skari appeared less than delighted at the prospect of another ocean voyage. After finding a suitable place from which to launch *Stormweaver* we made camp one final time on the ice, while Haddr had the presence of mind to set out some fishing lines overnight to replenish our stocks for the voyage. Although everyone was tired the mood in the camp that night lifted, people swapping stories and talking about what they would do when they returned to Laskar.

"I've not forgotten the Brotherhood's promise," Aerinndis reminded me. "I'm holding Etta to her bargain, even though she proved false. *Marl's Pride*, my mother's masterwork, belongs to us when all this is over and you'll ensure Johan makes good on that seat on the merchant's guild and those other trading opportunities for my parents."

"After everything you've done for the Brotherhood, they're yours," I said. "I can think of no finer person to captain *Marl's Pride* now Brunn Fourwinds is no longer with us."

It was the greatest compliment I could think of and Aerinndis' wry smile told me she understood.

***

We launched *Stormweaver* in the morning, her sail filling with favourable winds as we navigated around the sea of icebergs, Feyotra calling out orders to the rowers as they helped her manoeuvre the ship. I rubbed my shoulder, which still ached from time to time, as I sat at the stern with a groaning Skari, watching the towers of ice floating by, their massive weight somehow suspended in the freezing waters. Seabirds dived for fish, sharing their spring feast with seals and sea lions, who were also busy hunting. Further out to sea I thought I saw the shapes of orcas, busy pursuing their own prey. I glanced ahead and noticed dark clouds rolling across the horizon.

Meinolf looked up from his oar and followed my gaze. "The weather in early spring isn't always kind. Fortunately, the wind is taking that storm away from us."

I sighed. "Let's pray to Culdaff to speed us on our way and for Nanquido to calm the waters."

Meinolf grunted. "Pray all you want. We might have met with one of the gods but that doesn't mean the rest of them care. What will be will be."

We made good progress for the first week of our voyage as we sped southwards but Meinolf was proved right in the days that followed. The weather gradually turned against us, eventually forcing us to stow the sail to prevent the wind ripping it apart as the sky turned black with threatening clouds. Aerinndis' crew shipped their oars, plugging the gap in the hull with wooden blocks and hurrying to erect the oiled canvas to provide us with some shelter from the worsening storm.

"Looks bad," Meinolf shouted over the rising wind as Skari staggered to the side of the ship and retched.

"Come on," said Jolinn, waving at me to get under the canvas. I felt the tug of the wind on my cloak as I hugged it tightly around me, already damp and crusted with salt spray.

"Give me a moment," I told her, watching as Aerinndis

moved towards *Stormweaver's* prow.

I headed forward to join her and she shot me a bitter glance, jabbing her thumb over her shoulder at the runes of finding worked into the green dragon prow of her ship. "I hope your friend's handiwork delivers everything he promised. When this storm hits we'll be blown off course and there's no telling where we'll find ourselves."

I opened my mouth to speak, the words dying in my throat as the sea fell away in front of *Stormweaver*. We pitched downwards, riding the foaming crest, and I watched in horror at the mountainous wave of iron grey water rising up towards us on the far side. Aerinndis laughed at my expression and turned, whooping as she saw the towering waters.

"Relax, Rothgar," she told me, eyes wild with excitement as the wind whipped at her long red curls. "They call me Stormrider with good reason. Culdaff and Nanquido haven't yet conspired to make a storm that can sink me or my ship. At least, not unless today's the day when my legendary luck changes."

"How do you know today isn't that day?" I called, trying and failing to keep the note of fear from my voice.

Aerinndis' grin widened, white teeth gleaming. "Do you *really* want me to answer that question?"

I ducked back under the canvas, cowering with the rest of the crew as we huddled together. Outside, I could hear Aerinndis shrieking into the wind and the rain, yelling defiantly at the gods.

My eyes met with Meinolf and her first mate shrugged. "What did you expect? She's always been mad – which other captain would have agreed to come here with you in the first place?"

I closed my eyes and waited for the tempest to pass as *Stormweaver* began to pitch and roll. In the gathering darkness as the last rays of the sun were blotted out by the clouds I sought out Jolinn's hand, holding it tightly.

CHAPTER 75

Horns sounded and Norlhast Keep filled with fearful cries, running footsteps, shouted orders. Brosa argued fiercely with Nuna when she asked him to take her up to the walls of the keep. He should have known better – within a few moments she was wrapping her cloak around her as Katla fussed over her hair.

"Oh, leave it alone," Nuna hissed at her maid. "I'm going outside, not dressing for a banquet."

Katla apologised, pulling Nuna's golden hair into a simple ponytail, fretting over how it needed more brushing. "We're under attack and you want to style my hair," Nuna rebuked her, softening her words with a smile. Katla laughed nervously, brush held threateningly in one hand.

"This isn't a good idea," Brosa told her. *Again.*

"No, it isn't but we're doing it anyway," Nuna told him briskly as she checked her knife was tucked into her belt. Satisfied she was ready Nuna swept through the door and Brosa swore under his breath as he hurried after her, Katla locking herself inside Nuna's chambers.

Norlhast Keep lay in the centre of the port of Norlhast, surrounded by the low turf-roofed houses that formed the town. Those dwellings were defended by a low wooden wall. However, the towers of the keep provided a better vantage point to survey the surrounding countryside. As the sun began to rise, bright shards of yellow light peeping out amongst a gathering of dark rain clouds further out to sea, Nuna was able to see the cause of the disturbance. Orglyr's army had arrived. She could see the banners of the whale flapping in the breeze as the ranks of Orglyr's warriors formed up, long spears glinting in the morning light. Brosa peered out, trying to gauge their numbers.

"Perhaps as many as a thousand swords," he said. "It seems the earlier reports underestimated their numbers."

"It could be others have rallied to their call during their march east," Nuna mused.

"My lady." The words made her start – she hadn't heard Valdimarr approaching.

"Valdimarr. Dromundr. Well met. It seems the day of battle has finally come."

Valdimarr nodded, looking queasy, thick dark hair jutting out at odd angles around the back of his bald head and ears. Clearly Nuna wasn't the only one to have hurried from her bed this morning. Dromundr looked much calmer, dressed for battle in oiled chainmail, sword belted to his side and a heavy wooden shield with its bear sigil strapped to his arm.

"Where's Geilir?" Nuna asked.

"Getting ready to march out with Lefwine to meet Orglyr's threat," Valdimarr told her, wringing his hands. "He's left the defence of the town to me."

"You mean us," Nuna replied. "Remember we stand together. I'll not see Orglyr's rebels destroy our clan. We must put an end to the rebellion once and for all to prevent Norlhast being dragged further into civil war. My warriors are at your disposal."

"My lady, you have no idea what those words mean to me," Valdimarr told her, mopping at the sweat beading on his forehead with a small handkerchief.

Dromundr scowled, eyes bright with excitement. He'd spent years at the Norlhast court as Valdimarr's second and it was obvious he disliked all the boring politicking. Defending the town against attack – this was something he understood and he was relishing the moment.

"Your husband and his men are already heading towards the outer wall with my warriors," he told her.

"There's a small garrison stationed here at the keep to protect you but I doubt they'll be needed. There's no way Orglyr's army is going to get through Geilir's forces."

"I hope you're right," whispered Valdimarr.

***

Orglyr sat astride one of the few horses they had commandeered during their march east. No warhorse, the beast's main function was to enable him to move swiftly around his army as he gave his final orders before battle. Limping Tidkumi was in charge of their northern flank, Orglyr commanding the wedge of spearmen in their centre with Fundinn as his shieldman. To the south Hoskuldr was moving his archers into position on higher ground, trying to ensure the Norlhast warriors had some cover when the battle began. Soma was talking to Orglyr, discussing final tactics before heading back to stand with Tidkumi. She looked thin and tired, face pinched. Fundinn rolled his shoulders, trying to relax and loosen his muscles. *Not long now.*

The gates of Norlhast swung open to the sound of horns and drums and Fundinn watched as the Vorund army began to pour out onto the field. It quickly became obvious they were heavily outnumbered and a murmur ran through the ranks when the Vorund cavalry emerged. Fundinn could count hundreds of horsemen; the same forces that had run them down and turned the tide in the battle at Taur.

"Looks like he means to finish this," Orglyr observed. "It's better this way."

"Better how, exactly?" said Soma. "You'd prefer to die today rather than tomorrow?"

Orglyr gave her a wicked grin. "I'm not one to stretch things out and I don't relish the idea of attacking my own town and keep. Dealing with things out here on the field is much more ... civilised."

Soma exchanged a look with Fundinn. *No, I didn't know he knew that word either.*

Geilir's cavalry took up a position towards the rear

of the massing army, with two smaller flanks of warriors and archers flying the banner of the bear. Fundinn could see another group of warriors forming the vanguard of their enemy, their standards emblazoned with a hammer set above a pointed star.

"Riltbalt's warriors," he said to Orglyr, pointing at them. "On their own they almost match our numbers."

Orglyr nodded. "We'll have to punch through them to get to Geilir. He'll be in the centre of that group of cavalry, commanding his army from the rear. Gone are the days when a chief led his clan into battle."

Fundinn looked at the massed Riltbalt warriors, knowing they would never get near Geilir's horsemen. *We never had the numbers for this fight, not even last year. Once Riltbalt came to Geilir's aid we never stood a chance.* He glanced at the faces of the young men around him, knowing the same thought was going through their minds. Would some of them be contemplating retreat? Undoubtedly. He was thinking the same thing himself. *Retreat to where, though? It's too late to swear fealty to Adalrikr – there's no going back, not after all this.*

Orglyr rose up in his stirrups and lifted his axe high above his head. "Warriors of Norlhast, are you with me?" Not everyone heard his call and it was met with a muted response and a few half-hearted cheers. Orglyr turned his horse in a tight circle, puffing out his chest and beating his axe against his shield to gain their attention.

"I'll ask you again. Warriors of Norlhast, are you with me?" A firmer cheer went up this time, Fundinn lending his powerful voice next to Soma.

"That's better. I know you're thinking about the odds as you look at the army ranged against us. You'd be fools not to, but think on this instead. We've been under Vorund's rule for two years. Have you prospered under our king's benevolent leadership? Do you enjoy paying his taxes so he can live his life of luxury, paid for with our blood, sweat and toil?"

Nervous laughter drifted up and a few shouts of "Bollocks to that," met Orglyr's words.

"I didn't think so. This is our land, and the Vorund Clan have taken it from us. Well, today that changes. We're fighting for our homes and the right to rule ourselves. What are the Riltbalt and Vorund Clans fighting for? A king most of them have never met, who greedily gathers in the coin they collect. In battle the heart matters more than anything else, and we're fighting for our homes, our families and our freedom. They might outnumber us but we have the stomach for the fight. When we charge there's no going back, no surrender and they'll see it in our eyes and quail before our fury."

More shouts and cries went up and people began chanting Orglyr's name, loud enough for the sound to carry to the waiting Vorund army. Fundinn clashed his sword against his shield, others following his example and they built up their battle cry in a rising wall of sound.

Orglyr put his axe away and placed his hand over his heart, waiting for the crowd to quieten. "We're fighting for something and that matters more than anything else. Courage wins battles and we have the heart to take five Vorund warriors for every one of us. By the time the sun sets, we'll have driven our foes back into the Redfars Sea and Norlhast will be free once more."

Orglyr's speech was met with a deafening roar, shields and weapons raised in the air, pointing towards their enemies. Fundinn stared at the Vorund army and took a deep breath. Their thousand swords *would* make the difference today. *Live or die, they'll be singing about this for years to come. Who wants to live forever, anyway?*

Fundinn turned and put his hand on Soma's shoulder. "It's been an honour to fight alongside you. Your father was a great warrior, Soma Alvedottir. I know you'll make him proud today."

Soma put a gloved hand over Fundinn's, clasping it tight. "Keep your blade sharp and your wits about you. Oh, and don't let Orglyr do anything stupid."

Fundinn grinned. "I'll try. May Dinuvillan smile on you."

"And on you," Soma replied as she slid her helm onto her head and moved off towards Tidkumi's flank, while Fundinn took up a position next to Orglyr.

"What did you think?" Orglyr asked him as he dismounted from his horse.

"Good speech. Did you prepare it beforehand?"

Orglyr laughed. "No, of course not. Made it up on the spot."

"Bit like our battle plan, then?"

Orglyr grinned, pushing a helmet over his long mane of grey hair, which flowed down his back. "Attack the enemy. It's a good plan."

"I'm pretty sure Tidkumi wanted you to remember some other important points. There was definitely something about the lay of the land and not allowing Geilir to outflank us. You remember what happened the last time we did this and you almost got me killed?"

Orglyr slapped a heavy hand down firmly on Fundinn's shoulder. "Yet here you stand, the mightiest of Norlhast's warriors. Well, the mightiest after me, of course. Let's be honest, no tactical plan is going to make the blindest bit of difference to what's about to happen. All I'm interested in is getting as far as there." Orglyr pointed at the neat square of cavalry in front of Norlhast's gates. "I'm going to split Geilir's head open with my axe before all this is over."

"There's a lot of men between us and Geilir."

"Then we'd best start killing some of them," Orglyr replied before shouting out the command to advance.

Drums began to beat and the Norlhast army started to move at a steady pace towards the Riltbalt lines. The early morning sun was now obscured by dark clouds rolling in off the Redfars Sea and as they continued their march it began to rain. The raindrops sounded loud inside Fundinn's helmet, battering off his chainmail and shield and making the ground slippery. *That's great. That'll make the charge* much *easier. Now there's every chance I'll be trampled to death if I lose my footing. The bards don't sing about those kinds of heroes.*

"Least it didn't start raining until after my speech," Orglyr called out next to him, breath steaming out through his nostrils.

"Dinuvillan smiles on us," Fundinn replied with a wry grin, watching as they drew nearer the Riltbalt lines. He thought he could make out their commander; a tall, bearded man wearing a helmet with a long horse hair crest flowing from the top. He was pointing his sword at their direction, before gesturing to the Vorund lines to the right and left.

Looks like Geilir's going to make good use of his Riltbalt allies, Fundinn thought. *They'll bear the brunt of our attack and hold us in position, before the Vorund army flanking them move in. We needed heavy horse for this attack.*

Risking a glance over his shoulder, Fundinn could see Tidkumi's warriors keeping pace with them, whilst on the other side Hoskuldr's archers were advancing to get in range, needing a clear line of sight to avoid killing their own men. A horn sounded in the Riltbalt lines – three short, loud blasts. The noise was repeated twice more as Orglyr broke into a loping run, leading his men in the charge, Fundinn keeping pace as the rain began falling even heavier than before. The Riltbalt warriors uttered a war cry and Fundinn's heart began to hammer as he realised they weren't interested in holding their position. *They're going to charge us first ... wait, what's happening?*

With remarkable military discipline, the Riltbalt lines split neatly in two, moving off to the right and left, screaming a battle cry that drowned out the sound of the storm gathering above the battlefield. Shouts of alarm rang out from the Vorund army flanked either side of the Riltbalt force as they found themselves under attack from their allies.

"Charge!" bellowed Orglyr.

Heart hammering Fundinn tried to stay with him as the Norlhast warriors surged forwards through the gap left by the Riltbalt army. Arrows filled the air overhead as Hoskuldr's archers rained death down on the horsemen in front of them, who were milling around in confusion as the Vorund battle lines broke apart. Fundinn could see the more experienced warriors trying to form up to mount a charge, realising the danger they were in, penned in and trapped in front of Norlhast's gates. Wounded horses threw their riders to the ground as they bucked and reared in panic, the ordered ranks dissolving into chaos in places under the hail of arrows. A few wedges of riders broke away to charge Orglyr's men. Hoskuldr's archers turned their attention on this new threat, bringing many of them down before the two lines of combatants merged with a percussive *thwack* as they collided with the Norlhast spear wall.

Fundinn found himself forced forwards by the press of men at his back, swinging his sword wildly, cutting through horseflesh and rider alike. He blocked an overhead sword thrust with his shield, stabbing upwards and cutting into the groin of the Vorund rider towering over him. The man screamed and Fundinn held him off, shield forcing the warrior's sword away as he drove his own deeper. The rider slumped in his saddle, dropping his sword, his face pale under his helmet. Moments later he vanished under a swarm of Norlhast warriors as they surged towards the gates, using their spears to try and hem in the massed ranks of cavalry in front of them.

Fundinn hacked left and right, trying not to lose sight of Orglyr in the packed throng. A great mass of warriors were busy fighting, standing on top of the dead and the dying who lay tangled amongst a wavering wall of spears and broken wood. The Vorund Clan had lost their opportunity to crush them with a full cavalry charge but mounted combatants had a huge advantage over those on foot, even though the Norlhast warriors now had the greater numbers in this part of the field. The crucial thing was to keep them penned in, using the wall of spears to hold them at bay. The problem was Orglyr stood out and kept advancing beyond the spear wall, axe rising and falling as he hacked his way through man and horse alike, screaming now the blood lust was on him. With a massive effort, Fundinn followed him, calling for the rest of his men to gather round and protect their leader.

"Are you trying to get yourself killed?" he shouted at Orglyr as he drew alongside him, Norlhast spearmen gradually forcing the Vorund horsemen back. Orglyr turned and looked through him with wild eyes, face and helm flecked with blood.

There were more screams and another wave of arrows hammered into the Vorund army. Fundinn cursed Hoskuldr. *We're too close together. They're going to kill as many of us as they are the enemy.* Another wave of arrows hit and Fundinn realised they weren't coming from overhead. The walls of Norlhast were full of archers and they were inflicting serious damage on the trapped horsemen. Inside Norlhast itself Fundinn could hear fighting and he seized Orglyr's arm as the spearmen continued to press forwards, allowing them a moment's respite.

"Curren did it. He got word back to Karas. They're trying to retake the keep."

A glimmer of understanding flashed across Orglyr's blood-spattered face. "Then let's help them."

CHAPTER 76

"What's going on? I can't see properly." The pitch of Valdimarr's voice reflected his growing anxiety as the two warring armies battled in front of Norlhast's gates. Dromundr was standing next to him, shaking his head.

Nuna leaned towards Dromundr, adopting an innocent, confused expression. "What's happening? Is everything going according to plan?"

Dromundr swore. "No, it's not going to plan. Not at all. I'm sorry, my lady – please excuse my language but this is no place for a noblewoman."

"I've tried telling her," Brosa added, hand on the hilt of his sword as he watched Dromundr carefully.

"I have to get down there," Dromundr said.

"Down there? Why?" asked Valdimarr.

"We need to open the gates and allow Geilir to pull back. Those fools on the ... I'm sorry, my lady, I know they're your men ... They're not following their orders. They're continuing to fight when they should be helping our men retreat."

"Go, Dromundr," Nuna told him. "I'll be safe here in the keep with Valdimarr and Brosa."

Dromundr thanked her and hurried away, leaving two warriors to guard Valdimarr. Nuna watched as he took a score of men with him and left through the gates of the keep. Together the group ran through the streets of Norlhast, heading for the main gates as the battle outside continued to rage.

Valdimarr sighed, shivering in the persistent rain. "I suppose this is the safest place ... Wait, what was *that* noise?"

Nuna's heart began to hammer as she realised with Dromundr's departure the moment had come and Kalfr was attempting to retake the keep. One of the Vorund warriors drew his sword and turned towards the doorway leading up to the tower. Brosa stepped forwards and without a sound swung his own blade, connecting with the back of the man's neck with a wet crunch. The warrior dropped to the ground, face first, unmoving.

"My lord –" shouted the second warrior, his sword only halfway out of its scabbard when Brosa's blade sliced through his neck. He staggered forwards, gasping as he clutched at the wound, his blood splattering Nuna's clothes. Valdimarr gave a cry of fright as Brosa brought his sword down once more, splitting the guard's face in two.

"I'm sorry, my lady," said Brosa, looking apologetically at the blood stains on the front of her blue velvet dress. Nuna took a deep breath as she absently wiped her fingers over the expensive fabric, wondering what Katla would say when she saw the state of it.

"My lady ..." Valdimarr's eyes were wildly darting between the bodies of the dead guards and the doorway of the tower, with Nuna and Brosa barring his escape. Nuna felt a pang of pity for the man. She reminded herself of all the people who had died on his orders as he used the crude weapon of fear to rule her clan. The fact Valdimarr was no warrior didn't excuse what he had done – he was every bit as guilty as Geilir and Adalrikr for the suffering he'd caused.

"I'm sorry, Valdimarr," said Nuna. "Today is the last day you'll enjoy the hospitality of Norlhast Keep."

"My lady, please," Valdimarr cried, dropping to his knees, arms outstretched. It didn't occur to him to draw the sword he was wearing at his belt. "Please, Nuna. Please have mercy. I tried to do the right thing, you must believe me."

Brosa growled and his next sword swing took Valdimarr's head from his shoulders in a blur of steel. Valdimarr's twitching corpse dropped to the floor, dark blood gushing from his neck so voluminously Nuna had to take several steps backwards to avoid treading in it.

"You have no right to use her name," Brosa muttered, wiping his sword on the corner of Valdimarr's cloak. Nuna coughed, the smell of blood turning her stomach. She stepped away, trying to compose herself.

"My lady, I'm sorry you had to witness that," Brosa said in a gentler tone. "It's done now and we need to leave. It's not safe for the pair of us to linger when there's only one way down –"

His head snapped round as the door to the tower burst open. Brosa raised his sword, standing protectively in front of Nuna, who held her dagger with a shaking hand. The pair of them both gave a sigh of relief when they realised it was Kalfr hurrying towards them, a group of Norlhast warriors following close behind.

"The keep is ours," Kalfr declared with a wide grin, pulling Brosa into a firm embrace. "We thought you might need some help up here. Clearly not."

"Dromundr's gone to the gates," Brosa said. "Can we spare any men to help Karas and Sigurd down there?"

Kalfr shook his head. "His departure gave us the chance we needed to take back the keep. However, we've barely enough men to hold it and Karas may need somewhere to fall back if things don't go well."

Brosa pointed down to where the battle was raging most fiercely. "Lefwine turned against Geilir and the Riltbalt Clan fights for us. We might yet carry this day."

Kalfr leaned over the wall, peering through the heavy rain at the distant battle and Nuna could see he yearned to aid his brother and their chief. One house near the gates was on fire, thick smoke billowing out through the doorway as men and women fought the Vorund warriors in the streets. A huge roar erupted as the gates swung open, Vorund riders pouring through to escape their attackers.

"The day's not won yet," Kalfr muttered. "We have to

secure the keep and make sure we hold it. I don't want to give Geilir somewhere to run to."

Nuna nodded. "In that case we'll wait here. I want to see what happens."

"Go and I'll protect the lady of the keep," Brosa told him.

Kalfr nodded and ordered his men to follow him, patting Brosa on the shoulder as he left. Nuna turned back to watch the battle as it unfolded in front of her, praying Dinuvillan would protect her husband, who was fighting for his life somewhere down in the streets below.

***

Fundinn's shoulders ached as he fought back-to-back with Orglyr, gasping for breath as the rain battered down, harder than ever. The mass of horses and men fighting outside Norlhast had churned the ground in front of the gates into a thick, cloying mud, littered with the bodies of the fallen.

"They're retreating," Orglyr growled, nodding his head towards the town, where the gates were swinging open.

Fundinn felt a ripple around him as the mounted riders began to move backwards, hacking and slashing the Norlhast warriors as they fought to escape. Fundinn took advantage of the momentary respite in the battle, leaning on his sword. Behind him the fight between Lefwine's Riltbalt warriors and the Vorund men raged. Geilir's army was taking the worst of it, blocked off from retreat by the Riltbalt forces, whilst they were attacked on each flank by Hoskuldr and Tidkumi's warriors. As Fundinn watched the Vorund lines were already starting to waver, men panicking as their enemies closed in all around them.

"Geilir's getting away," snarled Orglyr. "Warriors of Norlhast, with me. After them."

Fundinn hefted his notched shield and stayed close to Orglyr as the Norlhast warriors spilled through the gates. Inside Norlhast Geilir's riders had scattered, people engaged in hand-to-hand fighting on every side. A number of houses were on fire, the smoke stinging Fundinn's eyes, rain hissing where it struck the burning buildings. Lightning flared in the sky above and the clouds burst, releasing a deluge over the streets as the wind picked up, buffeting them left and right.

"Where is he?" Orglyr was shouting, looking around frantically.

"The docks," Fundinn replied with a flash of inspiration. Together they led two score warriors in that direction.

"Would he be mad enough to launch a ship in this weather?" panted Orglyr.

"If he's desperate enough. Look at the keep – he's already lost the town."

Orglyr glanced up and laughed as he saw the banner of the whale flying from the nearest tower. A handful of Vorund warriors barred their path, distracted as they sought their own means of escape. Orglyr's axe rose and fell, tearing the first of them apart as Fundinn cut through the man in front of him and their company swept the rest of them away. Orglyr was cursing the delay as he pushed his way through the melee, roaring Geilir's name.

Down by the docks Fundinn could see men scrambling for the Vorund longships, crashing waves battering the quays. A number of vessels had been smashed against the stone dockside, backs broken as their timbers were torn apart with each pounding wave. Further out, more longships wallowed dangerously as they tried to row out to sea, their crews fighting hard against the tide and the raging waters threatening to sink them. Many men were in the sea, some trying to swim ashore from their sinking ships, others risking deeper waters in an effort to reach the fleeing fleet. A group of abandoned warhorses were watching indifferently over the fate of their riders, shying away from the spray that washed over the docks. Other horses had scattered throughout the town, frightened by the noise of the storm and the flashes of lightning.

With a cry, Orglyr led his warriors forwards, killing any straggling members of the Vorund Clan, showing no quarter and allowing no one the chance of surrender. Fundinn followed, watching his chief's back as they set about the grim business of freeing Norlhast. Several Vorund warriors threw themselves into the sea rather than face Orglyr, vanishing into the dark waters. Fundinn spun around, momentarily lost in his battle fury until he realised he had no one left to fight. Orglyr was standing a few feet from him, the heavy rain washing away the dark blood covering his head and chest.

"Too late," Orglyr gasped, removing his helmet, wincing as he tugged and freed the strap from under his jaw, which was black and bruised. He stared after the six ships still afloat, battling the waters as they plunged over the towering waves in the darkness of the storm.

"He might not be out there," Fundinn shouted over the wind. "Perhaps he was killed outside the gates."

Orglyr shook his head. "No, if he was dead we'd know it. We've missed our chance."

***

Nuna ignored Brosa's protests as her patience snapped and she made ready to leave the keep, wrapped in her cloak, hood up to try and ward off the driving rain. The wind almost knocked her over as she pressed on, holding tightly onto Brosa's arm, the pair of them soaked through within minutes.

"My lady, even though the battle is over it may not be safe," Brosa told her through gritted teeth. Several other warriors, including Kalfr, were accompanying them for that reason. It was obvious Brosa didn't think there were enough.

"My husband hasn't returned," Nuna replied. "He may need me and I won't stand idly by in the keep another moment."

Brosa grunted, not trusting himself to give a

respectful reply as they hurried towards the gates. Kalfr led the way, sword drawn and shield raised in case they met anyone intent on doing them harm. Instead, all they saw were the bodies of fallen warriors, both Vorund and Norlhast men, littering the streets alongside ordinary townsfolk. One man was crying over the body of his dead wife, not seeing Nuna as she walked past, oblivious to the efforts of his neighbours who were trying to put out the fire still smouldering in his house. The heavy rains were a mercy in that respect. Geilir's men had tried to torch Norlhast as they retreated, a final act of petty vengeance as they were driven out into the sea. Whilst several houses had been burned the rains had quickly doused the flames, preventing them from spreading.

Nuna heard Karas' voice before she saw him. In front of him were a group of warriors, defeated and disarmed, all of them on their knees, heads bowed. Next to him stood Orglyr the Grim, his long mane of white hair recognisable even when matted with blood and soaked by the rains. At his side his hulking second, Fundinn, was embracing Curren and patting him on the back as the two warriors were reunited.

Karas' eyes widened when he saw his wife and he hurried forwards to greet her. "Nuna. You shouldn't be here. Brosa, why isn't she back at the keep as I ordered?"

"Don't punish him, Karas, he's here on my instructions. I had to know for myself what had happened." Nuna stepped forwards and hugged her husband, ignoring the fact he reeked of blood and sweat. "That isn't your blood, is it?"

Karas shook his head. "No, I'm unhurt, although we lost many men trying to take control of the gates … I'm sorry to tell you …" He pulled away, turning to Kalfr who stiffened as he saw the expression on his chief's face.

"Sigurd's fallen," Kalfr said, eyes sweeping the bodies being laid out by the walls as people worked to separate the fallen Norlhast and Vorund warriors. By morning there would be a pyre for the Norlhast dead as they crossed with honour into Navan's Halls. Vorund's slain would be food for the crows and gulls.

Karas hung his head, putting a hand on Kalfr's shoulder as he steered him towards the rows of fallen warriors stretching out along the length of the walls. Sigurd lay among them, face white as alabaster, water beading on his cold flesh. There was no obvious sign of injury as Kalfr knelt next to his older brother, smoothing away strands of wet hair before kissing him gently on the forehead. Nuna put her hands to her mouth, shocked as she realised her husband's loyal friend would no longer be with them. Without Sigurd's support Karas would never have maintained his position as chief – they owed him everything.

"He fell from the walls during the battle," Karas explained. "He was defending me ..."

"Where's Geilir?" Kalfr asked, taking Sigurd's hand in his own, squeezing it tight.

"We think he got away," said Orglyr.

"There's no sign of Dromundr either," added Curren. "We didn't have the men to hold the gate. When Dromundr arrived he ordered them opened to allow Geilir's retreat and we weren't able to stop them as they made it down to the docks."

Nuna looked out at the raging seas, the skies overhead dark with storm clouds. "Could anyone have survived out there?"

Karas shrugged. "There are reports of ships being washed ashore further north, so he may not have slipped through our fingers after all. I've already sent out Vrand with some men to investigate."

Nuna walked over to Kalfr, who was still kneeling by his brother's body. "Norlhast is free because of the actions of brave men like Sigurd," she told him. "Your father should be very proud of both of you."

Kalfr took her hand, rising on unsteady legs. He wiped

his face, composing himself. "He'll journey to Navan's Halls as a true warrior and our jarl, the brightest and the best of our clan. I'll need to send word to Luta and the children. They should know what's happened."

A group of mud-splattered warriors were approaching them through the open gates, carrying the emblem of the whale on their shields. Nuna didn't recognise them and Karas leaned in close to introduce the new arrivals. "The thin bald man is Limping Tidkumi, one of Bekan's loyal warriors of old until he fell into disfavour with Orglyr. The woman next to him is his second, Soma Alvedottir, the daughter of his best friend and by all accounts every bit as skilful with a blade as her father."

"Fortunate for us Tidkumi and Orglyr have mended their differences," Nuna observed.

"For now."

"Karas Greystorm," said Tidkumi in a rasping voice, bowing low. "It gives me great pleasure to be welcomed to Norlhast by its true chief once more." There were roars and shouts at those words, somewhat dampened by the wind and relentless rain.

Karas bade him rise. "You're the welcome sight, my friend. Without you and your warriors Norlhast wouldn't be free."

Tidkumi jerked his head to the gathering of warriors behind him. Nuna took in a sharp breath as she saw the sheer number of fallen outside the town. Over to one side stood what was left of the Riltbalt army, their sodden banner flapping wildly in the gale blowing in off the sea. "You owe the day to the Riltbalt warriors led by Lefwine. If they'd supported Geilir as expected the outcome would have been very different."

"A welcome intervention," Karas replied. "However, a warrior who breaks his word doesn't make for the most trustworthy ally."

"He's asking to speak with you," Tidkumi said.

Karas frowned. "Tell him he and his men are welcome to take shelter in Norlhast after all they've done for us. I'll speak with him in the morning, once we've attended to the dead."

Tidkumi nodded and whispered something in Soma's ear. She gave a short bow to Karas and headed off towards Lefwine's men. The survivors resumed their ministrations to the dead and the dying, whilst the Vorund prisoners were taken away under Curren's watchful eye.

"You should go back," Karas told Nuna. "I'm going to be down here for a long time yet."

"Then I'll stay too," Nuna replied. She moved off to tend to some of the wounded, knowing that whilst she lacked the skill of a healer she could still offer some comfort.

She knelt down next to a young Norlhast man whose hideous open stomach wounds marked him down as someone who would soon meet Navan. She took his chilled, clammy hand in hers and spoke to him for a short while, feeling the life ebbing from him, his eyes going distant and glassy. As the poor man's grip slackened she looked up at the long lines of injured warriors. Those who stood a chance of survival were being carried on stretchers to makeshift hospitals that were being established throughout the town. Those who were mortally wounded were left out on the streets, tended by a few kind souls. Nuna did what little she could, aware of the costly price paid so her husband could call himself chief of Norlhast once more.

CHAPTER 77

"Wake up."

The stinging slap across my face dragged me away from Norlhast's gates. I could still feel the hand of the dying man Nuna was comforting, hear his sobs as pain wracked his body and death came too slowly as she called for someone to bring shadow root. I was back inside *Stormweaver*, the deck six inches deep in seawater despite being under canvas as a bright flash of lightning lit up the scared faces of her crew. At the rear of the ship Meinolf and Feyotra were desperately bailing out the vessel as another crashing wave poured more foaming saltwater over the shivering sailors. Only Aerinndis looked calm, curly hair encrusted with salt, as she peered over Jolinn's shoulder.

"Has he died?"

"No," Jolinn replied, helping me to sit up. "He's back with us."

Stormweaver was pitching and rolling in the wild seas, her next movement impossible to anticipate in the chaos of the storm. Water slopped over me and I screwed my eyes shut, head pounding from being dragged from the Path without warning.

"Rothgar, are you alright?" Jolinn asked me, taking hold of my face in her icy hands and looking straight at me. Her blue eyes looked different – for the first time I saw fear in them.

"Where are we?" I replied, tongue thick and clumsy in my mouth.

Jolinn had to shout over the raging storm. "No idea. All Aerinndis and Meinolf are concerned about is keeping

Stormweaver afloat, although I was wondering if you knew something about this."

Jolinn pointed at the runes covering the gunwale and the deck of the ship. Even though they were partially submerged I could see that they were glowing. It wasn't the ghostly blue light that signified the presence of the durath. Instead, the runes rippled with a cascade of colours that mirrored the nightly spectacle of the aurora of the Fire Isle, each one pulsing with magic.

"They're protecting *Stormweaver*," I told her, remembering my bargain with Molda and Tellian back in Romsdahl when I had promised to ward their daughter's ship. "They're releasing the magic they absorbed on the Fire Isle. As long as we can prevent her being swamped, she should hold together."

Another wave slammed into *Stormweaver*, shaking her timbers as we rose in the air before plunging down the other side of the towering wall of water. For a few moments I thought we were about to capsize before *Stormweaver* righted herself, spinning and turning on the churning seas.

Nearby, Aerinndis was laughing manically. "You hear that? The gods themselves protect us – no seas can tame Aerinndis Stormrider, no matter what the oceans throw at us."

I considered pointing out it was the handiwork of me and Joldir before deciding against it. What Aerinndis said sounded better. I wasn't sure the crew needed to hear their fate depended on how well I'd painted those runes.

There was a mighty crash as *Stormweaver* rolled onto her side, throwing her crew forwards. I lost my grip on Jolinn's hand as with an alarming creak *Stormweaver* juddered before rolling back onto her keel with a loud thud, lying at an odd angle. Water continued to pour in through the edges of the canvas as my shipmates scrambled to find their feet.

"We're grounded," shouted Meinolf, risking a look

outside.

"We need to get out," ordered Aerinndis, hauling Skari to his feet. "Move it before the waves pound us into pieces. Get outside and help drag her farther ashore."

Everyone scrambled out as *Stormweaver* rocked with the impact of another wave. Ulfarr was behind me, a bundle of oilskins clutched in his arms which he thrust into mine.

"Get these to dry land," he yelled over the howling wind. "We've come too far to lose them now."

I staggered under the weight of Bruar's gifts, up to my thighs in cold seawater, clothing soaked through and dragging me down. Aerinndis' crew took hold of *Stormweaver*, surrounding the ship and hauling her further up the beach as the runes on her outer hull gleamed, continuing to bind the ship together and repel the battering storm. I turned and waded towards land, fighting to keep my footing as a wave broke over my back, knocking me to my knees. I felt an arm around my shoulders and Myr and Jolinn were there, heaving me back up as I lurched forwards, gasping and shaking with cold. There was a crunch under my feet as we reached the edge of a shingle beach, the rounded pebbles shifting and making my footing treacherous.

"Come on," Jolinn shouted as the waters broke around us, salt spray stinging our eyes.

I looked back at *Stormweaver*, inching her way out of the waves like a beached whale, her crew straining to drag her forwards. Myr and Jolinn half carried me to a rocky outcrop which offered partial shelter from the wind. I watched them hurry back to Aerinndis and the others to help save the ship as I leaned back on the wet stone, water dripping from my clothes, too tired to move. *Stormweaver* gave off an ethereal glow, her crew dark shadows as they moved about her hull. I clutched the comforting weight of *Eagle's Defender* to my chest as I watched them work, leaning *Lightning's Fire* and *Death's Gift* against the rock, instantly feeling better even though I was holding them through layers of oilskins. Whatever else lay ahead of us, I knew I was never destined to bear either of those weapons into battle.

From my vantage point I was the first one to see the flickering torches approaching from inland. Everyone else lay insensible on the shingle beach, exhausted from dragging *Stormweaver* out beyond the breaking waters. By some miracle we had all survived being shipwrecked and the longship was intact. I called out a warning as I counted two dozen lights bobbing up and down as their bearers drew closer. There was no chance we would be missed, especially since *Stormweaver* still glowed dully with her own inner light as she rested on the shore. As I shouted again Ulfarr groaned and staggered to his feet, Myr, Skari and Jolinn joining him. Teeth chattering, I strapped *Eagle's Defender* to my arm, since there was no telling who these visitors might be. The party trudged down onto the beach, the crunch of their boots audible over the fierce storm as they drew near. They were armed and I felt a moment of panic until I saw the spouting whale emblazoned on their shields.

"Norlhast," I gasped at Aerinndis and Meinolf as they gathered with the rest their crew to greet our visitors. "We've landed in Norlhast."

"Meaning we're miles off course and we've delivered Bruar's gifts straight into Vorund's hands," Aerinndis replied with a groan.

I grinned at her, enjoying the giddy rush of knowledge I shouldn't possess. "No. Not any more – Norlhast is free from Vorund's rule."

"Declare yourselves," called out the leader of the warriors. I stared hard at him; the lower half of his bearded face under his helmet and his voice were both familiar.

"Vrand," I called out. "Is that you?"

Vrand hesitated at the mention of his name. "That's me. I asked you to declare yourselves."

"Look at the shield," one of his men said, gesturing at

me. "It's the banner of the eagle. They're Reavesburg sailors."

"Vrand, it's me, Rothgar Kolfinnarson. My companions and I need your help." Vrand looked doubtful, suspecting some trick and I realised I looked nothing like the man he'd first met when I came to Karas' court offering my sister's hand in marriage.

"You didn't approve of the Reavesburg alliance," I told him. "You set about me one night with two of your friends three years ago, trying to frighten me off. Sigurd had to intervene to break up the fight and that was the night I broke the hold of the coven over your chief. Am I right that Karas Greystorm is the Norlhast Clan Chief once more?"

"Aye, that much is true," Vrand confirmed, to shouts and cheers from his warriors. He peered at me closer, holding up his torch which hissed and spat in the rain. "You don't look much like the Rothgar I remember. Except your voice … That does sound right. I remember those honeyed tones as you treated with our chief."

I sank to my knees. "We're at your mercy. Please, I ask you treat us as your guests and allies, offering us sanctuary and shelter from this storm."

Vrand looked at me for a time, his cloak whipping in the wind as his torch guttered, threatening to go out. "Bring them with us. We'll see what Karas Greystorm makes of our visitors."

***

I lay on the soft feather mattress in my chamber, staring up at the ceiling. The day before had been a blur, exhaustion leaving me barely capable of exchanging formal pleasantries with Karas Greystorm after Vrand brought us to his feasting hall that evening. Orglyr the Grim had been named as Karas' new jarl, that much I did remember. Sigurd might have been dour company, yet he'd been an honest and honourable man whose support had made the alliance between Norlhast and Reavesburg possible. Orglyr was completely different – a man born for the single purpose of war. In these times he was the right choice to be the Jarl of Norlhast Keep. In the future? He had none of Sigurd's understanding and subtleties.

I sat up, finding someone had removed my travel-stained clothes and replaced them with a clean white nightgown. The cloth was smooth against my skin – luxury that was a world away from my journey to the Fire Isle. I felt naked without my cloak and furs as I slid forwards and peered at the end of the bed. To my relief *Eagle's Defender* was propped up against a wooden chest along with my sword in its battered scabbard. Next to them lay *Lightning's Fire* and *Death's Gift*.

There was a knock at my door and Styrman, Sigurd's old servant, entered carrying a tray of food. My mouth watered at the smell, even though whale meat soup was far from my favourite dish. When I mentioned through a mouthful of bread that this was unusual fare to break my fast Styrman gave me a withering stare.

"My lord, it is well past noon," he informed me as he laid out my clothes for the day ahead. Embarrassed, I finished my meal without further comment.

As Styrman cleared away the bowls and plates there was another knock and Katla, Nuna's maid, entered, escorting my sister. Brosa stood at the doorway, regarding me intently. Like Vrand, I realised he was trying to work out how the thin scarred man with a stoop fitted with his memories of the confident young warrior who had visited Norlhast Keep. I glanced at my sister and felt a lump rising in my throat as I saw she was thinking the same thing. As a reflex I began to reach out to her with the Sight, a gentle brushing of minds as I sensed her shock at my condition. With an effort I pulled away, not wanting to intrude on her private thoughts more than I'd done already.

"It's really you," Nuna said at last, Katla unable to stem her tears as she looked on whilst holding her lady's hand. "Myshall's bane … Rothgar, what have they done to you?"

I looked at Nuna. Her sky blue dress was made from the finest silks, matching cloak trimmed with white fur and her long golden hair was plaited together, falling to her shoulders in an artful cascade. Those deep blue eyes looked at me and I stared back, seeing her for the first time as a grown woman rather than my little sister. Nuna tugged at a light blue leather glove, removing it to reveal her pale skin as she took a seat next to my bed. She reached out and stroked my arm, fingers tracing the silver puckered scars, the marks of Tyrfingr's cruelty with me always.

"You've lost a tooth," Nuna observed, as if that was the full extent of my injuries.

My tongue probed the spot and I nodded. "It hasn't been the easiest couple of years."

Nuna burst into tears, ordering the rest of her retinue outside as she threw her arms around me, sobbing into my shoulder as I drew her close.

CHAPTER 78

For a time we sat there, wrapped in our tight embrace, afraid that if we let go we would lose each other again. Nuna was my last living relative, my blood, a connection stronger than the most powerful Sight bond. I hugged her tight, smelling the pungent scent of smoke on her hair.

"We lit the pyre for the fallen this morning," Nuna explained when I mentioned this after she had composed herself.

"I guessed as much – that must have been hard for everyone. I heard Sigurd fell in battle. I'm so sorry – he was a good man and a staunch friend."

"Many good men died yesterday," Nuna replied. "Almost half of Norlhast's warriors were slain, although they sold their lives dearly. I couldn't believe the mound of Vorund warriors piled high beyond our walls and more bodies keep being washed ashore. Kalfr tells me it's likely this will happen for the next few days until the sea surrenders all of its victims."

"Kalfr. It would be good to see him and Luta again. They made me so welcome when I was last here."

"In time, when you're stronger."

"And Geilir? The sea hasn't returned Adalrikr's golden-toothed jarl?"

Nuna raised a blonde eyebrow. "I didn't know you knew him so well."

"By reputation," I lied, wishing I didn't have to. Whilst I needed to broach the subject of the Sight with Nuna, today wasn't the day.

Nuna shook her head. "No, there's been no sign of him

since his defeat. That doesn't mean he escaped, of course. We've found two of the six ships that fled the battle wrecked on our shores. His longship could have sunk farther out to sea and we wouldn't know. On the other hand, the ship you arrived on is, by all accounts, in remarkable condition considering the seas you were sailing."

"*Stormweaver*."

"I'm sorry?"

"My longship. Her name is *Stormweaver* and her captain is Aerinndis Stormrider, the daughter of Molda, Gautarr's master shipwright in Romsdahl. She's earned her name all over again these past few days." I didn't mention the role my runes played saving the ship, deciding that Aerinndis deserved her own accolades.

"And what brought you to my shores, Brother, after all these years apart?"

"Ahh. Now, that is a long story."

Nuna rested her chin on her hands next to my bed, a playful look on her face that reminded me so strongly of home I felt a sharp pain in my chest. "Well, you'll be expected to attend a feast in your honour this evening. No doubt you'll be asked to tell your tale and recount the deeds of the Brotherhood of the Eagle that I've heard so much about. However, we have hours until then and I thought you would like to tell the whole story to me first."

"That's going to take a while," I said, wondering where to begin.

Nuna smiled. "We have the whole afternoon. Start at the beginning and while you're at it you can tell me who Jolinn is."

I stared at her, wondering what Jolinn might have said. "She attended your chambers most of last night and again throughout this morning," Nuna explained when she saw my confusion. "I sent her away at midday with Styrman to ensure the poor woman got something to eat."

I sighed, realising there would be no hiding anything

from Nuna as I began my story, starting with the night of my escape from Reavesburg. I didn't shy away from explaining how I came to possess the Sight and the only detail I omitted was the fact Nuna shared the gift. I listened in turn as she told me of everything that had happened in Norlhast, familiar with parts of it already, filling in gaps on other events I hadn't witnessed as her tale unfolded. It was only as Nuna was explaining how the alliances within the Norlhast Clan were playing out that I realised how I was approaching the whole conversation much like Etta would have done, leaving me with a disturbing sense of disquiet.

"The Norlhast Clan hasn't had any experience of fighting these creatures ... these skin thieves you've described," Nuna told me. "After seeing what Nereth was able to do with her magic I believe your story but it sounds so fantastical. Until we're at Vorund Fastness I wouldn't mention such things to my husband or his advisors. Let Johan and Gautarr persuade them concerning the true nature of our enemy."

"You really think they'll go to Johan's aid?" I asked.

Nuna nodded. "Yes, although matters are not straightforward. Karas' position has been weakened, despite his victory. We have less than a thousand warriors left after the battle and losing Sigurd was a huge blow. Both Orglyr and Tidkumi were Bekan's jarls and neither of them will forget Karas killed their chief."

I shrugged. "He could have ordered their deaths – they still owe him their lives, even if they weren't his original supporters."

"That's true. However, Karas is a changed man, there's no denying it. Sigurd played such an important role in maintaining his rule and now he's gone. Kalfr holds sway in Norlhast itself with one hundred warriors unswervingly loyal to their chief. However, Orglyr and Tidkumi have eight times that number. Whilst they're loyal to Norlhast and united in driving the Vorund Clan from our lands the balance of power has shifted. Karas had no choice other than to name Orglyr his jarl, although I know he would have preferred to bestow that honour on Kalfr or Curren. Orglyr's sworn to serve his chief and I'm sure that oath will hold whilst we remain at war. Afterwards, however ..."

"There's a long way to go before we get to *afterwards*," I assured her. My words were meant to be comforting. Instead they came out as a weary sigh, as if our challenge was insurmountable. "What about Lefwine?" I asked, changing the subject. "I heard his decision to side with us was decisive and he swayed the battle in our favour."

"He did," Nuna acknowledged. "However, this in itself is a problem. The enmity between Riltbalt and Norlhast runs deep and there's resentment brewing in some quarters that the Norlhast Clan needed his help at all. It doesn't matter that it's true; my people are proud. Lefwine is too, which is why he turned against Geilir, despite the fact his chief has bent the knee to Adalrikr. He wasn't prepared to die in the vanguard for Geilir's cause after sacrificing so many of his men that way in the previous battle with Orglyr. Lefwine saw an opportunity to turn the tables on his master in order to survive."

"Commendable, I suppose."

Nuna frowned. "It's dangerous. No one knows if they can trust him. However, without his five hundred swords my own people's army is less likely to turn the tide against Adalrikr. We need him, so our alliance has been built on some ... questionable foundations."

"You keep saying *your people*," I commented. "You really do consider yourself part of the Norlhast Clan now, don't you?"

Nuna looked at me intently. "This is who I am – who you and Etta made me. I still can't believe what happened to her. Such a betrayal – abandoning her to exile on that island was more merciful than she deserved."

Nuna stood and walked over to Bruar's shield, sword

and spear. “All those sacrifices and revelations to obtain these pieces.” She reached out and touched the black metal of *Eagle’s Defender* with a hesitant hand, snatching it back at once, rubbing her fingers. “It’s so cold. I ... There’s something ... unnatural about that shield.”

“The handiwork of the gods. There’s so much at stake, Nuna. This has gone beyond clan lands and our ancient feuds and rivalries. Amuran is slowly splitting apart as Adalrikr maintains his connection with the Shadow Realm. We have to stop him.”

“And we will,” Nuna told me, returning to my bedside and taking my hands in hers. “Karas holds sway as clan chief, at least for now. He’s determined to fulfil the oath he was forced to break the night Tyrfingr took Ulfkell’s Keep from us. Our ships will set sail with every warrior we can muster and we’ll lend our strength to the Brotherhood’s cause. The avatars themselves fight for us – we will prevail and bring Adalrikr down, I promise you.”

“I wish I had your confidence,” I replied, sinking down into my pillows.

“You’re exhausted. You should rest and I’ll send Styrman to get you ready when it’s time to join us. However ... before then there’s one more thing I’d like to know.” Nuna looked at me with a wry grin on her face.

“What?”

“Jolinn.”

“What about Jolinn?” I said, wishing there was somewhere I could retreat to. I was tired and I wasn’t sure I wanted to have this conversation with my sister.

Nuna folded her arms, looking at me severely as if I was her little brother. “You know perfectly well what I mean, so don’t dissemble. It’s obvious from what you’ve told me this young woman has liked you for a long while, well before your voyage north. I’m sure she’d like to see you now you’re awake but before I send for her I need to know what your intentions are.”

"You ... *You're* asking me this? Who do you think you are – her mother?"

Nuna frowned and I realised not getting her own way wasn't something she was used to. I was dealing with the Lady of Norlhast Keep. "You know perfectly well her mother isn't around and her father, who did precious little for her when he was alive, isn't in a position to help her either. Is this some brief affair for you, like how you treated Desta?"

I swallowed. Did *everyone* in Ulfkell's Keep know about me and Desta? We thought we'd been so discreet.

"Well?" pressed Nuna.

"Desta wasn't some ... fling," I protested. "I asked her to marry me – did you know that?"

That statement left Nuna stunned and she took a few moments to recover her poise. "You asked her to do *what*?"

"You heard me. I loved the girl at the time and back then I thought we could have shared a life together. We were both very young but I truly cared for her."

Nuna stared at me. "Rothgar, I wonder how you came to be the great hope of the Brotherhood if that's what you thought. Such a marriage would never have been approved of. There would have been uproar at the clan moot at snubbing so many young noblewomen."

"If there's a queue of young ladies at court waiting to make my acquaintance then perhaps you could introduce me," I replied, riled. "Should I tell Jolinn our relationship has to end so I can forge the next great alliance of the Reavesburg Clan?"

"No, of course not. Things are ..." Nuna's voice trailed off.

"Things are what, exactly?"

Nuna took a deep breath. "Things are different. You know they are. You're no longer the brother of the chief with a chance of rising to that position yourself. You told me yourself how you gave away any claim to lead the Reavesburg Clan when you made your oath to Johan. That means you're no longer a rival as Johan and Gautarr vie to become the next clan chief, so you have less power and influence. Yet with that change comes something else – something I didn't get much choice about. You have *freedom* and I'm asking how you intend to exercise it with that young woman."

"I'm tired," I told Nuna. "It's been good to speak to you and I'll see you again when I meet your husband later this evening. For now, perhaps you could let me rest and send word to Jolinn. I want to see her and I think we've kept her waiting long enough."

Nuna sat there, thinking for a time. When she rose she squeezed my hand tightly. "Alright. I'm sorry for being so forward. I'm pleased to have you back at my side and I don't want us to fight."

"It's alright," I replied. "Let me have another night's good rest and you can interrogate me on my love life as much as you want."

Nuna smiled as she left, opening the door to find Brosa and Katla waiting patiently for her outside. I lay in bed after they had gone, hands behind my head, staring at the canopy as I mulled over Nuna's words. I was annoyed with her not only because she had the nerve to challenge me but because she was right.

Sometime later there was another knock at the door and Jolinn poked her head inside my chambers. "Nuna told me you were awake," she said. "Are you up for more visitors?"

"I've always got time for you," I said, sitting up in bed.

Jolinn walked over and pulled up a chair, dropping into it with a heavy sigh as she placed her booted foot on the corner of my bed. Like me, she had changed her clothes, although no one could mistake her for a lady at court in her breeches and jerkin. She unbuckled her sword to sit more comfortably, dropping it with a thud onto the floor. Up close and with the late afternoon sun shining through the window I could see she was tired. There were bruises on her face and shadows under her eyes from our exhausting voyage and near shipwreck. Her hands were rough and scraped red raw from working the oars and hauling *Stormweaver* to safety. There was an undeniable strength to this woman, a quality that drew me to her and masked the vulnerability under the surface.

"What are you looking at?" she asked me, blue eyes staring hard back at me.

"I'm thinking about something my sister said to me earlier. Something we should have talked about long before. I was thinking about *afterwards*."

EPILOGUE

Humli sat in the comfortable chair of his cell, waiting for Lina and Desta to return, enjoying his pipe as smoke filled the air. The days and weeks of their imprisonment had turned into months, the exact span of time hard to measure, Djuri's promises of help almost forgotten. The warrior had been sent to Olt and there was no sign he would return any time soon. Perhaps it was a shrewd move by Tyrfingr to get him out of the way. Maybe Djuri's frequent visits to their cells had aroused suspicions in the keep.

Perhaps, perhaps, perhaps. What did any of it matter? They were stuck here, except for the times when Bjorr or Galin would call to escort the prisoners to exercise in the courtyard. Usually they went on their own and occasionally, such as today, walking in pairs was permitted. It was never all three of them – the unspoken truth was that if they tried to escape whoever remained behind in their cells would suffer the consequences.

Humli looked around at their room, which was no longer sparsely furnished with three lice-infested cots and a bucket. Although there were iron bars across one wall, so it was impossible to forget where they were living, Tyrfingr had made an effort to ensure their needs were met whilst the war with the Brotherhood dragged on. Allowing them to leave the cell under close supervision was a new perk. Humli told himself he shouldn't be pleased – he'd spent a life working outdoors and now here was Tyrfingr Blackeyes, the Jarl of Reavesburg no less, telling him when he could venture outside and for how long. *How's it come to this? It's ridiculous.*

He tried not to be grateful for the provision of the

bathtub that allowed them to wash once a week behind the privacy of a portable screen, with the guards told to turn their backs on pain of losing a hand if their eyes strayed. Enough people knew the story of how Galin Ironfist came by his name to know the truth behind that threat. He made every effort not to enjoy the hot food that came to their cell every day, complaining to Lina and Desta even as another part of him knew they were eating better than when they lived in his cottage by the river. *I thought I was coming here to die – instead they're fattening me up, like I'm in some children's story.*

They were being treated well, Humli had to admit. What was difficult was the lack of contact with the outside world. Their guards weren't permitted to speak directly to them, either when exercising or when they were watching over the cell. The whispered conversations as the guards changed over were the times when Humli could gather a scrap of news. That meant more than dishes of roasted meat, baked fish, thick crusted pies, warming soups or rich stews straight from the kitchens of Ulfkell's Keep. Through those snatches of conversation Humli knew Vorund still lay under siege and Norlhast was fighting back against their occupiers. There was more and more talk concerning this Brotherhood led by Johan Jokellsward, who stubbornly persisted in taking the war to their king, having wintered in Vorund and maintained enough supplies to keep his army fed and warm.

I hope he succeeds and breaks down those walls. If Adalrikr falls Tyrfingr has no reason to keep us all locked up. Humli reflected on that thought, turning it over and inspecting it from all sides. Either way, the outcome didn't look good for Humli and his daughter and Lina. If Adalrikr triumphed they would be shipped to Vorund Fastness. *And if Johan wins, it might not only be the good food from the kitchen that comes to an end if Adalrikr no longer needs us. Tyrfingr might decide to dispose of his guests too.*

He thought of Finn and Frokn, growing up in the

care of Tola and Boddi. He'd miss those boys if anything happened to him. *They're so small they won't remember us, which is just as well. Tyrfingr wouldn't stoop to hurt the children, would he? What would he have to gain?* Alone in his cell with his dark thoughts Humli shuddered. *It doesn't do to lack company in a place like this, waiting helplessly for things to happen. The end of this war can't come soon enough.*

When Lina and Desta returned Humli set his pipe on the table and got up from his chair, back creaking whilst he arranged his face to hide his feelings, smiling at both women as he walked to the door. It was his turn to exercise in the courtyard and Desta told him it was a lovely spring day. He walked out with Galin Ironfist at his side, three more guards surrounding him, determined not to be too grateful when he felt the sun on his face.

***

The scrying pool shimmered, the scene in Reavesburg's dungeons vanishing, only to be replaced with a view of Norlhast, where the banner of the whale flew proudly from the towers of the keep. Randall gasped as he saw the number of bodies lying outside the town, food for crows and seabirds alike, the might of Vorund's northern army spent and Geilir defeated. The scene shifted, moving inside a private chamber, where Randall recognised Rothgar the Cripple, sitting up in bed talking to a lithe young woman. After a while the talking stopped and the pair began to kiss, although Randall was spared from too much embarrassment as the view of the room moved towards the foot of the bed, where a plain shield, a beautiful sword engraved with runes and an exquisite metal spear, similarly decorated, all rested together. Randall couldn't explain why, but his eyes were drawn to those weapons and a chill ran up his spine.

The waters went dark and Heidr raised her head, blinking slowly, her grey eyes focussing on Randall as Adalrikr looked on, his expression thoughtful. The three of them were sitting in Heidr's private chambers within the

Inner Keep. The windows were shuttered and the room was lit by a single large guttering candle, set on the table next to the silver scrying basin.

"I can see no more today," Heidr declared, sighing deeply. "There is your answer, Adalrikr. Rothgar has returned and, as we feared, his quest to the Fire Isle has succeeded. *Eagle's Defender*, *Death's Gift* and *Lightning's Fire*. You will have to confront them all before the end."

Randall cleared his throat, glancing at Adalrikr. Would the King of Laskar be angry at what they had seen? *I guess I'm about to find out now Norlhast is free. Looks like Adalrikr was right to be worried about Rothgar, and now we learn from Tyrfingr's prisoner that Djuri Turncloak's heart is so conflicted. Humli and his family have their hooks into him and, if he's foolish enough to aid them against Blackeyes' orders, the Jarl of Reavesburg will have his head. Perhaps I shouldn't be surprised – does Heidr look into my own thoughts this way and see the same doubts?* Heidr was still staring directly at him and Randall swallowed, shifting in his seat.

"His thoughts were so clear," Adalrikr said in a hushed voice.

"A perfect connection, when the Sightwielder's mind, and thus those he touched, was unguarded in his exhaustion and relief," Heidr replied. "In such moments the scrying pool can see into the hearts of men when used by one possessing the old skills. This is what you needed to learn and understand. Rothgar will soon be at our gates with an army at his heels and the means of our destruction in his possession. This path was one he was always destined to walk and we must now follow it until the bitter end." Heidr offered Adalrikr a thin smile. "I can only begin to imagine what Nishrall will say when he learns of this."

Adalrikr bowed his head. "And what does the Prophetess see concerning Tyrfingr's prisoners?"

"That's much harder to say," Heidr replied. "Lina of Lake Tull remains a mystery."

"Once the battle with the Landless Jarl is won, she and, more importantly, her child must be brought to me," Adalrikr mused. "Rothgar's former lover is also a useful prize, although now we have learned there's someone else he cares for deeply. These are points of weakness, ones we can exploit."

"First we must defeat Johan and his Brotherhood on the battlefield," Randall observed, finally finding his voice. "I understand the arts of war well enough, but how do we deal with these mysterious magical weapons?"

Adalrikr turned to him. "We also wield powerful magic and, now we are forewarned, we can prepare for this threat. Leave such concerns to me, Randall, for when Rothgar arrives with the Norlhast army war will break upon the Fastness. When that time comes, you and your warriors must be ready."

Randall nodded and after being dismissed he left Heidr's chambers with a heavy heart, knowing the stalemate of the siege was about to end. The walls of Vorund were close to breaking and once the Norlhast army arrived Johan wouldn't hesitate to attack. *Our people will have to defend themselves as never before, against an implacable and determined foe.* Although predicting the final outcome was impossible one thing was certain. *Blood will be spilled.*

CHARACTER LIST

Square brackets around a [name] denotes that this character has already passed into Navan's Halls at the start of Lost Gods.

The Reavesburg Clan

The Brotherhood of the Eagle – an uprising of Reavesburg's warriors fighting occupation by the Vorund Clan

Johan Jokellsward – leader of the Brotherhood of the Eagle and jarl of Kalamar. His stronghold of Kalamar Castle on the northern border with Norlhast was sacked by Sinarr the Cold One. Also known as **Johan Landless** or the **Landless Jarl**

Damona Johanswyfe – wife of Johan and mother of Bandor and Reesha

> **[Reesha Jorikswyfe]** – Johan Jokellsward's daughter and Jorik Kolfinnarson's wife. Reesha, Jorik and their son, Kolfinnar the Younger were killed in the fall of Ulfkell's Keep, murdered by Tyrfingr Blackeyes
>
> **Bandor Johanson** – Johan's only son, married to Freydja
>
> **Freydja Bandorswyfe** – Egill's daughter, Gautarr's niece and Throm's sister, raised by Gautarr since being orphaned. Married to Bandor Johanson

Survivors of Kalamar and founding members of the Brotherhood

Petr Hamarrson – a warrior of Kalamar, Johan's second

Svan – a warrior of Kalamar, married to Dalla

Dalla Svanswyfe – wife of Svan

Maeva Brandrswyfe – widow of Brandr, serving as a healer for Johan's army

Eykr – a warrior of Kalamar

Faraldr – a warrior of Kalamar
Varinn – a warrior of Kalamar
Ingirith Ruggaswyfe – widow of Rugga and confidante of Damona
    Egill Ruggason – Ingirith's son
    Kitta Ruggadottir – Ingirith's daughter

Other warriors of the Brotherhood

Sigolf Admundson – elder of Falsten, the first Reavesburg town to answer Johan's call to arms. Clan moot speaker for western Reavesburg
Jolinn Hrodidottir – a shieldmaiden of Olt and the illegitimate daughter of Old Hrodi. Clan moot speaker for the mid-lands of Reavesburg
Beinir – a warrior of Olt, Jolinn's second
Ulfarr – the former leader of a band of outlaws, now a follower of Johan Jokellsward
Skari One Eye – the longest serving member of Ulfarr's crew
Myr the Silent – one of Ulfarr's crew
Ekkill – one of Etta's spies, now acting as a scout in Ulfarr's crew
Thengill – an exiled warrior from Vorund, loyal to their former chief Asmarr, now serving in Ulfarr's crew. He is immune to the powers of the Sight and cannot be possessed by the durath

Camp followers and Johan's advisors

Rothgar Kolfinnarson – second son of Kolfinnar Marlson, late chief of the Reavesburg Clan. Brother of Nuna Karaswyfe. Possesses the gift of the Sight and, together with Joldir and Leif, he has formed a powerful Sight Fellowship combining their abilities to serve the Brotherhood
Etta the Crone – aged former counsellor and spymaster for Reavesburg's clan chiefs until their fall to the Vorund Clan. Now acting as Johan's advisor
Joldir – a mage and advisor to Johan as well as one of Etta's agents. A gifted healer and the Brotherhood's artificer as well as a Sightwielder, he has trained Rothgar and Leif in the use

of this skill. Badly injured in the Battle of Romsdahl
Arissa – a former bard and adoptive daughter of Joldir, now serving as the chief healer in Johan's army
Leif Andersson – a boy rescued by the Brotherhood when they defeated the durath in Tullen. Possesses the Sight and part of Rothgar's Fellowship. His mother, Lina, has been possessed by the durath. The rest of Leif's family were killed during the occupation by Vorund
Curruck – a blacksmith serving the Brotherhood
Sinarr/The Weeping Warrior – Sinarr's shade, existing between life and death, sworn to avenge the deaths of Asmarr and Adalrikr when the durath took control of the Vorund Clan
<u>Fallen warriors of the Brotherhood</u>
[Gunnarr] – Kalamar warrior, killed in the Battle of Romsdahl
[Ragni] – Kalamar warrior, killed in the Battle of Romsdahl
[Yngvarr] – Kalamar warrior, killed in the Battle of Romsdahl
[Geirmarr Flint] – elder of Delving in the Baros Mountains, killed in the Battle of Romsdahl
[Geirmundi Flint] – cousin of Geirmarr Flint, killed in the Battle of Romsdahl
[Sir Patrick Wild] – one of Ulfarr's crew, a fallen Berian knight from Brighthorn Keep, killed in the Battle of Romsdahl
[Brandr] – Kalamar warrior, murdered after being betrayed by Hrodi Myndillson
[Harvald] – Kalamar warrior, murdered after being betrayed by Hrodi Myndillson
[Rugga, the Rock of Kalamar] – a good friend of Johan, killed in battle with the durath at Tullen
[Kimbi] – Kalamar warrior killed in battle with the durath at Tullen
[Ham] – Kalamar warrior killed in battle with the durath at Tullen
[Olaf] – one of Ulfarr's crew, killed in battle with the durath

at Tullen
[Callis] – one of Ulfarr's crew, killed in battle with the Vorund Clan

<u>The household of Gautarr Falrufson at his stronghold of Romsdahl Castle on the southern border with Vorund – now part of the Brotherhood of the Eagle</u>
Gautarr Falrufson – jarl of Romsdahl, father of Ragnar and uncle of Throm and Freydja
Jora Gautarrswyfe – the wife of Gautarr Falrufson
[Hroarr Gautarrson] – the late eldest son of Gautarr Falrufson, he drowned at sea during a storm
[Svena Gautarrdottir] – the late daughter of Gautarr Falrufson, died of a pox in childhood
Ragnar Gautarrson – younger son of Gautarr Falrufson and his sole surviving child
Asta Ragnarswyfe – called **Asta the Fair**, the wife of Ragnar Gautarrson
Hroarr Ragnarson – son of Ragnar Gautarrson
Halla Ragnardottir – daughter of Ragnar Gautarrson
[Egill Falrufson] – the eldest brother of Gautarr Falrufson and the leader of the Romsdahl household until his death at the hand of Joarr the Hammer. Father of Throm and Freydja
[Tora Egillswyfe] – the wife of Egill Falrufson. After her death her children were fostered by Gautarr Falrufson
Throm Egillson – Egill's son and Gautarr's nephew, raised by him since being orphaned
Freydja Bandorswyfe – Egill's daughter, Gautarr's niece and Throm's sister, raised by Gautarr since being orphaned. Married to Bandor Johanson
[Olfridor Falrufson] – the brother of Gautarr Falrufson. See Household of Jorik Kolfinnarson for further details
Domarr the Oak – the bastard son of Olfridor Falrufson, a mighty warrior, loyal to Gautarr
[Falruf] – the father of Gautarr, Olfridor and Egill

Adakan – a warrior of Romsdahl, clan moot speaker for eastern Reavesburg
Svafa – a warrior of Romsdahl, possesses the Sight
Tomas the Berserk – a warrior of Romsdahl
Karlin – the resident bard at Romsdahl and Jora's occasional lover
Molda Tellianswyfe – also known as **Molda the Shipwright**, she is the master shipwright of Gautarr Falrufson and wife of Tellian
Tellian the Samarak – a merchant from Naroque in Samarakand, married to Molda
[Haki] – a warrior of Romsdahl and Gautarr's second, killed in the Battle of Romsdahl
[Sigdan] – commander of Gautarr's archers, killed in the Battle of Romsdahl
The crew of the Romsdahl longship *Stormweaver*
Aerinndis Telliandottir – captain of Stormweaver also known as **Aerinndis Stormrider** and the daughter and only child of Tellian and Molda
Meinolf Saltbeard – Aerinndis' first mate on *Stormweaver*.
Feyotra – *Stormweaver's* navigator and Matthildr's lover
Aguti – One of Aerinndis' crewmates on *Stormweaver*
Fari – One of Aerinndis' crewmates on *Stormweaver*
Haddr – One of Aerinndis' crewmates on *Stormweaver*
Jonas – One of Aerinndis' crewmates on *Stormweaver*
Matthildr – One of Aerinndis' crewmates on *Stormweaver* and Feyotra's lover
Soren – One of Aerinndis' crewmates on *Stormweaver*

The town of Reavesburg, capital of the Reavesburg Clan and site of their stronghold of Ulfkell's Keep, now occupied by the Vorund Clan and ruled by Tyrfingr Blackeyes
Djuri Turncloak – a warrior of Ulfkell's Keep and Nereth's lover
Nereth – a mage of Mirtan who possesses the Sight. Adalrikr's agent in Norlhast until her plot was uncovered,

forcing her to flee to safety in occupied Reavesburg. Now Tyrfingr's advisor and Djuri's lover

Ulf – a warrior of Ulfkell's Keep

Desta Haarlswyfe – servant at Ulfkell's Keep and Rothgar's secret lover before its fall. Widow of Haarl

Finnvidor Haarlson – the infant son of Haarl and Desta, known as **Finn**

Humli Freedman – Desta's father, a widowed fisherman living on the River Jelt

Lina Anderswyfe – Leif's mother, now possessed by the durath and taking shelter with Humli after the Brotherhood destroyed her home in Tullen

Frokn – Lina's infant son

Darri – the resident bard at Ulfkell's Keep

Tola Boddiswyfe – a friend of Desta and a former servant at Ulfkell's Keep

Boddi – the husband of Tola. A fisherman

Drifa Boddidottir – the daughter of Boddi and Tola

Sissa Gamliswyfe – a fishmonger and wife of Gamli

Gamli – a fisherman and Sissa's husband

Rollef – leader of a group of Reavesburg refugees travelling west to try and start a new life in Vittag

Sunnifa Rollefswyfe – Rollef's wife

Almarr – a refugee travelling with Rollef and Sunnifa

[Haarl] – a warrior of Ulfkell's Keep, childhood friend of Rothgar and Desta's husband. Killed in the Battle of Romsdahl

<u>The merchant port of Noln, the town neighbouring Reavesburg</u>

Lundvarr – town elder

Ingunn – Lundvarr's mother

Dyri – a warrior of Noln and one of Lundvarr's guards

Elfradr – a captain of a small merchant vessel

The household of the late Hrodi Myndillson in Olt, occupied by the Vorund Clan

[Hrodi Myndillson] – former town elder of Olt also known as **Old Hrodi** or **Hrodi Whitebeard**, killed in the Battle of Romsdahl

[Radholf Hrodison] – eldest and only surviving son of Hrodi Myndillson, killed in the Battle of Romsdahl

Alfarr Radholfson – town elder of Olt, eldest son of Radholf and grandson of Hrodi. Loyal to the Vorund Clan

Jolinn Hrodidottir – a shieldmaiden of Olt and the illegitimate daughter of Old Hrodi. Clan moot speaker for the mid-lands of Reavesburg, loyal to the Brotherhood

Beinir – a warrior of Olt, Jolinn's second, loyal to the Brotherhood

[Karl] – a warrior of Olt and Jolinn's lover, killed aiding the Brotherhood

The fallen household of Jorik Kolfinnarson, ninth Reavesburg clan chief, murdered by the Vorund Clan

[Jorik Kolfinnarson] – ninth Reavesburg clan chief

[Reesha Jorikswyfe] – Jorik Kolfinnarson's wife and Johan Jokellsward's daughter

[Kolfinnar the Younger] – Jorik Kolfinnarson's son

Rothgar Kolfinnarson – Jorik's younger brother, a survivor of the fall of Ulfkell's Keep and now a counsellor to Johan Jokellsward

Nuna Karaswyfe – Jorik's sister, a survivor of the fall of Ulfkell's Keep. Married to Karas Greystorm of the Norlhast Clan

[Finnvidor Einarrson] – jarl of Ulfkell's Keep

[Olfridor Halfhand] – Jorik's weapons master. Brother of Gautarr and Egill Falrufson

[Brunn Fourwinds] – a warrior of Ulfkell's Keep. Bram's

father and captain of Kolfinnar's warship, *Marl's Pride*

[Bram Brunnson] – a warrior of Ulfkell's Keep, son of Brunn Fourwinds and childhood friend of Rothgar. Killed in battle at Noln at the hand of Tyrfingr Blackeyes, slain by an arrow meant for Rothgar.

<u>Former Clan Chiefs of Reavesburg</u>

[Reave] – first clan chief and founder of the Reavesburg Clan

[Sigborn Reaveson] – Reave's son and second clan chief, also known as **Sigborn Dragonslayer**

[Ulfkell Sigbornson] – Sigborn's son and third clan chief, the last of Reave's line

[Pengill Svennson] – fourth clan chief of Reavesburg

[Oli Pengillson] – fifth clan chief of Reavesburg

[Hroar Helstromson] – sixth clan chief of Reavesburg, Kolfinnar Marlson's grandfather

[Marl Hroarson] – Kolfinnar Marlson's father and seventh clan chief

[Kolfinnar Marlson] – eighth Reavesburg clan chief and father to Jorik, Rothgar and Nuna

[Alaine Kolfinnarswyfe] – Kolfinnar's late wife, mother of Jorik, Rothgar and Nuna

[Jorik Kolfinnarson] – Kolfinnar's eldest son and ninth clan chief

<u>Other fallen members of the Reavesburg Clan</u>

[Anders] – Leif's father, a farmer from Brindling, killed by the durath

[Halma] – Leif's elder sister, murdered by the Vorund Clan

[Gisla] – Leif's younger sister, murdered by the Vorund Clan

<u>The Vorund Clan</u>

Adalrikr Asmarrson – the **King of the North**, ruling from Vorund after murdering his own father, Asmarr, and his

three elder brothers. Adalrikr is one of the durath (see below)
Tyrfingr Blackeyes – Adalrikr's jarl, ruling the territory of Reavesburg from Ulfkell's Keep
Galin Ironfist – a warrior in Tyrfingr's service, Blackeyes' second
Bjorr – a warrior in Galin Ironfist's company
Randall Vorstson – Adalrikr's jarl, defeated in the Battle of Romsdahl
Kurt – a warrior and Randall's second
Meldun – a warrior in Randall's company
Joarr the Hammer – Adalrikr's jarl, defeated in the Battle of Romsdahl. Joarr killed Egill Falrufson, the brother of Gautarr Falrufson, in single combat
Hasteinn the Cruel – a warrior and Joarr's second
Valdimarr – a noble in Adalrikr's service, his emissary in Norlhast
Dromundr – a warrior in Valdimarr's service in Norlhast
Geilir Goldentooth – a warrior in Adalrikr's service, conqueror of the Riltbalt Clan
Tryggvi – a warrior in Geilir's company
[Sinarr the Cold One] – Adalrikr's jarl, killed in the Battle of Romsdahl
[Hrodmarr Hroarson] – a warrior of Vorund, leader of Adalrikr's forces in Olt. Killed in the Battle of Romsdahl
[Asmarr] – former chief of the Vorund Clan and Adalrikr's father

The Durath

Adalrikr Asmarrson – the first of the Sundered Souls created by Morvanos, known during the time of the War of the Avatars as **Baltus, First of the Sundered** and also **Vashtas, Flayer of Souls**. In his current guise he has declared himself the **King of Laskar** or the **King of the North**. Also known as **Adalrikr Kinslayer**
Hallerna – Adalrikr's lover, banished to the Shadow Realm at the end of the War of the Avatars and now restored to him

through the Calling

Heidr – called the **Prophetess** by her companions, she is a Sundered Soul and has the gift of scrying, through which she can perceive the present, past and future. Known as **Celembine** during the War of the Avatars

Nishrall – a Sundered Soul, he goes by his original name from the Age of Glory. He was the right-hand man of **Vashtas** during the War of the Avatars

Eidr – a Sundered Soul, Adalrikr's agent in Reavesburg

Kolsveinn – a Sundered Soul, Adalrikr's agent in Reavesburg

Orn – a Sundered Soul, sworn to protect Adalrikr as his shieldman

Finnaril – a Sundered Soul, who goes by her original name from the Age of Glory

Solvia – a Sundered Soul and Heidr's good friend

Vedisra – a Sundered Soul, sworn to protect Adalrikr as his shieldmaiden

The Six – Adalrikr's six undead warrior guardians

Lina Anderswyfe – Leif's mother, now possessed by the durath and taking shelter with Humli after the Brotherhood destroyed her home in Tullen

[Sandar Tindirson] – town elder of Tullen on the shores of Lake Tull, secretly one of the durath and slain by the Brotherhood

The Norlhast Clan

The Household of Karas Greystorm, who rules from his stronghold of Norlhast Keep

Karas Greystorm – Norlhast's former clan chief, now the jarl of Norlhast in the service of Adalrikr

[Katrin Karaswyfe] – the late first wife of Karas Greystorm she died in childbirth, her son stillborn

[Thora Karaswyfe] – the late second wife of Karas Greystorm, she died of the blood plague

> **[Gretta Karasdottir]** – the late eldest daughter of Karas Greystorm, she died in childhood of the blood plague

[Katrin Karasdottir] – the late youngest daughter of Karas Greystorm, she died in childhood of the blood plague

Nuna Karaswyfe – the third wife of Karas Greystorm, daughter of Kolfinnar Marlson of the Reavesburg Clan and sister of Rothgar Kolfinnarson. The marriage of Nuna and Karas was the foundation for an ill-fated alliance between the Reavesburg and Norlhast Clans

Sigurd Albriktson – former jarl of Norlhast Keep

Kalfr Albriktson – younger brother of Sigurd and a warrior of the Norlhast Clan

Luta Kalfrswyfe – the wife of Kalfr Albriktson

Thyra – Kalfr's eldest daughter

Tassi – Kalfr's eldest son

Gilla – Kalfr's youngest daughter

Varinn – Kalfr's youngest son

Albrikt the Wise – chief counsellor to Karas Greystorm, reinstated to his position after the fall of Nereth's coven. Father of Sigurd and Kalfr

Brosa – a warrior of the Norlhast Clan and Nuna's personal bodyguard

Vrand – a warrior of the Norlhast Clan

Katla – Nuna's maid, previously in her service at Ulfkell's Keep

Styrman – a servant at Norlhast Keep

Kofri – Norlhast fisherman

Skefill – Norlhast fisherman

[Bekan Bekansson] – the previous Norlhast clan chief, who was killed in single combat by Karas Greystorm

[Norl] – founder of the Norlhast Clan

Warriors involved in the Norlhast rebellion, led by Orglyr the Grim

Orglyr the Grim – the leader of the Norlhast uprising beyond Norlhast Keep. One of Bekan Bekanson's jarls until his exile by Karas

Fundinn – Orglyr's second. Possesses the Sight
Hoskuldr – a warrior in Orglyr's company
Snaga – a warrior in Orglyr's company
Curren Redblade – a warrior of Norlhast Keep and trusted friend of Brosa
Limping Tidkumi – a former ally of Bekan Bekanson and later Karas Greystorm, originally the jarl of Taur before his titles were stripped following Norlhast's occupation by the Vorund Clan
Soma Alvedottir – a shieldmaiden and Tidkumi's second
Vikarr – a former warrior of Bekan Bekanson
Nimm – a shieldmaiden in Vikarr's company

The Vittag Clan
Ingioy the White Widow – chief of the Vittag Clan
Valka – daughter of Ingioy and one of her jarls
Rasmus – a warrior in Valka's company

The Helsburg Clan
Falki Ruunson – the jarl of Helsburg, appointed by Finnaril to rule in Adalrikr's name
[Bothvatr Dalkrson] – chief of the Helsburg Clan, murdered by Finnaril

The Riltbalt Clan
Gunnsteinn Haddison – the jarl of Riltbalt, ruling in Adalrikr's name following his defeat by Geilir
Lefwine – the commander of the Riltbalt army sent to support Geilir in his war against the Norlhast uprising led by Orglyr the Grim
Vegrim – a defiant tribute from the Riltbalt Clan, taken as a thrall to serve Vorund
[Harvaan] – founder of the Riltbalt Clan

The Jorvind Clan
Onundr Arisson – chief of the Jorvind Clan, still resisting

Adalrikr from his stronghold in Rast

__**The Kingdom of Mirtan**__

Serena – Grand Mage of the Three Chapters and ruler of Mirtan

[Ramill] – mage of Mirtan and the tutor of Joldir and Nereth

Nereth – Joldir's former apprentice, now an agent of Adalrikr

__**The Fire Isle**__

Mendaleon – leader of the dragons and life partner of Alcor

Alcor – dragon and life partner of Mendaleon

Ralina – dragon and life partner of Sirion

Sirion – dragon and life partner of Ralina

Jade – dragon and life partner of Tanios, widowed when he was slain by Sigborn, her human lover

[Tanios] – dragon slain by Sigborn Reaveson after being betrayed by his life partner Jade

__**The Gods**__

The Creator – the god who, through his servants the avatars, created the world of Amuran

__The Avatars__

Altandu – avatar of light, sometimes referred to as the **Mother of Light**

Bruar – avatar of fire

Ceren – avatar of darkness, sometimes referred to as the **Mother of Darkness**

Culdaff – avatar of the air and winds

Dinas – avatar of time

Dinuvillan – avatar of good fortune

Garradon – avatar of defensive battle, general of Vellandir's forces opposed to Morvanos

Ilanasa – avatar of healing

Lamornna – avatar of nature and creation

Meras – avatar of love

Morvanos – avatar of chaos, leader of the rebellion that began the War of the Avatars
Myshall – avatar of misfortune
Nanquido – avatar of the waters and the seas
Navan – avatar who guards the Halls of the Dead in the afterlife
Rannoch – avatar of the earth
Rathlin – avatar of death
Vellandir – avatar of law and justice, leader of the avatars who opposed Morvanos

ACKNOWLEDGEMENTS

So many people have played a part in bringing this novel to life and ultimately into the hands of my readers. First of all, I need to give my heartfelt thanks to my wife, Liz, and my daughters, Emma and Megan. Writing a four book epic fantasy series has proved a far greater challenge than any of us expected, and I couldn't have completed this instalment without all their support and encouragement (and gentle teasing if my head ever gets too big).

Lost Gods was a difficult novel to write, mainly due to my inexperience as I struggled to keep control of the multiple strands of the plot and the various character arcs I'd set in motion during the first two books. Once I had an early draft, Laurence Keighley once again kindly volunteered to act as my test reader, as he's done for all my novels so far. It takes a very good friend to tell you when your book isn't up to the mark. Laurence's honest assessment of the various strengths and, more importantly, the considerable flaws of that early version of Lost Gods (written in 2019) was incredibly valuable. This prompted me to take a much-needed break before coming back to look at the whole novel afresh. That early feedback helped steer me back on course and Lost Gods is a far better novel as a result.

After an extensive rewrite, my agent John Jarrold provided his insightful edits on the next version, putting his finger on a few elements that needed further work. There's no doubt in my mind that John's input and sage advice over the years has made me a far better writer, helping me to turn out the best possible version of this book. It's always a pleasure to work with him and I look forward to doing so again as I get ready to complete this series.

Artist Anne Hudson has produced another lovely cover as she continues her great work on this series. When the final designs come together it's a really exciting moment in the creation of a book, knowing this is the first thing potential readers will see. She got the mood and atmosphere just right for Lost Gods and, as ever, I'm delighted with the results.

Once I published my work and writing stopped being my private hobby, my circle of literary friends widened considerably. I can honestly say my fellow authors have been nothing other than incredibly supportive and encouraging as I've moved into this much more public sphere. Special thanks are due to Holly Tinsley, Jacob Sannox, PL Stuart, Bjørn Larssen, Sean Crow and Krystle Matar. You're all incredibly talented writers and, between you, you've kept me sane whenever the pressure got too much as well as giving me lots of laughs along the way.

It's also important I thank my readers, since without you there wouldn't be much point doing any of this. I hope you've enjoyed this latest instalment of The Brotherhood of the Eagle series. If so, please do consider leaving a review on Amazon or Goodreads or simply tell your friends (after all, word of mouth is the best possible form of advertising there is!). Those recommendations, ratings and reviews give readers the confidence to take the plunge and try something new, which in turn makes my career as an author possible.

If you want to know more and keep up to date with all the latest news, you can sign up for my bi-monthly newsletter via my website. This will also give you exclusive access to my series of free short stories, which expand on the characters and history of The Brotherhood of the Eagle.

Twitter – @TimHardieAuthor
Facebook – @Tim.Hardie.Author.Public
Website – www.timhardieauthor.co.uk

Printed in Great Britain
by Amazon

18910389R00359